Guess Who

Chris lives in Durham and is a recent graduate of the Creative Writing (Crime/Thriller) MA at City University – *Guess Who* is his debut novel. He loves film and acting in an amateur theatre group, and can be found on Twitter at @crmcgeorge.

Guess Who

CHRIS McGEORGE

ORION

First published in Great Britain in 2018
by Orion
an imprint of The Orion Publishing Group Ltd
Carmelite House, 50 Victoria Embankment
London EC4Y 0DZ

An Hachette UK Company

5 7 9 10 8 6 4

A CIP catalogue record for this book is
available from the British Library.

ISBN (Mass Market Paperback) 978 1 4091 7808 8
ISBN (Hardback) 978 1 4072 5113 4

Typeset by Input Data Services Ltd, Somerset

Printed and bound in Great Britain by Clays Ltd, Elcograf S.p.A.

www.orionbooks.co.uk

for my grandfather John Board

The Players

Morgan Sheppard – Daytime television actor on *Resident Detective*. Widely known to have a drink and drug problem. Once hailed as the 'Child Detective'.

Amanda Phillips – Works at the *CoffeeCorps* in Waterloo station. Always serves with a smile. Dreams of becoming a journalist and working in the television industry. Often called 'sweet' and 'kind'.

Ryan Quinn – Hotel cleaner. Financially struggling and working to support family after move from Hong Kong to London. Takes pride in his work, but would rather be doing literally anything else.

Constance Ahearn – Famous West End actress. Currently playing the lead in the new musical *Rain on Elmore Street* at the Lyceum theatre. Regularly cited as one of the greatest actresses working in theatre today. Multi-award winner. Devout Catholic, often creates friction amongst people who don't share her beliefs

Alan Hughes – Decorated lawyer. Quickly rose up the ranks of the legal system, despite black lawyers taking up such a small fraction of London's courts. Never gives up and always offers legal counsel, sometimes even when it's not offered. Currently embroiled in a highly influential and career-making case.

Rhona Michel – Seventeen-year-old student. Keeps herself to herself. Likes listening to music using her large purple headphones. Suffers from crippling claustrophobia.

Simon Winter – Morgan Sheppard's therapist for most of his life. Prides himself on professionalism and an exceptional track record. Obtained a PhD in Psychology at a comparatively young age, and has worked as a private therapist in the suburbs ever since.

Guess Who

The school is quiet by the time I get back. My mum always used to say I was scatter-brained when I forgot stuff, but she never got round to telling me exactly what it meant. Looks like I've been scatter-brained again though. I knew it the second I looked in my bag, halfway home – I'd left it in the Maths room. My jotter, with tonight's homework on it. I don't want to let Mr Jefferies down, so here I am.

I slip back across the field and into the main entrance. There's something really creepy about school after dark – when all of us have gone. Usually it's loud and busy, but now the corridors are quiet and my footsteps sound like elephants stomping because they echo up and down, up and down. I don't see anyone but a man dressed in green overalls, using that weird machine to clean the hall floor. He looks like he's the most unhappy man in the world. Dad says if I don't study, this is the kind of thing that'll happen to me. I feel sorry for the man, and then I feel sorry that I feel sorry because pity isn't nice.

I start walking quicker and get to the Maths room. The door is half open. Mum always taught me to be polite, so I knock anyway. The door squeaks like a mouse as it opens.

I don't see him straight away. The door gets stuck on the papers and exercise books all over the floor. I recognise one and bend down to pick it up. Mine. Mr Jefferies had collected them in at the end of class.

1

I realise that something is very wrong, and I look up to see him. Mr Jefferies, the Maths teacher, my Maths teacher. My friend. He's hanging in the centre of the room with a belt around his neck. His face looks a strange colour and his eyes look so big he looks like a cartoon.

But he's not. He's real. And it takes me too long to realise what it really is that I'm looking at – too long to see that this isn't some kind of horrible joke.

But as I look, there he is.

Mr Jefferies. Dead.

And at some point, I start to scream.

1

Twenty-five years later . . .

A sharp, undulating tone – drilling into his brain. But as he focused on it, it separated into ringing. In his head or out there – in the world, somewhere else. Somewhere that couldn't possibly be here.

Bbring, bbring, bbring.

Brring, brring, brring.

It was real – coming from beside him.

Eyes open. Everything fuzzy – dark. What was happening? The sound of heavy breathing – taking him a second longer than it should have to realise it was his own. His senses flickering on like the lights in a hospital corridor. And then, yes – he could feel his chest rising and falling, and the rush of air through his nostrils. It didn't seem to be enough. He tried to open his mouth for more, and found it to be incredibly dry – his tongue rolling round in a prison of sandpaper.

Was it silent? No, the *brring brring brring* was still there. He had just gotten used to it. A phone.

He tried to move his arms and couldn't. They were above his head – elevated – slowly vibrating with the threat of pins and needles. He could feel a ring of cold around both of his wrists – something cold and strong. Metal? Yes, it felt like it. Metal around his wrists – handcuffs? He tried to move his limp hands to see what he was attached to. A central bar running down his back. And he was handcuffed to it?

Both arms were throbbing at the elbow – both bent at odd angles as he tried to manoeuvre himself. He was sat up against this thing, whatever it was. But he was sitting on something soft – and felt his current unease was most likely because he had slipped down a bit. He was half sitting and half lying down – an uncomfortable arrangement.

He braced himself, digging his feet into the surface and pushed himself up. His foot slipped, unable to keep any type of grip (shoes, he was wearing shoes, had to remember that), but it was enough. His bottom shuffled back so the strain on his arms was released. With the lack of pain focusing his mind, the blurs around him began to come into focus.

The objects to his left were the first to appear – the closest. He saw a table, between whatever he was sitting on and a white wall. On the table, a black panelled cylinder with red digital numbers on it. A clock. Flashing 03:00:00. Three o'clock? But no – he watched it and it didn't change, illuminated by the light of a lamp next to it.

It hurt his eyes to focus on the light, making him realise the room was rather dark. He found himself blinking away sunspots and looking up at the white wall. There was a picture there, framed. A painting of a distant farmhouse

4

across a field of corn. But that wasn't what drew him to it. The farmhouse was on fire, red paint licking at the blue sky. And in the foreground there was a crude representation of a scarecrow smiling. And the more he looked at it, the more the scarecrow's smile seemed to broaden.

He looked away, unsure why he felt so unsettled by the picture. Now, in front of him he saw his legs and feet – black trousers, black shoes – stretched out over a large bed. The plump duvet had slid down and he had been scrabbling against the bunched up sheets. Assorted dress cushions were scattered around him.

In front of him was a familiar scene – would have been to anyone. Desk, small flat-screen TV, kettle, bowl full of coffee and tea sachets, a leather menu standing open on its side. There he finally saw the phone – far and away out of reach. He moved his head slightly to see a walk-in wardrobe to the front left. To the front right, a window – curtains drawn with the ghost of light creeping through.

Unmistakeable. This was a hotel room. And he was handcuffed to the bed.

And it was all wrong.

Three sharp tones, drilling into his brain. Brring, brring, brring.

This was all wrong.

2

He didn't know how long he sat there, listening to the ringing. Forever and no time at all. But eventually there was a new sound. A voice. A female voice. Slightly robotic.

'Hello, Mr Sheppard. Welcome to the illustrious Great Hotel. For over sixty years, we have prided ourselves on our excellent hospitality and vast range of unique comforts that you can sample while staying in your luxurious surroundings. For information on our room service menu, please press 1, for information on our newly refurbished gym and spa, please press 2, for room services such as an early wake-up call, please press 3 . . .'

Mr Sheppard? Well, at least it was his name. They knew his name? Had it happened again?

'. . . information on live performances in our bar area, please press 4 . . .'

Had he had too much, *done* too much? Twenty years of using and drinking, and using *and* drinking, he had started to think that *too much* was a concept that didn't apply to him. But it had happened before. A grand blackout where he woke up somewhere else entirely. A rollercoaster of a fugue state, where he'd bought the ticket.

'. . . information on the local area, such as booking shows, and transport options, please press 5 . . .'

But he knew how those situations had felt. And this wasn't that.

Because —

It still wasn't there. Where had he been? Before. Where — the last time he remembered. Now, a hotel room, and then — a figure danced around on the edges of his memory. A woman.

He swallowed dry and ran his tongue over his teeth. There was something in them — the grey and rotting after-taste of wine along with something chemical.

'. . . for early check-out, please press 6, if you would like to hear your options again, please press 7.'

This was wrong. He shouldn't be here.

And the phone — the phone had gone silent. For some reason, no voice felt worse. If he could hear her, could she hear him? *It's a robot, just a robot.* But the line could still be open. Worth a shot.

'If you would like to hear your options again, please press 7.'

He tried again to move his hands, to get some feeling back into them. He made quick fists with his palms. And when he had enough control, he braced himself and moved his wrists quickly against the central metal bar. The centre of the cuffs clanged against it. The sound was loud, but not loud enough. *You're wasting your time. Just a robot.*

'If you would like to hear your options again, please press 7.'

He opened his mouth, his lips ripping apart as though they hadn't been open in years. He tried to say something, not knowing what. All that came out was a hoarse grunt.

'If you would like to hear your options again, please press 7.'

Silence.

He opened his mouth. And what came out was something like a 'Help'. *Just a robot.* Still not loud enough.

Silence.

And then the robot on the phone laughed. *Not a robot.* 'Okay, Mr Sheppard, have it your way. But you're going to have to start talking soon. Can't wait to see what you do next.'

What? He didn't have to time to think about the words because there came a terrible sound. The dull tone of a dead phone line. The woman was gone.

He tried to calm down – his heart racing in his chest. This wasn't happening – couldn't be happening? And maybe it wasn't. Maybe it was just some bad dream, or some kind of new bad trip. He had been hitting it pretty hard lately. But as he thought it, he couldn't believe it.

It felt too real.

Someone would come. Someone had to come. Because the staff obviously knew he was here, which meant the whole hotel knew he was here. And he couldn't have handcuffed himself to the bed, so . . .

Can't wait to see what you do next.

What was the point of the call? That was the thing about phones – you could pretty much be whoever you wanted to be and there was no way of knowing for real.

Why would this woman *robot/not a robot* be calling him? He couldn't reach the phone. So, this woman could be the one – the one who'd handcuffed him to the bed. The one who was playing some sick joke. And if she wasn't a staff member, maybe that meant no one would come.

No. This was a hotel. Of course someone would come. Eventually.

He shut his eyes. And tried to slow his breathing enough to listen for anything outside of the room. Any thundering past, any suitcases rolling. But there was nothing. Silence.

Except that wasn't quite true.

He felt it before he heard it. That prickling on the back of his neck. And then, very softly, the sound of breathing.

He wasn't alone.

3

He realised that it had always been there – such a natural sound that he didn't register it. But, as he held his own breath, it became louder. Breathing. Almost silent – like the breaths of a spectre. But it was there. Soft, shallow breaths.

And the more he focused, the more he heard. It was all around him. Not just one person. How many? He couldn't know. People – plural – in the room with him.

He knew he had to open his eyes, but they refused. His brain was starting to connect dots that weren't there – trying, fruitlessly, to make sense of it all. Was this some kind of PR stunt? His agent had warned him about stuff like this – the red tops paying for a scandal. What more of a scandal than some kind of hotel room orgy?

But it didn't sit exactly right. Would they really abduct him, cuff him to a bed, just for a story? Not their style. And besides he was fully clothed. The most disappointing orgy ever.

Against all odds, he almost laughed. He was going crazy now too. Add it to the long list of things that needed addressing.

But first – he wrenched his eyes open again. The hotel

room looked back at him. The breathing still there. He had to look. He leaned to the left with his wrists as far as he could. The ice-cold cuffs bit into his skin, but he tried to block it out. His body leaned left too, and he tilted his head so he could see over the edge of the bed.

He expected – *hoped?* – to see nothing but the carpet. Instead, he saw something he couldn't quite define. Until he realised he was looking at the back of a person, dressed in a brown suit, lying face-down on the carpet. As the thought clicked in his head, he hurriedly rocked back on his wrists and shuffled back to the centre of the bed.

A person. A real person. Face-down on the floor.

Silence again – the breathing still there. But now began something else. A skittering sound, like mice nibbling on cardboard.

He forced himself to look over the right side of the bed, straining on the cuffs again. There was no one there. The carpet was a muted purple. Looking down the slice of floor he could see, however, he noticed something. A small trail of something yellow towards where the bed ended. It looked too fine to be string, and as he looked it started to twitch. Hair. It was hair.

He returned to the centre of the bed. Hair? God.

He looked straight ahead, into the black mirror of the television. Couldn't see anything in it – not even himself. And he was glad. He didn't want to know how pathetic he looked. The blackness calmed him – the nothing. He would focus on the television until someone came to rescue him. He would refuse to accept any of this.

And even as he told himself that, he found his eyes drawn downwards to the edge of the bed, past the shine of his shoes, as something rose up. One finger. And then two. And then a whole hand gripping the duvet.

His heart sank. The shuffling grew louder and the breathing did too — all around him. And now —

They were waking up.

4

A face at the end of the bed. Blonde. A girl – twenties. Looking like he felt – confused and pale, her eyes filled with panic. She looked around first, her head rocking around on her neck, and then she saw him, rapidly ducking down again in surprise.

'H-Hey,' he tried to say. His voice was cracking in all the wrong places, making it sound like more of a threat than a greeting. He tried again. 'Hey.' A bit better that time.

The girl surfaced – just her eyes. They flitted to his handcuffs. They looked even more confused. But hey, he wasn't going anywhere, so maybe that helped her stick her head up again.

'What–? What's happening? Where am I?' Her voice was small and scared. 'What did you do to me?'

He looked at her, shocked. 'I woke up here, just like you.' He clanged the handcuffs to corroborate. It worked. There was something new in her face – understanding. For a moment, they were locked in each other's gaze, sharing their fear.

There was more stirring around her on the floor, and her eyes drifted down. He couldn't see. But whatever she saw made her jump up and back. Her hip collided with the desk and the room service menu toppled over. She gave a small, curt squeal.

He could see her more clearly now. Jeans. Light yellow hoodie. Just your average girl. As he looked, he saw that there was something on her left breast. A sticker of some kind. 'More people,' she said, gasping. 'There's more people.'

'I know.' Speaking was becoming easier, like an engine rolling over and starting up. 'How many?'

'I don't . . . I can't . . .'

'I need to know how many.' Why? Why was it important? Maybe because every extra person would make this so much worse.

Upon hearing his voice – his full voice – something must have sparked in her mind. She looked at him – her eyes wide and full. That look he saw nearly every day.

'Wait a minute,' she said. 'Aren't you—? Don't I—?'

Don't I know you? This was only going to delay things. He always existed on the fringe – he wasn't recognisable at a glance but a double-take would do the job.

'You're . . .'

'Yes, yes.' He usually would have loved it. But not now. 'How many?'

'Oh God . . . there's four people. A girl. Two men. And a woman. I don't know if they're . . .'

'Are they breathing?'

'I think so. They're moving – the woman and the girl anyway. I don't want to check.'

'No, no, you need to get to the door, okay.' He was

14

losing her again – she was shaking her head. Hysteria – the enemy of progress. He took in a deep breath. 'Just get out of here. Go and get help. You need to go and get help, okay?'

'What is this?' she said, her eyes darting around the floor. He was glad he couldn't see what was there.

'I don't know – but please, the door.' He was almost pleading. What had he been reduced to already?

Can't wait to see what you do next.

The girl kept her eyes up, not looking at the floor. She made her way across his vision, towards the alcove. She must've been able to see the door. He was right about where it was. Of course. The girl made two exaggerated movements, side to side. She was dodging bodies. He didn't have to be able to see them to know. She disappeared from view into the alcove.

He leaned on the cuffs, forward this time, and craned his neck, but he couldn't see her. He heard her try the door, fumbling with the handle. The shake of it. But he didn't hear the door open. Why did the door not open?

'It's locked,' she said. 'It's . . . The key card light's red. I can't . . .'

Another sound. Another scraping. The girl was trying the lock – the physical one.

'It's . . . it's stuck. It's locked.'

How could it be locked?

'Do you see anywhere the key card could be? Like a holder on the wall to activate the lights?'

'No, there's nothing. There's . . .'

'Look through the peephole,' he said, 'someone might

15

pass by. There may be . . .' *Someone. Anyone.*

A beat. And then, 'I just see the corridor.' Banging. She was banging on the door. Bang. Bang. Bang. She kept at it, louder and louder, until it sounded like she was punching the door. 'Hey. We're trapped in here. Someone! We can't get out.'

And above the banging, he heard and felt something else. Another presence. A mumbling. As if someone was whispering by his right ear. He turned and looked into the eyes of an old woman with blankets of long black hair. They looked at each other, and he wished he was able to block his ears, as she began to scream.

5

It felt like his ears erupted as the old woman emitted the shrill, coarse sound that seemed so loud it could alert everyone in the building. She jumped up and backed herself into the corner nearest to him, so it was hard for him to see her – his blind spot.

The banging stopped, or at least he thought it did. His ears were ringing. He looked across the room, to the alcove the girl had disappeared into, but he faltered along the way. There were faces – two new faces. Just like the girl had said.

A young girl – younger than the one at the door – at the end of the bed. Maybe she was 17 at most, and she was wearing some sort of black jumper. She had a large pair of purple headphones around her neck, a wire snaking down into her jeans pocket. She tried to stand up, but her legs gave way and she dropped out of sight again.

A young man, slightly to his left, fared better. He was slowly becoming conscious, but as soon as he opened his eyes, he snapped to alertness. He was wearing some kind of jumpsuit, pure white. There was something on him, a sticker, matching that of the girl's. Some writing. Impossible to read from the distance. He looked around, with more of a sense of wonder than confusion. When he saw Sheppard, he just stared at him.

The girl, the man, the woman – how many had the blonde girl said? Four. One more. The old man. The man he had seen when he looked over the left side of the bed.

The blonde girl appeared from the alcove, a look of dejection and shock on her face to mix with the panic.

The screaming woman must have seen her too, as she shot towards the girl, moving around the bed with a speed unreasonable for someone so delirious. The teenage girl darted out of the way of the woman, and Sheppard saw her decide to shuffle under the desk, wrapping her arms around her legs. A good but ultimately futile defence.

The black-haired woman grabbed the blonde girl by her arms and shook her, finally stopping screaming to utter, 'What is this place? Is this it – the consequence, the punishment? I must endure it.' She pushed past the girl and ran into the alcove, then a loud BANG, as if she had just collided full-pelt into the door.

The blonde girl, discarded by the woman, lost her balance and collided with the young man, who in turn toppled over, into something – or someone – new. There was a grizzly 'Ouch' from a new mouth.

The two responsible scrabbled up and away from the new voice. Sheppard knew the look – apologetic towards authority. He had seen it worn many times. They both made their way around to the right side of the bed, as though they were using Sheppard as a blockade to whatever was coming.

As the blonde girl came closer, Sheppard could see

18

what was on her sticker now – the sticker they all seemed to be wearing. It was white, with a red bar on the top – one of those stickers one would see on a team-building exercise at work.

HELLO MY NAME IS . . . over the red.

And then scrawled in black felt tip on the white – Amanda.

Sheppard looked at it, and then, by instinct, looked down at his own chest. It was the first time he had looked down and he was a little surprised to see he was wearing a white shirt, a dress shirt – and on his breast, his own sticker.

HELLO MY NAME IS . . . Morgan.

A fresh bout of 'What the hells?' burst in his mind.

He looked back up. The blonde, Amanda, was looking too. She looked down at her own sticker, and then they both looked at the young man's.

HELLO MY NAME IS . . . Ryan.

'That right?' Sheppard said, nodding to her sticker.

'Yes,' she said. 'How do they know my name?'

'Amanda.'

'Yes. But people call me Mandy. Mandy Phillips.'

'Yes,' he said, 'Ryan Quinn.' He pointed to his sticker on his – yes, it was a jumpsuit – and a rather strange one at that.

'Morgan Sheppard,' Sheppard said, but Ryan just nodded.

'I know. I've seen you on . . .'

'How is the door locked?' Mandy interrupted, thank God. 'Is this some kind of reality thing?'

'What?' Sheppard said. Reality thing?

Technically, everything's a reality thing.

Against everything, he almost laughed again. But Mandy had meant a reality show and hadn't he thought the same thing? And then it clicked. Why she'd calmed down when she realised who he was.

'Where're the cameras?' she said, looking around.

He frowned and Ryan looked at her, not quite getting what she was talking about. Mandy thought it was all some kind of stunt too. His TV studio was indeed pure evil, there was no doubt about that, but even they wouldn't stoop to kidnapping and, most likely, drugging.

'I'm sorry, Amanda – Mandy, but this is real. I woke up here, just like you.' An age where reality television was all but fantasy. Why not believe it? But this was real. He could feel it. And as he caught her gaze, he realised that, really, she knew it too. She could see it, but that didn't mean she wanted to.

Her smile dipped. 'No . . .'

He was going to lose her again. He needed her. Her and Ryan. He couldn't move, which meant they had to be his eyes.

'Mandy. Ryan. I need you to keep calm. And try to keep everyone else calm. You need to see if you can get me out of these.' He nodded upwards to the cuffs. His hands were almost totally numb now – limbs just along for the ride.

'A key,' Mandy said.

'Yes – a key. See if there's a key around.'

There was little chance of it just lying around. Whoever

had handcuffed him, handcuffed him for a reason. For a . . . Wait. A new question. A new big question. Why was he the only one handcuffed? They had chained up the famous guy – but no one else?

Mandy went around Ryan and started searching. But Ryan was still. He was looking at Sheppard, trying to puzzle out whatever was in his head. He seemed calm though, which was good.

As if to prove how he should be acting, the woman with the long black hair reappeared, only to charge into the alcove again. A slamming sound. She was going to hurt herself. 'Is sorry not enough?' in her shrill voice. 'This is hell. Hell.'

Sheppard knew better than that. Not hell. Hell wasn't a place. Hell was inside, deep inside. He had found it a long time ago.

'Hell. Hell. Hell,' the woman shouted, almost singing it. 'And you're all here with me. Why might that be, I wonder?' She slammed against the door again, and cackled. Insane. They were locked in here with an insane person.

Sheppard looked back at Ryan. He appeared to be wrestling with something, and the longer it took to come out, the worse Sheppard thought it was.

'Ryan.'

He almost jumped at his name.

Ryan leaned in and whispered in his ear, 'I need to tell you something.'

A clearing of the throat. Ryan and Sheppard looked at each other – the noise didn't come from them. They both looked around to see the old man steadying himself precariously against the wall and the bed, trying to get up. When he finally managed, his face changed to anger. 'What on earth is going on here?' Sheppard felt Ryan step back. 'Anyone? Tell me. Now.'

He was a smart man in an old-fashioned way, wearing a grey suit and a dulled tie. His dark skin was illustrated with a weathered way of worldliness and the flecks of a pepper pot goatee. His hair was black, obviously dyed, with patches of grey showing through. His face seemed to rest comfortably in a scowl and his round glasses were slightly askew. On his chest, above his left pocket, his very own sticker – HELLO MY NAME IS . . . Alan.

All eyes in the room were on him. Mandy had stopped what she was doing to look at the new arrival. Even the teenager under the desk was staring at him with wide eyes. It was clear that this man commanded attention.

'I – I . . .' Even Sheppard felt himself back down. He didn't usually do that. He usually stood strong against anyone. But the compromising position . . .

'What is everyone looking at?' Alan barked, and looked down. 'What?' He ripped his sticker off and crumpled it up. He smoothed the patch of his suit down. 'You can't stick things on this. It'll leave a bloody residue.' He threw the sticker into the corner and glanced around again. 'Well?'

Sheppard decided to be honest. 'I don't know.'

'You don't know?' Alan said. 'You don't know? Of course you don't. What is this, some kind of new telly show? Some Channel 4 rubbish. Dear God, tell me it's not Channel 5. Well, looks like you've included the wrong arsehole. I'm a barrister, idiot. I know my rights and the rights of everyone in this room. Look around. That's five lawsuits staring you in the face.'

'For the last time,' Sheppard said, out of frustration, 'this is not a television programme.'

'Of course it isn't.' Alan looked up to the ceiling. 'I want out now please. And I want everyone's name involved in this sham.' When no one answered, Alan stepped towards Sheppard again. 'I'm a real person, unlike you. I do important things. Like . . .' He looked at his expensive watch. 'Dear Christ, the MacArthur case. I have to be in Southwark by 2.'

Sheppard's blank look only seemed to rile Alan more. Everyone else was quiet, not wanting to incur any wrath themselves.

'The biggest case of my career and you people have put me here. Well, you are going to learn the harshness of the law when I get out of here. And I'm not talking about your studio, or your company. You. Sheppard. You.' Alan enunciated these points with jabs at the air.

Realisation by denial, by mania, by acceptance, by anger and, Sheppard saw out of the corner of his eye, by mere disapproval. The teenager, whose sticker was unreadable without his glasses, watched Alan while taking her headphones from around her neck and putting them over her ears. Sheppard suddenly felt a strong kinship to her, as she shuffled further under the desk – clearly trying to disappear into it.

'I'm sorry,' Sheppard said, although he didn't know why.

'Nonsense. Utter nonsense.'

Sheppard felt movement beside him. Alan seemed distracted too. Sheppard looked around. Ryan was moving over to the window. He realised what the young man was about to do. Ryan grabbed at the curtains, clutching them tightly, and with one swift movement, he flung them open.

There was a flash of sunlight, instantly stinging his eyes. After the relative darkness of the room, the light felt too much. He blinked once, twice, trying to blink the multi-coloured spots away. He looked to the window, looking outside. Buildings. Tall and thin. They were high up. The buildings were familiar, the backdrop he could so easily trace with his mind. He was looking out at central London. But why did that feel so wrong? Why did it all feel . . .

And then he remembered.

6

Earlier . . .

They barrelled into the room, in each other's arms. She was kissing him, deep and strong. A passion he hadn't felt in a long time. He managed to reach out and slot his key card into the light slot, and the lights turned on. They were back in his hotel room, upstairs from where he had met her – in the hotel bar. She pulled him back in and he was lost in her, and the night.

'*Pas maintenant, monsieur television*. Not now.'

She regularly lapsed into French. Drunk. Which only made her so much hotter.

She hadn't known who he was at first, and he found that endearing. He bought her a drink, and she spent the rest of the night Googling him on her phone, wondering why people were talking to him all the time. The Art Opening being held in the hotel function room eventually thinned out, and they were left at the bar with each other, talking into her phone. Foreign Siri didn't recognise his London accent.

She pushed him down onto the bed and crawled on top of him, hungry, nipping at his neck with her lips – sliding up him.

'Mind the tux,' he laughed.

'On s'en fout du costume!'

'You understand I have no idea what you're saying, right?'

She straightened up and got off him. 'Got anything to drink?' she said.

He gestured to the minibar. There were a few things left in there at least.

Her head disappeared into the fridge and she pulled out one small bottle of white wine and one of bourbon. They had known each other for all of two hours and she already knew his drink of choice. Was this what finding 'the one' felt like?

'Avez-vous de la glace?'

'One more time,' he said, laughing.

'Sorry,' she said, adjusting her language. 'Er . . . do you have any ice?'

He gestured to the desk, where he had put the ice bucket, already knowing it had all melted. She picked it up, looked inside and smiled. 'I'll go and get some then.' She lunged at him and kissed him rabidly – the ice bucket remnants sloshing onto his trousers. He didn't care. This woman was something else – something new.

She pulled back. *'Je reviens.'* And she rushed out of the room with the bucket under her arm, slamming the door behind her.

'Okay,' he called after her. He got up from the bed. 'I should have paid more attention in French class,' he muttered under his breath.

He walked over to the mirror and took off his bow tie,

undone and hooked around his neck. He took his suit jacket off and put it on the desk chair. He stepped forward and checked his eyes. The paranoia had set in a month ago. It had started when he had had to do a segment on liver cirrhosis on the show. The liver had the power to regenerate. A night of heavy drinking, and afterwards the liver works back to what it was before. But heavy drinkers (over years) damaged the liver so much that it would just give up. Therefore the damage would stick. Early signs included abdominal pain (which would have been dulled by the painkillers, even if he did have it); advanced signs included the whites of the eyes turning yellow. (At least, all of this was what he gleaned from the internet when he was curious after the show.) He had never considered himself a hypochondriac but . . .

You're not a hypochondriac if it's justified.

Said every hypochondriac ever.

He was just being cautious of his health. Anyway, he was fine. He was making something out of nothing.

'Je . . . mappale Sheppard. Mapelle?' He stepped back and smiled at himself. He only remembered one phrase from school. *'Je voudrais un serviette s'il vous plait.'* Meant 'I would like a towel please.' Wouldn't get him very far. *Merde.*

He went over to the window and drew the curtains open. The city looked back at him. He loved just watching the skyline, no matter where he was. There was something about staring out at a city, high up, making you think you're the king of the world. Seeing all the streets and the roads and the alleys and the highways all working together, becoming one organism. He had never

27

been here before, to this city. But it was the same feeling.

The Eiffel Tower was lit up, a beacon around which everything else emanated. He had been up there yesterday, lamenting the way he had decided to be a tourist. He was meant to go to the Louvre tomorrow with Douglas (his agent, who was staying somewhere '*a little more appropriate to an agent's salary*'), but now he was thinking he might have other plans.

After a late morning, and morning sex, he would probably just rest. Maybe get in a swim. Spend the day in the bar. Maybe she could do it with him.

This was the first real holiday he had had in years. *Resident Detective* had made him a household name, but at a cost – the intense filming schedule was crazy. When your series was on every weekday, you had to pump out ridiculous amounts of content, ridiculous amounts of lives he meddled in: affairs, stolen money, illegitimate children, misguided domestic lawsuits, more affairs – he had seen them all in the Real Life segment of the show. That was his favourite bit. That was the bit where he could really have some fun.

When you filmed five episodes a day, it was hard to remember specific cases. They all seemed to blend into one. And of course, he couldn't remember names. One time, he caught a *Resident Detective* episode and watched himself on screen as if he were someone else. He couldn't remember doing any of it. Part of it was because he didn't care. Part of it was because he was 'overworked'. Overworked and high all the time, he supposed.

Douglas had suggested the holiday. A chance to recharge the batteries. Come back a bigger and better Morgan

Sheppard. Sheppard hadn't been so convinced but one day, backstage, he had heard Douglas and the programming controller of the station having an argument. The PC said Sheppard was burnt out – heavily implying it was because of the substance abuse. The plan was for Sheppard to take 14 days, slow down a bit and come back 'refreshed'.

Sheppard didn't tell Douglas he'd overheard the conversation. He just agreed – and after that, he set about convincing himself. Maybe this was a good idea and maybe he had been hitting it a little hard lately. Douglas was overjoyed – so overjoyed he came too (which was probably why he was so into the idea all along).

So he'd come to Paris five days ago. And so far he felt great. Even more so now he had met this crazy-hot woman *who seems to be taking some time?*

He turned from the window and flopped down on the bed. Scrabbling around so he was finally lying down properly, his head between the two pillows. It was comfortable.

He closed his eyes. He didn't realise how tired he was. What time was it? He hadn't worn his watch either. He was on holiday – what would be the point? Now was for relaxing. But he didn't want to be asleep when she came back. He would probably ruin it if he was. And she was so hot. And it had been unreasonably long since the last time.

But he was so tired. And his eyes remained shut. And there was a soothing sound. Almost a hissing. He hadn't heard it before, but maybe it had always been there. And the more he listened, the faster he seemed to fall.

His thoughts fell away.

And he was gone.

7

How could this be real? How could this be possible? How could he be in Paris one moment and London the next? The woman. Had the woman done this to him? He hadn't just moved rooms, he had moved countries. How could you move countries without knowing it? He wouldn't call it impossible but not entirely possible either. It was in the grey area in between.

How long had it been? How long could he have been out? The red room. And here. How long between those two points? It could've been no time at all, could've been an eternity. But – no. He had his own personal way of knowing.

His last drink had been in the red room with the woman. Red room. Wine and bourbon. The stuff he had tasted in his teeth. And now, his throat and brain were dry. But there wasn't that gnawing feeling. That little scrambling on the edges of his brain matter, like something fizzing, whenever he didn't take his pills. So, all dried up but dosed enough. If he had to guess – six hours at the least but no more than twelve. That coupled with the fact that it was day – morning. Ten hours was a reasonable estimate. Ten hours all gone.

He looked away from London. Just in time to see Alan grunt in disapproval. He was walking over to the window. 'I'm supposed to be across the river for Christ's sake.'

'Oh shut up,' Ryan said. Alan looked taken aback and stepped away, crossing his arms and frowning at no one in particular. Ryan was looking out of the window, his eyes darting around the scene outside. 'We're near Leicester Square. Facing south.' He looked to everyone else, as if for approval. Sheppard just looked at him in amazement for figuring it out so quickly. Ryan looked back at the window. 'We're in Bank,' he said again, like he was confirming it.

'Try to open the window,' Sheppard said, stretching his arms, although Ryan was already reaching for the latch.

It was a sliding window, one that looked like it would only open an inch due to how high up they were. Ryan unlatched the window and pushed. Nothing. He made a confused grunt and then tried again, putting his full weight on the handle. Nothing. Ryan continued to try, until his hand slipped from the handle and he fell to the floor. Alan just watched him get back up, not bothering to try to help. Ryan righted himself and tried one last time.

'It's locked,' he said. 'Won't even open an inch.'

'Then let's try this,' Alan said, and before anyone could stop him, he picked up the chair which Headphones had pushed out from under the desk. Alan brandished the chair and thrust it full force into the window. The chair, and Alan behind it, bounced off the window like it was the wall of a bouncy castle. He was thrown to the floor and the chair flew into the centre of the room. Mandy, who was looking through one of the drawers of the desk, narrowly dodged it.

Ryan held his hand out to Alan. 'You couldn't break these windows. They're thick and anti-shatter.' Specific. Alan's eyes narrowed, as Sheppard's did. That was very specific.

'And even so, where would you go?' Mandy said, looking up from the drawers.

Alan chose not to accept Ryan's hand, reaching out for the desk to help him up. 'Well, I apologise for trying. You all seem to have made yourselves at home here. Ms Looney Bin might actually be the only sane one amongst you.' He looked around, catching sight of Headphones. 'What's your story?'

Headphones just looked at him, her eyes wide. Alan peered at her sticker.

'Rhona, what are you up to, Rhona? Just listening to some tunes waiting for the world to end. You teenagers are all bloody imbeciles.'

'Lay off,' Sheppard said, rattling the cuffs. A new pain and a glance upward confirmed what he thought – his wrists were red raw, the cuffs digging into his flesh.

'Oh, don't you start.' Alan rounded on him. 'You're a walking talking embarrassment. I read the papers. I know all about your addictions. But this is the worst addiction of all, isn't it – the lust for attention. Well, congratulations, you've got everyone looking at you. And now you've got us all stuck here with you.'

'For the last time, I don't know why we're here.'

'Bollocks. You television types always know when some idiocy is going on. Is this about the MacArthur case? You want me out of the way or something?'

'This isn't about your stupid case,' Mandy said, still rifling through drawers.

Alan laughed, looking from Sheppard to Mandy and back. 'Stupid. That's the word we're going with, is it? Stupid? Do any of you watch the news?'

'Let's not lose our heads,' Ryan said, 'we're all in this together.' He put a hand on Alan's shoulder – an act that wasn't entirely favoured.

Alan shrugged him off. 'Yes, but some of us are more in it than others.' He nodded to Sheppard. 'Why are you handcuffed, and no one else is?'

The same question he'd asked himself – Alan was just a bit behind him.

Sheppard gritted his teeth – shut his eyes and took a breath. 'I don't know.' Losing his temper wasn't going to help anything.

Mandy had finished searching the drawers but hadn't found a key. Now, she was just standing there, growing paler and paler. She had something in her hands. She put it down on the bed, and Sheppard saw the words glistening in the light. The Holy Bible. A hotel room's only constant. 'I need to . . . wash my face.' It looked like she was going to faint. She stumbled out of view, and Sheppard heard a new door open. The bathroom. How had no one thought to check the bathroom?

As Sheppard looked towards the alcove, he saw the woman with the black hair emerge from it. On her chest

– HELLO MY NAME IS . . . Constance. Sheppard watched her, wondering what she was thinking about.

'What I'm saying is this man may be dangerous. Maybe he's handcuffed for a reason,' Alan was saying. 'And I sure as hell know I need to be across London.'

Sheppard kept watching Constance. Her silence unnerved him. Her large, almost cartoonish eyes, accentuated by her panda mascara, fell to the bed and she snatched the Bible up, clutching it to her chest.

'Religious terms must not be taken in vain,' Constance said, in a low guttural tone, which probably escaped everyone else's hearing.

The situation was slipping from bad to dire in front of Sheppard's eyes – and he couldn't even move.

'Let's all just keep calm,' Ryan said.

'No, let's not. Let's not keep calm. This is not about keeping calm,' Alan said.

'Hell. Hell. Hell. Hell. Hell,' Constance said.

Headphones, mouth screwed up, looked at each in turn.

And then – a scream. A high-pitched desolate scream. One that seemed to bounce around the room, piercing everyone in the heart.

Sheppard glanced at Constance. But he already knew it wasn't her.

It was Mandy. In the bathroom.

And, just like that, things got worse.

8

The scream seemed to go on forever, but at some point it was over and then there was silence. And somehow the silence seemed much worse. No one moved – Alan and Ryan frozen in their conversation, Headphones peeking round the desk, and Constance looking towards the bathroom.

Sheppard's first reaction was to jolt forward at the sound. The handcuffs ground into his wrists and he yelped in pain. His flight response was overwhelming. He was not a man who wore panic and fear well. Even the moments when he woke up in a cold sweat, his heart beating three times too fast, and thinking that maybe he had finally overdone it, he always secretly knew he would pull through. But here, in this room, he was scared – genuinely scared.

There was a crashing sound as Mandy re-entered his field of vision, backing away from the alcove and bumping into Constance.

Constance pushed her away selfishly, like she was diseased.

Mandy looked to Sheppard. Her eyes were glassy reflections of themselves as tears streamed down her face.

She was a pale white colour and her skin was slick with sweat.

'What? What is it?' Sheppard said.

Ryan saw it before anyone else, and rushed to Mandy just as she was about to collapse. He caught her just in time.

'There's . . . in the bath . . .' Her voice was small.

'What?' Sheppard said, leaning forward as far as he could.

'A man. I think . . . a dead man.'

Sheppard felt the bed drop out from under him – freefalling through nothingness. But, of course, he wasn't.

A snort of derision. Not exactly the response he expected, but Alan seemed to be chuckling to himself. 'A dead man. A body in the bathtub. We've all been through a lot. We're all jumpy – we need to keep our cool here. The mind is a fragile thing.' He went over to Mandy and tapped her on the arm – a curt attempt at comforting her.

Through tears, Mandy looked at him. 'There is. A man. A man in a brown suit.'

'Well, if there is a man, who's to say he's not sleeping like we all were.'

Mandy gritted her teeth. 'You're more than welcome to take a look.'

Alan frowned. He straightened one of his cufflinks absent-mindedly and cleared his throat. 'Very well then.'

Sheppard watched Mandy as Alan disappeared around the corner. The girl was silently weeping and turned around to bury her face in Ryan's shoulder. Sheppard believed her completely. 'Alan, don't go in there.'

But it was too late. He heard the bathroom door open.

Sheppard's eyes drifted as he tried to focus his hearing on what was happening in the bathroom. He couldn't move more than two inches, and now the situation had changed. He found himself looking at the TV and had to look for a few seconds before he realised what was different. It was on – the TV was on. The last time he had looked at it, it had been blank. But sometime between then and now, it had started showing a gold mantra in the centre of the screen.

We hope you enjoy your stay! in a loopy, almost illegible, scrawl.

And there was something else in the corner. A little blue bar with white numbers, like something you would see when you connected a very old VCR. Sheppard had to screw up his eyes to see it. 'YOUR PAY-PER-VIEW STARTS IN: 00:00:57' Counting down – less than a minute. How did the TV turn on? And what was the pay-per-view?

Sheppard opened his mouth to tell someone – anyone. But at that moment, the bathroom door opened and Alan reappeared. His face mirrored Mandy's almost perfectly. He took off his glasses and wiped them with a cloth he took out of his upper pocket.

'It appears the situation is slightly graver than I first thought.'

Ryan detached himself from Mandy and started forward.

Alan put up a hand. 'Save yourself some sleepless nights, son.'

37

Ryan took a beat, and nodded.

'He's face-down, so I couldn't tell much, but there's blood – a lot of blood. Around the torso,' Alan said, plainly. Sheppard wondered if that was the tone of voice he used in court. 'No one else goes in there. Believe me, you don't want any part in this.'

Sheppard didn't know what to say, so a question slipped out. 'Did you recognise him?'

Alan's eyes snapped to him. 'Now that's an interesting question to ask.'

'There has to be a reason we're all here. I just . . .'

'What are you hiding, Mr Sheppard? I'm supposing you know all of this already. I'm supposing this is all some kind of sick game and I'm supposing we've all been roped into it against our will. Anything to say for yourself?'

Sheppard stared at him, walking the line between anger and fear. And he only half noticed the fact that the TV screen had changed.

And a new voice cut in. Slightly muffled. Coming through the TV speakers. 'No. Yes and yes.' Every face in the room turned towards the TV. A profile on the TV screen, but Sheppard's brain had to catch up to puzzle out who. It was a man, but his face was concealed behind a garish and colourful cartoon horse mask – like something you would see on Halloween. The eye holes were cut out, so this cartoon had big green human eyes. It was unsettling – gross, and Sheppard felt a shiver of disgust and fear.

The man on the TV laughed. 'Glad to see we're all getting along.'

9

'Hello everyone,' the horse man said. His voice was slick and smooth and the bad speakers on the TV gave it a detached, otherworldly cadence. 'Hello Morgan.'

Someone yelped. Constance – he thought it was Constance, although he couldn't really tell. His full attention was on the horse mask. He didn't know why, but he just knew. They were all in serious trouble, and he couldn't shake the feeling that he was worst of all.

'What is this?' Alan said, stepping forward to the TV. 'Who are you?'

Was this a conversation? Or a recording?

The horse mask reacted. A conversation then. 'You don't know me, not yet at least. But I know you. I know all of you. Especially you, Morgan Sheppard. I have been following your work very closely. It's hard not to.'

Eyes on him, like always. Was this a fan – a deranged, obsessed fan? Sheppard had had his fair share of oddball supporters over the years, and he had heard horror stories about others.

'What's happening?' Sheppard heard himself say. 'What do you want?' Something was very wrong here – more than it had ever been in his life.

The mask heard him. That meant there was a microphone. Maybe a camera. Somewhere — most likely watching since they woke up.

'How the mighty have fallen,' the horse mask said. Enjoying this — the sick bastard was enjoying this. 'Cuffed to a bed, with your mind racing to every eventuality — every possible way you could get out of this. With your instincts, I'm surprised you haven't bitten off your own hands and gone barrelling through the front door by now.'

Sheppard faltered. He hadn't exactly done that, but he had ripped at his wrists. 'What did you do to us?'

The horse mask ignored him. 'Do you ever look at yourself, Morgan Sheppard? Do you ever look in the mirror and see the drug-addled insipid attention whore you've become? A life governed by television contracts and YouTube comments. Stepping all over other people.'

'You put us here?' Trying to regain the conversation. Not wanting to hear anymore.

'And yet some still call you "Detective". Even after everything. You're the bastard child of a Conan Doyle nightmare. You're not fit for the word.'

'You put us here.' *Stop, please stop.*

'Of course I did, you idiot.' The horse mask twisted as the man crooked his neck. 'You see, I'm here to see if you can live up to your supposed reputation. Or more accurately, your self-proclaimed one. *Resident Detective*, rather gauche.'

'What is it talking about?' Mandy said, shooting Sheppard an unsure look.

40

Sheppard didn't hear. Thoughts, too many thoughts, swimming in a dead sea.

The horse mask cleared his throat, although he already had all the attention. 'As you probably know by now, you have been checked into a hotel room. The Great Hotel in Central London, to be exact. You are on the forty-fourth floor. It's not a luxury room but my people have made a few modifications.

'Firstly, they sealed the doors, the ducts and the window. There is no way out of the room, unless under my express orders. You cannot escape, unless I want you to. In the event of a fire, well . . .' He stopped to make a guttural chuckle. 'Secondly, they did some DIY and covered the room in soundproofing. You've already managed to make quite a noise with the screaming and the banging, but rest assured that no one will hear and no one will come. You could make the loudest noise in the world and not a soul on the other side of that wall would hear.

'It took a lot to get you all here. More than a few trips in luggage containers. Luckily none of you woke up. The point is the staff think that there is a very exclusive party going on in this room and have been asked to leave you alone. If for any reason you manage to contact the front desk, it'll be the woman you have probably already heard.'

'The woman?' Ryan said, looking to Sheppard.

Sheppard took a moment. 'There . . . was a woman on the phone. I thought she was one of those automated things, but . . . She . . . That's how I woke up.'

'She's one of my people. Of course she is. And now she

41

has disabled all calls going in or out of this room . . .'

'She said something about next. *Can't wait to see what you do next.* What's happening next?'

The horse mask stopped. No way he could tell, but he imagined a look of disdain. 'Today, we are going to be playing a little game of Murder. You've already found that one of your fellow guests is no longer with us. In fact, he has been brutally murdered by one of my associates. And here's the snap: that associate – the murderer – is in the room with you right now. One of these people is a murderer. The others are not – red herrings, macguffins, whatever you want to call them.'

What? The killer – of the man in the bathtub. The killer was in the room?

'Take a look around you, Morgan. Five people. Five suspects. One killer. One of these things is not like the other.'

Sheppard wasn't the only one glancing around. The others were too and now they were slowly separating – eyes darting as they moved into their own safe space.

He knew where this was going.

'So here's the deal, Morgan Sheppard. Seems you are the actual definition of *resident detective* in this room. I'll give you three hours. Three hours to solve the murder, to find out which of your fellow guests has killed a man in cold blood.'

'Why are you doing this? Why should I do this?' *It's my fault. It's all my fault everyone's here.*

The horse mask made that chuckle again – low and humourless. 'You never are a man to do something pro bono. Boring people need a reason to do unboring things. There's always got to be something to incentivise. Well, how's this? When it begins, a timer will start. The timer on the table next to you.' Sheppard looked down at it and then back to the horse mask. 'And there's no way to stop it until it ticks all the way down to zero.'

Sheppard was silent.

The mask was silent.

And finally, Mandy's voice came up. 'What happens at zero?'

'If Morgan Sheppard doesn't correctly identify the murderer in three hours, then you all die. And not just everyone in the room. Everyone in the hotel. My people have placed explosives around the structure of the building. I press a button and the Great Hotel becomes a Great Mess.'

Various cries of disgust rang out. Who from – everyone? He didn't know. He wasn't in the room anymore. He was somewhere else – a blank place with only him and the man on the TV.

'It's school holidays, Morgan. How many tourists do you think are staying here? How many young families – how many kids who just want to see *Wicked* and go to Hamleys? All going boom.'

'You're sick,' Alan said. 'Depraved.'

The mask twisted round again. 'Three hours. One murder. Should be easy for the good Sheppard. Really it would be a relief to have a few hundred deaths off my conscience. But rules are rules. And just like promises, they must be stuck to. Otherwise, there would be chaos.

Although I suppose this time there's chaos either way.'

He could use a drink right now. Some of his pills. Things were too real, and they always helped with that.

'Speaking of rules, there's a rule book in the bedside drawer, should you forget anything. But it's really quite simple. Three hours. Get the wrong answer, I blow up the building. Refuse to co-operate, I blow up the building. Cause too much of a headache, I blow up the building. You step one foot out of line – I. Blow. Up. The. Building. Got it?'

A sudden movement. Ryan pelted for the door. He disappeared around the corner and Sheppard heard him banging.

'Let us out. Let us out now,' Ryan shouted.

'Someone clearly wasn't listening,' the mask said.

'Hey. Let us out now.' More banging. 'Please, someone,' said Ryan, 'Let us out – now.'

The mask resumed, eyes front, talking to Sheppard directly. 'You can't do an investigation in chains. Forgive me for even handcuffing you in the first place. You're just a little . . . unpredictable. Addicts always are.'

That word. Addict. Not a good word.

'Besides, thought you might find a use for some handcuffs.'

Ryan reappeared.

'You're crazy,' Sheppard said. 'Insane.'

'Means a lot coming from you.' Sarcasm now? Impossible to tell in the mask's monotone. 'You'll find a key in the rulebook beside you. They'll unlock the cuffs. And then we can get this show on the road.'

44

'Please, let us go. Just let us go.' Straining on the cuffs. Thrashing out with his body. Until the real question came out. 'Who are you?'

The mask studied him for so long, he didn't think he was getting a response.

'I'll give you two minutes grace period before the games begin. Because I'm a good guy.'

The TV went black.

10

This wasn't real — it couldn't be. And yet it was.

In turn, they all faced him, looking like he had answers. The room seemed bigger now. They had all claimed their own place in it. They had been thrust together and then torn apart. Suspicion was etched on every face.

'What—?'

'I don't—?'

'But—?'

Voices running together. He couldn't focus. He had to focus. He shut his eyes, and took a deep breath. When he opened them again, Ryan was making his way down the left side of the bed. He opened the top drawer and took out a folder marked 'Rules'. He opened it. Sure enough, he took out a small key. He put the folder on the bed, and shrugged at Sheppard.

The key had been so close. Yet so far.

Sheppard gave him a sad smile, as the young man reached up.

'Now wait a second.'

Ryan stopped. *No, no, no.* He looked around.

Alan was watching them both, with his familiar scowl.

'Maybe it would be in our best interests not to let this man loose.'

'C'mon,' Sheppard shouted.

'Why?' Ryan said.

'I'm just saying,' Alan said, 'there's no reason why we should believe everything we're hearing. What if this man is behind everything? What did you . . .' He looked around to Mandy. 'Blonde, what did you say before?'

'What?'

'You thought this was all some set-up, some publicity stunt? Well, why not?'

'You went into the bathroom,' Mandy said, 'you saw that . . . man.'

Alan shrugged. 'I'm just saying, what if the only dangerous person in this room is already in cuffs?'

Sheppard groaned. He needed to be free. 'Are you serious? You heard what the TV said? You need to let me go now.' *And then what? I can't do this. I just can't.*

'We don't *need* to do any such thing,' Alan said. 'This whole thing is your fault, no matter which way you slice it. You television types are all the same. If this mask man is telling the truth, then you're the only one who can save us? Give me strength!'

'And what do you think is going to happen in three hours?' Ryan said, turning back towards Sheppard. *Yes. Just use the key. Use the key.*

'Empty threats,' Alan said. He actually believed every word coming out of his own mouth. 'We're supposed to take a man in a horse mask on his word?'

'It's all we have right now,' Sheppard said. 'He put us

here. He put us *all* here, and if you're all the same as me, here is goddamn surely not where I want to be.'

'God—' Constance started.

'Sorry,' Sheppard said. 'Who's to say his threats aren't real?'

Ryan nodded at him. 'That's good enough for me.'

'You're making a mistake,' Alan said, even as Ryan reached up to the cuffs again. *Yes. Thank you God.*

Ryan fiddled for a moment and Sheppard thought, for a horrifying moment, that maybe it was the wrong key. Maybe the mask was just toying with them. But then there was a *click* and Sheppard's limp arms fell down to his sides. Sliding down the bed, he took a moment to right himself.

He stretched his arms, getting the blood back into them. Peeking out from his shirt sleeves, he saw his raw, red wrists, crusted over with dried blood. They stung to the touch.

'Thanks,' Sheppard said, and Ryan nodded.

He tried to scrabble off the bed, fighting with the duvet, putting his legs over the side. He stood up too quickly. The world swirled around him. He put a hand on the wall to keep himself from falling.

The room corrected. Everything seemed smaller from higher up – the people less intimidating. He put a hand up to his chin and he found prickly stubble, longer than he remembered it.

They were watching him. He knew that. He needed a plan. *We need to get out of here.*

He turned slowly. Didn't want to upset his eyes again.

The bedside table. The clock. Still on 03:00:00. Hadn't started yet. The two minutes. How much time had passed? The binder saying 'Rules' on the bed where Ryan had put it. It was large. Ryan had only looked at the first one. He reached for it.

It was heavy – packed with pages. It would take over three hours to read it all.

But this thought was eradicated the moment he opened the folder. On the first page were four simple words – LISTEN TO THE HORSE. And then – nothing. He rifled through quickly. Blank page after blank page. Nothing. No more rules. A joke. Except one last sentence on the last page.

THE BOY LIED.

What the hell was that supposed to mean? Sheppard threw down the folder in disgust – it hitting the bed and bouncing off onto the floor with a thud.

'There's nothing – there's nothing else.'

What was he expecting?

'What now?' Ryan said.

Back to the room. All the lost faces, even Headphones, watching him. How much had she heard with those head-phones cupped on her ears?

Sheppard didn't answer. He pushed past Ryan, and towards the alcove. The head of the room was just as he imagined it. There was the main door, a closet on the right sitting open with bare coat hangers, extra blankets and a small safe and there was a door to the left which must lead to the bathroom. *Don't think about what's in there. Just don't.* A dead body – he couldn't face a dead body. Not until he knew he absolutely had to.

He ignored the bathroom and went to the main door – first seeing the fire escape information plastered on it, the rendezvous point of Floor 44. The door handle had a hooked message, Do Not Disturb or Please Clean My Room, whatever your preference. He tried the handle, relishing how cold the steel felt on his hands. To feel something again. He pulled. Nothing. Pulled again. Nothing.

Mandy was right. The key card light was red. Could it be overridden? Had the mask man hacked it somehow? He looked around. There was indeed a place to put the card to activate the lights, but it wasn't there. On a whim, Sheppard flicked the light switch. The lights came on. *What?* He turned them off again. That didn't make any sense.

He looked at the door again. It would be impossible to break down. It was a fire door and it opened inwards not outwards. He ran his finger across the edge of the door. He thought he felt the draught from outside – the corridor – but he could have been imagining it.

He looked through the peephole out into a hotel corridor in a fisheye lens. Muted carpet, nothing but more doors and doors left and right. Across from him, a door labelled 4402. He put his hand into a fist, and it made it halfway to the door before he stopped. There was no point hammering. It had already been tried and deemed pointless.

Claustrophobia crept in. No matter how big the room was, it felt suddenly very small. A drink would be great right about now and maybe a pill or two. He needed to get out – why was his mind on the mini-bar?

He wheeled around. All eyes were still on him, watching him with interest. No one looked like they could help – even Alan had nothing to say. He went over to the window and they parted for him. Maybe they were hoping he knew the way out. He had been in many hotels in his time and he had never entered or exited any way other than the main door.

He put his hands on the windowsill, looking out to the London skyline – a sunny day. The London Eye peeking up from the tops of buildings, Waterloo off to the left, Westminster to the right. They were high up enough that all these landmarks were framed by the window.

He wondered if they could get a signal to someone. A tall building was in the centre of the frame, running vertically against their own building, blocking out most of the sunlight. It looked like an office building. He screwed up his eyes to try and see in the windows. There was no one in the office – in fact, it looked all packed up. There was no one there.

Next . . . what was next? The main door was a no go. The window was impossible. The vents? Maybe the vents?

He looked to the bed and the wall above it. It took a few moments to locate it as someone had painted the vent the same shade of cream, but he saw it.

He climbed onto the bed steadily, hoping he wouldn't fall. His wrists protested as they rubbed against his cuffs but he maintained his balance and then went to the wall. The vent was large enough for someone to crawl through, it looked like. He managed to loop his fingers around the central bar of the grille and pull. No give. He looked at the edges. Flatbed screws on all of them. He tried getting a hold of them, but there was no way they were budging.

He turned. 'Does anyone have anything in their pockets?' Sheppard said. 'Like a penny? Some change?' Everyone checked. They were in their own little worlds. After a few seconds, they returned blank faces – turned up nothing.

Trust was gone. And it wasn't coming back.

'Here, try this,' Ryan said, and reached up and handed him the handcuff key.

Sheppard turned back, trying to work the key into the slots of the screws. It was too thick and he quickly lost grip.

Nothing. Door. Window. Grate. No way out.

There had to be something else – something he hadn't tried. Short of banging on the walls, he couldn't think of anything. He scanned the room, tossing the key back to Ryan. No other exit. Just a normal hotel room.

But it wasn't quite. It had stopped being normal a long time ago. Ever since the horse mask had decided to play a little game. But if the horse mask knew anything, he would know Sheppard couldn't do what he asked. Sheppard hadn't been a real detective in a long time. He was just a frontman. A man who talked about things that didn't matter, made bold predictions about *things that didn't matter*.

He wants to see you fail.

So what was he to do? Curl up in the corner and prepare to die?

Because as Sheppard looked around, he didn't see a hotel room.

He saw a coffin.

11

His life had gone too quickly. A blink of an eye and he was here, in this room. Fame rushed by, and now, for the first time ever, he wished he wasn't famous anymore. Even though that's all he had ever wanted. He had been fourteen when he met his agent for the first time. Three years, his parents had tried to keep him away from the limelight and that only made him want it more.

'Hey, little guy,' the man said. Decades ago. But very close.

Was it his fault – the man he would come to know as Douglas, the man who he considered his only friend? Was it his parents' fault? Or was it him, himself?

Douglas had taken him out for ice cream. He had asked if he was too old for ice-cream but being fourteen years old didn't make ice-cream taste any worse. People stared, they must have seen him on TV, people were still talking about what he did – it was awesome.

'What do you want most in the world, Morgan?'

'I want to be famous.'

'You already are, son. What you did a few years back – that boggles the mind. You want fame? You got it. Now, staying famous – well, that's something I might be able to help you with.'

And Morgan smiled. He always smiled.

Years later, in this room, and Sheppard thought he might never smile again. Fame? Wash it all away. Be done with it. The show, the book, the newspaper articles. *Just never let me end up here.* Because now he would be famous for a whole new reason. For killing people.

A sharp beeping noise pulled him out of his self-pity. Beeping somewhere in the room. Sheppard got off the bed and looked around, locating the noise – the bedside table. The cylindrical digital clock had started counting down. 03:00:00 had turned to 02:59:54. Six seconds. More – already gone. Slipping away in front of his eyes. The beeping stopped. The countdown didn't.

Three hours to solve a murder.

Sheppard looked around. Ryan was watching him intently, a dangerous look of hope in his eyes. He was probably thinking that Sheppard looked like this a lot on his TV show, but Ryan was mistaking blankness (reading the autocue) for thoughtfulness. The autocue was always Sheppard's best friend – behind the little black box was a team of people, the real brains. That's all television was. Smoke and mirrors.

'You can do it, right?' Ryan said. 'You can get us out?'

All that was behind Ryan was the others. And he could see that hope was infecting them all. Even Alan looked slightly less furious. Mandy was worst of all – she looked almost certain.

I can't get anyone out. There is no way out.

The murderer – in this room.

None of them looked capable of murder – but one was.

55

Sheppard looked down at his hands, unable to look at the others anymore. His hands were ever so slightly shaking – his body and his mind aching for a drink and some pills. His shoulders ached in response. But that wasn't his biggest problem, was it?

You can't do it.

His one real victory was twenty-five years ago. A lot could happen in twenty-five years, and a lot had. But as he thought back, not a lot happened of much consequence. Was his really a wasted life – only half lived? Maybe this was to be a fitting end.

He thought back to all the rookie books he'd read – books on how to be a detective. Most information gleamed from TV dramas and novels. A murder investigation was a big thing. Not for one person. There was no such thing as Sherlock Holmes, Miss Marple, Hercule Poirot. They didn't exist in the real world.

The hero saves the day. Every single time. Rubbish. *But then –*

What if he could actually do it? The odds weren't in his favour but – three hours. Five people. One dead man. That couldn't be impossible, right? Unlikely, but not impossible.

That's what I like about you, Morgan. You're a bastard. Douglas had said that once, and he had never truly understood it until now. The masked man was giving him a chance to become more than he ever could on his own. The chance to truly be a hero.

Sheppard looked up. The hope wasn't rotting people's faces anymore because he felt it too. He remembered a quote from some book he had read long ago: *'Murder is the greatest crime anyone can ever commit. But at least it gives you a good place to start.'* He had laughed at it at the time — but it was true. He had to do it — go into the bathroom and confront what he knew was in there.

He pushed past Ryan and rounded the corner into the alcove. He paused in front of the bathroom door. He put his hand on the door handle and took a deep breath.

'What are you doing?' Mandy said.

Time was escaping from the room. They were standing in an hourglass, with hands out trying to catch the sand.

'I'm going to solve a murder,' he said, and found that he had one last smile in him.

12

The bathroom was dazzlingly bright compared to the murky bedroom. Sheppard put up an arm to shield his eyes as he shut the door behind him and glimpsed under his elbow. As his eyes adjusted, he saw the marble sink, the pristine toilet, the towels hanging on the heated rail, with more stacked up above it. He had been here before, many times, all over the world. He didn't have to look to his right to see the bath that could double as a shower, with containers of shower gel and shampoo clasped to the wall. But he didn't see any of that – the transparent cream shower curtain was pulled across it.

He didn't want to think about what was in the bath yet, so he found himself staring at his own reflection in the mirror above the sink. He stepped forward, reaching up to his face to confirm what he saw. He looked older than the last time he had seen himself. He had deep black bags under his eyes like shadows. His hair looked duller and his patchy stubble shrouded half his face. There were a lot more wrinkles, around his eyes, his mouth, his brow. A stranger wearing his face.

As he rested on the sink, his hand crunched something. He looked down to the little bars of soap and tubes of toothpaste, but those weren't what he felt. He lifted his hand to find a pair of glasses.

His stomach dropped as he picked them up and turned them over in his hands. From any angle it was unmistakeable – these glasses were his. He was short-sighted, and he didn't wear them nearly as much as he should. He never wore them in public. Never. No one knew he needed glasses, not even Douglas.

He looked up to meet his own eyes.

Who is doing this?

He shook off the thought. Not now. He had a job to do. Just be grateful he had them. He picked up the glasses and put them on. He always thought he looked stupid in them. Never mind that now.

He rolled up his shirt sleeves, revealing the real damage the handcuffs had done. It looked like he was wearing two jagged scarlet bracelets.

He turned the tap on and put his left wrist under the stream of cold water.

An 'ah' escaped him. It stung. He put his right wrist under.

When he was finished, he reached down to the toilet paper. The end was folded into a triangle, just as he knew it would be. He dabbed at his wrists and the paper came away red.

He turned to the bath. He took a deep breath – there was really no escaping it now. It was large and the base was pure white, except there was a small line trickling down to the floor. It had only got halfway before drying up. It was red, a colour to match his wrists. Blood.

There was no blood on the shower curtain at least, but as Sheppard stepped towards it, he saw an ominous shape through it – a black mass, distorted by the curtain.

His nose picked up the unmistakeable smell – dark and metallic.

Before he could stop himself, he reached up and grabbed the curtain. Counting in his head – one, two, three. One quick motion, and he drew it across the bath.

The smell intensified as he forced his eyes down into the bath – and he saw. God, he saw. And he knew why Mandy screamed as he stifled one himself.

A man in a brown suit, lying face down in the drained bath. He looked uncomfortable, but you could be forgiven for thinking he was sleeping – if not for the blood. All the blood. It was pooling around his torso, snaking out from underneath him – frozen as the liquid hit the cool air. There was so much – too much. It seemed to have made its way around the length of the tub, giving the illusion that this man was bathing in scarlet.

All that blood. *Focus on something else.*

The man was grey-haired and balding – clumps of grey and white stuck out of his head at odd angles and Sheppard could see the scalp beneath. The man's hands were by his side, flecked with blood and wrinkled. Sheppard tried not to think about what he had to do next – he bent down and reached into the bath, slowly, trying to stay as far away from the blood as possible. He pressed a finger to the old man's ice-cold wrist. He waited thirty seconds. No pulse. Had he really expected anything?

An old man. Dead. But how?

The wound was in the front – Sheppard had to turn him over. He felt sick just thinking it but it had to be done. He awkwardly got to his knees using the side of the bath to steady himself. As he reached the floor, he lost his balance and his hand slid into the bath. He lurched forward and felt the cold thickness of blood.

He withdrew his hand in disgust. Before he could stop himself, he wiped his hand on his shirt, a smear of red down his chest, regretting it instantly as the smell travelled up from the smear, promising to stay with him.

He recovered. How was he going to do this? He reached both hands into the bath, one gripping the man's nearest side, the other reaching over to the furthest. *Do it quickly. Do it quickly. Do it quickly.*

In one quick motion, he pushed with his knees, lifting the man. Then pulled with his hands. He used the slope of the bath to lever the weight. And the man slid down, resting face-up.

Don't look at the face. He couldn't bring himself to do it. The half-congealed blood squelched as the body came to rest on the bottom of the tub.

He focused on the man's torso, thinking back to all the crime scene photographs he had seen on the show. Always still images. Taken in the past. Taken a long way away. Never right in front of him. Never there to smell and touch.

The man's suit lay open to reveal a light green shirt and a blue tie. At least he thought. The colours were all stained with red. The suit ruined. Hard to tell where the blood was actually coming from. Too much of it. But it seemed to be most around the lower area of the torso.

Looking closer, the shirt was ripped, lower left. Peering into the tub, as close as he dared, he could see the wound. Two wounds, two deep wounds above the waistband of the man's trousers. Gashes, so deep they probably hit some internal organ. Intestines, maybe? Sheppard didn't know. Straight gashes. Narrow. Stab wounds. Maybe a knife?

Two. Someone had buried a knife in this man, pulled it out, and buried it again. Schup. Schup. Once for safety. Probably aiming for the same place. A hell of a strong attack for so much blood.

That was it. That was all he could assume. A knife attack. Would a better person know? Know from this exactly who killed him? Who, out there, had the right MO?

As he thought, he found his eyes drifting up the man's chest. His old dusty suit. Clashing tie and shirt. To his face. His white stubble. His eyes shut. His –

Sheppard jumped back from the bath, slamming into the heated towel rail and falling on his arse with a great *thwack*. It was a pain he didn't even feel. He scrabbled with his limbs and found his way to the corner, squashing himself next to the toilet. He let out a long, drawn-out gasp.

No . . .

13

Before . . .

He was dropped off at the foot of the drive. They got out of there as quick as they could, speeding away as though they'd just dumped a broken washing machine. They didn't even look him in the eye anymore like he was possessed by something.

The house looked nice – big. The nice side of London. Not what he wanted when he grew up, but nice. A quiet neighbourhood.

He made his way up the gravel drive, making sure to crunch all the way. The front door opened before he even got there. Like the man on the other side was waiting.

He was old – wrinkly. He looked like he dyed his hair as some grey was creeping through the brown. His eyes were kind and green and framed by a round pair of glasses. He looked like the kind of man who read the paper every morning, grumbled at the weather and saw doing his taxes as an adventure. But he looked nice enough. A nice man, for a nice house, for a nice place. How boring.

'You must be Morgan,' he said, as he came to a stop on the doorstep.

He didn't say anything.

'Was that your parents in the car? I had hoped to talk to them.'

He was welcome to them.

'No matter, I'll catch them some other time.'

The man looked down at him.

'You're a quack?' he said.

The man laughed. 'I am a therapist, yes.'

'They said I needed to see a quack. That was the deal.'

'Well, sometimes we all need to talk through our problems. But I won't push you to talk about anything you don't want to. When you've been through something like you have, sometimes it's good to have an avenue to explore it.'

Morgan just looked at him.

The man seemed to visibly convulse. 'Silly me, I haven't introduced myself.' He held out a wrinkled hand. 'I'm Simon Winter.'

Morgan took it. The texture of a used tea bag. But he shook it nonetheless. And when he was asked inside, he went.

14

No ...

How long had it been? Five years? Six? Simon Winter lay in the bath tub – dead.

How was this possible? How was this happening?

Sheppard couldn't breathe. It couldn't be him. It just couldn't. He crawled over to the bath, fighting instinct all the way. He peered over the edge. Simon Winter. Unmistakeable. Lying there, his life streaming out of his gut.

Sheppard's vision blurred as tears gushed down his face. He gave out a sound that could easily be a dying animal. *No. No. No. Not him.* How did this happen – how was Winter here, in this room?

Questions – too many questions – but in front of his eyes, there was a constant fact. Simon Winter, his old psychologist, was dead. This had to be more than just a body – this had to be a message. The man in the horse mask knew him and knew what Winter had meant to him.

Sheppard covered his mouth with his trembling hand as a fresh whimper came out. Winter must have been so scared – dying all alone. He took off his glasses and wiped his eyes.

He looked at Winter again. A message – a message that

the horse mask didn't just know Sheppard. He knew him well — almost too well. The speech, the glasses no one knew he had and now Simon Winter, served up for him.

The tears just kept coming. No one knew he had seen Simon Winter for the better part of his life. But here the old man was. And Winter had almost certainly died because of Sheppard. When was the last time he had seen Winter alive? What were the last words they had said to each other? All he could remember is that they weren't kind.

The old man had his part to play. Every murder mystery needed a corpse. And every corpse is a fresh mystery. Would Winter still be alive if . . .?

No. *Can't think like that, Morgan*. Almost like Winter was speaking to him. *Think like that, and you're as dead as I am*.

Sheppard brushed his eyes, and reached down to check Winter's pockets, forcing himself to remember the time limit. He reached into the left pocket, which was soaked in blood. It felt like he was pressing his hand into the wound itself.

He felt sick.

There was nothing in the pocket, so he pulled his hand free, trying to ignore the resistance from the sticky, congealed blood.

Right pocket. Wallet. He took it out, looked through it. The usual cards — Oyster card, bank card, some reward card for a bookstore. Nothing to tell him what he didn't know already. Dr Simon Winter, sixty-five years old.

He put the wallet back and then paused, remembering

something he couldn't quite put his finger on. Instinctively, he took two fingers and clutched at the left side of the suit, lifting it up. The inside pocket. He reached inside with his free hand, to find what he had thought would be there.

He pulled out a small pocket notebook. After all these years, he still kept it in the same place. During their sessions, Winter would reach into his jacket to pull out the notebook, write a few words, and then replace it. It became a quirk that delighted and frustrated Sheppard in equal measure – why didn't Winter just keep it out if he was going to write in it every few minutes?

The notebook was relatively untouched with blood, although it did seem very shabby and old. Without a second thought, he opened it up and flicked through it expecting to find brand new notes. Instead, he found faded writing that looked years old. He flicked through notes on various patients, until he turned a page to find his name.

Morgan Sheppard. *Wait, what?* He hadn't seen Simon Winter in years, but he was carrying a notebook with notes from one of his sessions. The notebook had to be years old.

Sheppard glanced down at the notes – feeling as though he was violating some kind of privacy. The notes were dated 06/06/1997 and they detailed one session with him. Winter seemed to have written down standard things – Sheppard's mood, temperament, what he said. But somehow, in stronger pen strokes, certain words were underlined – dotted all over the page. 'Aggressive. Muddled. A new dream about . . .'

The words seemed to be underlined with no real purpose. Why underline 'A new dream about–' and then not underline what the dream was about? He was asking questions that were decades old. What was more important was why Winter had this notebook with him now? Was it another message from the man in the horse mask? Had he already tampered with the body? How could Sheppard trust anything in this room? How could he trust anything at all?

Sheppard slipped the notebook into his pocket, not being able to think straight while his dead therapist was staring at him. Winter had been more than that though – Winter had been his friend. A friend when he couldn't rely on anyone else, not even his parents. Did Winter remember Sheppard fondly? Or did all that happened cloud his perception? Because after all, Sheppard had taken him for granted. Just as he always did. Winter didn't look in pain – at least there was that.

'I'm sorry,' Sheppard said, choking on a fresh bout of tears.

15

Sheppard crashed out of the bathroom, losing his balance and almost going tumbling into the closet. The image of Simon Winter lying in that bath was imprinted on his vision – a photo negative seared into a life.

Sheppard. This puzzle was all based around Sheppard, and all he could think of were impossible questions with impossible answers. Winter, blood, sunlight, London, Paris, handcuffs, glasses and a horse mask – all swirling around in his head. A mess. And he had three hours to straighten it out – no, less than three.

Sheppard remembered something the French woman had said in the red room. She had called him a good man, and she had meant it.

A good man. But she hadn't known him – not even slightly.

Had she been in on it? Had she been tasked to get him into that room? What he'd felt for her had been real – or as real as he could manage nowadays – but was she stringing him along? He had made it easy for her – falling for it hook, line and arsehole.

Sheppard shut the bathroom door as though it might contain the horror within. But no, it was too late. He looked up to see it had infected the whole room – everyone a little paler and a little less alive.

Constance was sitting on the desk chair, silently clutching the Bible like her life depended on it, Headphones was still under the desk, Alan and Ryan were standing by the window talking in hushed breaths – Mandy was the only one to look at him as he came back into the room, waiting for him to come out.

'You saw him?'

Someone in here killed Simon Winter. Someone in here with him.

'Yes,' Sheppard said, his voice catching. 'I saw him.'

Was Winter killed in the bathtub – surely he had to be with all the blood? But there hadn't looked like any scuffle. Did that mean the killer had been standing in the bathtub too? That didn't make any sense. The blood was mostly dry – how long did that mean it had been there? Was Winter killed before or after Sheppard was taken? He couldn't do much without a timeline – something to measure everything against.

Someone laughed – a breezy chuckling. Sheppard and Mandy looked around to see Constance spinning around in the desk chair and laughing.

'Shut up,' Sheppard said.

Everyone could hear everything in the room. Sheppard could pick out what Alan and Ryan were saying. They were talking about the logistics of breaking the window, and what that would actually do for an escape attempt. No secrets. The room was an amphitheatre – you could hear every single word uttered from every corner.

70

'Mandy,' Sheppard lowered his voice as much as possible while taking Mandy aside, although he knew everyone could still hear. 'Do you know anything about that woman?'

'Her?' Mandy said. 'The crazy one.'

'Yeah.' He didn't expect much but Mandy nodded.

'Well . . . yeah,' she said, in a tone as though it were obvious, 'she's pretty famous. I mean, not like you famous, but still . . . You've never seen *Rain on Elmore Street*?'

A twinge of familiarity but nothing concrete.

'It's a musical on the West End. The Lyceum, I think. That's Constance Ahearn – she's the lead.'

Vague recollection of passing the theatre, the grand awnings, the sign lit up in the darkness while people queued around the block. *Rain on Elmore Street*.

Constance's laughing punctuated the memory. Sheppard guessed her acting was the flamboyant kind.

'I need you to go and try to keep her quiet.'

Mandy frowned. 'I suppose . . .'

'Please. I need to think.'

Mandy gave a curt nod. She went over to Constance and put an arm around her. She whispered something into Constance's ear. The woman stopped laughing, got up and followed Mandy around to the right side of the bed. They sat down, with their backs to everyone else. Mandy was good at this.

'You saw the body?'

Sheppard jumped at Ryan's voice. Ryan and Alan had turned their attention to him. 'Yes. I had to see it – him. I had to see him.'

You're not telling them. Why are you not telling them? Is it for them, or is it for you?

What would it accomplish – other than more needless speculation that would get in the way of actually escaping? 'It looks like he died of a knife wound. Well, two knife wounds – in his gut.'

Ryan looked at him. 'Who is he?'

And there it was. The choice – two paths, two possibilities. 'I don't know,' Sheppard said. *God, help me.* 'I – I'm still working out what to do here.'

'But I might know the guy,' Ryan said.

And Sheppard raised an eyebrow, as Alan clapped a hand on Ryan's shoulder.

As if he was summoned by the scent of unjustness, Alan cut in between Ryan and Sheppard. 'Wait, son. Usually my opinions cost seven hundred an hour but this one's a freebie. Don't talk. Or do talk – I'm not your father. We are in a highly volatile situation, and anything uttered in this room is suspect. I'm sure Mr Sheppard knows that that means anything said here will not stand up in a court of law.'

'I just want to help,' Ryan said.

'Get that window open, that's what would help.'

'How would that help?' Sheppard said.

'We need to get a message to the outside world. If we break the window, maybe someone'll see it. Call the police.'

'Forty-four storeys up, no one in the building across from us, and someone'll see it?' Sheppard said.

Alan snorted. 'Better than anything you're doing. What are you doing anyway?'

'I . . . I'm working things out.' Sheppard hoped that

sounded a little less pathetic to Alan.

'Yeah, that's what I thought,' Alan said, smiling. 'You see, I know people like you. I see them every single day. Difference is they're usually handcuffed in a box instead of on a bed.' Wrists stinging to punctuate this. 'Everyone's a liar – to the world, to other people, to themselves. But you put yourself up on a TV screen and spread your own lies out into the world, just to make it a little more insufferable.

'You're the definition of a joke, Mr Sheppard. And your big detective act is not going to fly here. You can't even save yourself. Why the hell would you be able to save anyone else? And maybe, as that clock runs down, you should remember that. Remember that you are the reason we're here.'

He could suddenly feel every inch of his skin, slick and sticky. Obviously worse than he thought. Drowning in sweat. What he wouldn't give for a drink right now – even half a pill? It felt as if the strength was pouring out of him.

'I have to try,' he said, his voice weak, and hitching. Suddenly he felt a buzzing in his head, in his cheeks – weak, tired. He needed to sit down. He needed water.

'I know,' Alan said, shimmering in front of him, pulled Sheppard close to whisper in his ear, 'and watching you bumbling around this room searching for answers like an idiot will be the last bit of enjoyment I get from this sad mess of an existence.'

Alan released him. He rocked back on his legs. They felt impossibly thin, not enough to hold him up.

Faces turning to look at him.

And then the floor coming up to say hello.

16

Before . . .

He stared at himself in the mirror. There was something about viewing himself like this, with his stage make-up on looking almost impossibly young – the wrinkles papered over, the pot holes under the eyes filled in. Looking like a cartoon version of himself. But under studio lights, he would look perfect. The immaculate man.

Not the tired, bored man he usually was.

'Why are you here, Douglas?'

Douglas sat in the far corner of the room, reading the pamphlet all the audience members got before the show. The rule book. He threw it aside. 'What, I can't visit my favourite client?'

Sheppard smiled. Couldn't help it. 'Mm-hm.' A kind of *cut to the chase.*

'Look,' Douglas said, jumping up and pacing in the mirror, 'I just wanted to make sure you were okay after our last conversation.'

'I feel fine.'

'Good, good – that's great.' A thumbs up reflected to him. 'Because you were kind of saying some crazy stuff.'

'I'm not going to quit, Douglas. If that's what you want to hear.'

'I want to hear that you're happy,' Douglas said. 'You don't look happy.'

'I'm fine.'

The door opened behind him. The dogsbody stuck her head around it. 'Three minutes, Mr Sheppard.'

He nodded and she left.

Sheppard stood up, fiddling with his cufflinks. Douglas stepped forward, and gripped him by the shoulders.

'You've really got something here, Morgan. You've built something for yourself.'

Sheppard smiled. 'I know.' Reached into his suit and brought out his hipflask. He took a swig.

'That's my boy.' Douglas beamed. 'How's your shoulder? You taking the medication?'

'Yes, boss,' Sheppard said.

'Knock 'em dead out there.'

Sheppard nodded, laughed and left the room.

Walking through the back corridors of a TV studio was a lot like walking through the trenches. He walked the narrow line. People stopped when they saw him, wished him good luck. He smiled back at them. But he was thinking.

He'd got drunk. Told Douglas he wanted out. Douglas called it cold feet. He'd only been doing this six months. The show was a hit. But it was too much. It wasn't what he had thought it would be. It was too . . . too something. Too raw?

He'd fallen on the stairs going out of the club. Where all

their business meetings took place. Slammed his shoulder something terrible. Douglas recommended a doctor. Who recommended the pills.

He took the little capsule out of his pocket and popped two out. He took them. Made the pain go away. Maybe a little too well.

He made his way around the back of the stage. It was dark. But he saw the dogsbody with a headset on, holding up a hand. Behind her, the light. She smiled at him, her fingers counting down from four.

Four.

Three. He felt the booze and the pills kick in, helping his mouth form that trademark grin. Already felt like he'd done this forever. And forever would do.

Two. And that was okay, wasn't it?

One.

He skipped out onto the stage. The light drowning out anything past the set. An audience of rabid fans back there, silent. Just wanting to see him do their favourite dance. And who was he to deny them?

'Camera one,' he heard the director say, in his ear piece.

He turned his gaze to the camera on a crane contraption, sweeping overhead. 'Today on *Resident Detective*: Is international pop sensation Maria Bonnevart sneaking around with *Red Lions'* lead singer Matt Harkfold whilst being pregnant with *FastWatch*'s Chris Michael's child? I'll be reviewing the evidence later in the show. Also, we head over to the Real Crime Board to see how police in South London are reacting to the latest spree of robberies where perpetrators only seem interested in nicking industrial radiators. Let's hope the trail hasn't gone cold on that one.' Pause for laughter. Plenty. *Christ*. 'But first, in our Real Life segment, we meet Sarah who has reason to believe her husband Sean, of five years, has been seeing their babysitter behind her back. Let's see if I can shed some light on the situation. I'm Morgan Sheppard. This is *Resident Detective*.' Applause. The kind you can only describe as rapturous.

Sheppard stepped aside as a TV screen lowered from the ceiling and the title sequence started to play, and then was followed by a short VT about Sarah and Sean. This was only for the live audience of course. For people at home, the video was spliced with the live footage in the control room upstairs. Sheppard didn't pay attention to the video. He had seen it all before – his producer made him watch every VT before the show.

It was hard not to see these things as all the same. A wife, a husband, sexual intercourse – sometimes not with the right person. His team did some rooting around and told him whether the guy was guilty or not.

At least, that was the deal. But what had prompted that drunken desire to get the hell out? Sheppard had found that nine times out of ten, what his team told him was guesswork. Fifty-fifty.

They didn't do lie detectors like other shows did because Sheppard's reputation meant he 'didn't need them'.

Was Sean guilty? The cue cards in Sheppard's hands said yes.

Is Sean really guilty?

The VT ended and the TV rose up to the ceiling. Giving

way to a row of chairs that the production crew put on during the VT. Silence.

Well . . .

He looked out to the crowd. Invisible shapes in the darkness.

Choose what you become.

'Sheppard,' the director said. 'Snap out of it.'

'Well let's . . .' Sheppard said. 'Okay. Let's welcome Sarah onto the stage. Everybody give her a big hand.' He raised a hand as a woman walked out onto the stage.

Applause.

'Jesus Christ, Sheppard. You want to give me a heart attack?' In his ear.

The woman sat down in the centre seat. As she was told, probably. Young, pale and sad. Not made for the limelight. A girl who worked in the behind-the-scenes of the world. She gave a small wave to the audience.

Sheppard sat next to her as the applause died down.

'Now, Sarah, how are you?' Sheppard said. Conversing with her, projecting pretty much everywhere but.

'I'm okay,' Sarah said. Voice small and timid.

'Now, Sarah, you contacted me–' *the show* '–and told me about this, and I've–' *the team* '–been out investigating this for some time now. It seems like a bad situation.' *War is bad, death is bad – this is busywork*. 'Could you maybe just tell the audience your story in your own words?'

Sarah started talking, basically repeating the entire story that had just been told on the VT. Repetition was a key part of the show – didn't want anyone getting lost, and that way the team didn't have to think up too much content.

'. . . and that's when I confronted him about the text messages . . .' The text messages already. He needed to slow her up.

'Unbelievable,' Sheppard said. 'So you found text messages on his phone from this babysitter and confronted him about it?'

'Uh . . . yes,' Sarah said. Like she'd just said that. Because she'd just said that.

'And what did these text messages actually say?' Talking slowly.

Sarah put her head in her hands, muffling the microphone clipped onto the collar of her top.

'I know it's hard, Sarah. But I'm here for you. All these guys are here for you, aren't you?'

The audience gave out something that sounded like a sympathetic whoop prompted by the guy holding up the sign at the side of the stage. This had all been rehearsed in the pre-show. Now the crowd were eager. Chomping at the bit.

Sarah looked up at Sheppard again, her eyes streaming. 'They were organising meet-ups. At hotels, at bars, everywhere . . . Holiday Inns, Premier Inns, you know the cheapest places.'

Crap. Did she really have to say the names? 'Lock it down, Sheppard,' the director said, 'we can't have anyone on our arse.'

'Cheap hotels in the centre of London,' Sheppard said. Companies didn't like to be referenced on the show. Negative connotations. Say the name of a place, and people will associate it with affairs. 'Now was there anything about Sean and this girl's relationship in these texts?'

Sarah looked at the audience. 'He said that she was the love of his life.' A collective gasp. 'He said that he loved her like he'd never loved anyone before and one day they would run away together and take the child too.'

Another gasp. Parrots echoing each other. His adoring public. Was this really what he wanted? But the little boy he once was spoke up. *Are you kidding? This is what you've* always *wanted. This is what we've been working for all along.*

Sheppard looked at Sarah. A real woman. With real problems. He thought he had the solutions. Not a team of white-collared idiots backstage. Him.

Sarah looked at him. Really looked at him. *Are you the person you say you are?*

'SHEPPARD!' the director shouted, making Sheppard jump, 'Jesus fu-'

'Well . . . um . . .' Sheppard stumbled, looking from Sarah to the crowd, 'he sounds like a complete idiot, but let's not take my word for it. Shall we bring him out, ladies and gentlemen?' The audience cheered with the severity of a lynching mob.

Sheppard stood up and strode out to the edge of the stage, turning his back on the young man, who was walking out from behind the right side. The audience booed ferociously, and he waited until they'd calmed down to spin around on the heels of his shiny pointed shoes.

Sean looked like a lost puppy in the middle of the A1. He sat down slowly, as though the seat may be booby-trapped. He wore a grubby white T-shirt and ripped jeans. Probably dressed by the production team. He had a snake tattoo peeking out of his V-neck and licking up his neck. He looked as though he should be intimidating, but all pretence of that had gone from his face. He was clean-shaven, but had missed patches. He seemed rather jittery. Not drug jittery, but a sleepless night jittery. But was this just nerves or was Sean really guilty?

He's guilty. They said so, didn't they?

Mouth open. On auto-pilot. 'Sean, welcome to the show.' Pause but no applause. This audience had already forged their conclusion. 'Sean, you've been hearing the accusations from backstage, what do you have to say for yourself?'

'They're not true,' Sean said. Thick Manchester accent. Eyes flitting – Sheppard, audience, Sheppard, audience. 'I would never cheat on Sarah. We have a baby together.' He wrenched himself around to look at his girlfriend. 'I love you. I love you, Sarah. I thought you knew that.'

'I don't know anything,' Sarah said. 'I'm stupid for believing you.'

You know where this is going . . . Morgan said in his mind. *It's your favourite bit. And don't lie and say it's not.*

It was time to ramp it up. This is what they wanted. This is what he wanted.

'Sean mate, what about these texts on your phone? Sarah found these texts, I've seen these texts.' Enunciating every point. 'You going to call her a liar, Sean? Are you going to call me a liar?'

Sean shuffled. 'No.'

'So you're going to explain it away? I suppose those texts were for your mother, right?'

Laughs. Sheppard looked down at his cue card. GUILTY.

This is what I've always wanted. The hundreds of people in the audience, invisible beyond the lights, and then the hundreds of thousands beyond the camera lens.

'Those texts were for Sarah,' Sean said, not making any sense. Maybe he actually was guilty? Fifty-fifty, right? *DO IT.*

Sheppard paced back and forth, and then turned to face Sean directly. He walked towards him. 'Those texts were for your girlfriend? Hmmph. That doesn't fly, Sean. That doesn't fly. You do not come onto this stage and lie to my face, Sean. Look behind me, you're lying to everyone in this room. You're lying to everyone watching this show, Sean.' Sheppard got in close, his face centimetres from Sean's. The audience liked when he did this – it all seemed so primal. A hundred pairs of eyes trained on him. And beyond them, infinity. *Always.* 'You know the worst thing, though? You're lying to that little lady sitting next to you, right there. And you're jeopardising a relationship where a child is involved for some little fling with a babysitter? Think carefully before you answer that, Sean. Remember who you're dealing with,' *YES* 'because now you're dealing with Morgan Sheppard, and you know what?'

Sheppard smiled in Sean's face before backing off. The audience erupted, nailing their cue. 'Nothing gets past him!'

And it all fell away. Sean – Sarah – the set.

Just Sheppard and his audience – loved. And that was when he knew that he could never walk away.

Sign away his soul. Because he didn't want to be saved.

17

He didn't know where he'd gone, but he'd managed to convince himself it had all been a bad dream. So, when he opened his eyes to see the five faces of the people trapped in the room with him, his heart freshly broke. Strangers who almost felt like home — Mandy, Alan, Ryan, Constance and Headphones. A bizarre family.

The lights seemed too bright and his body ached with longing. Pills, drink — if he didn't get one or both soon he was going to crash. Hard. And he wouldn't be useful to anyone when that happened.

How long had he been out?

He tried to get up but couldn't. Mandy held out a hand. He grabbed it, and she pulled him upright with surprising strength. The others took a step back as if he were contagious.

'Are you okay?' Mandy said.

'I don't suppose anyone here is a doctor or a nurse?' Sheppard rubbed the back of his head. He was getting a headache, especially where he'd hit it on the way down.

The room was silent, except Ms Ahearn, who was muttering something under her breath.

'You have a fever? Sit down,' Mandy said, gesturing to the bed.

Sheppard shook his head. 'I don't have time. I just passed out. It happens.'

'The rock 'n' roll lifestyle, huh?' Alan said.

Sheppard couldn't manage a retort. His body was shutting down . . . no, not shutting down. More like, going into SAFE MODE.

Where was he? Winter was dead and now what? He knew nothing of these people, but that would have to change. Right now, it was entirely possible that anyone in the room murdered Winter. Five people. Five suspects. A one in five chance of being the murderer. The fact that he had thought it was probably a man didn't mean anything – at least not yet. He was no expert. Everyone was guilty until proven innocent.

You still haven't told them . . .

He would have to. Winter's identity was the only real clue he had. But at least, he could do it one by one, reduce the fallout. Maybe these people knew Dr Winter too.

He looked across the room to the bedside table. The rulebook was gone. Glancing around, he saw that Ryan was looking through it. Then back to the table. The timer. He had passed out for almost five minutes.

Five fewer minutes . . .

When the wheels started turning, five minutes could be the difference between life and death.

He needed to start talking. But with no evidence and no clarification, anyone could say anything. They could've all been lying to him already.

The woman still lurked in the background, in the red room. In Paris. As though, if he turned his head quick enough, he might catch her. To be back there, with all this just a bad dream. It was almost too much – to hope.

The others went back to what they were doing. Alan was still staring at the window. Constance was muttering and looking down at her Bible. Ryan was reading the rules. Headphones was in her own little world. Only Mandy remained looking at him, concerned.

Sheppard took her aside, into the alcove by the door.

'I have to start interviewing people. Talking. Seeing if I can find anything that might give me a clue to who . . . who killed him. See if we can work out why we're all here.'

'Interviews?'

'Yes. We should really do them in private, but . . .' Sheppard's eyes skirted the bathroom door, 'I think over here will have to do.'

'Okay,' Mandy said.

'I need to start thinking about identities, possible motives, time frames.' All things he had learned reading his crime books. 'Everyone else should stay on the right side of the room. I need to try and make it so no one else can hear.' Even as he said it, he knew it was impossible. Alan's ears were twitching on the other side of the room, and he wasn't even facing them. Every single word any person said in the room could easily be heard by others – discounting Constance, who was spouting illegible nonsense.

'Okay. Who do you want to talk to first?'

'You?'

Mandy looked at him, and gave a smile. It was the same kind of nervous smile he saw on everyone who came on his television show. A smile that always looked like the smiler had something to hide. Under the spotlight though, everyone did.

Sheppard smiled too. And at that moment, he knew he was really going to try. He was a sham – a terrible excuse of a detective, hell, a terrible excuse of a man. But he was really going to do all he could to try and save them. To save the innocent ones.

Because they were the ones who didn't deserve this.

And, if he had the time, he might even try to save himself.

18

'I never usually come into central London, at least this side of the river, not if I can help it. When you just come here for a holiday, that's all you want to see, right? But the second I moved here, it seemed like the last place I wanted to go. All those people just rushing around but not really looking like they're doing anything – just there to get in your way. I hate it.'

Sheppard knew what she meant. It was always impossibly busy. He remembered going to Oxford Street for the first time as a child, when he didn't even know there were that many people in the world. 'You used to live somewhere else?'

'Manchester. It was much quieter. Even though I still lived in the city. I moved here for university and never moved back.'

'London's expensive, how do you get by?'

'I have a job as a barista in a coffee shop in Waterloo. I'm trying to get into the television business. My degree was in journalism, so not like you – I'm trying for behind the camera. My job supports me, mostly. Also, my brother gave me some money and well, I had a wealthy aunt who liked me,' Mandy said.

She put enough emphasis on the *had* for Sheppard to discern what happened.

'Still, the money is running out, and if nothing happens soon I'm probably going to have to move back up north. To have some fraction of savings left. Not that I want to move back. The centre horrifies me, but I love the quieter parts of London. The atmosphere of it, you know. Like anything's possible.'

Sheppard nodded. 'Where do you live?'

'Islington. A shared flat. I live with a struggling actor and a professional drug addict. Only one of them is great at what they do. I'm sure you can probably guess which. Times are tough, but we get by.'

'So what about today? Can you walk me through what happened?'

Mandy thought for a moment. He wondered if it was the same for her – like trying to recall a dream. The moment you thought you had it, it slipped through your fingers.

'It was pretty much the same as any other day. Number seventy three bus to Waterloo at some stupid time. It was about eight, but at this time of the year, it might as well be the middle of the night, you know. I work at the CoffeeCorps just inside the station. It's like a little kiosk on its own. If you've seen that film with Matt Damon, he runs right past it. What's it called?'

'Mandy,' Sheppard said, constantly aware of the timer over on the bedside table. He had a lot to get through.

'Sorry,' she said. 'So, it's a horrible little kiosk and it's really cramped in there. There's really only space for two people in the kiosk, but management always puts on three, because of first aid or something. Anyway, it was fine – as busy as you would expect – and it got to my morning break. I've always had this routine where, in my break, I walk down to the South Bank. It's nice. People are a little slower down there because it's just nice to be there. Looking out at the Thames, seeing the London Eye, seeing the rest of the city. Close but far enough for me. I go to this coffee place called Nancy's – small place, independent. I get the irony of that, but I really hate CoffeeCorps. I'm not a big small business warrior – I just don't like the coffee.'

'The South Bank's not far from here,' Sheppard said, more to himself than Mandy.

'No, it's not. In fact I remember looking at the Great Hotel building. I never thought . . .' She trailed off.

'So this coffee shop?'

'Yeah, sorry. I went into Nancy's as usual, and the guy who runs it has recognised me for a while so he knows my order and starts making it up for me. The place is always really quiet, which makes me sad. It's a small café – nice though. There's a few sit-in tables but they're never usually full. I remember a few people were there this morning, but not many.

'While the guy's making my coffee, I go in to use the toilet in the back. It's a hot day, so I wanted to wash my face. I locked the door, put the toilet seat down, and looked in the mirror. My hair was messed up in the heat, so I wanted to try and fix it. I propped my bag against the sink and was looking for a clip when . . . when something happened.'

'Something?' Sheppard prompted.

Mandy looked at him. She seemed to be rolling it through in her mind seeing if it made any sense before she said it. Sheppard could empathise, but wouldn't really care either way. Nothing made much sense yet. 'It was a smell – a weird smell. I started picking it up and I looked around to see. . . I don't know . . . if I could locate it, I guess. It grew stronger. I remember it burning my nostrils. It was a chemical smell, I think. And then my vision started going fuzzy. And then – I don't remember anything after that. Not until I saw you cuffed to the bed.'

Sheppard nodded. That was exactly in line with what he experienced. A chemical smell, a burning sensation, passing out. 'This sounds like you were gassed. Like *we* were gassed.'

'The same for you?' Mandy said.

'Yes. But why gas? It doesn't make much sense. Were they just waiting for someone to use that toilet and gas them? Or if they really wanted you, why didn't they just drug your coffee? Gassing someone is a hell of a lot more work.'

'The horse mask said we were random. Maybe I was just unlucky?'

'Maybe,' Sheppard said. 'I'm not entirely sure he was telling the truth though. At this point nothing's certain. You said you go to that coffee shop a lot?'

'Yes. Three or four times a week at about the same time. Ten thirty.'

'People know you go there? Can identify you?'

'The guy knows my order.'

Sheppard sighed. Gas – in a public place. How would

they get her body out of there? How would they get past the people in the café – let alone the people outside on the South Bank? Back up a truck to the shop maybe? But that would draw attention? This made no sense. 'We both experienced the same thing. This sounds like a plan, not random. They could've gassed you through the vents, like they did to me. I think someone knew you were going to be there.'

Mandy looked puzzled. 'But even I didn't know I was going to use the bathroom. I've never once used it before.'

It didn't make *any* sense at all. 'You had ordered coffee.'

'Yes.'

'And who else was in the café? Do you remember anyone?'

'There was hardly anyone in there, like I said. There was just one guy.'

'Had you seen him before?'

'The guy? No.'

'What did he look like?'

'I don't know? Normal I suppose.'

Mandy taken. Mere miles from the Great Hotel. Sheppard had to have already been taken at that point. The night before all this. So where was he as this was happening? A shiver. Not something he really wanted to know.

'Was there anything out of the ordinary?'

'There was something, I suppose. But it could be nothing.'

'I'll take what I can get at the moment.'

'From the moment I stepped in there, I felt eyes on me.

You know that feeling when you're convinced you're being watched? Yeah, it was like that. And I didn't really place it until I passed the guy sitting down on my way to the toilet. As I passed the guy, I saw that his eyes were almost locked onto me. He sort of smiled when I looked at him and I smiled back – like an automatic response during work hours. But he was creepy. I don't know what it was – I can't put my finger on it. Anyway, I just passed him and that was that. I didn't really feel it at the time, but looking back . . . it was kind of weird.'

'Can you describe him?'

'Like I said, he was just – normal. Um . . . he was thin, wiry. He had brown, short hair. Wore these thin glasses. He was a looker, pretty handsome. Probably about your age. He was wearing a black suit, with a red tie. He looked like some kind of banker or something.'

'It could be nothing,' Sheppard said. *Or it could be everything.* 'You said you were on your break? So people would know when you don't come back?'

'Yeah, definitely. And I'm not the kind of girl who slacks off – I've never missed a day in my life and I'm proud of it.'

Mandy was now officially missing. But a young girl disappearing in her break wouldn't be any cause for any real panic. There would be no calling the police or sending out a search party. Not at this stage anyway. People would just think she had decided to play truant. It was a lovely day after all.

Mandy seemed to have come to the same conclusion. 'The girls I was on shift with will think it's weird I'm gone. But they'll probably cover for me. We're friends. I'd do the same for them.'

No. There would be no rescue party. And even if the police did become involved, they would have no idea where to look.

Sheppard lowered his voice. Scanned the room to see no one watching. But how many of them were listening? 'You've seen the body, right?'

Mandy seemed to take his cue. Lowering her voice too. 'Yes. But only from the back. And I don't want to see it again.'

'No, you don't have to. Even from the back, did you think you recognised the man?'

'No.'

Sheppard frowned. He took out Winter's wallet, flipped to his driver's licence and held it up to Mandy. 'Do you recognise him now?'

Mandy looked at the picture for a long time. 'Simon Winter,' she said. Barely audible. 'No, I don't recognise him. But . . .'

'But what?'

'I work with an Abby Winter.'

Sheppard's brain turned over. Abby Winter. He hadn't heard that name in a long time. Simon's daughter. The same age as Sheppard. Sheppard remembered the first time he'd seen her. After a session. He left Winter's office. They were kids – just kids. She was sitting on the stairs.

'I know you,' she had said.

Little Morgan had smiled and sat down next to her.

'Sheppard?' Mandy said.

Abby. Now she was an orphan – because of him.

'I . . . do you know this Abby at all?'

'She's – I like her, but she's a bit of a mess. I think she's an addict of something – I don't know what – but she shakes a lot and she gets like that weird kind of slick sweat over her face. You know?'

Sheppard nodded. He did. More than she knew. But he was only half hearing her. His mind was on Abby– a girl he had cared about once. Now she was a drug addict, working a dead-end job. How long had it been since he saw her last? He remembered her as a bubbly, fun person, with one hell of a smile. And now –

'It's kind of sad – you know. She's a nice enough person, but she has her demons. I think our manager only keeps her on because he feels sorry for her . . . Are you okay?'

Sheppard nodded again. 'Okay,' he said, changing the subject, 'now what about the masked man? The horse mask? Did you recognise his voice?'

'No, not at all. Although . . .'

'Although?'

'I don't know, it's just – I might be wrong but the mask looked familiar.'

'The mask?'

'Yeah. I don't know why but I think I've seen it somewhere bef . . .' Her eyes searching and then . . . Something snapped into place. 'The theatre. The show. *Rain on Elmore Street.*'

'Constance Ahearn's play?' Sheppard said, looking into the room. Constance had backed herself into a corner

95

again, and was silent. Her eyes met Sheppard's and he looked back to Mandy. 'Are you sure?'

'No . . . not sure exactly. I saw it like a year ago.'

'Okay,' Sheppard said. 'Now I need you to think about that coffee shop – think of everything that happened this morning. If you think of anything else weird or out of place, you have to come and tell me straight away. I also need you to try and keep everyone calm – I need someone I can count on to try and keep the peace.'

'I can try,' Mandy said, and smiled that small sweet smile again. Almost too sweet.

There was something behind her words – something in the shadows. Sheppard thought it was fear, but what if it was something else – something with a slightly more ill intent?

'Thanks,' Sheppard settled on. He really couldn't trust anyone. But one thing he did trust was Mandy's scream when she first saw the body. It sounded so incredibly scared. That would be hard to pull off if it wasn't genuine.

'What are you going to do?'

Sheppard sighed again, and turned to the rest of the room. 'Looks like I'm going to have to talk to Ms Ahearn next.'

19

Mandy moved away from Sheppard, awkwardly moving around the bed, passing Alan and Ryan to sit down next to Constance. Constance shuffled closer to her and Mandy put her arm around her and whispered something in her ear. Alan and Ryan were both watching him now. He wondered how much they had heard. Everyone being in such close proximity was terrible. He could feel the fear seeping out of everyone else.

'You understand we can hear everything you say,' Alan said.

'I know this isn't ideal . . .' Sheppard started.

Alan scoffed. 'Ideal? That's the word you're going with? This is a waking nightmare.'

Alan started towards Sheppard.

'I need to talk to Ms Ahearn next.'

'No,' Alan said, 'you'll talk to me.'

'No, I will talk to Ms Ahearn.'

'No, Mr Sheppard. I personally think I am more equipped to deal with this investigation. You are a floozy, a human-sized bag of hot air. And you can only blow into bags so much before they pop.'

'Sit down, Alan.'

'You will talk to me next.'

'Yes. After Ms Ahearn.'

'You have no authority here,' Alan said, spitting vowels at him. 'The mask says this is all on you, so why even give you the time of day? Who's to say that you didn't kill that man in there? In fact, that makes perfect sense.' Alan's eyes sparkled with something Sheppard couldn't quite place. Had he heard Mandy talking? Or did he recognise the body?

Sheppard opened his mouth to say something to this effect, but . . .

'Stop it.' They both looked around. Ryan had stood up, the folder still in his hands. 'I'm going next.'

'And why's that?' Alan said.

'Because I've got something I need to tell Mr Sheppard. Something I should have said before.'

'Well, speak up, son. There's no secrets here,' Alan said.

'I heard you talking to Mandy. I need to tell you some things. Can we go into the bathroom?'

'Now wait a second . . .' Alan said.

Sheppard couldn't think. He didn't want to go back in there.

'You better think fast about what you're saying, son, because it's starting to sound like you're a murderer.'

'Shut up, Alan. I need to . . .'

'I didn't lie. I didn't,' Ryan said quickly.

Ryan held up the last page of the rule binder. THE BOY LIED.

'Someone tell me what is going on,' Alan said.

'Shut up, Alan.'

'No, you shut up. Son, what the hell are you talking about?'

'Why don't you butt out and let me do my job?' Sheppard rounded on Alan again.

'Your job?' Alan laughed, 'your job?'

He needed alcohol. Needed pills. Needed to not have a stupid old man telling him what to do. 'I am listening to you, okay. I am taking all your concerns on board. But right now, if you hadn't noticed, we're almost half an hour down and so far I'm coming up empty on the ideas front. So I'm going to do things my way.'

Alan stepped forward. 'You're only a detective because people like to label things. What you did however many years ago doesn't mean a damn thing.'

'Guys,' Ryan tried.

'You know what I'm detecting right now? I'm thinking that the only person who would actually want to delay me in this investigation is the murderer. Did you murder the man in the bathtub?'

'Guys.'

'No, I didn't. Did you?'

Ryan stepped between them, pushing them apart as they continued to fight, and shouted over them, 'I work here.'

This did the trick. Silence.

'Now please,' Ryan said, 'can we go into the bathroom?'

20

Sheppard went in first, and drew the shower curtain over the bathtub. He tried not to look, he really tried. But Winter was still there. Dead. With that look of sadness upon his face. It made him feel sick. He turned to the sink and splashed his face again.

Ryan took a tentative look towards the bathtub as he came in. Then focused his eyes on Sheppard.

'Start talking,' Sheppard said. The dull ache behind his eyes. That feeling at the back of his throat. That rumble in his chest. His hands were starting to shake. Why hadn't he checked the mini-bar yet?

'I'm sorry, I should have told you sooner,' Ryan said. 'I tried to tell you at the start.'

Sheppard vaguely remembered. 'Who are you?'

'Ryan Quinn. Like I said. I'm not lying.'

'You work here?'

'Yes. As a cleaner. That's why I'm wearing this.' Ryan gestured down to his white jumpsuit. Sheppard took a closer look at the young man. Black hair, short. Clean shaven, didn't look like he could even grow a beard. Mid-twenties, probably. The young man towered though. Was almost taller than Sheppard. 'It's not my ideal job.

But I do it. I come into the rooms, clean them, make the beds, give fresh towels, do that triangle thing on the toilet paper.'

Sheppard was thinking. 'That's how you knew where we were so fast. Between Bank and Leicester Square.'

Ryan nodded, sadly.

'Seems like a big thing to keep back from us,' Sheppard said. 'Where were you when we were trying to escape?'

'I told you, didn't I? There is no way out.'

Ryan and Alan talking at the window. Ryan convincing him that there was no way to escape.

'So you're a cleaner for the Great Hotel?'

'Yes. I have been for about a year now. Things are hard for my family. My mother and father moved here from Hong Kong just before I was born. They run a dry-cleaning business in Soho, but it's not enough to support them. I have to help them with their bills. I hate this job. But it's the only way I can keep our heads above water.

'I'm in the fourth quadrant with two other guys. That's three floors, this floor and the two below. There are thirty-five rooms on each floor.'

'That's a lot of cleaning.'

'Hotel this big has a lot of manpower. We start at nine in the morning and end by three. Then I have to go and clean the communal areas.'

'So you were cleaning this morning?'

Ryan seemed to visibly back away – his gaze slipped from Sheppard's.

'Ryan.'

'Don't freak out.'

'Ryan, where were you?'

'I . . .' Ryan said, trying to find the words, 'I think I was here.'

And that was that — why Ryan hadn't come forward. Simple. 'Christ, Ryan.'

The young man put his hands up in defence. 'It's not what you think. Nothing was wrong with this room, when I was in here before. The window was open. The door wasn't deadlocked. There sure as hell wasn't a body . . .' He looked toward the bath. 'Everything was fine. You have to believe me.'

Sheppard didn't know what to think — except now Ryan was the prime suspect, like it or not. 'You were in here?'

'Yes,' Ryan said, 'I came into the bathroom to change the towels and clean the toilet. I looked in the bath . . . and there was no one. There was nothing in it. You have to understand, I had nothing to do with this.'

'Tell me exactly what you did in here.' Trying to slip him up or rooting for him, he wasn't totally sure.

'Towels. Toilet. Bath. I even wiped it down and replaced the shower gel in the holder. Then I wiped down the mirror. And mopped the floor. And put a new toilet paper in the holder. That was all, I swear.'

'Wait, so if you were servicing this room . . . that means someone was staying here?'

'Yes.'

'Who?'

'I don't know. I don't usually see many people when I'm cleaning. They're usually out for the day by the time I come around. Sometimes I see people at the start. But this room is towards the end of my quadrant, so there's even less chance of them still being around.'

'Was there anything lying around? Anything that gave you a clue to who this person was?'

Ryan thought for a moment. 'No, it was all very clean. In fact, the bed didn't look like it had been slept in. There was no mess anywhere. But there was a suitcase next to the wardrobe. So I knew someone was staying here.'

'There's no way you could've heard this guest's name in passing or anything? Any way you could have seen him in the corridor?'

'Well, yeah, I guess it's possible,' Ryan said.

'Okay.' Knowing what needed to be done. But Ryan knew too. That's why they were in here, wasn't it? With the smell of blood and the thing looming behind the curtain. 'I need to show you the body now.' He could just show Winter's driving licence, but he needed to see how the young man reacted to the body.

That's mean. Maybe so, but necessary.

Ryan steeled himself and nodded.

Sheppard gripped the shower curtain. He didn't want to see again. He didn't want to have to look at Winter's face. But it had to be done. He drew back the curtain fast, before his brain could stop him.

Winter lay there. The blood grew stronger in the air. *Don't look down. Not at all the blood and the . . .*

Sheppard looked at Ryan instead.

He was clenching and unclenching his fists. In a calming technique that wasn't working. Ryan looked shocked, pale. But he didn't look away from the body. He stared at it, taking shallow breaths.

'His name is Simon Winter,' said Sheppard, his voice quieter than before. The stench. God, the stench.

Ryan looked at Sheppard, then back to the body. 'Out there. Out there, it is hard to believe. It is easy to think that this is all some kind of joke. But this . . . this is real. This poor man.'

'Do you recognise him – or his name? Was he staying here?' Sheppard said, a little too pushily. The image of Simon Winter was making him uncomfortable.

'I don't . . .' Ryan trailed off. He was thinking hard. Looking at Winter's face.

The young man was a wreck. There was no way he could have killed someone. Was there? If this was the reaction . . .

'I saw him,' Ryan said, in a whisper hard to catch.

'What?' Sheppard said.

'I saw this man.'

'This morning?'

Ryan shook his head slowly. 'No, not today. I . . . I suppose it was about a month ago.'

'What?'

'Here, in the hotel. It has been a long time. I can't say for sure where, but every room is the same. The same furniture, the same dimensions, the same contents. I think it might have even been this floor.' Ryan looked like he was about to break out in cold sweats.

'A month ago?' It seemed very strange that Winter would be in this very hotel a month ago and then turn up dead in one of their rooms – hijacked by a maniac.

Unless it's a big coincidence. Or you've all been in cold storage a hell of a long time.

There was something almost comic about that. The situation overwhelmed him and he didn't know if he was going to laugh or cry.

Ryan peered further into the bath, as if for answers. 'Yes. I remember.'

'Remember what?'

'This man . . . Winter, you said? Winter was here. And he was acting . . . strange.'

'Strange?'

Ryan tore his eyes from the body, back to Sheppard. 'I didn't remember before. It's a hotel. People act weirdly all the time. Especially the small amount of people who are still in their rooms when you come around to clean. They act like you're invading their space, when it was never theirs to begin with.'

'How was Winter acting?'

'It was towards the end of my shift. That's how I know it was this floor, even if it wasn't this room. Everything had gone fine with the other rooms, I was ahead of time. I thought I might even be able to get off early. I knocked on the door of the room as I always do. But there was no reply. So I just went in.

'That's when I saw this man. He was pacing around the room. He had a notebook in his hand and he was writing stuff down. He had something as well, some sort of bright yellow thing. It looked like he was . . . It sounds stupid, but it looked like he was . . .'

'Like he was what?'

'Like he was measuring.'

Sheppard was caught off guard. What – measuring? Why would he be . . .? Too many thoughts at once.

'I think that thing was a tape measure. And he was properly pacing, one foot in front of the other. And every step, he stopped to write something down. Maybe he was doing something else. Rehearsing for a speech, or mapping something out . . . but from the door, that's what it looked like.'

'Why would he be measuring a hotel room?' Sheppard said. More to himself.

'The moment he saw me, he quickly threw down the notebook and the yellow thing, and tried to step in front of it all. He was acting like he'd been caught doing something bad. For about five seconds. But it seemed longer. We were just staring at each other. I didn't know what to do. Then he came to his senses and apologised and just let me clean the room.'

'What did he do while you were cleaning?'

'He gathered up his things and left. I didn't see him again. It was definitely this man.'

Sheppard couldn't not look down at Winter. The man now seemed to be hiding something behind his expression. What was going on? 'Did you report it?'

'Report what? I didn't even know what I saw and it wasn't as if it was particularly suspicious. I forgot about it the moment I finished my shift. Until now.' Ryan's voice hitched. He put his hand up to his mouth. Took a few moments. Lowered it again. 'Sorry, the smell. And the blood.'

Sheppard nodded. 'I . . . you can go if you want.'

'You don't need anything else?'

Too much already. What was Winter doing in this room a month ago? What could he have possibly been doing? 'No. Just anything else you can think of, let me know.' Now, he couldn't take his eyes away. What was Winter hiding? The bathroom door opened and shut. He was alone with Winter again.

Sheppard took out Winter's notebook, and flipped through it again – not sure what he was looking for. He looked down at the old man. Measuring the hotel room? Why would he be measuring a hotel room. Unless . . . Did it mean that Winter was in on whatever plan this was? Was Winter in on the whole thing? But what led to him ending up dead in the bathtub? Surely that had not been part of the plan . . .

'What were you up to?'

Winter didn't answer.

21

Nausea washed over Sheppard as he returned to the room – he had to put his hand out to the wall to steady himself. Dizziness – the cold, hard crash was getting closer. How long had it been without pills? His hand shook violently, the dull throb of his head, the smell lingering in his nostrils and the itch – everywhere. A cocktail of awful – the usual symptoms.

'What's wrong with you now?'

He looked up. Alan had been waiting for him to come out. *Great*. The man was standing right in front of him, arms still crossed. His voice didn't sound caring – more irritated.

'Nothing, I'm fine,' Sheppard said.

Alan looked him up and down. 'Whatever, I'll keep this short and sweet. Not to mention loud,' he turned to the room and back, 'as I have nothing to hide.'

Sheppard looked over his shoulder to see the rest of the room, much as it was. Mandy and Constance were sitting with their backs to everyone. Ryan was pacing back and forth. And Headphones was watching them, with her ears still covered.

'I've heard all the questions you were asking Mandy

– hard not to – and I assume you asked the same of Ryan. So I'll give you the complete rundown of what happened to me. I was in my office when I was drugged by the same gas as everyone else. We all talked while you were in the bathroom – even Crazy Irish and Generic Teen. We were all gassed. I didn't only smell it, but I saw it pouring through the vents. It was some kind of colourless smoky gas, dissipating around the room very quickly. I tried to cover the vent, but it seemed like I'd already inhaled too much. I didn't even have time to call for help. I collapsed and then I woke up here.

'I was preparing, as I said, for the MacArthur case. A biggie. The kind of case to make or break a career. Of course, my career was "made" a long time ago, but it's always nice to have another notch in your belt.'

Sheppard was trying to keep up. 'Must be interesting for you to . . .'

Alan got him instantly. Could read him so easily. How did he do that? 'You're alluding to the fact I am black. Yes, Mr Sheppard, I am a black man. I worked damn hard to get where I am, and yes, I fought some opposition along the way. You know how many black lawyers are in London? We make up one point two per cent of them. So yes, to answer your question, it is "interesting".'

Sheppard nodded. Alan didn't seem like the type of person to let anything get to him. Sheppard wondered how old he was. Wrinkles under his eyes – tracing around to his cheeks. The wrinkles on his forehead seemed to be chiselled into a permanent scowl, making the man look more sinister. Fifties? Late fifties, maybe?

'Of course, none of this makes any difference. Because I'm here now. And that means the MacArthur case is ruined. Thank you for that, by the way.'

Sheppard frowned. 'Right.' Couldn't even be bothered to retort.

'I suppose you want to know about my connection with the body,' Alan said, nodding to the door.

'What?'

'You see I lied a little before. I did recognise that man. There was no point explaining it at the time – but now here we are. I see a lot of people in my line of work, so I pick up on all the details I can. My peers joke that I can recognise people by the backs of their heads – I guess I just proved that right. That coupled with the fact that I saw that man yesterday wearing the same suit – that made me sure. You showed something to Mandy, I assume it was his wallet. Anyway, that man's name is Simon Winter. He is a private psychologist operating out of his home in East London. The psychologist to my client, Hamish MacArthur. Winter is a key witness. That's all I can disclose.'

Sheppard was speechless and Alan seemed to relish that.

'You're wondering why I'm offering all of this up so easily,' Alan said, failing to hide a smile. 'You know how many clients I see try and hide the facts, even from someone who's trying to help them – just because they're scared of the outcome? It's pitiful and it's weak. Don't confuse this with me being co-operative.

'Now I believe I've answered everything from your

stellar line of questioning. Shall I see myself back to my window?'

'Wait . . .' Sheppard said. How could this man be so defiant, even in the face of death? That was the kind of person who was dangerous, the kind of person who found control in chaos. But still . . .

'Try to keep up, Mr Sheppard. Yes, I know Simon Winter. I haven't really ever talked to him,' Alan said.

'Because,' Sheppard said, 'he's not your witness.'

Alan scowled. 'No. I was rather looking forward to grilling the bastard in court.'

'What is this case?'

'I can't disclose any details of the case, Mr Sheppard. Much speculation has been made in the media. Maybe you could ring down to room service for a newspaper.'

Sheppard rubbed his eyes. 'If Simon Winter is here, is it possible that the person behind this is connected to the case?'

'Of course,' Alan said, 'that's why I thought it best to be as above board as possible. There is a possibility that this revolves around the MacArthur case.'

'But you still won't tell me anything about it.'

'No, Mr Sheppard. I won't. Because I think that I might be able to figure this out a lot better than you. I'm keeping my cards close to my chest, sure, but I'm doing what needs to be done. If that makes me more suspicious, so be it.'

Sheppard shook his head. 'Of course this makes you more suspicious. How could I take it any other way?'

'It doesn't matter,' Alan said, 'I am already a prime

suspect. You want a motive, Mr Sheppard? Well, I've got
a hell of a one. That man in there has been a thorn in my
side for the past year. I have dreamed of gutting him like
a fish, slicing him up into a million little pieces. But that
doesn't mean I would. It is clear what's happening here.
The horse mask is trying to pin this murder on me. And if
you take the bait, then you'll kill us all.'

'Pretty big ego, even when defending yourself against
a murder.'

'My ego is not the one on trial here.'

A lot of information, buried in not much at all. Alan
was presenting an account that surely the murderer
would want to hide. If it was true. Still, Alan did have
motive. And he knew how to play the game.

'So the MacArthur case was supposed to be today?'

'Yes. But none of the other details matter. They are not
related to this . . . this case, although calling this a case is
charitable to say the least.'

'Not related? Or you just won't tell me?'

'As a lawyer, I am bound by my station to keep certain
things between me and my client.'

'MacArthur?'

'Yes.'

Sheppard could see Alan was not going to budge. How
could he compete with a lawyer? Alan was really doing
what Sheppard pretended to do every day. 'Two people
involved with this case in the same hotel room. That can't
be a coincidence,' he said, more to himself than Alan.
Was there some way that Sheppard and the MacArthur
case were connected? The horse mask seemed to have had

only Sheppard in his sights, but maybe he had Alan too.

'No.'

'I really need that information, Alan.'

Alan smiled. 'You really are terrible at this, you know.' Alan was prepared to die for what he believed in. He knew people like that – so honourable they would fall on their own sword. He wasn't one of those people and didn't understand those who were.

'You're a very successful man, Mr Hughes, I can see that,' he said, picking his words carefully. 'You like being the leader of the pack, like all the attention . . .'

'Please spare me the psycho-analysis. You're embarrassing yourself.'

Sheppard held up a hand. 'You're a winner. You muscled your way into your business, didn't take no for an answer. You've won. Is this really how it ends? If the horse mask is correct, we all die.'

'You're asking me if I want to die? Of course I don't. But if I am to die, I will do it with dignity.'

'You don't want to die. You think we have nothing in common. But *that* – we have *that* in common. You don't want to die, and you're scared. Just like everyone else in this room. Just like me. I'm terrified. And when I look at you, I can see somewhere in there that you are too. Whether you like it or not, we're the same type of person, Mr Hughes. The kind of guy who busies himself and mouths off to forget his problems. But this problem, we can't walk away from.'

'No,' Alan said.

'The thing I keep thinking is that we were all put here

for a reason. But I haven't worked out quite why yet. Until you. You might be the key to the puzzle.'

'I was gassed in my office. I was alone. Yes, I may well have been targeted for my involvement with the case. But you're asking the wrong questions, Sheppard. You should be asking what connects all these other people, not me.'

Alan Hughes, the defence lawyer who conveniently disappears the morning of the trial. A key witness who disappears as well.

This had to be connected. Maybe the horse mask wanted to know who had killed Simon Winter. And Alan looked like the prime suspect.

Was the horse mask Hamish MacArthur? But Sheppard had never heard of him before. And MacArthur would have had to know Sheppard too well. And that theory discounted how involved Winter might be? Why was Simon Winter here? Maybe he was more than just the victim. His mind circled as though he were chasing his own tail. Too many loose ends . . . unable to be tied up. A good idea. But a wrong one.

'Kidnapping six people. To make a murder puzzle. What are we missing?' To himself.

So much so, he was surprised at an answer. 'Kidnapping five people. We have to assume the murderer and victim were already here,' Alan said.

Ryan. Ryan was here. But, that look when he'd seen Winter. That kind of look you couldn't fake.

Alan was playing? 'I think the horse mask wanted Simon Winter dead, so he enlisted one of us to do it.'

'So, how do I find the murderer?' Sheppard asked,

before he could stop himself. Weak. Weak. He was acting weak.

'Maybe it's just a question of simplicity. Maybe the murderer is the one with the simplest story. Murderers don't tend to be great storytellers.'

'Your story seems simple enough.'

Alan chuckled. 'Yes, I guess it does. That is all I have for you, Sheppard.'

'Okay,' Sheppard said. It had to be him. It had to. But he had two more people to interview and already too much to think about. He had to get everyone's story first. 'If you think of anything else, please tell me.'

'I will,' Alan said, not sounding very convincing.

'And, Mr Hughes, since you've been honest with me, I'll be honest with you. You're my prime suspect.'

The lawyer laughed again. A gruff, joyless laugh. 'And I'll be honest with you, Sheppard. You're mine.' He smiled and winked, before moving away. A glint in his eye. Easy to miss. Knowing.

A chill ran through him, that smugness. Alan had to know of Sheppard's link with Winter. Somehow, he knew. And he didn't know why, but that scared him more than anything else.

22

Two left. He looked at the clock. 2:14. Where was the time going? How could forty-five minutes have gone already?

He cleared his throat, trying to get attention. No one looked at him – they were all gone to their thoughts.

'Ms Ahearn?'

Slowly, Constance looked around. Mandy whispered to her and she stood up. She was wearing a black flowing dress that matched her hair. It was baggy, and Sheppard couldn't see her body underneath. She looked like a ghost, floating around and wailing. She was still clutching the hotel Bible, and as she made her way towards Sheppard, he could see the whites of her knuckles. On her face, her make-up had run so dramatically she looked like a mixed paint pallet. She looked old, but wore the years well.

Constance tucked one curtain of hair behind an ear, and Sheppard saw a fresh scratch down her left cheek. Must have done it to herself, with her long, clear manicured nails.

Sheppard guided her to the alcove. Not much point but the illusion of privacy at least. They were all, at least, pretending not to listen.

'I'm sorry we have to do this here. Limited space,'

Sheppard said. Taking Constance into the bathroom would be a mistake. She was bad enough out here. 'Maybe it's best if you just focus on me. Forget about everyone else, forget where we are.'

Constance looked at him and opened her mouth. He expected lunacy. But coherence came out. 'Yes.' Black hair, dislodged, cascaded down her face again. Like something from a horror film.

'I have to ask you a few questions. It'll all be stuff I need to know for the case. I need to know all about everyone in the room. I won't ask anything I don't need to know. You see?'

Constance peered at him, one eye out, one eye through hair. 'Yes.'

'Good.' Where to start? He'd only thought this far. He looked down. 'You're religious?'

Constance laughed. He thought he might have lost her. But then, 'Yes, Mr Sheppard. And now we are in Hell. And we are being punished. Not just you. All of us. We all must atone.'

'And what do you need to atone for?' Sheppard said.

Constance frowned at him. Looked to the floor. Needed to be softer.

'Okay, let's start a little simpler. Do you remember where you were, before you came here?'

'I was . . .' Constance thought. 'I was in my dressing room, I think.' Sharp voice. One built for singing. And projecting.

'Your dressing room? At the theatre? I understand you're the lead actress in a play?'

Constance looked angry. 'A musical. It's a musical. *Rain on Elmore Street*. Three years. Never missed a show. Eight times a week.'

'What were you doing there this morning?'

'A rehearsal. The male lead's off sick, so we had to run through some scenes with the understudy. Amateurs, both of them.' Constance stopped. Stuck her nose up, like a dog. 'Is that blood? I don't want to stand here.'

'Sorry, I'll make this quick. So you were on your own in your dressing room?'

'I have my own dressing room, but no one is truly alone.'

'Excuse me,' Sheppard said.

'I am receptive, Mr Sheppard. I am one of the few who can see those lost on their way to the next life. I see through people. I see their auras.'

Suppressing a sigh. 'Ah,' he made do with. 'Okay then.' She was crazy then. That proved it. Ghosts and auras.

'Your aura is very troubled, Mr Sheppard. Light and dark mixing all together. Tell me, do you think you are a good man?'

Sheppard fumbled. 'What?'

'I cannot tell yet, that is all.'

Tell me, do you think you are a good man?

One of the last things Simon Winter ever said to him.

'You're a Catholic. Devout, by the looks of it. But you believe in all of this stuff?' Sheppard asked. *Get away from the question. Get away.*

'There are more things in Heaven and Earth than can be dreamt of in your philosophy,' Constance said. 'Besides, I did not pick to become what I am. It just happened to me.'

'You can see everyone's colours, can you see the murderer in this room?'

Constance smiled, baring her teeth in an animal way. 'It doesn't work like that.'

'Of course it doesn't.' Before he could stop himself.

'You can choose not to believe, Mr Sheppard. That doesn't make it not real.'

Back on track. 'You were in your dressing room. And then?'

'I was getting ready. Mainly going through my lines. They had to change them a little bit for the understudy. In my line of work, performing is like breathing. You don't notice when you're doing it. Shows slip away with the days, and the weeks, and the months. I know my lines back to front, and then they went and changed them. Fully knowing that I would have to overwrite my instincts. They knew, but they still did it. All because of that bastard and his bastard cancer scare. I can't learn new lines in a day. I just can't. I won't, Mr Sheppard.'

'Okay?' Sheppard tried.

'I was livid. I threatened to quit, you know. I threatened to quit five times over. But I didn't. Because they want to replace me anyway. They want someone younger. So I stayed. And then I went back to my room to learn my lines. Like a good girl. And then I heard something. A . . . hissing. And then a bad smell.'

'Yes. A smell.' Sheppard was finding it hard to follow Constance's rambling. But seized on the bits he could discern. 'It seems that's how we were all knocked out and brought here.' New question. Was the murderer gassed as well? Or did they just pretend? Whoever would've done that would've had to be a good actor. And Constance was definitely skittish enough to fit the murderer's MO. She could even hide her nerves behind fake ones.

'Yes. Gas. That makes sense,' the woman said. 'I don't remember anything else until . . . I woke up here.'

'You think we're in Hell, but you accept we're still alive.'

Constance chuckled. A clucking sound. 'There is more than one Hell. This is a Hell on Earth. We must atone.'

'And you still won't tell me what you need to atone for?'

'No, Mr Sheppard,' Constance said, 'the bigger question you should be asking is what you need to atone for?'

Sheppard suddenly felt itchy, like something sliding under his skin. How did she do that? Manage to get to him. Past all his defences.

'Ms Ahearn.'

'No. I won't hear any more. I did not kill whoever is in that bathroom. I can't even stand next to the door without feeling like I'm going to vomit – that should tell you all you need to know. What makes you think I could kill a man? Just because I won't talk about my private life with you, a stranger?' Every word lavish. As though she was reciting Shakespeare.

A dead end. Sheppard knew she wouldn't budge. Constance was persistent. He took out Winter's wallet and waited for her to calm down. He showed her Winter's driver's licence. 'Do you know this man?'

Constance looked at it. For too long. 'I don't think so. I never forget a face.'

'His name is Simon Winter. Ring any bells?'

'Never heard of him.'

'Are you sure?'

'Yes, I'm . . .' Constance's eyes flitted back to the driver's licence. Another long pause. 'I've seen this man.'

'What, where?'

'I . . . I'm trying to remember,' Constance said. She really was. 'I saw him at the theatre bar after a show. A few weeks ago, I think. I go out to the bar after the show once a week to sign autographs. There's a lot of people usually. It was crowded.'

'What makes you remember Simon Winter then?'

'It wasn't him I remember specifically. It was the man he was with.'

'What?'

'They were talking at the bar. I don't know what they were saying. It was so noisy and people were rushing up to me. But, every once and a while, when the crowd parted, I saw them. This man was with a younger man, in a suit, red tie, with rectangle glasses. He had the darkest aura I've ever seen. I couldn't stop looking. This man was evil, Mr Sheppard.'

A man. Red tie. Glasses. The same man that Mandy saw. Was this him? Was this the man behind the horse mask?

'Can you remember anything else? Did you hear anything, anything at all?'

'No. But I kept watching. They were deep in conversation. They looked like they didn't belong there. This . . .

Winter was doing most of the talking, and the evil man was listening. The Winter man handed the evil man something. Something like a notebook, or a pocket book. They weren't drinking anything, so I wondered why they were even there. I got distracted signing autographs for a few minutes, and I thought that when I looked back they would be gone. I *hoped* they would be gone. But when I looked back, they were still there. And . . .' Constance gulped at air.

'And what?'

'They were staring right at me, Mr Sheppard. The Winter man and the evil man. Staring right at me. Like they knew I'd been watching them. The evil man's eyes. They looked so . . . like they were on fire . . . they looked so hot. I've never seen anything like it. I felt so scared. Like a little child. But for some reason, I couldn't look away. Until my assistant came and took me back to my dressing room. And all that time, he was looking at me.'

A shiver fluttered on Sheppard's spine. If this was the horse mask, this solidified that Winter was in on it. This plot, this plan. Winter knew. And was working with the horse mask. The evil man. *Handed him a notebook*. The notebook that Ryan saw him writing in? It was all getting clearer.

'I tried not to think of the man after that. I tried to forget the whole thing. But for the last few weeks, I haven't been able to sleep. Because when I shut my eyes, all I can see is him.'

'Do you think he's the one doing this to us?' A man in a suit and a red tie. Constance's 'evil man'. He seemed to be

a thread connecting them together. Sheppard thought —
had he ever seen anyone that fit this description? Maybe
— he saw lots of people in suits. There was no way someone like that would stand out to him. Also, most of the
time he wasn't exactly on 'high alert' — he was usually
a little 'washy'. He hadn't seen anyone who had seemed
particularly 'evil'.

Constance looked up at him, sadly. 'Of course he is, Mr
Sheppard. Because that man wasn't just evil. That man
knew what I'd done, just like he knows everyone else in
this room. He knows you. He knows what you're hiding.
He is the Devil.'

Constance took a few steps backwards. Moving away.
Sheppard couldn't move. The way Constance put it, this
man did seem evil. And he was talking to Winter. Constance had stared into the eyes of their captor. It had to
be.

Sheppard almost forgot. Grateful to change the subject.
'The mask the man is using? Do you recognise it? Maybe
from your show?'

'No. I don't . . . maybe. We did use horse masks for a
dream sequence once. Is it important?'

No idea. 'I don't know.'

'We have a prop department that makes everything
in-house.'

'So it would not be possible to acquire one elsewhere?'

'Why do you care about this? We have been put here
by the Devil.'

'I . . .' No good answer, except he had to stay grounded.
Would be all too easy to get swept away, with Constance.

And not be any use to anyone.

'Please hurry, Mr Sheppard. That man, he's coming. And he's coming for you,' Constance said, and stepped away.

Sheppard let her go. His breath caught in his throat. The evil man, behind the horse mask. The man who knew him all too well. The glasses, the show, the psychologist dead in the bath. The evil man knew him better than he knew himself.

And he's coming for you.

The devil didn't exist.

Why didn't that make him feel any better?

Constance found her way back to Mandy's side, while Sheppard stared out at the room. Her words still ringing in his ears.

Tell me, are you a good man?

He had no idea.

23

Headphones was watching him. He didn't know if he'd seen her blink yet which was slightly disconcerting. Sheppard wanted a break – to do as the others were doing, a period of silent reflection. But he couldn't. He had to move on. He beckoned to Headphones.

On her black hoodie, the sticker HELLO MY NAME IS . . . RHONA. Headphones stuck in his mind though. She looked at him for a moment longer and then shuffled out from under the desk. She got up and made her way over to Sheppard, keeping her purple headphones clamped to her ears.

They looked at each other, the silence unnerving, till Sheppard dared to speak.

'Hi.'

Headphones said nothing.

'Rhona? Is it?'

Standing still like a statue.

'What are you listening to?'

She just stared at him. Maybe she couldn't hear. But there was something in her eyes. A glint of understanding.

'What are you listening to?' he tried again.

Nothing.

Sheppard was suddenly very annoyed – everything

suddenly peaking. 'Okay, we'll just stand here for the next two hours. I wonder what exploding feels like.' He regretted it as he said it. It was all taking its toll on him, but that was no way to go about talking to a defenceless kid.

Headphones frowned, opened her mouth and closed it again. She looked around, probably to make sure no one else in the room was looking, and slipped her headphones off, hooking them around her neck.

'You're rude,' she said, her voice younger than she looked and softer than her expression implied.

'I'm not the biggest fan of talking,' she said. 'I'm listening to the Stones. Greatest Hits. Volume Two.'

'Ah, the Stones. What's your favourite song?'

'People like *Paint It Black* but I prefer *2,000 Light Years From Home.*'

Sheppard smiled. 'Unconventional choice, but I can definitely agree with that decision right now.' The evil man. Winter. And a hotel room full of truth or lies. He felt 2,000 light years from home too. 'You're a bit young to be listening to the Stones.'

'I'm seventeen,' she said. Defensive. As though she'd had to say that many times before. 'I also have taste.'

'Undoubtedly,' Sheppard said. 'I don't suppose that thing you're listening to can connect to the internet or make a call or anything.'

Headphones' mouth twitched at the edges. She pulled the device from the pocket of her hoodie – an old retro Discman. 'You're welcome to try and call someone on it if you want.' Kids her age would usually have an iPhone or something, and she must have seen his look because she added, 'Better audio quality.'

Sheppard looked from the device to her. 'Why are you not more freaked out by this situation? Have you heard anything that's been going on?'

'I heard the TV. When you were still cuffed to the bed. I heard there's a dead man in the bath. I heard there's a murderer here. Otherwise, I don't really care what these people have to say. I don't need to hear anymore. If I'm going to die, I want to sit in a corner and listen to my music. I can't think of a better way to go. At least not with the options available.'

'That's . . .' Sheppard struggled for the word. The more he thought about it, the more he thought it was the sanest thing he'd heard in the room so far. 'That's very grown up,' he settled with.

Headphones' face screwed up at *grown-up*. 'My dad taught me to prepare for the worst. Anything else is a pleasant surprise.'

'He sounds great at parties,' Sheppard said. 'But you know that I can't just sit in a corner and wait to die.' *Although that sounds enticing.* 'I'm not going to let anyone else get hurt, not if I can help it.' *Keep telling yourself that.* 'So I need to ask you a few questions.' Sheppard knew the type of girl Headphones was. A girl who hadn't seen the good in the world so just assumed the darkest parts were normal. Sheppard had seen his fair share of terrible but he knew that there was good out there, like the good he thought he saw in Dr Winter. Even if he didn't always feel that that good was inside himself. 'First off, do you remember where you were before you got here?'

'I was at home,' Headphones said, 'in my room on my laptop. My dad and some of his friends were downstairs, watching football. I try and drown it out with music but I can always still hear them cheering. Idiots. So instead of my stereo, I used my headphones. It works a little better. Then I heard them go to the pub after the match, as usual.'

'Do you live with anyone else?'

'You mean like a mother? Nope, I don't have one of those.'

'Everyone has a mother.' A flash of his own. A dreadfully insufferable woman.

'There was a woman. But she left.'

'Okay,' Sheppard said. Giving up. He scratched his chin. The backs of his hands were itching with want. 'So you just blacked out? And then you woke up here? Did you maybe smell something?'

A flash of recognition came across Headphones' face. 'Yes. There was. I smelt something weird, something chemical. And my head got all swimmy, you know. I couldn't focus on anything. And then I was here.'

'The same as everyone else.'

'Yes. I remember. But why did I forget?'

'It'll be the drugs. Making it all feel like a dream.'

'Right.'

'I need you to remember – I need to know if you were alone in that room.'

'Of course I was – it was my bedroom.'

'And you were alone in the house?'

'Yes,' Headphones said, like she were talking to a toddler.

'And you were sure everyone had gone out? You know these people?'

'Yes. My dad. His friend Bill and his friend Matthew. Although I have to call them Mr Michael and Mr Cline to their faces.'

'But how well do you know them?'

'I don't know them really, not very well at least. My dad does though. He's known them for years. They all work at an estate agency in Angel.'

'Do either of them wear glasses?'

'What the hell are you talking about?' Headphones said. 'No, neither of them.'

Stupid really. These people didn't sound important. But you never knew . . .

Sheppard had a picture in his mind. The evil man. Rectangle glasses. Red tie. Straight suit. The man that Constance described. The man that Mandy might have seen this morning. So he couldn't be in two places at once, right?

'It's always the same on a Friday. My dad and his friends get a half day. Isn't it weird how no one high up seems to work on Friday afternoons? Anyway, they always come back to our house and watch whatever sports are on, then they go to the pub. I go to college, go to therapy and then I come home.'

Sheppard froze. 'What?'

'I go to college. St Martin's. I'm doing a Foundation in Art and Design.'

129

'No. You go to therapy?'

Headphones narrowed her eyes. 'Yeah. What's wrong with that? Jennifer Lawrence went to therapy.'

'No. It's . . .' *Pick your words carefully.*

'I go mainly because of unresolved family issues. I also have claustrophobia, which I thought was getting better . . . until I got locked in a hotel room with five other people and a dead man.'

That explained Headphones' conduct a little more. Why she had squashed herself under the desk, closed her eyes and kept her headphones on.

He decided not to press the issue. 'Did you see your therapist today?'

'No, I went around his house as usual, but no one was home. It was weird, Dr Winter's never missed an appointment before. I guess it must have been serious.'

'Dr Winter.' *Of course, it's him. That's how everyone's connected, isn't it?* Surprised. Why was he surprised?

'Yes.' Headphones obviously saw something in his face. Maybe it was as pale as he thought. 'What?' She hadn't heard. She was listening to the Stones. She had no idea.

Sheppard took a shaking hand, got out Winter's wallet and opened it. Held it up to Headphones.

'Is this him?'

Headphones, confused, looked at the driver's licence. 'Yes. How did you . . .' She stopped. Her brain making connections it didn't want to make. She looked up at Sheppard with big eyes. And before he could stop her, she rushed into the bathroom.

Sheppard was taken off guard and rushed after her.

He was used to the bathroom now – the bright lights and the smell, but it was still revolting. Headphones had pulled back the curtain to see into the bathtub. When she saw Winter lying dead, she dropped to her knees, her hands gripping the side of the tub.

'What . . .' Headphones croaked. 'No . . .'

Sheppard stood behind her, not knowing quite what to do.

Headphones didn't cry. She just sat there on her knees and looked.

Any question that Headphones had murdered this man was immediately wiped from his mind.

Sheppard made his way around her and sat down in front of her . . . *No, the blood. No closer . . .*

Headphones looked down at Dr Winter as though he were someone very close. A father figure. Sheppard hadn't expected such emotion would appear on her face.

They sat there for a while. Until he knew he had to move her on.

'I'm sorry,' Sheppard said.

'Who did this?' Headphones said.

'That's what I'm going to find out.'

'I'll kill them,' Headphones said. And he believed her. 'I'll make it worse for them. Why would they do this to Dr Winter? He never did anything to anyone. He just tried to help.'

He didn't do anything. He was good and kind. And naïve.

'How long have you known him?'

Headphones dragged her gaze from Winter to look at him. 'I've been in therapy for five years.'

We could've bumped into each other. 'Do you mind me asking why?'

'I had social anxiety. Really bad stuff. That's why I don't participate much. I've got a lot better but it's still there. Dr Winter helped me. Showed me how to cope with it. He is . . . was . . . a good man.'

Tell me, are you a good man? The pangs of pain in his head accentuated with every word. He mentally swatted at the air trying to get them to disappear.

A jolt of confusion on Headphones' face. And Sheppard realised he had actually swatted the air. *Keep it together.*

'When's the last time you saw him?'

Her eyes back on Winter. 'A week ago. My normal session. He was telling me that I really didn't need him anymore. But I did . . . I do. He says I'm better. But I'm not. I need him.'

'Was there anything weird about the session? Maybe something he said?' *Maybe something he was planning.* Sheppard still couldn't comprehend Winter being involved in all of this.

Headphones wiped her eyes, although she wasn't crying. 'He cut the session short. I usually see him for an hour and about halfway through, there was a knock at the front door. His office is at the front of the house, so he looked through the window. He didn't waste any time after that. He told me something had come up and I had to leave. He was really apologetic. He said we'd make the time up this week. I didn't mind. He ushered me out the back way, into his living room. Then he shut the door to

132

his office and I heard him opening the front door to the next person. And that was that.'

'Did you hear or see who was at the door?'

'No, I just assumed it was another one of his friends . . .' *He called them friends because 'patients' was too clinical, too cold,* Sheppard remembered. 'Anyway, I thought, maybe someone needed to see him urgently. So I didn't mind.'

'But you were still in his house?' *He has an entrance door and an exit door. You know that?*

'Yes. Usually I go out the kitchen door and leave. The back door. But . . . I don't know why, this time I stuck around. I feel safe in his house. And my dad wasn't expecting me home, so I just sat down. I knew Dr Winter wouldn't mind. I was there about ten minutes. Just sitting. And then . . .'

'Then what?'

'I'm not a nosy person,' Headphones said defensively. In that way someone said something before saying another thing directly to the contrary. 'I don't know what came over me. But . . . after about ten minutes, the printer on a desk at the far side of the room started spitting out stuff. Maybe it was just instinct. But I got up. And I went over to it.'

'What was coming out?'

'Pages and pages of stuff. Loads of text. I didn't really read any of it. It looked like someone was faxing it over. I thought it was never going to stop. But then the last page came out or the first page I guess . . . I picked it up. It was a diagram of something. Filled with boxes, and measurements, and even coordinates, I think. Then I looked at the second page. It was a deed to some land somewhere. I remember being confused, like why Winter would want any of this. I thought maybe it was a mistake, but on the first page at the top, someone had handwritten, "TO WINTER". It was signed "C". I didn't understand any of it.'

Sheppard said nothing. A diagram. With measurements. Could it have been a diagram of this room? There was no question about it. Winter was deep into this. But what else had Headphones said? A land deed? What the hell did that have to do with anything?

'I just put the paper back. And I turned around. And I jumped. He was standing there. Dr Winter. He must have heard the printer or something. I thought I was going to get into real big trouble. But the strangest thing happened.'

'What?'

Headphones was silent for a moment, looking down at her dead doctor. 'He started to cry. Really. He rushed over to me, and was blubbering words I didn't understand. He saw what I was looking at. He saw it. And I saw it. Just some stupid document, but he was going crazy, saying something like, "No, not you". To me. I was still so shocked that I didn't know what to do. So I got my bag and I got out of there. As fast as I could. And I looked back, and he was there. Bawling. Sinking to the floor. And that was the last time I saw him . . . until now.'

Headphones bit her lip.

Sheppard didn't know what to say. Still thinking about what she'd seen. She made the connection before he could.

'Do you think that's why I'm here?'

Still not getting it. 'What?'

'Because I saw those things. He said, "No, not you". Like he wanted to protect me, but couldn't. I ran out of there, when I should have helped him. Like he always helped me.'

'We don't know anything for sure yet,' Sheppard said. But it fit. Headphones saw the plans. Constance locked eyes with the evil man. Alan stirred the wrong pot. Ryan walked in on Winter. Mandy worked with Winter's daughter.

The evil man had used Winter. To get information on the hotel room. And now, to be the murderee in a game of Cluedo. But who did it? Who killed him? Assuming it wasn't the evil man himself . . . that meant someone in the room was lying.

Sheppard got to his feet and held a hand out to Headphones. 'C'mon, you don't need to keep looking at him. It won't do any good.'

Headphones took a moment, then accepted it. He pulled her up and drew the curtain again.

'I can't quite believe it,' Headphones said. She seemed lost. 'I can't believe he's dead.' She gravitated towards the door – no real sense of purpose.

She turned back. 'I'm scared now. I'm really scared.'

And with that, she was gone.

24

He was alone in the bathroom once again. He turned to the mirror to see that he looked far worse than before. His skin seemed to be covered in some kind of slick liquid. His vision was blurred.

He tried to focus on his reflection but he was fuzzy around the edges. Cold jolts of electricity pulsed through him – his heart going three times too fast – enough to power an aircraft. He ducked down to the toilet as the urge to vomit rose up inside him. Opening the lid just in time, he threw up the entire contents of his stomach – a purple-tinged liquid mixed with small chunks of what was once food. It burned his throat and he choked as more came out. Three lurches of his stomach and it was done. The leavings floated on the top of the water. It stank of iron – of acid and The End.

He rested his head on the toilet bowl, blindly searching with his hand for the flush. He pressed it and the vomit swirled away. The smell stayed, mixing with the smell of blood. He closed his eyes and thought of how easy it would be to stay here, to just go to sleep.

His throat was on fire.

Somehow he pulled himself back up to the sink. He

turned the cold water on full blast and cupped a full handful of water into his mouth. He slurped it up and it slid down his throat, feeling better. A few more cups and he swilled the water around his mouth this time, spitting it out to get out the last bits of vomit. He turned on the hot tap, and after a few seconds, warm steam rose from the bowl. He closed his eyes, taking pleasure in the heat on his face.

He didn't know how long he stood there, sipping water from the cold tap and steaming himself. But he knew it was too long. He was feeling better – just had had to clear some space in his belly. But the Crash was still coming. He needed a drink, or pills, or both. The Crash would be worse than this.

Alan. Mandy. Constance. Ryan. And Headphones. *One of these is not like the other*. Who was the murderer? They had all given him reasonable stories. They all seemed genuine. No one had hidden the fact that they were connected to Winter. They were all linked together, in ways they didn't know.

Alan still seemed the most likely. He had a strong motive – even admitted it himself. But Alan didn't seem like a man to do something so brash. He was a terrible person, but he was also clever. Killing a witness would be irrational, stupid. But if it was all in service of some bigger plan . . .

Constance could've done it. She was an actress, so could've easily made him believe her story. And she was crazy, volatile. Who knew what she was capable of? He bet that getting her to murder someone wouldn't take too much. But there was something about her face when she was describing the evil man. He had seen something in her eyes.

Ryan worked here – in this building. He could've been a useful person to have on the inside of a plan like this. He knew things about the rooms that normal people wouldn't. And he also seemed to desperately need money to help his family. He was athletic, probably quite strong. Was it really too far a leap to think he could be responsible?

That left Headphones and Mandy. He couldn't see it. Headphones' reaction to Dr Winter – she saw the old man as a father figure. They were friends. And Mandy – there was one thing he kept coming back to with her. That first time she saw Winter. That first scream. When she had come into the bathroom. It was so loud, so scared, so devoid of hope. It was real. There was no way. Surely.

They're the least likely. So maybe they're the most. A strange thought, but he couldn't entirely dismiss it. After all, he was an entertainer, and on his television show producers regularly employed that tactic. They deflected suspicion from the actual perpetrator to make it a bigger shock when it finally came out. Maybe the man in the horse mask knew this. But still, Headphones? Mandy? Really? He still couldn't imagine they would be capable of such a thing.

Are you capable of such a thing? A strange thought, a sickening thought, but not unwarranted. After all, he was suffering some memory loss. But could he do such a thing? Especially to Dr Winter.

Winter and the evil man had been planning this for a

long time. Did Winter really hate Sheppard that much? To condemn hundreds of innocent lives. Is this what Sheppard did to people? He didn't mean to. Whatever Sheppard had done . . . he didn't mean it. *Maybe this is why you killed Winter. You found out what he was up to.* With a sickening feeling in his gut, Sheppard realised he couldn't rule himself out.

Could he totally blame Winter though? Sheppard knew he had probably meant to do whatever he did to make Winter hate him so much. The old Sheppard wouldn't have. The old Sheppard who thought that maybe things had gone too far. The old Sheppard that was going to quit his show, shrug off all the attention and go back to being nobody.

But he wasn't that man anymore. He was governed by the little kid he once was. The kid who wanted attention more than anything else. The kid that wanted 'it' so much, and reached out and got it. And then vowed never to be an unknown again.

Tell me, do you think you are a good man?

Things had happened too fast. The drink and the drugs. Making it easier to move. Forward. Always forward. He had grown into something terrible. And he hadn't even cared.

Self-pity gushed over him. He couldn't even look at himself. The bloodshot eyes, the slick skin, the look of disdain. He was broken. A shadow of the illusion that appeared on television. The man behind the mask.

The mirror was fogging up. His face disappearing in the mist.

He was not that man. Not now, not in this terrible bathroom. He was just another man with too many questions and no answers. He had ducked and dived all his life, trouble finding it hard to catch him. How had he not known something like this was coming? How one day the mouse would fall into the trap?

Was it enough to be sorry?

He turned the taps off to see the last of the steam swirl up and settle in the room, mixing in with the smell of blood and vomit.

At the door, he glanced around. The shadow of Dr Winter behind the curtain. He drew it back once more.

Tell me . . .

'I'm not a good man, I never was.' Finally answering him. After twenty years.

And Winter's face was cold – letting him know that it wasn't enough.

25

Before . . .

Brickwork was buzzing by the time he got there. He got out of the back of the limo and waved to the large queue of people waiting to get in. They waved back and a number of them screamed at him happily. He chuckled and nodded to the bouncer as he passed. The big burly man smiled and unhooked the cordon.

Sheppard made his way down the steps slowly. He'd already had a lot to drink, and had taken one too many pills. His limbs felt comfortably numb, as though they could float, and there was that familiar fluffy feeling in his brain. He was seeing the world through a cloud, but the drink was yanking him back down to earth. That was the coolness of the combo. He existed in the in-between. The new reality. Unfortunately, in the reality he had left behind, he could walk straight. He grasped the banister as he almost slipped on the carpeted steps. His heart fluttered. Stairs were the enemy of the drunk.

He prevailed eventually and emerged into the large open area of the club. It was incredibly dark, lit up incrementally by flashing strobe lights. The area was a fantastically crowded dancefloor with a raised bar to the side and booths placed around at the edges. The dance-floor was already packed with people, jumping up and down to some pop track.

He smiled and started to make his way across the dancefloor. As people saw him, they moved out of the way. Some people tried to talk to him, or grab him. He just smiled at them. In the light, he couldn't see anyone, pick out any distinguishing features, so he had no idea who anyone was. They were ghosts. And for that, he was almost glad. He didn't have time for real people.

He looked around the edges. For the VIP area. Found it by the bar. Familiar faces behind the barrier. The security guard spotted him and smiled.

'Mr Sheppard.' His mouth made the movements. 'Good to see you.'

He opened the barrier and let him through. Sheppard smiled back at him, slapping him on the back and covertly handing him three 20-pound notes.

The code for *No interruptions*.

The VIP area was slightly offset from the rest of the club. An alcove, small but long enough to channel the music coming from the rest of the room. Changing it. Making it quieter. It was also lighter, from small bulb lights embedded in the brick ceiling. The area was a round of comfy seats and Sheppard could actually see the faces of the people sitting there. It was largely empty but Sheppard saw his publicist, who was absorbed in conversation with two glamorous women who looked like identical twins, his director and PA who were not so enraptured in talking with each other and Douglas Perry, who was very obviously waiting for Sheppard to arrive while sipping on a strange-looking colourful drink, topped with a slice of orange and a small pink umbrella.

On the circular table, there were mountains of empty glasses, and as he looked, a pretty young waitress came along to clean up. The table was slick with alcohol and he thought he detected her grimace as she picked up the first glass to put on her tray.

As Sheppard slid down into a chair, happy to be able to stop worrying about falling over, Douglas looked up from his phone. With a straw hanging from the side of his mouth, he gave a great guffaw. Sheppard wondered how far gone he was. The agent had a penchant for cocaine and was rarely seen off it. He had even got Sheppard to try it a few times, and although it wasn't unpleasant, Sheppard didn't like the after-effects of it. He much preferred pills.

'Here he is, the man of the hour. Or should I say, the man of the year.'

Everyone in the area looked around at this bold statement, and saw Sheppard. They all turned, smiling and clapping. The girls talking to his publicist seemed to want to ditch him for Sheppard, although the publicist was so locked in conversation, they couldn't get away.

'Come on, what are you having? I'm buying.'

'It's an open bar, Doug,' Sheppard said, already slurring his words.

'Exactly. That's why I'm buying,' Douglas said, and laughed heartily. He raised a hand and waved over a woman in a short red dress. She was pretty, with long legs. Sheppard slowly looked her up and down as Douglas ordered him a bourbon and another monstrously colourful concoction for himself.

Once she had gone, Douglas returned his attention to Sheppard.

'So how are you, old mate?' Douglas always had the cadence of an older gentleman, one who might have seen wartime. In reality, he was fifty and as spineless as they came.

'I'm great,' Sheppard said, shuffling in his seat. Already thinking he could use another pill. He never felt sated by them – never content. He existed in one of two camps – too much or too little. He didn't know which one was worse.

'You look a little weathered, if you don't mind me saying, mate.'

Sheppard smiled at him as the woman came to give him his drink. He took it and downed it in one. A shiver through his brain, a jolt of energy. Better already. 'That better?' He replaced the glass on the waitress' tray and asked for another. She nodded and left.

'HA. Well, I guess you deserve it. You alone are putting my children through college, you know that.'

'Don't mention it.'

'Honestly, Sheppard, this is fantastic. Absolutely fantastic. Your numbers are going through the roof. The show is doing better than anything that has ever been in the morning slot. Have you seen the numbers? Did Zoe give you the numbers?'

'I've seen the numbers. She gave me the numbers.'

'I haven't seen Zoe here yet. When she comes, she'll give you the numbers.'

'Doug,' Sheppard said, laughing, 'I've seen the numbers.'

Douglas stopped talking and laughed too. 'I'm sorry, mate. It's just so fantastic. YOU are bloody fantastic. You remember when I took you on? You were—'

'Fourteen. Yes I know. I was there.'

'—fourteen. I never thought you'd get this far. I mean, I don't want to speak ill of the dead, but thank God that Maths teacher was murdered when he was.'

Sheppard didn't know how to respond. So just smiled. Douglas could always find the most tactless way to say something – it was his talent. It was why he had two ex-wives and four children who despised him.

Through his foggy mind, he thought of Mr Jefferies. The kind, rotund Maths teacher who had always helped him with his homework. The teacher who'd been found hanging from the ceiling.

'What did you want to talk to me about, Doug?' Sheppard said, as the woman with the legs came back with another drink and Doug's cocktail. This time Sheppard took his and held it up to the light. The crisp brown liquid looked inviting, silky. His life fuel. He took a sip and said to the woman, 'Don't let my glass get empty, yeah?'

The woman nodded. She looked dazed, excited. She was obviously a fan. Women did that weird fluttering thing with their eyes whenever they recognised him. He couldn't tell if they wanted to sleep with him or murder him. Either way, they looked invitingly dangerous.

Douglas took his new drink. 'I wanted to talk to you about new opportunities.'

'Sounds ominous,' Sheppard said. The drink wrapping round him, like a warm blanket on a cold evening.

'I've been approached by a number of parties about the possibility of you writing a book.'

'A book?'

'Yes, those things with words in.'

'Very funny, Doug. What would I write a book about?'

'Well, anything. Anything you like. As interesting or as dumb as you want. To be honest, it doesn't really matter. People will buy it because it'll have your name on it. Books are just like television. It's all about the man behind the glass.'

'I don't know how to write a book.'

'People will help you. Hell, people will write it for you, if you want. You just need to be the name on the cover. What do you say?'

Sheppard laughed. 'Easy as that, huh?'

'Think about what the book could be though. The Resident Detective Morgan Sheppard tells of his struggles solving the murder of his own teacher, when he was just eleven years old. I mean, Christ, Morgan, that's a sure-fire hit. That's *Times* bestseller list stuff.'

'It does sound enticing,' Sheppard said, swirling the bourbon around in his glass. He could almost see it. The book in the front window of Waterstones. A tasteful artsy cover maybe. His face on the back of the jacket, smiling out of thousands of copies. A nice thick volume, filled with the accounts of the child detective.

'So?'

'I don't very often say no, Doug,' Sheppard said, 'so it would be rather pointless to start now.'

Douglas almost jumped out of his seat. 'HA. Yes, sir, you are fantastic, Sheppard. We're going to be kings of the world. You and I. Morgan Sheppard at the top of every chart. You're a brand. And we're going to make millions. I've already got publishers willing to pay out the arse for the first one.'

'The first one? Let's not get carried away, Doug.'

'*Let's not get carried away,*' Douglas mimicked. 'That sounds like a Sheppard without enough booze inside of him. Waitress.' And he waved over the woman for another round.

The rest of the night was lost in a toxic fume of poisonous substances. Sheppard and Douglas talked a while longer about nothing in particular as they became steadily worse for wear. Many times, small groups of mainly girls came up to the VIP rope and asked Sheppard for an autograph. Although this was meant to be a TV company party, he didn't recognise any of them. Douglas insisted that he sign every single one and Sheppard didn't complain.

At some point, the music got louder and the lights got lower, so Sheppard could hardly see Douglas in front of him, let alone hear him. The two shouted to each other, but didn't get much of what the other was saying. Sheppard decided that he would have to cross the vast expanse of the dancefloor to find somewhere to urinate. He gestured to Douglas, and somehow the drunken man got the right end of the stick.

Sheppard stood up, the world around him rocking. It was the world that was unsteady, not him. He was the greatest he had ever felt. Child Detective. TV presenter. And now Author. He found his way out of the VIP area, patting the guard on the shoulder more for support than friendliness. The dancefloor looked bigger than it was before. It swelled and pulsated in front of him. The people all morphed together in his mind, so he was just looking at one dark mass. He kept his head down and walked through them.

A weird part of being famous was that people always seemed to want to touch you. It was rather bizarre. People didn't seem content with just seeing you – they had to make sure you were real. As he was crossing the dancefloor, Sheppard experienced this phenomenon in full force. People tapped him, shook his hand, and even hugged him. And Sheppard was drunk enough to let it happen.

It felt like an age before he finally got free of the dancefloor and looked up to see a neon sign saying 'John' and an arrow pointing down a narrow corridor. John? Well, it was a male name he guessed, so he followed it and finally found the toilets.

It was another half an hour before he finally got back to the VIP area. As he sat down, he noticed that Douglas had made his way through three more glasses of multi-coloured sludge. The groups had converged and Douglas was talking animatedly to the twins while the producer and the publicist were having a heated discussion. His PA, Rogers, was looking pale . . . like he might pass out or throw up or do both at any moment.

The others looked round as the waitress came up to Sheppard with another bourbon.

'Thank you,' Sheppard said, and downed it without a second thought. 'Another please.'

The woman smiled and nodded.

Douglas laughed. Gesturing to Sheppard. 'Now this mate really knows how to party,' he said, to the girls.

Sheppard smiled back. 'Just a little.'

'You alright, mate? You were a long time.'

'Ha, let's just say next time I want to take a piss, I might start out fifteen minutes early. You know what I think we need? I think we need to get far more drunk.'

Perry smiled. 'Well, I guess I better drink to that.'

As if on cue, and horrifically fast, the woman came back with another bourbon for Sheppard. He'd lost count of them – he remembered a time when he used to keep track. Now he didn't bother. Sheppard touched glasses with Douglas and the girls, just as PA Rogers finally passed out. The man's face hit the table and he collapsed on the floor.

The whole VIP area erupted into uncontrollable laughter.

Sheppard got up onto the table and the music dimmed as the DJ noticed something was going on.

'Three cheers for dopey Rogers,' he shouted.

And the entire club joined in in a round of hip-hip-hoorahs. Half of the people there probably had no idea why, but they joined in nonetheless.

Sheppard waved his drink around, sloshing it every-where, before collapsing back into his seat.

That was when he lost the night.

26

Sheppard left the bathroom so fast that he crashed into Mandy, who was staring at the wall beside the bed. They almost toppled over together, but Mandy grabbed and steadied him. The commotion drew everyone else's gaze before they went back to whatever it was they were doing.

'What is it?' Mandy said. She must have seen it in his eyes.

Sheppard opened his mouth, and thought better of it. He didn't know what to say. He was a fish gasping for air. Something about his admittance to Winter – *'I'm not a good man. I never was.'* – seemed to draw a line under everything. And the feeling that the evil man knew Sheppard's inadequacies better than he knew them himself. 'What are you doing?' he said.

'I'm looking at this picture. It's really weird, don't you think?' The painting of a farmhouse burning and a scarecrow smiling had almost smugly caught his attention when he'd first woken up but he hadn't thought about it since. 'Why the hell is this in a hotel room?'

'I don't know,' Sheppard said. He remembered thinking exactly the same thing.

Mandy reached up and ran her hand over the paint of the farmhouse. 'It's sad, isn't it? I like art, puzzling over what it all means. This painting freaks me out. Somehow I just know there's a family in that house, children burning. And that scarecrow with those eyes. They remind me of the eyes of the guy in the café.'

'What?'

'There have to be people in that house, right?'

'No, the other thing. About the eyes.'

'Oh,' Mandy said, putting her hand down, 'I remembered something. That man in the café who was looking at me? I know now what freaked me out so much. It was his eyes. They just looked like the eyes of a man who was up to no good. Like the scarecrow's.'

Sheppard looked up at the painting. The scarecrow's eyes looked oddly human. As he stared, they seemed to move and look at him. *No, just an illusion.* But this lined up with what Constance had said. Mandy had met the same man.

Which meant . . .

Sheppard put his arm on the wall to steady himself, as a pulse of dizziness threatened to topple him. 'We have to get out of here.'

Mandy's face was losing colour. 'But . . .'

You can't do it.

'I can't do it.'

All the interviewing, all that time lost, when he should have been doing the right thing. Trying to escape.

Alan's voice, far off. 'Well, nice to know he's on the same page as the rest of us.'

151

'Shut up, Alan.' Ryan.

Who was lying? Someone had to be? But all the stories fit together. They all had run in with Winter or Constance's evil man. They all ended up here because of it. But who was lying? Someone with more skill could tell. They could see it in their eyes.

Sheppard looked from Mandy to the timer. Under two hours to go. Too much time. If the evil man knew that Sheppard couldn't do it, why not just kill him straight off? Not place him here. In death's waiting room.

'Sheppard, what's wrong?' Mandy again. Scared this time.

Sheppard looked at her. And pushed past her. Ignoring her follow-up query.

There was only one thing for it now. One way to stave off the shakes, and the cold, hard crash. Take the edge off imminent death. Although maybe it would be the evil man's last laugh for it to be empty.

Sheppard almost fell to his knees in front of the television. The others were talking to him. Instead he found himself on Headphones' level. She had her headphones on again, and had shuffled back under the desk. He looked at her and she looked back. Running his hands over the cupboard underneath the desk in search of a handle, he hoped to God that he was right.

It was indeed the mini-bar. And even in the relative light of the room, the manufactured flickering of the fridge bulb was comforting. However, what was inside was not.

The minibar was almost entirely empty, just as he

feared. It looked pathetic, in the way barren fridges often do. There were only two items, on the top shelf — aeroplane miniature bottles. His favourite brand of bourbon.

It was almost worse than nothing.

Sheppard picked up one bottle — barely the size of his forefinger. One swig of alcohol, maybe two — barely enough to get a taste.

His favourite brand — best not to think about the implications of that.

Sheppard slipped one bottle into his pocket and took the other. He stood up and looked around, bottle in hand.

Alan was looking at him with something like confused disgust. The others were just confused.

'I don't think it's really time for a piss-up, Sheppard,' the lawyer said. An acid tone that could melt through skin.

'It's two bottles, Alan,' Sheppard said.

'I knew it. I knew the papers were correct,' Alan said. 'Shaky hands. Sweating like a pig. You're coming down with a nice case of withdrawal.'

Sheppard launched himself at Alan, grabbing him by the lapels of his suit and slamming him into the window. Alan let out an exasperated grunt, snarling at Sheppard.

'There he is,' Alan said, 'our real hero.'

'Can you shut your mouth for two goddamn seconds?' Sheppard said. 'It's two bottles.' Too close. He could feel the hatred running out of the old man. Almost burned him.

'Sheppard?' Mandy said, uneasy.

She was staring inside the minibar. Ryan was looking

too. Sheppard let Alan go, the lawyer readjusting his tie and dusting his lapels as if Sheppard was unclean.

Sheppard stepped back towards the minibar.

Mandy knelt down and reached into the small fridge, bringing out a small white box that was slotted into the lowest shelf. He hadn't noticed it before as it perfectly fit the dimensions of the fridge and was suitably camouflaged. She held the box up to Sheppard.

It looked like a first-aid box. But written in black marker, in the same handwriting as the rulebook, was 'With regards, The Great Hotel'.

He turned it over, but nothing was written on the bottom. The box rattled. It was heavy.

A first-aid kit? Was this another one of Sheppard's cravings? If the evil man knew Sheppard's favourite bourbon, surely he knew what else was needed. Maybe this box was a present.

Sheppard put the other bottle of bourbon in his pocket, and grasped the box with both hands, sliding the locks to open so it flipped open.

It wasn't what he wanted. And it wasn't food or water or sustenance. But even still, Sheppard couldn't quite believe it.

'What is it?' Ryan said, and Mandy echoed him.

Sheppard looked up at them, and emptied the box. They all looked down at the contents strewn out across the bed. Six mobile phones.

27

Mobile phones — what?

Sheppard looked around at everyone — they looked as confused as he felt. Even Constance had looked around from her seat on the bed and Headphones had stuck her head up from beneath the desk.

He looked down again — he couldn't see his own phone.

'What is this?' Ryan said.

Sheppard randomly grabbed one — a thin smartphone — and tapped the screen. It lit up with a wallpaper of a dog wearing antlers. It had a passcode. No matter. Sheppard saw what he needed. No signal.

Who would he call? The police? Never called the police before. Was it like on television?

999. What is your emergency?

We've been trapped in a room by a guy in a horse mask. I've got to solve a murder in the next hour and forty five minutes or he's going to blow up the building. No wait — don't hang up.

Sheppard went to put the smartphone down and someone whimpered He looked around — Headphones was staring at it. He held it up, the picture of the dog looking out to her. She nodded, and Sheppard gave it to her.

'Do you all see your own?' Sheppard said, but no one moved. So he picked up a flip-top phone that lit up as he opened it. Plain blue background. Old style. And in the corner – no signal.

Phone companies are really doing God's work.

He put the phone down, and Ryan picked it up. 'It's mine,' Ryan said, opening it.

Alan started forward into his view and snatched one of the phones up. 'Finally, I can tell Jenkins to prep my report.'

'I think we'll call the police first, yeah?' Mandy said, picking another one up. Hers had some kind of dongle thing hanging off it.

Two phones left. A BlackBerry and a smartphone. Neither one his. He picked up the smartphone. Slightly older than the last and cracked in one corner. Wallpaper – a young woman with a baby in her arms. Corner – no signal.

Wait.

Three phones with no signal. Looking around at Alan's and Mandy's faces, maybe more than three.

'How is that possible?' Ryan said, realising what Sheppard had already realised, holding his phone high in the air. Mandy too – whatever was hanging from her phone was swinging in the air.

'Goddamn it.'

There was a groan from Constance, as she digested the words. 'God doesn't need a phone mast.'

'Oh put a sock in it, Jesus-freak,' Alan spat.

Sheppard ignored them. 'Has anyone got anything?'

Blank faces all around.

'No signal,' Mandy said, 'but we're in the centre of London.'

'Bastard must be blocking it somehow,' Alan said. 'The reception. He's playing us like a damn flute. Getting our hopes up and then dashing them.'

'What are you talking about?' Ryan said.

'I see this all the time, son,' Alan told him. 'This is how you break people.'

Constance shuffled up the bed and gestured to Sheppard. He handed her the smartphone. She took it and recoiled, slinking back to her former position.

One phone left. The BlackBerry. One of the models that had an entire keyboard on it, with impossibly small keys for each letter. But whose was it?

He picked it up and pressed one of the keys at random. The screen lit up. On the screen, behind all the icons were two faces. A wife and a daughter. Younger than they must be now.

The drink and the drugs, they fogged him. They obscured the past. Made him live in nowhere but the present. They made it harder to remember, but it was still there. He just had to be helped in jogging his memory. Looking into Winter's daughter's eyes was more than enough. And he remembered how he had hurt them all. And now Winter was dead and they might never know. He shielded the screen from the others, as though he might contain what he had done.

Mandy faltered slightly. 'Is that yours?' she said, with a smile. Evidently this phone didn't look like Sheppard's style. Which was true.

'Um . . . yeah,' Sheppard said, looking up. 'No signal.' He put it in his pocket, next to the bottles of bourbon.

Lies can ruin a man, Winter had said – in one of his last sessions. *They can rot him from the inside out.*

Evidently he hadn't learned.

28

They fanned out to all corners of the room, holding up their phones, looking for any chance of a single bar. Sheppard watched them, knowing it would be no use. No point in putting on a show.

Because Alan was right. The evil man was toying with them, making them waste time.

There's more to it than that. Right? There had to be some reason why.

His phone wasn't in the box. Did that mean something? Had he had his phone on him in his pocket in his room in Paris? He couldn't remember.

So maybe–? Sheppard made sure everyone else was preoccupied with their own devices and took out Winter's BlackBerry again. It didn't have a passcode, so he was free to select whatever he wanted. He went to the messages to see none. They must have been deleted. He scoured through the rest of the applications on the home screen, to find much the same. No emails. No alerts. No notes.

Until he came to the calendar. The day was blocked out with a big yellow bar. A bar that kept on running. According to the phone, Winter was busy from now until . . .

He tapped the bar and it expanded with the details. The appointment ran from five am on 25 October (today – or at least Sheppard thought it was) to 31 December in the year 2999. The maximum the diary would allow. The appointment was titled in large block letters '4404'. And the location? Sheppard scrolled down to see: TGH.

Sheppard dropped the phone to his side. 4404. This room? The room Winter had measured out. If this was 4404 (and it had to be), the location was the Great Hotel. It all lined up. What was Winter doing with the evil man? And why would he willingly come to this room if he knew what was going to happen to him? Unless he didn't. The appointment running until 2999. Winter was all booked up until the end of time.

'Sheppard.' He looked up to see Mandy standing in front of him. How long had he been staring into space? Behind Mandy, Sheppard saw Alan trying to gain height by jumping up and down. It was almost funny. Almost. 'There's nothing. No signal anywhere.'

'No,' Sheppard said.

'How is that possible?' Mandy said, turning her phone over in her hands.

'I don't know,' he said, half-heartedly. 'Maybe a blocker like Alan said. Maybe he did something to the phones.' Tired of assumptions. Tired of shooting wildly in the dark. The running theme of all that had happened so far.

'That's not really how blockers work,' Ryan said, coming forward. 'Unless the horse man has a blocker taking out the entire floor. But someone would notice.'

'What about–?' Mandy started.

'We don't have time for this,' Sheppard said.

'I know,' Mandy said, almost smiling. 'I just thought you'd want this.' She held up a thin sliver of metal. It took Sheppard a moment to realise what it was. An army dog tag. It had been hanging off her phone. The name PHILLIPS pressed on it – a string of numbers underneath.

Sheppard looked confused. 'I'm not sure why I . . .'

Ryan seemed to be on Mandy's wavelength. His eyes lit up. 'Not a penny, but it'd do.' Mandy nodded.

Sheppard got it, and smiled. He smiled – because after everything, there was finally something. He took the dog tag and looked at it. 'The vent.'

'Can I have the other one?' Ryan said.

'Why?'

Mandy gave it to him anyway. He held it up. It matched the other perfectly. 'The bathroom. I'm not a plumber, but I know there's at least one way out of the room. The pipes.'

Sheppard wondered why he hadn't thought of it before. There were at least two things travelling in and out the room. The air in the vents. And the water in the toilet.

'If I can jimmy the toilet off the wall, maybe there'll be some kind of opening.'

'Yes,' Sheppard said, looking down at the dog tag in his hand. It might just work.

'There's one problem,' Mandy said, cutting into the hope. 'What do you think the horse mask'll do when he sees what you're up to?'

That was true. One press of a button on the evil man's

161

part and all this could be over. But Sheppard couldn't see any other way forward.

'I don't think the horse mask is done with us yet. I don't think he'd blow up his little game on a whim,' Ryan said. He looked at Sheppard and they both nodded in turn.

'What if you're wrong?' Mandy said.

'This is the best chance we have,' Sheppard said.

Mandy thought for a moment, growing quiet. Slowly she nodded. 'Okay.'

'I'll go through the vents while Ryan starts trying to find a way out in the bathroom. And I need you here. You need to keep the peace. Keep Constance quiet and keep Alan at bay and keep Headphones . . . I trust you.'

'Okay,' Mandy said. 'Will you be okay?'

'This is my problem,' Sheppard said firmly. 'It's only right that I go.'

Mandy nodded and went to sit with Constance.

Ryan watched her go. He lowered his voice to a whisper. 'She would have fit better in the vents. Or Rhona, even.'

Sheppard shook his head. 'Rhona has claustrophobia and Mandy doesn't owe anyone anything. This is on me. I don't want it to be her fault if the horse mask takes this the wrong way. I don't want it to be her fault if we all die.'

29

Ryan made his way down the right side of the bed and Sheppard followed, twirling the dog tag in his fingers. The name PHILLIPS shining in the light. Sheppard hadn't asked Mandy what the tags meant, but he assumed a family member. He resolved he would do it if . . . no, when he got back.

Ryan reached up to the vent, half above the bed and half above the bedside table where the countdown slowly ebbed away. Sheppard didn't look at it – if this worked, there would be no need. Getting out of here had never been so close.

'You'll have to take the whole unit off the wall. Behind the grate'll be a dehumidifier. It'll be heavy.'

'You seem to know a lot about this,' Sheppard said.

Ryan smiled. 'Perks of the job.'

Even now, his mind wandered. An intricate knowledge of the room. The perfect profession to set this all up.

But why? What motive did he have? What motive did any of them have?

'Thanks,' Sheppard said. 'We get out of this and I owe you a beer.'

Ryan laughed, for the first time. 'We get out of this

and you owe me a brewery.' Ryan clapped Sheppard on the shoulder and turned. 'I'm going to get started on the plumbing.'

Sheppard nodded as the young man rounded the corner and opened the door to the bathroom. He paused. Being hit with the smell. He pushed past it and disappeared, the door shutting behind him.

Sheppard started unscrewing the grate. When he had got both of the top flatbed screws out, he felt the grate wane with the weight behind it. He kept one hand pressed on the grate, pushing it in as he undid the bottom screws.

As he did so, he heard Alan somewhere behind him, finally giving up on his phone. 'Bloody hell, this is a day and a half.'

He slowed down, unscrewing so he could hear better. He stared straight forward at the grate. What would Alan be saying when he thought Sheppard was preoccupied?

Mandy stood up from the bed. As he felt the first screw come loose, Sheppard heard the muffled impact of shoes on carpet, then a little gasp and a shuffle. Like Alan had surprised Mandy somehow. Pulled her closer, maybe.

'We need to start thinking laterally here,' Alan whispered. As if to prove his point. However, he himself had been correct when saying that no one could have a private conversation. Now on the other side of one, Sheppard realised that everyone did indeed hear everything.

'Laterally?' Mandy said, with a tone that would have matched Sheppard's at that moment.

What was Alan's endgame? He was still suspect number one after all.

'This game is rigged, I bet you,' Alan whispered, harshly. 'There is no answer, or at least no answer that was presented as such.'

'What are you talking about?'

'Misdirection, Mandy. The oldest of tricks. The reason people think magic is real, or bombs were in Iraq. The simple art of misdirection.'

'I suppose you know all about it. Being a sleazy lawyer and all.'

'Of course. I use it all the time. And I'm seeing it here.'

Sheppard took the first screw out and the grate lurched again. How could a dehumidifier be this heavy?

Alan continued. 'What if this isn't *his* game?'

'I have no idea what you're saying.'

'Why is he the one who gets to call the shots? Because the TV said so, or because he's the one with the star power?'

'Hijinks.' A new voice in the conversation.

Sheppard looked around. Constance Ahearn was looking right at him. 'Even in your thoughts, do not curse the king, nor in your bedroom curse the rich, for a bird of the air will carry your voice, or some winged creature tell the matter.'

Sheppard glared at her. What was that? The Bible. Sounded more like *The Hobbit*. But her outburst made the two behind him stop.

'Shut up, Ms Ahearn, there's a good little lunatic,' Alan said.

Sheppard looked back as the final screw came loose. The grate launched at him as it came free and he gripped

165

it. It was too heavy. And he didn't have it. He pushed back with his legs, as he felt a body next to him.

Mandy had climbed onto the bed and quickly grabbed the left side of the grate, taking some of the weight. He smiled his thanks as he got a better grip. Between them, they managed to pull out the dehumidifier. They carefully levered it and put it down on the bed.

When Sheppard looked back up at the vent, he saw a long and narrow path. It carried on into darkness. 'We're at the end of the corridor,' he said. 'There's no way it could carry on for that long if we weren't. I'll have to make my way around.'

Mandy looked into the vent and frowned.

'I'll be back before you know it,' Sheppard said, 'hopefully having got someone's attention. Who knows, we could be ten minutes away from getting out of here.'

'If you're sure,' Mandy said.

Sheppard looked from the vent to Mandy. He wasn't sure about anything. But he wasn't about to say that.

'Keep the peace, okay. These people trust you.'

Mandy nodded and got off the bed.

Sheppard stepped back and looked into the vent again. He took out Winter's BlackBerry and looked at it. No. 'Does anyone have a torch on their phone?' he said and looked around. Mandy and Alan shook their heads, Ryan was gone and Constance had turned back into herself. But Headphones showed a glimmer of recognition.

The teenager slid out from the desk, dug into her hoodie pocket and took out her phone. She threw it to him.

He caught it and smiled at her. He thought that he

caught her blushing before she went back to her burrow under the desk. There seemed to be a lighter air in the room. Everyone seemed to be happier. Except Alan.

Sheppard was happier. The bourbon in his pocket and escape just a short shuffle away. This nightmare – almost over. The cold, hard crash seemed to have gone away for a while. That itching feeling on the back of his hands was sated. The ache behind his eyeballs diminished.

Sheppard turned the torch on, catching a glimpse of Headphones' dog again. He silently promised to bring the phone back safe.

He reached into the vent, hitching both his elbows into either side of the shaft. He placed a precarious foot onto the bedside table and the other foot on the bed, pulling himself up.

It took a few pushes with his elbows to fully get himself up into the small passageway. It was cramped. A small vent. His shoulders rubbing against the steel top. His legs flailing behind him. He wondered what the others were seeing in the room. Probably something comical. He took the smartphone and placed it in his top pocket. It illuminated enough for him to see ahead.

He felt the edges of the opening with his feet. The room behind him now. The room he thought he would die in. After this, he'd swear off hotels for life.

Because, finally, it was time to check out.

30

Sheppard shuffled forward, his knees already aching in response. More than ever, he felt like a mouse in a maze, chasing around to satisfy the horse mask, Mr TV, the evil man. Although maybe this maze could lead to freedom. And maybe the evil man slipped up, maybe this was something he hadn't thought of. He started forward again. His back scraped against the top of the vent, igniting it in a rush of pain. He would just have to worry about that later, drowning the agony in thoughts of escape.

He shuffled for a while longer, the torch in his top pocket bobbing up and down with each sliver of progress. The light showed the first intersection rather quickly, bouncing the light back to him. There were two paths – left and right. Both were tight corners – but they both looked able to support Sheppard's size. Sheppard got to the intersection, shut his eyes and thought. If the window was looking north (he decided, just for orientation purposes), the wall with the bed against it was the east wall. So he could either go north or south. Whichever way he chose, he would be making his way around the room – skirting the walls.

He chose north for no particular reason, slowly edging

around the corner. He got his torso around with little issue, leading with his arms, but when he tried to bring his legs around, the sharp corner of the vent dug into his shins. He briefly panicked, flailing with his arms and trying to pull himself around. He managed it and took a deep breath. He had never been a claustrophobic person, but he had never been in a situation like this before. It felt like the walls were closing in on him ever so slowly, as if he was going to get crushed in the slowest compactor ever.

The other thing he hadn't thought of was the smell. Not the smell of the vent, although it did slightly smell of burnt, hot air. The overpowering scent was his own – a sickly mix of severe body odour and recently jettisoned vomit.

Detectives don't smell.

He adjusted to the new direction. He got into a routine, slumping like a handicapped dog, moving his elbows and then his legs. Forward, back, forward, back.

The phone light was strong but only carried so far – he could only see a few feet in front of him. The air had an eerie feeling – the aluminium (or was it steel?) echoing conversations seemingly happening all around the building. Ghosts of voices seemed to come to him, although when he tried to focus on them, they disappeared.

Maybe you're just going crazy.

There were definitely a few voices he could hear. Alan and Mandy and another voice that sounded like Ryan's. It sounded underwater, the words impossible to decipher.

The vent sloped down and Sheppard found himself

gaining speed. He came to another turn – only one choice this time, left. He made his way around and saw that the vent grew visibly narrower, supposing it was running under the window. He had to flatten his stomach, flopping like a fish to get through the opening. It grew slightly larger – but only slightly. He was able to bend his arms again to gain some grip and propel himself forward.

The phone light was no help here, as it was pointed downwards. The darkness ahead of him loomed large. He became adamant there was something there in the dark, just out of his field of view, taunting him. He almost heard the shuffling of something, something that wasn't him – not allowing him to think it was just his imagination. Which of course, it was.

Probably . . . right?

After a while, another decision. Forward or left. Left would follow the room so he decided forward. This would mean he would be heading towards the next room, and towards rescue.

He repositioned himself and fished Headphones' phone out of his shirt pocket. He angled it ahead. The vent seemed to go on forever, or at least as far as he could see.

'Morgan.' A whisper in his ear.

He jumped, slamming his head on the top of the vent. The pain erupting before mixing in with all the rest. A voice. He had heard it. He had heard it, right? The hairs on his neck stood on end. Someone was right behind him. Someone had to be.

He realised the phone had a camera, and opened the camera app. He swapped to the front-facing camera. His face again. He could never escape it. He looked like he was dying. His skin, unreasonably pale, looking more like the scales of a snake than human skin. His hair seemed thin. His eyes, in the warm torchlight, almost looked yellow — the final curse of the alcoholic.

Get out of here, get to a doctor. Abridge the drinking history a bit.

Nothing behind him though. He tried to look over his shoulder to make sure, but couldn't manage it. The more he thought of it, the less he thought it had been real. Maybe it had just carried through the vents? Maybe someone in the room had said it?

No one calls you Morgan. Not anymore.

No one except him. He did. The masked man.

He started moving forward again, keeping the camera on just for peace of mind. But there was nothing behind him, and never had been — not really. He lowered the camera just in time to keep from slamming head first into the vent wall. Another corner? No, this wasn't a turn or an intersection. There were walls all around him. And there was something there, something white, on the vent wall.

He switched the torch back to front-facing. A sheet of metal was in front of him. And a piece of paper held up with a piece of tape. Sheppard looked at the words written on it, suppressing the sudden urge to retch up whatever was left in his stomach. No way forward. Air. There wasn't enough air. And all he could think of was the words on the paper.

THERE WAS AN OPENING HERE
IT'S GONE NOW
   - ☺ C

31

Sheppard stayed still. There was nothing else to be done. His eyes ran over and over the paper, reading the words again and again. A dead end? How could it be a dead end? The evil man blocked it off? He knew that they would get into the vents. All this time, he knew. And planned accordingly. Sheppard pulled his arms out in front of him and flattened his palms against the cold metal. He pushed. Nothing. No give. It had been blocked off.

Unless this had never been a way around. Maybe the evil man was just toying with him. Maybe he had got turned around somehow. Because how could someone block off a vent – make it look like there was never an opening to begin with? Maybe he had just chosen a wrong turn.

He shuffled backwards, replacing the phone in his top pocket. Soon, he was back at the previous turn. This time, he went left. This meant he should be running parallel to the west wall of the room and the east wall of the next room. Sheppard stopped for a moment, listening. He couldn't hear anything, apart from a low mutter of familiar voices that was surely coming from his left. Nothing from the next room.

What if no one was there? What if he couldn't get anyone's attention?

Then you keep going. You keep going until you do.

It was exhausting. Dragging himself along. And as he brought his knee up for another shuffle, he felt and heard the two bottles of single-serving bourbon in his trouser pocket. That would give him some more strength – a little pick-me-up. But he didn't think he could reach them even if he wanted to.

He pressed on, the dark closing around him and the pain coming in waves. Knees, back, shoulders. All feeling raw and tender. He continued until he thought he must be nearing the edge of the room.

Sure enough, he came to the edge. Left, right or up – straight up, vertical. He angled the torch and looked. Up seemed like a hard task to accomplish so he went right.

As he travelled down the passage, he tried to focus on the low voices he heard, just to distract him from the pain. Mandy and Alan. He wondered what they were talking about, and remembered what he had heard just before he went into the vent. It felt like hours ago. He severely hoped it wasn't.

Alan was clearly up to something, and even if he didn't murder Simon Winter, he was a dangerous man. Unscrupulous. Never thinking he's wrong. A talker.

Remind you of anyone?

Maybe that was why he was so wary of Alan. Because they were so alike.

He hoped Mandy was keeping him at bay.

About a minute later, the torchlight hit on something

white ahead. He took the torch and almost dropped it. Another piece of paper, the same message . . .

THERE WAS AN OPENING HERE
IT'S GONE NOW
- ☺ C

How? How was this happening? Another dead end, just as closed off as the last. He looked carefully at the sides of the vent but he saw no join or connection where the evil man (this C?) closed it off. It was just as if the vent ended here. But how was that possible? Was he turned around again? No, he was running along the south wall of the next room, he had to be. He retraced the route he'd taken in his mind. Yes, that was it.

He banged on the side of the vent with his right hand, the sound bouncing around him. 'Hey. Hey. Anybody. Can anybody hear me?'

No sound apart from his own voice echoed back to him. No voices. No shuffling of movement beyond the vent. Nothing. What he had come to expect – the worst possible outcome.

'Hey. Anyone? Come on,' he shouted. Trying to convince himself he had some optimism left.

He tried the left side too – facing the corridor. But nothing.

He looked back at the message on the piece of paper. C. Was C the one who was doing this to him? Was C the man behind the horse mask? The man who had known he would go into the vents. The man who seemed to know him better than he knew himself. The smiley face seemed to broaden its grin, and then it winked.

He was sure it did.

But it didn't. He imagined it. He must have.

And all of a sudden, it drew closer. The feeling of it all getting too much. The cold, hard crash shuffling into him. He could feel his skin — all of it, itching, like thousands of spiders running over him. He could almost hear them — could almost see their silky webs in front of his eyes. He shut them. He was so tired. And it would be so easy to let them consume him.

He moved backwards. Had to move on. Had to get out of here. If not away, then at least back to the room. Because he wouldn't do this here. He wouldn't die in a vent — refused to.

He kept his eyes closed until he felt the pressure let up. He opened his eyes to see the pathway up. He decided to take it, panicking now. He steadied himself and brought his legs around to the front of him. Reaching out with his hands, he managed to slowly stand up. His legs howled with pain as they tried to support his weight. Looking around, he found another offshoot — only one, to the left. This meant he would be going back towards the room. He didn't care anymore. He clambered into it, pulling himself up and pushing off with his legs.

He tried to think about where he was. He had to be over the room. It had to be the ceiling. And as he finally got his full form into the vent, he looked ahead and saw light. Yellow strips of light.

He wondered if he was coming to another opening, but

as he got closer, he realised it was a grate in the bottom of the vent. It looked down into the room. And as he reached it, the voices inside were easier to hear.

'. . . crazy.'

'Am I? Or am I the only one who actually has a brain in this room?'

He looked down. To see the mess of covers on the bed. Couldn't get an angle to see anything else.

'Let's hear him out, Mandy.' Ryan. 'At least then he might shut up.'

'That man has the power of the devil behind his eyes.' Constance. Impossible to tell who she was talking about.

'Shut up.' Alan.

He could see shadows of them. Could picture them all standing around talking about him. Alan. Mandy. Ryan. Constance. Maybe even Headphones.

When the cat's away . . .

'Are you hearing what I said?' Alan said. 'That man cannot be trusted.'

'He's trying to help,' Mandy said.

'Help who? He's trying to help himself. Why do you think we're all still here and he's off gallivanting around in the vents? We don't even know if he'll come back.'

'Of course he's going to come back. You're not making any sense.'

'How's this then – we're not going to pretend we didn't hear everyone else's story, right? Everyone has a connection to either Simon Winter or this horse mask guy, everyone except him. Why hasn't he told us anything about that?'

'We don't know it's the horse mask guy. And why would Sheppard need to tell us? We already know who he is.'

'Yes, Mandy,' Ryan said, 'but how much do we know, really? Maybe Alan has a point. An incredibly laboured point, but a point. Anything could be going on here. This could be all some kind of weird set-up.'

'This man is not a detective. Not in any real sense of the word. He's a TV phony. They crave attention. Especially him. And I'm quite sure he'd do anything to stay in the limelight.' Alan's voice.

A sigh. Sounded like Mandy. 'Will you two listen to yourselves, please? Mr Sheppard is stuck here just like the rest of us. Right now, he's trying to get us out of here. Why would he kill anyone? It doesn't make any sense.'

Sheppard's stomach turned over. What? That was what they were talking about? How in the hell could they think . . . Alan. Alan was turning them against him. And it seemed like it had already worked on Ryan.

'Why is him killing Winter any weirder than one of us killing him? I know for a fact that I didn't, and I'm not sure anyone else here right now did. What did you say before – misdirection?'

No. No. No. This couldn't be happening. Not Ryan.

'Exactly,' Alan said, not bothering to hide the triumph in his voice. 'What if this isn't his game at all? What if it's ours?'

Sheppard didn't want to hear anymore. He had to get back in the room as quickly as possible. The vents were a washout – a dead end before they'd even started. And if he didn't get back, things could get a whole lot worse.

He shrugged off the itching feeling and carried on, moving faster than he thought he could. Mandy could only fight his corner for so long.

Alan did it. He had to have done. This was his plan all along. Convince everyone else that Sheppard killed Winter. But why? What was in it for him?

And there it was. Another wrinkle in the plan. One so obvious he didn't know why he hadn't seen it before. Why was the murderer even going along with this? Why had no one just owned up to it? Because surely they were going to die too if Sheppard got it wrong. Unless he/she had been promised safety. But how would that work?

Alan killed Winter. The why didn't matter. Probably something to do with his precious case. Or maybe not even that. If he had been in on the plan from the start, it could have just been to set up the game. He would get back to the room, and declare Alan the murderer.

Before he knew it, he came to another turn. His head awash with theories.

Down or left? This layout made no sense – down would put him back to where he started and left would have him re-treading the east wall albeit from higher up. He didn't know for sure, but he didn't think this was how vents worked. Why were there none going to any of the other rooms? It was almost as if this was all there was to the vent system. Did every room have their own system?

But he knew better than that. The dead ends. C, the evil man, had done something to the vents. He had foreseen Sheppard's little expedition and planned it all out.

He probably rigged it all – the discovery of the phones, finding something to unscrew the grate. Maybe he even hoped it would happen. To waste time.

Oh God, *time*. How long had he been in here?

Ahead there was some kind of widening. He could see the vent turn but also carry on. As he got closer, he saw that it was a wide junction. He pushed himself into it and immediately stretched out. The phone light flailed and caught on something in the centre of the junction.

A flicker of white.

He focused on it, crawling forward. Something else was there – something reflective, bouncing back the light. And then, as he moved forward arcing the torch, he saw it. The red – the blood that had dulled and dried on it. It was a knife, a wide knife – sharp, one that looked like it was to flake fish or something. The moment he saw it, he had no doubt that this was the knife that had killed Simon Winter. It had to be. And it had been hidden in the vents because that was always where Sheppard was going to go. This was just another part of the plan.

An unreasonable sadness burrowed into him. The knife sat in a pool of blood, which had dried and clotted and now looked more like jelly than something that came out of a human. Next to the knife, slightly stained in scarlet, was a message on another piece of paper.

THIS IS A
MURDER WEAPON
  - ☺ C

That smiley face again. That signature – C. This was the knife that had killed his psychologist – the knife that had been thrust into his gut, pulled out and thrust in again. Who had put it here? The murderer or C himself? Maybe the murderer was C? Making his way through all the vents just to leave the knife here. C was guiding him – had been all this time. And time was ticking away.

C wants you to fail. The murderer wants you to fail. The masked man wants you to fail. He wants you to die. And he wants you to kill them all.

He had to get the knife back to the room. There could be a clue to it, but there was no way he could see well enough to notice it here. This wasn't over. With no exit, all he could do was carry on. With any luck, he hadn't been in the vents as long as it felt.

He reached forward and touched the knife. He ran a finger slowly down the blade. It was definitely sharp. Sharp enough to pierce skin, muscle, organs. Sharp enough to end a life. He grasped the knife's wooden handle with his thumb and forefinger and pulled it out of the mess of congealed blood. He tried to ignore the ripping squelch that accompanied it. He put the knife down now it was free of its trappings and wiped some Simon Winter on the breast of his shirt. He instantly regretted it.

As the situation seemed too much, he remembered the tiny bottle of bourbon in his trouser pocket. As good a time as any, he thought. With some difficulty, he reached a hand into his pocket and brought out the bottle. It was even smaller than he remembered. He unscrewed the top and looked down at the knife. He gulped the liquid down and it was gone in less than a second.

The feeling of salvation was so fleeting that he had to question if he had felt it at all. It subsided the pain a little at least. But it couldn't touch the dejection. He had come into the vents with thoughts of escape.

But now he knew that this was far from over.

C was nowhere near finished with him.

Silently, he placed the bottle down and picked up the knife instead. With one last look at the pool of blood and his bourbon bottle sitting next to it, he shuffled back towards the room.

32

Sheppard felt sunlight on his face as he stuck his head back into the room. He tried to climb out of the grate as gracefully as possible but ended up falling face-first onto the bed. The knife fell down next to him, dangerously close to his eyes.

He scrabbled around and sat up. Alan was staring at him, arms crossed and face stern with focused rage. Next to him, on either side, were Ryan and Constance. Mandy stood off to the side, next to Headphones who was looking worried. Both of them were looking nervously at the knife, while the others seemed not to have noticed it.

'The Good Sheppard returns,' Alan said, with all the triumph still in his voice.

Sheppard quickly got off the bed – the left side. The bed between him and everyone else.

Ryan looked down at the knife. 'What is that?'

Sheppard spluttered. 'It's the murder weapon. I found it in the vents.'

'What about a way out?' Mandy said.

'There is no way out. He knew someone was going to go in there. He blocked it off.'

Sheppard went to pick up the knife, but Ryan jumped forward.

Sheppard suppressed a groan. 'Are you serious?'

'No sudden moves, Detective,' Alan said.

He threw his hands up in disgust. 'Are you hearing what I'm saying? There's no escape. You have to let me do what I can to get us out of here. The knife is the next clue. I'm closer to solving this thing.'

'And how did you know where to find it?' Alan said.

There was a murmur from Constance, who seemed to be hiding behind Alan now.

'I didn't know where to find it. I was in the vents trying to get us all out of here. That's what I've been doing ever since we woke up here.'

Alan smiled. 'You were being reckless – endangering everyone in this room. And you were so adamant that it had to be you, weren't you? You had to be the one who went into the vents. See, we've decided something while you were gone. Because from the very beginning this was always about you – the big shot television man stroking his ego just a little bit more. Well, maybe this was more about you than I cared to admit.'

'No. No,' Sheppard said, 'it's you. I know it's you. And I'm going to prove it.'

'Ramblings of a drunk and a drug addict and a piece of human waste. Don't try and confuse things now. Go out with a little dignity, huh?'

'You're insane,' Sheppard said. Panicking. 'This is insane. I'm trying to . . .' But he trailed off. Not knowing what else to say. He shot a look at Mandy. She looked away. Not her too. If she believed it, then that was it. It was over. Headphone's, Rhona's, eyes were shut, her face screwed up.

'Why did you go and get the knife?' Alan continued. 'So you could off another one of us. Stab us in the back.'

'If you just listened to yourself, you'd see that this made no sense.'

They were advancing now. Closing the gap between them and him.

'I think this actually makes perfect sense,' Alan said. 'You killed Simon Winter, didn't you? What secrets would he have told us if he were still alive?'

Ryan stepped around the bed. Sheppard looked at him pleadingly. 'Ryan, please. We don't have time for this.'

Ryan looked guilty, but not for long. 'It does make sense. You being all secretive, keeping things from us. We don't even know anything about you. Not really.'

'I'm being the detective,' Sheppard said, in the same voice as a child playing dress-up. 'I can't tell everyone everything. That's not how it works. And besides, the murderer is here with us.'

'Yes,' Alan said definitively. 'He is.'

Ryan put his hand around Sheppard's back and before he realised what he was doing, he felt something cold lock around his wrist.

Not again.

No, not again.

Ryan forced Sheppard's other arm around and cuffed the other wrist. There was no point in struggling. There was nowhere to go.

'You're making a terrible mistake,' Sheppard said, to anyone who'd meet his gaze. 'I have to solve this murder or we're all going to die.'

Ryan brought him around – still weak from the vent crawling – and pushed him in the back. Forcing him forward.

'Don't worry about that, Morgan,' Alan said. 'I've just solved this murder.'

Morgan.

Sheppard looked into Alan's smug face. 'What did you just call me, you bastard?'

Ryan pushed him again. Towards the bathroom.

This was all happening too fast. Ryan jabbed him again and Sheppard stumbled forward. He glanced around to the bedside before it disappeared from view.

The timer. 01:02:43. Ticking down and down.

'No, you can't do this,' he shouted. 'He's playing games with you.' He couldn't fight it – too exhausted, too thirsty, too wanting. It was all he could do not to crumple in a heap. It was over. It was all over. Alan had brainwashed them all, and there was barely an hour left.

Ryan went around him and opened the bathroom door. He nodded inside. 'Make it easy, yeah.'

'Ryan.' A harsh whisper. 'It's Alan. Alan killed him. I know he did. You have to trust me.'

'I can't trust anything anymore,' Ryan said. And he grabbed Sheppard by the wrists and shoved him into the bathroom. He tripped on the first tile and went barrelling into the room, crashing into the sink. He turned to see Ryan staring dumbly at him.

'For what it's worth,' Ryan said. 'I didn't think it would be you.'

He shut the door.

33

Before . . .

He was sitting on his hands – didn't know what else to do with them. He looked around the room. Winter was staring at him like a bespectacled praying mantis and he tried not to meet his eyes. There was only twenty minutes left on the clock and this meeting was cutting into his valuable drinking time. He was currently in the throes of a managed addiction – a day without drinking seemed like a wasted opportunity although he could hold off if he needed to.

Winter cleared his throat. Sheppard just tried to focus on the items on Winter's desk. In the twenty years he had been coming to this room he didn't think anything on the desk had ever moved – not even a millimetre – even down to the pile of papers and pen positioned neatly in the centre.

Winter cleared his throat again. Sheppard finally gave in and looked at the old man sitting in the red armchair he always did for his sessions. 'We're twenty-five minutes into the session, Morgan, and you don't seem to be as open as usual.'

Not a question, a statement. *Just putting it out there.*

Nothing to really respond to – apart from calling him Morgan when he had very kindly asked Winter not to. Everyone called him Sheppard – to the point where when someone called him by his first name it took him a second to remember they were addressing him.

'How's work?' Winter said.

'Fine,' Sheppard said. It was fine. The show had been picked up for another two series, which would see it run for at least another two years – another 120 episodes. If life were measured in content, he would have won a long time ago.

'I watch you on television when I don't have a session. There was a rather interesting one on yesterday.'

'What do you think?' Sheppard said.

'It's . . . good.'

He was lying. Sheppard didn't need a psych degree to tell that. 'What do you like about it?' he said, just to have a little fun.

Winter seemed to visibly squirm for a second (*bluff called*) but then realised what Sheppard was doing and snapped out of it, straightening his glasses. 'You've been doing a lot of work.'

'Twelve hours a day. I have to be at the station in the morning for any live cuts to *Morning Coffee* . . .'

'Wait, your show is called *Resident Detective*, is it not?'

Sheppard sighed. 'Yes, but it's on after *Morning Coffee*. Sometimes the presenters of *Morning Coffee* throw it over to me to do a "Today on the show . . ." kind of thing.'

'Why do you have to do that live? Could you not just record them?'

'I've been fighting the bosses over that one. Their response is they want to do it live so that it feels genuine. Like if *Morning Coffee* had just had a news story or a feature on socks for cats, I could comment on it.' *I hate it. I hate it. I hate it.* Sheppard hated *Morning Coffee*. He hated the smug presenters. He hated his stupid live links. And what was worse, it meant he had to get up two hours earlier than he would have to normally. 'We start filming the actual show at half ten. We usually run till about eight at night, four days a week and shoot about four, maybe five episodes in a day.'

Winter looked visibly impressed, but then that could just be a trick. Over the years Sheppard had become wary of the old man. Winter understood human behaviour very well and mimicking it for a cheap revelation was not above him. 'That *is* a lot of work. How do you keep going?'

I pop pills like a lunatic and I wash them down with liquid only a few rungs down from paint thinner. 'A positive attitude.'

Winter laughed and then grew silent. He put his pen down on the notebook he always had in his lap – a sure sign that things were about to get serious. 'I cannot lie – I am slightly concerned about you, Morgan.'

Sheppard suppressed a sigh.

'Throwing yourself into your work is good, but you must achieve a balance between work and leisure time. You look like you haven't slept since our last session.'

I have slept – if fragmented drunken dozing can be called sleep. Sheppard remembered a conversation with

Douglas – ironically, over beers – where Douglas said that heavy drinkers pretty much forget what normal sleep is like, and what feeling truly awake is like. He could now confirm that. Sheppard drifted through life constantly half unconscious, just going from one scene to the next because there was nothing else – it was something to do.

'I just want to make sure that you are not doing yourself any harm by taking too much on. You have to stop sometime, Morgan. Why don't you take some time for yourself?'

It was Sheppard's turn to laugh. 'Do you have any idea how television works? Hmm? You can't just take time off whenever you want. I'm at the forefront of one of the biggest morning shows in the country. I'm making money out my arse. And if nothing else, I'm contracted for two years. I can't drop everything for some spirit journey.'

Winter inched forward in his chair – his usual stance when he was expecting a fight. 'No one's talking about a "spirit journey", Morg—'

'Sheppard. Sheppard. Sheppard. My name is Sheppard,' he shouted, and got up. He went towards the door. *This is over*. He reached for the door handle.

'You never talk about it anymore,' Winter said, behind him. He willed his hand to clasp the handle, for his legs to carry him out the room, for his mind to give over to the pills and the drink so he couldn't go back. Back to that time.

For all Sheppard's willing, he found himself turning around and looking towards Winter, still sitting in his chair. '*It?*'

'You know what I mean,' Winter said softly.

Sheppard ran a hand down his face – sleek with sweat. 'What more do you want from me, old man? You want me to cry again? You want me to scream again? You want me to recount every detail of the nightmare again? I am not some broken machine to fix, some puzzle to solve. It happened – Mr Jefferies happened. Not everything has to have some cosmic significance. Maybe I did what I did purely because I did what I did. Maybe all your psychology crap isn't worth a damn because humans are simply spontaneous. I did what I did and now I live with that. Chisel it on some stupid stone somewhere because it's never going to change. I am the person I made myself. And the world carries on. Just like it always does – always will.' For some reason, his eyes were welling up with tears. He choked, cleared his throat and repeated finally, 'I did what I did because I did what I did.'

Winter got up at this. 'You solved a murder. You caught a killer.'

'Yes,' Sheppard said, 'and wasn't it amazing? But that doesn't mean I want to micro-analyse it with you every week.'

'I still feel we haven't fully explored . . .' Winter stepped towards him. Sheppard stepped back.

'You know what? I'll see you next week.' Sheppard said, turning and opening the door.

'We have ten more minutes,' Winter said.

'Take that ten minutes to think up a few more original questions for next time, yeah?' And Sheppard slammed the door behind him.

In Winter's front hall, he breathed. He didn't like to argue with Winter, but the drugs had made him impatient, and he needed to be out of this house. But that didn't excuse Winter's behaviour. Talking about something, yet again, which he would never truly understand. Sheppard was trying to bury it down deep – forget all about it. The drink and drugs were helping with that – as if every night he was shovelling one more mound of dirt into the grave of his memory. Soon it would be all gone and he would be free of it. But for now, all he wanted to do was have some fun.

A quick thundering down the stairs surprised him and Abby Winter appeared in front of him. Sheppard had first met her after his first session with Winter; they were both children then. Now she was nineteen and beautiful. She blushed when she saw him. 'Sheppard, sorry, I heard the door and I thought you would have gone by now.'

He didn't know if it was his lingering resentment of what had just happened with Winter or the fact he just wanted to forget everything but he found himself saying, 'Do you like cocktails? I know a good place not far from here that does amazing cocktails. Wanna go?'

'I . . .' Abby laughed uncomfortably, squirming slightly, 'uh . . . yes of course. Of course, I'd love to.'

Of course. Well of course of course. 'Great.'

'I should just tell . . .' Abby gestured towards Winter's office.

'Ah, don't bother him. He's busy doing paperwork anyway.'

Abby looked unconvinced, but equally didn't seem to

care. 'Okay. I'll just go get ready.' And Abby retraced her steps up the stairs.

Sheppard smiled to himself and took a pill. He sat down on the stairs and waited. This was going to be good – there was no way that this could be a bad idea. Sheppard didn't really care even if it was. Abby was beautiful and fun and he wouldn't sleep with her. He just needed a companion. Drinking alone was never fun in public, even for him. He tapped on the steps while he waited, making up a rhythm. And then for good measure, he took another pill.

Another shovelful of earth fell into the abyss.

Five weeks later . . .

It had been five weeks since he first asked Abby out. They had been out nearly every night since. He had no doubt Winter knew, but he didn't really care. Abby was worth it – she was a lot more fun than he thought a daughter of a stuffy psychologist could ever be. She fit in well on his arm as he showed her the best clubs in London. She could hold her drink, and she even tried some pills. She was great, charging forward with a youthful energy that sometimes made it hard to keep up with her. It was almost like she was trying to rebel against something – maybe a strict, rigid, old stick-in-the-mud of a father (*just a guess*).

He put his shaky arm around her and pulled her in for a kiss. She wrapped her arms around him, whilst also managing to rummage in her bag for her keys.

How long had they been standing here? He didn't know. It felt like forever and no time at all.

'I can't find them,' she said, slurring slightly. She couldn't handle it as well as him. And, as if to prove the point, the bag sprang out of her hands and hit the floor, the contents spilling out over the welcome mat.

They both erupted into laughter. Until he realised they were being way too loud for this time of night. He held a finger to her lips, barely able to stifle his own laughs, let alone hers.

She bent down and picked up the keys, which had miraculously revealed themselves. She held them up in triumph, smiling that smile − the smile that made him forget about all the badness in the world, all the badness inside everyone. There was only her. And he wanted to be with her always.

She lurched forward, searching for the lock on the door. A fumbling as she failed to find it, scraping the door, leaving fresh scars on the metal, and then success.

But before she could turn the key, the door seemed to open of its own accord. He was amazed . . . until he saw the old man stood there in his dressing gown, with eyes like thunder, arms folded and a frown on his face that could sour wine. He looked at her and then at him.

'Go upstairs, Abby,' he said.

She pouted. 'But . . .'

'Go upstairs.'

Abby took one long look at Sheppard, and went to hug him.

'Don't you touch him. Just go upstairs.'

Abby passed her father and disappeared into the house without another word. Sheppard heard her taking the stairs two at a time, then slamming her bedroom door.

He looked at Winter and wondered how long he had stayed up just to make this little show. He wondered if it would be worth it.

'Simon,' he started, after a long silence.

'Don't Simon me, son. Do you even care what I have been through tonight, waiting for my little girl to come home? You took her after our session, didn't you? This afternoon. Where the bloody hell have you been for fourteen hours?'

Fourteen — So that meant the time was . . .? Wait, so the session this afternoon was . . . Nope, he lost it. Instead he decided on, 'Here and there. She came because she wanted to.'

'She is nineteen years old. Too young for whatever you have on your mind.'

'Last I checked, nineteen was plenty old enough,' he said, realising when it was out there that he'd meant to keep that bit in his head.

Winter was silent. In response, he reached into his dressing gown pocket and brought out two little tubs. He held them up to the light, in his open palm. 'You know what this is?'

Sheppard looked at them, really trying to concentrate. One looked like a capsule of some kind and the other looked like a pill bottle. That was all he could manage. 'Should I know?'

'This is ketamine. Found in Abby's room, son.'

'The horse tranquiliser?' he said, suddenly proud of himself for knowing that.

'No,' Winter said, 'a common misconception. Ketamine can be used to sedate animals but it is mainly used on humans.' Sheppard turned a sudden laugh into a hiccup. Even in blind rage, Winter couldn't turn the doctor in him off. 'What's important is Abby has been taking this.'

'I don't do ketamine,' Sheppard slurred.

'No, but you've taken and drank everything else under the sun. And you introduced my daughter to the prospect, so you'll be okay if I go and blame you anyway. This life you're leading? It's not for my girl, son. I wouldn't wish it upon anyone, so not my little girl.'

Sheppard snorted. 'I get it.'

'Good.'

'No, not that,' he said, holding the doorframe for support. 'I get IT. You get to sit in your chair all day and lord yourself over other people's lives. Well, here's my turn. You love your daughter. You love her so much you want to wrap her up in cotton wool and keep her indoors away from the baddies, and the criminals, and the Disney villains. She's all you've got. Because your wife went to that hospital, all fat and busting, and only little Abby came back.' Somewhere in his brain he knew the line was being crossed.

Winter let out a small wheezing sound, but was silent for a long time. His eyes swam. A gust of wind threatened to up-end Sheppard and he tried to grab the doorframe again. Winter smacked his hand away.

'I don't think I can treat you any more, Morgan.'

'What?' It caught him off guard. Punched him in the stomach. But what had he expected? Winter was the only constant in his life, and he had done nothing but abuse that fact. How could he say things like he did and expect Winter to take it? It wasn't the old man's fault.

That's how he felt the next morning when he found the fragmented memories of the night nestled in amongst the empties around his bed. At the time, however, he found Winter nothing but a selfish old coot.

'Oh shut up. Really?' Sheppard said, shouting a little too loud. 'Because of Abby? You understand how stupid that sounds? You're going to stop seeing me, just because you're so anal about your daughter? You're supposed to be helping me.'

'No, son, you're meant to be helping yourself. But you won't. You're simply refusing to change. You're the most stubborn boy I've ever met.'

'I'm not a boy.'

'I should have stopped this long ago. Our relationship has become volatile, and yes, part of it is your fraternising with my girl. If we continue, my personal feelings will affect my job.'

'And what are your personal feelings?'

'I've known you since you were eleven, Morgan. I've known you since before you knew yourself. That scared little boy sitting in my waiting room. I was always able to look past what you've become and see that little boy. But now—'

'Say what you have to say,' Sheppard spat.

'You disgust me.'

Sheppard didn't know what he had expected. He was suddenly frozen, an uncontrollable shivering taking over his whole body. Winter meant more to him than he had ever known, meant more to him than his own father. And now – he was disgusted by him?

'Wait,' Sheppard said, wanting to rewind the last ten minutes and go about everything differently – the drunk version of him finally realising the significance of what was happening. 'I need you.'

'I'm sorry, Morgan. But you can't be here anymore.' Winter went to shut the door, but Sheppard slammed his palm against it.

'This . . . can't . . .' He couldn't even think.

'You know,' Winter said, relenting on the door, 'a third party came to me, purely by coincidence. That was the final nail in the coffin for us. Just another patient, telling tales of what a man called Morgan Sheppard had done. I didn't believe it at first – part of me simply couldn't believe it. But over time – well – it all makes such perfect sense.'

'Who came to you?'

'I'm a psychologist, Morgan. I know how people work. And I've always thought there was something deep down in the heart of you. And now I know. And I can't un-know. And that is why I can't possibly treat you anymore.'

Winter tried to close the door again, but this time Sheppard thumped the wood with his fist. 'No,' he choked. Even drunk-Sheppard understood that when the door closed, it wasn't going to open again.

Winter stepped forward and wrenched Sheppard's fist off the door with a surprising amount of force and Sheppard toppled back. 'You know the worst part?' Winter said, hissing. 'You don't even remember, do you? All the substance abuse has just turned you rotten. You can't even remember who you really are. It's a coping mechanism, you know – you don't have to be a doctor to see that. You drink and take all that rubbish because you're running away from yourself. From what you did.'

'And you're going to turn your back on me?' Sheppard said. He felt like crumpling to the floor.

Winter's face flamed, and he lunged at him. Sheppard dodged back, managing to keep his balance by stumbling down the porch steps.

'Get out of here,' Winter said, almost sadly. 'Before I call the police.' And he shut the door.

The walk from the door to the gate seemed to stretch on. Sheppard's feet felt heavier with every step. This was it. He knew he would never come here again, forgetting Abby at that moment. Because Winter had been important to him. And for some reason, he had forgotten that. But now he had pushed him away. Just like everyone else.

He didn't want to look back, but as he opened the gate, he couldn't stop himself. The house was quiet and dark, as though nothing had ever happened. He knew every detail of this house. He could almost see the eleven-year-old Morgan standing there on the doorstep, shuffling his feet nervously. He had been coming to this house forever. But he couldn't quite remember why.

Forever and no time at all.

34

What was happening to him? Time was fluctuating all around him – rocking the bathroom back and forth. Things went in and out of focus at random. His mind dashed from thought to thought. The spiders had him now.

One thought – how long had he been here? Had he ever been anywhere else?

Another thought – the doctor said not to exceed the recommended dose. Unless you were awesome.

Another – he couldn't remember her name, the one from Paris. She was so pretty. He didn't even get her number. How would he find her again? After . . .

This brought on a bout of uncontrollable laughter. Going crazy, or maybe coming down from it. Something a little appropriate medication would fix. Nice and easy. One little pill. Or maybe two.

Treat yourself.

Did he say it or did he think it or both?

He wanted to laugh again, but stopped himself. Instead he straightened up, trying to stretch his arms behind him. They had cramped up.

Just like before. Just like when it began.

He'd never been one for talking to himself. Whenever

he had tried, he felt like one of those idiots talking to themselves in movies. The kind that only talked to themselves to make sure the audience knew what they were doing. The kind of bad writing Sheppard could not advocate even when he was alone.

'Sheppard is thinking of dying now,' he said aloud. And cackled.

Things were happening outside. In the room. Echoes. He couldn't focus on them enough to hear what they were saying. It was as if out there didn't exist – at least not in the same way as in here. Two separate realities connected by the greatest invention of mankind: the humble door.

He suppressed another laugh. Until he heard something. Shouting. His ears perked up slightly, like a lethargic meerkat. Someone was shouting really loudly, almost loud enough to penetrate the fog that had settled around him.

It was Alan, or at least he thought it was. Still couldn't make out what he was saying.

Something was wrong.

A sound. A horrible sound. How to even think of it? It was a grunt, but louder and more urgent, halfway between an acknowledgement and a scream. And then there was a scream. Not just one but two women's screams.

The sound startled him so much that he jammed his shoulder against the toilet trying to get up.

This game is not over.

No, no, he couldn't do it. He couldn't carry on. This was it. Had to be.

But Mandy and Headphones were in there.

He pushed on his palms until he was as high as he could go and then tried to lever himself up the toilet. Surprisingly, he managed it and before the screamers had even drawn breath, he was sitting on the toilet lid. He got up, feeling his head loll on his shoulders. He thought he would never get up again, but it hadn't been too hard, right?

His need for the things he desired had to be filed away. The spiders had to go away. Come again another day.

NO. No laughing.

Another scream. By the same person. One of them at least. There was a commotion. Raised voices cursing and shouting.

He staggered around his small space. What was happening out there? Why were they shouting? His cuffed hands got caught around the towel rail and he face-planted the wall, his forehead erupting into pain.

He recovered. And looked at the bathroom door. He had to get out. He had to know what was happening. He stumbled forward and turned around, feeling with his hands for the door handle. Grasping it, he pushed it down.

Nothing. It didn't open. Even though the lock was on this side, they'd found a way to keep it shut.

'Hey,' he tried to shout, but his throat was so dry it wasn't louder than a whisper. He forcefully cleared his throat and tried again. 'Hey.' Better this time. But the voices outside kept screaming and shouting.

'Hey. What's going on?' he said, slamming his shoulder into the door. He backed up and kicked the door repeatedly with an unsteady foot. 'Hey. What's happening?'

Bang. Bang. Bang.

The sick sense of humour that resided in his head punctuated these three bangs with three rings of a phone. *Press 6 for early check-out* . . .

'What's going on out there?'

He raised his foot again. Bang.

They were being too loud. Something was very wrong. He could hear a scream that was not Mandy's, but was still youthful. He thought it must have been Headphones. He could hear Mandy's incoherent sobs. He could hear Ryan shouting at someone, telling them to calm down, telling them to . . . put down the knife.

And Sheppard realised what had happened. He had brought a weapon into a room with a murderer. Alan had seized his chance and had obviously been backed into a corner where he had to do it again.

Another murder. No.

He had to get in there. He had to know.

With a renewed strength, he slammed his entire body weight into the bathroom door and continued to do it even as his right arm became numb. 'Hey,' he shouted, over and over again.

Finally, outside, the conversation subsided and someone moved, close enough to the door for him to feel it. There was someone standing right on the other side.

'Come on. Come on,' he said, deciding to slam once more into the door. 'Come on.'

There was no response, and it seemed so long that Sheppard thought maybe the person had moved away again. Maybe he was still deemed the murderer even though something else had just very obviously happened. Maybe locking Sheppard up had been the best decision they ever made. No, Sheppard thought, that's Winter talking.

Sheppard backed up and slammed his entire side into the door one last time. Silence. And then . . . a click. And then the bathroom door opening very slowly.

He stepped back as it swung wide.

Ryan stood there, very pale and very uncertain. He didn't look at all like the cavalier guardsman he had played whilst throwing him in there earlier. 'I'm . . . I'm sorry,' the young man said, not daring to meet his eyes. 'I thought it was you. I . . . He got into my head. You know . . .' Ryan was blaming himself as much as Sheppard was, and why not? At that moment, he wanted the young man to blame himself for everything. Because now Alan had killed again and Sheppard would have to clean up the mess.

Sober. Straight and clean. A miserable existence.

Sheppard stepped forward but couldn't manage a friendly look towards Ryan no matter how hard he tried. Sheppard turned around and showed Ryan his handcuffs.

'Oh,' Ryan said, patting himself down, 'of course.' A few seconds later, the cuffs were off. Sheppard made sure to keep hold of them and Ryan looked at him sadly.

'We're going to need them,' he said, and turned into the room.

More death in a room that needed none at all. Alan Hughes, the murderer. Sheppard walked out of the bathroom, picturing what the scene would look like when he turned clear in his mind.

He looked – and it was different.

As he expected, Ryan, Mandy and Headphones were all standing back, visibly shaken, trying not to look at the body that was making a mess on the carpet in front of the television.

Alan Hughes lay face down on the carpet, the knife protruding from his upper back, around about where the heart was. He looked rather pathetic, lying there – a molecule of his former self. Blood was slowly leaking out of the wound, on either side of the knife.

There was a trail of blood leading off to the window and Sheppard followed it with his eyes, not quite ready to believe who was going to be standing at the end of it. But it all made sense, in a kind of odd way. It all sort of added up.

Because at the end of the blood trail, with blood staining the torso of her dress and a big grin on her face, was Constance Ahearn.

35

Constance? How could it be Constance? But in some ways, it made sense – in an odd sort of way. It all added up. He had to act quickly. He threw the handcuffs to Ryan, who advanced on Constance. Sheppard went to Alan and checked his neck for a pulse. None. He checked his wrist. Nothing either. Alan was dead. The knife was sticking out from under his shoulder blades. Must have threaded through two ribs, pierced his heart. The big, bad lawyer didn't seem so scary anymore. As he looked up, he saw Mandy and Headphones, squashed into the furthest corner, holding each other.

Constance was moaning as Ryan tried to put the handcuffs on her. Sheppard helped him by grabbing one of Constance's flailing arms. She wasn't making any sense, spouting rubbish about Jesus and God and Hell. Pretty much par for the course there then.

'The promised land is filled with traitors. The promised land is here.'

Ryan managed to slip on one handcuff and then stopped. 'We should cuff her to a chair.'

Sheppard nodded and took the chair that was slotted under the desk and held it as Ryan wrestled Constance down. Sheppard took the other handcuff as Ryan pushed Constance's right arm through the back of the chair so they could be sure she wasn't going to go anywhere. Not easily, at least.

Sheppard and Ryan straightened up and stepped back from Constance. She regarded them with those wide eyes of hers. The kind of eyes you could get lost in, that's what he had thought, right? Now those eyes looked like somewhere he was afraid he would get imprisoned.

'What happened?' Sheppard said, turning to the others.

Mandy and Headphones seemed unable to respond. But Ryan cleared his throat and managed to speak, although it seemed like he was fighting himself the entire way.

'We were just talking. That's all. Just talking. We hadn't kept track of the knife – we should have done, but we didn't. Putting you in the bathroom, we were all a bit shaken up. Alan said that we had finally solved the puzzle. He was so sure, so adamant, that you had killed the man and that you were the answer to the question that the horse man asked. He kept saying that – over and over.

'So he just shouted for a while. Looking at the TV, looking all around. "We've got him. Morgan Sheppard is the murderer." All around the room. But there was no kind of answer. No kind of sign that the horse man had even noticed him. Alan said that he was playing games with us. So he got annoyed and shouted louder. Then he started screaming some incoherent rubbish, just venting you know?

'We were all just watching him. I admit that he got to

208

me. He made me think it was you. But I wasn't happy about it. But Alan was almost gleeful. I sat on the bed, watching the TV. I mean, watching the letters flicker up and down. "We hope you enjoy your stay." I can't help but think it means something. Anyway, Rhona was where she always was and Mandy and Constance were sitting on the right side of the bed.'

Sheppard looked to Mandy. She silently nodded.

'So nothing happened for a while. Alan calmed down for a bit. We all kept to ourselves. Me and Mandy had a talk and I understood maybe I was a bit hasty putting the cuffs on you and throwing you in the bathroom. I told this to Alan and obviously he wasn't best pleased. We had a talk; all of us gathered around and that was when it happened. She stabbed him, like it was nothing. She must have slid it in his back like she was cutting a cake. Alan gave out this kind of yowl and then keeled over. Dead.'

Sheppard sighed. It wasn't as if Alan wasn't a thorn in his side the entire time he'd been in the room, but that didn't mean he should die. He looked from Alan to Constance, who was rocking the chair left and right, almost looking like she was enjoying it. Her own little fairground ride.

He looked down at what was once Alan Hughes.

'We need to move him,' Sheppard said, 'he's only going to make people uncomfortable here.'

Sheppard stepped over Alan to get the man's feet while Ryan got his shoulders. On three, they hoisted him up. They slowly carried him to the bathroom, attempting to not drip too much blood on the carpet. They mostly succeeded, with only a small trail tracking to where he lay – Ryan backed into the bathroom, pushing the door open as he went and Sheppard followed. They lowered Alan onto the floor – blood dashed across the white tiles as they let go.

Two dead bodies. It didn't feel weird anymore. Being around all this death. That kind of day.

'Should we, you know,' Ryan said, nodding to the knife, 'take it out? Just doesn't seem right to leave it in there sticking out like that.'

Sheppard didn't particularly want to touch it, but knew that it was probably the right thing to do. With one glance at Ryan, seeing that the young man had no intention of actually doing the deed, he stepped forward.

He bent over the body. With a deep breath, he grasped the wooden handle of the knife, standing up to attention. The spiders were still there, on the back of his hand, but he tried to forget about them. He pressed down on either side of the wound with his other hand, knowing that this was how they did it on those Saturday evening hospital dramas. He yanked the knife. It didn't move. It was stuck in tight. Sheppard yanked again and it gave way slightly. On the third pull, it came free and in its place a fresh fountain of blood spattered Sheppard's shirt. He flinched away, but too late.

Ryan looked at him, freshly coloured in Hughes. 'That's gross.'

'It was stuck in there tight,' Sheppard said, trying to connect two dots that he couldn't see, at least not at first. But then he got it. The wounds in Winter's gut had been deep, really deep. That was why he thought that it was probably a male. But if Constance could manage to plunge a knife so far into Alan's back, she could easily have killed Winter.

'What?' Ryan said, reading his expression.

'Nothing, or maybe something.' Sheppard went to the sink and washed off Alan's blood. It all blended in – Winter's, Alan's, creating a pinkish stain on his torso.

He studied the knife in the light, stuck it under the sink, and saw Ryan staring at him. 'I'm going to hold onto this,' Sheppard said. 'Do we have a problem with that?'

Ryan shook his head.

'How long was I in here?' Sheppard said. 'How long do we have left?'

'I'm sorry I put you in here.'

'How long do we have left?'

'It's just Alan was so . . .'

'Ryan. How long?'

Ryan said nothing but walked out of the bathroom, holding the door open for him. Sheppard stepped forward, knowing that he had to look, but couldn't bring himself to do it. He managed by shutting his eyes and looking in the direction of the timer. He opened his eyes and felt his stomach lurch.

He had seventeen minutes left.

36

Constance Ahearn was humming some inconsequential tune as Sheppard turned back into the room. She looked at him and smiled. He did not smile back.

He barely registered that Mandy and Headphones were now sitting on the side of the bed in each other's arms. Ryan looked like he didn't know what to do with himself. The room suddenly seemed a lot more empty – Alan's ego had filled the room full of something, at least. Now everything was quiet. The horse man hadn't been around for a long time. It was only them now. Him and the young people and a killer. It had to be her. She had to have killed Winter too.

Sheppard walked up to her, got level with her, got up in her face like he was on his TV show. Like the lights had just come on and the audience was rabid.

Because you know why?

NOTHING GETS PAST HIM.

He heard it, behind him. The audience shouting it out, prompted by some dogsbody holding up a card saying 'Catchphrase'. Not real. He was still hallucinating. Needed to get more of a grip. He couldn't lose it now.

'What did you do?' Sheppard said to Constance, a lot

sadder than he thought it was going to come out.

Constance's eyes snapped to his. There was madness there now. It wasn't there before, right? He would have seen it. She smiled. 'I saved you. I saved you all.'

'What do you mean?' Sheppard said. 'You killed a man.'

'He was a liar. He was an adulterer. He was a glutton.' Constance tensed up in the chair and the handcuffs rattled as she tried to move her hands. 'No man resided there.'

'How do you know all that?'

'I just know.'

'You're crazy,' Ryan said, beside him.

Constance's eyes shot to him. Then back to Sheppard. Sheppard held a hand up to Ryan. He was thinking exactly the same thing. But crazy people didn't know they were crazy.

'So you saved us,' Sheppard said. 'Is that because you thought Alan killed Simon Winter?' After all, he had thought the same himself.

'Yes and no.'

'Did you kill him? Simon Winter.'

Constance looked at him for too long. 'No.'

'You're religious. What happened to "Thou shalt not kill"?'

'I don't need to be talked down to by you, Mr Sheppard. I know what I've done, but He will see it differently. He will forgive me, when I am come to the kingdom of Heaven. He sent someone to tell me what to do.'

'What are you talking about?'

'You could see it. You could see it in his eyes,' Constance said, widening her own. 'He had evil in them. And

213

I was told that I must act. To save everyone in this room.'

'Who told you to kill Hughes?'

Constance looked around, as though she was trying to avoid the question.

'Please, Constance,' Mandy said, 'just answer him.'

Constance looked at Mandy and softened slightly. It seemed she trusted the young girl more than Sheppard. Obliging, she leant forward on her chair and whispered, 'The Mary Magdalene.'

Sheppard chuckled and nodded. What else had he expected? 'The Mary Magdalene. You're insane. You killed a man in cold blood. Do you understand that, Ms Ahearn?'

'I saved the soul of the man the devil resided in by setting him free. She told me to kill him. She told me to take the knife and plunge it into his back. She said only I had the power – because I had the Holy Spirit on my side.'

Sheppard felt that fire. The fire he felt when he was on set, but this time he wasn't acting. This was a real burning anger. An emotion free of the drugs and the drink. He hadn't felt one of those in a long time. Apart from fear of course. 'You killed a man. And that means you had it in you to kill Winter too.'

'Why would I kill Simon Winter?' Constance said, defensively. As though her integrity was still something she could fight for.

'I honestly have no idea. Maybe because you saw him with your Evil Man. Maybe because he was one of the Four Horsemen of the Apocalypse. Maybe because he cut you off in a bike lane once? I don't know anymore.'

'Demons, Mr Sheppard. We are already enduring our punishment.'

And that made him remember. Constance's initial outbursts in the room, when she had been running around and throwing herself into the walls. What had she been saying?

Is this the punishment I must endure?

We're all in Hell. And you're all here with me.

'You said things, when we first woke up in the room. You said something about this being your punishment. What did you mean by that?'

'What?'

Sheppard looked around. Ryan was nodding, remembering it too. 'She was talking rubbish about this being her atonement.'

'I don't know what you're talking about,' Constance squealed. A little too readily.

'Who are you, Ms Ahearn? Who are you really? What's your secret?'

'We all have secrets. That doesn't make them relevant.'

Sheppard sighed. 'The first thing you said to me. You said you were being punished.' Just two hours ago, but it might as well have been a lifetime. If Sheppard didn't work this out, it was indeed a lifetime.

'My family is strongly Catholic, Mr Sheppard.'

'Really? I hadn't noticed,' he said, sensing the sarcasm would probably be lost on her.

'My daughter got pregnant, and she had an abortion. I disowned her and she moved halfway across the world to America. California. She tried to contact me but I never talked to her. One day, I got a call from her husband. My baby girl had been hit by a drunk driver, killed along with a new unborn child. I prayed for the safety of one child and ended up killing another.'

Sheppard frowned. He didn't want to be cruel but the first thing that sprang into his head was *Is that it?* He was sure it was very horrible but he was expecting something a little more . . . All he found was a dead end.

'I told you I had nothing to do with your investigation,' Constance said. Constance was crazy, but he couldn't help thinking that in some ways, it wasn't her fault. She obviously had some severe mental problems, but right here and right now, that didn't matter. Unfortunately for her, if Heaven and Hell did exist, Constance had earned herself an en-suite in the latter, hotter one.

Sheppard paused. 'I'm sorry. But I think you have everything to do with it. I think you killed Simon Winter.'

37

Sheppard turned to the rest of the room, and raised his voice, just as Alan had done an age ago. 'Constance Ahearn. The murderer is Constance Ahearn.'

He waited for a moment. Nothing happened. Ryan looked around, expectantly, while the two girls just looked on, bewildered. This had to be it. It had to be her. He was looking for something, maybe some kind of acknowledgement. Some kind of hope. A reason to keep going – if only for a few more seconds.

Constance Ahearn gave out a fresh splutter of laughter. 'Not quite, Mr Sheppard.'

Sheppard wheeled around, looking towards the timer. It was still counting down. Five minutes.

What had gone wrong? Constance was the murderer. She was the only one that made sense. But the game was still going. They were still dying one second at a time.

'Why didn't it work? How could it not work?' Ryan said.

This wasn't over. This couldn't be over. 'Maybe we haven't worked it out right. Maybe she needs to say something.' Sheppard kneeled down and was face-to-face again with Constance. The woman looked normal, as if nothing was happening at all. She smiled at him and tilted her head to the side, as though she were greeting a family pet.

'You know something,' Sheppard said, 'I know you do.'

'I know everything and I know nothing,' Ahearn said, almost singing it in her tuneful voice. 'It depends what type of everything you want to know.'

'You killed a man. You killed a man like it was nothing. Like slicing butter. You've done it before. I know it's you.'

'As I've already said, Mr Sheppard, I didn't kill Dr Winter. Why would I kill him? I have no motive.' Constance winked at him. 'But I do know who did.'

'I knew it,' Sheppard said, through clenched teeth. 'Why didn't you say anything?'

'Because I cannot dishonour by telling.'

Sheppard laughed in her face. 'You understand we're dying, don't you? That when that timer runs down, we're all exploding? We're all going to die in a mess of fire.'

Constance smiled. 'Rapturous.'

Sheppard stood up in annoyance and felt someone at his side. It was Ryan – anger flared in his eyes. 'Why won't you tell us, you bitch?' Ryan said, and Constance smiled at him too. Ryan turned to Sheppard. 'We can make her talk.'

'What do you mean?' Sheppard said, but he thought he already knew. He could see it in Ryan's eyes. 'No, we can't . . .'

'You said it yourself. We don't find out and we all die. I

just have to hurt her a little bit. She'll crack easily.'

Sheppard opened his mouth and closed it again – had he discounted Ryan so quickly?

Ryan made his way behind Constance. She tried to follow him with her eyes but he was in her blind spot. She looked back at Sheppard, with confused eyes.

'We can't do this,' Sheppard said. *Could they?*

'Yes, we can,' Ryan said, bending down behind Constance. 'Just ask her the question.'

'What is he doing behind there? Demon.' Constance looked at Sheppard, as though she could see him entirely. She could see all his secrets, all his bad decisions, all his failed relationships. She could see *him*, the real *him*, beyond all the clutter and the bad blood.

Mandy stepped forward, seeing what Ryan intended to do. 'No, you can't do this.'

'We need to do this. Whether we want to or not. We don't do this and we're all going to die,' Ryan said. He had clearly justified it to himself. He nodded with such a conviction, it was exciting.

'Sheppard,' Mandy said, 'please stop this.'

'When are you going to see, Mandy?' Ryan said, 'Sheppard failed. He doesn't know who did it, so now it falls to the rest of us.'

'This is what he wants,' Mandy cried, 'this is exactly what the horse man wants. Don't make him turn you into this.'

'I'm confused,' Ryan said. 'Are you saying this because of the well-being of Ms Ahearn here, or because you're scared of what she'll say?'

Silence. Ryan's gaze darting from Mandy to Sheppard and back.

'Ryan,' Sheppard said, as Mandy gave an exasperated sigh, 'come on, this is lunacy.'

'Just ask the question.'

'Ryan.'

'Sheppard, ask the question.'

'I . . .' Sheppard said, unsure how to start the sentence, let alone finish it. With a glance at Mandy, he got down in front of Constance again.

'Sheppard, no,' Mandy said.

Sheppard looked at Constance and tried a sad smile. She smiled back. 'Ms Ahearn, I need to ask you, who killed Simon Winter?'

Constance looked at him, then at Mandy and Headphones, even trying to look at Ryan although she couldn't manage it. 'I won't tell you. But God will forgive us in the kingdom of Heaven.' She gave a yelp of surprise and struggled. 'What are you doing back there? Don't you think about hurting me.'

'Ryan,' Sheppard said.

Ryan disappeared behind the chair for a few long moments. Sheppard could only see what was happening sketched on Constance's face. She looked slightly uncomfortable and he thought that maybe Ryan had a hold of her fingers. But her expression didn't change. And a moment almost became a minute, when a sorrow-filled yelp came from behind the chair, and not Constance.

Ryan stood up behind her, tears in his eyes. 'I can't do it,' he said, with all the defensiveness of a child who had been caught stealing pic 'n' mix. 'I can't do it. It's over. We're all going to die.'

Mandy let out a skittering breath, sounding as though she was holding back a cry. She sat on the bed with her back to them. Ryan wiped his nose with his hand and looked at Sheppard.

'I'm sorry,' he said, before going to sit down as well.

Sheppard got up, looking at Constance with one final, long glance. Their last hope. Not much of a hope anyway. It was indeed all over. *Time always runs out in the end.*

Sheppard walked over to the wall beside the TV and slid down it. As he hit the floor he was struck by one final opportunity. And the more he thought about it, the more it made sense. His heart rose in his chest, he had worked it out. It was all so simple, and he had finally worked it out.

'Horse Mask,' he shouted, almost sounding happy, 'the murderer is Horse Mask.'

He waited a few seconds.

Nothing. Nothing at all.

The timer slid to two minutes left.

38

Sheppard looked from Ryan to Headphones to Mandy. Behind him, Constance had started chuckling about something. Most likely, the prospect of dying. Looking at the others' faces, they were contemplating it too.

He had to try again. 'Constance Ahearn. The murderer is Constance Ahearn.'

He waited again. Nothing happened. The seconds slipping away too fast. This was it – it was over. They were really going to die.

Why not? He was already a joke. He couldn't protect himself, let alone the others.

'Rhona Michel,' Sheppard said, turning away from her as he said it. He couldn't look her in the face. 'The murderer is Rhona Michel.'

Again, a few seconds wait yielded nothing.

'Ryan Quinn, the murderer is Ryan Quinn.'

One, two, three. Nothing.

One name left. That meant . . .

'Amanda Phillips. The murderer is Amanda Phillips.'

One, two, three. Nothing.

Had he expected that to work? He had at least hoped for some kind of response. Maybe a comical err-err 'No' noise? That sort of seemed like the horse man's style.

He looked up to the television. It was still showing the flickering, putrid-coloured words 'We Hope You Enjoy Your Stay'.

Sheppard grabbed it by the corners and stared into it, as if he could summon up the horse man. 'Hey, hey. You. I need to talk to you.' The words flickered. 'You. You bastard. Come on.' Nothing.

Frustration welled from his stomach. In a swift move, Sheppard – not thinking – leapt up and picked up the television. He lifted it over his head and was poised to throw it on the floor, but at the last second, he felt a hand on his shoulder. He turned to see Mandy giving him a sad smile. He looked to Headphones and Ryan, and he saw something like acceptance in their eyes.

Sheppard sank to his knees, feeling the carpet rub against his sore knees. The timer slid down to one minute. He looked up to the ceiling as if to ask a higher power for help, but instead he just said, 'Morgan Sheppard. The murderer is Morgan Sheppard.'

39

'What's your biggest fear?' Winter had once said, sat in his high-backed chair assuming his usual therapist pose. His legs crossed, his glasses down his nose, his notebook in his lap – there was no confusing the profession Winter was in.

'To be forgotten,' Sheppard said, after a moment's deliberation.

Winter regarded him and leant forward. 'Most people say their greatest fear is death.'

'Death is inevitable; being remembered is a courtesy.'

Winter took off his glasses and tapped them against the arm of the chair. 'You're an interesting man, Morgan.'

Sheppard smiled, 'Thank you.'

Winter smiled too, albeit a bit too late. 'I don't know if I meant that as a compliment.'

The only thing Sheppard could take with him now is that he'd never be forgotten. No matter how this played out, he would go down as a tragic figure held hostage in a hotel room. But sitting there, looking into the faces of the people he had failed, he wished it could end any other way. He wished he could have saved them.

Saying his own name had done nothing. Had he really expected it to? Did he really think in some warped way that he had killed Winter, and forgotten it? No, he was clutching at straws.

But now there were none left.

Sheppard looked from his hands to Ryan. The young man who worked at the very hotel he would die in. Now, Ryan seemed a lot younger than he was. A scared child trying to put on a brave face, he peeked out from his hands occasionally to see that everything was still in its place. Ryan would never see his family again, the parents he was working to support.

Next to Ryan sat Mandy. The blonde who had stuck her head over the bed when he had only just woken up handcuffed to the bed. She had looked so scared then, but now she was wearing a stoic expression, almost resigned. Sheppard knew from the brief time he'd known her that she wouldn't be one to die crying and screaming. She was noble, someone with a set of morals to live by. And one of them was dying silently.

On the floor was Rhona, her headphones around her neck. She had her hands dug deep into her hoodie pockets. She was silently crying, tears falling down her cheeks erratically. She took a hand and jabbed at the tears sporadically, as if angry that she had even created them. When she had finished mopping them up, she quietly stood up and walked over to Constance Ahearn. She didn't even look at the woman cuffed to the chair but instead walked straight past her to the desk. She climbed under the desk and resumed the position she had been in for most of the three hours. She caught Sheppard's eye and hollowly looked at him. She took her headphones and slid them onto her head.

Constance Ahearn seemed to be all out of lunacy. She was finally quiet and looking down at the bloodstain on the lap of her dress. The woman had turned herself into a monster and this was the first time that Sheppard thought she might have realised it. Her faith had got her nowhere in the end, a means to facilitate her worst fears. Sheppard knew that faith was not always like that, but it only served to help Constance in her conviction. Gone was the woman whose biggest problem was her estranged daughter, now she was a murderer. Maybe, if there was a God, she could make up for it somewhere else.

Sheppard looked at his four roommates in turn, and still didn't know which one did it. Maybe his first hunch had been true. Maybe it was Alan Hughes who had killed Simon Winter, it all being something to do with the MacArthur case. Somehow though, this didn't really fit. This wasn't what it was about, couldn't be. Because they weren't the biggest clues. And who killed Simon Winter wasn't the biggest mystery.

Thirty seconds on the clock and how many people? How many children and families would there be in this hotel? How many around the building? What would the body count be? Would they blame him? All the families who knew that the building exploded just because he couldn't solve a simple puzzle?

The simple fact was one that he had been running from for as long as he could remember – a fact that he was forever scared that someone would find out. 'I'm not a detective,' he said into the quiet room. No heads turned, no one acknowledged it. It just hung there in the air. An epitaph of a nightmare.

Because that was what the horse man had wanted, wasn't it? That's what this whole thing had been about.

Ten seconds, and Sheppard thought of his mother for the first time in a long time. She was rotting in a care home in North London. And he thought of his agent, who would probably lament the loss of a revenue stream. The two people who might possibly miss him. Yes, there may be fans who would weep for him, but they would move on to bigger and better things, often without even knowing it. The living were much more interesting than the dead.

Eight.

'I'm sorry,' he said. Again, no one responded, but he knew he had to say it. He had failed them. He had failed them all. And now they were dead because of him.

Seven.

The Great Hotel becomes the Great Mess.

Six.

A funny place to die.

Five.

Would there be an investigation? Would they hunt the horse man down?

Four.

Or would they all dance on his grave and say 'Good Riddance'?

Three.

He was so, so sorry.

Two.

Sometimes all we want is to be seen, said Winter, in his ear, and he told him to shut up. He wanted to die in peace.

One.

He closed his eyes. Would it be quick? Would it be painless?

Zero.

The sound of the explosion and the piercing white light was his only answer.

40

1992

The body was hanging there in the centre of the room. A strange mass in a strange place, almost like a spectre of something impossible. It was ever-so-slightly moving, swaying. At first, he thought it was because of the breeze coming from the open window. Later, however, he would come to realise that it was probably from struggling.

He stood in the doorway, unable to move. The room was a mess: upturned desks, scattered papers, forgotten chairs. It was nothing like the neat and normal room it had been two hours before in Maths class. He could even still see the equation they had been working on, on the whiteboard. To step inside would be to step into a deeper, darker world – a world where he had no desire to be.

He was scatter-brained. His mother had always told him so. And this time, he had forgotten his jotter. He was halfway home when he realised and couldn't do without it. He had written down the Maths homework he had to do that night, and for the life of him, couldn't remember what it was.

The halls were quiet as he returned, the ghosts of laughter and shouting in the air. His classmates were long gone and it seemed that most of the teachers were too. The only person he saw was a caretaker, who didn't look familiar, who was unenthusiastically buffing the hall floor. The man looked up at him as he passed and smiled sadly, like he was apologising for his mere existence.

The door to his Maths classroom had been ajar. Not wishing to appear impolite, he had knocked. There was no answer, apart from the door slowly creaking open.

Mr Jefferies looked almost comical, like he was hung up on a coat rack – a discarded and empty anorak. His eyes were lifeless, his face a pale aubergine colour, his arms hanging at his sides. The belt around Mr Jefferies' neck was barely visible under his chins but he eventually saw it. The leather was strained, cracked and discoloured. It was wrapped around an exposed pipe in the ceiling. The same pipe he had always complained about because it made a weird hissing sound whenever someone flushed the toilet on the second floor. Now that pipe was holding him up. Mr Jefferies was dead.

At some point, he started to scream.

He heard footsteps behind him – running, and then someone clutched his shoulders tightly. He couldn't rip his eyes from the scene in front of him, but he smelt the familiar perfume of Miss Rain and heard his name in her soft voice.

'What in the heavens is wrong?' she said.

He couldn't speak; he just pointed into the room.

He saw the outline of Miss Rain turn and look. And then he heard her scream too.

The next few minutes were a rush of colours and lights.

He was so disorientated that he didn't know what was happening. He heard more people rushing around him and then he was picked up by someone and rushed away into the staff room. When he opened his eyes, Miss Rain was sat across from him, smiling sadly, her eyes red with tears.

'Do you want a glass of water?'

Before he could reply, she got up and crossed over into the kitchen area. He looked down at his hands as he heard the tap – they were shaking. He tried to stop them but he couldn't.

Miss Rain put a glass of water down in front of him and then sat down again.

'Drink this. It'll help.'

He picked up the glass of water. It sloshed around in the glass as he held it to his lips. Ever so slightly swaying in the glass. A wave of nausea as he took a sip. The water was cold and very real. Inviting. He took a sip and put it down again.

'How are you – feeling any better?'

A silly question, and from the sound of it Miss Rain knew it was. He didn't know. He couldn't know. There weren't enough words in the English language to explain how he felt, at least of the ones he knew. It wasn't fair. It wasn't fair to ask him that.

'Please, sweetie, can you talk to me? I need to know what you're feeling.'

'I . . .' So many words – too many words. Why did the human race need so many words? 'I've left my jotter in the Maths room.'

'That's why you're back?'

'I just need to go get it and everything . . .'

'No . . .'

'. . . everything'll be okay.'

He grew silent – his little brain was going too slowly. He couldn't think. He couldn't even . . .

'Mr Jefferies . . .' he said slowly.

Miss Rain was crying now. He didn't understand. He didn't understand why she was crying. She dabbed at her eyes with the sleeve of her cardigan. 'Yes, I know. It'll all be okay. It'll all be fine. You just have to be strong now.'

Miss Rain moved round and sat next to him. He lay his head on her shoulder and she wrapped her arms around him. Soon they were both crying silently.

More people around him. He shut his eyes – screwed them up tight like they did in the movies. He heard bodies around him, he heard sharp whispering. Miss Rain was talking to the headteacher. Then there were sirens, slowly getting closer, and someone else ran into the staff room. He felt strong arms grasp him.

He opened his eyes. His father's face – very close. His father pulled him into a hug and he started crying more.

'I was outside waiting for you in the car. I saw the police cars. I'm so sorry.'

His father hugged him for a long time, gripping him so tight that he found it hard to breathe. But at that moment, that was exactly what he needed. He felt safe there, he felt calm. He felt like a child being comforted by his father. But somewhere in the back of his mind, he knew that the child in him had died along with Mr Jefferies. The child in him was hanging there in the Maths room with his teacher.

His father pulled away and looked him in the eye. 'Talk to me, son. Are you okay?'

In his father's bright eyes, shadows glinting – the image of his teacher hanging from the ceiling. Would he see that everywhere now – forever and no time at all?

'Say something.' His father looked worried. 'Please say something, Eren.'

41

1992

The next few days passed in something of a fog. Before he went home that day, Eren had to talk to the police for what seemed like hours, although it was probably more like minutes. Time was not working like it usually did. His father held his hand in a tight grip throughout as he told of finding Mr Jefferies' body. He left the details as fuzzy as the police allowed. He didn't want to think about it. And he could already feel his mind closing around the memory, like a chrysalis, protecting him from the horrors inside.

In the following days, the information started to come out. George Jefferies was dead. He hanged himself with his belt in the Maths room. Police said that Mr Jefferies' parents had said their son had been unhappy for a long time. Eren had never even thought that Mr Jefferies would have parents. They said that he had money troubles and he was very lonely.

The police visited Eren and told him this. They said that his teacher had taken his own life, not thinking that a student would find him. They said they were very sorry.

Everyone apologised. 'We're sorry this happened to you.' 'I'm sorry you had to see that.' 'The school is sorry for everything and understands if you need some time to collect your thoughts.' He didn't understand why everyone was sorry. They hadn't done anything. When he told his father this, his father said that people just apologised when they didn't really know what to say, which was ironic as he was the one who said sorry the most.

He wasn't allowed to go to school for the next week and his TV privileges were gone. His father didn't want him seeing anything on the news. Eren learned from friends that it never reached the news though. It wasn't interesting enough. Mr Jefferies, his kind, fun Maths teacher killed himself and the world didn't care.

His world had grown quieter. He no longer heard the birds in the trees or the traffic outside. He only heard silence. Colours were not as bright as they once were. His world was no longer exciting, no longer hopeful. Why bother with hope when one can just die, anytime or anywhere. He slept a lot. His father rang a psychologist – not telling him, but he snuck out of his room and listened on the stairs. Food didn't seem to be edible anymore.

On the Wednesday after the incident, he heard a knock at his bedroom door. He didn't answer, he just looked at his clock. It was 4 pm – when did it get to be 4 pm?

The door opened and his father stuck his head around the door.

'Eren, there's someone here to see you.'

Eren just turned his back. 'I don't care.'

His father ignored him. 'It's your friend. Here he is.'

And Eren turned around to see Morgan standing there. Morgan Sheppard with a big smile on his face. Morgan could usually cheer him up, but today Eren could see that he was forcing that smile.

'I'll leave you two to it.' The door shut.

Morgan dumped his backpack in the centre of the floor and school textbooks spilled out. 'How are you?'

'I'm fine,' Eren said, never feeling further from fine.

'You're the talk of the school,' Morgan said. 'Are all the rumours true? You found Mr Jefferies in the Maths room?'

'Yes,' Eren said, the image flashing through his mind quickly. 'I found him.'

'We've got a substitute for Maths. She's a real hard arse. I also don't think she can count. And we have to have our lessons in the library which is annoying. No one's allowed in that room.'

'Hmm,' Eren said, not really listening.

'Sadie said that room's haunted now. She said that's why we can't go in,' Morgan said, picking up one of Eren's action figures and sitting down at the edge of the bed. 'She said that Eric said that Michael's sister saw Mr Jefferies in the window last night. But I think she's lying just to get attention because . . .'

'Because he's dead,' Eren said, sitting up.

Morgan fiddled with the action figure's arm, making it wave at Eren. 'Yeah,' he said, in a small voice.

'Do you . . .?' Eren started, sliding his bum to the edge of the bed so he was sat next to Morgan. 'Why do you think he did it?'

Morgan was silent.

'What can be so bad that someone kills themselves?'

'Maybe he did something wrong,' Morgan said, handing

Eren the action figure. It was a knockoff superhero toy, a generic man in a cape with a big toothy grin and strong muscles.

'Everyone does wrong things — we don't all kill ourselves.'

'Maybe he was just too sad.'

Eren thought about this, but it didn't make any sense. Mr Jefferies was always so happy. He was always smiling and joking with them. There was never a hint of sadness there. Maybe he was just good at hiding it.

'I'll miss him,' Morgan said, 'we all will. He was nice.'

'Yes.'

'And funny.'

'Yes.'

Morgan was quiet for a moment and then chuckled, 'You remember the time he let us watch movies instead of do work . . .'

Eren's eyes were on the action figure. There was something at the back of his mind. Something gnawing at him. And it was only getting stronger when he looked at this stupid toy. But he had no idea what it was.

'. . . or when he told jokes all lesson. Even that dirty one, haha.'

Eren's eyes went down the action figure to the superhero's utility belt. Something . . .

'You remember when he lost all that weight a month ago? And he kept having to pull his trousers up all the time. He was a good teacher.' Morgan looked at Eren and nudged him on the shoulder. 'You want to play some SNES? It'll take your mind off it.'

Eren looked up at Morgan, his eyes wide. 'Say that again?'

Morgan smiled. 'SNES. I've got really good at World 2.' Morgan looked around. 'Where'd your TV go?'

'No, no,' Eren said, 'say what you said before that.'

Morgan looked confused. 'What? About Mr Jefferies? His trousers falling down. Surely you remember all that? He even made a joke of it.'

Eren looked at Morgan, holding up the action figure. Morgan looked confused. 'I remember,' Eren said. 'I didn't, but now I remember. I remember perfectly.'

'What's wrong, Eren? You look like you've seen a ghost.'

Eren jumped off the bed.

'Okay,' Morgan said, 'poor choice of words.'

'I'm going to need your help, Morgan.' Eren said, picking up the other boy's backpack and throwing it at him.

Morgan caught it. 'What are you doing?'

'I need to get back to school,' Eren said, looking at Morgan. Somewhere in his mind, a spark lit. Memories of Mr Jefferies came flooding back. He was happy. He was kind. He wasn't sad or miserable. He would never do what he did.

Colours and sounds flooded back into his world again. And also, in the darkest moment, a little bit of hope. Hope that his world was not entirely wrong.

Eren slung his backpack over his shoulder and turned back to Morgan, still looking bewildered on the bed. 'Mr Jefferies didn't kill himself. Someone murdered him.'

Eren threw the action figure to the ground.

*

It took Morgan a few minutes to catch up with him, although he was on his bike and Eren was only walking. Eren didn't really know where he was going – he was walking towards school taking the back alleyways he knew so well.

Morgan rode up alongside him. 'What are you doing?'

'I'm not sure,' Eren said truthfully.

'Why did you say Mr Jefferies was murdered?'

'Because he was.'

'He killed himself, Eren.' Morgan was half riding the bike and half walking to keep pace with him. They emerged from the alleyways onto a big football field.

'He didn't. He didn't kill himself. He wouldn't do that.'

'Eren, you're freaking me out.'

Eren stopped abruptly. Morgan hit the brakes and almost fell as the bike went crashing to the ground.

'The belt. He hanged himself with a belt. I saw it. But Mr Jefferies didn't have a belt.'

'Yes he did.'

'No, he didn't because of his trousers.'

Morgan's face showed a flash of understanding. The same understanding that was fuelling Eren now. 'But that was weeks ago. He could've got a belt since then. Was he wearing a belt that day?'

Eren tried to think. He couldn't remember. It was a detail that you wouldn't actively forget but also one you wouldn't think to keep. It was a detail that could slip through the cracks. Eren wondered if adults could make the same mistake. If it could slip through the cracks of an investigation.

'I can't remember if he was,' Eren said, and Morgan was looking similarly perplexed, 'but that doesn't matter because I know Mr Jefferies didn't do it.'

'How?' Morgan said.

Eren thought for a moment. That was a good question. But he had a strong feeling that Mr Jefferies really didn't do it. He knew there was something else. Some clue that he was missing. Something had happened that was out of place. But he couldn't put his finger on it.

'We have to find out who killed Mr Jefferies.'

Morgan scratched his forehead. 'Eren, I can't even reach high shelves. I'm pretty sure I can't solve a murder.'

'We owe it to him.'

'I dunno. Maybe if you really think something's up, we should go to the police.'

Eren put a hand on Morgan's shoulder. Morgan looked at it ominously. 'You're always talking about how you want to be famous. Cricket, video games, acting – what if those things don't matter. What if you're going to be famous for this instead? What if we actually do solve a murder?'

A moment was all it took and Morgan's eyes lit up with possibilities. The boy was easy to talk around. Ever since Eren had known him, Morgan had had a desire to be known for something. Quite what it was, it didn't seem to matter. Morgan just wanted to be someone. 'Okay,' the boy said, 'but are you sure? What if we find out that Jefferies did really kill himself?'

Eren started walking again. 'He didn't.' There was no way. Because that would mean that the world wasn't what he thought it was. That would mean everything would be different. He couldn't have killed himself. Or more accurately, he mustn't have. And as Eren stomped across the field, it became apparent that a little boy's psyche depended on it.

Eren and Morgan walked around in circles for the rest of the evening. The school was shut — locked up. There wasn't really anywhere else to go. They walked in silence, Morgan pedalling his bike alongside him. They returned to Eren's house around six o clock and Eren's dad ordered pizza. They ate and played SNES until it was time for Morgan to go home. Neither of them mentioned Mr Jefferies.

For the next few days, nothing much happened. Eren returned to school and was harassed by other kids wanting to hear all the gory details. The teachers tried their best to stop this, but Eren still found himself repeating the same brief story over and over — they seemed to be content with that. Soon it was old news.

But it wasn't old news for Eren — far from it. The death of Mr Jefferies weighed on him even more than it had on the fateful day. More than ever, a single thought burned at the back of his mind — he didn't do it — and he still felt that niggling feeling that there was something obvious he was missing.

Nearly a week later, Eren and Morgan were in the park after school. It was the first time the two of them had been alone since Eren had made his assumption. Morgan was tightrope-walking on a small, short brick wall that belonged to a house that had been knocked down on the edge of the park. Eren was sitting on the grass, picking at the blades.

'You want to go to the cinema?' Morgan asked, putting his hands out to steady himself as he walked along the wall. 'My cousin got a new job there. If I ask him really nicely, he might get us in to see *Reservoir Dogs*. Someone's ear gets cut off and you see everything.'

Eren ignored him. He kept on picking at the grass. He was thinking about that day again. He was always thinking about it. There was something to be found there, in his memory.

'Eren. Eren. Eren. Eren. Eren,' Morgan continued. 'Eren. Eren. Eren.'

'What?' Eren said, annoyed.

Morgan smiled. 'What's wrong with you? You're super-quiet.'

'I'm just thinking. Thinking about when I found Mr Jefferies.'

Morgan jumped off the wall and slumped down on the grass splaying his arms out dramatically. 'You're still talking about that? That was like–' Eren could almost see the gears whirring around in his little friend's head, '–That was like two weeks ago.'

Two weeks felt like a lifetime and Eren's memory was starting to fade. The chrysalis around the memory was destroyed. He didn't want to forget. Because he knew that was where the answer lay. It was the strongest feeling he'd ever had.

'I'm trying to remember,' Eren said, pulling up a fresh clump of grass, 'but it's hard.'

'Why don't you say it out loud?' Morgan said, 'Maybe that'd help.'

Morgan was usually a rather simple boy but even Eren couldn't deny that this made a lot of sense.

'Okay,' Eren said and for some reason, he stood up in front of Morgan, almost as if he was about to perform a play.

'So start at the beginning,' Morgan said, 'unless you're sure we can't just try and go see *Reservoir Dogs*.'

'Morgan, focus.'

'But the ear, dude. The ear.'

Eren ignored him. 'Okay, it started about halfway home. I looked in my bag trying to find the sweets we'd bought at the shop, and I knew I'd left my jotter behind. Me and Benny Masterson were playing noughts and crosses with it in Maths, and I just knew that I didn't put it back in my bag. I don't know why. I just could see it lying there on the table. I don't know how but I always do it. I always manage to leave it somewhere.'

'Like that time you left it at the aquarium,' Morgan said, laughing.

'Yeah, I guess,' Eren said, dismissing Morgan so he could continue. 'So I doubled back, and went back to school. It was quiet. Quieter than I'd ever seen it really, even at parents' evening. There was no one there apart from this caretaker guy I didn't know. He was using that thing that shines the floor. Mr Jefferies' room was open. And I went in.

'And there he was. Then I shouted . . .' Eren somehow didn't want to admit he screamed and cried, at least not to

Morgan. '. . . and Miss Rain came and other teachers too, although my eyes were closed so I don't know who. We went to the staff room, and then my dad was there. And then I had to talk to police for ages.'

'Hmm,' Morgan said, scratching his chin, most likely to look intelligent.

'Yes?'

'I think maybe you need to take your mind off this,' Morgan concluded.

'I don't need to do anything. Apart from find out who killed Mr Jefferies,' Eren shouted. It was so loud that a few boys playing football across the field looked over in their direction. Morgan shuffled around so he blocked Eren from view.

'Eren, dude, calm down. Maybe you just need some more time. Mr Jefferies killed himself. And it was really sad. And we'll all miss him. And it was really messed up that you found him. But he did kill himself. And going around saying that he was killed maybe isn't the best thing.'

'You still don't believe me?' Eren said, trying not to cry.

'I believe that you've seen something messed up. And maybe you need to take your mind off it. By seeing something equally messed up. Like an ear severed from a man's head. Where you see everything.'

'Morgan, I'm not going to the cinema,' Eren said defiantly, shuffling away from him. It wasn't fair. If he couldn't persuade his best friend that Mr Jefferies was killed, then what hope did he have of convincing anyone else? 'Do you not want to know what happened? Do you not feel it?'

'Feel what?' Morgan said.

'He didn't do this. He couldn't have.'

'I dunno, I guess it's possible. But the police can't be wrong. They're never wrong. That's what my mum said.'

'But what if they are? What if there's a killer out there free right now? And I know there's something I'm missing.' Eren threw up his hands in disgust, soil and grass going everywhere.

'Maybe you need one of those cleaning machines for your mind. You know like that caretaker was using. You need to wash the memories away.'

'That's dumb—' and Eren trailed off. That was it. That was what he was missing. He looked at Morgan intently.

'What?' the other boy said.

'The caretaker. I didn't recognise the caretaker.'

'But the caretaker's Freddy,' Morgan said. The caretaker at their school was referred to only as Freddy. He was a small mousy man with huge jam-jar glasses. He was often seen pottering around school during the day, fixing light fixtures or mumbling angrily at children who brought dirt in on their shoes. The school could only afford one caretaker, so he was always really busy.

'This wasn't Freddy,' Eren said, the colour draining from his face.

'Then,' Morgan said slowly, as he matched Eren's expression, 'who was it?'

They were both silent for a very long time.

42

'So this caretaker guy, you're sure you haven't seen him before?'

They were back in Eren's room sitting on his floor. Eren doodled on a piece of paper while Morgan watched. Downstairs, Eren's father was watching football. They could hear the chanting of the home team and various cheers as someone scored.

Eren had never been one for sports, much to the disappointment of his father. When his mother had died, his father tried to get him into football. Eren had seen it as some kind of attempt to get closer to him. They went to a couple of games, Eren pretending to be enthusiastic when Arsenal, the team his father supported, scored. But over time, he couldn't keep it up, and eventually he told his father he just wasn't interested.

'I didn't recognise him at all. I've never seen him around school before.'

'What did he look like?' Morgan said.

'He had brown hair. He looked big, not like fat, but big like muscly. He had like a brown overall thing on and he was using that thing to shine the floor of the hall.'

'Couldn't he have just been a cleaner? Like someone who comes in when all us kids have gone home?'

Eren thought for a moment. He wished he could remember the man a little better. 'I guess he could've been. But he looked more like a caretaker. And he definitely wasn't Freddy.'

Morgan rubbed his eyes and sighed. 'So what does this mean?'

'If this guy wasn't a caretaker, and he wasn't a cleaner then what was he doing there?' Eren asked, with a degree of finality. He'd found it, that one strand of thread that didn't fit in the picture. He felt happy for the first time since he had gone into that room. He was getting somewhere.

There was a fresh cheer from downstairs and the sound of Eren's father shouting 'Get in!' Arsenal had scored.

'You're saying that . . .' Morgan didn't finish, but Eren knew exactly what he meant.

'Yes. I think it was him. I think he killed Mr Jefferies. I think he went into that room and he . . . he killed him. Made it look like Jefferies had killed himself to get away with it. Then he left the room, maybe heard people coming, and had to work out how to blend in. Maybe he found that shining machine and decided to pose as a caretaker. Then when I had passed by, he ran away.' Eren put his pen down, in resolution. 'What do you think?'

Morgan scoffed. 'I don't – I mean it makes some kind of sense, I suppose. And it sounds like it could've happened. But . . .'

'Yes?'

'. . . that doesn't mean it did.'

Eren had known Morgan all his life. The two of them had met at kindergarten and had stayed together since. They'd never once fallen out. Even as an eleven-year-old, Eren had a basic understanding of how people worked, and he knew how Morgan worked more than anyone. If his friend was going to help him, he would have to appeal to his more exciting side. Eren needed to know what happened to Mr Jefferies for his peace of mind, but Morgan had no such issue. Morgan was just a kid who wanted life to be more like it was in the movies.

'Morgan, imagine if Mr Jefferies was murdered, and we caught the killer? Imagine how famous we would be? The two kids who caught a dangerous man, who had killed their own teacher. We could be better than everyone else. We could be better than the police. We would be superheroes.'

Eren slid the action figure across the carpet, in front of Morgan. It had still been where he'd thrown it a week before.

Morgan looked at him, his eyes alight. He picked up the action figure. And smiled. 'Okay. So what do we do?'

'We need to make sure that that guy wasn't just a cleaner.'

'How do we do that?'

'There's a book with pictures of all the staff at the school in. I saw it once – it was out at parents' evening. They probably have it in the office. We need that book to see if that guy's in there. I'll know it if I see him, I just can't describe him.'

'And what if he is in there? Hell, what if he isn't in there? What then?'

'We'll work that out when we've found out.'

Morgan nodded, not looking entirely convinced. 'Okay, I guess.'

'One more thing, we have to keep this totally quiet. Only you and I can know we're doing this. We could be in danger if it gets out that we're investigating.'

Morgan looked insanely happy about this. The more danger, the more exciting it was to him, no doubt. 'Okay.'

Eren put a fist out. 'Pard'ner,' he said, in an old-timey voice.

'Pard'ner,' Morgan said, bumping his fist with his own.

Downstairs, Eren's father howled. The other team had scored.

The next day during break, Eren and Morgan went to the school office, and were confronted with a rather crotchety Miss Erthwhile. She was an old woman who had worked at the school since the dawn of time, and famously hated children. She was always in the office, dunking biscuits into her coffee and typing slowly on the computer. She was also the qualified nurse for the sick room, and since she had taken up that particular job, the number of children who went to the sick room had gone down by more than half. No one wanted to be faced with her.

Eren and Morgan walked up to the desk slowly as if approaching an almighty dragon. Similarly to a dragon, Miss Erthwhile could be defeated if you knew her weaknesses.

'Hello, Miss Erthwhile,' Eren said, sunnily.

Miss Erthwhile peered down at the both of them. Her face was just a pile of wrinkles. Many scholars had died attempting to figure out how old she was. 'Yes?' she said.

'Me and Morgan here were wondering if maybe you had a book with pictures of all the staff at the school in?'

Miss Erthwhile regarded them with her small squirrely eyes. 'The alumni book? Now, why would you want that?'

Eren and Morgan looked at each other. 'We, uh, we're doing a project,' Morgan said – he was always far quicker with the excuses. He'd had plenty of practice.

'Project for what?'

'Geography. We're doing a map of the city, and the teacher says we can get pictures of everyone to stick on the map. Like which areas they live in.'

Eren looked at his friend, with something like admiration. Even he had to admit that that wasn't a bad save.

'Hmm.' Erthwhile thought, while looking down her nose at them. 'If you bring me a note from the teacher, I'll let you have a look.'

Morgan smiled. 'We don't really have time for that, Miss Erthwhile. Our project's due tomorrow and we really wanted to do the project now.'

'Sorry, but you can't see it without a note,' Erthwhile said, not even attempting to hide her happiness that she had disrupted someone's day. 'That book is not for children to see.'

Morgan and Eren looked at each other again. Eren shrugged, not knowing what else to do. Morgan got in close and whispered in Eren's ear, 'Watch this. I saw this thing called reverse psychology on a TV show.'

Morgan straightened up again and cleared his throat.

Erthwhile watched him, bemused.

'Don't give us the alumni book,' Morgan said, confidently.

Erthwhile chuckled, 'Righto.' She went back to typing very slowly on the computer.

Morgan looked confused. He leant in to Eren again. 'Okay, there may have been more elements to it.'

The two boys walked out of the office, dejected. Eren needed that book, it was the only way he could know for sure if the man he had seen worked at the school or not.

Out in the corridor, Eren slammed his fist into a locker. 'Ouch,' he said, instantly regretting it. 'We need that book.'

'Is there no other way?'

'No,' Eren said, rubbing his hand.

'Okay then,' Morgan said, 'then there's only one thing for it.'

'What?'

'One of us has to go to the sick room.'

During English, Morgan suffered an intense and concentrated stomach ache. The teacher rushed him off to the sick room, telling the class to re-read the opening of *Of Mice and Men*. Eren waited as long as he could, which was about two minutes, and then snuck out the back of the class.

The corridors were quiet, reminding him of that fateful day, but this time he could hear the muffled sounds of classrooms full of children all around him. He took the shortcut through the courtyard, nodding to Freddy, who was clipping a bush, as he passed. He emerged into the office corridor. The sick room was just down the hall from Erthwhile's office and Eren could hear the howls of his friend. He was either overacting his stomach ache or Erthwhile was torturing him. No one knew the horrors of the sick room.

Eren stuck his head around the office door. It was empty. He went round Erthwhile's desk and started rummaging. The top drawer had packs of sweets in.

The next drawer down had random papers all heaped together. They all seemed to be spreadsheets filled with more letters and numbers than Eren knew existed.

To Eren's dismay, the final drawer was locked. He tried pulling on it three or four times before he noticed that there was a sticky note on the upper right corner of the drawer. In Erthwhile's unmistakeable scrawl, it said, 'Key on monitor'.

Eren looked up at the bulky computer monitor but couldn't see a key. All he found was another post-it note, this time reading 'Cactus'.

Eren almost laughed as he realised that this was Erthwhile's version of enhanced security. He reached across the desk and picked up the small potted cactus in the corner. Just below a layer of soil was the key.

Eren unlocked the drawer and opened it. Piles of books were in there – big luxury embossed books. Most of them were yearbooks, dating back as far as 1985. But under them all, he found what he was looking for. A large leather book with 'Alumni' embossed on it in gold lettering.

Eren opened it, flipping through the pages of staff. He saw Miss Rain smiling out at him and next to her, he saw the kind face of Mr Jefferies. He looked so alive. But now he was dead. He turned the page quickly, and finally found the Cleaning Staff section. No one was smiling here, just a bunch of older women looking stern and very unhappy about having their photo taken. They were all women, not a man among them. Eren turned over the page, but saw that that was the only page for cleaning staff. The man wasn't there. He wasn't there.

Eren calmed down. He decided to go through the entire book, looking at every picture. He realised for the first time that he almost wanted to see the man. Because the alternative would be horrifying. He looked through the entire book, but he wasn't there.

Eren shut the book and put his head in his hands. Who was that man? How could he be there, in the hall, when he had walked past. Was this man the murderer? It was the only lead he had.

Eren put the book back in the drawer, locked it and replaced the key in the cactus. He didn't know what to think anymore. This was too real.

He looked up and almost jumped out of his skin.

Miss Rain was in the doorway, watching him.

Miss Rain was nice – she didn't even really ask what Eren had been doing. She said that all the teachers were worried about him. He'd been acting distant, not been working very well. That was mostly because he had been drawing diagrams of the Maths room and thinking about how someone could stage a murder to look like a suicide, but Eren didn't tell her that.

'I understand, Eren. It's horrible. It really is. And no one would blame you if you needed to take some more time off.'

'No,' Eren said firmly, 'I can't just sit around and do nothing.' He was talking about his investigation, but Miss Rain obviously took it to mean school work.

She smiled sadly. 'You're very strong and intelligent, Eren. More than most eleven-year-olds. You could achieve such great things.'

Eren smiled at her, trying to ignore Morgan, who was standing outside the window, pulling funny faces.

'So this mystery man is our guy,' Morgan said, at lunch.

It was a nice day and Eren and Morgan had walked all the way down to the far side of the field, where no one ever bothered to go, so they could have a conversation in peace.

'Maybe. Possibly,' Eren said, thinking. He was think-ing about what had happened after he screamed on that day. After he had reached the edge of his sanity and just howled. Who had come for him?

'What?'

'We have to consider . . . other possibilities.'

'Other possibilities? What other possibilities? You see a mysterious guy on the day Mr Jefferies is killed? That seems pretty good to me. He's our guy.' Morgan was climbing the fence and stopped about halfway up, perching precariously on an iron bar. Eren was always impressed by Morgan's energy – he could never stay still.

'We need to look at every possible avenue. We don't want to make a mistake.'

'Eren, if the police couldn't solve this, what makes you think we can? What are we actually doing? Even if this guy did kill Mr Jefferies – or someone else, or whoever – what do we do then?'

'Then we go to the police. If we don't have concrete proof, they'll never believe us. It's just like you said, we're eleven. We can't even reach high shelves.'

'Exactly,' Morgan said, jumping off the fence and stumbling on the landing. He put his arms out anyway, like the gymnasts you saw on TV. 'We're eleven. We can't figure this out.'

'Why not?' Eren said. 'Eleven-year-olds solving a murder. Maybe we'd be the first.'

'It sounds great, Eren. But can we do it?'

Eren thought for a long time. 'I have to try.'

'Okay, so what now?'

'We have to get into the Maths room.'

'More rooms, huh?'

Eren and Morgan stayed behind after school, pretending to study in the library. They waited until five o clock, when they made their way down the quiet corridors towards the Maths department.

They found the door to Mr Jefferies' classroom closed – a wrapping of police tape around it. POLICE LINE – DO NOT CROSS.

'I heard the Head talking,' Morgan said. 'They're just keeping the tape there to stop kids wandering in. The police are long gone.'

Eren nodded. He looked at the door, suddenly unable to move.

Morgan nudged him. 'C'mon, it's just a room.'

'I know, it's just . . .' Eren trailed off, not knowing what it was just.

Morgan pushed the handle. The door creaked open wide of its own free will, revealing the perfect classroom behind. Someone had tidied up, of course. The chairs and tables were all set out in an immaculate symmetrical pattern. It was all ready for learning.

Morgan ducked under the tape and walked into the room. He stopped in the centre, right under the exposed pipe, and looked back.

Eren was watching wide-eyed.

'Come on then,' Morgan said, and seeing Eren's horrified face looked up to the pipe. He side-stepped quickly.

Eren shook himself out of his paralysis and ducked under the tape. He shivered as he entered the room. It was as cold as it had been on that day. Someone had left the window open again.

'So what are we looking for?' Morgan said, picking up an exercise book that had been left on one of the desks and flipping through it.

Eren looked around. It was like nothing had ever happened in here. No one had died. No one had even lived. There was no hint that Mr Jefferies had ever been here at all. His desk was scrubbed of any character.

Eren walked around it and expected to see the framed photo of his dog, or the weathered copy of *The Catcher in the Rye*. People used to ask him why he had become a Maths teacher if he loved books so much. Eren remembered his answer word for word.

'Maths is mechanics. You can work at it and get better, until you are the greatest mathematician to ever live. To write like Salinger is a gift, a gift you cannot teach, and one which I sadly do not possess.'

It wasn't there. The book wasn't there. It was always there, at the end of the desk, perfectly lined up to the edges. But it wasn't there. It became imperative that Eren found it. Why would someone take it? Why was it not where it belonged?

Eren yanked open the desk drawers. They were all empty. There was nothing left. There was nothing of him. He slammed them shut.

'Careful,' Morgan said, stepping towards Eren, 'we don't want to make too much noise.'

Eren's eyes were filling up with tears, and he didn't think he could stop them this time. He buried his head in the sleeves of his school jumper. 'He's gone, Morgan. They got rid of him. All of them. All the grown-ups.'

'Turn around, Eren.'

'It's like he never even existed.'

'Eren, turn around.'

'He's gone. He's all gone.'

'Eren,' Morgan said, in a sharp whisper, 'he's not gone, not quite.'

Eren finally heard his friend, looking up from his sleeves. He looked around.

Although the room was spotless, the whiteboard had remained untouched. It seemed whoever had cleaned the room had not been able to wipe away the last things Mr Jefferies ever did. Eren saw the equations that his class had been working on, Mr Jefferies' convoluted explanation of Pythagoras, and in the upper right corner his name, which he had written the very first day they had met him and never erased. Eren looked at it and smiled sadly. It was almost like a mural to the forgotten.

Morgan stood next to Eren as they both looked at the diagrams and the numbers.

'I still don't bloody understand it,' Morgan said, and started laughing.

Eren laughed too, as his eyes scanned the equations. His eyes fell to the bottom left corner of the board where, in Mr Jefferies' scrawl, there was a three-digit number.

'Wait,' Eren said, 'what's that?' He pointed to the number.

391.

'That?' Morgan said, confused. 'It's just a number, Eren.'

'But it's not got anything to do with the other stuff. It's not connected at all.'

'It's a number. He was a Maths teacher.'

'Do you remember him writing this in the lesson?' Eren said, examining the number closer.

Morgan chuckled and threw his arms up at the whole

board. 'I don't remember him writing any of this. I wasn't paying attention.'

'I don't remember him writing this,' Eren said, taking a step back and looking behind him at where he was sitting in that lesson. 'And it's in the bottom corner. None of us could've seen it.'

'So he didn't write it in the lesson. So it was already there. Or so it wasn't. Eren, you're starting to sound a little crazy.'

Eren rounded on him, suddenly angry. 'What if this is Mr Jefferies' last message? What if it's a clue to who murdered him?'

'Seriously?' Morgan said, reverting to harsh whispers as the boys heard someone pass the room. The footsteps didn't stop and then they were gone. 'So Mr Jefferies' last words were 391. Three, nine, one. What does that even mean? It means nothing, Eren. And no one would ever think it did. You have to stop obsessing over this.'

'No. No, I don't,' Eren said, feeling the prick of tears in his eyes again. 'Everyone else needs to start obsessing over it. Someone killed Mr Jefferies and they're going to get away with it.'

Morgan was silent for a moment and stepped back from Eren, shaking his head. 'I thought maybe being in here would help you.'

'What are you talking about?'

'He killed himself, Eren. Mr Jefferies killed himself and he left the rest of us behind. He is not coming back. We just need to forget him.' Morgan was stony-faced, but Eren could read the sadness on his face.

Eren saw red. 'You don't believe me. You've never believed me. You're just like everyone else. You're an idiot.' Before he could stop himself, Eren pushed Morgan hard. The boy fell back into a desk, and took a moment to regain his composure.

He went to his backpack, unzipped it and pulled out something. He held it up to Eren.

It was a photo. A photo of the man – the man Eren had seen that day cleaning the hall floor.

'Is this him?' Morgan said.

Eren couldn't talk, he couldn't manage a word.

'I saw him the other day in the PE department. His name's Martin. He's the new caretaker.'

He threw the photo at Eren. It bounced off his chest and fell on the floor. The man's face stared up at Eren. He couldn't take his eyes from it.

Morgan picked up his bag and slung it over his shoulder. He went to leave and then turned back, looking at Eren with a seething anger in his eyes. 'You know what, I am an idiot. And so are you. We're kids. We're allowed to be.'

Morgan left.

Eren fell to his knees, picking up the photo. He looked at it and he cried – he didn't know for how long.

43

The investigation, as short-lived as it was, was officially over. Eren and Morgan kept their distance from each other. Morgan didn't even look at him. Eren felt as though the only friend he had had betrayed him. No one believed him and maybe he didn't even believe himself anymore. After all, he had no suspects – not now. He started to believe that maybe Mr Jefferies was just a sad, sad man who couldn't think of anything else to do but kill himself. Eren threw himself into his school work, having a lot to catch up on, since he had spent all his free time on an investigation that went nowhere. He felt stupid, he felt embarrassed.

He didn't talk to anyone at school. From afar, he watched Morgan's new scheme to get famous. The boy had started a band. All the other kids and teachers carried on as normal, like nothing had ever happened.

The school and Eren's father agreed that Eren should go to see a therapist, which he did without any argument. He talked more in the sessions than he did anywhere else, but he never brought up what he thought had happened to Mr Jefferies. He actually liked his therapist a lot – a young man called Simon who the school had recommended. It was funny — the tricks he pulled to make Eren explore himself. Eren often looked back on the sessions fondly.

Christmas went by without much consequence. Eren sat at a table with his father, his aunt's family and his grandmother. He laughed and joked with his cousins, who were his age. There was still nothing from Morgan, and Eren began to be glad. Maybe this was just a fresh start. He had extra helpings of turkey and sprouts. He liked sprouts.

1993 came around and Eren and his father ate chips on the beach, watching the New Year wake up. It was bitterly cold and the sea lapped against the sand like water on velvet. They walked five miles, tracing the coastline.

At the end of January, Eren started working a paper round. It had been a freezing month, and he trod out in the snow every morning and delivered people's papers. He had fifty-five papers on his route. He passed the time thinking to himself.

He never thought of *that* anymore. Simon said that the mind was a magical thing and although it hurt now, there would be a time when he didn't have to actively *not* think about it. *He would just forget?* Not really, it would always be there, but for all intents and purposes, day to day he would forget.

And he was starting to feel like maybe he could carry on. The rest of the world was, so why couldn't he? The morning sun in the January air was so strong, why couldn't it wipe away the past? That was why, when he went into the newsagents on the first Saturday in February, he was shocked when Mr Perkins told him he had a new house to deliver to. He knew the address well. It was Mr Jefferies' old house.

Eren didn't think much of it as he went on his round, but when he rounded the corner to Mr Jefferies' house, he found that his legs had grown heavier. Every step he took towards the house was slow and lumbering. He had to fight himself to get there, and after he had put the newspaper through the letterbox, he just stood there and looked at the house sadly.

There was a sharp sound at the door, as the newspaper got pulled through the letterbox. A dog barked and an elderly lady shushed it. Before Eren could turn away, she had opened the door.

'Hello dear,' she said, not appearing the slightest bit confused as to why he was standing there in the snow.

'Sorry, ma'am,' Eren said, 'I . . .I just used to know someone who lived in this house. My teacher.'

The old woman smiled at him. 'You mean George?'

Eren was taken aback. 'Um . . .yes, ma'am. Sorry, but how do you know him?'

'Oh, poor child, I'm his sodding mother,' the old woman said, laughing as a cocker spaniel poked its head around the doorframe with the bundled up newspaper in its chops. 'Come on, you'd better come in for a nice cup of tea. You look like you're much about to catch your death.'

'I really can't, ma'am. I've got more papers.' He nodded to his sack full of undelivered newspapers.

The old woman shook her head. 'Nonsense. No one

263

ever missed a bit of bad news. They can wait for their papers.'

And before Eren knew it, he was ushered into the small house. It smelled odd – not unpleasant but strange and the place looked like a traditional old person's house. It was very compact and there was a putrid red carpet running throughout the place. Eren spotted a tiny kitchen branching off from the living room – the sideboards cluttered with things all stacked on top of each other. The living room was equally small, with two hideous brown fabric sofas and a chair. Eren perched on one of the sofas, putting his bag down. *What am I doing here?*

'There you go,' the old woman said, 'so a tea, yes?'

'I don't drink tea, ma'am,' Eren said, apologetically.

The woman laughed and went into the kitchen. 'You will,' she said.

Eren looked around the room. It was hard to believe that Mr Jefferies used to live here. It all looked so – old. He stared at his reflection in the small television. He looked uncomfortable. Most likely because he was. He couldn't meet his own eyes, so looked down to the glass coffee table. There were a few gossip magazines, along with a paper with an unfinished crossword.

The clock was very loud.

A few minutes later, the old woman came back. She carried one cup and saucer very shakily, handing it to Eren. The tan liquid slopped over the side as it changed hands and pooled in the saucer. Eren smiled at her as she went back into the kitchen to get her own.

'What did you say your name was, my dear?' she said

as she came back, and slowly lowered herself into the armchair.

Eren's mouth worked faster than his brain. 'Morgan Sheppard,' he said. If this was Mr Jefferies' mother, it was possible that she knew Eren's name. It wasn't likely, but Eren was already uncomfortable enough – he didn't want her knowing he was the one who found her son.

'Morgan. Now that's a nice name. And you were George's student?' the old woman asked, raising the cup to her lips and slurping.

'Yes. I was in his Maths class. I . . . I just want to say how sorry I am, about everything.'

The woman put the cup down on the table and smiled at him. 'We can't change what happened, dear. It's no one's fault – let alone yours. I'm sure it's harder for you than anyone else. I mean, all you children. To be faced with something like that at your age. How old are you, dear?'

'Eleven,' Eren said, taking a sip from the cup, swallowing and then promptly putting the cup down reminding himself never to touch it again. He coughed. 'Twelve in two months.'

'You're just a baby,' the old woman said, and her voice cracked with sadness. 'Oh dear, what a mess. But we all must carry on. That's all there is to do.'

'Do you mind if I ask a question?' Eren said.

'No, dear. You must have so many.'

Eren spoke slowly, picking his words very carefully. 'Do you . . . Do you know why Mr Je– George – did what he did?'

The woman pursed her lips and picked up her cup again. 'None of us can really know, dear. That's the curse – the curse of the ones left behind. I can tell you why I think he did it. I think he did it because he saw no other way out. There're two types of people in this world and you don't know what type you are until it's too late.'

'Two types of people?'

'Yes. Say you're running through the forest. It's dark and you don't know exactly where you are. All you know is you're far from home, far from everyone you've ever loved. And you're running. You're running because things are chasing you. The most ferocious and hideous monsters you can think of are right behind you. So you run. You run and run because you won't let them get you. The trees start to thin and suddenly, you find yourself at the edge of the forest. You come to a rise and beyond it, you find you are at the peak of a cliff. You turn back but the monsters are coming out of the treeline. You are cornered. There is no way past them. You look down and hundreds of feet below you are jagged rocks and the unkempt sea. The monsters are creeping up on you slowly but they are gaining ground. You have two clear choices placed in front of you – you submit, let the monsters get you and do whatever they want with you or you jump off the cliff, giving yourself to the rocks and the sea.'

'And Mr Jefferies jumped?'

The woman looked at him, with her old eyes. He thought she was about to cry. But then she snapped out of it and slurped at her tea again. 'Yes. George jumped.

Figuratively, of course. That was a metaphor – you know about metaphors?'

'Yes. Saying something *is* something else.'

'Yes, you are a smart child. George taught you well.'

Eren didn't remind her that Mr Jefferies taught Maths and it was in fact another teacher who had taught him about metaphors.

'George had monsters?'

The woman chuckled, an almost entirely humourless sound but still kindly. 'We all have monsters, dear. Even me. Even you. There's always something chasing us in the forest, even if we don't want to admit it. But to answer your question, yes, George had monsters. They just caught up with him.'

'What were they?' Eren saw the old woman physically recoil. 'I'm sorry if that's rude,' he said quickly, 'but I think I need to know why. I just need to know why someone would do that.'

The old woman settled back into her chair and looked at him. 'I forget what it's like to be eleven. I've lived your life eight times over. There's a thought. I was once inquisitive. Life'll beat it out of you though.

'The truth was, George was always a very lonely man. He lived here with me his whole life. He kept saying that it was because he wanted to look after me, wanted to make sure I had a good life. Along the way, he forgot to have his own. He never had any partners. He used to say that he didn't need anyone, but I could see the loneliness in his eyes – always there.

'He loved his job. He had always wanted to be a

267

teacher. He put everything into his work. When he came home, he did all his marking and then watched sports. That's how it started, you see. He started to bet on all kinds of sport – football, rugby, cricket. He didn't even know how cricket worked, but he still bet on it. And then there were the horses. He went down the betting shop of a Sunday. That was where he fell in with the wrong crowd. Before long, he was betting too much. Addiction, dear, is a cancer, but it's a cancer that tricks you into thinking you want it. I tried to talk George around, but the addiction talked back.

'He borrowed money – money from the wrong people – thinking he would make it back. But of course he didn't. He lost it. He lost it all. People started coming round, to this house. Unsavoury types, you know. People who looked like they were right out of the movies – shady people. They threatened George, they manhandled him and I couldn't do a thing. There was one man who came around a lot – he used to be as nice as nice could be with me. I even thought he might be different from the rest of them. But one night when it was very late, I heard him come over and assault my George. George wouldn't do anything of course, and I'm not stupid, I knew that something had to be done, but done in the right way.

'The next time this man came round, I had George sitting at the table with me. I told this man to sit down and we would civilly talk things out. He sat down, but he didn't seem happy about it. Neither of them did. And I said, "Now look, George, Martin, you have to sort this out—"'

Eren froze. He suddenly had shivers down his spine. It took him a moment to realise why but when he focused, it came down on him like an anvil. The woman was still talking, but he couldn't hear her anymore. What had she said—? She couldn't have—?

'I'm sorry, ma'am.' He wrenched the words out of him through tingling lips. 'What did you say this man's name was?'

'What? Oh, um, Martin. Yes. I thought he was a nice boy, different from the rest of them. Turns out he was the worst of the lot though.'

Eren's head swam. The man. The man cleaning the floor, with that stupid machine. The man in the caretaker uniform. The new caretaker. Martin.

Before he knew it, he was standing. The old woman was still talking. 'I have to go,' he interrupted.

The old woman looked at him, confused. 'Alright then, dear, it was nice to meet you.'

Eren was out of the room and down the short hall, before she could even get up.

'Please come back any time,' she called after him. 'Morgan is such a nice name.'

And he was out the door, slinging his coat on as the cold bit at him.

He made it around the corner before he vomited into the snow.

Eren found Morgan in the main hall at lunch. He was on stage with his band, a mismatched group of kids who had no business being anywhere. There was a fat boy on guitar, and a nerdy-looking girl on drums. Morgan, of course, was the lead singer.

They had just been making a terrible racket, but Morgan stopped them. He walked over to the fat kid with the guitar in his podgy hands.

'Eric, you were totally off.'

'Sorry, Morgan,' Eric said nasally.

'You remember how it goes right?'

'I think so.'

'Okay, I'm sorry, Eric, but I think you might actually have to learn how to play guitar.'

'Do I have to?' Eric said.

'I'm sorry, mate. You should have picked drums. You just hit them and it's fine.' Morgan turned his attention to the girl on drums, and gave her a wink. 'You're doing fabulous, Clarice.'

Eren cleared his throat. Morgan and the others looked around. Morgan grimaced when he saw it was Eren. Eren had expected as much.

Morgan seemed to resign himself to it and clapped his hands. 'Okay, take five. That's five minutes, not five chocolate bars, Eric.'

The other two mumbled and grumbled and made their way off stage into the wings. Morgan jumped down from the stage and walked up to Eren.

'Well, it's Eren,' he said, looking him up and down.

'Yes,' Eren said.

'You like my band? This is going to take me straight to the top. We're going to be the next big thing. We're called The Future in Italics.'

'You mean *The Future*?'

'No, I mean The Future in Italics,' Morgan said, like it was the most obvious thing in the world. 'You need an edgy band name if you're going to go places. Edgy like Blur . . . or ABBA. Actually, maybe not ABBA . . . or Blur now I think about it.'

Eren smiled, and was surprised to find it was genuine. He'd forgotten how much he'd missed Morgan's schemes, and just the boy in general.

'What'd you want?' Morgan said. 'As you can see, I'm super-busy.'

'I need to talk to you,' said Eren and he quickly relayed what he'd learned from Mr Jefferies' mother. To his surprise, Morgan was actually intrigued by it, but he was still sceptical.

'I thought you'd forgotten all this, Eren.'

'But you have to admit it's weird.'

'Martin's a common name.'

'But that guy was there. That day. That Martin.'

Morgan scratched the back of his neck. 'Yeah, I suppose it's a bit weird.'

Eren smiled. 'I just need you one last time. And then if I'm wrong, I'll drop the whole entire thing forever. I'll accept it and move on. But we just need to do one thing. One last thing.'

Morgan looked around at the stage with all his band equipment on. He looked back at Eren.

'Okay.'

*

The plan was simple – watch for Martin when he left school and follow him home. There, there had to be some incriminating evidence proving that he killed Mr Jefferies. Eren hadn't even considered the possibility that he didn't have any. There must be something linking him to the murder. Eren was more confident than ever that he had found the man who'd done the deed, and with Morgan's help, he could finally catch him.

Morgan didn't seem quite so convinced, but he was excited to break into someone's house. Maybe a little too excited.

They were in Eren's room the night before they planned to follow Martin. Morgan was playing SNES, while Eren was rummaging around under his bed.

'I know I saw them around here somewhere,' Eren said. He was looking for a pair of walkie-talkies that his aunt had gotten him for Christmas. At the time, he hadn't really thought much of them – he'd had no one to call – but now they seemed essential. What was a tailing mission without the right tech?

'Have you checked in the cupboard?' Morgan said, with no attempt to actually help his friend.

'Yeah,' Eren said, sliding out from under the bed and slumping down on it. 'I think they might be in the attic.'

Eren watched Morgan play Mario until he heard his father go out to the pub. He always did on a Thursday night, every week since his mother had died. Eight o'clock on the dot.

'Morgan, come on, I need help.'

Morgan moaned all the way to the garage as Eren

enlisted him in helping to carry the ladder up the stairs. Five minutes and a few future bruises later, Eren propped the ladder on the landing in front of the attic hatch.

He went into his father's room and found two torches in his tool cupboard. He threw one to Morgan. 'The walkie talkies should be in a blue plastic box.'

Morgan smiled. 'Right you are, guv'nor.' He raised his hand in a little salute.

Eren laughed. He had definitely missed Morgan's special brand of immaturity.

Eren climbed the ladder and pushed on the attic hatch until it gave way. The attic was pitch black, and Eren shone his torch inside. A shaft of light etched out a few boxes near the hatch, as though they were only there when the torch was on. There was no blue box nearby. He looked down to Morgan.

'I'm going to have to go up there. You stay here and hold the ladder.'

Morgan laughed. 'You really think I'm going to stay down here, while you have the time of your life up there?'

'It's just an attic, Morgan.'

But Morgan followed him up into the attic anyway. The ladder was not quite tall enough for Eren to easily get up. He had to push hard with his elbows to fling the rest of him inside. He helped Morgan up into the attic.

The two beams of torchlight explored the room as Morgan and Eren looked around. The attic was incredibly cluttered, with piles upon piles of cardboard removal boxes stacked on top of each other. Eren had no idea that his father and he had so much stuff, and he couldn't see his blue box anywhere. He walked over to a mound of boxes, careful to pick his way over the wooden beams.

Morgan's torch lay on a clutter of loose items. He went over to a big monitor and started poking at it. 'Is this a TV or a computer monitor?'

Eren ignored him, putting the torch in his mouth as he shifted boxes over in his great pile to see what was behind them. There he found the blue box, depressingly, at the bottom of the biggest pile of boxes he had ever seen.

As Morgan looked around, his torchlight dancing around on the edges of Eren's vision, Eren started to shuffle boxes around so he could get to the pile he wanted. It took him ten minutes to finally lift all the boxes down and get to his blue box. He breathed out with exhaustion – his arms ached with the ghost of how they would feel in the morning. He opened the lid and there was the pack of two walkie-talkies still in their impenetrable plastic womb. Eren picked them up, and expected some sort of fanfare for all the trouble he'd gone to. Instead he got one word.

'Eren.'

Morgan's voice, but not like before, not excited or enthusiastic. It almost sounded . . .worried.

Eren looked around, but Morgan was nowhere to be seen. There was a crest of light coming from over a sea of boxes.

'Eren, come here.'

Eren started to pick his way around the attic, getting worried himself, until he found Morgan at the very back of the dark space, with his torch fixed on an old wooden chest.

'What?' Eren said, trying to laugh it off.

Morgan looked at him and then looked back at the chest.

Eren looked too.

The chest looked old and rather rickety. Painted across the front of the chest in chipped and weathered letters was the name 'Lillith'.

'That's your mother's name, right?' Morgan said.

Eren nodded silently. He had never seen this chest before, didn't even know it existed. His father had never told him about it, but had in fact said that all his mother's things had been left behind when they moved. His father said all the things were just too heart-breaking so he got rid of them. But here was something. A chest with his mother's name on it.

Eren kneeled in front of the chest, running his hands over the top. Just touching it made him think of her, her warm touch, her soft hugs. It made him feel closer to her, this wooden thing he didn't even know was here. He remembered the day she left, walked out of the house. She said she'd be back – she never was. Not that she could've known. Not that she could've predicted that car would barrel off the road and hit her. They said she had died almost instantly. His father comforted himself with the *instantly*, but Eren horrified himself with the *almost*.

Now, in the darkness of the attic, illuminated by Morgan's torch as well as his own, he felt more like a child than he ever had. A child who just wanted his mother.

He went to open the chest, but the lid was stuck. He moved his torch along the seam of the lid to find a padlock.

There was no keyhole, but instead three tumblers with the digits 0 to 9 on. He sighed.

'It's locked,' he said, looking past the torch beam to where he thought Morgan's face was. 'A three-digit number.'

'Can we just guess it? Or try every combination?' Morgan said. Eren knew he was trying to be helpful, but that didn't offset how dumb it sounded.

'Three numbers. Ten digits on each. That's a thousand combinations.'

'Whoa,' Morgan said, briefly moving the torch to his face to show his impressed look. 'How did you do that?'

Eren sighed. 'We literally did that in Maths this morning.'

'Oh, I—'

'—wasn't listening,' Eren finished, 'yeah, no surprise there.' He waved his torch around. 'There must be something around here we can use to break the lock.' He got up and went over to the pile of stuff that Morgan had been looking in previously.

'But if we break it open, your dad'll know we've been up here,' Morgan said.

'I don't care.' Eren moved the bulky monitor aside, looking for something sharp and strong.

'But maybe it's not something you should see. Maybe he kept it from you for a reason.'

'I don't care,' Eren shouted, rounding on Morgan, pointing the torch in his face so it made his eyes squint. 'This is my mother's. And I'm her son. And I deserve to know what's in here.'

'Okay, okay,' Morgan said, pushing Eren's torch down. 'It would just be easier if we knew the three-digit number. I mean, maybe your father wrote it down somewhere. I have to write stuff down or else I forget it.'

'Write it down?' Eren said, something in his brain clicking into gear.

'Yeah. Like passwords for SNES and stuff.'

Eren rushed back to the chest. He kneeled down in front of it again and fiddled with the padlock. 'Shine the light here again.'

Morgan did.

Eren moved the tumblers quickly. It couldn't be–? This couldn't work. It made no sense. But it was the only three-digit number in his head. He finished. The padlock clicked open.

Morgan looked confused. 'What the–? Did you just–?'

'Think, Morgan. You have to write stuff down to re-member it. What's the only three-digit number we've seen out of place these past few months?'

'I don't know what you're talking about.'

'Yes you do. 391. On the board. In Mr Jefferies' class-room. The code for this padlock was 391.'

'Wait, what?' Morgan said. 'That doesn't make any sense. Why would a code for a chest in your attic be on Mr Jefferies' board?'

'I don't know,' Eren said, touching the lid of the chest as a tingle prickled his spine. 'I don't know.'

Eren remained motionless, feeling the edges of the chest lid with his fingers. What was this? How could this even be possible? This couldn't be a coincidence.

A thousand combinations and it just so happened to be that one. That one number written on the board by his dead teacher – the answers to all the questions swarming around in his head must be inside this chest, which was why he couldn't open it.

A shuffling beside him. Morgan sat next to him and put his hands on the lid too. He started to open the chest, and Eren found himself pushing too. The chest opened, the lid springing back. Inside was darkness.

The two children shone their torches into the box, at first afraid that it was completely empty. But the chest was not. It was about half full with scraps of paper all bundled together with paperclips. There were also a few photos of Eren's mother, smiling out at them.

Eren picked up one of the bundles of papers and took off the paperclip. He looked through them slowly. They were letters from his mother to his father. They were love letters. They all started *My love* and were signed *Your Lillith*. They were long, all over a page and some spanning two or three. They talked of how much his mother loved her father, detailing their encounters in minute detail.

Do you remember the café on the lake? one read. *We fed the ducks, and ate carrot cake until the sun set behind the trees. I don't think I've ever been as happy as you make me. When I'm with you, my soul is peaceful. Life is drowned out with how much I love you. Why do I have to keep you secret? I hide our love in a chest in the attic. The password is the room number of the hotel we stayed in that first night, you remember – you can't not.*

Eren blushed, and he put up his hand to mask his face

from Morgan even though it was probably indecipherable in the dark of the attic. He felt like he was intruding on something private, but he couldn't stop himself. He had never felt that his mother and father shared this level of affection although they must have at some point.

He shuffled the letters and read another.

My love, how much this mundane existence can be ignited by just the mere chance of meeting you. My life would be so boring if not for you, and I know I have made some choices I am not proud of. If only we could be together. But one day, we will be. We'll be together forever. I promise I will do it soon.

This one seemed odd. Do what? What choices? He scanned the rest of the letter, but there was nothing more of any interest. He went on to the next.

My love, I'm sorry. I just need more time. Please you have to allow me time. I'm stuck, I'm stuck in this place and I don't know how to get out. But knowing you are there at the end of the road is what will give me the strength to break out. I promise you, I will tell him soon.

Eren's stomach knotted, although he didn't know quiet why. This letter was strange, weirdly urgent. And what was his mother talking about? He read the rest and came to the bottom of the page. She signed off in her usual way, but added a PS.

Your Lillith. P.S. I have included our photo overleaf. Look how happy we are, let's be this happy forever.

Eren saw a little sketched arrow in the corner of the page and he turned the paper over. Paper-clipped to the top of the page was the photo.

279

Eren dropped the letter in plain shock and scampered backwards, hitting a pile of boxes so the top one fell off causing a small avalanche of boxes.

Morgan looked up from some of the letters and looked at Eren. 'What?'

Eren was too busy processing what he'd seen in the photo. And now things were slotting into place. Things were becoming clear – for the first time in a long time. For the first time in forever.

That feeling he had had on that day, that terrible day when he had found Mr Jefferies – that feeling that he had missed something, an important detail. He thought it had been the caretaker. He really thought it had been the caretaker. But it hadn't been, not at all. He had spent the last few months chasing the wrong man.

Morgan picked up the letter with the photo on it and shone his light at it. His face dropped, his trademark smugness falling away. 'Oh,' was all he could say. 'What the hell does this mean?'

He turned the photo to Eren and Eren saw it again. A photo taken in a park, by a pond. His mother smiling, looking happier than she ever had when she was at home. And with his arm around her, smiling too, was Mr Jefferies.

It was so simple. What he had been missing. But sometimes the simplest things were the things that got lost. He'd been walking home when he realised he'd forgotten his jotter, so he went back to school, back to the Maths room where he found Mr Jefferies hanging from the ceiling. Miss Rain took him to the staff room where he cried and cried. And then his father came in. His father, who said he had been waiting for him outside. But his father wasn't meant to be picking him up. Eren was walking home.

391. His mother's chest where she hid her love for Mr Jefferies. The number on the board was Mr Jefferies' last clue. The number was his final declaration – to get justice.

Silent tears fell down Eren's face.

Morgan looked at him. 'Eren, what does this mean?' The boy was almost pleading.

Eren opened his mouth and only a raw cry of anguish came out. It was all so simple. So real. 'I don't think Martin killed Mr Jefferies,' he said, amidst sobs, 'because my father did.'

'I still don't understand,' Morgan said. They were still in the attic and both of them had been quiet for a very long time.

'My father,' Eren said, his voice devoid of any emotion, as though he were answering a question in class, 'my father killed Mr Jefferies.'

'But how do you know that?'

'He was there, that day. But he shouldn't have been. That's what I'd been missing. It was nothing to do with the caretaker, but someone else who was there that shouldn't have been. My father.'

'But surely there's some other explanation for all this,' Morgan said, staring at the photo as though trying to find another secret that wasn't there.

'My mother was in love with Mr Jefferies, this is his

chest. The code, Morgan, the code on the board.'

'What does this mean, look?' Morgan said, holding up the letter with the photo. '*See you on the 24th*?'

But Eren didn't even need to hear it. He had worked it out. He was clever. He was cleverer than anyone knew. Mr Jefferies, his father, his mother, even Morgan. They didn't know. Because it was all laid out in front of him. And he knew with a burning certainty that his father killed his teacher.

'My father told me what happened. She said she was going to a conference at Bank in the City. I kinda remember it − I remember my father was annoyed and they fought about it. It was Sunday 24th October.'

Eren looked at him. The world was warped and wrangled through his tears. He thought it might never look right again.

'She wasn't going to a conference. She was going to see him. And that was how she died. Got run over by a car, whilst going to him.'

Eren wiped his eyes and sniffed.

Morgan looked down at the picture again. 'But . . .'

Eren gathered together all the papers on the attic floor, suddenly spurting into life. He threw them back into the chest and snatched the piece of paper out of Morgan's hand. He took one last look at the smiling faces of Jefferies and his mother and threw that in the chest as well.

Morgan got up. 'Eren, I . . .'

'Shut up.'

'Did he really do this?'

'The window was open wide. The Maths room window. He could have easily got out, snuck around to the car and waited there.'

'How did the police not find out?'

'I don't know,' Eren said, hating how his voice sounded as it came out. He sounded . . .broken.

'But the police are supposed to know everything?'

'I don't know. It all lined up. He was a sad man. He had problems. It looked like he killed himself.' Eren shut the lid of the chest. It felt more final than it should have. It felt like the whole world had been contained in that chest, and he was trapping it. His father's guilt, all locked up.

Eren replaced the padlock, spinning the numbers around to some random combination. After that, he made his way downstairs like a zombie, not really understanding what he was doing.

Before he knew it, he was back in his room. He threw the torch down and sat, leaning against the bed. Burying his head in his knees, he cried. He cried and cried for his mother, for Mr Jefferies, for his father and for himself.

When he finally looked up, the light in the room had dimmed. It was dark out and Morgan was sat in his desk chair staring at him.

'He killed Mr Jefferies,' Eren said, somewhere between a statement and a question.

Eren sat with his head in his hands. The revelation hung in the air — he could feel it. His own father — a murderer. He knew it was true, but willed it not to be. His father wrapping that belt around Mr Jefferies' neck, stringing him up on the pipe in the middle of the room, disappearing out the window. His own father.

'Imagine how famous we're going to be,' Morgan said, softly.

Eren looked at him. 'What?'

'I mean, your own dad. We're going to be famous, Eren, the talk of the city. The Kid Detectives.'

'What the hell are you saying?' Eren said.

'We solved the murder. That's what it was all about, right, finding out who killed Mr Jefferies and getting famous?'

Eren found another emotion nestled amongst the despair, a white-hot rage. 'What the hell are you saying?' he hissed.

'When we tell people, we'll be famous.'

'What is wrong with you? I was doing this because it was the right thing to do.'

'Oh.' Morgan seemed genuinely surprised – like it had all been fun and games.

'I guess I knew that at the start, but after Christmas? I thought you were just doing it for the same reasons.' And Eren saw the real Morgan for the first time. A horrible, vapid creature, so immature and careless. The kind of creature who would see the tearing apart of his friend's world as an opportunity. Morgan was not his friend.

'No one can know about this,' Eren said, through clenched teeth.

'What?'

'No one can ever know what my father did.'

'But, Eren . . .'

'No one. You understand? No one. My mother's gone. I can't lose my father too.'

'But, Eren . . .'

And there it was – a moment. A moment Eren would remember for the rest of his life. He remembered how lonely he felt, how small he was in relation to everything else in the world, how far anger governed everything. He remembered his hot tears splash against the navy of his jeans creating dark blue spots, he remembered Morgan's childish face. But most of all he would come to remember the next five words out of the idiot's mouth.

'. . . I want to be famous.'

Eren's vision crackled blood red, as he launched himself at his former friend. Morgan jumped out of the desk chair sending it careening backwards into the wall. Eren connected with the desk, banging his head and shrieking in pain.

Morgan looked down at him, dumbfounded, as he propped himself up with his arms.

'Get out,' Eren said, in a voice that was not his own.

Morgan looked down at him.

'Get out,' he shouted, launching himself once again. Morgan ran out of the room and Eren slammed the door. He heard the boy rushing down the stairs and the front door bang.

Eren fell to his knees and wailed, a strange and painful sound. He crawled into his bed and put the covers over himself – protecting him. He lay there, as still as he could, the tears pooling on his cream-coloured sheets.

Mr Jefferies was dead and his father had killed him.

The evidence was all there, in the attic. Why had he done it? Because he blamed Jefferies for Eren's mother's death? How could his father do it? How could anyone do it? Kill someone? These past few months felt like an endless stream of questions.

'I'm sorry, Eren. I'm so sorry,' his father had said that day. Now he knew what it really meant.

Over and over and over he had said it. At the time, he didn't know why – not really. But now he did. And he wished he didn't. He wished he had dropped the whole investigation thing. What was it all to achieve anyway? But he knew why. It was to prove that his teacher wouldn't have killed himself, to prove that the world wasn't a certain shade of dark. But now it was darker than ever.

As he lay there, he wondered how he was going to carry on. He wondered that if he tried really hard, if he willed it, he could just die, lying there in the warmth of his bed. If he wanted so much to die, could he will it so? Probably not, and anyway he knew that it was not to be.

He had to carry on. He had to find some kind of strength, even if it felt like he couldn't. No one could know what he had found, least of all his father. He would put the information away, in his brain – lock it up and throw away the key. He would force himself to forget. His father was still his father because he had to be. For Eren to survive, he had to be.

He lay there for longer than seemed possible, his breathing becoming more regular, his tears drying. He was staring at his hands, thinking of them wrapping a belt around Mr Jefferies' neck, tying it to the pipe in the ceiling. And after a while, he thought of his mother. He thought of how happy she looked with Jefferies, how kind she was. And with his mother's face in his mind, he found enough peace to lapse into a gentle sleep.

And at about 1 am, he heard the front door open and shut as his father returned.

He had bad dreams, so bad that he thought the sirens were in his head. But when he opened his eyes, they were still there. He sat up, the covers falling away from him. It was light in the room, the sun shining in through the window and stinging his eyes. He jumped up and looked out the window, and his stomach immediately turned.

The scene was abhorrent. Two police cars parked on the kerb — two officers standing by the cars, talking to each other. Over the road, Eren's neighbours peered from their windows, watching. The old couple directly opposite had even come to the front door, not even disguising the fact they were being nosy.

Maybe it was something unrelated. Maybe this was just a coincidence. But as the police officers reached into their respective cars to turn their sirens and lights off, he knew it couldn't be for anything else. They knew. And the police officers started walking down the drive to his house.

He panicked but couldn't move. He didn't know what was happening. The fog of sleep was still wrapped around him but he knew that his father was in trouble.

He watched out the window as the two police officers went to their door. Eren heard it open. His father's voice.

And then shouting. And then they had him. They cuffed him. What were they doing? They cuffed him and he tried to struggle, but one of the officers pinned him down on the grass.

More neighbours were coming out of their houses to see what was going on. He wanted to scream at them to go away. He didn't want them to see. But he was still frozen there. At the window.

The other police officer disappeared, and Eren heard him inside the house. What was happening? How – how was this happening? How did they know? How did they find out?

And as Eren heard the other police officer come up the stairs, taking each step one by one, the answer came to him, fully formed and crystal clear. Two words. One name.

Morgan Sheppard.

44

Sheppard took a breath – in and out. Curious – he shouldn't be doing that. Because he was dead. Breathing stopped when you were dead – that was how it worked. And there was no way he was still alive. He'd been blown up.

Although, he had to admit, it hadn't hurt a bit. Dying. But it was meant to, right? It had to. But it hadn't.

And now he thought about it, something about that explosion sound had been strange too. It had been almost tinny, like it wasn't actually happening. Like it was being played through a speaker.

He opened his eyes. The room was still there. The same as it had always been. Mandy, Headphones, Ryan and Constance all still there – looking as confused as he felt.

Could they really be still alive? Was that possible? Or was death very similar to life? He held up a shaky hand and looked at his palm, just to check it was still there. It was – he was. He felt fine – better than fine. Alive.

He looked towards the bed. Towards the timer. It was flashing 00:00:00.

'What happened?' Ryan said, pale and small.

'It didn't work,' Mandy said.

Nothing had happened. The explosion sound, the lights, they had both gone off at the exact moment the timer had hit zero. An illusion? The illusion of death?

Sheppard got to his feet, on legs that thought they were never going to stand again. Even the fact that he was still breathing air was joyous – a cause for celebration. But there would be time for that later. The explosion had failed – the horse mask man had finally shown his hand. They were alive. They were blissfully alive. And now, it was time to make a break for it.

They had been played – all of them.

'There was never going to be any explosion,' Sheppard said, fighting back his sheer glee. 'Mandy was right all along.'

The others seemed to be two steps behind. Headphones' eyes were still shut. Constance was abnormally still. Ryan was staring at him with wide eyes. Mandy cleared her throat of sadness. 'That this was all for television?'

'Yes,' Sheppard said, 'or no. Maybe not TV, maybe the internet or something like that. I'm betting this was all staged. I'm betting the horse man has been filming this entire thing. And now he's got what he wanted, we can leave.'

'But what did he want?'

Sheppard looked into the corners of the room, seeing if he could see anything that looked like a camera. He knew the horse man was watching. It didn't take a leap in logic to think he was recording it. 'He wanted to watch me squirm. He wanted to show the world I couldn't solve a murder. Well . . .' He threw his arms up, 'you got me.

You've done it. I don't care. I refuse to care. Whoever you are. Because now the bell's rung. And it's home-time.'

Mandy got up and Ryan wasn't far behind. They both stepped around the bed as though wading through treacle.

'Has it stopped?' Mandy said.

'It's over,' Ryan said.

Sheppard turned to them. 'He got what he wanted. The ending he assumed. Reality 101, no one actually likes a happy ending. The horse man's story ended with us dying.'

'But we didn't,' Mandy said.

'It doesn't matter. It never did. In the narrative of the thing, we die and we fail. That's what the cameras got. Just a game.'

'This still doesn't feel right,' Ryan said taking a step back and observing the room.

Mandy looked from Ryan to Sheppard as if wondering who to believe. She seemed to settle on Sheppard and smiled. 'Then what are we waiting for?'

Headphones got out from under the desk and joined them. Even behind them, Ahearn seemed to be happy – she sang some kind of upbeat hymn. Sheppard almost joined her.

Sheppard went to the door, followed by the others. It was all over. Finally. And how stupid of them all to go along with it anyway. A murder in a hotel room – a body in the bathtub. Blowing up the building. A set-up – all an elaborate way of stringing them along. Sheppard fell for it – feared for his life and everyone else's. Exploding in a bout of fire. But what kind of work would that have been to orchestrate? Committing mass murder just to get back at one man? That would have been too much, no matter who the horse man was.

But Winter? Winter was dead. There was no doubt about that. Winter had died for what? A sham. A joke. Some things still didn't add up – but it was hard to think about them when there was an overwhelming feeling of relief. Once Sheppard got out of here, he would not rest until he found Winter's killer, but he had to get out first.

Sheppard reached for the door handle. The light was green now. Just as he knew it would be. Go down the corridor, down to the lobby. Call the police. They had to know what was going on. And then get some fresh air, go outside and live. 'Who's ready to go home?' he said, with more hope than he had ever felt.

There was a positive response behind him. Everyone.

Sheppard depressed the handle.

He took a deep breath in and out. Still alive.

And swung the door open.

To reveal a wall of concrete on the other side.

45

They were silent – not quiet, but completely and utterly silent, as though they had been frozen in place. On the other side of the hotel room was a wall of grey concrete. Nothing else. Directly on the other side. He didn't understand – couldn't wrap his head around it.

No.

'No,' he said, out loud this time – breaking the silence. He reached out to touch the concrete. It was cold and rough against his fingers. It was real – very, very real. He pushed on it, hoping it might give way to something – but it didn't. It stayed strong and steadfast. 'No, no, no, no, no, no, no, no.' He hit the concrete with his fist and sharp pain erupted in his hand. 'Ah . . .'

'What is this?' Mandy said – it seemed to be all she could manage. 'How is this possible?'

'I told you,' Ryan said. 'I told you something wasn't right.'

Mandy shook her head. 'How is this in a hotel? Why would a fake door be in a hotel? Sheppard, please, what does this mean?'

'We're not in a hotel,' Sheppard said, 'everything was made to trick us. To . . . keep us busy.'

'But I saw the corridor. I saw the corridor in the peep-hole,' Mandy said, questioning reality – questioning what was right in front of her.

Sheppard swung the door back and looked through the peephole. Surprisingly, he could see a hotel corridor, distorted and odd in the way a fisheye lens was. He looked away and looked back a few times just to make sure he wasn't seeing things. 'It must be a small screen showing a corridor somewhere. The corridor is there – it just isn't here.'

A small sound emanated from Headphones and she backed up.

'What is this?' Ryan said, angry this time. 'You said the game was over.'

'I thought it was.' Sheppard touched the concrete again, searching for anything – any little bit of hope. But he didn't find any. The wall seemed strong and steadfast – no way there was another side.

'How is this in a hotel?' Mandy said again, as if they were all stuck in a bewildered time loop.

'We're not in a hotel,' he said again, softer this time, and turned to Mandy and the others. 'We never were. It's the phones.' Mandy looked confused. 'That's why he gave us them. He wanted to give us a clue. None of us got any signal even though we're high up in the centre of London. Or at least we're supposed to be.

'And the vents. The vents didn't lead anywhere. Because there's nowhere else to go. Maybe everything we know was wrong. We were led down the garden path. Maybe we're not in London at all.'

Mandy and Ryan looked at him, their faces looking more desperate.

'The timer,' a voice behind them. Headphones. 'The timer's restarting.'

Sheppard's mind racing. 'The thing Headp– The thing Rhona saw in Winter's office. The whole reason she's here. The land deed. We're not in the Great Hotel. We're where . . .'

'Sheppard,' Mandy said, touching his shoulder. He jumped, but gave her a sad smile. 'Where are we?'

'We're where we've always been,' he said. 'Underground.'

46

Underground. Trapped in a box. With a killer. Maybe
with two killers.

'Underground?' Mandy said. 'How is that possible?
How can we be underground? London's out there.' She
pointed to the window. Constance Ahearn followed her
finger and laughed.

Sheppard looked to the window as well. And went
over to it. He gazed out of the glass. Central London at
the peak of day. Nothing out of place. He could almost
feel it – the city all around him. The electricity of being
part of something bigger than you could possibly imagine. But it couldn't be real. And the closer Sheppard
looked, the more he could see it. It was only very slight
– you couldn't see it if you weren't looking for it – but
the image looked grainy. Made up of pixels. The highest
quality he had ever seen, but fake nonetheless. How had
he done it? Sheppard looked down as much as he could. It
really looked like he was looking down from a hotel room
window. The perspective was perfect.

'I should have realised,' Sheppard said, putting a hand
on the window. He reached up to the edge of the window
and ran his finger along the seam where the glass met the

frame. 'There were enough clues. He didn't even hide it sometimes. But I didn't get it. Of course I didn't. We never were in a hotel room.'

'But . . .' Mandy started and Ryan put a hand on her shoulder to stop her.

'He's right. I didn't understand it until now, but . . . the toilet's locally plumbed in. It's not hooked up to a bigger pipe system like it would be in the hotel. I didn't think much of it at the time . . . but it all makes sense.'

'This is insane. You two are insane,' Mandy said.

'Insane, yes, but that doesn't mean wrong,' Sheppard said, slapping the window when he couldn't find a way through. It gave a soft clink. 'If this isn't a hotel window, I wonder if we can break it.'

'Can someone please explain what is going on?' Mandy shouted.

And the familiar sound of feedback. A sound that he had heard once before in the room, but couldn't place it. He didn't remember until he heard the voice.

'Hello everyone,' the horse man said.

Sheppard wheeled around. Headphones jumped out of the way in surprise. They were all looking at the television, showing the same shot of the man wearing his horse mask.

Who is he? The horse mask, the horse man, C, the evil man. So many names – but none that count.

It looked like he hadn't moved for three hours, had probably been watching everything. No doubt enjoying the show. Making them think they were getting out, then flipping the script.

We're all in danger. More danger than we ever were before.

Now the killer knew there was no way out, what was to stop them killing again? Killing them all? Maybe the masked man wasn't the main enemy any more.

'Where are we?' Sheppard said, stepping forward.

'You're underground, as you said. Exactly where really doesn't matter for your current predicament, does it?' the horse man said, in that familiar muffled voice.

'Why are you keeping us here? You've got what you wanted,' Sheppard said, pointing to the corners of the room where he presumed the cameras were. 'Your little game went exactly as you planned. I failed.'

Mandy stepped forward, slightly unsure of herself. 'We named everyone in the room. How did we fail exactly?'

The horse man shifted his never-ending gaze from left to right, plastic eyes glinting in the light – Sheppard to Mandy and back. 'It's not enough just to name everyone. You could have done that at the start, for God's sake. You had to *know* who killed Simon Winter and why. Captivity seems to have made you all brain-dead. Maybe I should have done this experiment somewhere more airy, more public.'

'Who killed Simon Winter?' Sheppard said.

The horse man laughed. 'Well, I'm not going to tell you, am I? That's the whole point.'

'The game is over. And I'm done with you. So just tell me.'

The horse man seemed to actually consider it. 'Hmmm. No. You see your problem at the moment, Morgan, is that you're not looking on the bright side. You're still alive, ergo you still have time to find out.'

'What do you mean? You're not going to blow up some-where underground. I doubt that you even ever planned to. What's the point in us co-operating now?'

'Because you haven't exactly found an exit, have you? And because for about six hours now, I've been pumping air into your little room (at great expense I might add). So about two minutes ago, I stopped.'

Quiet – processing the information.

'Wait . . . what?' Ryan said.

Unease settled over Sheppard again – control slipping away. 'What do you mean?'

'I mean just that. I stopped. I cut off the air supply. If you look at the timer, it should be showing you your new countdown. Courtesy of the Great Fake Hotel.'

Just as Headphones had said. Sheppard looked to the bedside table. The timer displaying a new number – counting down again. Twenty-four minutes.

'It should be somewhere around twenty-five minutes until there's no air left in the room. That's an extra twenty-five minutes. You should all be thanking me. Al-though after about fifteen minutes, areas of brain function will probably start to shut down, so . . .'

'Liar,' Sheppard shouted at the television.

The horse man stopped. 'You don't have to take my word for it. Just listen. I've been circulating air in the room for the past three hours – that makes a sound. That sound you thought was the air-conditioning? Is it there anymore?'

Everyone was silent. Sheppard strained to hear – anything. But he couldn't.

'You're sealed up all tight now.'

Mandy gave out a squeaking sound – suppressing a scream. Ryan looked like he was about to vomit, and Rhona clutched her headphones around her neck, as though for comfort. Only Constance seemed unperturbed.

Suffocating. Worse than being incinerated.

This had been part of the plan all along. Another step in breaking him down.

'You know, I think I'm done here,' Sheppard said, saying the exact opposite of what he was thinking. Inside, he was wondering how to get out of this. He was still wondering who killed Winter. But even if he worked it out, who was to say the horse mask would let him go? Maybe this was all for naught. 'Who are you?'

'You still haven't worked it out? Even after all this time, you still don't know. That's one of the reasons you're here in the first place. You've bewitched everyone – most of all yourself. That's exactly why I did this.'

'What?' Sheppard said.

'You don't even know. I bet now you're thinking and thinking about who I could be, but you'll never work it out. Because you don't function like a normal person. You don't think, or feel, how normal people do. You're a disgrace.'

His mind flitted from person to person – the protective shell around which he'd put his deepest, darkest memories finally chipping away. But it still wasn't enough. His memory had fused a long time ago. All the drugs and drink had made him forget things. Especially things he repressed. Or, no, it couldn't be called repressed when you forced it down to the back of your memory and left it there to rot.

'I told you right at the start, Morgan. I'm your best friend,' the horse man said, reaching up to grasp the mask. And Sheppard didn't even get it then. That was who he was – he didn't live in the past, couldn't bring himself to. People came and went within him. It wasn't strange to think he'd lose track of them all.

The horse man reached back behind his head. And pulled the mask away.

A man he didn't even know he remembered. But he did. It was unmistakeable. He was twenty-five years older than when Sheppard had last seen him. Now he was a man, his piercing eyes, wrinkles, his big smile. It was the smile that made him so familiar. That smile hadn't changed. In a quarter of a century, that smile had not changed a bit. Sheppard found himself speechless, rasping for words to come out. The man on the television just smiled that smile.

The smile of Eren Carver.

47

'Hello again, Morgan,' Eren said.

What? How . . .?

Sheppard's knees buckled. He fell to the ground – mouth wide.

How is this possible? And the more pertinent question – *how did I not know?*

Twenty-five years – it had been twenty-five years. And now he was here. How could he have forgotten him – how had he not known straight away who it was? Could he really be so naïve? All the memories he had buried deep with booze and pills suddenly surfaced. Mr Jefferies. Eren's dad being taken away by the police. It had made little Morgan Sheppard famous (what he had always wanted) but it had left Eren without a father. Eren was the only person the masked man could have ever been – and he hadn't thought once about him.

Calling him Morgan. That was the first clue. No one ever called him by his first name anymore. His publicist, his agent, even his array of girlfriends – everyone just called him Sheppard. He had talked to his agent about it – it wasn't like he hated his first name, but rather fell back on his last one. *Sheppard is a good strong name, it's a name you can hang your hat on. Biblical – if with a few typos.*

The glasses. That had been the next thing. Sheppard hadn't worn glasses in public, probably since his school days. He hated having them, so didn't wear them much, preferring to strain his eyes. He was badly short-sighted, but he had learned to live with it. When he got older, he got contact lenses, but always had his glasses for around his flat where no one else would see. He remembered the first time he'd got glasses. His mother forced him to wear them every day, which he did. But he always took them off by first period – sick of them. He'd put them in his back pocket – joking (but not joking) that he hoped he would sit on them and break them.

It all made sense, but even now, as he looked at Eren's face on the television screen, he couldn't bring himself to believe it. Even with all the clues there in front of him and the truth staring him in the face.

'Eren?' he said, his face incredibly close to the television screen.

'Hello, old friend,' Eren said, smiling, 'but it's not Eren anymore. I found Eren a bit too homely, and a bit too ingrained in bad memories. It's Kace now. Kace Carver. You like it?'

'Kace? What is that?'

'That's my name.'

'No, it's not. Your name's Eren.'

Eren frowned. 'We may have a history, you and me. But, I'll warn you now, Morgan, do not attempt to pretend you know me. You left me all that time ago, and I have changed since then. So have you, although in your case it's rather for the worse, I'm afraid (if that was even possible). Who would think that this is the way it would work out?'

'Wait . . .' Ryan. At least he thought it was. All he heard were the words. Couldn't discern who it was anymore. 'What is he talking about? Who is that?'

How to explain . . .

'Sheppard.'

'It's come to the point in proceedings that I've been looking forward to the most,' Carver said. 'It's time for our hero, our protagonist, to explain himself.'

'Eren,' Sheppard said, holding his hand out to the screen, 'stop this, let us out. Please.'

'No. I won't. Because it seems throughout this whole charade, you haven't learned a thing. You didn't even know who I was.'

'But I know you now, Eren. I know you. I remember you. I remember everything we did together. And I'm sorry. I'm so sorry. We were best friends. I remember everything. Just please – let us go.' A tear rolled down Sheppard's cheek. Crying – he hadn't cried, he could never remember crying. Crying wasn't something he did – that was for other people. 'Please, Eren.'

'Don't call me Eren,' Eren said. 'I am not Eren.'

'Please let everyone else go. Please, this is between you and me. These people have nothing to do with it,' Sheppard said, sweeping his arm across the rest of the room.

Eren faltered slightly, peered closer at the screen. 'That is uncharacteristically selfless of you. Are you okay? Do you have indigestion? I can only assume it's to save some kind of face. You still think you're getting out of this, don't you?'

He didn't anymore. He didn't know anything.

'But no, I will not be letting any of you go. At first, I just thought I'd put you in there. Plop you all in there like flies in a jar and watch you buzzing around, not knowing what to do. But now I have the bite, the bite of curiosity. I want to see if you can do it. And more than that, I want to see you die. So keeping you in there to rot sounds good to me. But if you do it, if you manage it, I'll let the others go free.'

The others . . .

'So I solve this and you let everyone else go?'

Eren looked frustrated. 'Is your brain already that starved? I just said that, didn't I?'

'Can someone tell me what is going on?' Mandy this time. But he couldn't think about anyone else. Not right now.

'And what happens to me?' Sheppard said.

'I think we need a nice little chat,' Eren said, smiling again.

Sheppard didn't move except to nod. 'Okay.'

'Solve it, Morgan, or die with your roommates. It's your decision. But can you please do something for me?' Carver said.

'Yes – of course.' What a snivelling little hermit he'd become. He knew that Eren was his only way out. Didn't Eren see that? Didn't Eren see that he would do anything?

'Tell the truth, Morgan,' Eren said. 'Just for once in your life, tell the truth.'

Sheppard collapsed on the floor, finally admitting to himself he was crying. Eren Carver. The boy who had been his best – his only – friend.

But something was different. Something had happened to him.

And as his eyes stung with tears, he realised that what had happened to Eren was Morgan Sheppard.

48

'Sheppard. Sheppard.'

Who was it?

The air felt thicker. Was that a real thing or was it just because he knew the air was in short supply – the oxygen decreasing by the second? He and his roommates were dying one breath at a time. He didn't need a timer – he didn't need a countdown – to know that they were in trouble – more trouble than they had ever been in. Death by suffocation – death worming its way around your body, gripping the heart and squeezing the life out of it.

'Sheppard. Damn it.'

It was the image of himself choking in a corner, his eyes becoming redder, which made him get up. He pushed himself up by his hands and then tested his legs. They seemed okay and he got up on them.

Eren Carver. He had been right.

Sheppard had forgotten all about him. He had turned the memory of Mr Jefferies' death into a little ball and stuffed it at the back of his mind. He had written his own narrative of how those few months in 1992 played out – and started to believe them. And that made it all the worse.

Sheppard held out a hand to skirt the bed as he got

his balance back. Ryan and Mandy were still standing around, Headphones had somehow got back to her place under the desk and Constance had resumed rocking on the chair. It wasn't enough to fail them once, or even twice. Eren was going to humiliate him as many times as he could.

'Sheppard?' Ryan said. The young man was halfway between anger and panic. Didn't seem to appreciate being kept out of the loop. 'What the hell is going on? Who was that? And what did he mean by telling the truth?'

'Please, Sheppard,' Mandy said. Looking at her, he realised there was no more hope in her eyes.

Headphones stared across the room, watching the timer. She appeared to be breathing through the sleeve of her hoodie, as though that might use less air.

Constance had shut her eyes and even looked asleep. She obviously didn't care anymore.

Sheppard looked at them all. All he had been running from, his entire life, etched across their faces. He remembered how he had been back then. He had just wanted to be famous. He smiled when he thought that that was no different to how he was now. All he wanted was to be known.

Sometimes, all we want is to be seen. An old thing Winter said once. He remembered it because when it got stripped down, that was all he ever wanted. To be seen.

Was this it? And as he thought about it, he was relieved. It was more than time. 'I'm a liar. A fraud. That's the simplest way of putting it.'

'What?' Ryan said.

'I am known as the Child Detective. But that's not true.

I did not solve the murder of George Jefferies in 1992, didn't even have much of a part in it. The person who solved the murder was Eren Carver, the son of the man who did it. He was brilliant and fantastic in all the ways I could never be. He was my friend. And I betrayed him. And, for all intents and purposes, I assumed his identity. For twenty-five years. I told everyone I solved it. And Eren didn't come forward because it had gone too far. Everyone truly believed it was me. Morgan Sheppard means nothing.

'That's the reason we're all here. That man on the TV is Eren, or whatever he calls himself now. He's torturing me, proving to everyone else that I'm not who I say I am. And he's right.'

His eyes fell, not able to hold anyone else's gaze any more. Eren was watching, and for all he knew, so were others. He hoped they were. It was time for Morgan Sheppard to die, or at least what Morgan Sheppard had become. The man was gone, cast away like a snake's shed skin. It wasn't by choice, but by need. And Sheppard didn't know if that kind of made it forego the point.

No one moved around him, but he had one last job to do. If he'd never done anything selfless in his entire life, let him do this. He had to rescue three of the four people in the room— one of them killed a friend of his, and the other three deserved to live. Hell, they all deserved to live.

The killer. We're in here with a killer.

Sheppard had gone too far — he knew that too. He had gone beyond the bounds of his particular abyss to something bigger than killing and something bigger than mere deceiving. He was the man who fooled the world. And he guessed that he'd at least have that accolade right up until the very end.

Atonement was on a timer and dependent on shallow breaths.

'What the hell are you talking about?' Ryan said.

'It's all true.' He breathed in and out – savouring it. And promised it was the last time he would do it. From now on, he would only breathe slightly. To give them enough time to maybe get out of this.

Mandy still looked like she was trying to process everything. But it seemed to have finally clicked for everyone else. Headphones was watching him with shifty eyes. Constance had regained a little bit of interest too, staring around. Ryan seemed like he was about to explode, going a reddish colour.

'Are you serious?' he said, striding forward, like a peacock showing his feathers. 'That's what all this is about? I'm going to die because of you? Ever since the beginning, this has all been about you. Me, Mandy, Rhona, even Constance and Alan. We've all been nothing. Just things to get in your way.'

'I'm sorry,' Sheppard said. It was all he could say.

'You're a joke,' Ryan said. 'A sick, sick joke. How did you live with yourself?'

Very easily. 'Ryan, I'm sorry. I didn't want any of this to happen.'

'Well, yeah, of course you didn't. But still . . .'

'Ryan, I need all of you. I need you to help me. I'm going to save you. I'm going to save you and Mandy and

Headphones and Ahearn. Hell, I'm even going to save Alan's body so he can have a proper burial. I know it's the end for me. I know I'm a dead man walking. Eren isn't going to let me walk out of here.'

'How do you know that?'

'Because I know Eren and he is resolute – but he's something more than that. He's just. You see that?'

'Why would any of us listen to you anymore? Why would we trust you?'

'Because this is not over. You can hate me all you want – later.'

'He's right,' Mandy said, dully.

'Thank you,' Sheppard said to her. He tried a smile. It felt like lifting weights piled on the ends of his mouth. He didn't get very far. Not when he was interrupted.

Mandy slapped him straight in the face. It was stronger than he ever thought would be possible from such a small girl. His face flew to the side and he felt a hand-mark developing on his cheek.

Mandy, the sweet girl who had always been by his side, now looking so angry. 'Why would you do that? Why would you do that?' and again, just because it seemed she couldn't think of anything else, 'Why would you do that?'

Sheppard looked at her, his tears drying on his right cheek and his left cheek stinging.

The air definitely felt thicker now – it drooped around them almost visibly. Sheppard could see it in the corner of his eye. Like reflections of a time never lived. His cravings kept on a shelf in the back of his mind with the other lives.

And some kind of new feeling manifested itself. He mistook it for the need to vomit again.

'I just need some water,' Sheppard said, still watching Mandy intently. She was watching him, as though he was the devil, but he thought he detected an element of softness coming through. 'I need some water. And then I'll get you all to safety.'

He started towards the bathroom, but a hand shot out from under the desk to grab his leg. He looked down. Headphones looked at him and pointed. To the timer. It seemed to be going faster than before. Accelerating.

Fifteen minutes.

Sheppard looked back to Headphones and nodded. Smiled.

Headphones frowned at him. 'Also, my name's Rhona . . . dick. Who the hell calls someone Headphones?'

Sheppard dropped the smile and nodded dutifully. He passed Ryan without looking.

'You better know what you're doing,' Ryan called after him as he walked towards the bathroom. He pushed the door open, and chanced a look back at them. They were all watching him – of course they were.

Behind the others, Constance was still shackled to her chair – she wasn't smiling, or rocking back and forth. She was actually looking scared – the first time Sheppard had ever seen her look scared in all her time in the room.

Sheppard stumbled through the bathroom door – no closer to knowing how to rescue them all.

49

Sheppard almost forgot where Alan had been placed. He walked into the bathroom and felt something squish under his feet. He looked down to see one of Alan's hands. He jumped back against the door.

When he had regained some kind of composure, he manoeuvred around the lawyer, trying not to step in any of the blood, and went to the sink. He turned the hot tap on. Winter's body was still there in the tub – he saw it in the mirror. Winter, a pawn in Eren's plan. He felt even sorrier for the old man now, being manipulated so easily.

Sheppard cupped water into his hands and splashed it on his face. It felt good. He had to stay awake, and stay alert. All his sordid addictions would have to be kept at bay. He had to save everyone else – that was all that mattered now.

He leant over the sink and shut his eyes as the steam rose – overriding the cold, slick sweat on his clammy skin.

He opened his eyes.

The mirror had steamed over. As if nothing behind him existed any more. But he could feel Winter.

Winter had always been such a strong figure in his life. He remembered going to his house on Saturday afternoons for his therapy sessions. He had protested to start with, but after a while, he relied on them. Winter always had a way of explaining things to him, making them seem more entertaining than they actually were. He taught Sheppard how to deal with his increasing fame, told him which thoughts were harmful and which were beneficial. He taught Sheppard how to be a better man.

If only I had listened.

Sheppard reached into his pocket and took out Winter's notebook. He still had no idea why the old man was carrying it – an old notebook with old session notes in. He flipped to his own notes – looking at the underlined words. Was this what Winter really thought of him? Aggressive? Muddled? Important words, he guessed – but then why had Winter also underlined 'A new dream about . . .'? Not even a full sentence. He read on: 'A new dream about a field of corn. Out in the distance there is a barn – a farmyard. It's on fire and it's burning down. Morgan is out in the field looking at it. As he watches, a scarecrow rises up out of the field of corn. Morgan just knows that it was the scarecrow who set the fire. The scarecrow smiles at him. And that's when he wakes up.' Sheppard read this, enraptured. He'd forgotten all about the nightmare. He used to have it every night – waking up in cold sweats, sometimes even having wet himself. It began just after – just after he did what he did.

But the painting on the wall? The painting on the wall was depicting the dream almost to the letter. Such a strange painting to have in a hotel room – he had thought that when he saw it. Now even just thinking about it made his skin crawl. And Mandy had said it looked creepy too.

He read on: 'I need more information to really understand this nightmare. It sounds like a classic "created destroys creator" thought stream, but I don't know how that pertains to Morgan exactly. Also – NB – IMPORTANT POINT Morgan says that the worst part of the nightmare is he knows the children upstairs are burning alive.'

Sheppard almost dropped the notebook. Children upstairs? Why was that so shocking? Had someone . . . He looked at the page – at the underlined words, at the wording of the dream. And suddenly, it all clicked.

Sheppard looked at the words. What did they mean? How could they mean anything? He traced his finger over them. Too broad. Too—

He stared at the words. And he thought.

No.

It all came back. The air was solid now. He couldn't breathe.

No. Not—

But it all made sense.

50

Before . . .

She clutched the invite tightly, making the card crease down the middle. She had arrived far too early – couldn't just sit around at home. Besides, she knew she would have to scan the entrance and pick the opportune time to make a move.

Her brain was already trying to convince her this was a bad idea. *Suppose the bouncers know this woman? Suppose they know what she looks like? What then? Will they call the police?* What would she do then? Hold up her hands, call 'fair cop' and walk away? There was too much riding on this for that.

They wouldn't know her. She had to get in.

It was simple. She was going to wait for the time when it was busiest. Then even if people did know the woman, no one would notice. The bouncers would be flustered – more capable of making mistakes. She would slip through the cracks. And through the door.

She checked her watch. Far too early indeed. So she propped herself up in a café across the street. It was just gone five – the party didn't start till eight. Party rules dictated that people wouldn't be arriving until about ten.

She ordered a coffee and waited.

She checked her Dictaphone was working – switching it on and off. Full battery. When that was done, she spent most of her time thinking, or gazing unenthusiastically at YouTube videos on her laptop. For a while, they were on-topic – watching his smug face on that damn show, watching him lord himself over everyone else, watching an audience lap it up, but soon they just became whatever came up on the sidebar – top 10 English Haunted Hotels, Nyan Cat Remixes, the funniest things babies have ever done, the stuff that kept the internet rolling on its endless journey to ruin the world. Still, she was part of the problem – she was hypnotised by this crap just as much as everyone else. She looked through the window to see no one had arrived at the club yet.

At seven, the café closed. She asked to stay a little longer, but seeing as she had only ordered one small coffee in two hours, she knew she wasn't going to win. She moved to a pub down the road, opting for a window seat. She could still see the club, although not as well.

She ordered a diet coke at the bar and got the Dictaphone out of her pocket again. Off and on. Light flashing. It was still fine.

The internet was to blame for him. He could've been a daytime television anomaly – a person that most of the population weren't even aware of because they all turned their televisions off at nine when they went to work. But it was the age of the internet, where every show could be chopped up and put online and farmed out for millions and millions of views. This was his home and he wasn't

317

even the one who made it. The television channel made him his own website, where clips of his show were put up. His YouTube channel quickly flooded with ten-minute segments – Celebrity Cuckold, The Truth About You, Sleepin' Around and Around. Eight million subscribers were the audience, a pack that grew incredibly quickly as they enjoyed his brand of Sherlockian hilarity. If Sherlock had been an idiot, that is. Most of what he deduced wasn't even true. He was a detective who couldn't really detect anything. But above that he was a personality – a television personality, an internet personality, it didn't really matter. He was right even though he was wrong.

As the light in the sky dimmed, she put her laptop away and made sure the external mic on the Dictaphone was working. She recorded herself reading the fact on a beermat – *A blind chameleon still changes colour to match the environment*. She played it back. It sounded fine. It was going to be far noisier in the club, but she thought it would still pick voices up if she held it close enough. And she would. Because too much was riding on this to make a simple little mistake like that.

It had only been two weeks since . . . since . . . People were calling it the tragedy. The tragedy – so cold and distant. Maybe that's why people called it that, to put space between themselves and what happened. But that wasn't what she wanted. She wanted to understand why. And she was ready. Her anger fuelled her most – it was what got her out of bed in the morning, what saw her through the day. Her brother had always hated when she was angry, could see in her eyes how it wrapped around her and consumed her. Her brother had always said that she could never let her anger control her – put a lid on it while there is still a lid. Because if she didn't, there would be nothing else.

But she was alive and he was dead. And it was all Morgan Sheppard's fault.

And, now, sitting in the pub, she was angry. She was so very angry. But she was also resourceful. Her journalism degree was almost over and she had signed the recorder and mic out at the desk. She was ready.

Because she was alive and she didn't understand why he had to be dead.

She watched out the window and by eight-thirty, a slow trickle of people started entering the club. Brickwork was an underground nightclub just around from Leicester Square tube station. It was notoriously expensive and notoriously exclusive. She had never set foot in there before, and by all account, had no right to set foot in there now. This was a private party for television people and their high-class friends. The invite she had swiped had been from a low-level employee working on his show.

She watched as the gaggle of women who walked up to the door pulled out their invites. They were all stopped at the door by a burly bald man dressed in black. The bouncer had a list. The women were checked off and disappeared inside.

At nine, a limousine pulled up and she saw him get out. He had a tuxedo on and was already swaying. The bouncers didn't ask him his name.

She wondered if she should go in, but there was no

queue and she didn't want to risk it. She waited another thirty minutes, until she couldn't wait any longer. A queue of about thirty people had built up and she swallowed the rest of her diet coke, checked her hair in the bathroom and went out. She joined the queue and noticed the crease on her invite. She tried to straighten it out but only made it worse.

The queue moved slowly and she tried to blend in with the women waiting in line. She noticed that there was only one man in the queue, a straightened-up button-down type who seemed rather stoic and out of place. He didn't say a word as the women around him laughed and joked, sometimes about him. The women were the usual glamorous, 2D type – the kind of women you couldn't see from side-on. They were what her brother would've called 'Extras from *The OC*', a dumb programme they used to watch together when they were younger about pretty people with pretty problems.

When the woman ahead got to the door, the group became very flustered and high-pitched. There were three of them and the one in charge of the invites had not brought them, instead electing to bring more drink. They were stupidly drunk, considering they hadn't yet entered the club. It seemed like their names were on the list though as they were allowed inside – probably nothing at all to do with how slutty they looked. Self-doubt seeped in.

What was she doing? Really? Starring in her own little espionage thriller? This was stupid. She turned and saw a wall of sexy young women coming down the stairs, blocking her exit. She felt the recorder in her hand.

You're a lot more than you think. You're strong, stronger than him. And you've read the papers — he'll be worse for wear, you just wait and see. You're cleverer than he could ever dream of being. It was her brother's voice. Her thoughts often came to her in his voice. He was always more confident than her.

A fresh pang of anger flared in her mind.

You've come this far.

See it through.

Without another thought, she entered the club — the doors spitting her out onto a bustling, dark dancefloor. The place seemed to be far more crowded than she expected, given she had watched everyone enter. People were everywhere, blocking her view of the rest of the club. She made her way over to where she presumed the bar was, dodging all the featureless silhouettes of people, lit up occasionally by a flash of multi-coloured light. The dancefloor was densely packed and progress was slow. Getting through it was like an impossible version of *Frogger*, sometimes having to double back on herself to avoid people swooping by with drinks. Finally, she made her way through and got to the bar.

She ordered a gin and tonic. She often thought nightclubs were intolerable without at least something coating your judgement. A sober her could see the absolute insanity of a penned-in drinking factory. She got her drink and paid an astronomical amount for it. The price of being thirsty in London.

She looked around. The dancefloor was the majority of

the club but there were booths to the left and right sides. She scanned around and found what she was looking for – the booth nearest to her on the left-hand side had a partition around it. It was the VIP area. And behind the theatre-esque ribbon, was him. She watched him smiling and talking, swaying even though he was sat down. He had this look of joyful bewilderment. He was drop-dead drunk. The others in the VIP area she didn't recognise, apart from one person who she thought might be a host of *Morning Coffee*. The rest of the men looked like business types and they were peppered with scantily clad women, who looked as though they had won a prize just by being there. Add smug, subtract self-respect.

Propping herself up against the bar, she watched him. She hated him. It was red, raw, unbridled hate. She had never felt anything like it before. She understood why people equated hate to love. It felt the same. Wherever you were, whatever you were doing – it was there. Love pulled you to someone else, and so did hate. But for the exact opposite reasons. You looked at someone you loved, and saw a whole life spread ahead of you – a life that could be. But in hate, you just looked at someone and saw devastation – a life that once was. But both could drive people to terrible things.

Anger is not you. Her brother had been able to see it within her, before she had herself. And he had seen the dangers of it.

Three gin and tonics later and the world was shifting, as though a wave lapping against an unknown beach. He was still in the VIP area, drinking amounts that seemed illogical. She hadn't stopped watching him but no one seemed to notice. The music was deafening and the lights were low, so the chances of someone even seeing her were slim. She wondered if this was it. If he wouldn't leave the VIP area at all, and she had gone to all this effort just to spend a night staring at him . . . Would it all be for nothing?

The middle of the fourth drink and someone tried to talk to her. A young man who looked too confident for his own good. Bad news.

'Wow, I love your outfit,' he said, with the enthusiasm of a self-help coach. 'You seem quiet. You haven't talked to anyone all night. Are you on your own?'

This made her shiver slightly. The idea that he had been watching her all night was not particularly enticing. 'I'm here with some people,' she said. 'I'm just waiting for them.'

'What's your name?'

'Zoe,' she said, without hesitation.

'I'm Tim,' the man said. Tim was a boring name even if you made it up. 'I work with a Zoe. She's not here though.' He seemed lost as he looked around.

She didn't notice. She was watching as he, him not Tim, stood up on two unsteady feet. He whispered something into one of the women's ears and she laughed for an unreasonable amount of time. He stepped over the cordon, tripping as he brought up his right foot. A fresh bout of laughter came from the VIP area and he turned to them and gave them a thumbs up. He staggered off and got swallowed by the crowd of dancers.

'I wonder if I could buy you a drink?' Tim was saying, as she slid off her stool and left the bar. She didn't really care for Tim's feelings – leave it for the other Zoe to clean up.

She followed the dark mass she thought was him through the dancefloor. It didn't really matter if it wasn't him. She knew where he was going. The only place a man who had spent an hour heavy-drinking in a nightclub would go. The toilets.

She tore her eyes from the mass to look up at the walls. There were two neon signs. One said 'John' and she didn't really understand until she saw the other at the other end of the large area – 'Yoko'. She started towards the 'John' arrow, but a dark figure appeared in front of her. In the next flash of lights, she saw it was the guy from the bar – Tim. The stalking creep – but she had underestimated him at least. 'I would really like to buy you a drink.'

'I'm not interested,' she said, sharply. She tried to step around him, but he stepped too. She didn't have time for this – Sheppard would be in and out quickly, he was a man after all. She was going to miss her chance.

'It's weird, "Zoe". I only know one "Zoe" on the set.' Tim was slurring – he was drunk.

'I'm new,' she hissed, and pushed past him. Tim responded in kind by grabbing her arm. She turned. 'Let. Me. Go.'

'I will, if you have a drink with me,' Tim said happily – probably thinking all of this was flirty sparring.

'Don't take this the wrong way, but I'd rather kill myself.'

324

'Don't be like that.' Tim grabbed her other arm – he had her now. This was bad. And the opportunity she wanted was slowly slipping away. Her anger suddenly flared – she thought in that moment, she could kill this little minnow just to get her chance at the big fish. 'Aren't you here to have fun?'

'You want to know why I'm here?' she said, before she could stop herself. 'I'm here to have a little word with your lord and saviour Morgan Sheppard. You're all pathetic little idiots partying with that monster, latching onto him just because he can get you to the top. You don't care what he's done, do you? In fact, you probably helped him do it.'

Tim was struggling to comprehend what she was saying, and his grip on her arms was loosening. What she wanted to say – what she came here to do – was spilling out, and she couldn't stop it now. The fact that Tim was not her intended target didn't seem to matter anymore.

She started to cry. 'Morgan Sheppard ruins people's lives. And you all stand there, and film it for television. For what? Personal gain. Do you remember him? Do any of you remember my brother? Sean Phillips? He was on Mr Sheppard's, on your, show. Three years ago. He was on with his girlfriend, the mother of his child. Morgan Sheppard proved that Sean was having an affair. When he wasn't. I can prove it – I have solid proof that he was not having an affair. And Morgan Sheppard ruined his life.'

Tim was looking uncomfortable. She was screaming now but the volume of the music meant everyone else around them was oblivious.

'He killed himself,' she shrieked. 'My brother killed himself.'

Tim let go of her.

'He killed himself,' she said, finally. She buried her face in her hands and cried. She hated it. How he got to her. She hated the tears.

Sean was quiet in her mind. Had nothing to say. Was that it? Was she alone?

Tim was still staring at her. 'Okay then,' he said, 'you know what, I prefer my girls a little less – you know – psycho. So I'm going to go have a drink alone and you have a nice night.' And with that, Tim disappeared – becoming another black mass in the room.

She dried her eyes and thought she still may have a chance to catch Sheppard. She turned towards the bathrooms, and her heart stopped.

There he was, in front of her. The smug bastard, looking glazed and happy. He was walking through the crowd towards her. She had missed him at the toilets but now he was coming for her. This was her chance. So why would her voice not work? She had seconds. He got to her – they were centimetres from each other – and then he passed her. She could almost feel the smugness coming off him like steam.

She wheeled around. He was disappearing into the anonymous crowd. This was it. Her last shot.

'Sheppard,' she found herself shouting.

Sheppard stopped – he had heard her – and turned around. He didn't know it was her of course, and his eyes moved around the room as he tried to find out who shouted.

She held her breath as his eyes fell on her. How long was it? It can't have been for more than a second, but for her it felt like an hour. All that time, all she had to do was open her mouth – open her mouth and say what she came here to say. But she couldn't. Whether it was her exhaustion, or Tim, or seeing Sheppard's face, she just found she couldn't do it. It suddenly became real.

And then it was over. He looked for another moment and then turned. He got swallowed up by the dark. And just like that it was all over. She suddenly felt dizzy, and staggered to the wall. She slid down and buried her face in her knees, becoming as small as possible. And the tears began. And they carried on.

Some time later, she looked up to see two men laughing at her. She ignored them and got up, pushing past them with a force that stopped them laughing. She pushed her way across the dancefloor. Not looking to the VIP area, not looking for him. She couldn't.

She got to the bar and ordered another gin and tonic. Just another to add to the collection. Sean used to say that their family was born with iron livers.

She toasted to nothing, and everything. Drank it in two gulps. She stared at the empty glass, thinking about how she had failed. Maybe she would just get drunk – that seemed like a good way to forget. It was working for his holiness Morgan Sheppard.

'Can I buy you another?' said a voice. Had Tim lucked out with every other woman in the club and decided the crazy one was better than nothing? But when she looked up, she saw a different man. The smart man she had seen in the queue to get in.

'Gin and tonic,' she said. Abruptly.

The man didn't seem to mind. He flagged down the barman and ordered. She regarded him a bit more. He was young, but not as young as her. Thirty, maybe thirty-five. He wore rectangular glasses and had on a suit with a red tie. He looked stern, but inviting. To most people, he would be disregarded as normal. But there was something about him. Something that she had noticed before in the queue – a sort of presence.

He slid her her drink – he had ordered a pint.

'You seem distraught,' he said.

'I'm fine,' she said.

'These things are always despicable,' he said, throwing his hands up all around him. 'A monument for the self-involved.'

'Then why are you here?' She sipped at her drink.

'Because it's always good to keep tabs on people. Otherwise you just get left behind,' he said, and she totally understood. And everything he said seemed to make perfect sense. 'Why are you here?'

She smiled sadly. 'I had to get some answers.'

'And did you get them?'

'I had my chance to get them. And I didn't take it.'

And he must have read her sad face, because he said, 'Well, you mustn't take it out on yourself – answers aren't always the end. Sometimes they're just not worth the wait. Bad things happen to good people. That's the way of the world.'

He was right. She touched his glass with hers, not loud enough to make a sound but enough to show the sentiment.

There was a loud commotion over in the VIP area. Sheppard's colleague had passed out and the man himself was creating quite a fuss about it. He gestured to the DJ and the music cut out.

Sheppard got up onto a table, liquid sloshing visibly off as if he'd landed in a puddle, and produced a microphone. 'Three cheers for dopey Rogers!'

She didn't know who that was, but assumed it was the passed out colleague. The entire club erupted into hip hip hurrahs. She did not join in and neither did the man.

When it was all over and the music turned back on, the man said, 'Now, that Morgan Sheppard, that's a man who needs taking down a peg or two.'

She looked at him and he looked back.

'Kace Carver,' he said, putting out his hand.

She started to say 'Zoe' and stopped herself. She cleared her throat and said 'Mandy', shaking his hand.

She smiled for the first time all evening.

51

The red string connections in Sheppard's mind were working overtime. Winter had made it so simple for him – and he still hadn't seen. But now it all made sense. It was all clear. The only possible conclusion. Winter laid a trap – maybe he saw the situation going south and decided to make a breadcrumb trail for Sheppard. If he was a better man, he would've seen it earlier.

He staggered out of the bathroom and looked up at them all. The notebook in his hand. A finger still marking the page, where the underlined words were – and where the description of the nightmare was. 'Aggressive, Muddled, A dream about . . .' The answer he was searching for. And even if Sheppard didn't understand what Winter was getting at, he spelled it out too. A word puzzle – an incredibly easy one.

'It was you,' he said quietly, not wanting it to be true.

Ryan looked around.

The first letters . . . spelling it out . . . spelling out AMANDA. The trap that Winter set for Mandy, telling her about the dream no doubt – hoping that she would let something slip. And she did.

Headphones jumped up. But she jumped up too late.

Mandy had realised and grabbed the teenager, restraining her. To his surprise, Mandy brandished the knife – she must have slipped it from his back pocket – and held it to Headphones' throat. The teenager didn't make a sound – just looked at Sheppard with eyes that didn't fully understand.

'No one move,' Mandy said, looking at them each in turn. 'Move and I'll cut this emo's throat.'

Movement didn't seem to be an option. He was too busy processing it. Mandy, the sweet young girl who'd always had his back.

Ryan seemed to be in a similar state of bewilderment, holding his hands up in surrender.

Mandy started backing to Ahearn, who screamed gleefully. Mandy took no notice of the mad old woman, sidling past her and resting her back against the window so Sheppard or Ryan couldn't get behind her.

'Mandy, what are you doing?' Ryan said.

'Go ahead, Sheppard,' Mandy said. She didn't even sound like the same person anymore. She sounded cold and hard and inhuman. 'Explain it to him.' She waved the knife in front of Headphones' neck as if impatient for blood.

'What? You?' Ryan said, to Mandy.

'I was wrong,' Sheppard said, wondering how to manage to get to Mandy before she did something insane. He tried a short step forward, holding his hands up too. Mandy didn't seem to notice, too focused on his eyes. 'Ever since the start, this has been designed to fool me.

'It was the wounds – the wounds in Winter's gut that

were so deep. I didn't think it could have been Mandy because of that. But there were some things that I missed, at least not enough for me to notice at the time, but she was more than capable of plunging a knife deep into the body of Simon Winter.'

She pulled me up, one of the first things she did. I remember thinking she was strong.

'Right at the start – you pulled me up off the floor. If I had been a proper detective, I would have seen it, I would have noticed straight away.' Another step forward.

She slapped me. My face flew to the side, because it was so strong. Anger. The anger in her eyes when she had done that. Like anger she had had to keep pent up for days, months, years even. Setting her eyes on fire.

'*The worst thing is the family in the barn, the children upstairs burning.*' The ultimate slip-up that she wouldn't even know she was making. Winter was clever – he was very clever – and Sheppard had almost missed it entirely.

Ryan was incapable of helping – he still didn't understand. It would make him slow and unsure – not useful. Headphones was squirming in Mandy's grip, her eyes following the edge of the knife hovering at her throat. He couldn't be sure Mandy wouldn't do it. He didn't know her – not anymore. Another small step.

'You're strong, but that doesn't mean you're a murderer. But then there were more clues, weren't there? More reasons to suspect you,' he said, edging closer. 'Like how you woke up first and seemed to know information about everyone. You probably would have told me more if I'd asked, but you told me just few enough details to get away with it.'

She knew plenty about Constance. Her name, where she worked. She got away with it because Constance was famous. But he was betting she had known about everyone in the room.

Step, a small breath, Mandy looked from him to Ryan, smiling to herself, as if she was pleased at what she had accomplished. Sheppard had never expected to see her face look that way.

He was level with the television now. Headphones watched him — she saw everything, she always did. She was the silent observer. She had said about ten sentences in the past three something hours. She'd be able to see things others didn't, just by virtue of being silent. Sheppard gave her the quickest and smallest nod he was able to manage. His head hardly moved, tilting forward maybe a few centimetres. She watched him for a few moments after and then mimicked the motion.

Mandy was too busy, probably feeling proud of herself, to notice.

'I don't understand,' Ryan said, 'that doesn't explain what she did?'

'She's been playing us off against each other, Ryan. When Alan was stabbed, Constance was behind him, right? And who was next to her?'

Ryan didn't answer. He didn't have to.

'Constance here killed Alan, seemingly unprovoked. At least at first.'

He chanced a look at Ryan. Finally, something in his eyes.

'All that rubbish Constance spouted wasn't rubbish at all. She *was* told. I looked her in the eyes and I knew she believed it herself, but I just thought she was mad. Sorry, Ms Ahearn, but you have been lied to. We all have.'

'How could Mandy get someone to kill someone? I saw – Ahearn did it.'

'Do you want to field that one?' Sheppard said to Mandy, and when she shook her head, he continued, 'Have you said two words to Constance, Ryan? No, there was only one person who spoke to Constance in the entire time we've been in here – whispering so no one else could hear.'

Sheppard looked to Mandy, to make sure he was getting it all right. It appeared he was.

'You knew about her religion, and you used it against her. Mary Magdelene – really?'

Mandy smiled, an ugly-looking thing that reeked of positivity. 'I embellished it a bit. Gave myself a nice title.'

'You used a poor woman. You made her into a murderer,' Sheppard said.

Mandy tilted her head and gave a pout. 'Try and say that like you're not proud of me.'

'All for what? Just to make things a bit more interesting?'

'Oh come on,' Mandy sighed, 'Hughes was eternally boring. Walking around like he was king of the world. He had to go.'

Sheppard ignored the ease with which she dismissed a human life. 'You set this whole thing up, didn't you? You and Eren and Winter. You lured Winter down here and killed him. Used him too. You're sick.'

Mandy laughed. 'Winter was in it all along, Sheppard. He knew what he was getting into. Winter hated you as much as we do. You ruined his life, just as you ruined ours, remember?'

'I don't know you. I've never seen you before today.'

'No, but you knew my brother. You probably don't remember him, do you? You don't even remember Sean Phillips? How you drove him to kill himself?'

Sheppard faltered, stepping back a bit defensively. The name rang a bell, he thought he might have been briefed about the situation in some production meeting or something. But he couldn't remember Mandy at all. But that didn't say much when you couldn't remember what happened yesterday. 'Whatever I did, it's not a reason to kill an innocent man.'

'Sean Phillips was innocent. Winter was different. He had a darkness inside him – the burn for revenge. Just like me and Kace. Winter walked down here of his own accord. He was so very wanting to see your face when you woke up. When you realised what we'd done. Unfortunately for him though, his time came before then.'

'You used him.'

'Yes,' Mandy said. 'Rather stupid for a psychologist, don't you think?'

'I think he was more intelligent than you gave him credit for. I think he worked it all out. Albeit too late. He left me a message. Telling me exactly who killed him. I don't think you're as perfect as you think you are.'

'Fantastic, wonderful,' Mandy said, 'you worked it out all too late. You really are pathetic, Sheppard, and now the whole world knows it. You are a fake, and you have blood on your hands that will never wash off. We've beaten you.'

'Eren knew how to play into my hand,' Sheppard said. 'He knew I would never expect the young blonde. He knew you were just my type.'

Mandy frowned at this. 'What? Don't be disgusting. Kace and I are in love. There's no way he would use me like that. My reason for hating you is just as valid as his. Why don't you think I'm the mastermind of this whole thing, huh?'

'You're not the mastermind because you're here in the room. I almost feel sorry for you.' Sheppard stopped. Mandy had to notice he'd moved now. He was almost within an arm span of her. He could probably reach out to grab Headphones. At least he hoped he could.

If Mandy had noticed him, she didn't show it. 'You don't get to feel sorry for me. Why do you feel sorry for me? Stop it.' The knife was quivering in anger in front of Headphones' throat.

Sheppard poised himself, ready. 'I feel sorry for you because we got played,' he locked eyes with Headphones and did the small nod they had communicated before, 'and so did you.'

Headphones didn't falter — she sank her teeth into Mandy's wrist.

52

Mandy howled with pain, pulling her wrist free. Sheppard ducked forward, just avoiding Mandy's blind swing of the knife and grabbed Headphones, pushing her onto the bed and free from harm. Ryan had reacted to the move as well, jumping over the bed and moving up towards Mandy.

Mandy had other ideas, however, as she clutched her wrist which was blossoming with colour, and with a primal scream, she launched herself at Sheppard. Sheppard dodged too late, and the two went sprawling into the alcove near the main door.

They both fell to the floor, Mandy on top of him. He grabbed her wounded wrist and she growled in pain, losing grip of the knife. It clattered off to the side and as Sheppard followed it with his eyes, he saw Ryan at the other end of the room, taking Constance's handcuffs off. Headphones was still on the bed, stunned.

A second later, Mandy was back, her hands around his neck. Her grip was strong and he rasped for the thick air that had enveloped the room, but her frame was still light. He forced her off him and she went flying into the closet, which stood open. She slammed against the wall and he lunged for her. She dodged and her nails plunged into his leg. Sheppard went careening forward. His fist struck the wall and kept going. It was plasterboard, thin and slight, a weakness in the walls of the room. His motion stopped as a shard of board dug into his wrist. It was stuck.

Mandy panted behind him. She reached behind her, no doubt picking up the knife. He pulled at his wrist, but the more he pulled, the more it seemed to get stuck. He looked over his shoulder as Mandy advanced towards him, knife in hand.

'Mandy,' Sheppard said, pulling and pulling but getting nowhere.

'You don't know how long I've waited to hear you beg, to hear you scream,' Mandy said, lifting the knife.

'No,' Ryan shouted and lunged at Mandy.

Mandy was surprised by the noise and turned as Ryan collided into her. Sheppard saw what was going to happen before he heard the scream. Mandy turned the knife on Ryan, sweeping it around. Ryan grabbed Mandy, as the knife plunged into his stomach.

Ryan howled.

Mandy looked shocked. 'I – I . . .'

Ryan clutched at his stomach, blood pouring out from between his fingers. He sunk down to his knees.

Mandy held the knife up – now decorated with Ryan's blood. Her eyes seemed to be processing what she had done.

Sheppard took his chance pulling as hard as he could on his wrist. It came free, along with half of the plasterboard. He lunged at Mandy, bending down to pick up the cuffs and he barrelled into her. Mandy yelped and raised the knife again. Not caring anymore, Sheppard ignored it and as the knife came down, he just got to her free wrist first. The knife lurched back up as Sheppard got the handcuff around her wrist. *Click* – as it locked into place.

Mandy squawked. She slashed at him, but wasn't able to reach him. Even so, the blade ripped through the shoulder of his shirt, grazing his skin. He lunged at Mandy's free arm between slashes, forcing it around the back of her to meet the other. Even as he closed the second cuff, she tried to slash at him. But when the cuff touched her bitten wrist, she dropped the knife through pain. It clattered off the wall and fell to the floor.

'No,' Mandy screamed, over Ryan's grunts.

'Is he okay?' Sheppard said, looking round to Ryan's fallen body. His head was propped up by the bed box-spring, looking down at his stomach. Headphones had taken the edge of the duvet and was pressing it to his stomach. It was already turning red, even through the thick layer.

'He's losing blood,' Headphones said.

Mandy had given up any discernible language and snarled at Sheppard, alternating whoops and growls.

What to do? What to do?

Sheppard opened the bathroom door, trying to push Mandy towards it. She didn't budge, obviously seeing the dead bodies of Simon Winter and Alan Hughes. He pushed her harder and she went careening into the room, her hands locked behind her back.

'Sheppard,' Mandy shouted, and he would never forget

339

the cold, murderous way she said it – she really wanted him dead. Was she like that before, or was this what Eren did to people? 'I might not have done it, but you know he will. Kace is going to kill you. And then he'll come back for me.'

Sheppard slammed the bathroom door and almost instantly there was hammering on the other side. He held his foot against the bottom of the door, ignoring the screams. Until they subsided. He took his foot away. There was nothing – she was stuck in there.

He went to Ryan. 'Ryan, are you okay?'

He looked up at Sheppard and moved his mouth but no sound came out.

'He's dying, Sheppard,' Headphones said, her hands slicked red. 'We need to stop the bleeding. We need to get help.'

Sheppard pressed his hands down around the area too. 'We can't do that. There's no way out.'

'We know who murdered Winter. Isn't it over?' Headphones said.

'I don't know.'

But as he said that, he heard something. Where there was nothing before, there was a small whirring sound.

Sheppard slowly released his hands and got up. He went around Ryan and Headphones to look at the timer.

Three minutes. Twelve seconds.

He watched it. It didn't change. It had stopped.

Sheppard breathed out forcefully, expelling all the panic. 'I think it's stopped. I think the air came back on.' He looked down at Headphones and Ryan, his head lolling from side to side, a hum escaping his lips. Headphones wasn't looking at him. She was looking into the cupboard.

He went around to her, looked her in the face. 'What?'

Inside the cupboard, the fake plasterboard wall had crumbled away to reveal a brick wall behind it. One of the bricks had come free, and in the gap, Sheppard saw an opening. 'I think it's loose,' he said, peering at it. He lifted his leg and kicked at the brick wall. The dust of old concrete and brick showered down, but nothing moved.

He ignored the slight jolt of pain in his foot and did it again. Still nothing.

Ryan's moans drove him to carry on, kicking the wall again and again until finally the wall collapsed in a satisfying *thud*.

There was a small opening behind the wall, an opening with a ladder. He stuck his head into the hole he'd made and looked up. It was dark, but the ladder seemed to carry on climbing into the darkness. He turned back to Headphones.

'It's a ladder. I think it's a way out.'

Headphones couldn't look happy – a ghost of relief was barely there, but he saw it. She moved the segment of duvet down so she could press on Ryan's wound with a fresh piece. 'You need to go,' she said. 'Get help. Ryan's not going to last much longer.'

'But I can't leave you . . .'

'Sheppard,' Headphones snapped, looking older than she ever had, 'you have to go. You wanted to save us. So save us.'

Sheppard reluctantly nodded. He took one more look

341

at Ryan, who met his gaze only briefly. He might have imagined it but he thought he saw the young man nod too.

'I'll be as quick as I can,' Sheppard said. 'I'll be back for you.'

'Go,' Headphones said, impatiently.

Sheppard turned away. He walked into the cupboard, fitting into the dark section behind the wall. He grasped the first rungs of the ladder – feeling cold and strong. This was it – the end. So why wasn't he more relieved?

As he started to climb, the overwhelming feeling was one of fear.

53

Before . . .

Kace Carver entered the lobby of HMP Pentonville at 9 am. The place had become too familiar to him. He knew the drab walls, the stained carpets, the weathered fabric of the chairs as if this were his own home. The lobby was small and cramped, with a reception desk masked in a sheet of thick plastic. Kace went up to the desk and slipped his visitor's permit through the small slot on the desk.

'I'm here to see Ian Carver,' he said, not bothering to look at the specimen behind the desk and behind the plastic. This always played out the same. He had no need for pleasantries. Next, there would be a spell where the pass was verified and then the great charade would begin. Kace would be searched, his belongings scanned and then he would be ushered into a room even shabbier than this one. A room filled with tables and chairs and hopeful prisoners looking for their loved ones. He hated it. It was pitiful and it was weak. The lack of hope sealed them all in a vacuum.

'Hmm . . .' the woman behind the plastic said. A new sound. That wasn't the sound they usually made. Kace looked at her. Through the plastic, she looked slightly distorted, but she was an elderly woman, wearing a drab dress. She had a peacock brooch above her left breast. Probably against code. 'I'm sorry, Mr Carver, can you wait a second?'

She gestured to the seating area and Carver drifted off. He didn't sit. He wondered what that 'Hmmm' was all about.

The woman behind the plastic picked up the telephone and dialled. Kace couldn't hear what she was saying and she'd brought her hand up to mask her mouth.

He stood still, not lifting his eyes from the woman, as she had her silent conversation. She put the phone down and smiled to him.

'Just a few minutes, Mr Carver.'

'Can I go through?'

'One of the officers on duty is coming to meet you, Mr Carver. Have a seat.'

Kace didn't sit. He stared at the receptionist for a number of minutes before a short skinny man in a suit came around the corner. He looked uncomfortable, as though he may spontaneously combust at any second. There was no way that he was a guard – this man couldn't police a slice of toast.

'Mr Carver,' the man said, holding out a shaky hand.

Kace took it. It was cold and clammy. Something was very wrong.

'I am Evan Wright, the family liaison officer for Pentonville. Would you follow me to my office?'

'I'd rather like to see my father instead.'

Evan Wright offered a short smile. 'Please.' And he gestured down the hallway.

Without any real alternative, Kace followed the officer into a small office, filled with filing cabinets and stacks of paperwork.

The man slid behind the desk and sat down, instantly seeming to calm down. Now there was a desk between them, everything was okay. Kace sat.

'When was the last time you saw your father, Ian Carver?' Mr Wright said.

'Last week. During weekend visiting. Has something happened?'

'How did he seem to you?' Mr Wright said, ignoring Kace's question.

'He was fine. He was in prison. He was as fine as he could be. Can you tell me what is going on?' Kace was starting to get agitated, and he knew what he got like when he was angry. Dr Winter's voice echoed in his head, 'Use the anger. Don't let it control you. *You* control *it*.'

Wright held up a hand, as if predicting Kace's outburst. He put it down and smiled that short sad smile again. 'Your father seemed very odd this past week. He is usually obedient. He usually keeps his distance from the, let's say, more colourful characters we have here at Pentonville. But suddenly, he started getting on the wrong side of those very same people.

'Prisons are weird places. There's no real concept of time. Things can change at the drop of a hat. Your father started to make enemies. Powerful enemies.'

'Why?'

'We were hoping you knew.'

'No. He. He . . .' Kace said, trying to grasp words just out of reach, 'he was fine.'

'As far as we can tell, he was going through some kind of psychological crisis.'

'As far as you can tell? You run the prison. Just ask him, for God's sake,' Kace said.

That smile again. That was the moment Kace knew. They hadn't asked Ian Carver because there was no Ian Carver to ask.

Mr Wright cleared his throat. His eyes flitted away from Kace every few seconds, as if looking at an invisible checklist of things to tick off. 'We are to understand that this is around the anniversary of your mother's death? Maybe that was why Mr Carver was . . . unpredictable. I'm afraid he was involved in an altercation.'

'An altercation?' Kace said, almost laughing. How cowardly this man was, this Mr Wright. Wright couldn't even look him in the eyes, let alone put a name to what had happened to his father.

'Yes,' Wright said. 'Your father and some other prisoners fought, and . . .'

'He's dead,' Kace finished, begging for the other man to correct him.

Instead, Wright just looked at him. 'I'm very sorry.'

'Sorry?' Kace said, expecting to shout but instead whispering. 'Sorry? Where were the guards?'

'There will be a full investigation into how this was possible.'

'Who did it?'

'I'm sorry?'

'Who killed my father?'

'I'm afraid I can't tell you that.'

'I want you to tell me who killed my father.' Something uncurled inside Kace, some creature which had been asleep for a long, long time. An insatiable anger. And he wanted to laugh. He wanted to howl. And now his father was dead.

'We will do everything in our power to figure out the facts of the situation. On behalf of HMP Pentonville, you have our condolences. Everything will be done to support you at this difficult time.'

Kace got up. 'My father is dead,' he said, tucking his chair in to the desk. 'I have no further business here.'

He walked out of the office, ignoring the fact that Mr Wright was shouting to him about details and follow-ups and inquests. He walked out of the reception, even as the receptionist begged him back to sign some forms and check out. He walked across the parking lot and made it to his car, as other visitors were arriving to see their, no doubt living, loved ones.

He sat in his car for a long time. He sat there in silence, barely moving, barely even breathing. It was a cold day but it felt even colder now. His father was dead. He was a thirty-seven-year-old orphan. Why did that bother him as much as it did? He was alone. He sat in his car for a long time.

He just sat there.

And at some point, he started to laugh.

54

It went on forever. Up and up and up, like he was climbing out of Hell itself. His calf throbbed with pain every time he put his left leg down on one of the steel bars of the ladder. His leg ached where Mandy had dug her nails into him. Somewhere below him, he could hear Ryan and Headphones. It felt wrong to leave them, but what could he do?

It felt like he was back in the vents. The air was thinner here than it had been in the room. It took a lot of effort to heave himself up the ladder.

He had just got used to the cycle of effort and pain when he almost slammed head-first into the hatch. It seemed invisible in the darkness – a nondescript lid on all the terrors happening below.

He sensed it just in time and stopped, putting a hand out to feel above him. It felt cold and strong. He ran his fingers across it and found a steel wheel in the centre. He redistributed his weight, making sure he wouldn't fall, and grasped the wheel with both hands. It was stiff but after a few seconds it started to turn. He steadied himself and turned until he felt the seal open. He pushed on the wheel and it started to come free.

He felt the hatch move – start to open above him. It was heavier than he expected – requiring all the strength he had left to push it. Finally, he wrenched it up and over the hinge. It made a dull scraping sound as it rested open against something.

He took a deep breath of cold fresh air and stuck his head out. He was in what looked like a small stone outhouse. Tight and narrow, and somewhat hastily built. He could see sunlight through the gaps between the wonkily placed stones of the four walls.

He pulled himself out of the hatch and finally set his feet on solid ground, a sigh escaping him. He ran his hand over the stones of one of the walls, cold and rough against his fingers. They felt real, more real than anything he'd experienced today.

The door was wooden and rotten, hanging slightly off its hinges. On the back of it was a mouldy poster of a soldier talking to someone. 'They talked . . . this happened. Careless talk costs lives.'

World War II. A World War II bunker. That must have been where he was – what the place was built for. A repurposed World War II bunker made up to look like a room in the Great Hotel. He had been fooled, hell, even the man who worked at the hotel had. The level of detail was astonishing. It really had been a hotel room in central London. A very public place. But it wasn't. Really, it was just some nondescript bunker in the ground. Sheppard wondered how long it had taken to make something up like that and kept coming back to how much effort it had all been. The repurposing of the bunker, orchestrating everyone's kidnappings, keeping them all under until it was ready for them to wake up, placing the clues.

The one, horrible thought.

Eren must really hate me.

Hate didn't seem an adequate word.

Sheppard reached the door and slowly pushed it open. Sunlight flooded the outhouse. So bright, it blew out his vision for a few seconds. He shielded his eyes and looked out. A field – lush and green. Not quite the bright, airy summer's day he now knew to be manufactured down in the bunker. More dull and cold. The wind greeted him, whipping across his face as he stepped out. Seagulls cawed and he smelled salt in the air. He looked towards the noise as a couple of seagulls emerged from beyond the field. There, the grass grew longer and more disparate. Were they near the sea?

He looked the other way and saw only more fields. He decided the hill was the way to go and started walking. Following a hunch. Although he couldn't really rely on hunches anymore. He was a fool, and everyone knew it. Especially Eren.

But where was he?

He knew he was in Britain. He could feel it, smell it, sense it in the way you can do when you are home. But quite where he was, he had no idea.

More seagulls and as he climbed the hill, he looked up to see the birds making their way across a sky plagued with dark clouds. Two of the birds dipped and swirled through the sky, keeping pace with each other. Free. Together.

He was at the top of the hill before he knew it, the ground becoming more uneven and unstable. He looked down to see it was sand.

What he expected. The land cascaded into a beach that stretched as far as the eye could see. The tide was coming in, making the beach narrow, quickly dipping and getting swallowed by the sea. Even in the dingy light, Sheppard didn't think he'd seen anything more beautiful or ever felt so alive.

The scene was perfect.

Until . . .

There was someone. A small figure standing on the beach. Possibly about a mile away. He knew who it was.

And he knew the figure was waiting for him.

55

Before . . .

Winter didn't like them in his house. Eren had obviously been there before, but it was something about him and the girl together. They were sitting around his kitchen table, with documents spread out all over it. In front of Eren, there was a large hand-drawn diagram of the hotel room that he himself had drawn when he had stayed in the Great Hotel.

In front of him and Phillips were fanned out profiles of people – real people – that were candidates. A couple of them were about to become players in a game they could never hope to understand. Winter had been sorting through the profiles for the last five hours.

'Are we done?' Phillips said, sounding bored.

Eren smiled. 'I think so. Simon, you want to run down the list of England's luckiest?'

There was a bad taste in Winter's mouth. 'I'll let you do the honours,' he said, and slid the pile over to Eren.

'I was secretly hoping you'd say that.' Eren laughed and picked up the first sheet of paper. He turned it round and showed it to the other two as though he was showcasing it in front of a class. The sheet had a picture of Phillips clipped to it. The rest detailed her backstory – like some crib sheet for a fantasy game.

Phillips smiled.

'Here we have our very own Amanda Phillips, our snake in the rough. Her task is to keep the game going along its intended path. You, Mandy, are the most important piece of the puzzle. You have to become Morgan's ally, he has to believe you are his friend. He'll like you – you're young and pretty. And he's stupid. As long as you don't do anything to reveal your position, there's no way he'll ever suspect you.'

'I won't let you down,' Phillips said, and she put a hand on Eren's arm. Winter had noticed this happening more and more. They had tried to keep it from him but he knew. They had entered a romantic relationship – maybe it had been going on for weeks. He was sure that at the start they had probably been using each other for their own ends. But now it wasn't hard to see that Phillips had become truthfully infatuated. Eren saw it too.

'Up next,' Eren said, picking up the next piece of paper. 'Ryan Quinn. The boy that works at the Great Hotel, so it's going to be hardest to convince him. But he is an important player – he will provide legitimacy if anyone else starts to question if they are in a hotel. We need to fool Ryan Quinn and if we fool him, we've fooled everyone else.'

'Next is Constance Ahearn. Me and Simon were on the lookout for someone who could incite some trouble in the room. We might be able to bring out Morgan's dark side if he's faced with lunacy. Ahearn will be desperate and that'll bring everyone in the room down with her. For you Mandy, this will be a tricky one. Ahearn is massively unstable, which means that you should be able to lean on her and make her do things if things get a bit too quiet. One of your priorities is to stick to Ahearn, be the little angel on her shoulder whispering into her ear. Whispering whatever you want. Sheppard doesn't like instability and he sure as hell doesn't like dealing with problems himself. If he trusts you, he'll surely palm off Ahearn to you.'

Eren and Phillips laughed. Winter tried to smile too. But he couldn't. This was all becoming very real.

'Next, we have Alan Hughes.' Winter held his breath — he had put Hughes' name into the mix to throw a spanner in the works. Hughes was a dedicated lawyer, he had seen that through his involvement with the MacArthur case. Hughes could solve the murder, even if Sheppard couldn't. *And that's what you want now, is it? You want Sheppard to win?* He didn't know anymore. But this was all going too fast, and he was starting to foresee this whole thing spiralling out of control. Yes, it looked like Eren had a handle on it. But . . .

Go on, think it.

But Eren was insane.

He had seen it too late. The man was a good play-actor, maybe even better than Morgan. He was not surprised they had been friends at school. They were two sides of the same coin.

'. . . Hughes is going to be a pillar of strength in the room. He's undoubtedly going to be an antagonist to

354

Sheppard. It sounds like a lot of fun.' Eren looked at Winter and beamed. 'Good shout, Simon.'

Winter scraped his chair back and got up. 'I need to get the land deed documents from upstairs.' A worthless lie as everyone knew why he had to leave the room. The next piece of paper hovering in Eren's hand. *Rhona Michel . . . itsallyourfault itsallyourfault.* Why had he told Eren?

'Fair enough, Simon,' Eren said. 'You know we have to do it though. She's the one who's seen the most. If only you had locked the door, huh? Poor little Rhona . . .'

'Don't say her name,' Winter said quickly, 'just don't.' And he stepped around the table and got out of the kitchen as quickly as possible. Out in the hall, he shut the kitchen door and leaned against it, as silent tears started rolling down his cheeks.

What had he gotten himself into? What had he got them all into? Those poor people were going to go through hell because of him. What could he do? Did he really have the power to stop this? He was in far too deep to go to the police – he couldn't reveal Eren's plan without revealing his own part in it. And he couldn't go to prison.

'Is he gone?' Phillips' voice. Very quiet. Through the door. 'I think I heard him go upstairs.'

'He won't be back for a while.' Eren. 'All because of this Michel girl. He can't deal with the consequences of his actions. I think he's faltering. We need to deal with it.'

Phillips. 'Do we need to remind him why he's here?'

Eren cleared his throat and lowered his voice even more, so Winter had to strain to hear. 'No. He's working against us now. I'm not sure why he chose this Hughes man as a candidate.'

'So we just take Hughes out the room.'

'I'm afraid we're a little too far along for that. Besides, we can spin this Hughes situation to our advantage, I think. What we can't spin . . . is Simon's mindset.'

'So what do we do?' Phillips said.

'I think you know really,' Eren said, and Winter could tell he was smiling. 'After all, we still haven't picked a body.'

Winter started uncontrollably shaking, so hard he had to step away from the door. They were going to kill him. His part in the game had changed. He had to get out, he had to leave, he had to be anywhere but here. He was going to die.

But where would he go? They knew where he lived – they were sitting in his kitchen, for God's sake. The wrath Eren was bringing down upon Morgan – did Winter really think it would be any less for him? Winter had known Eren for years, knew his deepest, darkest secrets. Eren would find Winter wherever he went. And if he couldn't, he would find Abby. Hell, he already had. He'd already overheard that Phillips had scored a job at Abby's coffee shop.

Eren had him.

Winter's silent tears were now ones of fear. How was he going to get out of this? How was he going to stop Eren doing this to these poor people? And then – a thought, an almost impossibly warped thought. He couldn't do both – but he could help Morgan. Yes, because no matter how much he knew Eren, he knew Morgan more. He could get a message to him somehow.

But that means – Yes. It did. *That means you have to die.* And maybe that was his sacrifice – no – not sacrifice. Maybe that was his reward. For being so consumed by anger. For being moulded into something despicable. A monster of his own. Eren and that insipid Mandy Phillips. He wanted to say they used him, but really he had been with them. Running so fast his conscience had to catch up. Maybe this is how it ends.

Abby would be safe. That was the main thing. And, at long last, he would have done the right thing.

But can you do it? Can you go down there knowing you're going to die? No. But he could go down there knowing it was right.

Winter wiped his eyes with his handkerchief and felt a light finality drape over him like a thin bedsheet on a summer's night. This was it.

All he needed was a plan.

And by the time he was ready to re-enter the kitchen and rejoin the people who were going to kill him, he had one.

Carver straightened the pad of paper slightly closer to the bedside lamp. Impressions were the most important thing, and anything out of place would ruin the whole thing. That was why he had been extra careful. He had been to the Great Hotel many times, taken thousands upon thousands of photos that would seem dull to even the most enthusiastic photographer. He had even measured everything: the space between the pad and the lamp, the space between the television and the room-service menu, banal things that wouldn't matter to anyone in isolation. But together, they might matter – they might spoil the whole illusion.

Amanda was 'outside' positioning one of the screens that would show the centre of London out of the window. She hadn't believed it would work, but Carver had convinced her when he'd created a scale model. Now she was back to being sceptical. A large screen curved down around the window creating a sense of depth. Amanda was positioning a screen adjacent to that which would pipe in the exact same image but would create an illusion of depth. It was like those old TV sets – say a kitchen with a window looking out to the garden – you had to account for every possible way an audience member could view that window and create enough garden to accommodate that. It would give the illusion there was a garden beyond the window – just as his creation gave the illusion of the London skyline. It was a live feed and they were piping in the high-quality audio feed from the real room in the Great Hotel so all the faint traffic sounds, aeroplanes and city hum was there. It was all smoke and mirrors but it looked good – more than passable.

'Are you sure about this?' Mandy said, hopping over the 'window' and taking a look at her handiwork. 'All I see is a bunch of screens of London. Yes, they all join up and they all look and sound alright. But it's just screens.'

'You see screens because you know they're screens,' Carver said. 'These people will be stressed, as stressed as they've ever been in their lives – their brains will work against them, fill in the blanks. And you're going to have to pretend.' Carver went over to Mandy and carefully put his hands over her eyes. She giggled like a schoolgirl (it made his skin crawl). 'Now think,' he said, before taking his hands away. 'What do you see?'

'London,' she said, altogether too triumphantly. She jumped up and kissed Carver on the cheek.

He forced a smile. Of course he wasn't sure about this – not any of it really. Any part of the plan could fail at any moment. The screens. The body. The knife. The phones. And Mandy. He trusted Mandy – no matter how much he despised her – and he thought she could pull it off. That first night they had met in Brickwork he had known she was the right person for the job – but he would be lying if he said he wasn't a little worried.

Dr Winter was hammering a nail into the wall. He picked up a painting he had specifically asked for himself and hooked it on the wall. Carver had signed off on it of course – it appealed to his warped sense of macabre. Dr Winter had said that the real painting in the room he had visited was one of a peaceful stream on a summer's day. This one was far more apt.

Mandy looked at it. 'Where the hell did you find this?'

'Car boot sale,' Winter shrugged. 'Thought it looked a bit weird.'

Mandy reached up her hand and ran her fingers over the dried paint. 'You're right there, doc.'

Dr Winter laughed. 'I can't help but keep looking at it. I'm not sure what I find more horrible – the scarecrow's smile or the fact there are probably children upstairs in that house, burning alive as the scarecrow just watches.'

Carver raised an eyebrow. Mandy seemed similarly affected. 'You know, I might nick that,' she said.

'Be my guest,' Dr Winter smiled.

Carver cleared his throat. 'Simon, can you go into the bathroom and double-check everything again?'

'Eren, I've already done that three times over. Everything's fine. It's going to be fine.'

'Please, just do it.'

Winter frowned but scuttled off to the bathroom. He heard the door open and close. Winter was not wrong – he had already been in that small bathroom for about six hours. The man had proven himself to be rather adept at plumbing, believe it or not. Carver had always known that he would need a flushing toilet and working sink. The bathtub was fine, as no one was going to want to get in there. But the other luxuries had to be plumbed. Even if no one actually needed the toilet, Sheppard would be suffering from alcohol and drug withdrawal. So, odds said he was going to throw his guts up.

Carver centred the pad of paper and took the pen out of his pocket, resting it next to the pad. Next to the Holy Bible. Because that was the one staple of all hotels, no matter what the star rating. Every hotel presumed Christianity. Carver always thought how disgustingly offensive that was. Hopefully the Bible would at least help trigger Constance Ahearn's lunacy. Just to help things along.

'It looks like we're all set,' Mandy said, looking around and checking everything.

'Yes,' Carver said, 'just one last thing.'

Silently, he pulled the knife out from under one of the pillows on the bed. He handed it to her – handle out.

'This is it then,' Mandy said. Carver thought she sounded almost excited. 'After all we've planned.' She took the knife and looked at it in the light.

'You don't have to be the one who does this, you know. I can do it and make it look like you.' She looked at him and he saw her mistake his concern over the plan going awry as concern for her – just as intended.

'I can do this,' Mandy said. 'You believe in me, don't you?'

'Of course I do,' Carver said, and kissed her.

'Everything seems fine in here,' Dr Winter's muffled voice came through the wall.

Mandy and Carver just looked at each other. He nodded. She nodded back.

No more words were needed.

56

Sheppard thought of turning away; walking in the opposite direction. But he knew that he couldn't. He knew that he had to face the man at the end of the beach – he knew that that was the ending to this story.

He made his way down the dunes onto the beach below. Sand kicked up under his feet and he almost fell, moving faster to get to solid ground. The sand on the beach was firmer and easier to walk on than on the dunes, but it was no less inviting. Exhaustion was lapping at him like the waves on the beach, but he knew he would be able to make it to the figure in the distance.

Sheppard took Winter's phone out of his pocket – no signal. He swore under his breath – still no signal even though he was finally out of that hole. He dialled 999 anyway – but nothing. Where was he? He needed to find a phone quickly or Ryan was going to die. And the best chance of a working phone was Eren himself – so Sheppard started walking towards him. Because he knew that, in some way, he deserved this. No one else would have to suffer because of him.

He'd hidden Eren away in his mind for so long. Hiding what he did under all the good memories, all the substances, all the late nights and later mornings, all the television episodes. Eren was a ghost in the machine of his mind.

If he survived this, could he recover? Bury the fake hotel room like he buried Eren? Everything that happened on this day was a nightmare, buried deep inside him. The people there – like figments of a troubled imagination, fractures of a sub-conscious. Did he think that, in time, he would come to believe that? Just like, in some way, he had truly believed he solved Mr Jefferies' murder? What life was there left for Morgan Sheppard after this?

Maybe dying here, in the sand, would be a fitting end. A footnote on a life. He dragged his legs along. They seemed to want him to stop – lie down in the sand. Lie there and die. This was it and this was always where it was going to end.

He was just happy to have been able to get out of the room. To come outside and see the sky again. He had always liked to be outside – needing freedom. Most likely because he loved an exit strategy. But now, he wasn't going to run away. Quite the contrary.

He thought of all the mistakes he made. The parties, the painkillers, the drink and all the bits in between. Every single day was incredibly hazy. The last few years just melded into each other – the same things over and over again. And nothing of any consequence. Not remembering much of anything. And it all began that day he went to the police about Eren's dad.

But everyone would remember this. The Lying Detective. A hell of a headline – one that would no doubt sell a few copies. The red tops finally taking him down.

The figure was slightly closer now, yet still far enough for him not to be able to make out any features. A black sliver against the dull yellow sand. The only thing Sheppard knew for certain was that the figure was watching him, and had probably been waiting for him for quite some time.

Just keep on walking.

What would happen at the television studio? Would they all weep for him, or would they cry not really knowing why, mistaking grief for their jobs as grief for him? Someone would probably organise an expensive funeral and wake. It would be high profile – good publicity for the network. An open casket with a side of caviar. Lobster toast. Champagne to toast the great brute off.

The show would probably go on without him. It would be stupid not to use the publicity to their advantage. A fresh face would be ushered in. Hell, maybe even Eren himself or someone like him. Someone who deserved it. There would be a memorial episode before handing over – a changing of the guard – to a random, a non-entity. The entertainment business stopped for no one – cash the cheques and move on. He'd be forgotten in a week.

He didn't have many friends. Couldn't think of a single person he would call one. There was Douglas, but that was different. It was in Douglas' best interests to get along with him – he was getting paid through the nose for it after all. There were a few people at the television studio he talked to. He didn't know them well enough to put a name to them. And as he thought more about it, he didn't know if he hadn't made those names up as well.

There were a few ex-girlfriends. Michelle, from college, was a plucky young English student. Sheppard had dumped her the minute he signed the TV contract. Last time he'd Googled her, she was happily married and pregnant. Her Facebook photos were bright and airy and she wore a smile that he'd never seen on her. He pictured her at a breakfast table with her husband, and a baby in a high chair, reading the paper. 'Huh, I used to go out with him.' And that would be it. Next came Suzie, a woman who didn't respect anything, least of all herself. She wasn't interested in the world, and the world wasn't particularly interested in her. She was a celebrity chaser, which Sheppard found out when he found her in bed with a boy band – all five of them. Sheppard dumped her and she took what little self-respect she had left with her. He fell down a hole of unnamed rendezvouses, the ones of which he could remember being particularly sordid and fuelled by drink or drugs or both. There were so many, it was a blink-and-you-miss-it type of life. All of them had names like Crystal, Saffron, Rouge – things that could be adjectives. None would mourn him, unless it garnered them some attention.

No, the person who would probably miss him most was his dealer. He had plunged a lot of capital into the ventures of a certain young druggie (who just so happened to be a bad medical student) with an eye for business etiquette. When the prescriptions ran out, he had had to rethink. He didn't know how many pills he had bought over the years – probably enough to kill a small army– but he was sure he was the reason that that dealer had kept afloat. What was his name? Sheppard could remember his face, but his name escaped him. He was always hyperactive, his medical degree very obviously in the toilet, and wanted Sheppard to stay and play *Call of Duty* with him. Sheppard always appreciated why he had never just upped and sold him out to a newspaper. That's what he would have done.

Sheppard looked up to see that he had covered a lot of ground. The man in front of him was wearing a suit, with a red tie. When Sheppard saw this, he knew it was impossible that he could have been wearing anything else. The elusive man with the red tie from Constance's story. The evil man.

The man was holding a pair of black, shiny, pointed shoes – his feet were buried in the sand. He wasn't looking at Sheppard but out to sea, with a glazed expression of wonder on his face. Sheppard had seen that expression many times on him when he was younger. It was a look of excitement.

Sheppard walked up to him, keeping his slow and plodding pace, and only when he was directly beside him did the man turn his head.

Kace Carver smiled, not horribly or wickedly, but genuinely as if he was indeed happy to see his old friend. 'Hello Morgan,' he said.

57

He said it as if nothing had happened — as if they'd bumped into each other on the street years later.

'Eren,' Sheppard said, feeling the fresh air gush down his throat, drying it up. The name came out as a small rasping sound.

He didn't respond — not at first, but his smile dipped slightly. His eyes became less kind. He broke eye contact and looked back out to sea. 'No one's called me that in a long time. I'd really prefer it if you didn't either. It's Kace now.'

'Why?' Sheppard said.

'Because the boy you knew is gone. This is the new me. The Carver that you created. So, what do you think?' Carver held his hands up and spun around, like someone trying on clothes in a shop, primed for inspection.

Sheppard wanted to punch him, smash his handsome face in, mash it into something unrecognisable. 'You're a monster,' he settled on instead.

Carver chuckled. 'Well, you've looked better as well.' Carver looked him up and down. 'You really are a state. I didn't think you'd look this bad. I mean, Jesus. You're pathetic.'

'You locked me in a bunker to die,' Sheppard said,

resenting himself at how much it sounded like an excuse.

'Yes I did, but here you are. Isn't it a marvel – the human being's resilience, the need to survive? Or, of course, maybe this was all part of the plan.' Carver winked.

Sheppard looked out to sea. He couldn't bring himself to look at that face anymore. 'Where are we?'

Carver looked around. 'We're on Luskentyre, a beach in the Outer Hebrides. You're in Scotland, Morgan.'

'How is that possible? How was I in Paris and now I'm in Scotland? How was everyone else in London and now they're here?'

'Nothing supernatural, Morgan. No magic. Just a matter of science. Science and a private jet.'

Sheppard genuinely laughed at this, looking back at Carver, but quickly saw that Carver was not joking. 'A private jet?'

Carver cleared his throat. 'Seeing as you are going to ask me all these questions, I might as well just tell you. I think I owe you an explanation before you leave.'

Before you leave.

Sheppard had no fight left in him. He had no will to run away screaming. He just nodded. He wanted to know. 'Okay.'

Carver nodded too. 'You don't know how long I've waited for this moment. I have been harbouring a special kind of resentment for you, Morgan Sheppard, and if you have to ask why, then you really haven't been paying attention. I've been watching you, watching all your feeble relationships, your vapid television programme, all your enigmatic substance abuse. Sometimes I have been right behind you, so much so I could whisper in your ear – but you never noticed me. I'd been content being the observer, but something changed.

'Three years ago, my father died in prison. I visited him every week, ever since my aunt let me. I never missed a visit – and then one day I went and he wasn't there. He was never built for prison. In some ways, I'm shocked he lasted as long as he did. Two guys blinded him with sharpened plastic cutlery, cut his throat. When the guards found him, half of him was spread out on the floor. Some people say the guards were in on it. You see, I think my father was killed because he was too nice.

'That's the first time I really knew the extent of my hatred. That was when it was over and when it had just begun. I knew the one man who had ruined my life was out there, popping pills like Tic-Tacs and barrelling through lives like they were nothing. I knew I had to stop you. I knew it was my duty.

'My father left behind not an unreasonable estate. But it wouldn't have been enough to support me. I sold everything. Even . . . no *especially* . . . the family house. It gave me enough to start anew. I bought a small flat in Milton Keynes. Not very grand, but enough.

'I used the rest of the money to invest in stocks. A risky venture, you might say. But it was easy enough for me. As you remember (or don't, as the case may be) I've always been gifted with a rather special mind. I treated the stock market like I would, say, a murder. I analysed every inch, every eventuality, every outcome. It was almost fun. But it was also too easy. I still do it – but I've lost interest.

Once you have so much money – well, even that seems boring.

'So I needed a new venture. And that is when I got the idea. To finally find you. And make you see what you'd done. I had the capital, all I needed was the plan.'

'What about the others? Mandy and Winter,' Sheppard said.

'I knew very quickly that I would need help on this venture of mine. It was a lot of work. I found one of my helpers at one of your God-awful parties. She had snuck in to try and get you to confess to killing her brother. Not directly killing, of course. You never do anything that could actually get you in trouble, do you? You prefer the indirect route.

'Amanda Phillips seemed keen – she was almost as eager for revenge as me. You have probably seen it – that fire behind her eyes. Did you know that you could do that to people? Anyway, Amanda was on board almost immediately, but I couldn't let there be a slight chance that she would disappear. So I let her fall in love with me. It was pretty easy – she was vulnerable, and I've always been blessed with a certain charisma. We bonded over you. Soon enough, she would do anything for me. Even kill, and even die. Of course, she never actually thought I would let her die down there. Even when we were planting the explosives, she thought I would somehow swoop in to save her, in the event of us blowing the place sky high. She was so clever, but what is it they say? Ah yes – love makes fools of us all. I didn't ever believe that, but it turns out it's true.

'Dr Winter was a little harder to bewitch. Even though you messed up his daughter and he knew the truth . . .'

'It was you,' Sheppard said, 'it was you who told him. That's what he was talking about that night.'

'I'll let you into a little secret, Morgan,' Carver said, 'I was there that night.' He laughed. 'In the kitchen. It was quite a show.'

Sheppard felt a shiver go down his spine. Eren had been there – had really only been one step behind him.

'Anyway, even after all that, Winter was still reluctant. The old man had a code. The terrible thing about codes though – the wording's always terrible, no one really knows how far they can go before they get to their breaking point, so how is one to know when to stop? Winter was a fragile soul. Eventually, he snapped. It was that night – you remember it. He was very useful in providing information about drugs that could knock someone out for long periods of time, for instance. And he was good at doing the things I didn't want to do. Like going to the hotel and buying the land on which the bunker is based. It's always nice to have a partner after all. Well, half partner, half scapegoat.

'See, I had to make sure that things went how I wanted. So we had to make sure anyone who could possibly rumble us was taken care of. Luckily we needed people inside the room so that worked out well. We didn't have to choose random people. In a way, they chose themselves. And Mandy fit in perfectly as one of them – and after all, she could easily play the pretty young thing. The girl that just so happened to be entirely your type. It was perfect – almost like it was destined to be.

'There was one person who was never in my plan though. One person who was never meant to be in the room. Alan Hughes. Dr Winter went off-script, used my plans for himself. So I changed mine.

'See, we knew Mandy was going to be in the room as your temptress, but the body was never meant to be Dr Winter. I wanted him with me, watching everything, providing his professional opinion. But he decided to get personal, do things he didn't tell us about. He got very angry towards the end – not just towards you but towards the world. It was about his daughter – he found out I had Mandy take a job where she worked, just to check on her. I knew that he might lash out again at a point I couldn't predetermine. So I knew we had to get rid of him – and we did need a body for the bathtub. Of course he didn't know – the old fool.'

No, Sheppard thought, *Winter was worth more than you gave him credit for. He worked it out straight away. He knew he was going to his death – and decided to tell me exactly who killed him*. This was what he thought, but he found he still couldn't speak.

'Of course, with Winter being in the bathtub, I knew the whole structure of your investigation would change. People would recognise Winter and you would start to piece together some kind of truth. I thought about it for a long time, but in the end I knew you wouldn't have enough of the facts to get to me, and even if you did figure it out, you couldn't do anything. In a way, having Winter there was better. I could see the look in your eyes when you saw him.'

Carver smiled. Sheppard felt sick. An old man died and the only way his friend could think of it was as a cog in his machine.

'I was planning to pick the corpse at random so it would be more difficult. So really, you were playing my game on Easy mode. And you still couldn't do it.'

A gust of wind threatened to blow him over. Carver stood steadfast.

'Far less easy was actually getting everyone into the room. The stage was set, but we needed the players. We extracted most people without incident – we used the gas to knock a person out and then got them into a van where we gave a general anaesthetic that could be applied at regular intervals on the trip. We used my private jet to get here, transferring you first and then all the London people. Mandy stayed with you to make sure you didn't wake up while we got everyone else. You think that it has only been a matter of hours since you fell asleep in Paris. But in truth it's been two days.'

'Two days,' Sheppard said, 'how is that possible?'

Carver smiled. 'People seem so astounded at this, but hospitals keep patients asleep for hours upon hours, sometimes days. You know that the longest surgery ever was four whole days. The human body is a wonderful thing, Morgan. You should know that. How much alcohol have you poured into that liver of yours? And you're still standing. The body adapts, repairs itself, forgives and forgets.'

They were quiet for a moment. Sheppard didn't know what to say – there was nothing left.

Carver seemed to agree. 'I think that's it,' he said. 'I know it's probably not what you had dreamed up in that head of yours, but there it is. The cruel hard truth I have found over the last three years is that money really can buy anything. But anything isn't enough for me. No, I just want one little thing in particular.' Carver put his hand into the waistband of his suit trousers and brought out a small compact pistol. Sheppard had never seen a gun in real life before, but even the sight of it sent him into uncontrollable shivers. 'Do you have any more questions?' He clicked the safety off, and held the gun at his side. 'Or shall we begin?'

He had to force the words out. 'Begin? What have we been doing up to this point?'

'Playing.'

'Playing? People died, Eren.' Fear in his voice, impossible to mask. 'What else do you want? You wanted to hear me say it? I said it. You deserve everything that I have. I admit it. I am nothing. I never was – not without you.'

Carver's face suddenly turned a shade of red. However, when he spoke, his voice was still calm. 'You know you're only here because of yourself. You have waded through life without even the slightest sniff of consequences. I am the man at the end of the road. This is the path that you set us on twenty-five years ago, Morgan. And you have to be held accountable for that.'

Sheppard opened his mouth and found that he could

talk again, or that he was allowed. 'I was a child. I was eleven years old.'

'And it seems like you still are. I guess I have to give you a bit of credit. Not many eleven-year-olds manage to deceive the world. All these years, you could have owned up, come clean, but you never did. You're pathetic. You just wrapped yourself up in all your rubbish and started to believe it yourself. You – a detective? You can't even save yourself. How are you meant to protect other people?'

'I've saved people . . .'

Carver laughed. 'You're talking about those people down in the bunker? Ahearn and Quinn and Michel. You saved them from what exactly? You?'

'No. I saved them from you.'

'You didn't save Hughes. You didn't save Winter. Ahearn is going to prison now, for the rest of her life. So will my little helper, Amanda. And Quinn – he's down there dying right now. Because you couldn't protect them.'

'How could I have stopped it? I was locked in . . .'

'Oh shut up. Hughes and Winter are dead because of you. Ahearn and Amanda are killers because of you. What part of that don't you understand? This was all because of you.'

Sheppard's strength was low, and Eren's accusations hit him harder than the gusts of wind. He found himself looking down. Because of him – that was undeniable. But this had all happened because of Eren too, and somehow his old friend was blind to that fact.

'So this is the end of your plan? The ending of your story? You're going to kill me?' Sheppard said, meeting Eren's eyes.

Carver looked at the gun in his hand and waved it at him. 'Yeah. Kind of poetic. I was thinking about drowning you, but even I have limits.'

For some reason, this made Sheppard smile. Was this even happening? The delirium, the withdrawal, the exhaustion. It was all making it seem like a dream. Maybe he was still stuck down in the bunker, gasping for air as the timer ticked down to zero. Was this just all the final brain gasp of a dying man? He wasn't sure which prospect was better, but it seemed that the outcome was going to be the same.

Maybe it was for the best.

People had died. Alan Hughes. Simon Winter. Mandy's brother. He'd messed up Winter's daughter. He just took from the world – take and take and take. Maybe it was time to give back – a debt repaid.

'So,' Carver said, 'are you ready, old friend?'

He held the pistol to Sheppard's head.

58

'Get on your knees,' he said, placing his shoes down on the sand, so he could hold the gun up with both hands.

Sheppard did what he was told.

Why fight it?

'Why didn't you just kill me? Why didn't you just do it at the start? Why all this? Why all this theatre . . .?'

Carver laughed, standing over him, holding the barrel of the gun to Sheppard's forehead, death just a millimetre away. 'Do you remember back in school? You were always so sure of yourself? Just like you were all your life. Just like you aren't now. See, I had to show you what it felt like to fail. You were always such a bastard,' Carver said. 'I should have known you would do something like this. Like all this. Your entire life has just been one big joke. I needed to make you understand that.'

'What happened to you, Eren?'

'You happened to me. And don't call me that.'

'Your father was guilty, Eren.'

'Never call me that. My father was guilty of protecting his family.'

Sheppard almost laughed at that – somehow. 'Protecting his family? Really? Did you ever ask yourself why your father waited so long to kill Jefferies? He wasn't protecting anyone; he was just a time-bomb that went off. The only person he did it for was himself.'

'That doesn't matter,' Carver hissed.

'No, Eren, it's the only thing that matters. This wasn't a crime of passion. It was a well thought-out and co-ordinated plan. Your father just plucked up the courage one day to do it. Pathetic. Looks like you really take after him.'

'My whore of a mother was going to see Jefferies the night she died. My father was devastated. He took an acceptable measure.'

'He took a measure six years later,' Sheppard said. 'I pity him.'

'Shut up,' Carver shouted.

Sheppard looked at him, into his eyes – and saw that Eren Carver was indeed gone. This was something new – someone new. The person standing over him was so sure of himself he hadn't even thought about what he, himself, had done. And yes, maybe Morgan Sheppard was the beginning of the path, but the trail he followed had been his own – that of Kace, not Eren.

Maybe Carver saw this flash of realisation in Sheppard's face because he spat at him. 'You did this,' Carver said, standing over him, waving the gun around as though it were a conductor's baton. 'You. Did. This. And as you lie there dying, your blood flowing out onto the sand, you just remember you wanted this. This is the end of the path you started us on. This is on you.'

Sheppard breathed, spluttered. 'No, Kace, this is on both of us.'

Carver stopped, rested the barrel of the gun in the centre of Sheppard's forehead. 'Morgan, it's over.'

'You think . . .' Sheppard said, stopping to splutter, 'you think I stole your shot at being a hero. You think I ruined your life. But I can't have done both. You were never a hero. You were always a monster. You would have ruined your own family, or you would have condoned a murderer. Which would it have been? You're the villain.'

'Say that again and I swear to God . . .'

'You're the villain. And I'm a terrible excuse for a human being. I've sat back and wreaked havoc with other people's lives. I've done some, no, a lot of things that I am deeply ashamed of. But I can change. You, you'll always be a monster.'

The butt of the gun came hurtling towards Sheppard. His nose plumed into a mess of blood and hurt. He howled.

Carver was laughing. 'You are the parasite. You think the world will miss you?'

'No,' Sheppard said, nasally, spitting blood this time. 'Not in the slightest.'

He saw his parents, his ex-girlfriends, his colleagues. All people he had driven away. The only real friend he'd ever had was moments away from putting a bullet in his brain.

This isn't the end.

With the last of his strength, Sheppard charged forward, taking Carver by surprise. He collided with the man's legs just as the gun went off. The bullet passed millimetres from Sheppard's right ear, ripping into the top of it. Carver went sprawling on the ground. The gun fell an arm's stretch away from both of them.

Sheppard reached out for the gun, but Carver punched him in the face. His vision blurred and he scrabbled around in the sand with one hand. With the other, he slammed Carver's head into the sand.

Carver yowled as Sheppard pressed the man's nose into his face.

Sheppard blinked away the blur and grasped the gun. He pinned Carver down and his friend roared with unbridled hatred. Without thinking twice, Sheppard threw the gun into the sea. It sailed through the air and landed in the water with a plop. Sheppard watched it and Carver took his chance to send his fist ramming up into Sheppard's chin.

Sheppard went sprawling and Carver got up, going over to Sheppard and grabbing him by the scruff of the neck of his shirt. He pulled him over to where the water was coming up against the beach. Carver bent down and gripped Sheppard by the neck. 'I don't need a gun to kill you.'

Sheppard realised what was going to happen too late. Carver forced his head up then plunged it down into the cold, cold water. Sheppard didn't have time to breathe before water filled his lungs. He struggled – his life draining out of him. How many seconds could he last? How long did he have?

Carver wrenched him out of the sea. 'These are consequences, Morgan.'

Sheppard swung around at Carver blindly. It was no-where near connecting but it was enough for Carver to lose his grip around Sheppard's neck. His face planted into the sand and he kicked out with his legs. They connected with Carver's shins, and the man groaned.

Now. You have to get away now.

Sheppard fell into an oncoming wave and scrabbled around to get up. Carver was staggering away from him, sinking down onto all fours. Sheppard got to him and grabbed him by the shoulders, pulling him up by his tie. Carver choked and snarled at him through clenched teeth. He'd cut his lip, so it was a bloody scowl.

'Thank you, Kace, for showing me people can change,' Sheppard said, spitting seawater at him. 'Maybe there's hope for me after all.'

Carver looked at him, an unwavering gaze. 'This isn't over, Morgan. If it's not today, it'll be another. Wherever you go, I'll be there. No matter how much you feel protected. I would burn the world down to get to you. So, kill me now.' An animal voice that didn't even sound human.

Sheppard smiled. 'No, I don't think so. It's not my style,' he said.

He head-butted Carver as hard as he could.

59

Before everything . . .

'You know, when you convinced me to skip class I thought it was for a reason,' Eren said. He and Morgan had been walking around central London for about two hours. It was two thirty on a Friday and Eren was missing Maths with Mr Jefferies. He liked Mr Jefferies and was already building up a guilty conscience for missing it.

Eleven years old and they were out on their own in London. Morgan had got them out of school by saying that his mum was taking them to a science exhibit. Morgan's mum hadn't ever taken them anywhere, so Eren agreed only because he thought it wouldn't work. But, it did and here they were.

Morgan was giddily skipping along the pavement, ducking and weaving through the crowds of tourists. They had found their way to Leicester Square and beyond, and Eren was starting to believe that there wasn't actually an intended destination.

'You feel that, Eren,' Morgan said, turning to him. 'That's what freedom feels like.'

Eren was still hung up on the Maths class issue. 'I just think – like, what if we get homework? We're going to be behind and everything. Maybe we should just go back.'

Morgan stopped, 'Just chill, Eren, okay. It's one Maths class. School isn't everything.'

'It kinda is,' Eren said.

Morgan sighed and turned to Eren holding him by the arms. 'Eren, mate, we're gonna be fine. I have a foolproof plan to success.'

'What is it this time? Olympic gymnast? Writer? Weatherman?'

'I don't know what it is yet, but I just know, Eren, that one day you and me are going to be famous.'

'Mmhmm.'

'Look,' Morgan spun Eren around. 'Look at this place.' They were standing in front of a hotel. It looked like a pretty expensive one too. There were men on the large glass doors. One of them opened a door to let in a man in a business suit and Eren saw a flash of the lobby. Beautiful clean marble floors and people in crisp uniforms.

'You see this place? All fancy and stuff. Someday we'll be able to stay somewhere like this, Eren.'

Eren looked around at his friend. 'Okay, but how?'

'Because we'll be able to afford it. We'll be able to get rooms in cool places and actually be able to use minibars and drink beer at ten in the morning and say stuff like "It's five o clock somewhere."'

'You hate beer. You had that bottle you stole from your mum's fridge and you threw up.'

'Yes, but I'll drink it till I like it,' Morgan said.

Eren sighed. 'I'm a little confused what we're doing here.'

'We're living in the moment, Eren,' Morgan said. 'You always act so ... old. You're always thinking things through too much. Can't we just for once go "We're going to be awesome" without having to plan out our entire future? I'm just being ... in the moment ... that thing that Miss Rain said?'

'Spontaneous?' Eren said.

Morgan clapped his hands and beamed. 'Yes, I'm being spontaneous.'

'Okay,' Eren smiled too, 'I'll make a deal with you. You use your spontaneity and I'll use my thinking and we'll see where it gets us. The winner is the one who gets the furthest. The loser has to get the winner a room in that dumb hotel.' He nodded to the entrance of the building.

'That, my friend,' Morgan laughed, 'is a deal. Now, c'mon, I think there's a good noodle place round here.' And he started off walking again, so fast that Eren had to jog to keep up. 'My mum took me once when she was feeling guilty for leaving me at the supermarket that one time.'

'Is that why we skipped class? For noodles?'

'Nope,' Morgan said, nudging Eren, 'we just so happened to be here. See, Eren, spontaneousity.'

'That's not how you say it. You know what, never mind.' Eren dodged a large clump of tourists who were crowding around a map. 'You never did tell me your new big success plan.'

Morgan jumped and laughed. 'What do you think about being in a band?'

'I think that's the dumbest thing I've ever heard,' Eren

said, and they both burst out laughing.

Once they had finished, Morgan skipped across the road (without waiting for the green man of course) and beckoned to Eren. 'It's through an alley up here.'

Eren crossed the road when it was safe, and as Morgan disappeared around a corner, he looked back at the hotel they had been standing in front of. It looked even more intimidating at a distance – a sleek, rectangular building stretching up into the sky. On the front, the name 'The Great Hotel' shone in muted gold.

Eren made a mental note and followed Morgan to the noodle place.

How would Morgan put it?

Ah yes – he followed Morgan to the future.

60

Sheppard screamed with pain as Carver went sprawling on the sand and lay still, his head bleeding. Unconscious. That had been a lot more painful than it looked in the movies. He dipped his hand into the sea and wiped his forehead. His legs gave out and he fell backwards into a wave.

Crawling out of the sea, he vomited — the same purple sludge as before.

Was it over? The nightmare? He couldn't bring himself to think that. Maybe this was all just another step in the plan. Maybe Carver was pretending.

But no. His old friend was lying still, breathing shallowly, eyes closed. The cut on his forehead oozing blood at intervals. Now, he was still and quiet, Sheppard could see Eren in there. The little boy who played SNES and snuck into movies with him — the boy who was the kindest and the smartest person he'd ever known.

How did this happen? How did we get here?

Blink. He was back in Eren's room. Back in time. The children, them, sitting there. He wanted to tell them.

Just don't go in the attic.

Blink. He was back on the beach. And the sky started

to spit out rain. Drops fell on his face.

Ryan and Headphones. They need help.

He held himself up by his elbows and looked over to Carver. With some trepidation, he reached over and checked his trouser pockets. Nothing. But in the right pocket of his jacket was a smartphone.

He pulled it out and unlocked it. Falling back into a lying position. He had to sleep – had to rest. But not before . . .

He pressed the 9 button three times and held the phone to his ear.

It took a while to connect and he thought it wasn't going to work, just like the one he had brought out of the room. But eventually, faintly, it rang.

Beside him, Carver expelled a deep breath. But he was still out. And the sky gave a loud clap of thunder.

As Sheppard listened to the ringing, he saw one lone seagull travelling across the sky, trailing behind the others. Probably on his way home. Sheppard breathed in, feeling the air hitch in his abdomen. He had never felt worse. Or better.

The ringing stopped. He heard a voice.

'Hello?' Sheppard said, and closed his eyes.

61

Three Months Later . . .

Paris was hot in the summer, but not insufferably so. He strolled through the city, regarding the crowds of tourists and locals mixing together. This time, he didn't bother with the tourist locations but instead enjoyed walking around the back alleyways and roads, finding obscure cafes and shops. Fractured discussions in French and English came to him on the breeze. He even understood some of it.

His leg was much better now, and although his slight limp was still noticeable, he barely paid attention to it. People here didn't recognise him as much as they did in London, for which he was thankful. Besides, he didn't really look the same anymore. He'd changed.

He made his way to La Maison around 12. She was already there, sat at the bar. He recognised her immediately. His memory of her was blurred, as fractured as the conversations he heard around him. When he looked back, she was not there, not fully, in his memory, in his mind. But he had spent a long time thinking about her. So much so that now, she seemed so familiar. Her brown hair tucked behind her ears, her kind, youthful face. The very things that had attracted him to her in the first place.

'*Bonjour*,' she said, with a smile.

'*Bonjour*.' He sat on the stool next to her.

The same place they had first met – almost exactly.

'You look different,' she said, regarding him with a very precise stare – those wistful eyes.

'Yes,' he said. 'And you look captivating.'

'Can I get you a drink?' she said, gesturing to her cocktail.

He could smell it. Alcoholic – sweet yet sharp. He wanted nothing else.

'Soda water,' he said, and when she looked at him strangely, he added, 'I'm trying to quit.' One day at a time.

'*Vous allez faire une boisson de femme seule?*'

'*Je le crains*,' he said, after a moment of thinking.

She was surprised.

'*Tu parle francais?*'

'Just a little. I'm taking a class.'

She gestured to the barman and he came over instantly. She wasn't the kind of woman you kept waiting. '*L'eau petillante s'il vous plait*.' The barman quickly put a bottle of chilled sparkling water in front of him with a glass. The man waved off the offer of her money. It looked like he was smitten. Hard not to be.

'Why are you learning French?'

'Doctor says it helps to keep the mind busy. Also, there's this girl I like who inconsistently lapses into French, so I thought it might be useful.'

'How gallant of you. She must be a lucky woman.'

She took a sip of her cocktail. 'I'm surprised you found me. We didn't really know that much about each other when . . . you know . . .'

He chuckled. 'Yeah well . . . I had a few favours to call in from the television show.'

'I looked you up – heard you quit.'

He poured a glass of water. 'Yeah. I guess I did. Just didn't seem right to carry on, you know. They wanted me to stay – turns out any publicity really is good publicity – but I couldn't. You heard everything?'

'Yes.'

'And you don't mind.'

'My grandmother used to say *"Un homme sans demons est pas un homme du tout."* A man with no demons is no man at all.'

'Yeah. No, I got that one. It was pretty easy.'

She laughed. 'So what are you going to do now?'

'For the first time in my life, I have no idea.'

'Scary,' she said, smiling at him.

'Yes.' He cleared his throat, took a drink. The bar was filling up with afternoon tourists, and the temperature was rising. 'I need to ask you something – why I needed to find you.'

'Yes.'

He looked at her – looked into her deep blue eyes and wondered if she wanted to know what secrets lurked there. 'Did you know what was going to happen? Did you know Eren – Kace Carver?' The name still fell heavy on his lips. He was back on the beach, the salty water in his stubble. Wiping blood off on his shirt. 'I just keep thinking – maybe he had got someone to get me back to my room.'

'*Non*. The last I saw of you was when I went to get ice. I came back and knocked on your door but there was no answer. I stayed there for about thirty minutes – just knocking. I thought you must have gone – or fallen asleep. It was not the first time someone had run out on me, I'll have you know. But there was nothing to be done. So . . .'

'So you forgot it ever happened.'

'Yes. Until I saw the news. And then I knew.'

'You could have come forward, you know. Sold your story.'

'I could have. I didn't.'

He nodded. She was telling the truth – didn't seem like the type of person who didn't.

'How are the others?' she asked. 'The people you were with?'

He thought for a moment. He hadn't seen any of them in a while. Any time he had, it had been awkward. He'd gone to see Ryan in hospital a few times, but it was strange. Like their story together was over. They would always be bound by what happened in the Room. But that was done. 'They're okay, as far as I know,' he decided on. 'Hughes' funeral is next week. I don't know if I'm going to go though.'

'You should go,' she said, 'you owe him that.'

What he had been wrestling with. Spoken aloud. He knew he had to go.

'Is he in prison?' she asked. He knew who she was talking about.

'He's going to trial soon. Amanda – I mean Phillips . . .' (they were all referred to by their last names in the newspapers) ' . . . has already been sentenced. And Ahearn got sent to Broadmoor. Turns out she'd been skipping out on a lot of medication.'

'The *mechants* are behind bars. *Une fin heureuse?*'

'No, I think my *fin* will not terribly be *heureuse*.'

'That doesn't make any sense.'

He took another sip of water. Nervous, for some reason. He thought maybe it was some kind of PTSD. His doctor said it was a side-effect of being normal and sober. He decided to go for it. 'Have you eaten? I know a good place.'

'Are you asking me out on a date?'

'I guess I am.'

She mused for a moment. 'Okay. *J'adorerais.*'

'Good. Great,' he said, and then chuckled. 'It occurs to me that I still don't know your name.'

She laughed, and put out her hand. 'I'm Audrey.'

He shook it. 'Morgan Sheppard.'

She laughed, 'I know.'

Acknowledgements

Firstly, I wouldn't be a writer without my grandfather who encouraged my love of books and inspired me to start writing my own. Given that this novel was written as my thesis for the MA in Creative Writing (Crime/ Thriller) at City University London, the number of people who have been part of it is rather astronomical. Firstly, I would like to thank Claire McGowan, the course leader, who was always there when I needed a helping hand, and my personal 'celebrity guest' tutor A.K. Benedict, who believed in me from the very start, even when I didn't believe in myself. Without the guidance of these two people, this book would not be in your hands today. They were always there to pick me up when I was down (one time, literally). To William Ryan, who offered help in the early stages of the novel's life. Of course, to all the wonderful people I met throughout the MA course and helped me along the way. I couldn't have asked for better classmates. To the #SauvLife crew (simply put, we're a crew and we like sauvignon blanc), Fran Dorricott, Jenny Lewin and Lizzie Curle, some of the most talented and kind people I have ever met. To my wonderful agent Hannah Sheppard, who is incredibly dedicated and didn't mind having to explain incredibly simple things to me about business. To my amazing editor Francesca Pathak, who was behind this book from the second she read it and sourced a horse-head mask in record time to attempt (and succeed) to wow me. And finally, to all the people at Orion, who have made me feel perfectly at home. An incredible thank you to everyone.

If you enjoyed **GUESS WHO**, you will love the next
thriller from the new King of the Locked Room Mystery,
Chris McGeorge.

NOW YOU SEE ME

Six people went in. Only one came out . . .
In 2014, six students were on a barging holiday on the
Huddersfield Narrow Canal. They came to Standedge
Tunnel, the longest canal tunnel in England. Six
students go in, and two and a half hours later, the
boat reappears on the other side with only one of the
students, unconscious, and the dog.

Five years later, Robert Ferringham, a middle aged
and jaded journalist, decides to write a book about the
Standedge Six. He sees the case from every angle – the
law, the conspiracy theorists, the supernatural cultists.
But what is he really searching for? And do the answers
he's looking for lie deep within the darkness of the
tunnel?

Turn the page for an early extract now.

Chapter One

YOU ARE RECEIVING A TELEPHONE CALL FROM 'HMP New Hall'. THERE MAY BE REVERSE CHARGES ASSOCIATED WITH ACCEPTING THIS CALL. IF YOU ACCEPT THE CALL, PLEASE PRESS 1

— '... ... ...'

YOU ARE RECEIVING A TELEPHONE CALL FROM—

— 1.

— *'Hello?'*

— ***Feedback***

— 'Hello? Who is this?'

— '... Hello ... I've been calling ...'

— 'Who is this? What do you want?'

— '... Is this Mr Ferringham? Robert Ferringham?'

— 'Who is this?'

— '. . . I didn't do it, Mr Ferringham. I didn't kill them.'

— 'Who is this?'

— '. . . I didn't do it . . .'

— 'Tell me who this is or I'm hanging up.'

— '. . . I didn't do it, Mr Ferringham. We went through, all six of us. And only I came out. But I didn't do it.'

— 'Last chance, I'm going to hang up.'

— '*WAIT* . . . my name is Matt McConnell. My aunt calls me Matthew. You have to help me, Mr Ferringham. Help me, please.'

— 'I have no idea who you are.'

— '. . . I'm Matt McConnell. My aunt calls me—'

— 'Yes I got that, your aunt calls you Matthew. But I have no idea who you are. Why the hell would I help you?'

— 'We went through, Mr Ferringham. Standedge. It's a canal tunnel. The longest in Britain. We went through on a narrowboat – me and my friends. I was driving. But

I can't remember anything after we went in the tunnel. And – they're gone, Mr Ferringham.

— 'What do you mean?'

— 'My friends. Five friends. Five people. They're gone. Vanished – inside the tunnel. I was found knocked out on the deck. Alone, with only the dog. There's no way they could be gone. But they are.'

— 'What?'

— 'Five people. My friends. Disappeared. Into thin air. I don't know where they went. But they think I killed them. And I didn't, Mr Ferringham. I didn't.

— 'Wait . . . Why did you call me?'

— 'What?'

— 'Why did you call me?'

— '. . . because she said I could trust you. She said if I ever needed help, I should come to you.'

— 'Who told you?'

— '. . . She did . . . your wife . . . Samantha.'

— 'My wife has been missing for three years.'

— 'I know but . . .'

— 'What? You're breaking up?'

— *Feedback*

— 'Hello? . . . Hello?'

— *Feedback*

Don't miss out – order your copy today.

LES ANGES
ET LES FAUCONS

Du même auteur

AUX MÊMES ÉDITIONS

Les Flamboyants
roman, prix Goncourt 1976; « Points Roman » n° 377

La Diane rousse
roman, 1978; « Points Roman » n° 331

Le Dernier Viking
roman, 1980; « Points Roman » n° 58

Les Forteresses noires
roman, 1982; « Points Roman » n° 122

La Caverne céleste
roman, 1984; « Points Roman » n° 246

Le Paradis des orages
roman, 1986; « Points Roman » n° 263

L'Atelier du peintre
roman, 1988; « Points Roman » n° 360

L'Orgie, la neige
roman, 1990; « Points Roman » n° 461

Colère
roman, 1992; « Points Roman » n° 615

L'Arbre-piège
coll. « Petit Point » n° 57, 1993

CHEZ D'AUTRES ÉDITEURS

La Toison
roman, Gallimard, 1972

La Lisière
roman, Gallimard, 1973
« Folio » n° 2124

L'Abîme
roman, Gallimard, 1974

Bernard Louedin
Bibliothèque des arts, 1980

L'Ombre de la bête
Balland, 1981

Egon Schiele
Éditions Flohic, 1992

Georges Mathieu (*en coll.*)
Nouvelles Éditions françaises, 1993

PATRICK GRAINVILLE

LES ANGES
ET
LES FAUCONS

roman

ÉDITIONS DU SEUIL
27, rue Jacob, Paris VIe

IL A ÉTÉ TIRÉ DE CET OUVRAGE
VINGT-CINQ EXEMPLAIRES
SUR PAPIER VERGÉ INGRES DE LANA
DONT VINGT NUMÉROTÉS DE 1 À 20
ET CINQ HORS COMMERCE
NUMÉROTÉS DE H.C. I À H.C. V
LE TOUT CONSTITUANT
L'ÉDITION ORIGINALE

ISBN 2-02-020604-8 ÉD. BROCHÉE
ISBN 2-02-021597-7 ÉD. DE LUXE

A cette époque, personne ne parlait des faucons de Notre-Dame de Paris. Ni le journal, ni la télévision. Ces oiseaux n'étaient pas encore médiatiques. La cathédrale visitée par les touristes du monde entier restait l'île mystérieuse, une forêt de pinacles et de gargouilles sauvages. Moi, j'avais repéré les faucons avec émerveillement, car je m'y connaissais depuis l'enfance en bestiaire de tout genre, je me cherchais des totems, des filiations ailées, monstrueuses. Ce rapport de la madone et des rapaces me fascinait. De mon poste, sur la tour sud, j'avais vu un faucon fondre du haut d'une flèche dans la main du grand ange vert et central, à la croisée du transept. Là, un moineau expira, pantelant, éventré sous le bec du prédateur. Un battement d'ailes, une courte piaillerie. L'ange souriait toujours. Le faucon s'envola, mince, véloce et courbé sous la voûte céleste. Je le vis tout là-haut, vif et brun dans l'azur. Il planait. La grande cathédrale dormait dans le tollé des ponts, des îlots, des boucles et des eaux.

De nos jours, il n'est pas rare qu'on installe, comme au printemps 1991, un système vidéo dans le jardin de l'arche-vêché, ce qui permet aux visiteurs d'admirer les faucons et

d'espionner leurs nichées. On peut même, moyennant une pièce, diriger une lunette sur un trou de boulin ou la cavité trifoliée d'un pinacle et avoir en gros plan le bréchet du rapace.

Vingt ans plus tôt, il n'y avait que mon regard et, de loin en loin, un ornithologue discret qui venait compter les oiseaux. C'était avant que j'apprenne que Notre-Dame, en fait, avait été restaurée de fond en comble par Viollet-le-Duc. Je croyais que j'avais élu domicile sur le temple originel. Tel était mon rocher, mes racines dans le passé mystique. J'étais étudiant. Je venais les après-midi d'automne lire au sommet de la tour sud. J'y emmenais Anny pour flirter. Le toit de plomb n'avait pas encore été isolé des visiteurs par le grillage quadrangulaire que l'on voit aujourd'hui. Les gens circulent dans une sorte de cage métallique. On ne peut plus toucher la madone et la mère. Jadis, Notre-Dame était nue et j'étais son enfant contre son sein gothique, dans une robe d'ogives. Je ne connaissais pas encore Wolf et Ehra, je n'avais vu que leurs noms énormes inscrits dans la matière plombée du toit, au milieu d'un brouillard d'initiales et d'autographes, la nébuleuse des signes qui coiffe la tour sud. Grand grimoire où les voyageurs du globe avaient déposé leur empreinte superstitieuse comme sur le corps de la Vierge.

On lisait Wolf, Ehra mais aussi Amador et Rawi. On les déchiffre encore aujourd'hui. J'ai vérifié. Certes, il y a Bébert et Alice... La poésie n'a pas de limites. L'avantage de la grille est qu'elle empêche d'effacer les noms du passé sous des signatures, des entailles neuves. Ainsi le toit de la tour m'offre intact le manuscrit de mes vingt ans. On y avait, Anny et moi, fiancé nos prénoms.

C'était l'époque de ma logeuse manchote. Oui, Marguerite était manchote. Un jour elle me dévoila pourquoi. L'horreur fut sur moi. Je devais entrer dans la vie sous l'augure de cette

vieillarde et de la Vierge. Oserais-je entrer dans cette vie immense comme la ville ? La formule me remplissait d'effroi. Je sentais physiquement que je longeais le bord de l'avenir comme celui de l'abîme. Nulle évidence ne m'habitait. J'étais comme au paroxysme d'un désir de vivre et de mourir, tout au fond d'une peur qui ne m'a jamais quitté. Mon angoisse étincelait dans le vide du monde. Et ce feu intérieur pouvait me sauver ou me tuer.

J'habitais 9, rue Pavée, juste devant la synagogue. Aujourd'hui le 9 est un bâtiment officiel, signalé par un drapeau tricolore. Naguère, il abritait des logements dévolus à des gens problématiques et pauvres. L'immeuble a une histoire puisqu'il constitua une dépendance de la prison de la Force. Ma chambre possédait encore des barreaux. Ce qui apparentait un peu mon destin à celui de Fabrice del Dongo. Surtout quand, à travers les barreaux, je contemplais une très jeune Juive qui, une fois par semaine, venait suivre un cours dans une école religieuse qui jouxtait ma façade, côté cour. Elle me regardait et je la regardais avec toute l'impossibilité, la nostalgie causée par les barreaux et quelque chose de plus grave encore, une tonalité plus triste que je ne pouvais expliquer. Tout cela est trop précis pour mentir. Je ne pense pas que la vérité littérale dans le roman soit d'une essence supérieure aux fables de l'imaginaire, mais j'ai besoin de dire que Marguerite a vécu et moi dormi dans la geôle de ma chambre où je faisais l'amour avec Anny. Des prisonniers avaient souffert et s'étaient langui là où nos corps s'étreignaient dans la jeunesse et la liberté. Des fous avaient été ligotés sur leur lit là où tous nos désirs s'étaient donné licence.

J'avais trouvé l'adresse sur une petite fiche d'un service universitaire qui dépannait les étudiants en quête d'une chambre et j'avais débarqué au métro Saint-Paul, faubourg Saint-Antoine. La rue moutonnait dans l'effervescence du soir. Mais l'espace me parut grand ouvert, balayé par un autre flux : quel souffle, quel miroitement, quelle onde de vie dévalaient largement, se resserraient plus loin, au bout du faubourg dans une sorte de défilé où le grouillement des gens devenait noir ?

Le porche du 9, rue Pavée était ouvert. Je traversai un couloir gris et galeux et l'escalier dédalien s'offrit à ma vue, avec ses paliers branlants, ses rampes tortueuses, ses appartements suspendus, mal alignés sur des plans irréguliers, troués de petites portes. Grosse baraque zolienne décrépite et tordue, vieux bagne échafaudé dans l'ombre, tout feuilleté de plafonds et spiralé. Telle était la carcasse de cette geôle antique convertie en habitat des pauvres. Tout en haut, au cinquième étage, la porte de Marguerite L. était close. En face, une autre porte pareillement verrouillée, bosselée, s'encadrait dans une cloison elle-même pourvue d'une fenêtre intérieure donnant sur le couloir. Il me sembla voir un rideau bouger. J'eus le sentiment d'une compartimentation extrême, comme si la bâtisse se divisait, se démultipliait en agrégats de logis contigus ou décalés, réminiscences des anciennes cellules dans la voltige du grand escalier.

Je redescendis et le vaste courant de la rue me saisit de nouveau. J'étais éclaboussé par son déferlement en pleine travée où pétillaient les braises du soir sur les grappes humaines. Je perçus, tout à coup devant moi, la bousculade ponctuée d'exclamations, un trottinement qui rameutait le voisinage, le coloriait de nuances familières, c'était un chahut, un sillage allègres. Je sus que c'était Marguerite. L'intuition m'assaillit à regarder ce feu follet sexagénaire tirant son sac

10

bourré de victuailles, d'un pas véloce et tressautant. Petite, bouclée, lunettée et pas jolie du tout, le menton en galoche et une raideur le long du flanc droit... bancale comme sa maison, mais leste, volubile, aiguillonnant tout sur son passage, interpellant son monde, ravie de rentrer chez elle, de s'exhiber et de lancer des blagues : Marguerite. Elle me vit hésiter devant le porche. Et elle non plus ne douta guère à voir ce gringalet anxieux à la mine de papier mâché. Elle m'arraisonna, me dévisagea avec cette vivacité curieuse composée de méfiance et de flair gourmand. J'étais son étudiant, nouvelle recrue, son locataire pour une ou deux années. Jeune homme entrant dans la vie, frais émoulu de sa province, fragile, maigre, malhabile, se profilant au seuil du monde, anguleux dans son rôle, timide et âpre dans cette tension, cette question du devenir.

— Venez ! me dit-elle avec entrain.

Car elle était heureuse. Ses étudiants successifs conféraient une originalité à Marguerite L., un prestige qui la distinguait des voisins. Elle arborait ses étudiants comme les échantillons d'une faune surprenante et changeante. Chacun possédait son histoire tragique ou comique. J'entrai dans l'appartement, microcosme vieillot et tarabiscoté qui reproduisait à son échelle l'allure fantastique de la maison globale. Plans disjoints, lignes instables. Pourtant, les rayons du soir éclairaient le papier fleuri, le mobilier Henri II, le linoléum rosé, les napperons, le tourne-disque sur le buffet qu'elle mit en marche tout de suite, choisissant une indicible ritournelle d'un certain André Dassary, qu'elle surnommait : « mon Dédé »..., une sorte de Georges Guétary en plus naïf et boute-en-train. Elle filait d'une pièce à l'autre, appelant sa chatte, l'aguichant de louanges amoureuses et j'avais l'impression que sa seule présence ravivait la lumière, provoquait la musique, faisait luire les meubles, le rouge des

géraniums dans les jardinières sur cour. Dans ce décor râpé, objectivement sinistre, elle distillait un enchantement. Marguerite, c'était l'allégro malgré ses déficits, une accumulation de ratages et de malheurs fantastiques. Mais à travers ce fracas vital, parfois son œil fixait un autre horizon, on ne savait quelle scène qui la hantait, la happait dans un élan avide et coupable. Son œil devenait morne et neutre, puis étincelait d'un éclat vicieux. J'ignorais encore la dualité de ma logeuse, ce combat acharné entre deux tentations, deux convoitises. Marguerite adorait la vie, elle était fascinée par la mort. C'était un mélange de désir et de peur. Sa curiosité était plus forte que sa terreur. Elle n'avait de cesse de s'approcher au plus près du foyer béant. Elle se penchait en avant. Elle regardait. Elle buvait des yeux l'horreur avec une excitation quasi sexuelle. Passionnée, bariolée de verve et de vie mais nécrophile dans les coulisses, aimantée par l'extrême limite, la bordure noire du néant. Voilà ce que je devais découvrir très vite.

Et tout à coup, pour ne rien me cacher et me mettre à l'aise d'emblée, elle attrapa de son bras vivant l'autre raide et tombant. Pris depuis le début dans sa farandole, je n'avais rien vu. En me révélant son infirmité elle déboîta la prothèse. Je vis la manche de sa robe se vider soudain et surgir un bras de celluloïd rose, membre de poupée articulé à une main factice qu'elle déposa d'abord sur la table. Le tour était joué. Elle me lorgnait pour voir si je tenais le coup, acceptais les données... C'était tout naturel pour elle, mais moi j'étais surprise. Plus tard, je m'habituai à ce qu'elle enlève, en débarquant de son travail, la totalité de sa robe avec le bras arrimé dans la manche. Elle enfilait la panoplie sur le dossier d'une chaise et tourniquait en combinaison miel dans la salle à manger. C'était sa tenue favorite et séductrice. Car Marguerite se voulait vamp et c'était le prodige, en dépit de

ses disgrâces. Pour un peu elle se serait trouvée belle. A tout bout de champ, elle découvrait ses jambes aux mollets fermes et roses. Et sous prétexte que la peau était vierge de varices, elle vous fichait ses guibolles sous le nez comme des trésors. Mais peut-être que le bras manquant revalorisait et vivifiait, par compensation, les membres intacts. Mutilée, mille bras, mille jambes lui fleurissaient, des myriades de mouvements l'élançaient. Elle montrait les deux jambes saines et courtes, les contemplait avec ravissement comme si elles venaient de lui pousser, de naître, tandis que la robe et son bras postiche se découpaient sur le dossier de la chaise, à contre-jour.

Cette vision bouffonne et lugubre perdit bientôt son aspect maléfique, je n'y fis plus attention. La robe ankylosée du bras rejoignit le buffet Henri II, le papier fleuri, les napperons, les disques de « mon Dédé adoré », les accessoires d'un décor amical et chaleureux où dissonait la chatte.

Elle me présenta Toufflette, rousse et blanche, créature malingre, revêche et tachetée comme une hyène. La bête me prit en grippe aussitôt. Toutes les réserves d'amour de Marguerite avaient reflué sur ce monstre. Armée de ciseaux, ma logeuse découpait une part de rognons de porc puants et violacés que la chatte déchiquetait avec des rafales de miaulements et des convulsions hystériques, et gardait l'autre part pour sa propre consommation, car elle adorait ces abats bon marché, bien gras et rissolés. Elle ignorait qu'ils regorgeaient de cholestérol et lui ruinaient le cœur. A moins qu'en secret elle eût pressenti le péril et choisi de l'affronter par défi, sans vraiment croire à la mort mais pour toiser la camarde et la chasser.

Marguerite m'entraîna dans un couloir suffisamment élargi pour contenir une machine à laver d'un côté et, de l'autre, une douche dans un recoin. C'étaient deux merveilles enviées

13

par les voisins. La jeune crémière du faubourg, tous les samedis, venait prendre une douche et Marguerite dans ses moments de générosité fourrait dans sa machine le linge de ses amis... Ses étudiants, sa laveuse électrique, sa douche d'émail, son grille-pain automatique la plaçaient au-dessus du commun et fortifiaient une renommée de fantaisie et de singularité.

Ma chambre était peinte en blanc, large, fraîche, donnant sur une autre cour intérieure. Un dessus-de-lit à carreaux rouge et noir de belle qualité et des rideaux de même couleur égayaient tout ce blanc. La chambre d'étudiant était la surprise de l'appartement, son fleuron. Marguerite la faisait visiter à ses nouvelles connaissances comme le Sacré-Cœur. Chaque étudiant préludait une aventure gonflée de promesses et de rêveries, car Marguerite berçait son content de bovarysme. La chambre recevait chaque année un nouveau prince adolescent, plutôt désargenté, pâlichon, exilé mais paré d'un lustre intellectuel qui propageait dans l'appartement les subtiles vibrations de l'esprit ! Ma logeuse participait de ce principe lumineux, s'y ébattait avec exubérance et vanité. Quand elle prit conscience qu'en ces matières, harcelé par les doutes et l'angoisse de foirer, je ne lésinais pas, en rajoutais plutôt dans la saga universitaire, elle se prit d'un véritable intérêt pour moi... Lorsqu'elle disait « mon étudiant », il ne s'agissait plus d'une allusion à tel ou tel locataire du passé, mais bien de moi et de moi seul. Toutefois, Marguerite nourrissait un rêve plus personnel encore et qui m'éclipsait tout à fait. Je le livre comme tel. Elle désirait accueillir un grand étudiant noir. C'était sa chimère d'Afrique. Je ne suis pas sûr qu'elle y mettait un vœu de cosmopolitisme et de coopération désintéressés. Non, c'était surtout un fantasme où couvaient des appétits fous. Je ne puis plus douter qu'elle imaginait une idylle superlative, dénigrée par les voisins et dont elle se fût nimbée, auréolée

14

comme d'une légende lascive et quasi barbare. Ainsi, les prouesses supposées de mon intelligence fascinaient moins Marguerite que les féeries d'un désir tabou. Cet étudiant, elle l'eut enfin, car elle le demanda expressément au service universitaire. Je puis maintenant dévoiler qu'il fut mon successeur. Mais il se révéla introverti, un beu bègue, adorable et rêveur, un être en pointillés, tout en spéculations évanescentes, l'étudiant le plus délicat, le plus effarouché et le moins dionysiaque qu'on pût imaginer. Quand l'année suivante elle arriva chez moi, flanquée de son nouveau locataire, je compris, au premier coup d'œil, la déception de Marguerite, l'écrasement de sa belle utopie torride. Mais une autre impression plus sournoise m'effleura. La robe de Marguerite me lançait de petits appels mystérieux et quasi excitants. Je cherchais la raison de ce phénomène magique. Et tout à coup, me revinrent les étreintes avec Anny sur le dessus-de-lit à carreaux rouge et noir. Tel était précisément le motif de la nouvelle robe de Marguerite, qu'elle venait de tailler dans l'étoffe de notre amour. Il me sembla voir en transparence nos corps adolescents et nus, affamés, agrippés dans les plis, le roulis du dessus-de-lit rouge et noir. Marguerite arborait le drapeau de nos jouissances comme un trophée de nostalgie.

Quelque temps après mon arrivée, j'appris qu'une étudiante m'avait précédé, anorexique, délinquante et belle. Mais elle mourut en juin d'une overdose d'héroïne. L'atmosphère de ma chambre en fut altérée. Je ne pensais plus qu'à la trépassée splendide. Bientôt prit corps ce pressentiment de jouer, en cette dernière année d'études, une partie serrée, vertigineuse, sous l'œil de Marguerite dont je ne savais s'il me

serait faste ou funeste... Très vite, au 9, rue Pavée, j'eus la conviction que je devais franchir la ligne, passer dans la vie mais que ma réussite était incertaine, que des embûches se mettraient au travers, des épreuves épineuses, que cette ligne se déroberait, s'éloignerait, que je connaîtrais des trébuchements, des chutes plus graves, peut-être irrémédiables et que ce faubourg Saint-Antoine où j'avais vu un soir crépiter, rouler une vague de lumière ne m'entraînerait pas forcément avec lui, dans l'essor de l'épopée collective. Car c'étaient bien l'aventure de la foule, le souffle de la destinée humaine qui me parurent si beaux, si désirables, pourtant inaccessibles.

Quand je sortis de chez Marguerite, à la nuit, les cafés brillaient le long du faubourg, il faisait tiède. Des couples rentraient chez eux avec des airs câlins, quelques silhouettes plus solitaires se croisaient, se hâtaient. Les automobiles moins nombreuses glissaient vers les prochains feux rouges. La station de métro Saint-Paul, dont j'aimais le nom biblique et dépouillé, s'ouvrait calmement lumineuse. Je sentis mon cœur se serrer. Je savais bien que tout allait commencer ou finir. La joie et l'effroi s'enflaient partout dans la ville, serpentaient, passaient dans le grondement, l'éclat triste et jaune des métros, leur chuintement à l'arrêt, ce sifflement morose, épuisé. Je voyais la tête de mes semblables, figures butées, égocentriques, gardant jalousement leur destin, indifférents à la lueur blafarde des compartiments. Il fallait donc entrer dans ces tunnels, rouler, parcourir ces labyrinthes, traverser sans cesse des séquences de ténèbres que coupaient, à intervalles plus ou moins longs, les stations, leurs quais éphémères, soudain clairs comme des apparitions, des sursis, des cavernes aux rivages hallucinés. J'étais emporté et je craignais de n'aborder jamais.

J'étais installé depuis un mois. Anny, chaque week-end, venait de Lorraine pour me voir. Nous nous aimions et nos rencontres avaient pris un tour assidu. J'allais la prendre tous les samedis, gare de l'Est, à midi. Je scrutais la foule du train, cherchant sa fine silhouette. Je redoutais toujours quelque contretemps imprévu, quelque fatalité. Des colosses lorrains, des affairistes pressés, des chariots submergés de bagages la planquaient. Enfin ses cheveux courts et blonds perçaient au sein du pullulement, leur couleur clignait, s'éteignait, ressuscitait. J'étais sauvé par ce sillage clair. J'embrassais Anny avec avidité. Nous allions au restaurant. Mais le repas me restait en travers de la gorge tant mon désir d'Anny me spasmait. J'étais d'une hystérie totale et charmante... J'avais envie de vomir et souvent je le faisais. Je finis par expliquer à mon amante l'impossibilité où j'étais d'avaler quoi que ce fût, car ma fringale était tout autre. Elle fut compréhensive et nous courûmes désormais nous coucher dès la sortie du train. Elle était toute brûlante et béante. J'entrais dans son ruissellement. Une impression de chaud, de fusion, de joie goulue, fulgurante. J'éjaculais presque tout de suite. A peine une pause et nous reprenions longuement. Nous partions

17

enfin déjeuner. Cette fois, la nourriture restait. L'après-midi, nous traversions le faubourg jusqu'au Pont-Marie. J'aimais ce pont, la simplicité de son nom, c'était un joli pont ingénu, ignoré. Quand nous y passions enlacés, Anny et moi, nous sentions toute la limpidité et la beauté de notre amour. Ma peur de la vie diminuait un moment. Mais tout à coup la possibilité, la proximité du bonheur me l'arrachaient. Un vertige me saisissait au cœur de l'évidence. Je savais que pour Anny la vie allait de soi et qu'elle était entrée dans notre amour sans angoisse. Tout uniment, comme dans la transparence. Alors je redoutais de n'être pas au diapason, d'être inférieur à son sens du bonheur, de le gâcher par ma peur, de flancher, de déraper et de dévoiler ainsi à Anny mon incapacité, ma tare. Comme si j'étais ailleurs que dans le plein courant de la vie, à côté, en dessous, instable dans les ressacs, sur une crête qui menaçait de rompre. Je craignais surtout de perdre Anny, de l'effrayer en lui avouant ce gouffre. Pourtant l'île de la Cité composait un royaume d'objets parfaits, tranquilles, éternels qui auraient dû me rassurer, me dérober la prémonition du désastre. Je noyais mon regard dans la Seine, sa longue faille sombre et mouvante, et mes appréhensions renaissaient à la vue de ce fleuve un peu faux, urbain, qu'on imaginait mal venir de la nature mais dont le bouillonnement semblait sécrété par les salissures des avenues et du métro.

Ce jour-là, comme d'habitude, nous rejoignîmes Notre-Dame et ses tours. Une escalade de quatre cents marches. La première partie dans l'escalier nord, puis nous traversions la grande galerie et la dernière étape s'effectuait dans la tour sud. En effet la tour nord était interdite. Mais justement elle me manquait. Au moment où nous débouchions dans la grande galerie, on apercevait la petite porte close derrière laquelle l'escalier conduisait à la tour inconnue...

18

Au cours de notre ascension, nous nous arrêtions souvent dans les encoignures percées de fenêtres d'où l'on voyait Paris, les fines vertèbres des ponts sur la Seine moins proche et dont les eaux perdaient leur aspect noir et profond, allongeaient une lame ciselée qui s'harmonisait bien avec la texture des pierres et chassait l'idée de flux et de mort. Fouettés par les courants d'air, serrés l'un contre l'autre, dans chaque niche nous échangions des baisers et des caresses. On montait vite exprès, l'essoufflement était un jeu, un pari. Les murs s'enroulaient en un cornet de plus en plus exigu, couvert d'autographes, de noms du monde entier, de paraphes qui annonçaient ceux du toit, tout là-haut. Pantelants, on touchait du doigt la colonne fourmillante des mots qui battaient à la cadence de notre sang. Tous ces voyageurs et ces amants nous avaient précédés, avaient gravé des cœurs, des serments, des flèches, des rébus dans la patine du mur couleur cendre et lisse comme un os. La cage de l'escalier géant nous parlait comme les bas-reliefs d'un pharaonique tombeau, un goulet de pyramide entièrement revêtu de hiéroglyphes... Et nous savions que tant de noms coulés dans le cou de la tour, formant des charabias et des imbroglios, vocables étrangers emmêlés, nous aspiraient sur leurs ailes vers les sommets, vers le toit où Wolf, Ehra hérissaient leurs entailles si fraîches, si étincelantes qu'on les eût dites inscrites dans le plomb par un bec de faucon. De l'autre côté, aux antipodes, Amador et Rawi offraient des caractères plus épanouis, plus anciens, dont l'éclat tendre rayonnait doucement, tourné vers le chevet de Notre-Dame, vers le jardin cerné d'eaux, à l'Orient du monde.

Ehra et Wolf, eux, faisaient front et corps avec la façade de la cathédrale, sa rosace, son œil écarquillé, son grand porche, ses rangées d'anges longilignes aux bréchets de hérons gothiques. Nous nous sommes penchés, Anny et moi, sur ces

19

prénoms polaires, échevelés, qui nous subjuguaient comme des étoiles.

Vers le soir, nous vîmes deux silhouettes s'approcher du toit et s'incliner exactement sur les prénoms gravés. La surprise nous saisit. Le jeune homme et sa compagne contemplaient les signatures avec voracité. Ils souriaient et semblaient s'assurer de la prégnance des lettres vitales et de leur union. Une prémonition nous envahit, Anny et moi. Immédiatement. Wolf était-il ce grand jeune homme aux cheveux courts et blonds, au regard bleu très clair devant Ehra, la brune, si longue, si élancée, au visage immaculé, charnu ? Ils se ressemblaient en dépit de la différence des cheveux. Ils admiraient les astres jumeaux de leurs noms. Ils se tournèrent vers le vent vif et Wolf montra son visage d'une virilité ambiguë, voluptueuse. Pommettes hautes, lèvres minces, prunelles de chat enfoncées sous des arcades sourcilières brusques. Ehra se pencha vers son cou et l'embrassa, ce qui nous émut. Oui, nous étions sûrs qu'il s'agissait des signataires célestes, car ils revenaient à leurs noms qu'ils touchaient, qu'ils couvaient de regards superstitieux.

... Alors un faucon dessina une vrille autour de la tour nord, la tour fermée, inaccessible. Quels signes étaient inscrits sur son toit de plomb ? L'oiseau descendit en flèche et se posa sur l'épaule du diable bosselé et cornu, accroupi en dessous de nous, le long de la grande galerie médiane. Personne ne l'avait vu, hormis Wolf. Le garçon montra l'oiseau à sa compagne. Ehra riait. Sa poitrine s'enflait sous son tee-shirt noir. Wolf passa son bras autour de la taille de la jeune fille. Leur couple ne quittait pas des yeux le faucon.

Nous n'étions donc plus les seuls, Anny et moi, à partager le secret des rapaces et des anges. Nos rivaux, Ehra et Wolf, venaient de se découvrir à nous, à la cime de Notre-Dame. On les trouvait trop beaux, trop cristallins. On voyait des

frissons nerveux filer sous le visage de Wolf, sa peau trop sensible et trop pâle, veinée de bleu. Sa pomme d'Adam montait et descendait dans son cou et donnait une impression d'âpreté et d'étranglement à cette figure où brûlait une convoitise froide. Ehra le regardait avec adoration. Ils disparurent. Était-ce vraiment eux, narcissiques, orgueilleux, qui avaient sculpté ces lettres capitales dans le plomb, sur le crâne de la cathédrale ?

C'est en redescendant que j'éprouvai l'élancement douloureux, un fer ardent au genou. Je m'arrêtai un instant, puis en boitant, au bras d'Anny, rongé par l'inquiétude, je repris le chemin de l'ancienne prison de la Force. Ce fut le premier signe du combat. Je ne savais pas encore que la bataille avait commencé, qu'il faudrait disputer le terrain, pied à pied, à la maladie, au mauvais œil, à Marguerite, qu'Anny m'accompagnerait, présente, confiante toujours, se demandant ce qui m'arrivait, pourquoi j'attirais tant de foudres, étonnée, mais attentive, clémente. Sa cohérence me protégeant dans l'enceinte du mal qui me cernait, me hantait, grandissait.

En rentrant, nous avons croisé, dans l'escalier, Johann Neuzil, un voisin. Il me vit boiter et s'enquit de ma douleur. Il nous regardait avec bonté et sa gentillesse nous toucha. Il nous invita à venir chez lui boire un thé. Son appartement était bourré de vieilleries dorées, avec deux gros fauteuils profonds, aux ramages luxuriants et fanés. On entendait Neuzil s'affairer dans sa cuisine. Il revint avec un plateau, une jolie théière d'argent, dodue, cannelée et trois tasses de porcelaine pâle. Le thé sentait bon. Neuzil aimait servir le breuvage chaud et roux. Il nous regardait avec bonté. Mais cette bonté était intelligente et précise. Elle imprimait sur son visage une attention lucide et douce. Une certaine interrogation se lisait aussi sur ses traits, comme une question gentille. Mlle Poulet qui habitait juste au-dessous de l'appartement de

Marguerite, et qui était une ancienne infirmière sexagénaire mais vierge, avait inventé la plus belle formule pour baptiser Neuzil. Elle l'appelait « l'homme gentil ». Pourtant Mlle Poulet ne pratiquait guère une langue édulcorée, sa virginité allant de pair avec un verbe rude et cru. Quant à Marguerite, elle surnommait Neuzil : « Soudain », sous prétexte qu'il agrémentait ses phrases de soudain multiples et intempestifs. Anny et moi n'allions pas tarder à vérifier cet usage immodéré quand Neuzil nous dit :

— Les enfants, vous pouvez boire, soudain !

Mais ce soudain sonnait comme un à présent, un désormais. C'était un mot bref et doux, engageant, qui, loin de marquer une action brusque, ouvrait plutôt sur l'avenir, un mot de dialogue et de liaison que Neuzil rendait délectable et familier. Anny et moi étions tombés amoureux du petit adverbe de Neuzil, car nous pressentions que son tempérament y révélait ses inclinations les plus suaves et les plus singulières.

Alors il me parla de mon genou :

— Vous avez toujours mal ?...

— Oui, c'est un pincement tenace et cuisant.

Il me regarda avec une vigilance aimable. Il avait l'air de me sonder, de remonter à la source de mon mal, de le situer, de le replacer dans la totalité de ma personne. Puis il me dit :

— Ça ne devrait pas être grave... Au pire, c'est un petit rhumatisme inflammatoire, à votre âge on guérit de ces choses-là.

Mais Neuzil ne paraissait pas se débarrasser du problème par un optimisme de commande, non, j'avais le sentiment qu'il disait sa vraie pensée.

Il nous regardait avaler le thé avec un évident plaisir. Les joues d'Anny étaient roses. Elle avait chaud. Il nous resservit une tasse de liquide plus noir, en s'amusant de notre

légère grimace qui accusait le changement de saveur :

— Ce n'est pas si désagréable que ça finalement quand la saveur s'altère, presque à sa limite, qu'elle bascule dans ce qui la corrompt... hein ! C'est un petit moment amer et rigolo.

Et je compris que Neuzil était un homme plein de finesse et que la moindre circonstance était pour lui l'occasion d'une expérience, voire d'une révélation. Un gros album de peinture était posé sur une console. Mes yeux furent attirés par la couverture qui montrait le portrait d'un jeune homme aux cheveux courts et bruns, aux pommettes saillantes et aux yeux fulgurants. Le personnage exhalait quelque chose de sauvage, de passionné, comme une colère lyrique. On sentait aussi une provocation orgueilleuse. Mais c'est le dessin qui frappait par sa violence et sa sûreté. Quelques coups de pinceau en soulignaient le tracé avec sensualité. Le peintre s'était gardé de saturer son dessin de matière colorée, bien au contraire, avec une sorte de négligé génial il s'arrêtait dans certaines zones. Mais cette incomplétude, loin de frustrer, de donner une impression d'inachèvement, renforçait la vivacité du portrait, son caractère véloce et spontané. L'accomplissement suprême tenait justement à cette puissance de l'ébauche qui n'avait nul besoin d'être continuée et se dispensait royalement de prouver davantage, car il avait fait mouche d'une seule flèche. Et son œuvre était saisie dans cette convulsion immédiate et sanglante, comme la proie du faucon se débat dans un paroxysme de vie, écartelée, rougie, hérissée de plumes avant que la mort n'immobilise la transe, n'éteigne la roue du sacrifice.

Neuzil fut touché par ma fascination. Il me révéla le nom de l'artiste :

— C'est un autoportrait d'Egon Schiele.

Je ne connaissais pas. Et c'est dans mon imagination vierge

23

que s'inscrivit ce prénom dur et courbe, tel un bec, une serre d'oiseau, et ce nom rougi par ces voyelles centrales qui l'éclaboussaient dans un chuintement, un échevèlement de consonnes.

Neuzil ouvrit devant nous l'album et fit défiler des dessins inouïs d'adolescentes nues, cuisses ouvertes, pubis noirs, écarquillés, tandis que leurs visages juvéniles et beaux regardaient le peintre avec franchise, avec enfance, sans le moindre sourire aguicheur ou pervers. L'une d'elles, le menton appuyé sur un genou dressé, montrait sa fente et sa belle fourrure et regardait Schiele avec une évidence lisse où l'on percevait toutefois une légère pointe interrogative comme si, en pensée, elle s'était adressée à l'artiste pour lui dire : « Ça va comme cela ? C'est bien... c'est ce que vous vouliez... Je vois que vous êtes content. » C'est cet accord innocent et paisible avec l'attente de Schiele que le visage offrait. Puis arriva un portrait. Une jeune femme rousse était assise par terre, une main dans les cheveux. Ses grands yeux noirs et charbonneux fixaient le peintre, elle portait une chemise carmin, sa jupe très courte se retroussait sur les cuisses relevées dont on voyait la chair festonnée au-dessus du genou par les volutes d'une paire de bas rose orangé.

— C'est Valérie... Egon l'appelait Wally... Wally Neuzil.

Surpris, Anny et moi nous attendîmes la suite.

— Oui, Neuzil, mon nom... Wally était ma mère. Elle fut, à dix-sept ans, la maîtresse de Schiele, elle posa pour lui et il l'abandonna un peu plus tard pour se marier.

Neuzil attendit un peu et reprit :

— Ma mère est morte de la scarlatine en 1917, à vingt-trois ans. Elle était devenue infirmière, à la guerre. Elle resta donc pour moi cette jeune adolescente que vous voyez, le modèle préféré de Schiele, sa petite favorite.

— Pourquoi ne l'a-t-il pas épousée ? demanda Anny.

— Parce qu'elle n'avait pas très bonne réputation, qu'elle s'était peut-être prostituée, qu'elle avait sans doute été l'amante de Klimt avant de se jeter dans les bras de Schiele. Parce que ce dernier est tombé probablement amoureux de l'autre, la bourgeoise, Edith Harms qui devint sa femme. De toute façon l'aventure fut courte pour tous les trois. Edith, l'épouse, meurt de la grippe espagnole en 1918. Elle est enceinte. Egon meurt peu après, il a vingt-huit ans. Et Wally, ma mère, était morte l'année précédente. Ils meurent tous, très tôt, fauchés dans l'éclat du désir, la jouvence, le génie. C'est terrible. Des adolescents encore, innocents et violents... Il y a un doute sur l'identité de mon père. Avant son mariage, Schiele revoyait encore ma mère malgré l'interdiction d'Edith, sa fiancée. Il pourrait donc être mon père. Mais cela n'a pas été prouvé. Je rêve d'être un bâtard inconnu d'Egon Schiele. Ma mère disparaît deux ans après ma naissance. Orphelin, je suis placé chez une nourrice, puis dans une institution pour enfants abandonnés. Ma mère a-t-elle fréquenté d'autres hommes que Schiele, au moment de ma conception ? Ce n'était pas une fille effarouchée soudain.

Je remarquai au passage ce soudain impromptu... comme la signature de Neuzil, son tempo à lui et si beau.

— Voyez-vous, jeunes gens, j'adorerais être le fils d'Egon et de Wally, de leur passion presque taboue qui fit scandale à l'époque, car ma mère était mineure, car Schiele faisait poser nues ses modèles dans son jardin, au vu et au su de tous, car les adolescentes amoureuses et fugueuses venaient trouver refuge chez lui. J'aurais aimé être l'enfant de cette légende, avant la guerre, avant le mariage, avant l'épidémie de grippe, avant leur mort à tous. Aujourd'hui je ne possède presque rien de lui et de ma mère soudain, hormis quelques rares photos collectées plus tard par les historiens de la peinture. Mais heureusement, il y a ces autoportraits et ces nus de ma

mère. Je suis né de cette adolescente audacieuse et nue. Elle sera toujours nue pour moi. Il me semble qu'elle est morte ainsi et qu'il n'est pas de transition entre ma mère heureuse, exhibée devant son amant, et sa mort...

Après un silence, Neuzil murmura :

— Tous moururent au tout début. C'est comme si Egon Schiele avait d'avance compensé l'hécatombe par cette convoitise, cette contemplation insatiable des corps et de la chair.

Neuzil se ressaisit, s'excusa :

— Ah mais je suis trop lyrique et trop triste ! Tout cela, c'était jadis. Aujourd'hui, il n'y a ni guerre ni grippe espagnole. La mort n'existe plus, les enfants... Pour vous, c'est tout à fait inconnu, impossible...

On frappa à la porte. Deux hommes entrèrent, David et Maurice, flanqués d'un grand chien doux : Anchise. C'était un couple d'homosexuels qui occupait un appartement au rez-de-chaussée. David était vendeur dans une boutique du faubourg et Maurice garçon de café. Ils bricolaient volontiers et rendaient des services à tous les locataires de la maison. Anchise, leur chien policier, différait de ses congénères par sa taille géante. De quelles mutations ou autres manipulations génétiques procédait cette démesure ?... Mais le plus étonnant, c'était la tendresse d'Anchise, un chien qui ne gardait rien, qui n'aboyait que de plaisir dans une sorte de gémissement roucoulé. Marguerite le soupçonnait d'être débile.

— Il n'a pas de cervelle, le cabot des deux... (c'est par ce raccourci qu'elle désignait les amants). Un chien si doux que cela, c'est un peu écœurant. Vous pouvez lui enlever un os d'entre les crocs sans qu'il morde. Eh bien, moi, je préfère ma chatte, ma Toufflette. On la dit nocive mais elle n'est pas servile !

Marguerite avait des adjectifs, des mots choisis parfois.

26

Elle aimait bien parler, s'écouter parler, user d'expressions élégantes qui épataient la galerie. Neuzil regarda sa montre :
— Ah oui, c'est notre heure !
Puis s'adressant à nous, il s'expliqua :
— Ce sont mes pieds, il faut que je marche tous les jours, pour mes pieds... mon diabète vous comprenez, il faut que le sang circule.
Neuzil partit encadré de David et de Maurice, leur parlant avec calme. Anny et moi, suivions du regard l'homme gentil qui était peut-être le bâtard d'Egon Schiele. J'étais au courant de la maladie qui pourrissait Neuzil. Agé de cinquante-huit ans, il en faisait dix de plus. Son diabète lui causait une artérite sévère. C'étaient surtout les orteils qui étaient enflammés, comme me l'avait expliqué Marguerite, experte en maladies. La gangrène menaçait les pieds violacés. Il fallait donc que Johann Neuzil marche chaque jour et le plus possible. Souvent je l'avais croisé sur le Pont-Marie, le long du quai Bourbon, accompagné de Mlle Poulet ou de la concierge, de la jeune crémière encore qui prenait des douches dans l'appartement de Marguerite. Ma logeuse ne manquait pas non plus de faire une promenade avec « Soudain », qu'elle trouvait cultivé et délicieux.
— Il est délicieux n'est-ce pas ? C'est un homme on ne peut plus exquis ! Je pouffe quand il dit soudain... J'en meurs ! Et sa jeune mère nue et morte, cette histoire du peintre, qu'est-ce que vous en pensez ? Moi, je préfère les impressionnistes : Monet, Renoir surtout. Son peintre, c'est trop tordu, c'est mal léché, un peu obscène aussi, trop cru, sans préalables...
Outre sa douche, sa chambre d'étudiant, son grille-pain automatique, sa machine à laver, Marguerite conservait un gros album sur Chatou, et la cité concentrait toute sa nostalgie. Pelouses, lacs et cygnes blancs, villas cossues,

allées ombragées, verdoyantes et peinture impressionniste.
« Je serai enterrée à Chatou ! » Peut-être retrouvait-elle dans
la consonance du nom comme l'écho de son chat, son grand
amour. Marguerite prononçait Chatou avec adoration. Sa
voix en caressait l'or lisse, le bijou, et la dentale claquait avec
douceur comme un fermoir de sac précieux. Le monde
comportait aux yeux de Marguerite quatre « pures merveilles ». C'était son expression pour la beauté. Il y avait ses
jambes, Toufflette, Chatou et l'escalier du Palais de justice
qu'elle entendait bien me montrer. Elle me promettait cette
visite qui devait marquer un point d'orgue.

— Nous irons tous les trois avec « Soudain », ça le fera
marcher.

Marguerite possédait un ultime trésor dont je n'ai pas
encore parlé, une encyclopédie Larousse en trois volumes
qu'elle avait achetée par correspondance. Dès qu'elle hésitait
sur un mot ou cherchait un nom propre, le doigt levé dans un
effet de suspense, elle adoptait un air gourmet, émoustillé et
m'entraînait au trot dans sa chambre. Toufflette somnolait
sur le lit, l'œil entrouvert et grincheux, et les trois tomes de
l'encyclopédie s'étageaient sur un tabouret comme un objet
d'art, une sculpture sur son piédestal. Marguerite s'émerveillait, à chaque fois, de trouver chez elle la réponse à tout ce
qu'elle cherchait. Elle se redressait avec un frémissement de
voluptueuse fierté, comme si l'encyclopédie lui avait réservé
à elle seule le sens des choses et la primeur du monde.

Si Marguerite avait vécu plus vieille, elle aurait vu le nom
de son étudiant dans la grande encyclopédie et c'eût été pour
elle un bonheur absolu. Identifiée à son locataire, elle aurait
eu le sentiment qu'une part d'elle-même avait été reçue au
royaume des noms, des « pures merveilles », en compagnie
de l'escalier du Palais de justice, de l'impressionnisme à
Chatou... Ainsi, ma logeuse, au sein de la divine encyclopé-

die, de la Jérusalem des noms, aurait lu en filigrane, à travers celui de son étudiant, son propre prénom comme une étoile : Marguerite, fleur magnifique ! Elle n'aimait pas L., qui était le nom de son mari alcoolique et décédé.

En retrouvant l'appartement, je racontai à Marguerite le thé chez Neuzil. Avec le petit air entendu de celle à qui on ne la fait pas, elle déclara :

— Mais vous savez qu'il possède un dessin de son peintre, un vrai ! Si ! Si ! C'est David et Maurice qui me l'ont dit, il le leur a montré.

Nous avons fait l'amour, Anny et moi. A chaque élan, mon genou rampant sur le drap me renvoyait l'aiguillon de la douleur. Je n'osais confier cet inconvénient à mon amante. Mon plaisir, étrangement, n'avait rien perdu de sa force, mais une douleur parallèle et parasitaire le côtoyait... comme un double. Et c'est vers cette époque que je compris peu à peu que toute souffrance est notre sœur, oui notre mal : un jumeau, un reflet noir de nous. Pendant l'amour avec Anny, ma souffrance était cet autre, cette présence. Au cours de la nuit, alors que mon amante dormait, j'apprivoisais lentement l'intruse, elle devenait un personnage moins tentaculaire et plus familier, comme un enfant. Je faisais un berceau de ma douleur, un nid endolori... Et je pus recenser les prodiges de cette journée où j'avais retrouvé le corps et la complicité d'Anny qui doucement dormait. Dans l'après-midi, Wolf et Ehra s'étaient soudain incarnés au sommet des tours. Pour finir, j'avais découvert l'existence d'Egon Schiele, l'ardent jeune homme qui dénudait les jeunes filles. L'idée que le dessin secret du peintre était en la possession de Neuzil me ravissait. Ainsi, dans les profondeurs de la maison, au cœur

de l'ancienne prison, il y avait ce dessin authentique, non pas une reproduction mais le chef-d'œuvre sorti de la main, de l'œil du créateur. Un dessin vierge, vivant. J'aurais accepté de souffrir encore plusieurs mois de mon genou pour mériter de savoir et de voir le thème de l'œuvre. Me revenaient la danse des nus, des filles ouvertes, anguleuses, l'innocence de leur regard, ces falbalas de soie verte, rouge, des bas, des volants, des culottes béantes où surgissaient, toujours, le sombre pelage des sexes et souvent leur fine brèche dorée. C'était un jeune homme au bord de la mort qui peignait des nus, foule d'adolescentes nues, chaque jour, sur chaque feuille, une proie très nue. Je sentais que j'avais partie liée avec cette aventure primordiale. Schiele regardait ce qu'il fallait regarder. Il ne démordait pas de l'essentiel, il ne s'en laissait pas distraire, faute de quoi il risquait de mourir. Et peut-être bien qu'en épousant Édith, qu'en bannissant Wally la maîtresse mineure et taboue, qu'en entrant un peu trop dans la vie, dans le temps ordinaire et social, il avait trahi la vraie vie des sexes, de leurs levers noirs, éblouis, chaque jour, toujours, dans l'éventail heureux des cuisses. Ce jeune homme vif, angoissé, me hantait, je ne pouvais douter d'un lien secret entre lui et moi. Dans la nuit et le souffle d'Anny, j'entendis de nouveau les vagues sœurs de la vie et de la mort, je voyais leur écume de feu, cet échevèlement de crinière noire, immaculée : Wolf, Ehra, Schiele, Anny. Quels signes ? Et Marguerite ? Où étaient le passage, la plage qui me protégeraient de la déferlante, de sa horde bruyante, lumineuse, de ses naseaux gonflés, de sa mousse éclatante où jubilaient le désir et la mort ?

J'arrivai chez le spécialiste en début d'après-midi, avec cette douleur, ce glaive ardent qui bloquait l'articulation. L'appartement était grand, opulent, vétuste, pas loin de la place Victor-Hugo. Un parent, familier du milieu médical, m'avait conseillé le Dr P., « un intuitif, un artiste... il fait des miracles ! ». J'attendis dans une pièce aux rideaux épais, éclairée par des lampes. Il faisait doux, cela sentait la cire, les vieux objets, tous les dépôts du temps recueillis dans un halo. J'étais déjà presque rassuré. J'entendais de l'autre côté de la cloison la voix forte d'un vieillard un peu sourd auquel le médecin répondait sur un ton amusé. Tout à coup, la porte s'ouvrit. Je vis le vieil homme surgir, torse nu, bouclé de poils blancs, un manteau sur les épaules. Et le docteur lui indiqua le grand escalier : « Voilà, mon cher, vous montez lentement, tranquillement, en respirant bien et vous redescendez. Ensuite, on fait l'électrocardiogramme ! » Le génie du Dr P. tenait à ce bricolage singulier. Nulle bicyclette pour tester le cœur des clients, l'épreuve de l'escalier suffisait. Et le vieillard immense et chenu s'engagea avec calme, non sans un certain apparat, dans la volée des marches. On eût dit quelque David ou Salomon, patriarche barbu au manteau de

31

sacre. J'imaginais la tête des locataires et des propriétaires qui occupaient les différents paliers, quand l'escalier craquait, que le vieillard s'arrêtait, repartait, croisant les enfants effrayés, les femmes de ménage partant faire des courses, les bourgeoises pomponnées revenant d'une visite. Car, comme je m'en rendis compte plus tard, le carrousel des cardiaques se déroulait à longueur de journée dans l'escalier. Le Dr P. devait éprouver un plaisir mystérieux à lancer les malades à l'assaut des marches. Ils montaient, descendaient, subissaient l'électrocardiogramme tandis que déjà le suivant se préparait, se déshabillait, gardant, selon la saison, une chemise béante, un imperméable ou un pardessus, amorçant l'escalade. Joie sereine ou sadique du Dr P. La résidence devenait un temple gravi par des grands prêtres ou des victimes expiatrices. Les cadres orgueilleux, stressés ou trop lourds, les P-DG mis à nu, les seigneurs de l'industrie connaissaient le calvaire de l'ascension, la pause des paliers bénis, décorés par l'antique grille noire de l'ascenseur. Ils étaient pris dans une spirale d'ombre, muets, soumis à la volonté du maître, en bas, qui attendait, allait prononcer le verdict. Certains étaient saisis de vertige, tout là-haut, dans les solitudes. Ils haletaient, se demandant ce que ferait P. s'ils ne redescendaient pas... S'élancerait-il à son tour pour les rejoindre, les soutenir et les sauver ?

Et moi, à vingt-trois ans, j'étais le client le plus jeune du Dr P., spécialiste des rhumatismes et des troubles du myocarde. Je me sentais angélique, dans l'adolescence du temps, presque vierge en comparaison de ces colonnes d'alpinistes surannés et magnifiques. Car les barbons bien mûrs et les vieillards de P. me semblaient beaux. Je les admirais, je les enviais d'avoir ainsi parcouru leur vie, jusqu'au bout ou presque. C'étaient des vainqueurs. En haut de l'escalier, ils pouvaient se retourner sur le gouffre comme

sur leur destinée domptée. Leur marche se métamorphosait à mes yeux en triomphe. Et, lorsqu'ils repassaient devant moi, à l'issue du périple, je croyais voir des Ulysses constellés de lentigo et d'immémoriales poussières. Ils étaient chauves ou hérissés de toupets épars et fantasques, pâles, sourcilleux, visages creusés de rides, l'air hagard. On les eût dit sortis d'un naufrage. Cependant, la chair de leur poitrine était souvent restée intacte, lisse et douce. Ils me regardaient avec un sourire gentil comme si j'étais un enfant, comme si mon sort leur inspirait une compassion. De quel mal précoce ne devais-je pas souffrir pour hanter le cabinet de P !

Il me reçut dans une pièce garnie d'instruments et d'appareils multiples. Car le docteur vivait en autarcie. Il s'était équipé d'une radio, d'une machine pour les électrocardiogrammes, d'une pharmacie complète, de seringues de toute nature. Il possédait tous les produits. Ce fourmillement hétéroclite, rafistolé, dégageait cependant une impression de vaillance. On sentait que P. faisait face sur tous les fronts, qu'on ne le prenait jamais en défaut, qu'il disposait sur place de toutes les réponses. Parfois, il réfléchissait, cherchait l'outil, le médicament approprié, ouvrait une armoire, farfouillait dans une trousse de cuir et brandissait les remèdes. Il condamnait cette médecine moderne qui consistait à faire circuler le malade entre les mains de spécialistes divers. P. était polyvalent, il ajoutait à ses compétences de rhumatologue, de cardiologue, des qualités de pneumologue, de dermato, d'oto-rhino... Rien n'échappait à son acuité. Ce dont il jouissait justement, c'était de repérer un symptôme sur un terrain éloigné de ses spécialités officielles, de produire un diagnostic imprévisible, de vous nommer la maladie rare qui eût échappé à ses confrères. Ainsi, dès qu'il me vit entrer en boitant, il me lança :

— Êtes-vous allé à Malte, cet été ?

Interloqué par ce Malte, saisi par la crainte, hésitant, je répondis que non... J'avais peur de le décevoir, je sentais que Malte l'électrisait et l'eût comblé, comme ça, d'emblée, au premier coup d'œil : Malte !

— Cela ne fait rien. Par précaution, vous ferez une prise de sang, car il y a une fièvre, un rhumatisme spécifique et virulent qui s'attrape à Malte.

Ensuite, P. passa à un plus ample examen. Il inspecta mes amygdales qu'il trouva fort rouges et dilatées.

— Vous faites des angines à répétition, vous !

J'opinai. Aussitôt P. assena son hypothèse mirobolante :

— C'est un staphylocoque doré !

Le diagnostic exerça sur moi une fascination immédiate. Il m'expliqua qu'il ne fallait pas être bluffé par le rhumatisme au genou. En fait, c'était ma gorge la clé du problème, un microbe baladeur qui d'abord s'attaquait au pharynx, puis passait au genou et demain pouvait bien gagner le cœur. Aussitôt il me fit subir un électrocardiogramme et une radio. J'aurais bien voulu moi aussi tâter de l'escalier. La fois suivante, timidement, soulevé par une secrète espérance, je lui demandai si le test ne serait pas utile et révélateur. Mais toujours il me refusa l'escalier. J'étais trop jeune. Mes coronaires étaient larges et souples. Non, le microbe atteindrait directement le muscle et le paralyserait. Voilà ! Il n'attendait plus que ça le Dr P., l'intrusion du staphylocoque dans le muscle. A chaque visite il lorgnait la radio pour voir si la raideur n'était pas advenue enfin, ce trouble du rythme, ce dysfonctionnement typique vérifiant la thèse d'un microbe hémolytique.

Terrorisé, mais en proie à cette dose de masochisme et de fatalisme qui fait penser que le malade est souvent complice de sa maladie, j'imaginais mon cœur subissant le même clou douloureux que celui qui me tenaillait le genou. Cœur cloué

donc, comme une chouette ou un corbeau, quelque oiseau maudit, écartelé sur la porte d'une grange, chauve-souris peut-être, dont le plumage gigote encore dans un spasme d'agonie. Mon jeune cœur d'étudiant, d'amant livré au microbe rapace et que le Dr P. et sa horde de vieillards quasi immortels me paraissait couver d'un désir sacrificiel.

Je rentrai chez moi avec cette idée que ma gorge était chroniquement et anormalement écarlate, que c'était la crypte cramoisie du staphylocoque doré. Tant d'excessives couleurs marquaient mon destin d'un panache mortel. Je révélai à Marguerite l'existence de la bête nomade, dont le raid tôt ou tard harcèlerait mon cœur. Aussitôt, je perçus combien l'aimantait, elle aussi, mon staphylocoque. Car il était doré, le monstre, comme un scarabée d'Égypte. Rare oui, coriace, et cet or devait tuer. On se précipita sur le Larousse pour authentifier le microbe. En effet, sa virulence était dûment attestée. Marguerite me regarda avec ce mélange d'admiration et de suspicion qui lui venait dans les moments critiques. Elle aimait les maladies, elle adorait ces prémices de la mort. Ainsi, moi, son nouvel étudiant, étais-je touché par la grâce d'un mal précieux. En même temps, elle louchait un peu de côté, avec un air faux jeton, secrètement vicieux, oui, aviné. Elle me humait, me flairait par en dessous, esquivait, revenait à ma fragrance de victime inédite et novice. Et son jeu signifiait non seulement une connivence entre elle et moi, puisque Marguerite était vieille, atteinte d'une kyrielle de maux, mais aussi une différence qu'elle semblait savourer : au moins, elle était quitte, elle, d'un tel staphylocoque sinistre, caparaçonné d'or, plus dangereux, plus expéditif sans doute que son cholestérol, ses œdèmes, sa tachycardie, son diabète, diverses saloperies banales, universelles, avec lesquelles on vit jusqu'à cent ans. D'ailleurs, Marguerite, un jour, avait prononcé un mot sublime sur sa santé :

— Vous savez, avec toutes les maladies que j'ai, il me faut une santé de fer pour être en forme comme je le suis !

C'est vrai, Marguerite était tonique. Ses maladies étaient le ressort de son énergie, le moteur de ses rebonds multiples. Elle réagissait au défi avec bravade, alacrité. Ses maladies, elle vous les arborait comme une ferraille de médailles, de titres tintinnabulants. Elle jubilait d'en triompher toujours. Depuis la perte de son bras, rien de pire ne pouvait lui arriver. Elle avait d'un coup, à dix-sept ans, épongé ses dettes envers la mort. Et je crois qu'elle se sentait immortelle. Cependant, elle avait un flair infaillible de la mort comme je devais l'observer plus tard, elle était sœur et fille de la mort, elle en connaissait tous les nœuds, les replis, les venins. Sa vitalité, loin de se fonder sur l'ignorance et l'inconscience, procédait, au contraire, d'une intense proximité avec le trépas. C'est de l'avoir frôlé jadis et de convoler sans cesse avec lui que Marguerite, perpétuelle fiancée de la mort, ne l'épousait jamais. Elle était immunisée et mon staphylocoque doré entra dans sa vie comme un nouveau fleuron de l'épopée.

Je téléphonai à Anny, à mes parents, à mes amis pour les informer de mon investiture dorée. J'avais été choisi par lui, oui... et tous s'intéressaient au microbe comme à un insecte royal, coléoptère d'Orient, mobile et courroucé, quelque peu barbaresque, avide de mon sang et me visant le cœur. Ma mère sombra dans l'épouvante, mais Anny manifesta une crainte plus modérée. Elle n'adhérait pas tout à fait à ce mythe du staphylocoque doré. Cela lui paraissait presque trop beau, en accord avec ma prédilection pour l'or et le rouge. Mais au lieu d'être blessé de la voir si distante, si sceptique, je me sentis protégé par son incrédulité. Celle-ci ne faisait que rejoindre une impression qui m'habitait tout au tréfonds, moi aussi : je ne croyais pas définitivement

au microbe mortel. Des vagues d'angoisse m'agitaient en surface, mais dans la caverne centrale de mon moi et de mon cœur, je restais invulnérable, intact, inaccessible au scorpion.

Au fond, je ressemblais à Marguerite, tous les deux nous faisions la paire. Mais lorsque, chez le Dr P., je voyais les cadres somptueux, les dirigeants pleins de morgue, les grands vieillards offrir leur buste nu, ennuagé de poils blancs sous l'aile de leur manteau, avant de monter l'escalier, ils me semblaient formidablement libres et sains. Ils n'emportaient dans leur voyage qu'un cœur fatigué et non ce myocarde menacé d'une flèche d'or. Comme il me paraissait sobre, incolore et désirable, le cœur flétri des patients de P. ! Le mien battait, jeune, appétissant, serti dans l'écrin d'une convoitise fatale. Le Dr P., armé d'une robuste seringue, m'administrait une dose de cortisone qui soulageait la douleur. En effet, c'était miracle que de sentir dans la demi-heure suivante mon genou délivré de son étau cuisant. Ingambe et leste, je n'en revenais pas de marcher, d'accélérer, de galoper. L'avantage des maladies c'est de donner du prix, par contraste, au bien-être de la guérison. Seulement, je n'étais pas guéri, je ne jouissais que du répit imposé par la cortisone à l'action du staphylocoque. Et puis, au sein de ma rémission se passait un phénomène étrange. Je ne sentais plus le rhumatisme mordant. Mais au lieu même où la brûlure avait été gommée, j'éprouvais un vide, une douleur en blanc. Je n'irais pas jusqu'à dire que j'avais la nostalgie de mon mal mais, sachant qu'il allait revenir dès que la cortisone arrêterait son effet, je l'attendais déjà, je préparais pour lui un créneau, j'étais dans l'impossibilité de faire mon deuil de la douleur, je restais uni à elle avec une complaisance morbide. Au fond, la vie qui commençait devant moi creusait un trop grand vide, trop d'inconnu. Il me fallait tromper cette peur immense de

l'avenir par une angoisse locale et tangible. Absorbé par mon microbe, agrippé à lui comme à une bouée, j'oubliais l'océan de la vie. Peut-être même que j'espérais fuir cet infini et rebrousser chemin vers l'hôpital, une régression, un sursis m'évitant de me jeter à l'eau... Car Paris, c'était bien la mer que j'avais toujours redoutée, marée de pierres, houles des hauts édifices, des rues sans fin, balisées de signaux et de feux. La ville n'étendait pas pour moi un échiquier minéral et solide, bien au contraire, elle bougeait, fourmillait, me pressait, m'étranglait ou se dérobait sous mes pieds comme en des fosses marines, métro, places trop vastes, boulevards gris et sans fin où je n'avais nul havre.

Par où fallait-il aborder la ville ? Comment me situer, m'inventer des repères dans cet univers étranger, glissant, étiré, disloqué, sans frontières ? Au moins, dans mon enfance, l'espace était délimité par des faits de nature : coteaux, bois, arbres, rivières. L'estuaire de la Seine signait le paysage d'une entaille bien nette. Et l'on n'était pas obligé de fixer des yeux la mer, cette grisaille fluide. Mais là, dans la ville, tout était répétition serrée, palpitations des mêmes pierres, des foules et du bruit. Un grand vacarme se tissait dans le maillage étouffant des façades salies, des trottoirs et des avenues qui donnaient sur d'autres avenues, des horizons pétrifiés par de nouvelles rangées d'immeubles. Et ce qui aurait pu fournir des axes, des pivots symboliques à cette jungle — l'Arc de triomphe, les Champs-Élysées, le Panthéon, la Concorde — n'appartenait pas à ma mythologie intime, j'y étais affronté comme à un monumental spectacle dont je me sentais exclu. Les grandes vagues de la ville venaient battre contre ces architectures, ces quartiers célèbres, trop universels pour être annexés. Ils se dressaient devant moi, comme des objets froids et splendides. J'étais donc repoussé, renvoyé au chaos urbain. Les gens me

semblaient courir là-dedans avec une brutalité, une assurance de leurs buts qui m'écrasaient. Ils étaient donc tous devenus des adultes. Même mes camarades étudiants avaient la volonté de l'avenir et s'ébattaient dans cette perspective avec un optimisme, un appétit, des projets qui me sidéraient. Les adolescents que je dévisageais dans le métro accrochaient leur main à la barre d'appui, plaisantaient entre eux, chahutaient, exhibant l'orgueil d'être jeune dans la ville, au diapason de sa force monstrueuse. Quand retentissait le signal du départ, ils choisissaient le dernier moment pour bondir dans le wagon. Les portes claquaient sur leurs épaules qui bloquaient les panneaux métalliques. Cela faisait un choc, un tressaillement brillant d'armure qui les enveloppait, les sacrait chevaliers de la ville, de ses coursiers. Tant de fanfaronnade m'éblouissait...

Le soir tombait. De la fenêtre de ma chambre, je voyais, une fois par semaine, s'allumer une salle de classe dans le bâtiment d'en face, au-delà de la minuscule cour. C'était une école juive. Des enfants ou de très jeunes adolescents venaient y suivre des cours d'instruction religieuse. Je m'étais attaché au visage d'une très jeune fille, assise près d'une fenêtre assez rapprochée de la mienne. Ses traits étaient beaux et réguliers, sa chevelure très noire. Il m'avait semblé une ou deux fois qu'elle avait repéré ma présence et mon regard et qu'elle n'y était pas insensible. J'aimais beaucoup retrouver l'adolescente comme à un rendez-vous. C'était un moment de calme, de contemplation, de rêverie au cœur de ce Paris bruyant, mobile, que j'avais tant de mal à accepter. La lumière en face s'éteignait au bout d'une heure. La jeune Juive tournait son visage vers moi, elle se levait lentement et disparaissait dans l'ombre. Je me retrouvais plongé dans une solitude mélancolique.

Bientôt, heureusement, Anny venait. Nous traversions le Pont-Marie. Je recevais aussitôt cette caresse de l'air plus léger. Je sentais mon âme s'adoucir et comme verdir dans le parfum du fleuve. Je quittais le désert de la ville et son caillou stérile. Puis le chevet de la formidable cathédrale se dévoilait, cette couronne d'arcs-boutants pareils aux arêtes énormes et courbes d'un Léviathan. Mais je n'avais pas peur. Bien au contraire, je m'approchais encore du vaisseau caréné. De cette corbeille de pierres les ogives jaillissaient, fleurissaient sous mes yeux, les pinacles lancéolés, les rosaces. Notre-Dame de Paris, à la différence de l'Arc de triomphe, du Louvre, du Panthéon, des autres monuments, ne m'excluait pas. La grande Brocéliande de vitraux, de jambages et de piliers montait de mon enfance, s'enracinait dans mes réminiscences. Elle était l'arbre de vie, la forêt toujours vierge de mes chasses adolescentes. Je voyais les gargouilles bondir, multiples et béantes comme des mufles de chiens dans les arceaux, les fougères, les trèfles, les acanthes sculptés. Tous ces abois couraient, fusaient, m'auréolaient. La cathédrale balançait ses vertèbres, ses épaules et ses voûtes tel un cerf couronné d'andouillers gigantesques, dressé au sein d'une médiévale futaie. Je la sentis plantée devant moi, sur l'île, derrière la muraille de son quai harnaché de lierres, entourée par son fleuve et baignée par lui. Elle croissait, se subdivisait, s'étoilait, déployait sa ramure, sa grande gerbe d'ogives. Tout à coup, dans le ciel je reconnus le vol du faucon crécerelle. Alors, je serrai Anny contre moi et lui racontai l'oiseau, la cathédrale était son nid, son chêne ramifié. Notre-Dame des faucons, mon perchoir enfin, dans la clairière de l'île et la boucle des eaux. Oui, j'eus le sentiment d'entraîner ma fiancée dans un immense fais-

ceau de branches. Je l'embrassai là, sous les oiseaux, les saints, les apôtres... dans l'odeur de vase du fleuve, toutes ses écailles de poisson. La langue de mon amante s'enroulait à la mienne dans l'accolement étroit de nos lèvres. Enfin, j'étais au centre, j'étais ancré.

Marguerite nous emmena, Neuzil et moi, voir l'escalier du Palais de justice. Elle avait des mimiques exaltées, une concentration d'énergies comme si nous allions nous lancer à l'assaut d'un pic ! Neuzil jeta un œil à son orteil et très gai s'écria : « Ça va me faire du bien, il faut que mon sang circule ! » Et nous partîmes tous les trois par temps clair et vent léger, vers l'île Saint-Louis, plus loin. Ma lucidité était exaspérée et je nous voyais : Marguerite en tête avec son bras postiche, le corps cahin-caha sur les pattes courtes. Neuzil qui boitait dès que son orteil rongé touchait le sol. Mais le bâtard d'Egon Schiele ramassait son courage et ses forces pour se propulser en avant, effectuer un nouveau pas et lutter contre la gangrène. Enfin, « mon étudiant » avec son genou gommé. Il me venait une crispation au souvenir de la douleur, j'ébauchais toujours un mouvement réflexe d'esquive pour la contrôler alors qu'elle avait disparu. J'avais l'air de marcher sur des œufs. Nous étions les héros d'une escapade sinueuse par les ponts et les quais, comme des manants mutilés, des moines mendiants. Je crois qu'on nous regardait passer, bancals et disparates. Marguerite s'exclamait, s'enthousiasmait devant les arbres du square

Jean-XXIII qui ceignaient Notre-Dame d'un blason automnal. Les arcs-boutants rugueux fusaient d'une turbulence de feuilles lentes et rouges. Marguerite commenta le charme singulier des saisons...

Plus tard, j'osai demander à Neuzil quel métier il avait pratiqué avant de prendre sa retraite.

— Représentant en cosmétiques, mon ami, me répondit Neuzil.

Il se tut un instant, puis reprit :

— Marchand de rouges à lèvres, pour être précis !

Marguerite émit un petit rire fripon à l'idée de ce négociant en produits de beauté, rompu à tous les subtils ressorts de la séduction.

— Hein ! qu'il est beau, mon rouge à lèvres, Johann !

Et elle avança la bouche dans un grand sourire béat, puis la regroupa en trognon, fière de ses lèvres dont elle faisait valoir l'incarnat sensuel. En réalité, le rouge était mal appliqué. Il débordait, se fendillait dans les fines rides qui raturaient le pourtour de la bouche. Neuzil parla des lèvres des femmes, évoqua ses souvenirs de représentant de commerce dans la beauté. Il avait sans doute connu des passions auprès d'amantes auxquelles il offrait la gamme précieuse des rouges. On ouvre l'étui cylindrique et doré, on visse et le bâton surgit, sa pâte brillante, cramoisie, dont le lobe biseauté vient enduire la lèvre. Neuzil avait vu cela des milliers de fois, la métamorphose des bouches, leur sourire entrouvert et figé pendant la délicate manœuvre qui les empourpre, les irise. Ensuite, la femme se regarde dans un miroir, sourit, cette fois en fermant les lèvres, en les étirant un peu, puis les avance comme pour donner un baiser, tester l'adhérence du produit, sa fusion avec la pulpe des lèvres. Alors la belle matière amoureuse et luisante s'épanouit, c'est une seconde bouche.

— Je ne voudrais pas vous choquer, déclara Neuzil avec une pointe de suspense et de malice, mais savez-vous, au moins, avec quoi c'est fait, le rouge ?

Marguerite, qui adorait les devinettes, s'arrêta, campée sur ses mollets costauds, frisée, excitée de curiosité, coquette dans son frémissement d'impatience.

— Eh bien, les enfants... c'est du chien... Le rouge à lèvres, c'est du chien !

Marguerite poussa une exclamation d'horreur, en jetant d'instinct les doigts vers sa bouche.

— Du clebs ! Vous êtes répugnant, Neuzil !

— Oui, du chien mort... mes amis, du cador ratiboisé...

— Ce n'est pas possible ! Pourquoi justement du chien, pourquoi pas du renard, du coq, du bœuf, du gorille pendant que vous y êtes ? protesta Marguerite dans un élan de révolte.

— Parce que le chien, c'est plus courant et c'est meilleur, le chien éviscéré, c'est la carcasse idoine. Avec les nerfs, les tendons triturés, broyés, traités, on obtient une texture soudain résistante et souple, parfaitement adaptée à la bouche. Oui, chère Marguerite, la bouche des femmes arbore du chien mort. Elles séduisent, attirent leur amant avec ce précipité de chien égorgé...

— Vous employez de ces mots, Neuzil ! J'aime les images, mais là je n'apprécie pas. Ça n'arrive pas à faire passer la marchandise... C'est écœurant !

Or Neuzil n'était pas cynique, il disait la vérité, c'est tout, en provoquant pour rire, mais sans méchanceté. Neuzil était bon mais il n'était pas bête. Sa bonté était si profonde, si étendue qu'il lui fallait l'aiguillon de l'intelligence pour ne pas se diluer dans une béatitude trop éthérée. C'était une bonté saturée de présence lucide. Tel était son prix. Cette histoire de chien mort converti en bâton de rouge m'épatait et me terrifiait. Ainsi, la fascination exercée par la bouche

adorable des femmes, son rouge hémorragique et vernissé, n'était pas étrangère au massacre clandestin et crapuleux des chiens. Ils erraient dans les rues. Les flics, la fourrière s'en emparaient, une brigade de médecins exécutait des tests, des expériences, puis des carcasses écrabouillées on tirait la quintessence de ce rouge lascif et magique. Nous croisâmes une belle fille élancée dont les lèvres flamboyaient.

— Celle-là, Neuzil, c'est du setter, du caniche, du bouledogue ou un gros chien des Pyrénées tout désossé ?

On longeait le quai des Orfèvres, Marguerite haletait un peu et Neuzil tirait son pied. On s'arrêta pour digérer la révélation du chien. La Seine se gonflait des pluies d'automne, elle bouillonnait dans sa masse pleine et fluide. Marguerite plaça de belles réflexions sur l'écoulement du temps, des êtres...

— Je ne comprends pas les suicidés par noyade... ça, Neuzil, je ne comprends pas ! Dégringoler volontairement dans ces remous, toute cette eau qui s'engouffre dans la gorge et les poumons, vous emporte, vous bascule, vous enfonce dans la vase, vous livre aux anguilles, sans compter les péniches qui vous butent, vous éventrent... Alors qu'on dispose aujourd'hui des moyens d'en finir propres et médicaux.

— Mon amie, songez à ceux qui grimpent au sommet de Notre-Dame pour faire un piqué jusqu'au parvis. C'est pire, à mes yeux, impensable... Voyez-vous, l'eau c'est tout de même la vie, le flux, ça vous enveloppe et vous prend. Mais atterrir sur le pavé par le plus court chemin, sans parachute, c'est tout à fait horrible !

— Dans quel état ils doivent être ? Tout ratatinés, compressés...

Marguerite, en énonçant l'horreur, trahissait une fois encore une curiosité fascinée. Je ne doutais pas un instant

que si quelqu'un en sa présence accomplissait le saut fatal, elle ne fût la première à se précipiter pour voir. Il y avait ceux qui, épouvantés, se détournaient, fuyaient, et ceux qui accouraient pour voir : car c'était voir vraiment. Voir tout et crûment, sans maquillage. L'intime chaos. C'est cela que Marguerite convoitait au tréfonds : l'horreur sans fioritures. J'imaginais, oui, sa courte silhouette obscène, déhanchée au premier rang, bouche bée, l'œil tendu et gorgé, gavé d'horreur. Elle resterait debout jusqu'au départ des ambulances et des pompiers. Hypnotisée par ce paroxysme de vérité. Alors, je cessai d'aimer Marguerite. Elle me faisait peur. Elle était trop avide. Elle se régalait du sang des morts. En première ligne et gratis ! Elle évitait le cinéma, « il fait trop chaud et c'est trop cher ! », tandis que le spectacle d'un suicidé en plein air l'eût subjuguée, le suicide d'un jeune surtout : le comble !

L'escalier du Palais de justice qui s'offrit à nos yeux chassa la vision des chiens assassinés et des kamikazes de Notre-Dame. Marguerite nous avait amenés à l'arrière du Palais. Mais je ne comprenais pas ce qui élevait le fameux escalier au rang de chef-d'œuvre, de « pure merveille » comme elle disait. Margot joignait les mains sur sa poitrine comme devant une apparition de madone, elle rayonnait, déversait des chapelets de louanges, transfigurée par la beauté. Neuzil se taisait, contemplait l'escalier, affectait un sourire admiratif de courtoisie. Certes, l'escalier dessinait un dédale compliqué semblable à celui du palais de la Suprême Harmonie dans la Cité interdite, dont j'avais vu une reproduction. Mais ce n'était pas tout à fait cela, quand même... Manquaient la pourpre des murailles et les toits recourbés. C'était du marbre sans doute, mais l'éclat en semblait terni. L'ensemble ne me paraissait ni ciselé ni sculpté. Neuzil et moi nous demandions par quel mystérieux concours de circonstances

47

Marguerite en était venue à élire comme parangon du beau cet escalier profane et entortillé. On restait là à attendre que s'apaise son extase.

La marche et l'émotion avaient fatigué Marguerite qui résolut de rentrer par le métro. Neuzil ne se fit pas prier, son orteil avait eu sa dose d'exercice. Notre trio baroque clopina vers la prochaine station, Margot en tête ! C'est alors que, se penchant vers moi, Neuzil me souffla :

— Marguerite a dû se tromper d'escalier, celui qu'elle nous a montré est sans intérêt soudain.

L'usage qu'il fit de l'adverbe me fit ciller encore. Neuzil continua :

— Le seul escalier qui ait quelque valeur est peut-être l'escalier Louis XVI qui longe la cour de Mai, à l'intérieur du Palais. Personne n'a jamais admiré le machin qu'elle nous a montré. Peut-être même qu'elle confond avec un tout autre escalier d'un autre édifice. Voyez-vous, mon cher, les choses ne sont que ce que nous projetons sur elles. Nos illusions seules les font exister. Je crois que Marguerite est sincèrement émerveillée. Il suffit de croire, et c'est vrai pour tout.

Moi, je me sentais horriblement déçu. J'attendais une révélation solide, indubitable, un monument légendaire, un joyau, et ce n'était qu'une chimère. Le discours de Neuzil portait atteinte à mes autres croyances, à toutes mes admirations. Je me révoltai contre cet anéantissement et lui objectai l'exemple de Notre-Dame, intacte depuis huit cents ans ! Je crois que Neuzil ignorait les liens passionnels qui m'unissaient à la grande cathédrale sororale et maternelle. Sans penser à mal, il me livra l'information suivante :

— Oh ! Vous savez, Notre-Dame n'est qu'un simulacre. Viollet-le-Duc l'a tellement retapée au XIXe siècle qu'on ne sait plus qui est quoi.

J'étais écrasé de stupeur :

— Enfin, c'est bien Notre-Dame ! Ce n'en est pas une autre...

Neuzil me fixa soudain du regard, étonné par mon expression de détresse.

— Mais mon petit, c'est quand même Notre-Dame, bien sûr... Ça reste Notre-Dame. Viollet-le-Duc a restauré quelques statues, décalé une rosace, érigé la grande flèche, mais...

— Mais vous venez de me déclarer le contraire tout de go ! Que c'était une cathédrale postiche.

— Oh ! Je n'ai pas dit ça ou alors j'ai exagéré, le socle reste le même, il y a là-dedans des morceaux authentiques, médiévaux... le portail Sainte-Anne ! Les racines sont là, le soubassement robuste, immémorial !

Je sentais bien que Neuzil avait compris et qu'il cherchait à me rassurer. Mais le doute s'était insinué. La cathédrale était minée, toute son architecture me paraissait fabriquée et suspecte. Les faucons eux-mêmes étaient dupes des anges rafistolés par ce Viollet-le-Duc dont le nom à rallonge suintait le faux-semblant, le replâtrage prétentieux. Alors Neuzil me révéla le pire :

— Voyez-vous, Viollet-le-Duc, quand il a reconstruit la flèche et restauré les statues de cuivre à la croisée du transept, n'a pas manqué de se représenter parmi les apôtres. Hein ?! Ce vaurien de Viollet-le-Duc dans la cohorte des saints, coucou c'est moi !

Cette incrustation du bricoleur profane au milieu des anges et des saints me parut une incroyable pollution. J'aurais voulu que les faucons des tours allassent lui chier dessus jusqu'à recouvrir sa tronche d'excréments. Marguerite s'étonna de ce vain débat :

— C'est normal de restaurer, il faut bien la moderniser un peu la cathédrale, la faire évoluer, regardez Malraux comme il vient de la rafraîchir !

Or, je n'approuvais pas vraiment le nettoyage exécuté sur l'ordre du ministre mégalo et convulsif en diable. La cathédrale était trop claire et trop propre maintenant. Je l'avais vue sur des reproductions noircies par la poussière des siècles. Comme elle était plus romantique, plus sombre et plus sainte alors, oui, alchimique ! Notre-Dame d'Hugo et de Quasimodo. La grande église caverneuse, voilée, fissurée de ténèbres. Elle était si neuve aujourd'hui qu'on l'eût dite truquée. On avait lessivé son mystère qui couvait sous la crasse des âges, leurs sédiments hantés. J'étais convaincu qu'en étrillant Notre-Dame on avait attenté à son aura secrète et déréglé ce magnétisme lié au vieillissement des pierres sacrées. Je m'ouvris de mon opinion à Neuzil qui m'écoutait avec intensité, avec amour. Margot haussait les épaules :

— Vous êtes cinoques !

Elle grimpa dans le métro. Je sus plus tard que c'était là qu'elle avait perdu son bras, jadis, à dix-sept ans. Son bras arraché, au départ ! Le compartiment était encombré. Alors, avec une mimique de jouissance sadique, Marguerite sortit sa carte d'invalide de son sac. Dans la hiérarchie des martyrs, elle arrivait juste après les grands infirmes de guerre, et surtout elle devançait les femmes enceintes ! Elle venait justement d'en aviser une, bien ronde déjà, assise en paix aux places réservées. Marguerite, levant sa carte de son bras unique, fonça sur la future maman. Neuzil et moi en restâmes pétrifiés de honte. La jeune femme incrédule voyait Margot brandir sa carte comme un couperet. Pour bien se faire comprendre, ma logeuse tapota et toqua sur son bras de celluloïd. Alors la jeune femme entendit le son artificiel, identifia la matière rosâtre, se leva et alla se caser ailleurs. Je la regardai en coulisse. C'était une jolie jeune mère encore adolescente. Brune, cheveux courts, garçonnière, lisse et

50

peau claire. Je l'avais vue décroiser ses longues jambes musclées quand elle s'était levée. Elle restait debout, la main agrippée à une colonne métallique, avec son ventre haut et protubérant. Elle n'avait pas pris de graisse aux hanches ni aux cuisses, de telle sorte que son abdomen se détachait comme un gros œuf, tout seul, indépendant du corps resté indemne et sportif. Je pensai à l'amour, au type qu'elle désirait et avec lequel elle avait fait l'enfant. Je n'arrivais pas à imaginer Anny enceinte. Une descendance m'eût rempli d'effroi. Il aurait fallu entrer dans la vie à trois !... et cela m'eût alourdi d'un nouvel handicap. Assurer le bonheur d'Anny et de notre enfant, voilà qui me paraissait inaccessible. J'enviais le courage de la jeune femme, son inconscience. Elle avait oublié Marguerite. Elle regardait machinalement le tunnel du métro. Mais moi, dans ses yeux, je saisissais les mille petites encoches et secousses d'accommodation de sa prunelle. C'était d'une vélocité étourdissante, comme si l'œil de la voyageuse ne voulait rien perdre du parcours, l'enregistrait à vitesse fulgurante. J'en avais mal aux yeux rien que de penser à cet effort continu et monstrueux. C'était cela aussi, vivre : s'adapter automatiquement à toutes les aspérités du réel, les répercuter, encaisser tous les chocs... Rien que d'y penser, d'envisager la complexe machinerie de réflexes, oui, déjà je clignais des yeux, j'allais tout détraquer...

Marguerite ravie triomphait, installée sur la banquette ornée d'une bite bien dessinée à l'encre. Ma logeuse était donc capable de ce coup de force, de cet abus sordide ! Marguerite possédait deux cartes qui lui ouvraient des portes et des places : sa carte d'invalide et sa carte du parti gaulliste, carrée, éclatante et tricolore, qui lui valait des chocolats à Noël, une réunion annuelle qu'elle appelait « son meeting », et différents avantages ténus dont elle faisait état avec des airs de privilégiée introduite dans les hautes sphères.

J'allais passer un moment dans l'appartement de Johann Neuzil tandis que Marguerite s'apprêtait à rentrer chez elle. Elle cueillit au passage Mlle Poulet qui avait ouvert sa porte. Je vis la vieille fille, infirmière à la retraite, énorme, toute bouclée et blanchie, voix douce mais qui pouvait vous tutoyer soudain de la façon la plus crue. Vierge timide en apparence mais directe, vaillante, d'une texture militaire en vérité. Elle lançait des « merdes », et des « cons ! » qui vous braquaient. C'était une vierge de choc. Grande et propre dans ses tabliers fleuris. Faute d'avoir pu déflorer son corps immense, elle ne cessait de dépuceler son langage à coups de jurons. Pendant la dernière guerre, quand elle soignait les jeunes soldats, elle devait les apostropher ainsi pour ne pas se laisser impressionner par leur virilité. Elle piquait les jeunes fessiers épiques et musculeux, badigeonnait les gonorrhées. La vierge furieuse face aux verges !

Marguerite soudain se retourna vers moi :

— Si vous avez besoin un jour d'une piqûre, on ne sait jamais... Mon Petit Poulet fera l'affaire !

Mlle Poulet émit un rire doux en me toisant :

— Je te piquerai le cul ! Hein !

Pour le moment, c'était le Dr P. qui m'administrait la cortisone. Mais « mon Petit Poulet » se profilait, candidate à la succession, déjà armée jusqu'aux dents, virginale et sanguinaire. Elle pourrait bien affronter avec succès mon staphylocoque doré, cet oiseau de feu qui vivait dans le fleuve bleu de mes veines. Je voyais la Demoiselle, comme le saint Georges de la légende, pourfendre l'éblouissant parasite. J'aimais imaginer cette scène où la Vierge terrassait le démon de mon corps.

Marguerite et sa copine ont déguerpi. On a parlé longtemps, Neuzil et moi. Il affectionnait les paradoxes, les grandes énigmes de la vie... des choses qui, pour le commun,

paraissent aller de soi mais dont il révélait la contingence miraculeuse. Ainsi, la vision de la femme enceinte nous avait amenés sur le terrain de l'amour. Neuzil me dit alors avec un air de perplexité infinie :

— Voyez-vous, c'est une question qui m'a toujours fasciné : pourquoi la jouissance s'accompagne-t-elle d'un sentiment d'immortalité ? Hein ! Ce n'est pas si évident que ça... On pourrait n'éprouver qu'un certain plaisir, un vif plaisir, admettons... bon, mais l'extase ! Hein ? Schopenhauer explique qu'il s'agit là d'une ruse de l'espèce pour nous inciter à sa perpétuation. Ensuite, peu importe notre mort puisque la descendance est établie... En quelque sorte nous serions dupes d'une jouissance qui nous cache la mort sous le couvert de l'immortalité... Mais que les seuls hasards ou nécessités de la biologie inventent l'extase, avouez que c'est improbable ! Car, n'est-ce pas, l'espace de quelques secondes nous nous sentons immortels, soudain ! — ce soudain-là était à peu près légitime —, nous traversons tous nos déterminismes, l'opacité du temps, de la matière, nous franchissons le mur des choses, nous débouchons de l'autre côté, dans cet ailleurs de l'extase, nous voilà en lévitation sur les vagues de l'immortalité... Pourquoi ?... Comme habités par la prescience d'un au-delà, proche, accessible. Nous baignons dans son sein. Ce décrochement est fantastique ! Nous sommes à dix mille lieues de l'expression banale des plaisirs. Un saut qualitatif se produit, sans commune mesure avec le quotidien de la vie. C'est une rupture illuminée, l'enchantement de la transcendance. Mais pourquoi ? Le déterminisme biologique ne saurait expliquer cette surabondance lyrique ! N'est-ce pas l'avenir de l'homme, de l'humanité qui se préfigure ainsi dans ces flashes ? Le signe d'une éternité future qui n'est nullement à mes yeux le paradis religieux et céleste, mais une éternité de l'homme devenu dieu, de son esprit, je ne

sais... au terme de l'évolution peut-être. Ah ! Je m'égare...

J'adorais Neuzil de s'envoler si haut à partir d'une éjaculation. Je rentrai dans ma chambre avec cette idée de l'immortalité. Je la portais dans mon cœur. Une espérance me venait d'elle, un avenir d'amour. Demain, Anny arriverait de Nancy et nous allions connaître l'immortalité. La vie m'épouvantait et me submergeait de délices. Et c'est pendant cette nuit-là, avant de m'endormir, que mon intuition naquit, à propos de Johann Neuzil, une lueur merveilleuse...

Le samedi, je savais qu'Anny et moi entrions dans un temps sans limites, nous jouissions longuement de midi, puis l'après-midi s'étirait, bien plus tard viendrait le soir, la nuit immense, et ce seraient des étapes suivies d'autres moments, matinée du dimanche, déjeuner... J'étais avec Anny pour toujours. A deux heures du matin, notre intimité vigilante se prolongeait encore. Le temps s'élargissait, paradisiaque, intarissable. Mais quand elle repartait le dimanche soir, soudain la durée écoulée se contractait, tenait dans notre main, dans notre souvenir, révolue à jamais. C'était fini...

Par bonheur, le week-end ne fait que commencer. Le crépuscule vient. Et nous sortons, nous allons vers les îles sur la grande rivière. Vers le square Jean-XXIII que nous préférons appeler par son ancien nom : square de l'Archevêché. Les faucons reviennent de leurs chasses diurnes. On les voit traverser le ciel et se poser dans les lucarnes. Ils ont tué des moineaux, des rongeurs, des campagnols dans les bois de Vincennes ou de Boulogne. Ils peuvent ainsi quitter leur perchoir mystique pour rejoindre les arbres roux et verts. A la vision des toits séculaires, des verrières et des vitraux, des dentelles de pierre succède le dédale vivant des branches, des

clairières et des lacs. Les troncs, les écorces moussues remplacent les hautes statues gothiques. Les faucons voient le monde, détectent le campagnol furtif entre les herbes. Leurs ailes battent sur place, cou tendu, œil fixe. L'oiseau se laisse tomber d'un coup sur un sursaut de bestiole percée, ensanglantée. Il sent la vie, cet effroi de la boule de fourrure griffée, déchiquetée par son bec et ses serres. L'oiseau dévore les entrailles de sa proie au fond des grands bois. Il dresse son bréchet, surveille le voisinage, tient ferme entre ses pattes la dépouille éventrée. Il regarde encore une fois, puis son bec avide plonge dans le grouillement de chair, à petits coups de pique nerveux. On devine les tendons de l'oiseau, la force de son cou.

Les faucons rentrent au crépuscule, après une journée d'espionnite, de tuerie, de girations et de rapines. Ailes tachées de sang, becs rougis, serres souillées de poils. Ils sont gavés de vie douce, ardente. Ils se blottissent dans la haute basilique de pierre. Ça ne bouge plus comme le feuillage sous l'impulsion du vent et les moirures de la lumière. C'est plus dur, plus articulé. Au milieu des anges et des gargouilles, les faucons rêvent. Le crépuscule coule. Ce sont des rapaces... Ils sont précis, ils sont cruels. Chacun de leurs rouages intimes est conçu pour le meurtre. Ils vivent de la mort. Ils s'envolent pour tuer. Leurs ailes parfaites sont courbées à cette fin. Les voilà tous tapis dans les recoins de la grande cathédrale, à différents niveaux, plus ou moins haut. Leur regard saisit l'édifice sous des angles insolites. La cathédrale se ramasse, se tasse, aligne ses arêtes, les enchevêtre de profil ou élargit son ample panoplie haussée d'un coup. Tantôt elle est ronde, cabossée, tumultueuse, ou bien tranquille. Ils voient les apôtres, leur face en gros plan, la madone du transept sud tenant l'enfant Jésus. Ils voient la Vierge sous leur bec. Ils voient ce qu'on ne saurait ni surprendre ni

contempler. Car ils vivent dans la cathédrale, dans la complicité des saints, des statues, des âmes et des démons. Et parfois ils se posent sur l'épaule de la Vierge ou le crâne d'un loup, d'un aigle dont le cou fait saillie. Ils ne savent pas que c'est la cathédrale divine. Ils font partie de ce corps sans savoir. Personne ne sait, ni les statues, ni les apôtres, ni les rois. Et pourtant tout est là... matière hérissée, plissée, ciselée, fignolée dans son détail mystique. Les faucons clignent dans le crépuscule. Ils nettoient leur livrée. Ils sont maniaques, très scrupuleux. La moindre saleté restée dans les plumes freinerait leur piqué, ralentirait d'un cil l'impact fulgurant. Tout doit être lisse et rapide, d'un trait. Impondérable et parfait. C'est ainsi dans le ciel, rien ne pèse. Faucons du soleil. Ils tuent comme des rais de feu.

...Le couchant rougeoie sur la grande rose de la façade. Des pans de cathédrale s'empourprent, des flancs palpitent sous la lance des pinacles. La bête immense saigne comme un trophée sous le bec des faucons. Ils somnolent dans les rayons du soir qui dorent le visage des vierges. Ils se réveillent, aigus ils observent un moineau, un pigeon... des hommes en bas qui vont et viennent, glissent dans le jardin de l'archevêché, enjambent la palissade qui isole le transept sud. Les faucons ne savent rien mais ils sentent la présence, l'approche, la menace éventuelle. C'est pourquoi les oiseaux se tiennent haut dans la cathédrale, hors de portée. Ils veillent, dispersés, chacun dans son repaire, son territoire sacré, son trou. Ils habitent Notre-Dame de Paris. Dans son corps, dans sa chair, dans sa multiple membrure. Ils sont les parasites, les squatters de la divine Mère. Tout est paisible au sommet des falaises, des aplombs, des corniches, des redents. C'est là qu'ils élèvent, au printemps, leurs petits. Des familles, des nichées dans la Mère. Ils s'envoleront, à l'aube, quand Paris dort encore dans le ronron cadencé des péniches

qui descendent la Seine. Ils s'ébrouent, cinglants à l'aurore. Ils vont chasser au Bois. Certains restent autour de Notre-Dame, voltigent tout le jour autour de sa flèche. On dirait des sentinelles, des janissaires de la Vierge. Ils ne veulent pas quitter la Mère. Ils préfèrent tuer des moineaux dans sa robe et se nourrir à même son corps.

... Le rouge a disparu. Le crépuscule noircit tout. Au pied de l'ombre gigantesque, la Seine luit encore pareille à du cambouis. L'eau fourmille, insomniaque dans l'ouïe des faucons.

Il y a soudain une grande panne d'électricité sur le quartier. Les projecteurs qui mitraillent la cathédrale et l'enferment dans une clarté criarde, continue, lâchent prise miraculeusement. Pour la première fois de notre vie, Anny et moi, nous voyons Notre-Dame plongée dans la nuit et nous nous serrons l'un contre l'autre avec un frisson de bonheur. Les faucons ont saisi l'obscurcissement brutal. Nerveux, à l'écoute, car les plans de lumière dure, les miroitements artificiels ont disparu. Les faucons retrouvent la grande nuit cosmique. La nuit nue. Ils sentent cette métamorphose comme le lever des ténèbres. Dans leur cœur, dans leur sang passent un courant scintillant et plus fort, une rumeur d'étoiles.

Le temple colmaté et comme pansé par les ombres me fait oublier les retouches sacrilèges de Viollet-le-Duc. La nuit unifie le grand œuvre gothique. C'est Notre-Dame du Moyen-Age, du fond des âges. Mes doutes s'estompent devant les deux hautes tours dressées pareilles à des oreilles vigilantes, un peu démoniaques. On ne voit plus les rois de Judée de la première galerie ni les évangélistes du transept. Les clochetons, les pinacles, les gables, les arcs-boutants semblent planer, délestés, affranchis par la nuit. Et les astres peuvent enfin apparaître, ils ne se noient plus dans le halo des

spots. On les voit éclore, un à un, pour couronner la Vierge, consteller le vide entre les tours, piqueter la cime d'un pinacle. Pour la première fois, le firmament enlace la cathédrale, la parsème de ses lueurs, de ses reflets. Notre-Dame n'est plus cet objet piégé, stérilisé dans le carcan des projecteurs. Elle renaît à la nuit, elle frémit dans le vent des étoiles et peut-être qu'elle gravite, qu'elle voyage et que les faucons tournent dans son voile.

David et Maurice passèrent devant nous, dans un frôlement presque silencieux. Ils nous reconnurent et s'arrêtèrent pour nous parler. Ils s'étonnaient de la panne de secteur mais s'émerveillaient comme nous de la grande ombre paisible. Ils nous sourirent. Puis apparut le guide et le gardien des tours. C'était un Martiniquais surnommé Osiris. Nous le connaissions à force de monter là-haut. Il filtrait les visiteurs à l'entrée des escaliers, il leur faisait voir le bourdon Emmanuel. Il était prolixe et mythomane, il inventait à Notre-Dame des scandales et des secrets dont on ne savait jamais démêler le vrai du légendaire. Ainsi, au chapitre des suicides, il aurait vu, un soir, tard, alors qu'il finissait sa journée, une très jeune fille blonde se jeter du sommet, planer comme un ange, atterrir en douceur et partir miraculeuse comme une fée au bord de la Seine. La cathédrale inspirait Osiris. Il la considérait comme une pyramide millénaire. Il faisait d'abord allusion à l'église Saint-Étienne qui s'élevait au même endroit aux Xe et XIe siècles, puis il évoquait ce sanctuaire antérieur dont on ne savait plus bien s'il était mérovingien, gaulois, romain... Cela se perdait dans les racines du temps. Là, sur l'île, ça ne s'arrêtait jamais... paysans, sorciers, guerriers, chasseurs sur leurs pirogues. On avait retrouvé des armes, des poteries, des signes dans des cryptes... Osiris dérivait devant les touristes étrangers. Il racontait les destructions commises sous la Révolution. Il

filait vers Saint-Louis, affabulait, enluminait à loisir, ensorcelait Notre-Dame, en faisait tout un vaudou.

Anny et moi savions qu'Osiris, David et Maurice chas-
saient, la nuit, dans le jardin de l'Archevêché. C'était un lieu
de rendez-vous, de galanterie virile. Les mecs prenaient en
enfilade les quais de Seine, montaient par les petits escaliers,
s'infiltraient à la pointe de l'île, sous les arbres, dans les bos-
quets. Ils rappliquaient de partout. Le jour : les faucons, la
nuit : les anges... Notre-Dame a toujours attiré les amants.
Une maman éternellement vierge et naïve n'a rien à voir avec
une marâtre dont l'œil épie sa progéniture. Mère d'un Dieu,
sans coït, son cas est assez incongru, surnaturel et quelque peu
pervers pour que tous ceux qui hantent les marges de l'amour
trouvent des affinités avec cette sœur monstrueuse fécondée
par un ange, et viennent se réfugier dans les plis de son voile.

Tout à coup, ce fut Wolf, là devant nous, sa stature, son
front et sa gorge nue. Il serra la main de David, de Maurice et
d'Osiris. Wolf sans Ehra. C'était le visiteur de la tour sud,
son signataire céleste. Anny et moi aurions voulu lui poser
mille questions, mais nous étions paralysés de surprise et de
timidité. Il avait un accent du Nord. Il paraissait lent et
calme. Je sentis en lui cette résolution du désir que rien ne
limite. Il avait la nuit devant lui. Il prenait son temps,
écoutait Osiris, souriait à Maurice et David, tantôt il jetait un
œil sur une silhouette vagabonde puis le ramenait sur nous.
Émanaient de sa personne, de sa chair entrevue, quelque
chose de soyeux et d'impulsif, un lyrisme froid. Nous ne
savions rien de lui. J'avais peur d'en apprendre trop, je
voulais préserver la légende et son graphe sur le toit du
monde. Il nous quitta comme il était apparu, sans nous serrer
la main. Il fit un geste léger et s'envola. A peine avions-nous
entendu sa voix, reconnu l'arrogance de ses traits dans les
ténèbres.

— Qui est-ce ? demanda Anny qui voulait une confirmation.

Je redoutai en un éclair qu'on nous réponde Frédéric, Kurt ou Charles.

— C'est Wolf, répondit Osiris.

Anny et moi étions muets de bonheur. Nous avions un peu peur. Car ce Wolf qui s'ancrait ainsi dans la réalité, correspondait à l'autographe de la tour, était trop proche tout à coup, trop vrai, trop pressant. Nous n'avions plus ce recul de l'improbable et de la rêverie. Wolf, là, carré dans la nuit.

— Qu'est-ce qu'il fait dans la vie ? demanda Anny cette fois à Maurice.

— Il vit avec sa sœur dans une péniche, derrière la cathédrale, là-bas, sur le grand quai sud, au-delà de l'île Saint-Louis. Mais vous êtes très curieuse, Anny ! Il vous plaît, il est très beau n'est-ce pas ?

— Il a un métier ?

Maurice s'esclaffa devant l'entêtement de mon amante. Elle ne lui laissait nul répit.

— Il est photographe.

— Et sa sœur ?

— Ehra recueille des graffiti, elle fait une thèse sur les graffiti de Paris, c'est magnifique, n'est-ce pas ? Elle en dresse l'inventaire, elle les classe, les interroge, les commente... voilà ! Et elle remballe tout ça dans sa péniche.

Comme nous avions aimé, Anny et moi, la fin de la phrase !... cette idée d'emmagasiner dans une péniche la moisson des signes et des noms, des marques mystérieuses. Le frère et la sœur, Wolf, Ehra gardiens des hiéroglyphes. Osiris se taisait dans la nuit. Son silence était rare. S'il s'était agi d'autres personnages, il eût enchaîné et brodé une histoire extraordinaire. Mais il y avait un interdit, ou presque. Osiris

n'osait se lancer dans le sillage de Wolf et d'Ehra. Pourquoi ?
Il semblait grave, peut-être ému. Wolf était beau, immaculé.
Osiris se taisait dans l'ombre de Notre-Dame...

Oriris, Maurice et David ont décidé soudain de partir et
nous nous sommes retrouvés, Anny et moi, remplis d'une
connaissance dont le relief, le prestige nous obsédaient. Il
fallait tout récapituler, savourer les détails. Nous sommes
restés un moment là, debout, puis nous avons repris notre
chemin, nous écartant des jardins de l'Archevêché, par égard
pour Wolf et ses frères qui déambulaient, glissaient, se
croisaient autour du colossal chevet. Mais la lumière revint
d'un coup. La cathédrale jaillit des ténèbres. Jaune, entièrement éclairée, livrée dans toute sa matière nervurée. Comme
une carte postale profane. Une grande tristesse nous submergea. Nous regrettions la madone des ombres. Nous étions
pleins de nostalgie. Deux crimes avaient été commis : le
nettoyage de Malraux et l'éclairage des spots ! Dans les deux
cas, Notre-Dame était dévoilée, violée, mise à l'encan, à la
retape du spectacle. Rendre visible la beauté, l'exhiber sans
trêve, c'est ça le péché. Pourtant, les faucons dormaient
malgré l'éblouissement. Derrière l'image phosphorescente de
Notre-Dame, on devinait encore sa part cachée. Anny et moi,
nous nous convainquîmes que la lumière, en quelque sorte,
n'était qu'un déguisement, une façade qui permettaient à la
cathédrale profonde de s'éclipser dans sa nuit à elle. De la
cathédrale, les spots ne montraient que l'écorce sous laquelle
se dérobait le noyau mystique, son peuple d'anges et d'oiseaux.

Anny se déshabilla. Fine, précieuse, dorée encore depuis
l'été. Un triangle étroit et plus clair se détachait à la place du
slip et dans cet angle nu le pubis brun se bombait. J'adorais

cette imbrication du corps bronzé, de la peau blanche soudain et du sombre pelage. C'était une succession de frontières savoureuses. L'épiderme ensoleillé sentait le musc, suggérait le sable, l'oisiveté, il se reliait aux autres corps dénudés sur les plages. Sa beauté, loin d'être individuelle, était solidaire d'un rite collectif, comme d'une contagion qui mêlait Anny et les filles de l'été. Bronzage nomade, visuel et prostitutionnel. Là-dessus tranchait le triangle de peau immaculée. C'était Anny qui surgissait alors, sa vraie chair pâle et veinée, sa délicate texture et ses aines diaphanes. Enfin le pubis, tout ce poil bouclé, renflé sur la fente mouillée. Et là, je n'avais plus de mots, le corps cessait de se conjuguer à celui d'autres filles. C'était Anny, devant moi seul. Un sortilège. La présence nue, l'ombre... Je ne me lassais pas de regarder, de refaire le parcours, de franchir les limites vers le centre, cette clarté du ventre, sa pâleur d'icône et sa fougère noire. Me fascinait le poil oui, le mot brut et velu. Neuzil, lui aussi, se fût étonné de ce pelage, lui qui excellait à poser les vraies questions, à démasquer les fausses évidences. Pourquoi? Là, ces reliques, ce trésor d'une bestialité miraculeusement intacte, dans cet angle, à la fourche de l'être, à l'intersection de ses courants, de ses forces. Comme si la grande vie sauvage n'avait pu déserter tout le corps, mais s'était resserrée dans sa zone violente, dans sa fente féconde. Sur la rive belle du fleuve. A la source parfumée. Les poils, le joli bois d'Anny, sa forêt en forme d'ogive.

J'admirais aussi ses épaules larges et minces. Les longues clavicules dont le dessin divergeait. Son dos fin et musclé. Ses seins au galbe ferme et rond, les bouts foncés. Son visage doux et enfantin. Ses yeux très bleus, d'un bleu qui s'agrandissait parfois pour m'absorber tout entier dans sa luminosité.

Elle se mit à quatre pattes et je la pris ainsi longuement. Le dos se relevait, s'éployait, équilibré par l'envergure des épaules droites. La nuque oscillait sous ce frêle joug. Et les fesses s'offraient lisses et ovales, s'écarquillaient vers le bord du pubis que je retrouvais inversé, en retrait, plus à l'étroit entre les lèvres brouillées. Ce n'était plus l'impeccable emboîtement du triangle de chair blanche et de son angle noir, c'était moins circonscrit, plus anarchique et turbulent. Cela convenait mieux à la ferveur de l'action. C'était plus cru. Je ne voyais presque plus. J'étais dans le sexe d'Anny, amalgamé à sa chair. Elle émit son chant familier : « Je sens tes couilles... je sens tes couilles... » en litanie toute simple, sa chanson d'orgie d'amour.

... Je m'en souviendrai toujours : un beau soir, lors d'un dîner entre amis, la conversation tournait autour des mots dont s'accompagne volontiers le coït. Alors, je trahis le secret d'Anny. Je ne crus pas mal faire. Je savais que ces hymnes étaient universels : « Je sens ta bite » est une variante, plus banale encore... Moi, c'étaient mes couilles qui carillonnaient au derrière d'Anny. Excité par l'alcool, je le dis, je révélai la phrase d'Anny en la mimant peut-être. Personne ne fut vraiment surpris, chacun reconnut la musique de l'amour, son livret efficace et senti. Anny ne parut pas se formaliser outre mesure de mes aveux. Mais je ne l'entendis plus jamais prononcer la phrase qui célébrait mes couilles d'amant. Elle se tut désormais là-dessus. J'avais sans doute galvaudé le secret. Je compris trop tard qu'il ne faut pas tout dire mais garder les mots clés, les mots du désir. Il est un langage de l'ombre, tout imprégné de magie et comme mêlé aux corps, exhalé de leur fièvre... oui la langue du triangle d'or, langue de nos sueurs, de nos pelages ébouriffés, de nos sexes enfilés l'un dans l'autre, langue du fleuve d'amour. J'avais prononcé la formule sacrée en dehors de la fusion qui la produisait.

Coupés du délire d'immortalité dont parlait Neuzil, les mots perdaient toute leur aura, se fanaient maigres et plats. En les entendant, lors du fatal dîner, Anny ne les avait pas reconnus, n'en avait perçu que le déchet trivial. Depuis, elle ne pouvait plus les dire. Car elle ne les avait jamais dits. En vérité, ces mots montaient de nos corps, nous enveloppaient, nous comprenaient tous les deux dans leur matière onirique et sonore. Ils fusaient de l'étreinte, ils poussaient de nous comme des fleurs obscènes et splendides. Ils étaient embellis, transfigurés par leur grossièreté même, leur naïveté sexuelle, leur énergie, surtout, nourrie de tous les magnétismes du désir.

Il ne faut pas tout dire. Il faut savoir garder le secret, taire et protéger nos cathédrales dans la nuit, respecter nos madones, nos anges et nos faucons de feu. Les regarder, les reconnaître dans la lumière de l'âme. Pour nous-mêmes, sans l'ébruiter, sans gâcher le trésor dans le chaos et la rumeur du monde. Ce sont les œuvres de l'amour. Elles germent lentement, croissent et s'épanouissent dans le silence. Ce sont, dans la pénombre du fleuve, les grandes, les belles forêts de la nuit intérieure.

J'eus des vomissements, des vertiges de future accouchée. La cortisone m'attaquait l'estomac et la tambouille des restaurants universitaires ne pouvait plus passer. On me donna l'adresse d'un restaurant de la Sécurité sociale réservé aux étudiants valétudinaires. On y faisait le régime, on y chouchoutait les infirmes. Après une visite médicale, je fus autorisé à fréquenter ce lieu privilégié. C'était à Saint-Germain-des-Prés, dans une rue longue et calme, un peu dérobée. Dès l'entrée, je fus surpris par un climat de gaieté, tout un tapage vaillant. Des gaillards de tous pays dont beaucoup — je les revois dans ma mémoire — étaient bruns, barbus, à belle trogne, plaisantaient, se bousculaient, s'envoyaient des bourrades familières. J'avais redouté à tort que l'endroit ne fût trop confiné, ravalé au diapason de la maladie. Les gros mecs se servaient des pichets de lait entier — c'était là un des avantages du régime offert — qu'ils avalaient comme des rasades de vin. J'avais beau les scruter, je n'arrivais pas à les croire décalcifiés. Le patron du resto, une sorte d'intendant, manifestait lui aussi des marques de pétulance indubitable. J'enviais son teint fleuri, ses chemises écossaises et laineuses, ses pulls douillets, sa barbe, son

embonpoint, sa jactance. Ils avaient tous une barbe, je le répète, c'était le signe de leur vitalité et de leur luxuriance. Je me demandai si tous les planqués, tous les tire-au-flanc de l'Université ne s'étaient pas donné refuge ici pour se régaler de rations supplémentaires et mieux équilibrées...

Cependant, à bien observer les tables, de temps à autre, je repérais une fille plus fragile, un visage cireux, des joues trop pâles, une efflanquée au milieu des rangées d'ogres cramoisis, velus comme des singes. D'instinct, j'allais m'asseoir à une table où figurait justement l'une de ces figures chlorotiques. Je m'incrustais dans une enfilade de convives bouffant comme quatre, gorgés de lait frais, émoustillés, juteux. Jamais je ne me suis senti plus faible, plus fluet qu'au milieu de ces hommes colossaux dont certains avaient dix ans de plus que moi, étudiants à vie, logeant à la Cité internationale, dont plusieurs, comme je devais l'apprendre plus tard, étaient des agents, des barbouzes, des activistes surentraînés, des trublions musclés, bourrés de vitamines et d'énergie militante. Au restaurant des malades, ils étaient moins en vue que dans les services ouverts au tout venant. Grâce à des combines, pistonnés par leur ambassade, ils avaient obtenu un passe-droit. Et je puis révéler aujourd'hui que cet asile de la maladie servait en réalité de repaire aux sagas du Proche-Orient. La chute du chah s'est concoctée sous mes yeux, sans oublier les échauffourées du Sinaï, les attentats de l'OLP... Après coup, j'ai recollé tous les morceaux jusqu'à une perception nette des faits. J'étais tombé dans un nid de types suralimentés, surmotivés qui, entre des brocs de lait, préparaient des raids et des révolutions enturbannées.

Une nausée me saisit dès la première bouchée. L'odeur du lait surtout me révulsait, avec sa crêpe de gras plissé à la surface du pot. Les mecs touillaient la peau, la creusaient et faisaient gicler le liquide dru dans le verre. Cela me rappelait

les vaches, les grosses laitières de ma Normandie natale. J'en aurais dégueulé de réminiscences rustiques. L'herbage, la viande, les pis, le lait, la bouse bien étalée, rousse et fluide. Il me semblait que les géants pompaient directement toutes ces matières gluantes, ces déjections des génisses et des truies.

Ma voisine d'en face, à laquelle ses déficiences prêtaient un flair particulier quant à la détection des hystéries d'autrui, reconnut immédiatement son frère morbide en ma personne. Elle posa sur moi un délicat regard de compassion où j'entrevis tout un dosage d'amitié, d'encouragements, de connivence. Elle arrivait à manger, elle, par petites bouchées pingres, du bout des lèvres, on eût dit un grelottement. Les gros mecs échangeaient, de temps en temps, une mimique railleuse, des coups d'œil noirs, étincelants de mépris et peut-être même de lubricité. En coin, ils guignaient la chèvre. Moi, l'agneau, je lui rendis un sourire timide. Ainsi, la maladie agglutine l'un à l'autre les natures débiles ou blessées pour des idylles médicamenteuses, des sérénades de la souffrance. Ma nature imaginative me dépeignit en un éclair des amours évanescentes, entrecoupées de prises de sang, de piqûres et de pilules. Et nous arriverions, dans des instants de rémission, à des extases d'épaves, exaspérées par la menace du trépas.

Je ne pouvais plus rien absorber. Ma voisine continuait de mâcher avec patience et résignation pour survivre, pour faire plaisir sans doute à ses parents, obéissante jusque dans le désespoir. Elle levait sa fourchette, attrapait un petit bout de viande, le découpait avec ses dents, le malaxait et l'ingurgitait. J'imaginais le parcours de l'aliment dans ce dédale lassé. Elle était jaune, très jaune, l'œil jaune, l'épiderme de banane morfondue, c'était le foie sans doute. A me voir aussi rétif et dégoûté devant la bouffe, elle redoutait de rechuter dans ses propres nausées. Car elle connaissait parfaitement mes

spasmes et ma lucidité de malade sceptique devant l'aveugle acharnement vital des convives. Les grands porcs se servaient des monceaux de nouilles au gratin dont les filaments de gruyère étiraient leurs tendons élastiques entre leur assiette et le plat. Ça ne pouvait plus se décrocher, c'étaient des stries arachnéennes innombrables qui faisaient reluire la matière visqueuse du fromage, tout le gluant des nouilles, de la pâtée pour les cochons. Avec des rires goulus, les saligauds faisaient tourner leur cuillère et enroulaient la mélasse jusqu'à leur bouche ouverte. Ils se resservaient un grand verre de lait. Il me semblait que je les voyais grandir, grossir, se charger de vigueur et de sang. Ma voisine en avait mal au cœur elle aussi.

Nous sortîmes tous les deux avant le dessert : des yogourts aigres, ce n'était plus possible ! On se promena au jardin du Luxembourg. Elle s'appelait Nicole. Elle avait vingt et un ans et faisait une maîtrise de psychologie. Elle était douce et faible. Des traits réguliers, assez beaux, sans éclat. Elle s'économisait en respirant, en marchant, en parlant, en me regardant. Pris de paranoïa, je crus qu'elle voulait m'identifier à elle, me rabaisser à son débit languide. Je vis aussi qu'elle avait perçu et compris ma peur et qu'elle cherchait à m'assurer de ses bonnes intentions à mon égard. Elle sentait tout, la maladie avait affûté ses moindres fibres, tous ses organes de perception. Toutefois elle fut un peu éberluée quand ma cyclothymie naturelle me fit soudain passer de la déprime à l'effervescence prolixe. Elle ne reconnaissait plus l'adolescent diaphane et nauséeux du restaurant. Elle se demandait aussi d'où me venait soudain une telle débauche énergétique, puisque je n'avais rien mangé. Je devinai qu'elle diagnostiquait la crise maniaque, forte de son expérience livresque et psychiatrique. Mais un instable, un surchauffé de ma trempe ne pouvaient que fasciner la belle décavée,

rongée par l'anémie et dont le foie se décomposait. Elle avoua, en effet, qu'elle souffrait d'une hépatite rare, d'une dégénérescence chronique. Son foie pourrissait lentement et sûrement. Elle avait cette éponge vénéneuse sous les côtelettes. Je vis ce nénuphar malodorant et la pauvre existence attelée à l'organe croupi. Elle m'admira, m'envia avec cette impulsion chimérique qui pousserait chaque malade à échanger ses affres contre celles d'autrui qui lui paraissent plus confortables. Dans le même genre d'idée devait me frapper, des années plus tard, le dialogue de deux mères dont l'une avait un enfant trisomique et l'autre autiste. La seconde s'extasiait sur le mongolisme. Comme elle aurait bradé son petit prostré incontinent contre un bon trisomique autonome, gai et râblé! L'horreur est toujours relative et l'enfer une question d'échelle. Nicole m'eût cent fois refilé son hépatite contre ma fringante cyclothymie. Sans doute retombais-je épuisé de mes paroxysmes, mais ces accélérations soudaines avaient bel air. Je pouvais ainsi faire illusion pendant trois heures, voire quatre, cinq heures d'intempérance cataclysmique au grand dam de mes amis qui redoutent encore aujourd'hui mes coups de téléphone. L'autre avec son foie ne parvenait même pas à décoller pendant dix minutes. Mais elle avait une haleine douce et discrètement fétide, de grands yeux gonflés, délavés par la jaunisse et la mélancolie. Je dois avouer qu'un résidu de sadisme animal, au tréfonds, était excité par cette extrême fragilité. Le faible est cruel avec plus faible que lui. Hélas, oui, je m'en repens, mais l'anémie de Nicole me fit bander soudain. Elle éveillait en moi je ne sais quel loup archaïque. Ainsi n'étais-je pas d'une essence bien différente de celle des barbus triviaux et congestionnés qui assaillaient en parasites espions le restaurant des déconfits. Et peut-être même — je sais que je dis une horreur — que si Nicole, par le jeu de la providence, était tombée sur un

malade plus démoli qu'elle, sa déliquescence se fût reconvertie, revivifiée d'un coup, et qu'un désir prédateur l'eût fait fondre sur le comparse malingre.

Un pâle soleil éclairait notre rencontre. Les feuilles dorées du jardin flambaient d'une lumière qui semblait émaner de leur intime essence. Dans l'agonie de l'automne, elles diffusaient un feu ultime. Et ce luxe, cette splendeur dans la mort me fascinaient. J'enchaînai là-dessus quelques belles métaphores qui achevèrent de séduire ma nouvelle amie. Elle me répondit que son foie, lui-même, brûlait de cette lueur mourante. J'avais beaucoup de peine à comparer au foie de Nicole les hauts marronniers secs et solaires, leurs rousseurs qui crépitaient à l'air. Le sol était jonché de larges feuilles dont les dos brillaient, une saute de vent les houspillait et soudain elles s'envolaient en bande, faisaient des farandoles brasillantes. On était pris, Nicole et moi, dans le cerceau des flammes. J'adorais cette danse et Nicole me vit me propulser en avant, soudain dionysiaque, vers ces volutes ardentes comme pour les étreindre et m'en parer d'un trophée de gloire. J'eus tout de même un vertige, ma tension avait dégringolé d'un zeste, je titubai et basculai contre l'épaule de Nicole. Elle me prit dans ses bras. Je reçus son haleine fanée, je me noyai dans ses grands yeux jaunes pareils à des mares. Je m'appuyai sur sa cuisse. Agrippée, la jupe se retroussa un peu et je sentis sous mes doigts la chair nue. Je me mis à bander, à flamber crûment comme au bord de l'évanouissement, incroyablement dur, marronnier rouge, érigé... La sensation de la peau vierge débusquée des coulisses de la maladie, le contact de cette chair très lisse, inconnue, comme cueillie sous les liasses de l'automne, m'avaient brandi vif. C'étaient la vie de cette fille au tréfonds, la beauté de sa cuisse intacte pour ma jeunesse avide. J'avais envie de baiser, de baiser à en crever, de nous faire gueuler de plaisir sous la

couronne incandescente des arbres et de pourfendre ainsi la mort, de terrasser son dragon de feuilles rampantes et mouillées au bord du bassin où les enfants jouaient.

Nicole et moi nous séparâmes. Je ne pus lui cacher tout à fait mes liens avec Anny. J'étais à un âge où l'on ne compose pas encore dans les affaires du cœur. Nicole fut déçue par mon engagement, mais, en même temps, me savoir pris la soulageait, la renvoyait à la maladie, à ses rites lents et réguliers, à ses macérations pareilles à une drogue douce où l'existence somnole.

Le soir, j'avais rendez-vous avec le Dr P. L'idée de mon staphylocoque obsédait de nouveau mon esprit. Je redoutais que le médecin ne constate un progrès de la maladie, un bond vers mon cœur poignardé. On me fit patienter un peu. La porte du cabinet s'ouvrit. J'espérais voir surgir un beau vieillard anxieux ou un quinquagénaire stressé, P. leur montrant la porte, leur indiquant le grand escalier et le client entreprenant l'escalade, passif, résigné, mal rhabillé ou encore dénudé, en vue de l'électrocardiogramme qui suivrait. Mais au lieu d'un patriarche ou d'un barbon, parut une petite vieille alerte et papotante. Quand, tout à coup, P. étendit le bras, je sus qu'elle allait subir le test de l'escalier. Elle se fit répéter cette exhortation insolite. Piquée, elle se raidit, toisa le Dr P. :

— Quoi ?? vous voulez que je grimpe là-haut, toute seule, vous n'avez pas d'autres moyens ?!

Et elle fut prise d'un fou rire :

— Vous êtes un excentrique, docteur ! Un médecin bohème ! Si ! Si ! un farfelu... Je ne monterai jamais dans votre escalier, j'ai mal aux genoux rien que d'y penser. Trouvez un autre truc, mais moi jamais ! Je suis claustrophobe, docteur ! Je ne tiens pas à faire des rencontres tout là-haut, dans les étages, dans l'inconnu. Jamais !

71

Médusé, le Dr P. hésita, puis capitula. Dès qu'il me vit entrer, marcher, je crois qu'il reçut sa nouvelle intuition et qu'il abandonna l'hypothèse du beau staphylocoque doré. Toutefois il me fit passer une radio et observa le cœur. Non, le muscle fonctionnait normalement. Le microbe n'aurait donc pas bougé... Il me lorgna, m'ouvrit le bec, trouva la gorge moins rouge. Il me sonda encore. Ça l'embêtait tout de même d'abandonner le grand staphylocoque. Alors il s'écria :

— C'est un ménisque !

Je tressaillis, j'ignorais tout de ce mot. Je crus à quelque mal virulent et plus irrémédiable que mon staphylocoque. Et le docteur lança :

— C'est rien ! c'est rien, ça s'opère !

Mais moi, cette idée d'opération me remplit d'effroi, je préférais encore mon microbe nomade et mordoré.

— C'est rien ! C'est un petit cartilage tout mince, un bracelet qui soutient l'articulation du genou. Et vous l'avez brisé, voilà ! Je n'y ai pas pensé d'abord parce que vous n'avez pas l'air d'un sportif et ce genre de pépin arrive surtout aux footballeurs et aux joueurs de rugby. Mais c'est ça ! Je le sais.

Pourtant, moi, je craignais que P. ne soit la dupe d'une nouvelle illusion. Le ménisque ne m'inspirait pas. Alors il procéda à un nouvel interrogatoire, me demanda si je n'avais pas subi un choc, fait une chute. Nulle collision...

— Cherchez ! Cherchez ! m'encourageait P., de toute façon on va faire une radio des cartilages, voilà, c'est un peu douloureux, on instille un liquide dans l'articulation, le genou triple de volume, il quadruple comme un ballon, alors on voit tout, on peut faire la radio ! Mais c'est courant, c'est banal, c'est rien ! C'est bien mieux que le staphylocoque doré ! Cherchez ! Il y a eu un traumatisme, c'est sûr... ménisque externe en plus ! C'est rare ! Ça ne se pète pas tout

seul, cherchez plus loin, dans votre enfance même. La lésion peut couver pendant des lustres puis ça se fissure, ça se disloque d'un coup...

Je cherchais un traumatisme dans mon enfance. C'était du Freud, mais le Dr P. ne l'entendait pas de cette façon, il voulait du physiologique, du mécanique, un bon bris d'os, pas une fêlure de l'âme. Rien ne venait. Il me prescrivit la fameuse radio.

Le soir, dans mon lit, des réminiscences naquirent, à la faveur de cette griserie qui monte à la lisière du sommeil, chez ceux-là mêmes qui le refusent et reculent devant l'anéantissement. J'aimais ce moment-là, cette lutte contre la léthargie par un ballet doré d'images. Peu à peu s'évanouit le sentiment du temps irréversible et de notre finitude. Le moi chauffe et s'enivre, irrigué par les courants de sa vie propre, de toute sa destinée. Narcisse se renfloue à ses sources, plus vives, plus profondes qu'il ne l'imaginait. C'est une résurrection et une reviviscence. On vole, on lévite, on tournoie dans des vagues d'euphorie. On se sent circulaire, immortel, mais pas comme Neuzil en observait le miracle dans l'orgasme. Non, l'insomniaque plonge dans une immortalité moins aiguë, moins extatique, il nage, il baigne dans le fleuve de sa vie qui s'enroule autour de lui, placentaire et constellé. Le lit est un retour au ventre originel, l'imaginaire surexcité vous nourrit de son sang, de son courant brûlant. On plane dans les étoiles, l'infini rond, saturé de vigilance, de sens, de rayonnement.

C'est alors que certains épisodes de mon passé sont remontés à la surface. Oui, je m'étais bien pété un ménisque et je compris comment, avec cette lucidité et cette indulgence qui caractérisaient l'état où je me trouvais, à minuit... Lycéen, j'avais coutume d'amuser la galerie par des vols planés dans les escaliers. C'était un jeu, une farce, un défi.

J'avertissais mes copains. Je bloquais à l'intérieur de moi toute sensibilité, j'occultais tous les accès à la souffrance. C'est une technique que je pourrais faire breveter et diffuser pour les adeptes de la marche sur les braises ou les fakirs, voire les candidats à la torture. Je réussissais d'un coup à paralyser mes circuits. Je ne clignotais plus. J'étais à la fois tendu, tout engouffré dans une concentration paroxystique, et gommé. Et hop ! Je sautais dans l'escalier, je valdinguais sans un cri, tout ramassé entre mes bras, mes jambes, encoconné, rebondissant. La douleur m'enveloppait de chocs gourds, à la périphérie, sans m'atteindre, sans percer mes barricades intérieures. C'est ainsi que j'ai dû casser le ménisque. Ça correspond. J'étais aussi un as de l'escalade. Quand nous sortions le soir, mes camarades et moi, j'avisais un lampadaire et je me hissais avec vélocité à la force des bras, des genoux et des pieds jusqu'au sommet. Un peu comme les indigènes gravissent les cocotiers. C'était mon exotisme. J'adore les îles… Je sentais bien que la colonne de métal cognait contre mes genoux. Pire, en redescendant, pour abréger le retour, je me laissais tomber de haut. Mes articulations, à l'arrivée, répercutaient le choc du trottoir…

Or, en y repensant, ces exploits de kamikaze dévoilent à l'adulte des postulations adolescentes et suicidaires quelque peu inquiétantes. Je me lançais dans le vide avec avidité. Je me sentais invulnérable tout en tentant le diable. Au bout de cette logique, je nourrissais secrètement la certitude que même la mort ne m'aurait pas fait mal. C'était là l'idée abyssale, la tentation de fond. Je la redécouvre aujourd'hui. Se tuer sans frémir et jouir de la mort en un éclair et lui crever la panse et passer au travers. J'ai toujours admiré la cérémonie du *seppuku*, ce charcutage souverainement orgueilleux et narcissique qui consiste à s'inciser sans hésiter, à entrer dans la mort en ouvrant soi-même la porte de son

corps. Travail précis, juste, sans bavure. Pas tant de l'héroïsme que du boulot d'artiste et de grand prêtre. Je trouve cela un peu têtu mais d'un culot exaltant. Il faut ce qu'il faut pour ne pas mourir idiot. Une sûreté d'écriture et de style en quelque sorte, une signature en paraphe écarlate. Bon, je vais peiner et apeurer mes proches. En tout cas, cette nuit d'insomnie, j'adhérai soudain à la thèse du Dr P., c'était bien un ménisque ! Et je troquai mon staphylocoque romantique et doré contre un mince bracelet d'ivoire, tel l'anneau de ma destinée.

Le lendemain, au téléphone, je déballai la vérité au Dr P. Il se réjouit d'entendre la confirmation de son hypothèse, sans pour autant s'étonner de mes cascades dans les escaliers ni m'inciter à me poser quelques questions radicales sur cette pulsion étrange.

L'arthrographie fut moins pénible qu'on ne me l'avait prédit. Je n'éprouvai strictement rien pendant l'impressionnante dilatation du genou. Mais peut-être était-ce, là encore, un tour que me jouait mon aptitude à neutraliser la douleur en fonçant droit sur elle. Car voilà l'explication : je me ruais en chantant contre le mal que j'avais provoqué et choisi. Oui, et ce n'était pas sans élan lyrique ! Un ami, vieux romancier, m'a surnommé un jour : « le clairon », sous prétexte que j'ai le verbe fort. Il ne croyait pas si bien dire. L'adolescent chargeait, piquait des deux, clairon en main et célébrait son hallali.

J'achetais un journal dans une petite librairie fourre-tout, gommes et crayons, quand derrière la vitre, sur le trottoir, je vis la jeune Juive qui venait une fois la semaine prendre un cours d'instruction religieuse dans la petite école sur laquelle

donnait la fenêtre de ma chambre. Je la reconnus tout de suite. Pondérée, timide, avec ses longs cheveux. Une femme très belle l'accompagnait, sa mère sans doute... On pouvait présager que la fillette l'égalerait plus tard. Elles s'approchèrent et soudain entrèrent dans la librairie. Nous nous saluâmes. La fillette me reconnut, rougit, esquissa un sourire léger, la vapeur d'un sourire qui lui embua les traits. La mère perçut le trouble de sa fille et me considéra. Elle avait une chevelure énorme et profonde, de grands yeux noirs, ardents, qui vous prenaient le visage. Un jean pâle et moulant gainait ses cuisses et ses fesses charnues. Un court blouson de cuir un peu voyou s'arrêtait au ras d'une ceinture à clous. Le vêtement était ouvert sur un pull brun. L'on voyait les mamelons gros et calés dans la laine. La petite fille regardait sa mère me regarder. Elle perçut mon saisissement devant la belle femme musquée, ses gestes câlins, la façon émouvante dont elle se penchait sur les magazines pour les feuilleter du doigt. Nonchalante, puis nerveuse soudain, plantée devant sa fille, lui montrant une image, lui proposant une revue, autre chose... flâneuse le long des étagères, rêveuse. Puis précise, attirée par une photo de mode, elle élevait la page près de ses yeux, la contemplait longuement, la scrutait, se confrontait au modèle, l'étudiait, imaginait la parure sur elle, demandait à sa fille son avis. Et cette dernière découvrait une toute petite robe de jersey qui épousait le galbe d'une fille dont s'exhibaient la gorge, les hanches, les plis sensuels. La fillette cillait devant tant de hardiesse, de sûreté dans la féminité et elle se recroquevillait d'un mouvement frileux, comme éclipsée par la magnificence et la convoitise de sa mère qui désirait le sacre de la robe d'amour.

Avant de quitter la boutique, elles me saluèrent de nouveau. La petite fille sourit encore, de ce sourire évanescent qui était moins dessiné sur les lèvres que reflété par

l'ensemble de ses traits. Elles se retournèrent. Le cul de la mère concentrait dans le jean un maximum de chair lente et lascive. Je ne pus m'empêcher de le fixer des yeux, la petite fille jeta un bref coup d'œil en arrière et saisit la direction de mon regard que je déviai aussitôt. La mère partit la première dans la rue, la petite la suivait, son magazine à la main. Elle ne put éviter comme moi de regarder très vite, avec un air presque apeuré, le derrière de sa mère, riche et remuant, pétri par l'étoffe délavée, dilatée à l'excès, sous la bande noire et gluante du blouson de loubard qui dansait. La petite fille portait un manteau bleu foncé qui masquait son corps.

J'allais sortir à mon tour quand je vis Johann Neuzil qui avançait lentement le long du trottoir. L'apparition du bâtard d'Egon Schiele me surprit. Neuzil clopinait avec une mimique douce, un peu douloureuse. Il s'arrêta pour regarder un couple qui galopait, sautait sur le trottoir, retombait... La femme et l'homme se bousculaient, cognaient leurs épaules l'une contre l'autre dans un chahut léger. Ils s'enlaçaient, s'embrassaient, l'un en contrebas, l'autre planté sur le trottoir, titubaient. Ils jouaient les amants, car on les sentait conscients de leurs gestes, de leurs joutes capricieuses. Neuzil contemplait la scène, arrêté dans la rue, un peu penché, courbé sur son pied malade. Il buvait des yeux le couple adorable et juvénile. Mais son regard ne manifestait aucune curiosité érotique, seulement le bonheur de la contemplation. Neuzil baignait dans la beauté des amants. Ils le dépassèrent et Neuzil resta là, un peu sidéré, immobile sur la chaussée. Il ne repartait pas. Il n'avait pas de but, de rendez-vous précis. Il était bien où il était. Il ne sentait plus la douleur de son pied. Il humait l'air, un souffle frais. Un rayon déchira les nuages et toucha la rue, l'éclaira tout en long. Neuzil sourit à la lumière. Son visage réverbérait une infinie douceur. Il restait là, debout, offert, abandonné au

pâle soleil, absorbé dans une écoute intérieure mais ouvert en même temps aux choses, aux gens de la rue. Il devenait diaphane, sa silhouette surnaturelle allait s'évanouir, s'envoler dans un mirage. Puis, tout à coup, il reprit sa marche, le visage porté en avant, toujours empreint du même ravissement, dans cette rue de sortilège que le bruit semblait avoir soudain désertée... couloir vacant, élargi, allongé dans sa phosphorescence... Neuzil rayonnait. Et je fus pris d'un frisson quand je le vis passer de profil, j'apercevais les veines fragiles de sa tempe et de sa joue comme des sillons de souffrance mais apaisés, délivrés dans la lumière.

Cette vision de Johann Neuzil me préoccupa tout le jour, m'obséda. Je tentais de détacher ma pensée mais l'image revenait de Neuzil porté par la lumière, ouvert et rayonnant. Le soir, j'essayai d'expliquer la scène à Marguerite qui chantonnait en découpant des rognons pour Toufflette. J'insistai. Elle se redressa, me scruta en haussant les épaules. Soudain, je la trouvai grotesque, bancale et ballonnée, puis elle lança :

— Eh bien oui ! C'est un délice, Neuzil ! Il est un peu dans les nuages... bon !

Comme je savais gré à Marguerite de cette image céleste.

— Oui, justement... il marche sur les nuages...

— Ah ! Je n'ai pas dit ça ! Il est dans la lune ! repartit Margot.

— Non ! C'est mieux, c'est plus intense... Neuzil est lumineux !

Marguerite ne me suivait pas jusque-là. Elle trouvait même un peu louche mon enthousiasme. Je n'avais pas les yeux en face des trous, j'exagérais !

— Mais qu'est-ce que vous voulez me dire, avec Neuzil ? ! Qu'est-ce qu'il y a ?

Elle était suspendue à ma réponse. Ce fut plus fort que

moi, je savais que j'avais tort et qu'il fallait me taire, garder scrupuleusement mon intuition, mon illumination. Mais débordé, ébloui par l'évidence, je m'exclamai :

— Johann Neuzil est un saint ! Voilà ! C'est un saint ! Marguerite, c'est extraordinaire... C'est un vrai saint transpercé par la lumière. Oui, il était radieux !

Marguerite n'appréciait pas du tout. Elle était profondément réaliste, éprise de faits palpables. Va pour un soleil radieux, va pour l'escalier du Palais de justice, pure merveille d'architecture, va pour Toufflette, va pour les engouements normaux. Idolâtrer un chat, d'accord. Mais délirer sur Neuzil et, pire, évoquer le surnaturel ! Je savais que si elle croyait en Dieu, se réclamait du catholicisme sans pratiquer, c'était justement pour juguler tout mysticisme et pour garder les pieds sur terre. Marguerite respectait les normes. Affirmer tout de go que Johann Neuzil était un saint, voilà qui la choquait, me faisait suspecter de déséquilibre mental. Marguerite méprisait les illuminés, les « fadas » comme elle disait.

— Soudain n'est pas un saint ! Vous déraillez... Dans son jeune temps, je sais qu'il fut très cavaleur, un sauteur ! Oui ! Oui ! Il tenait ça de son père, son supposé papa ! L'autre, le Schiele, avec ses filles à poil, tout le temps et partout, à la renverse, écarquillées, si ! Mal fichues même et malingres, phtisiques, syphilitiques, des putes et des gamines en plus... des mineures ! Je les ai vues dans l'album qu'il a chez lui, sur sa table, comme la Bible... eh bien merci ! Et il paraît que le dessin de Schiele que Neuzil détient en secret est tout à fait obscène et sacrilège. Maurice et David l'ont vu. Il le leur a montré en catimini. Alors, remballez votre sainteté ! J'en sais quelques autres sur lui, ses tendances... En gros, c'est un brave type, si vous voulez, globalement, mais il a des failles, voilà ! et pas des petites, des grosses comme ça !

79

Comment osait-elle profaner Neuzil avec ce grotesque surnom de Soudain et ses ragots fétides. Révolté, je m'écriai :

— Je ne vous croyais pas si bégueule ! Et je me fiche du passé de Neuzil, c'est pas ça qui peut l'empêcher d'être un saint à mes yeux ! Car ça s'est vu, des saints qui ont vécu une jeunesse très libre ! Moi, je l'ai bien regardé dans la rue, je l'ai contemplé même et je sais ! L'avez-vous déjà entendu dire du mal de quelqu'un ? Non ! Jamais... Il est patient, plein de bonté. Il écoute avec attention, avec amitié. Il donne beaucoup de gentillesse, d'amour ! Et justement, quand il m'a montré l'album de nus d'Egon Schiele, il l'a fait sans rien d'ambigu ni de salace. C'est à mille lieues de lui ! Au contraire, il était respectueux de tant de beauté, scrupuleux ! Émerveillé ! Il commentait le dessin fulgurant de Schiele, son art précis, surnaturel, son amour des corps, de leur beauté vulnérable et mortelle, voilà ! De leur beauté sainte ! C'est un saint ! Il est éthéré, voilà ! Je cherchais le mot. Ah ! c'est ça : éthéré !

— Éthéré ?

Marguerite, interloquée, hostile, releva le mot comme un outrage, une pièce à conviction :

— Éthéré ! Ça ne veut rien dire, ou alors c'est que vous ne tournez pas rond !

J'aboyai :

— C'est un saint !

Alors, ma logeuse découvrit un trait de son étudiant qu'elle ignorait : la colère, la crise qui montait, la voix qui avait changé, le timbre soudain métallique et tonnant. Elle n'aimait pas ça du tout. Qu'est-ce qui me prenait de faire l'énergumène ?

— On ne parle pas sur ce ton à une vieille dame ! dit-elle au comble du déplaisir. Vous me faites de la peine, je vous trouvais plus... mieux que ça ! Ne m'emmerdez plus avec la

sainteté de Neuzil et toutes les cochonneries de son Schiele. Vous êtes fanatique ! Fanatique ! J'ai horreur de ça ! Les saints, ça n'existe plus ! Depuis sainte Thérèse, il n'y en a plus ! Ça n'est plus moderne, c'est terminé !

Je remâchai mon échec dans mon lit. Je n'avais pu communiquer la révélation à ma logeuse. Il fallait ne rien dire, attendre Anny qui comprendrait.

On fit l'amour, une fois tout vite et la seconde lentement, en savourant tous les méandres. Puis on alla déjeuner, puis on revint dans ma chambre. J'attendis, j'hésitais... Anny se demandait ce qui me rendait si perplexe.

— Tu es tout drôle, ça ne va pas ?

— C'est une scène de la rue. Voilà ! J'ai rencontré Johann Neuzil. Il marchait, puis il s'est arrêté le long du trottoir. Un brusque rayon de lumière a baigné son visage. Neuzil a souri d'un sourire surnaturel, voilà ! Il était transparent. Il devenait tout lumineux. Il était complètement éthéré !

— Oui, c'est vraiment un homme gentil. Je l'aime beaucoup, moi aussi.

— Mais non, Anny ! c'est mieux que cela ! Neuzil est un saint. Ça m'a frappé soudain, une évidence éblouissante : Neuzil est un saint !

Anny se tut. Elle se garda de me contrarier, mais elle n'abonda pas dans mon sens. Elle était étonnée de cette sainteté qui arrivait ainsi sur le tapis, par un week-end comme les autres. Elle ne sentait pas tout à fait cette sainteté, sans l'exclure à priori.

— Tu es d'accord, non ?

— Je ne sais pas... Je ne me suis jamais posé cette question...

Non, Anny ne partageait pas ma conviction. Mais elle n'avait pas vu Neuzil auréolé en pleine rue, nimbé de pâle soleil. Cette expérience n'était pas communicable. Si j'avais été à la place d'Anny, la chose m'aurait sans doute intéressé, attaché, sans me pourfendre, m'éclabousser d'une certitude miraculeuse. J'espérais qu'Anny m'interrogerait, me demanderait de raconter encore, de développer mes impressions. Mais elle restait coite. Car la sainteté échappe à la conversation ordinaire, à l'enquête. On ne peut dialoguer là-dessus. Et surtout, la sainteté fait peur. Je compris soudain ce malaise, cette peur face à l'irrationnel, à la déflagration du spirituel. C'était trop dangereux. On risquait de décrocher, de se perdre...

J'embrassai Anny avec une telle intensité, un tel émerveillement pathétique qu'elle se raidit un peu. Car nous n'étions tout de même pas des saints. Elle aurait préféré que j'atterrisse plus vite, que je lui attrape les fesses bien crûment, le sexe dardé, collé contre elle. Ça l'aurait rassurée un peu. Elle m'eût branlé en m'embrassant, se fût déculottée en une seconde, les jambes encore garrottées par son Levis... Nous deux bientôt haletants, encombrés par le pantalon, excités par l'entrave, le slip plus clair, plus suave, tirebouchonné au fond, ma ceinture me battant les mollets... Anny plus nue, plus lisse d'être ainsi dégainée de l'étoffe froissée. Parfois, comme la transe nous prenait au moment de partir, elle n'avait pas le temps de s'essuyer, elle sautait sur ses jarrets, se dressait d'une volée, remontait directement le slip, fermait avec autorité les boutons de son pantalon. Et je trouvais cela leste et coquin, ce pantalon bouclé sur un coït furtif et son sexe trempé. Moi-même j'escamotais mon phallus parfumé sans m'essuyer. Et nous partions dans la rue lumineuse, vers le Pont-Marie, les îles, la cathédrale sainte, tout imprégnés d'odeurs. Il nous arrivait de croiser Osiris, le

guide et le gardien des tours. Il nous dévisageait. Il souriait avec malice, nous frôlait, et ses narines humaient notre odeur d'amour.

Hélas, ce scénario charmant venait d'être bloqué par l'intrusion du sacré, de cette sainteté trop vaste, trop périlleuse. Donc, je fis un retour sur moi, je me tançai sévèrement. Neuzil était peut-être un saint. Mais il ne fallait plus m'exalter là-dessus. Au contraire, je devais me concentrer sur Anny, sur le monde, dans les limites de nos forces et de nos vies. J'eus peur soudain moi aussi, peur pour Anny et pour moi. Car si, dans le grand vide de la vie qui s'ouvrait, la sainteté m'obnubilait, ce serait sans doute pire, plus vertigineux encore, il n'y aurait plus de garde-fou au désir d'infini, à l'ivresse, à la chute dans l'immensité.

Mieux valait parler de mon ménisque brisé. Ce petit cartilage-là était utile et concret... Je ne pouvais envisager une ablation pendant cette année universitaire. C'était trop risqué avant le concours. Il fallait compter quinze jours de clinique et une rééducation... Anny m'écoutait, était du même avis. Soudain, elle m'embrassa la joue. Je perçus sa tiédeur et la lueur de son collier nacré. Nous étions de nouveau au diapason, deux étudiants, jeunes amants dont la vie commençait. Neuzil, lui, marchait dans la lumière, rayonnait vers sa mort, emportant sur son cœur l'icône d'Egon Schiele. Anny et moi étions si loin du bout des choses, du fin mot de l'affaire et de l'éternité.

Je sautai dans le métro, les portes claquèrent. J'avais une vision encore très vague des gens qui m'entouraient. Tout à coup, devant moi : DE GAULLE EST MORT. En lettres capitales. Énormes et noires. Un journal déployé. Le message occupait toute la page. Incrédule, je regardais les passagers sans réaction. Mêmes expressions gommées, bringuebalées dans les tunnels. Je n'avais jamais été gaulliste ni rien du tout. Ni mao ni gaullo. Un désir sans objet, une révolte sans thème ni drapeaux. Des nerfs, des spasmes, des chimères. J'avais choisi Rimbaud lyrique plutôt que les doctrines à panoplie et petit livre brandi. Puis, l'Autre, le Grand, sabré soudain. Fin du totem. De Gaulle est mort. C'était haut, majuscule. Ça allait bien avec le nom, le blason un peu froid du nom. Grandiose, épique et funèbre. Une muraille croulait comme le donjon d'un château qui ne me concernait pas directement, ancestral et lointain. Mais rapproché d'un coup. De Gaulle est mort. Chaque lettre taillée dans le roc s'effondrait de tout son poids, de toute son altitude. Le grand donjon crénelé s'abîmait. Vieille épopée rugueuse. Emphase écrabouillée. Décombres là, tout noirs.

J'arrivai chez Marguerite. Elle était assise sur une chaise et

85

pleurait. La voyant, je fis comme elle. Je pleurai beaucoup sur moi et peut-être sur le roi. Je ne sais sur qui pleurait Margot… Un horizon tombait, une montagne dans son cœur, une grosse rêverie d'enfant, de petite fille. Je ne sais pas… car d'habitude les morts attisaient plutôt sa curiosité et son plaisir de se sentir toujours en vie. Ce jour-là, Marguerite n'était pas curieuse, mais elle s'abandonnait à une grande lessive de larmes et de hoquets. Elle regardait la télé et avalait les images, toutes les images, de tous les temps, du monde entier, de ses appels, de ses promesses et de ses volte-face. C'étaient les attentats, les discours, le comique des improvisations dans les langues étrangères. L'air bourru, hautain. Le ventre colossal pointé au-dessus des peuples. L'allure, la tronche grise, ravinée, austère, puis la gouaille, les roulements caverneux, les facéties de singe géant, les entourloupes, le style, la phrase pétrie dans notre histoire, les secrets mijotements, les ressassements vindicatifs et les fanfaronnades, les défis.

On revoyait tout, Lear errant sur les grèves d'Irlande, la France grondée comme un gosse, houspillée ou chantée, exaltée dans des légendes qui s'envolaient au-dessus de nous dans un éblouissement gothique. Vieux soldat homérique, vieux sire, Graal recru, patriarche obèse, plein d'orgueil familier. Dragon des origines, monumental gourou des Gaules, vieux gui, vieux tronc, antique ramure rouillée par les tempêtes. Vitrail. Et tout ça culbuté. Ruines.

Margot me demanda de rester dîner avec elle. Elle courut dans ma chambre, ouvrit une sorte de placard long et bas, une vraie planque dérobée derrière un rideau. Une niche apparaissait, avec des bouteilles de vin et divers objets au rebut. On aurait pu dissimuler dans le trou un terroriste, un de ces mecs du restaurant médical pétant de projets apocalyptiques. Là, chez Margot, dans ma piaule, au secret. Comme à

l'époque du Vieux, des réseaux cachés, des complots sublimes contre la botte nazie. Margot prépara un poulet... « Vous aimez bien un petit poulet ? » J'acquiesçai. Elle s'activait, y allait d'un nouveau torrent lacrymal, s'arrêtait, une assiette à la main, pour regarder l'Autre à la tribune, tonnant contre les généraux félons, furieux soudain, fulminant... Et il changeait de forme suivant les époques, les documents, plus ou moins gros, lisse ou parcheminé, flétri. Je le trouvai un peu obscène en 58, luisant et gominé alors que l'Histoire le reprenait. Ni vieux ni jeune, gonflé, baudruche superbe et sûre de son droit, époux, maître de la France, content de son couple. Mari heureux de Marianne. Il devait me fasciner plus tard, dans les attentats, Petit Clamart sous la mitraille, les orages, les harangues, les anathèmes et les railleries. Et plus loin encore, surtout, mon favori fut le très vieux bougon, grommelant, gris, à bajoues, fanons de préhistoire, grande archive lasse et monstrueuse. Il n'y avait plus que les yeux brillants, aigus, dans la peau incroyablement cartonnée, son écorce mâchonnée, cabossée, décrépite. Vieux caïman de gloriole et de chevalerie. Les yeux dans le nid des rides, leur pétillement encore sans merci, entêté, avec ce rictus déçu vers la fin, cette fêlure d'amertume dans tous les plissements de sa figure paléontologique... Tout au bout, poudré, la poudre craquelée sur les failles, les bourrelets, autour des petits yeux luisant dans le cuir des paupières poudreuses elles aussi... Car cette poudre qui était nécessaire pour passer à la télévision devenait la poussière du temps, le sable millénaire, limon où s'était roulée sa statue vert-de-grisée, piquetée, lézardée, maculée par les bains, les chimies de l'histoire.

Margot me servit le vin. Elle sanglotait : « Il est bon mon petit poulet, pas vrai ?... » Je disais oui. Je mangeais le blanc. Elle préférait les cuisses, les parties grasses et musculeuses,

les os qu'on suce, le croupion, petites cochonneries de carcasse, lambeaux bien accrochés. Moi, les grandes plages de blanc homogène et moelleux. On se gorgeait de vin. Elle trottina vers la planque, en rapporta un second litre et hop ! Maintenant je pleurais avec Margot dès que l'Autre surgissait... L'Auguste, le fantastique Matamore monté sur des échasses, bedon protubérant et képi héroïque, le gladiateur des Gaules... L'augure du 18 juin valsait dans notre ivresse. Puis, soudain, ça nous prit, on se mit à rigoler en pleurant, on ne pouvait plus se retenir, ça nous prenait malgré la tristesse de le voir en gros plan, en majesté, moche quand même, le pif impossible, gondolé, brioché, les joues de cachalot, son air de chêne de Dodone, de Bourbon suffisant, plein de morgue et grognon. On pouffait, on y allait d'un nouveau verre de vin, on torchait le poulet jusqu'aux petites esquilles, rogatons rissolés.

Marguerite avisa Toufflette : « Ah ! ma pauvre Toufflette, le grand Charlot est mort ! » La chatte pointait sur nous son œil resplendissant et nul. Puis, devant les deux ivrognes, émit un maigre petit miaulement et se trissa dans la chambre voisine.

De Gaulle hurlait : « Vive le Québec... » et on se marrait, on reprenait en chœur : « libre ! libre ! » Morts de rire... Les foules s'époumonaient, le hélaient, s'agenouillaient. « Je vous ai... » Et nous, bras dessus, bras dessous, en duo : « compris ! compris ! »... « Un quarteron de généraux à la retraite ! »... Et nous en ricochet : « Hélas ! Hélas ! Hélas ! »... Toutes ces maximes, tirades bien astiquées... « Le con ! s'extasiait Margot, ah le con ! » Mais c'était de l'admiration. On pleurait, on s'esclaffait, pissant dans notre culotte devant l'épopée. En Amérique latine, il ressemblait à quelque potentat populiste de là-bas. Sur les affiches et les banderoles, on le représentait toujours beaucoup plus jeune,

88

sorte de barbon aux cheveux enduits de brillantine, sans âge, mélange de coiffeur, de colonel inoxydable. En Union soviétique, il prenait l'air russe et slave, sa dégaine Tolstoï. Il n'y avait qu'en Angleterre et en Amérique qu'il n'arrivait pas à faire british. Puis la perfection : au Togo, au Cameroun, au Sénégal, là, un mélange de sultan paternaliste, de saint Louis, de Lyautey, avec un zeste de Fidel Castro. Roi de France, surtout, formidable fétiche, maître griot glorieux, de marbre et plein d'aménité. Très bon en Afrique noire. Il fut le meilleur là-bas, catholique, colon volontairement défroqué, chef de tribu et cacique de tous les clans. Fellah faramineux et pacha inspiré. On avait envie de lui amener des caravanes d'or et des harems. Nabuchodonosor... Et puis soudain bonhomme, rustique, tout simple, Lorraine...

Margot qui était saoule se bidonnait à le voir encore et encore. « On ne peut pas dire qu'il était beau gosse... C'est pas Alain Delon, pour sûr ! » Et on se tapait sur les cuisses de rire, en rotant le poulet dont la sauce était grasse, affalés sur la table, parmi les miettes, entre deux bouteilles vides. L'Autre nous lorgnait, sa trogne comme postiche enfoncée dans la salle à manger, comme une tête de gros calamar en colère ou de dindon à caroncule, écarquillant son œil patriarcal. « Moi, la France !... » Nous, on n'était que du menu fretin, on n'y comprenait mie, piétaille, petite ferraille dans la poche des dieux et des rois. « On n'est que de la merde, c'est sûr ! » pleurait de rire Margot. « C'est vrai que de Gaulle, lui, en avait deux ! » Celle-là, c'était le bouquet ! Toute la France l'avait faite, refaite, épuisée. On ne s'en lassait pas, vautrés sur la toile cirée, à imaginer l'engin éléphantesque, le manche dont tout le monde parlait... Mille histoires drôles, devinettes sur le chibre de Charlot, sur la massue du mec. La France rêvait au sceptre dont on savait qu'il n'abusait jamais, son côté vierge ainsi, catho, époux

fidèle, immémorial... ce qui conférait à l'outil impollué on ne savait quel éclat, quel prestige d'incorruptibilité.

Le jour des funérailles, Marguerite s'était levée à six heures du matin et m'avait réveillé, emmené de force sur le parvis de Notre-Dame. Elle ne pouvait rester seule debout trop longtemps, il fallait que je la soutienne un peu. En récompense, elle reverrait le prix de ma chambre. Je la suppliai, lui expliquai mon horreur des foules, des messes collectives. Rien n'y fit, elle insista, me menaça, me cajola, exerça mille chantages... Sans moi, elle aurait un malaise. Je n'avais pas le droit de la priver de Charlot. Je capitulai.

Margot adorait les grands spectacles, surtout quand ils étaient gratis. A Cannes, un été, elle s'était levée à quatre heures du matin, installée à la plage, pique-niquant, campant jusqu'au soir minuit où se donnait un festival de feux d'artifices. Margot, c'était ça ! Aux premières loges pour la curée, le cataclysme en technicolor. Je crois qu'elle eût assisté aux exécutions publiques : décapitations, derniers guillotinés au grand air. Bouche bée, ravie... Louis XVI, Capet, coupée cabèche. Une larmichette pour Marie-Antoinette.

On nous contenait derrière des barrières métalliques et des piquets de flics en cordons sans faille. Marguerite avait apporté une paire de jumelles qu'elle gardait pour les grandes occasions : éclipses, comètes, sacres... Au premier rang, grâce à sa carte d'invalide, moi derrière elle, factotum à son service, elle s'appuyait sur une barrière, allongeait le cou, bouclettes au vent, l'œil immensément fasciné...

De longues bagnoles arrivaient sur le parvis, tournaient, allaient se placer en file indienne devant le porche central de Notre-Dame. Cela sortait : les reines, les rois, les princes, les

princesses, les maharadjas, les colonels, les présidents à vie, les généraux musclés, les potentats de l'Orient, de l'Oural, de l'Ouganda... de pays dont on ignorait l'existence, petits États perdus, caniculaires, tyrannies de l'Équateur, oligarchies. Il y avait la terre entière. Tous s'engouffraient dans ma cathédrale, accueillis par une sorte de prélat diplomatique et onctueux, l'équivalent d'un secrétaire général de la présidence de la République, chef du protocole, un type très doux, très distingué qui s'inclinait devant les majestés et les guidait à l'intérieur. Margot me passait de temps en temps les jumelles, elle s'énervait, elle ne reconnaissait presque personne. Elle confondait les Turcs, les Russes, les Sud-Américains, les Japonais et les Chinois. D'où ça venait ? Le monde immense, tous les pouvoirs, les maîtres. Là... le porche avalait leur serpent monstrueux. Ils prenaient un air droit et solennel et se noyaient dans l'ombre, à l'intérieur.

Pendant toute la messe, on attendit. On ne pouvait que les imaginer tous bien serrés dans la cathédrale bourrée à craquer de sommités. Un empilement de destins fracassants, de leviers féeriques, tous les ressorts de la planète, son horlogerie précieuse. Bokassa et Mobutu pleuraient, se mouchaient à qui mieux mieux. Agneaux, cœurs tendres. Et l'ogre de l'Ouganda, Idi Amin Dada, était-il déjà là ? Moi, j'avais peur pour Notre-Dame des Anges et des Faucons. Que devenaient les oiseaux dans leur lucarne ? Entendaient-ils les chœurs, les hymnes, les orgues ? Devinaient-ils le fourmillement sacré sous la voûte gothique ? Anges et oiseaux farouches, indifférents à la mort des hommes. Excités, apeurés par le boucan, le carrousel des voitures, la foule alentour, l'éclat des chromes, des uniformes. Cela pouvait ressembler à un géant hallali, à une chasse colossale aux faucons, quelque tuerie royale. Carnage d'anges et de rapaces. Les faucons guettaient, écoutaient du fond de leurs

fissures, dans la grosse bogue des pierres sculptées. Ils entendaient la rumeur mystique comme le bruit de la mer.

Alors le glas retentit. Le glas du bourdon Emmanuel. Osiris devait commander le déclic. La cloche qui sonne de loin en loin sur Paris. Pour les catastrophes et les grandes euphories. A la Libération de Paris, le même de Gaulle altier, libérateur avait entendu ce carillon. Tout à coup, Margot s'exclama : « Nixon ! » Elle me tendit la paire de jumelles. C'était bien Nixon sorti devant le porche, attendant sa voiture. Sourire opaque et discret. Sa tête carrée, ses joues en boules de chaque côté. Nixon. Et sa bagnole ne venait pas. Il fallait écouler d'abord des tapées de rois, reines hollandaises et suédoises et d'ailleurs, la blondeur entrevue de la princesse Grace, ducs dorés, dédorés, grands vizirs, croquemitaines du cap Horn et de la Corne d'or, bourreaux médaillés, certains mal en point, branlants, gâteux, venus ici humer leur futur trépas, d'autres fringants félins, l'œil carnivore encore, douchés du sang d'un putsch. Et Nixon souriait, gommant toute mimique trop narquoise ou glacée, affichant à présent un air contemplatif, patient, apprivoisé. Margot me disait : « J'aime bien Nixon ! » Elle ne le quittait plus de ses oculaires. Elle s'en ressasiait. Moi, je redoutais l'homme, je préférais Kennedy, juvénile et donjuanesque, à quenottes allègres. Nixon, on sentait que c'était vissé par le X, la consonne centrale, écrou noir, impérieux, cloué dans le nom. Il n'aurait jamais couché avec Marilyn Monroe. C'était ce qui le rendait nocif.

Margot chuchotait : « Quand je pense qu'Il n'est pas là ! » C'est à de Gaulle qu'elle revenait quand même, au géant paradoxe. Tous les puissants planétaires n'adoraient qu'un absent. De Gaulle avait renié ma cathédrale. Et je lui en voulais un peu. Mon rêve eût été qu'on organisât des funérailles privées à Notre-Dame. Rien que la famille et les

résistants de la dernière guerre, en compagnie des anges et des faucons. Voilà. Pas de tralala. La cathédrale et le Général. Seul à seul. Fils et madone. Et dix faucons de feu.

Pendant ce temps-là, on l'enterrait à la campagne, dans la terre de la guerre et des bergères hallucinées, gorgée de morts depuis toujours, féerique et funèbre. Des types de son village, musclés et rougeauds, sortaient de l'église en portant le cercueil sur leurs épaules. Douze gaillards de la glèbe. Douze culs-terreux sans phrases. Il préférait ce sacre rugueux aux fastes. Ma grande cathédrale était vide, saturée d'un grand fracas vide. C'était la faute de Viollet-le-Duc ! De Gaulle n'aurait jamais voulu d'une cathédrale en simili-gothique, avec Nixon sur le parvis et son sourire de Ku Klux Klan. Il y avait, à Colombey, le village du Vieux, ici le temple de Nixon. Horreur... Tout au fond de moi, vague d'amer-tume horrible. Notre-Dame sous le joug de Nixon, sous scellés de la CIA. Le tympan du porche, les arcs-boutants, les pinacles, la flèche, tout dégénérait en simulacre et carte postale factice. Je voyais fondre ma légende et mon amour, pollués par tant de rois et de reines et par l'Al Capone attendant sa Cadillac. Notre-Dame de Chicago... ou quoi ? d'Hollywood, et encore ? Grand décor de B. De Mille... John Wayne et Ford attendant sur le parvis eussent été dans la veine héroïque et cavalière ou le vieux Négus Haïlé Sélassié, roi d'Éthiopie, empereur du pays de Saba, de l'or, squelette momifié, rabougri, despotique, eût convenu au mythe. Où était-il donc, celui-là ? Sans doute fourgué illico dans sa bagnole, à bout de forces, déjà aux prises avec des soulève-ments multiples, des rumeurs grandissantes de révolution. Et le chah, le chah ! Le loup d'Iran, Margot et moi l'avions raté, elle se plaignait : Nixon, ça allait un quart d'heure, mais les autres, les plus vieux, les artistes, les alchimistes de la tyrannie et des Mille et Une Nuits ? Le Négus et le chah, un

vrai couple cruel et luxuriant, dans un bruissement légendaire d'or et de sang. De Gaulle aurait brillé par une simplicité romane et soldatesque auprès des deux empereurs d'Orient. Mais Nixon emportait le morceau, souriant, immobile, impavide. Déjà, les potentats somptueux et carnassiers, c'était de la vieille pacotille, rebuts rassis, pharaoniques déchets. Partout fermaient les antiques opéras des crimes royaux. C'était la fin des mythes.

Margot avait tenu six heures debout contre sa barrière. Elle suçait de temps à autre un sucre ou croquait un petit biscuit Lu et m'en refilait des morceaux pour les glucides... Car elle se méfiait, à présent, de ma santé. Elle connaissait mon restaurant pour infirmes. J'étais faible quoique impétueux comme elle, un fond de vitalité dans un vertige continuel. On grignotait nos sucres en couvant des yeux Notre-Dame. Puis Marguerite se lassa d'un coup, sans prévenir. Elle se retourna vers moi : « On y va ! »

Le soir à la télé, en voyant l'enterrement à Colombey, elle ne pleurait plus. On raconta que lorsque le cercueil sortit de l'église, un grand vol d'oies passa sur la campagne. Ça me ramenait aux chasses, aux neiges de mon enfance. De ce jour, au fond, je ne me souviens vraiment que du sourire vissé de Nixon et des oies déployées qui l'effaçaient, là-haut dans le ciel du voyage, de l'éternelle migration.

Anny était saine, donc peu sensible au trépas du dernier roi franc. De Gaulle les avait toujours enquiquinées, elle et sa sœur, quand, petites filles, elles devaient se taire dès qu'il apparaissait à la télé, apostrophait, pérorait, paterne et pontifiant. Anny ne vibrait pas à la grandeur, à l'emphase, elle y reniflait une senteur dangereuse. Elle n'aimait pas non

plus que je m'échauffe dans le panache épique. D'instinct, elle y voyait l'œil du gouffre, l'éclipse de nos amours.

Nous avions mal dormi, mon amante et moi. Mon genou me faisait souffrir, je m'étais retourné sans cesse dans mon lit, excité, vigilant, si bien qu'à l'aurore on fut debout avec le sentiment d'une toute petite nuit rognée par les deux bouts, effilochée, de rien du tout. Pourtant, j'étais grisé par l'insomnie, extralucide. Anny redoutait un peu cet accès qui serait suivi d'un lamentable reflux. Il émanait de Paris, quand nous sortîmes, un bruit de fond, homogène et sourd, pareil non pas au grondement de la circulation automobile mais à une rumeur naturelle de mer sur les rochers, de vent dans la forêt. Cela devait être dû à l'heure matinale, à la présence presque cosmique des brumes, d'une lumière rougie, glacée, qui voilait le va-et-vient des hommes. Le fleuve avait retrouvé une odeur de source et d'estuaire.

Le parvis de Notre-Dame était redevenu calme. La cathédrale venait d'encaisser les ors et les gloires sans rien prétendre. Elle en avait avalé d'autres depuis des siècles, des sacres, des pactes et des déconfitures, et toujours les funérailles pour conclure, le même train lent et noir, les gisants pour l'éternité. Ce matin, Notre-Dame était vierge des fastes et des deuils.

A la cime de la tour, au débouché de la grande galerie, nous vîmes Ehra. Elle semblait seule et triste. Au lieu de nous approcher, nous sommes restés à l'écart, confinés dans un angle, le regard dirigé vers le sud-est, tandis qu'Ehra était assise au nord-ouest, sur la bordure plombée du toit. Les prénoms orientaux et ardents d'Amador et de Rawi étaient inscrits sous nos yeux. Mais leur chaud rayonnement ne parvenait pas à nous toucher, tant était grande notre stupeur de contempler Ehra sans Wolf. On l'eût dite endeuillée et

blême. Sa silhouette demeurait sans mouvement, rigide. Elle ne paraissait rien attendre, rien regarder. Elle n'aimait plus le monde. L'absent terrible, Wolf, lui manquait.

Un faucon s'est posé soudain sur le museau d'une gargouille lycanthropique, non loin d'Ehra. L'oiseau restait calme. Il regardait Ehra sans peur. Cette dernière l'avait vu, car son visage était orienté de biais vers lui. Le profil blanc d'Ehra et l'œil du prédateur ailé. Anny et moi étions saisis par le silence et la mystérieuse beauté de la scène. L'oiseau s'envola, tourna, piqua vers la nef et ses rémiges brillèrent dans le soleil. Il se posa de nouveau, mais au-delà, sur la légère pointe du toit de la tour Nord, la tour inconnue, vierge de tout regard. Et on eût dit qu'il regardait encore Ehra. Surtout, celle-ci me paraissait toujours dans l'aura et sous la coupe de cet œil d'oiseau. Je ne pouvais plus déceler si ce qui unissait ainsi la bête et la jeune fille était de l'ordre de la confiance ou de l'emprise. Je chuchotai dans l'oreille d'Anny mes impressions. Mon amie avait été frappée d'abord par la proximité du faucon et d'Ehra, par cette coïncidence dans le matin de Notre-Dame. Mais elle ne pensait pas que le faucon continuait de regarder Ehra. Elle trouvait que j'exagérais un peu, inventant des signes là où il n'y avait que hasard et quotidienneté. Anny ne voulait pas détecter partout des indices. Elle aimait le monde tel qu'il était, dans son apparence naturelle. Mais moi, je rêvais à la tour Nord, à son silence où l'oiseau veillait.

Un peu gênés de chuchoter dans le dos d'Ehra, nous sommes redescendus et nous avons trouvé refuge dans un bar, derrière le chevet. David et Maurice sont entrés peu après et sont venus s'asseoir à côté de nous. Une pudeur nous interdisait d'aborder trop vite la question qui nous préoccupait. Un tabou, le respect d'Ehra. Nous parlâmes de choses et d'autres, encore du général enseveli. David et Maurice

l'abominaient. Ils étaient nés en Algérie, petits pieds-noirs, issus d'une classe pauvre. Il ne fallait attendre aucun éloge de leur part. Alors, soudain, électrisé par leur violence, je me jetai à l'eau :

— Nous avons vu Ehra, la jeune fille, là-haut. Elle était seule. Elle était triste.

David et Maurice, un peu troublés, hésitaient.

— Oui, c'est toute une histoire... Wolf a disparu. Enfin... on ne peut pas le rencontrer actuellement. Quelque chose est arrivé. On ignore de quoi il s'agit exactement. Il y a des rumeurs. Il aurait eu un accident. Mais c'est confus. Il n'y a pas eu de témoins. C'est tenu secret. Ehra se tait.

Et voilà. Le silence sidéral de la sœur s'élargissait autour du frère. Puis David, pour racheter un peu tous ces mystères, se mit à parler d'Ehra, de ses recherches, des graffiti qu'elle glanait dans les plis de la cité.

— Elle va partout, dans le métro, les chiottes, les vieilles églises, les gares, les cimetières, le long des murs. C'est incroyable, c'est infini ce qu'elle recueille, disait David.

— Et elle arrive à tout classer ? demanda Anny.

— Oui, elle établit des fichiers, des familles de thèmes qu'elle analyse, relie.

— Vous avez vu son boulot ?

— Elle m'a montré ses carnets... Il y a des signes innombrables, certains sont communs, pornographiques ou des slogans, d'autres sont barbares, atroces, racistes. Ehra m'a avoué aussi qu'elle s'était inventé un signe personnel qu'elle s'amusait à dessiner dans la forêt des graffiti.

— Quel est ce signe ? demanda Anny.

David l'ignorait. Ehra en gardait le secret.

Dix ans plus tard, je visitai la crypte archéologique sur le parvis de Notre-Dame. Au bout d'une galerie l'on retrouve les fondations du grand rempart gallo-romain érigé à la fin du IIIᵉ siècle et qui protégeait l'île de la Cité. On peut appuyer à volonté sur des boutons qui éclairent les vestiges. Or, exactement dans la zone marquée par la lettre G, on voit d'impressionnants blocs quadrangulaires mélangés à des pierres d'aspect plus chaotique et souvent striées de gribouillis et de signes. Alors, dans l'éclat solaire d'un spot, à la base de l'immémoriale muraille, je crus reconnaître la forme d'un faucon. Dans un lacis de lignes sombres se dessinaient l'œil, le bec, l'aile longue et la griffe. C'était un oiseau de cendres. L'intuition qu'il s'agissait du signe d'Ehra me frappa tout à coup.

L'oiseau est tatoué sous le talon de Notre-Dame. Car si l'on s'avise de suivre l'alignement du rempart, il conduit tout droit à la cathédrale et bute sur le portail Sainte-Anne, le troisième de la façade, le dernier au sud, le plus ancien, le plus beau, avec sa Vierge de la première moitié du XIIIᵉ siècle, encore romane, en majesté, assise sur son trône, immobile et frontale, cardinale et cosmique. Notre-Dame prenait ainsi racine dans l'œil solaire d'Horus et sur son bec de faucon.

Par la fenêtre de ma chambre, à travers les barreaux, je voyais la jeune Juive. Maintenant nous nous connaissions mieux. Depuis que je l'avais surprise dans la librairie. Je la savais éclipsée par la trop grande beauté de sa mère. Le silence de la cour grise nous séparait et j'avais envie de lui envoyer un billet, de lui dire qu'elle serait un jour plus belle que sa mère, plus svelte, plus lucide. Belle dans son âme et dans son corps délié. Je cédai tout à coup à ce désir. Je pris une feuille de papier à dessin, très large et j'écrivis dessus : « Espoir, confiance au soleil. » C'était ronflant et ridicule. Et comment prétendais-je insuffler un quelconque encouragement à une petite fille, moi qui avais tant crainte de l'avenir. J'aurais voulu écrire : « Vous êtes plus jolie que votre mère ! » Mais c'eût été sans doute maladroit. Les autres élèves pouvaient me voir. Alors je renonçai au message, à la banderole du bonheur, et je me contentai de lui adresser un léger salut de reconnaissance, la main ouverte vers elle. Un sourire vif assaillit son visage. Et, n'osant me répondre d'un geste trop manifeste, le coude appuyé sur sa table, elle agita lentement vers moi ses doigts minces et pâles. Ce signe m'obséda longtemps... Dans le gris des murailles, il se levait fantomatique et délicat.

Je connaissais maintenant quelques figures du quartier. Souvent, par la fenêtre de la cuisine qui donnait dans la rue et sur la synagogue, je voyais passer un type sinistre, une sorte d'épave beckettienne en pardessus sombre, visage hâve, teint de plâtre, cheveux gris collés au crâne en mèches rares et grasses. Sa vision me remplissait toujours d'angoisse. Un jour, il me fit rire malgré lui. Il baladait son éternelle chienne, une saucisse informe, quand surgit un bâtard de mâle apparence qui se mit à sauter au cul de la chienne. Mon type tirait tant qu'il pouvait. Mais le mâtin gaillard leur tournoyait autour et s'acharnait. Dans la rue l'homme restait en panne, empêtré de sa chienne dans la danse du cabot bachique. Je le voyais grimacer, gémir, se lamenter, accablé par l'obscène vitalité du clebs et la docilité de sa chienne qui remuait à peine. Je m'esclaffai devant ce Job chagrin, en butte à son destin crotté, car la chienne tentait à présent de déféquer en plein pavé, avec le chien surexcité par la bête accroupie.

Mais le reste du temps, j'appréhendais de rencontrer ce promeneur de mauvais augure. Je redoutais de finir un jour comme lui, écrasé, lent, poussif... Pourtant, un mois après la pantomime des deux chiens, je regardais par la fenêtre de la cuisine et je le reconnus, tout métamorphosé. C'était encore lui, la même physionomie de toute évidence. Mais cette fois l'homme était allègre, bronzé, en gros pull jacquard, sans chien, sans laisse ! Il remontait la rue d'un pas vif, tenant à bout de bras l'étui d'une raquette de tennis. Détendu, gai, libre, prospère. Que lui était-il arrivé ? J'étais abasourdi. Un héros de Beckett mué en tennisman positif et pétulant. Le soir, je racontai l'affaire à Marguerite qui rigola sans me croire. Elle ne voyait pas de qui je parlais. Le week-end suivant, Anny crut elle aussi à un canular, une nouvelle affabulation de mon cru. Et pourtant c'était réel. Ce type

100

abattu, fléchi sous le fardeau du temps, s'était miraculeusement redressé, transformé, avait voyagé, s'était mis au tennis. C'était lui, des traits identiques, et c'était un autre, un nouvel homme. J'aurais voulu qu'on me révèle les circonstances, les médecines qui pouvaient expliquer cette résurrection. Quelles vitamines ? Cure hormonale, testostérone, secrètes radiations, gourou génial ? Quelle conversion, quel amour ?

Quand je le revis plus tard, il gardait toujours cet air sportif et dispos. Je craignis qu'il ne retombe dans sa décrépitude antérieure. Peut-être même que je l'espérais un peu sadiquement, afin de renforcer le caractère cruel et contrasté de sa destinée. Mais il demeura en pleine forme, à l'épreuve de la durée. Alors, je me dis qu'un jour, peut-être, les habitués du restaurant médical me verraient surgir, reconnaissable mais grandi, musculeux, tanné par le soleil, gaillard ferrugineux, impétueux, tonitruant, plaisantant avec tout le monde, allongeant des bourrades aux barbouzes en planque, m'asseyant auprès de Nicole affolée, sidérée, la pelotant, lui fourrant des doigts partout et lui promettant, à elle aussi, une même métamorphose dionysiaque. Pour sûr, bientôt elle serait haute, mamelue, rousse, épanouie en un jour, gonflée de sucs et de sèves, dans un jean moulant, cachant une large toison bruissante, béante sur les phallus des terroristes éberlués. Puisque j'avais été témoin une fois du miracle. Ça pouvait recommencer. Et telle perspective me requinquait.

Marguerite prit Anny en aparté et lui dit qu'après le coup de Neuzil et de sa sainteté, voilà que je me fendais d'un nouveau miraculé : « Il fait le zig ou quoi ? Il se fiche !? Surveillez-le un peu. Il dévie, ma petite ! Il dévie. Il est surmené. » Anny me répéta tout. Elle n'était pas inquiète. Elle me croyait. Neuzil n'était peut-être pas un saint

incontestable, canonisable dans l'immédiat, mais le pouilleux au sombre manteau avait bel et bien changé d'aspect. D'ailleurs, je le montrai à Anny, nous le croisâmes dans la rue et nous le regardâmes avec avidité. Il nous gratifia d'un long sourire fiérot de connivence indubitable. C'était la preuve ! Après tout, l'ère des miracles peut-être commençait, faisait enfin pièce à mes ombres, à mes prémonitions noires. Mais je n'avais pas la recette du type, me manquait son élixir. Alors, quand je le voyais dans la rue, je m'approchais de lui en catimini jusqu'à le frôler pour humer et saisir son secret, pour recueillir par contagion l'éclat de ses vertus. Et, en effet, de près, il était presque effrayant de bonheur, tant sa chevaline santé rutilait, avec une sorte de rire continu sur son visage pommé qui lâchait des vagues de félicité. Cette allégresse me parut si excessive, tout à coup, qu'une nouvelle angoisse m'envahit. Décidément, ce type était à fuir !

Anny et moi étions friands d'un petit resto marocain où nous mangions un couscous pas cher et luxuriant. J'oubliais pour un soir le restaurant hygiénique et médical. La salle était étroite, pourpre, rouge pisé. On l'eût dite toute enduite d'harissa cramoisie et de pilipili partout. Une serveuse s'occupait de nous. Elle avait des bras blancs où sinuaient des veines d'une coloration verdâtre. Son visage offrait une densité de chair pâle et ourlée qui traduisait une volonté, un quant-à-soi puissant. Ses cheveux étaient riches et sombres, un duvet noir embuait la nuque, les avant-bras. J'adorais cette fille robuste et pure, le bel abus de sa fourrure.

Le couscous me remplissait d'un ravissement qui rachetait toutes les carences et les précarités de la vie. Arrivait d'abord

la semoule mamelonnée, gironde et fumante. Puis les bols, les soupières, les jattes pour le bouillon, les sauces, d'autres assiettes pour les viandes. Il y avait des écuelles partout. J'aimais ce plein, cette multiplicité. Le chou, les carottes, le mouton couillu et odoriférant, tous ces remugles poivrés, ces rafales parfumées montant des grands plats caniculaires. Le poulet très cuit au gras rissolé et jauni, racorni sur les os, les pois chiches, secs et coriaces, telluriques oui, grenus, farineux et craquants, dont la sensation tranchait sur les giboulées de semoule plus douce que ponctuait le raisin moins sec que gommeux et sucré. Les merguez légèrement cannelées, martelées dans leur matière rousse, se cassaient sous la dent comme un glaive torride. Les boules de viande compactes, bourrées d'herbes hachées et d'effluves, les légumes du bouillon bien touillés parmi les graines trempées, assaisonnées, les guenilles de poireaux, les fouillis, les succulentes rognures, mille petits rogatons, jusqu'à la soupe du fond, salace bouillie et quintessence juteuse des carottes, du chou et des viandes moulinées. Tout cela gouleyant dans l'œsophage, varapant au fond du bide, vous brûlant les tripes, vous bombant, vous fichant des envies de péter, de bander, vous ravalant au diapason doré de la bête gourmande. Mais surtout, le caractère inanalysable de cette nourriture, patchwork tissé de bouts, de fibres, de moelleuses ramures, les méandres et les mélanges du grand couscous tentaculaire, la démesure, le côté Missouri de la mangeaille, safari des saveurs. Nil limoneux, crue de bouffe ! Oui, je me fourrais avidement au sein du couscous, ventre, oreilles, babines et narines béantes dans le brouillard ardent. Et ça n'en finissait pas, tribulations, surprises, péripéties... Il y en avait toujours, il en venait encore, des merguez cramoisies, des lamelles de poireau et du rab de semoule moutonnant encore et encore. J'ai toujours eu peur de finir,

de m'interrompre, de manquer, de mourir... Baroque, oui j'étais, déjà, dès l'origine. Horreur du vide qu'il fallait parer, habiller, revêtir de myriades de plis. Le prodige, c'était que l'abondance orgiaque du couscous était sécrétée par la terre ascétique. Je me savais aussi maigre que ce Maghreb ailé. C'était ça le génie du couscous qui extirpe toutes ses secrètes ressources, sa chair, ses condiments de l'humus rare, de l'âpreté des tiges, des épines broutées par les moutons, oui cette sorcellerie tirée du climat sec aux effluves de bouc et d'agaves, de mules et de figues. Trésor jailli des rocailles pour les aspics. Je voyais des oueds et des ergs brûler au cœur du piment, des tartines d'harissa que je dévorais. Des vagues fauves me poignardaient, des déferlantes ardentes m'enveloppaient, me nappaient et je les apaisais avec des louchées de semoule blanche et nubile.

Couscous ample et cosmique, arabe et rouge et bordélique, lupanar de la langue, je te salue et t'encense. Belle mosquée immaculée d'amour, grand coursier du désert. Pur-sang ! Couscous colossal et glouton, tu m'arrondis, tu me satures et me combles enfin, me constelles... solaire, je suis, planté dans ton bedon et ta bonté géants.

Anny consommait avec modération la semoule et les pois chiches. Un rien la nourrissait. Elle n'en pouvait déjà plus. C'était surtout les côtelettes de mouton qu'elle prisait, leur petit cœur tendre et rose. Mes débordements feuilletonesques la divertissaient sans la contaminer. Et je ne détestais pas cette distorsion entre nous, ce décalage nécessaire à la séduction...

Souvent, le samedi au restaurant, quand nous finissions notre dessert, un grand type surgissait, échevelé, en paletot noir. Beau visage, bleu et dément, mais surtout une abondante chevelure grisâtre, éparse. Tout se déroulait selon le même scénario qui confinait à la chorégraphie. Le type

104

faisait deux pas en avant d'un mouvement vif et ample, reculait, tournoyait, arrivait devant le bar où le tenancier le fixait des yeux avec un air de souverain mépris. Pleine d'appréhension, Anny me soufflait : « Ça recommence, le couple infernal ? » Soudain, le type, d'un geste théâtral, ouvrait son paletot noir et en sortait un gros revolver dont le métal brillait. Il levait l'arme, la passait sous le nez du tenancier, recommençait son galop, deux ou trois pas en avant, très allongés et fulgurants, reculade, girations, le bras levé visant les lustres. Alors, le tenancier sortait de son bar, fonçait sur le dingue, l'étreignait en lui serrant le bras. Une brève échauffourée ponctuée de halètements et de chuintements musclés. Puis, miraculeusement, l'homme au revolver se dégageait, prenait du champ, s'effaçait dans la rue, d'une entourloupe. Anny et moi avions assisté à la même scène trois fois de suite. Le type et le tenancier devaient être liés par une ancienne et rituelle inimitié. Personne ne pipait dans la salle. Seule la belle serveuse aux bras nus, à la chair blanche et duveteuse, frémissait dans son coin, palpitait, les narines légèrement dilatées, ses beaux nichons soulevés. Elle trahissait une tension soudaine, une fringale de violence mal contenue qui s'opposait à l'idée que l'on s'était faite d'elle.

Ce soir-là, l'homme au revolver fit sa virevolte habituelle, mais dès qu'il se défaussa pour replonger dans la rue, nous vîmes son bras et son poing soudain dressés vers le ciel dans la lueur des lampadaires où il tira deux coups. J'eus le sentiment d'une danse, d'une voltige extraordinaire, couronnées par les détonations de western qui se répercutèrent le long du faubourg Saint-Antoine. L'homme s'évanouit dans les ténèbres.

C'est un peu plus tard que je me suis senti bander de façon anormale. Je ne reconnaissais pas la sensation. C'était douloureux et brûlant. Était-ce le cocktail périlleux du

couscous et de la cortisone que je continuais de prendre qui me mettait dans cet état, ou bien n'avait-on pas subrepticement glissé dans mon verre de Sidi Brahim quelque substance chimique, aphrodisiaque ? Je n'éprouvais pas de plaisir mais une barre de sang me dardait, me poignait.

Nous étions couchés, Anny et moi, sur le lit. Nous avons d'abord essayé de faire l'amour pour soulager la tension morbide, mais nulle amélioration n'advint. Nulle éjaculation, nulle vivante, euphorique montée de l'excitation. C'était du fer, de la matière sans âme et ça allait casser, péter, veines et artères. Me revenaient à l'esprit des histoires atroces de priapisme, les types au-delà de quelques heures d'érection subissaient des accidents de circulation, vaisseaux foutus, gland virant au noir, gangrené... Un crépuscule d'amour dans un final paroxystique. Je bandais à en mourir. Anny observait la chose avec un réel étonnement et une pointe d'humour voilé. Elle ne croyait jamais à la gravité de mes symptômes. Son incrédulité m'irritait tout en me rassurant en profondeur. Ils avaient injecté une dose de papavérine dans mon Sidi Brahim, c'était sûr ! Mon amante hésitait encore à me dire d'appeler un médecin mais une grimace de déplaisir me déformait le visage et la bite prenait une drôle de forme dure, légèrement incurvée, la métamorphose empirait. Un vertige me prit. Je revoyais la transe du grand satan noir, son revolver braqué, crachant la mitraille. Il me semblait que mon sexe allait partir ainsi d'un coup, tout seul, s'arracher à la pesanteur, à ma peau, se déraciner et fuser tout entier, météorite rouge et dure, là-haut, dans le ciel, la bacchanale des astres et des comètes. D'instinct je le retenais, la main au ventre, de peur de l'envol cosmique chez les anges. Anny me conseilla l'eau tiède, un bain émollient. Mais dans la flotte, ma torpille pointait, dirigée vers le ventre de destroyers imaginaires. Puis une fatigue me submergea, un affaissement

de la pensée. Je sentis graduellement la déflation, la régression des forces. L'outil se relâcha, s'avachit, retomba. Jamais je n'avais débandé avec un tel enthousiasme. Mon visage restait empourpré, mes tempes battaient fort, ma chamade n'avait pas décliné. Le poison agissait encore dans le cerveau. Couscous à l'harissa, cortisone, Sidi Brahim, aphrodisiaque clandestin, quel poivre ? papavérine... oui j'aime bien ce nom de héros russe, espion et suicidaire. Nous avions noté depuis longtemps l'allure émoustillée des clients en fin de repas, leur air excessivement érotisé. Ils repartaient bras dessus, bras dessous, écarlates et empressés. Donc, mon soupçon sur le petit coup de pouce donné aux sauces n'était pas arbitraire. Nous avions même surpris, Anny et moi, un couple à la sortie, dans une voiture garée le long du faubourg, qui était passé à l'empoignade sérieuse et dévêtue, sans attendre le retour en chambre.

Même après le reflux, je suais, je suintais encore, le muscle de mon cœur me tiraillait comme charcuté par des pinces d'acier. J'avais une cagoule cramoisie sur le visage et mon torse était pantelant, trempé. D'où cela m'était-il venu ? De quelle secousse nerveuse déclenchée peut-être aussi par la valse vengeresse du mec dément et noir, revolvérisant le beau ciel de Paris, à minuit ? Cela avait jailli comme un chant, une détresse lyrique qui fusillait les astres.

Le dimanche après-midi, une érection nouvelle apparut. Nous nous sommes penchés, Anny et moi, dans l'angoisse... Peut-être fallait-il détourner mon attention, songer à des idées funèbres ? Mais le phénomène ne s'accompagnait d'aucun signe de douleur et de raideur minérale. C'était une belle et chaude érection de jeune homme amoureux et nous avons fait l'amour comme chaque week-end, sans lésiner. Le lundi, pourtant, je payai le prix de nos tendresses. J'avais la queue un peu râpée, surtout la peau si fine, si transparente

dans la partie qui précède la bosse du gland quand la verge est bandée et le prépuce retroussé en entier. Cette peau devait souvent émouvoir mes amies au fil du temps, car le pénis révèle là toute sa fragilité, son caractère originel, délicat et tourmenté, satin guilloché de grosses veines qui gonflent pour un rien. Pénis blessé, semé de petites écorchures dès qu'on laboure dans le coït... Or, l'on ne peut pas dire qu'à vingt ans, Anny et moi profitions des week-ends pour hanter les musées. Nous avions nos usages à Notre-Dame, c'était à peu près tout. Le reste du temps se déroulait en étreintes goulues. Mon lundi consistait donc à panser les excès de la veille. La queue entaillée d'imperceptibles griffures me brûlait. J'ai mis du temps à trouver la parade. Maladroit, la première fois, et prétentieux, j'avisai une bande Velpeau, m'en enveloppai le membre comme d'un cache-nez. Mais la vision du manchon disproportionné par rapport au sexe flapi me remplit de malaise. La mythologique peur de la castration me revenait dare-dare. J'imaginais des taches de sang souillant la texture neigeuse du pansement. Immédiatement l'image de la guerre de Sécession jaillit dans mon esprit. Allez savoir pourquoi ? Je pouvais en effet puiser sans peine dans nos boucheries nationales. 14-18 collait bien, baïonnettes et tranchées... Non, la castration dans mon inconscient évoquait d'abord la guerre de Sécession, en raison de l'idée de rupture et de scission ! Dans quel film avais-je assisté à ce déploiement de bande Velpeau sur quelque amputation sudiste ?

Je renonçai à la bande trop emphatique et me rabattis sur une modeste pommade gluante et camphrée. Son contact était doux et j'en profitai un peu pour me masser, ce qui eut pour effet de déplier le membre et de faciliter l'étalement. Quand je me soignais, mon pénis devenait mon double, mon rejeton, mon jumeau métonymique, mon bébé en un mot.

Ainsi se vérifiaient sur moi les fortes thèses de Freud. J'étais expérimental en diable, un festival de viennoiseries. Il n'y avait qu'à observer les avatars. Donc, je chouchoutais et dorlotais mon phallus décousu, mais la pommade trop grasse qui gommait la douleur ne permettait pas aux fines plaies, tout en biffures secrètes et sanglantes, de cicatriser. Il fallait essuyer la crème et le frottement m'irritait de plus belle. J'ai enfin découvert le remède, ses étapes, et c'est un traitement que je puis communiquer à mes pareils, mes frères ! D'abord laver à l'eau fraîche les subtiles lésions, tamponner avec une serviette sans appuyer. Attendre que cela sèche, utiliser non pas un onguent visqueux mais une poudre antiseptique et cicatrisante, genre Exoseptoplix — je n'ai pas d'énoncé moins gaulois... Cette poudre a le mérite d'être sèche. Il faut en saupoudrer le membre uniment. Ce n'est pas déplaisant, on a le sentiment de s'enfariner, de devenir boulanger de sa bite et cela occupe un bon bout de temps, pendant lequel on s'aime, on se réconcilie avec soi-même, on remédie au mal de naître et d'exister dans l'exil et l'absurde. On pouponne et pomponne son pénis blanchi. Un accident bénin peut assombrir le rituel, lorsqu'une perle de sang sortie d'une plaie vient colorer la blancheur de la poudre. Ce mélange du sang et de l'immaculé a quelque chose de défloré et de pénible. Dans ces cas-là, arrêter les fâcheuses associations d'idées, laver de nouveau, sécher, saupoudrer à peine, attendre que le sang se coagule et reprendre le poudrage complet. Le miracle est qu'il n'est pas nécessaire de nettoyer la poudre après usage, ce qui risquerait de rouvrir les estafilades. Il est impératif de la laisser s'évacuer d'elle-même. Sa nature volatile la dispose à s'égailler, à se dissiper peu à peu dans le slip et jusqu'aux chaussettes. Ce n'est qu'après une parfaite cicatrisation que l'on pourra recourir à une pommade grasse et protectrice pour nourrir la muqueuse et prévenir de nouveaux dégâts.

Toute solution alcoolisée, même pour désinfecter, est à proscrire sous peine de jongler, de sprinter *illico* en émettant des cris de Sioux.

Anny était attendrie par ces blessures auxquelles elle contribuait dans nos élans. Mais l'agaçait la cure cérémonieuse, un tantinet narcissique et masturbatoire à laquelle je me livrais. Jalouse, oui, de cette bite à la toilette, de cette intimité maniaque que j'entretenais avec mon phallus meurtri et renaissant, tige au centre de mes métamorphoses, enjeu de mon image de moi-même, de mon identité, de mon être, de ses crises, de ses conflits... Tout ce cocktail d'élégie et d'épopée pour un vit ! Anny avait toujours été curieuse de lui, de ses déclics, ses effusions, ses déploiements, ses entêtements, ses aurores merveilleuses et ses couchants ratatinés, ses ratés et ses retours si rubiconds. Ça l'amusait de le toucher, de le sentir raidir et s'allonger. Je n'irai pas jusqu'à dire qu'Anny illustrait la fameuse thèse si sexiste, si machiste, si totalitaire de l'envie du pénis ! Oui, Anny me manifesta souvent le fantasme qui lui venait d'en avoir un ou une, et pas symbolique du tout, mais organique et consistante. Plutôt une qu'un d'ailleurs... Je ne saurais expliquer la nuance. Elle en avait envie d'une, voilà. Parfois ça la prenait, c'est tout, pour jouer ? Je ne sais... pour s'en servir et pénétrer à qui mieux mieux le tout venant, les uns, les unes, les autres. Elle était bien capable, sous ses façons limpides, de couver des appétits, des truculences, voire des extravagances. Un pénis joli pour Anny.

Nous avons rencontré Osiris dans l'escalier de la tour. Aussitôt, je suis revenu sur Ehra, sur son regard désespéré. Osiris adopta une mimique de mystère. Il en savait sans

110

doute plus que David et Maurice. Anny le pressa un peu.

— On ne voit plus Wolf ! Wolf a disparu.

Et le gardien martiniquais, le passeur de la tour Sud, se taisait, muet tout à coup, ce qui était exceptionnel chez lui, contraire à sa nature loquace.

— On ne peut pas tout dire, Anny...

La phrase nous parut merveilleuse. Il savait donc. Osiris savait tout !

— Mais on peut laisser deviner, insinua mon amante.

— Pas aujourd'hui, pas encore...

— C'est une belle histoire, Osiris, comme vous aimez les raconter ?

— Oui, une belle, une terrible histoire... ma plus belle histoire.

Nous n'y tenions plus.

— Et vous n'en direz jamais rien ?

— Pour le moment non... c'est interdit. Motus, Anny !

Il n'y avait nul visiteur à cette heure matinale. Osiris nous entraîna dans la grande charpente du bourdon Emmanuel, la prodigieuse cage de poutres et de piliers. Ça sentait le bois, la forêt, mon enfance et mes cavales aux lièvres. Ainsi les tours de pierre recelaient ces entrailles ligneuses, cette formidable ossature de chêne où le vent vibrait, où valdinguait Quasimodo, jadis. Anny préférait Osiris, le beau Martiniquais svelte et prolixe. Le grotesque et le gothique n'émouvaient guère mon amie, tandis que — comme elle me l'avait avoué un jour — la dégaine noire d'Osiris rieur lui plaisait. Jaloux, je lui avais expliqué qu'elle n'avait aucune chance de séduire un amateur de garçons. Alors, arborant un sourire conquérant, Anny opéra une élégante torsion du buste et frappa joliment de la main son cul tendre et gourmand, si mignon, si hermaphrodite, en pavane oisive sous le velours serré. Je fus abasourdi par ce défi obscène. Fou de jalousie...

111

Osiris parlait du bourdon. Je l'y encourageai.

— Treize tonnes, mes amis, un gosier de treize tonnes. Il a été refondu au XVIIe siècle et là j'ai un bel épisode... si vous avez une miette de temps.

Osiris excellait à créer le suspens, à se faire désirer.

— Nous avons la journée, lui déclara Anny tout miel.

— Eh bien ! Quand on a refondu ce monstre, les princesses, les dames, les comtesses, tout le gratin de la noblesse la plus belle et la plus pure, ont versé dans le bronze bouillant leurs bijoux, leurs clairs anneaux, leurs bagues d'or au fond du creuset, pour l'amour de Dieu, vous comprenez, par sens du sacrifice et du don, pour gagner le ciel, des indulgences divines... une fontaine d'or dans le volcan du bronze... Les belles voulaient tinter avec la cloche géante, entrer dans ses sonnailles, ses carillons et ses tocsins.

— J'avais entendu parler de ça, en effet, c'est connu, c'est historique !

J'étais méchant soudain avec Osiris, je diminuais la portée de sa révélation.

— Ça c'est connu, c'est vrai, mais mon histoire en fait est plus particulière, plus précise, et celle-là tout le monde l'ignore, je la tiens d'une filière discrète, d'un religieux spécialiste de Notre-Dame.

Osiris attendit, dressé sous la charpente, dans l'entrecroisement des poutres planétaires où le vent grondait. On était sur la mer, dans le gréement de l'Arche de Noé. Osiris nous regardait, entrouvrait ses lèvres charnues sur ses quenottes immaculées. Il émit un petit rire grêle et doux, un filet qui montait de sa gorge lisse et noire. Osiris nous convoitait. Jambes écartées, il étirait son torse, balançait ses épaules, fanfaronnait, mais sans forcer, avec une sorte de délicatesse musclée. Il était le Narcisse et le corsaire du colossal clocher.

112

— Il est quand même plus mignon que Quasimodo, me chuchota Anny.

— Oui, l'histoire, la véritable, la clandestine, la délectable ne concerne pas tant le bourdon que son battant ! Pas la corolle mais le pistil, mes amis !

Oh, comme il avait distingué avec sensualité la corolle du pistil ! Osiris prononçait pistil en affûtant les i.

— Le subtil c'est le pistil !...

Anny laissa échapper un rire dont l'écho vint ricocher contre la gorge nue d'Osiris qui fut parcourue d'un gloussement aigu, ensorcelé. Osiris fut tout parfumé, tout pimenté de son rire, pétri de petits couinements qui sonnaient, roulaient plus bas dans sa poitrine. Il allait s'esclaffer carrément. Mais il se retenait. Le rire se baladait de haut en bas sans exploser, mué en écumes assourdies, éternuées, en pétillements dorés. On eût dit qu'il voulait garder ce rire pour lui, pour se délecter de son sel.

— C'est un pistil de cinq cents kilos mes amis, c'est pas mini !

Rires d'Anny.

— Donc, quand ils ont fondu le bourdon, ils ont fait la même chose pour le battant. Mais à part ! Et les dames ont remis ça, froufrous de soie et chuchotis : la cascade des anneaux, des bracelets, des colliers d'or pour ce pistil géant, c'était plus excitant encore... Or, personne n'a raconté l'histoire de la comtesse Jeanne, ce qu'elle versa, elle, au sein du battant, pour le faire battre et palpiter plus fort. Voilà l'histoire ! L'amour qui unissait Jeanne, une jouvencelle de seize ans, à son amant, un évêque de trente-six ans, un aristocrate ardent.

Osiris se tut pour allumer Anny, bien l'attiser. Il avait l'air de dire : « Ça se mérite, une histoire pareille, ma jolie. » Il s'appuya contre la bordure cuivrée de la cloche, fouilla dans

sa poche, on voyait par en dessous ses doigts tripoter quelque chose pas loin de son slip, sortit enfin une grosse pièce de cinq francs, la cogna contre le bronze. Ce dernier réagit par un cri clair et mélodieux, toute la musique des anneaux d'or réveillés soudain. Comme si tant de bijoux purs et secrets, enfouis au sein du bronze, ne demandaient qu'un coup d'archet pour vibrer. Et Osiris tapait avec sa pièce brillante. Ses yeux s'élargissaient à l'écoute de l'écho. Son visage alors devenait doux, plus charnel, une tête de Bacchus amoureux tandis qu'il frappait toujours, faisait chanter le bord du bourdon.

— Alors, la comtesse Jeanne ? suppliait Anny.

— C'est une histoire belle et triste, répondit Osiris, car l'évêque mourut d'un accident de cheval. C'était un évêque bien de son temps. Il cultivait coursiers et catins plus souvent que la confession... Alors, voilà... Je m'excuse, c'est très singulier. Ça reprend d'une autre façon l'histoire d'Héloïse et d'Abélard, mais cette fois, c'est Héloïse qui agit. Ça reprend même des rites plus anciens, le don d'Atys à la déesse Cybèle, si vous voyez ce qu'Atys lui offre comme gage absolu de fidélité. Enfin bon ! L'évêque était mort. On ne pouvait plus rien en tirer. Alors, Jeanne, par amour, a coupé son phallus, l'a fait enclore dans une gaine de marbre, puis de bronze et, avec la complicité d'un maître artisan qui fondait le battant, l'a fourré au dernier moment dans le bronze, juste quand il se solidifiait. Voilà, mes amis, comment le phallus de l'évêque amoureux de Jeanne s'est logé dans le pistil !

— Vous avez inventé ça de toutes pièces, Osiris !

Anny me lança un regard réprobateur, je gâchais tout. Osiris écarquilla les yeux, outragé que je puisse le soupçonner d'affabuler.

— Cette histoire m'a été confiée par un religieux haut placé, un cardinal, j'ose le dire, très célèbre, très mondain,

académicien et sensuel, mes amis. Un jésuite. Je le jure... sur mon île !

— S'il le jure sur son île... me dit Anny. Moi, je crois à votre phallus, Osiris !

— En effet, c'est plutôt le phallus d'Osiris ! déclarai-je à mon tour.

— De l'évêque, mes amis !

— C'est aussi un peu le vôtre, Osiris, puisque vous êtes le seul dépositaire de ce pénis chantant !

Osiris souriait, hésitait, chancelait. Il lui plaisait que ce fût un peu son phallus confondu à celui de l'évêque qui occupât le cœur du battant. Il se tut avec un air mystique et gourmet.

Nous devenions rêveurs, Anny et moi. Ainsi, l'autre jour, quand on enterrait de Gaulle et que les potentats du monde remplissaient Notre-Dame, le glas qui retentit fut le phallus d'Osiris cognant le calice béant du bourdon. C'est toujours le phallus d'Osiris qui carillonne à Pâques, baigne Paris de ses échos ensoleillés. La Sainte Vierge et Osiris : n'était-ce pas le couple le plus nécessaire, le plus féerique qu'on pût imaginer ? Oui, Osiris sonne dans la tour de Notre-Dame, au secret de sa robe surnaturelle. Voilà la nouvelle paradisiaque. Tous les faucons le savent.

Margot revint de son travail vers six heures. Elle faisait un boulot un peu mystérieux, réservé à des cas sociaux et des handicapés. Elle était employée dans un centre de recrutement de la fonction publique, je crois, je n'ai jamais vraiment élucidé la question. Mais elle classait des dossiers où figurait pour chaque candidat le résultat d'un entretien avec un psychologue. J'avais jeté un œil aux fiches. On parlait du regard phobique d'untel, de l'aspect introverti de celui-ci, de l'agressivité latente, de l'instabilité de cet autre... de profil psychopathe, maniaco-dépressif, obsessionnel, de morphologie longiligne et asthénique...

Margot, le soir, quand elle voulait prendre de l'avance sur la tâche du lendemain, étalait la paperasse sur la table à même la toile cirée et se mettait à trier les tests, très affairée. Ainsi défilaient sous son œil les cas, les candidats. Elle s'exclamait soudain avec compassion et condescendance : « Ah celui-ci n'ira pas loin... Oh le pauvre, qu'est-ce qu'on lui passe ! » Cette hécatombe de la jeunesse l'épanouissait. Frétillante, elle humait les feuilles, relisait, commentait, poussait des soupirs, des petits rires de complaisance. Elle était importante soudain, elle régnait. « J'aime mon travail ! Ah mon travail ! C'est tout... »

117

A la sortie du métro, elle trottinait avec ses dossiers sous le bras, montait l'escalier en haletant, s'arrêtait chez Mlle Poulet, exhibait son paquet avec des airs d'intellectuelle. Et les voisins étaient jaloux.

Ce jour-là, pourtant, elle ne trimbalait nul fardeau mais arborait une coiffure vibrionnante et gonflée, incroyable. Elle se débarrassa de son sac et de sa prothèse en les jetant sur la table. Elle mit son disque préféré d'André Dassary : « mon Dédé », alluma l'électricité, partagea des rognons avec Toufflette en la submergeant de mamours, avala une giclée de citron pour digérer les rognons. Elle prétendait que le citron faisait passer la nourriture. Il la faisait roter et elle prenait cela pour le signe de la digestion. Elle chantonnait, ouvrait la télé, s'enthousiasmait des moindres nouvelles, y allait d'un gémissement éphémère quand l'information expédiait les décès du jour, les guerres, les raz de marée. Puis s'ébrouait, piaffait dès que la gaieté revenait avec Pompidou, son blabla et sa bobine réjouie.

— Et vous ne me dites rien ! Vous ne remarquez rien ! me lança-t-elle enfin, en tapotant sa chevelure gaufrée.

Je lui répondis qu'en effet sa coiffure était remarquable. C'est alors qu'elle me confessa avoir une ruse pour ne jamais payer le coiffeur. Elle servait, en effet, de cobaye aux apprentis et aux stagiaires. Les jeunes types, les shampouineuses en mal de promotion s'exerçaient sur sa tignasse. Ils s'épanchaient sans scrupules, tour à tour lyriques, farfelus ou concis. Ils cisaillaient, bouclaient, tressaient, torchaient, fomentaient d'extraordinaires mises en plis. Chaque fois, ils la rataient mais avec des surprises, une invention dans le saccage et des caprices, des tournures inédites, des improvisations savoureuses, des bouffées de kitsch... Mais Margot était fière d'offrir sa chevelure à ces artistes novices avec lesquels elle plai-

santait, si féminine, mutine, lançant des œillades entre ses touffes ébouriffées. Elle était le centre, elle adorait ça ! On la rinçait, on la séchait, on la frisait. On lui envoyait n'importe qui, les stagiaires les plus nuls, les coupeurs de bambou caractériels, les instables, les champions de la tonte des brebis, les rois du sécateur, les Caligula du cheveu. Les postulants se bousculaient pour tenter un shampoing, une teinte, un petit reflet... comme ils disaient par euphémisme, des mèches, des franges, des guiches, des accroche-cœurs coquins, des crinières léonines ou des coupes Jeanne d'Arc, des sabrages pour la guillotine. Elle ne se plaignait jamais, se trouvait ravissante, renouvelée, galopait de porte en porte pour montrer le chef-d'œuvre, la coiffure qui serait à la mode au printemps prochain. Et tout le monde opinait, renchérissait, avec un sourire neutre, que c'était, oui, original...

Ces soirs de fête, Margot m'invitait à dîner. Vin et poulet toujours. Elle me confiait ses nostalgies.

— Ah... mon rêve, voyez-vous ! Ce serait d'avoir un compagnon !

Et elle joignait les mains, comme si le compagnon apparaissait devant nous. J'aimais ces accès de romantisme contre la solitude.

Elle passait à des épisodes de sa vie qui sont à peine dicibles. Des abominations. L'histoire de son mari alcoolique et maçon qu'on lui avait conseillé d'épouser quand même, car son infirmité et sa prothèse n'allécheraient pas forcément des légions de prétendants. Le type mourut vite et je ne sais comment, laissant à Margot une fille qui épousa, à dix-huit ans, un ingénieur dans le pétrole, si bien que Marguerite ne revoyait presque jamais son unique descendante. Un jour, pour toucher une assurance, Margot fit déterrer son mari. Il s'agissait de prouver qu'il avait trépassé des suites d'un

accident du travail. C'est alors qu'elle m'avoua ce détail horrible.

— Quand on a ouvert le cercueil, je me suis penchée et j'ai regardé Roger. Il avait des poils noirs poussés partout sur la figure avec plein de gros vers rouges dedans.

Je retranscris littéralement. Ce portrait m'a cueilli au seuil de la vie. L'art de Margot et sa curiosité. Ce dévoilement de vérité sévère. Comme elle avait dû se pencher et lorgner ! C'était ainsi qu'on finissait. Margot vous soulevait le couvercle, vous découvrait le pot aux roses et le précieux fumet. C'était sa botte secrète, son sens de l'authentique, des destins véritables. Margot de l'horreur.

Le même soir, sur sa lancée, elle me raconta son accident. Comment elle avait perdu son bras ! Pourtant, elle s'estimait heureuse et gratifiée, car elle aurait dû mourir. Un miracle ! Elle s'extasiait... Elle avait toujours été comblée dans le malheur. Le métro était arrivé. C'était avant la guerre. Elle avait dix-sept ans. Elle était vive et gaie. Un optimisme à faire peur, animal, intempérant. Le métro déboule du tunnel noir et s'arrête tout contre le quai. Margot papote avec une amie, traîne trop, s'élance au dernier moment, rate le coche, mais son bras se coince dans la porte refermée. Et le métro repart, véloce... grosse besogne de chaque jour.

— Alors, j'ai hurlé, j'ai été bousculée, cognée, happée... J'ai hurlé... J'avais dix-sept ans, j'étais vierge... Mon amie m'a parlé bien plus tard de ce hurlement. Ça l'a glacée, c'était un hurlement d'égorgée, ça me sortait du ventre, un beuglement d'épouvante. C'est le mot qu'elle a répété : épouvante. Comme si, je ne sais pas, un python m'était tombé dessus pour m'avaler vivante. Voilà ! Le cri que l'on pousse quand notre être nous est arraché, qu'on le perd, qu'on vit cela... Voilà !

Marguerite, je l'ai dit, avait un don verbal, un sens inné de

l'expression, des intuitions et des trouvailles. Son « j'étais vierge » était inopiné, impressionnant. La vision entra dans ma cervelle de jeune homme. Je m'initiais à la vraie vie. J'imaginais la scène, je la voyais... le polichinelle aspiré, plaqué contre le métro, claqué, secoué, martelé, démembré. Et ce cri originel et horrifié, cri des cavernes, soufflé, ventral, gavé d'horreur... Quelqu'un qu'on viole et qu'on vide. Oui, j'entendais ce cri de vérité.

On lui avait fait une des premières transfusions sanguines. Elle ne parlait plus de sa jeunesse à partir de l'accident. Elle se taisait sur les années qui suivaient. Elle se mariait plus tard. Elle était mère. Le maçon mort, exhumé, la prime touchée. Veuve et voilà.

— Il n'était pas méchant, mon mari, mais il buvait.

Ça résumait toute l'affaire, du Zola ! Je découvrais cela comme *L'Assommoir*. Naturaliste et cru. Ça existait donc. Le mélo bien bas, bien noir et sanglant. L'alcool et la fatalité. Moi, j'étais provincial. J'ignorais la ville, ses faubourgs. Un ivrogne à la campagne reste pittoresque et rigolo. Plein air ! Il vous garde un petit aspect champêtre de chemin creux, de fenaison. Mais l'alcool à Paris, chez les pauvres... c'est une tout autre histoire, ombreuse, étroite, sur le pavé, chez les prolos. J'écoutais, j'imaginais, je comprenais la ville, ces commencements tristes du monde, cette odyssée de la foule lugubre. Et j'étais dedans, rue Pavée, chez Margot, au tout début. Et j'avais peur de son bras et de sa gaieté obscène, du faubourg moche et familier déjà. La station du métro Saint-Paul était peinte en marron. C'était la seule, toute marronasse et merdeuse. J'allais bouffer au resto des malades et des planqués. C'était le soir. J'en avais marre de l'avenir, de mon genou meurtri. J'étais si effrayé. Rien que de penser que j'étais dans Paris. Vertige. J'allais rater le grand concours, décevoir Anny, finir par lui foutre ma peur. On serait à la rue

sous l'œil de Margot qui attendait, qui savait tout depuis toujours.

Notre-Dame seule me consolait, et les récits d'Osiris, Ehra. Le jeu des signes. Horus, le soleil. Puis Egon Schiele, mes exotismes déjà.

Je regardais Johann Neuzil avec le maximum de discrétion et de doigté. J'essayai de capter sur son visage, dans ses gestes, des signes indubitables de sainteté. Un saint sait-il qu'il est un saint ? Sans doute pas, car son humilité souffrirait d'une telle complicité avec le ciel. Je lui demandai des nouvelles de sa santé. Je savais que son artérite prenait des proportions désastreuses, la circulation se faisait de plus en plus mal dans l'orteil malade. On parlait d'une amputation préventive pour empêcher la gangrène de monter. Neuzil me répondit sur le ton d'une fatalité douce :

— C'est le pied qui empire. On parle de me couper ça, mais depuis si longtemps. Il faut que je marche davantage pour activer l'irrigation. Alors je marche, je marche. Les gens du quartier se demandent quelle mouche me pique. Pourquoi je tourne ainsi. C'est étrange d'aller, d'aller... Le mouvement sans fin, une expérience, une aventure vous savez. L'esprit y trouve son compte... on voyage, on découvre la Seine, les quais, les petites rues, tant de vieux noms. Je m'amuse à les identifier, des noms célèbres mais oubliés du xviie, du xviiie siècle. Je les note et je cherche dans des dictionnaires. Je découvre des vies complètement effacées de nos esprits. Je vis un peu avec ces fantômes amicaux. Mais vous ! C'est vous que je veux entendre. Vous travaillez à votre concours, vous avancez...

Je bredouillai que oui. En fait, j'avais envie de parler de

Schiele, de Wally Neuzil, la mère de Johann. Je désirais par-dessus tout voir le fameux dessin secret. Mais je ne savais comment aborder la question. Je n'osais pas. Alors, tout doucement, je me suis mis à feuilleter l'album exposé sur la table. Je retrouvai les jeunes filles rousses, sœurs du soleil, leurs cuisses heureuses et leur fente dorée. Car Schiele avait tendance à colorer d'or le sexe des femmes. Dans la sombre fourrure se profilait la brèche, la mince faucille de feu dont la couleur semblait s'étendre aux cheveux roux, à la pointe rouge des seins et aux bras orangés.

Je regardai Neuzil et me jetai à l'eau :

— On dit que vous détenez un dessin secret d'Egon Schiele ? Est-ce vrai ?

Neuzil me rendit un regard long et limpide :

— C'est vrai !

— Mais comment vous est-il parvenu puisque votre mère, comme vous me l'avez confié, est morte quand vous aviez un peu plus d'un an, je crois...

— Elle est morte de la scarlatine en 1917, elle s'est vue mourir, comme Schiele de la grippe, comme Edith la femme de Schiele, tous trois coupés dans leur fleur. Et les plus beaux modèles de Schiele ont dû mourir aussi de la grippe espagnole en 1918. Elle a donc remis le dessin à un cousin qui me l'a restitué plus tard, à la fin de mon adolescence. Ce dessin a une histoire extraordinaire soudain... Car Schiele, en 1912, est installé dans un village, à Neulengbach. De très jeunes filles posent pour lui. Une certaine Tatjana s'éprend de lui, fuit ses parents et se jette dans ses bras. Aussitôt, la famille accuse Schiele de détournement de mineure, d'atten-tat à la pudeur. Les policiers débarquent, confisquent des dessins érotiques exposés dans sa maison, et celui qui est jugé le plus scandaleux est brûlé le jour du jugement, au tribunal et en public ! Inouï ! Mais ce que peu de gens savent, c'est

que Wally a réussi à substituer ce dessin officiel au vrai chef-d'œuvre, au dessin tabou et beau. Elle a su convaincre ou tromper ou séduire les auteurs de la perquisition. Wally, ma mère, était une femme d'une grande nature, d'une grande liberté. Schiele, lui aussi, était hors du commun. Ils ont réussi à détourner l'œuvre. On n'a brûlé en public qu'une chose mineure. Du coup, Schiele par gratitude a donné à Wally l'œuvre sauvée, elle l'a conservée après leur rupture et je l'ai recueillie à mon tour. Ce chef-d'œuvre a échappé au bûcher ! C'est le phénix, mon ami... Mais Schiele a tout de même fait vingt-quatre jours de prison !

Neuzil se tut, il n'avait pas proposé de me montrer le dessin.

— Et que représente ce dessin ? demandai-je troublé.

— Vous me le demandez avec tellement de sincérité et de gravité que je vais vous le dire. Ça représente le couple non pas d'Egon et de Wally, mais d'Egon et de Gerti, sa sœur, qui fut son premier modèle nu. Elle fut, oui, la première à poser nue pour lui, en 1910. Et c'était d'une audace inconnue. Elle avait seize ans et lui vingt ans. Ils étaient adolescents et ils s'aimaient. C'était une passion fondée sur une ardente précocité, sur la tendresse possessive et l'admiration, la fascination encore et toujours.

— Wally, votre mère, ne fut pas jalouse de cet amour ?

— Je n'en sais rien, mais je pense qu'elle en voulait beaucoup plus à Edith Harms qui épousa Egon en 1915. C'est Edith qui sépare Egon de Wally. Pas Gerti.

Et Neuzil, ouvrant les premières pages de l'album, me montra le portrait de Gerti nue. Grand corps maigre, hermaphrodite et rouge. Egon se peint presque de la même façon, en fusion avec sa sœur. Tous les deux écarlates, asexués, anguleux.

— C'est un peu Adam et Ève, pour moi, voyez-vous... les

jumeaux de la Genèse. Leur chair à vif et radicale... des écorchés de l'Éden.

— Et votre dessin secret les représente donc ?

— Oui... J'ai compris que vous voulez le voir. Je sais qu'il ne s'agit pas d'une curiosité superficielle. Je le sais bien. Je sais que ce dessin vous concerne soudain, qu'il est essentiel pour vous.

Neuzil me contemplait avec intensité, cette alliance de calme et de concentration, et toujours cette transparence paisible qui prévalait sur le reste. Son regard m'englobait et me centrait, me comprenait. Et cette spiritualité bienveillante souriait avec humour. Elle n'était pas austère mais légère. Neuzil, l'homme gentil, était léger, angélique et léger.

— Quand je vous vois avec Anny, votre petite amie... Je pense toujours à Egon et à Gerti. C'est vrai, cela me touche. Votre air nerveux, presque violent, et elle si vraie. Elle est là, toute. La présence et l'adéquation. Elle est juste. Vous à côté d'elle, elle auprès de vous. Cela va de soi, ça ne se discute pas. Vous savez, ces choses-là comptent beaucoup pour l'homme que je suis. Contempler cela. Je resterais penché sur vous deux pendant des heures, sans me lasser. Regarder !... L'autre jour, je faisais une visite au musée de Cluny. Je suis tombé en arrêt devant une tête d'ange qui provient du portail de la Vierge de Notre-Dame... La tête a survécu aux sévices de la Révolution, avec les têtes des rois de Judée. Or, cet ange gothique sourit. C'est le premier sourire de la sculpture gothique. Cet ange est colossal. Il n'a rien de gracieux, d'ailé. Il est massif, oriental. Le nez manque. Ce qui donne à sa face un aspect aplati, effacé, de mage camus et mystérieux, mais le sourire s'esquisse, à peine un sourire secret éclos dans la pierre. Vous devriez aller au musée de Cluny pour voir cela poindre à l'origine. La religion qui sourit. C'est Dieu qui nous sourit. Le ciel qui s'ouvre, s'allège. Tout le cosmos plus

doux. Je suis resté longtemps, longtemps. C'était presque fou, car je ne pouvais plus me détacher de ce printemps de la sculpture. Ce n'est pas de l'hypnose, mais je regarde, je regarde... sans me perdre pour autant, sans m'absorber. Je suis devant. C'est étrange ? De plus en plus. Je suis bien, là, le monde est là. Et cela me comble...

Moi, je sentais que c'était là le signe indubitable de la sainteté de Neuzil, cette capacité spirituelle d'écoute et de contemplation infinie. Je jubilais au fond de moi : « C'est donc un saint ! » Quelle flambée de joie. Et dans l'élan je lui lançai :

— Montrez-moi le dessin secret !

— Ah j'aime cela ! J'aime que vous me le demandiez avec cette joie-là.

Et Neuzil, sans hésiter, quitta la pièce. Je l'entendis ouvrir une porte, puis tourner une clé et s'activer assez longuement à petit bruit. Il revint avec le dessin nu, énorme, sans étui, comme cela, déployé devant moi. Sauvage. Et je le dis comme cela fut, un rayon traversait la fenêtre. Alors, Neuzil plaça le dessin dans le soleil. Et les rouges et les ors d'Egon Schiele éclatèrent comme du sang. Puis Neuzil posa la feuille sur la table, tout en long.

— Je l'ai dégagé de son cadre et de sa plaque de verre exprès pour vous, pour qu'il vous apparaisse sans écran ni reflet.

Egon et Gerti offraient leurs corps longilignes et gothiques dans une étreinte immense. Leurs hauts corps écarlates et solaires, conjugués et cosmiques. De cet agglutinement émanait une impression de douceur et de sérénité. Mais la cellule irisée d'Egon et de Gerti restait précise. La fusion du frère et de la sœur, leur inceste ne les noyaient dans aucune confusion originelle. Ils étaient deux, ils étaient un, leur dualité demeurait dans leur commune et claire adoration. On

reconnaissait dans ce dessin rehaussé d'aquarelle et de gouache toute la force, la violence concentrée de Schiele, son œil intense, son âme individuelle et libre. Mais l'œuvre était ample, délivrée. La matière vibrante, heureuse. Les visages d'Egon et de Gerti se ressemblaient. L'œil noir et dévorant d'Egon, son sourcil noir, ses pommettes dures, et Gerti anguleuse, plus fine et rousse. Cette rousseur surtout distinguait la sœur, ainsi qu'un casque de cheveux un tout petit peu plus fourni. Leurs mains longues, effilées — tout le style de Schiele, son paraphe ciselé — se caressaient mutuellement le visage. Les faces étaient prises, épousées dans la flamme amoureuse des mains. Les torses étaient semblables, maigres, taillés comme des coffrets de sacre, des reliquaires où tressaillent les cœurs. Et les ventres se bombaient en avant, pareils à ceux d'un Adam et d'une Ève gothiques. Les ventres se touchaient. Lui bandant, elle béante. Incurvés l'un vers l'autre et soudés dans une sinuosité lascive, un agrippement de fièvre. Mais tout cela, oui, affranchi de la soif. Leurs culs étroits et musclés étaient d'une symétrie parfaite. Les cuisses d'Egon s'éployaient plus grosses et plus velues que la fragile chair de Gerti. C'était la seule différence un peu marquée : les cuisses. Mais dès que l'on s'abandonnait à la contemplation de l'œuvre, le frère et la sœur, le roi et la reine basculaient l'un dans l'autre et se transverbéraient de sorte que Gerti phallique semblait étreindre Egon, son frère fendu, puis ce dernier redevenait plus dur et se fourrait avidement dans sa sœur ouverte et plus tendre.

Et Neuzil se saisit de la grande feuille qui se creusa, ondula au bout de sa main. A nouveau, le rayon de lumière vint tremper l'union des enfants incestueux, du peintre et de sa sœur. Leur amour était pris dans la matière et le dessin de Schiele, dans sa ferveur, dans l'encre qui les sertissait comme dans un nid. Frère et sœur à l'écrin, jeunes pharaons sculptés

dans le limon du Nil, vivifiés d'un rai rouge, d'un Orient ailé. Le dessin avait échappé au bûcher par l'entremise et la ruse de Wally et il avait été transmis. Johann Neuzil, l'infirme, le déterrait, splendide et secret. Le tabou de l'étreinte et de l'éternité.

Neuzil revint. Et je me répétais inlassablement : « C'est un saint. »

A la fois, je savais et j'ignorais la mesure de cet énoncé évident et voilé. Neuzil me regardait. Son regard visait mon essence et mon être. Mais était-ce encore moi qu'il contemplait ainsi ? Il aurait porté le même regard sur Anny. Je me demandai si subsistait encore dans ce regard une perception de ma réalité concrète et de ma différence. Que voyait-il si loin ? Tout ne devenait-il pas égal et transparent ? Le regard de Dieu est-il encore un regard porté sur la créature personnelle ? Neuzil n'était ni ange ni Dieu, mais peut-être un saint dans la rue pauvre et la maison lépreuse. Non loin de la station Saint-Paul, du Pont-Marie et de ma belle cathédrale. Il marchait... David et Maurice se relayaient sans cesse pour le conduire dans le dédale des rues, le long des quais, des îles, dans l'allant du fleuve vers la mer. Son orteil était noir. Et sur ce pied pourri, Neuzil souriait. Je n'avais rien connu de plus beau que cette marche sans trêve, sans espoir. Qu'avais-je vécu alors d'aussi intense, sinon les chasses de mon adolescence dans l'ouragan de neige et de pluviers dorés, sinon l'éblouissement dans la fente d'Anny, sous son baiser brûlant ? Rien que le lyrisme des faucons... Puis l'apparition du vieillard lumineux, bâtard d'Egon et de Wally, qui marchait autour du grand dessin de l'étreinte ensorcelée comme pour l'entretenir et le protéger, et dont le corps frappé de gangrène tournait sans fin, se corrompait, oui, autour de ce trésor intact et central. Egon et Gerti. Et l'agonie du gardien.

Nicole m'a téléphoné. Nous n'irons pas au resto médical assister au gavage des rares malades et au festin des parasites. Nicole ne supporte plus la vue des beaux bruns plantureux et lubriques qui n'arrêtent pas de rigoler entre eux en lui faisant de l'œil. Elle baisse les yeux, elle jaunit, elle se fane dans ce resto de carnaval. Elle voudrait chasser les escrocs, dénoncer le scandale et ramener ces lieux à leur vocation première et protectrice : isoler les faibles, les recrus, les morfondus de la terre dans un havre de paix, autour d'une table familière, d'une nourriture moins corrosive... Mais les barbus sont apparus, un tollé de gros boucs baraqués qui boivent tout le lait, étanchent leur soif insatiable, font honte aux pâles agneaux, aux brebis efflanquées, bâfrent, s'empiffrent, squattent et monopolisent le resto des maigres.

Je l'invite donc dans un petit resto chinois. Elle aime l'Asie, les fluettes créatures pépiantes qui nous servent dans des culottes floues, leur androgynie pâle. Les aliments translucides et abstraits servis dans de petits raviers. Pousses de soja, vermicelle de riz, étroits pâtés qui n'ont d'impérial que le nom, crevettes. Nicole savoure notre dînette d'anorexiques. Elle m'annonce qu'elle quitte Paris, la Faculté, en

raison de son foie qui empire. Elle s'est fait inscrire à Rennes, dans sa province natale. Elle retourne vers son père et sa mère. Elle les avait quittés pour ressusciter, s'affirmer, s'affranchir, être enfin ! Et voilà qu'elle abandonne, régresse dans sa famille, son nid, son foie. Elle n'émergera plus jamais. J'ai pitié d'elle. Mais d'une pitié profonde, sagace et bouleversante. Que dire ? Que faire ? La supplier de rester, de tenir. Mais quel allié trouverait-elle en moi, mon amitié lointaine, intermittente, fuyante ? La laisser faire, partir, se replier, s'atrophier dans le cocon de sa famille et de la compassion. Je n'ai rien à dire, rien à donner. Je ne suis pas un saint. Je ne peux même pas lui parler d'Egon et de Gerti et du dessin de vie. Ça l'écraserait.

On part dans la rue. La Seine brille froidement. Nicole tremble. Toute la grisaille urbaine pèse sur elle. Même les îles sont moins belles et les quais semblent déchus. Un bateau-mouche clairsemé et clinquant passe devant nous, rangées de chaises vacantes. Et dans le gouffre du quai Voltaire, toutes les bagnoles dures, chromées, accumulées, se jettent sans un écart, sans une pause, imbriquées et rapides, avec voracité, tressant des chaînons métalliques, des éclats de pare-brise et de pare-chocs, agglomérées comme les pièces d'un Lego. Coriaces, assourdissantes, elles foncent dans l'entaille du quai, le long de la grosse rapière des eaux. Nicole est saisie de vertige, d'une envie de vomir devant la frénésie. Je la prends dans mes bras. Je la cajole. Une lueur blême traverse les nuages, remue tous les gris de la Seine. Nicole lève les yeux vers moi, tout à coup frileuse et belle. Elle a la chair de poule. Elle est toute grenue de frissons qui la rendent charnelle. Je la serre longuement sans rien dire. Je saisis sa main pâle que je plaque contre mon sexe. Il me semble que je suis renaissant et que je puis transmettre à Nicole ce viatique, ce contact superstitieux de ma bite droite

d'un soudain désir d'elle. Je sens Nicole respirer, palpiter. Elle garde la main longtemps contre ma tige vivante. Elle la caresse, la cerne, la tient doucement à travers l'étoffe. Et toute la Seine verse ses vagues, ses nuages, ses pierres, ses voitures, embarque les quais, emmêle les lumières et les corps, les masses, les flux, les énergies dans un chaos qui valse autour de nous.

Je lui dis : « Serre... » Elle n'ose pas. Je répète : « Serre fort. » Et elle serre tout à coup entre ses doigts, contre sa paume, s'empare du sexe, l'écoute et le savoure. Et je lui souffle : « Prends, prends. » Et elle le prend avec force et fringale. J'aurais voulu qu'elle se l'enfourne, qu'elle en mange, qu'elle parte avec dans son pays natal. Et que la barre la coupe de sa tribu, l'arrime et l'arrête au bord de l'abîme. Nous aurions dû aller nous coucher dans quelque hôtel. J'aurais dû accomplir la prouesse. Mais c'était là, dans la rue, que ça m'avait pris et qu'elle me serrait, presque dure elle aussi. Et très pâle. Chercher un hôtel et parler nous aurait séparés. Il aurait fallu tout reprendre. De tels instants ne se répètent pas. Elle s'est détachée au bout d'un moment, sans brusquerie. Elle a levé la bouche vers moi et déposé sur mes lèvres un baiser auquel j'ai répondu. Puis elle s'est détournée. Elle est partie. La recouvrit toute la matière morcelée des quais, des berges fuyantes, des gris, des pierres chancelantes et verticales, des eaux, des nuées chamboulées, avec les deux tours de Notre-Dame dressée, grise elle aussi, de la même couleur anonyme et flétrie. Je ne la revis jamais.

Je suis revenu vers Notre-Dame. J'ai escaladé la tour pour rêvasser. A peine étais-je installé sur le toit et son bourrelet de plomb que j'ai vu un vieux pigeon Bizet se poser,

souffreteux et pelé. Il se traînait. Son plumage, à la longue, avait pris la couleur ardoisée et salie des gouttières. Ces oiseaux, à mes yeux, n'étaient plus des animaux sauvages. Les ramiers de mon enfance étaient fleuris de plumes mauves et rosies. Les Bizet étaient ternes et noirâtres. Et celui-là était venu mourir sur le toit de plomb, dans la constellation des noms et des paraphes. Alors, le faucon a tourné dans le ciel, aigu et précis. Sa vrille nous coiffait, sa couronne de mort. Il s'est immobilisé dans un frétillement d'ailes et d'un coup a fondu sur le Bizet. Les serres se sont agrippées sur l'échine, labourant les pauvres rémiges convulsées. Et le bec a attaqué le crâne, l'a perforé sans merci. Le faucon a ensuite retourné sa victime pour l'éventrer et piller ses entrailles chaudes. Je regardais, saisi de crainte, l'horrible fierté du faucon. Hérissé, farouche. Son œil dardé de côté. Ses pattes minces et fermes. Ses griffes. Les petits soubresauts de ses ailes en équilibre sur la carcasse. Au fur et à mesure qu'il déchique-tait les chairs de son cou tendineux et de son bec tenace. On eût dit le faucon d'Ehra. Je croyais reconnaître sa couleur, son galbe exquis et cruel. C'était lui qui s'était posé non loin d'elle pour l'observer. Nous avions assisté à la scène, Anny et moi.

A la fin de la semaine, je revins avec mon amante. Et nous l'avons revu. Il avait perdu son arrogance. Il se voûtait un peu. Nous l'avons reconnu de dos, à sa nuque haute et fine, à son cou immaculé, à sa glotte outrée et saillant de profil. Puis, quand il a légèrement pivoté, à sa gorge féminine et courroucée dont la ligne pure s'offrait. Il a fait volte-face, les bras appuyés en arrière sur le bourrelet du toit dont il semblait pétrir les noms par essaims, dans ses mains ner-

veuses et lasses. Nous avons vu son visage barré d'un bandeau sur l'œil droit. Wolf aveuglé.

Nous nous sommes enfuis. Nous l'avons laissé, là-haut, solitaire dans le ciel froid. Nous sommes rentrés dans ma chambre et nous avons échafaudé les hypothèses les plus folles sans trouver une explication plausible. En fin d'après-midi, à l'heure de fermeture des tours, nous avons intercepté Osiris. En nous voyant, il s'est un peu rétracté. Notre curiosité insatiable l'agaçait, mais il subissait en même temps la séduction de notre extrême jeunesse, de ce mélange d'exaltation et d'ingénuité. Nous n'osions aborder la question. Bien sûr il nous avait devinés. Alors, on employa les grands moyens, on l'invita carrément à dîner. Osiris était libre pour un couscous sur le faubourg. Poivre rouge et Sidi Brahim viendraient à bout du mystère. Osiris admirait notre condition d'étudiant, un prestige intellectuel, des compétences littéraires pourtant légères encore. Notre amitié le flattait un peu. Ses relations étaient variées et dispersées, mais un poil de Sorbonne enrichissait l'éventail. Parfois, il nous interrogeait sur tel ou tel auteur. Et lorsque nous lui fournissions une réponse précise et ample, nous le sentions conquis. Il fallait déployer un beau volume de mots méticuleux, ponctué d'images, de surprises, de petits renseignements succulents, de détails coruscants. C'était justement ce type d'adjectifs qu'Osiris raffolait de découvrir. Son œil brillait de convoitise en captant le vocable... coruscant ! Il le balancerait aux visiteurs des tours, évoquerait le battant d'Emmanuel, central et coruscant dans sa corolle de bronze et de vermeil. L'on devait attiser Osiris avec des mots précieux, en distiller dans la conversation, l'air de rien, l'appâter avec ce grain doré. Il se parait de ces plumes irisées. La manœuvre consistait à lui faire sentir qu'on en possédait encore des kyrielles en réserve... mots mordorés, moirés,

ciselés dans le métal rare. Là, il n'en pouvait plus. Il nous aurait donné sa sœur contre le talisman d'un mot.

Anny se lança :

— Nous avons vu Wolf, là-haut !

Osiris cramait doucement dans le piment, le vin violent. La question ne déclencha aucun réflexe particulier. Il semblait la boire, l'absorber au même titre que le reste, l'ambiance, la nourriture, nos deux visages adolescents et notre science du langage. Mais cette passivité un peu stuporeuse nous fit craindre qu'il ne prenne même pas la peine de répondre et se contente d'esquiver, de flotter dans son rire sensuel, déboussolé. Alors il dissolvait tout. On n'avait plus de prise sur lui, chacune de nos charges se réfractait en un surcroît de gaieté pétillante et paresseuse. Il nous noyait dans son ivresse rieuse. Au mieux, il nous regardait avec amour et lasciveté, comme assailli d'une envie de baiser. On éludait, déguerpissait presto. Inquiets tout de même. Nous qui ne possédions que la science des mots. Il s'agissait de le freiner sur sa pente.

— C'est horrible, Wolf avait l'œil crevé.

J'avais fait fort, sans savoir rien encore, pour exciter Osiris, provoquer un sursaut.

— Qui vous dit que c'est un œil crevé ? Peut-être ne souffre-t-il que d'une blessure passagère... Wolf a toujours eu les yeux trop clairs, sensibles à l'excès, il ne supporte plus la lumière.

— Voyons ! s'exclama Anny, il porterait des lunettes noires. Or il avait un bandeau et un pansement dessous. L'œil était opaque, obturé, c'était horrible. Pourquoi nous cacher la vérité, Osiris, je ne comprends pas ?

— C'est parce que vous désirez savoir et que vous manifestez à outrance ce désir. Alors, je mesure soudain le pouvoir que je détiens sur vous et j'ai la tentation d'en jouer,

de vous tenir par cela. C'est instinctif. Je n'ai même pas à le vouloir, c'est ma sensibilité qui me porte. C'est délicieux même.

— Osiris, je vous révélerai des mots merveilleux, presque inconnus... Vous pourrez les emporter.

— C'est trop général, me répondit-il, et je puis lire le dictionnaire.

— Beaucoup trop long et hasardeux ! Vous capitulerez au bout de trente pages dans l'encombrement, sans tri, pêle-mêle. Un mot ne brille que dans l'usage qu'on en fait, il faut le prononcer, le modeler dans la parole... le colorer sous la langue... Moi, je vous situerai mes mots, je vous les mettrai dans des phrases comme des écrins. Je vous les offrirai chatoyants dans leur éclat, leur consistance, leur grain lourd ou plus sec, velouté ou guilloché. Vous comprenez, ça dépend de leur texture, de leurs nervures...

Ah comme je le sentais mordre, mon Osiris, à ce chapelet de qualifications... sortis de mon sac à magie, nervures et guilloché surtout... Je le voyais poindre et s'aiguiser...

— Donnez-les-moi donc, ces mots d'abord !

Anny intervint :

— Non, on vous les enverra dans une belle missive, par la poste, joliment, calmement calligraphiés. Vous les lirez, vous les découvrirez. Puis on viendra les prononcer, les illustrer oralement, pour vous !

Ce rituel subtil électrisait Osiris. Il cuvait les épices et l'alcool. Il se sentit comblé d'avance par ces mots rares, ce trésor pour lui. Ses belles lèvres charnues déjà les suçaient, les mangeaient. Ça faisait chair et jouissance, jus de langage en lui.

Alors il lâcha le morceau :

— Wolf a été tout simplement agressé, la nuit, dans le jardin de l'Archevêché, par un voyou. Un coup de couteau.

— Mais on n'a pas retrouvé le type ? demanda Anny.

— Non, il ne l'a pas bien vu dans le va-et-vient nocturne, vous comprenez, il ne s'est pas méfié.

— C'était peut-être un amant jaloux ?

— Je ne crois pas, Anny, pas jaloux à ce point. Il n'y a pas trop de jalousie dans le jardin. Les rencontres ne sont pas fondées sur l'appropriation. Tout est fluide...

Anny poursuivit :

— Mais quelqu'un peut souffrir de cette mobilité, de cette disponibilité, et venir y mettre brutalement fin.

— Je ne crois pas à ce scénario mélo... D'ailleurs, lui !...

— Lui quoi ?

— Lui, il tient un tout autre discours. Il déraisonne.

— Il dit quoi ? demanda Anny.

— Il dit qu'il a entendu dans la nuit un soudain bruissement d'ailes, un claquement noir au-dessus de sa tête. Et que c'est un faucon qui lui a crevé l'œil.

Osiris presque tremblant savourait l'écho de sa révélation. Anny et moi restions silencieux. Une pensée nous glaçait, nous brûlait : le couteau de l'oiseau dans l'iris bleu de Wolf.

— Vous aurez toujours envie de m'envoyer la moisson de mots ?

Je répondis :

— Un peu plus tard, Osiris, on vous le promet. Mais pas tout de suite. On est sous le coup, les mots ne viendraient pas. Ils seraient indécents.

Osiris était ivre d'avoir bu et tout dit. Dans le faubourg, il dressait sa stature. Ses longues cuisses s'incurvaient dans ses jeans, arcs-boutants de mec du grand bourdon d'Emmanuel. Il murmura :

— Pourquoi a-t-il inventé cette histoire de faucon ? C'est ce que je n'ai pas compris. Il s'est envolé soudain dans cette

histoire. Il ne veut plus rien entendre d'autre. Il n'accuse personne. Il dit : « Le faucon a crevé mon œil bleu. »

Dans la chambre, je n'arrivais pas à trouver le sommeil. Je pris deux ou trois Imménoctal. Ce somnifère a été interdit depuis. Et pourtant, je lui devais visions, délivrance et griseries. L'Imménoctal ne m'endormait jamais mais produisait en moi une effusion lyrique, une élation quasi cosmique qui me démultipliait, me répandait dans un amour sans limites qui me réconciliait avec moi-même et le monde et comblait tous mes vides. Anny ne m'aimait pas sous Imménoctal. Je lui faisais peur. Il paraît que mes yeux s'égaraient, que mes prunelles glissaient contre le bord des paupières supérieures dans une sorte d'extase, et je ne tardais pas à débiter des propos délirants. Je devenais oblatif. J'annonçais ma mort bienheureuse. Je nous fondais, Anny et moi, dans une cellule angélique et radieuse. Il n'y avait plus d'altérité, d'accroc, d'angoisse ni de manque. Les vagues sourdaient d'un fond de félicité océanique. Notre-Dame se dilatait, immense, ensoleillée, portait sur ses ramures gothiques tous les faucons au poitrail flavescent. Les magnifiques janissaires nous émouvaient, érigés et tutélaires, sentinelles du cosmos. Et la Seine cernait de son fleuve notre clan d'amour. Elle nous baguait de sève noire, de grandes épées et de larmes d'amour.

Je m'imménoctais. Vingt ans plus tard, je me souviens encore de l'effet, cet affaissement de mes défenses, de mes cloisons, cette délicieuse évanescence. Cet à-vau-l'eau de l'être entier, éboulé, diffusé, soudain traversé de hautes

flammes lancéolées, de purs accès de joie, d'éternité. La semaine du grand concours, ayant perdu complètement le sommeil, je m'imménoctais, mais le produit ne daignait pas m'accorder plus de deux heures de sommeil. Toutefois, ma vigilance au fil des longues nuits était transfigurée. Au lieu de compter les heures et de me désoler, je voguais illuminé par une foi indestructible. J'étais guidé par la nef de la folie et toutes les lampes de la beauté.

Et le miracle, c'était mon arrivée, le matin, dans les salles de l'examen. Mes camarades étaient frappés par ma pétulance, ma volubilité. Le seul en forme, c'était moi, l'insomniaque intempérant. On aurait pu redouter un écrit cafouilleux, halluciné. Bien au contraire, mes vues étaient claires, ma mémoire souveraine. Je voltigeais en écrivant. Marivaux était tombé. Et je saisissais les plus fines nuances, les aveux mouchetés des amants. Des phrases me revenaient, je découvrais leur musique intime, étourdissante... des allégros voilés, des surprises alambiquées, des anicroches, des enchantements obliques, des clairvoyances et des tropismes... J'étais dedans, je nageais dans les ruses, les moirures du cœur, les duplicités, les calculs tamisés... Je gagnai quatre-vingts places d'avance à l'écrit. Mais l'oral m'abattit. L'Imménoctal diminua d'effet. Une dépression puissante m'accabla, une anorexie presque totale. Alors je m'efforçai de manger par petites bouchées, une pour Giono, une pour Proust, une pour Céline, une pour Freud, une pour Saint-John Perse, une pour Jean Genet, une pour Arthur Rimbaud et la dernière pour Brigitte Bardot.

Je dégueulais souvent. On en riait, Anny et moi, dans le malheur. Et j'avalais derechef quelques broutilles. Ça ne pouvait être pire, je n'étais menacé après tout que de gerber encore. Et de rire dans la nausée et le noir. Marguerite ou Anny me forçaient d'aller passer l'oral. Je n'avais plus envie.

Je calais devant la vie, sa perspective ouverte, juste à la porte. Le concours réussi allait me flanquer dans le temps irréversible. Sans y couper. L'horreur. Et je cherchais à fuir. Mais elles m'encourageaient, me ramenaient coûte que coûte à l'oral de la vie. Je perdis cinquante places. Mais l'avance du bel écrit béat, imménocté, me permit d'occuper le juste milieu de la liste des reçus. Et c'est ainsi qu'on entre dans la fonction publique par la porte de la névrose hallucinée. L'accès est rigoureusement le même pour la littérature...

Cette nuit-là, avec Anny, après la révélation de Wolf et du faucon, je planais dans les vallées luxuriantes et les firmaments me berçaient. Le couteau de l'oiseau dans l'iris bleu de Wolf se changeait en une aiguille de neige sur le fond de l'azur. Je bandais d'un phallus dont je ne sentais ni la raideur ni le poids. Un phallus voyageur et volant, un ange lévitant que je fourrai entre les cuisses d'Anny. L'amour était fusion au sein d'une symbiose plus vaste. J'éjaculai sans rage ni ahan. Une vague à peine plus vive rayait mon euphorie.

Anny me préférait conscient, corsaire de son cul, l'éperonnant, haletant, éructant des petits mots furieux, fervents, des louanges bien crues, plutôt qu'ainsi noyé dans une marmelade céleste où mes yeux révulsés devenaient blancs comme ceux des moribonds de la Méduse, des immolés du Colisée ou des extasiés du Bernin, au choix...

Je devais tout de même un peu l'écœurer, la saturer avec ma cortisone, mon ménisque morcelé, mes effrois, mes convulsions, mon obsession de la sainteté de Neuzil, mes couscous priapiques, mes Notre-Dame, mes nus de Schiele, mes faucons faramineux, ma phobie de l'avenir, mes fièvres, mes fringales et mes débagoulis, mon verbe intarissable. Je

l'enlianais dans cette jungle. A la longue elle devint un peu claustro quand même, elle eut besoin d'ouvrir les fenêtres, de grapiller un petit coulis. Forcément je la submergeais, je lui pompais l'oxygène et j'occupais tous les créneaux avec mon évent de baleine, tout ce potin de mes poumons et mon fracas vocal terrible pour les tympans du voisinage, mes amis délicats. Elle eut, oui, toujours besoin d'air et de silence à cause de moi, d'un jardin calme et muet.

Osiris reçut la missive promise, le don des mots. D'abord « lancéolé et flavescent ». En duo, pour tout l'or hérissé, dansant. Puis, par contraste, « acuminé et obombré ». Mots plus durs et plus sombres. Ensuite nous vint « obi », joli mot vif et nu, cette large ceinture japonaise et antique. J'avais toujours eu envie de posséder une femme d'Asie uniquement ceinte d'un obi de soie. Nous eûmes l'idée d'une maxime talismanique, sorte de formule magique dédiée à l'imaginaire d'Osiris. Après plusieurs essais, permutation des mots, cela surgit : « obi et branlerie d'amour ». Le néologisme à partir de branler nous ravit. Branlette est si petit, canin, anecdotique. Mais comme branlerie roule et brille dans la nuit du désir.

Quelques jours plus tard, Marguerite invita à dîner quelques amis. La meute était bariolée. Neuzil, la concierge et son mari, David et Maurice et Anchise leur grand chien si con, Mlle Poulet et Osiris. Ce dernier en entrant se pencha vers Anny et moi et souffla : « Obi et branlerie d'amour. » Nous fûmes gênés par l'indécente formule que nous avions

pourtant ciselée. Mais le passage de l'écrit à l'oral créait un effet de proximité lubrique assez périlleux. Osiris nous signifiait notre appartenance à la société secrète des mots ensorcelés. Mlle Poulet, l'ex-infirmière immense et vierge, assenait toujours ses propos de soudard. La concierge était moche, acariâtre. On la soupçonnait de racisme. Son mari était gratifié d'une réputation de virilité insatiable. Marguerite m'avait rapporté qu'il harcelait sans cesse sa femme et qu'elle s'en plaignait. Or, le type était petit, malingre, l'œil faible, le poil usé, le teint pauvre. Mais sa voix était dotée d'un timbre net, métallique. Était-ce l'indice de cette virilité de fer ? Marguerite, qui ne faisait pas dans la dentelle, l'avait surnommé : « pine d'acier », elle abrégeait en « pine d'ace » dont elle faisait siffler la finale. Ce fut toute une affaire de séparer Anchise d'avec Toufflette. Des deux, c'était elle l'enragée, chuintant, sifflant, dardant son poil à la vue du clebs géant. Margot n'avait pas mégoté sur la vinasse. Elle nous présentait des bordeaux bien aigres comme s'il s'était agi de crus célestes. Elle servit son éternel poulet, l'homonymie avec la demoiselle entraîna de vieilles plaisanteries.

Mlle Poulet parla des vacances qu'elle passait à Louviers chez sa sœur. Il n'y avait rien à faire ni à voir à Louviers, me semblait-il. Mais c'était la migration annuelle de la demoiselle. La maison se situait le long d'une route nationale dont elle était séparée par un jardinet. Les deux sœurs s'y installaient pour regarder les voitures passer entre les barreaux de la grille et en surveillant le cerisier. Dès qu'un vol d'étourneaux surgissait, elles houspillaient les pillards avec des cris, du tintamarre. C'était une espèce d'épopée, *Les Sept Samouraïs*... Quand les étourneaux s'attaquaient à un autre arbre, elles s'ennuyaient un peu. Mais c'était justement la qualité de cet ennui estival, si différent de celui qu'elle connaissait rue Pavée, qui constituait pour Mlle Poulet le sel

de ses vacances. Toute l'année, elle rêvait à cet ennui délicieux, dans le jardin de sa sœur, à l'ombre du cerisier menacé. Je ne sais pourquoi j'insiste sur la villégiature de Mlle Poulet à Louviers. Mais secrètement elle m'émerveillait. J'enviais la sérénité de l'infirmière à la retraite qui n'avait plus à entrer dans la vie, à affronter l'avenir, mais passait des vacances douces et vides. Elle savourait le temps ramené à son pur écoulement. Cela devait être long, infini, sans danger. Le bonheur, sans doute, puisque Mlle Poulet ne désirait plus rien de particulier mais se laissait flotter au fil de ces journées d'été, en compagnie de sa sœur. Elles vivaient. Elles ne faisaient plus que cela. Et brusquement elles sortaient de leur sieste, se dressaient, hurlaient, se démenaient comme des Apaches au premier raid des étourneaux. Tout le voisinage assistait à la crise. Les oiseaux décrochaient en voilier déployé, glapissant et noir. Leurs ailes vibraient, brillaient, bruissaient dans une fuite oblique.

David et Maurice buvaient avec modération, se tenaient bien et considéraient les convives avec aménité. Marguerite, très allumée, faisait le pitre. Elle adorait les farces et les fanfaronnades, les lazzi. Elle se levait sans cesse, gesticulait, allait voir chaque invité, troussait des phrases pour la concierge analphabète. Elle frôlait le mari qui réagissait mollement, mais l'on voyait Marguerite sursauter comme si le bonhomme l'avait pincée. Elle coulait un regard entendu à Mlle Poulet, puis levait les yeux au ciel, l'air de dire : quel obsédé ! Elle affichait une mine blasée. Son rêve eût été d'être draguée dans la rue par de beaux hommes. Elle compensait sa frustration en interprétant le moindre regard, la moindre bousculade comme des entreprises libidineuses dont elle était le pôle.

Neuzil ne mangeait pas trop mais buvait normalement. Margot en profitait pour le resserver ostensiblement en me

jetant un regard de victoire qui signifiait : « Vous voyez bien que ce n'est pas un saint, il boit comme un trou ! » Puis, sacrilège, elle parodiait son tic : « N'est-il pas exquis mon petit pinard, soudain ! »

Au bout d'un moment, je pris le commandement de la conversation, si l'on peut appeler ainsi ce chaos de blagues, d'ébriété pour des riens. J'aimais faire rire, broder des manières de sketches qui les faisaient pouffer. Et ce n'était pas difficile. Maurice et David s'esclaffaient, postillonnaient. Cette hilarité liée au vin, à la bouffe, au babil effréné, nous mêlait dans une confusion bon enfant, bienheureuse, pas si éloignée des effets de l'Imménoctal. Même la concierge en oubliait sa vacherie. Osiris jetait dans cette euphorie des volutes plus suaves, des roulades de rires qui sonnaient, ricochaient, cuivrées, intarissables. Nous admirions alors ses dents éclatantes, tout un clavier de squale ! L'ambiance était si chaude qu'il suffisait d'un trait, d'une mimique, d'une bouffonnerie pour alimenter le brasier, lancer une nouvelle flambée. Avec une jubilation presque sadique, j'y fourrais la paille d'une nouvelle plaisanterie pour les voir aussitôt se plier et se tordre, haletant, pâmés, oui martyrisés, n'en pouvant plus, à bout de respiration, me suppliant en se tenant le ventre : « Non... non... arrêtez ! arrêtez ! » Larmoyants, apoplectiques. Je jouissais de leur infliger la torture du bonheur. Quelques années plus tard, devenu professeur, j'abusais ainsi de mes élèves par le rire. Ils se débraillaient, s'écarquillaient, fendus de rigolade. Jeunes mecs et jolies filles, écarlates de gaieté, moussant, éclaboussés de pleurs compulsifs. J'adorais ce naufrage de mes petits drilles, ce raz de marée de rires orgastiques. Il me semblait alors que mon métier était le plus beau du monde, mon pouvoir d'incendiaire bachique ! Oui je les embrasais, je les tisonnais et je me chauffais à ce feu de jouvence, de licence à satiété.

Une accalmie se dessinait. On émergeait, ravagés encore, illuminés par le supplice. On rentra par degrés dans le temps quotidien et le monde sérieux. On s'ébroua. D'ultimes vestiges s'évanouirent des visages. On se sentait un peu gênés, honteux de redevenir normaux, mortels, de dire adieu au délire.

Osiris alors se mit à raconter ses fables. On ne savait jamais s'il mentait totalement ou si ses récits s'appuyaient sur un noyau de vérité. Il nous parla du Christ caché de Notre-Dame. Neuzil, un peu gris, l'interrompit dans son élan en s'émerveillant des Christs gothiques et d'ivoire du trésor de Notre-Dame.

— Je les adore... Ils sont si hiératiques, si tourmentés, taillés dans la matière blanche. Le temps n'a pas de prise sur eux. On est tellement habitués aux Christs de bois et de pierre qui vieillissent, se fendillent, tout rongés et noircis, que ceux-ci semblent vernis, quasi factices. On dirait des faux tant ils brillent!

Osiris arrêta Neuzil.

— Mais justement, c'est d'un autre Christ d'ivoire que je veux parler, pas de ces deux-là qu'on exhibe, mais un Christ...

— Mais qu'est-ce qu'il a de sorcier, votre Jésus, Osiris? s'exclama Marguerite.

— Un détail, un petit grain dans l'engrenage, si vous voulez... un grain de trop. C'est un Christ d'ivoire à peu près de la même taille et de la même époque que ceux du trésor, du XIIIe siècle donc. Mais la paume de sa main gauche serre un grain de blé. Un mince grain allongé et c'est ce petit détail païen des semailles qui lui a valu d'être escamoté!

— Où est le mal? lança Margot.

— Un soupçon de rusticité, de mythologie agraire, sans doute... observa Neuzil.

— Ce n'est plus un Christ, c'est Dionysos ! fit remarquer le gardien des tours. Vous comprenez, le Christ a été inventé pour sublimer toutes ces affaires de paysans superstitieux et sacrificateurs. Ce n'est pas un dieu des bacchanales et des moissons, quand même ! Alors, ils l'ont planqué. En outre, il a une drôle de mine... trop orientale, trop hybride. Il a déplu, si vous voulez. Louche ! versé au milieu des autres comme un trublion !

— Et on vous l'a montré ? demanda Anny intéressée.

— Oui, bien sûr...

Et c'est là qu'on devinait à quel point Osiris était capable d'en rajouter, de tricher. Cela se voyait dans son regard trop limpide. Il devenait tout lisse d'innocence. C'était trop bien ajusté.

— Il y a le trésor officiel pour les badauds, les dévots, et l'autre, un trésor moins orthodoxe, inclassable, embrouillé... Il faut voir ce qu'on découvre actuellement sous le parvis de Notre-Dame... Les archéologues ne déterrent pas que des poteries. Il y a des emblèmes et des objets de culte gaulois... des statuettes assez truculentes. Le sol est bourré de figures d'aigles, d'éperviers, j'en passe, et des faucons... Ça plonge dans l'animisme, les symboles phalliques de fécondité, si ! si ! le chamanisme et tout le tralala des transes. Notre-Dame pose son pied sur un fameux bestiaire ! Alors, ce Christ un peu mêlé et trop agreste, avec sa promesse d'épi, on l'a mis de côté. Il y a assez des tripotées de gargouilles de Notre-Dame, à trompes et becs peu recommandables, grimaces simiesques et ventres protubérants. La Dame hausse ses deux tours sur un carnaval sauvage.

Et Marguerite éméchée, prise d'un fou rire :

— On ne peut pas dire, mon cher Osiris, que vous soyez le plus réglo de la farandole. Hein ! Vous avez l'air d'un roi mage un peu bariolé. Un de ces quatre, ils vont vous mettre

145

au rancart comme votre Jésus trop printanier. Méfiez-vous !
Et tous vos copains de l'Archevêché, leur ronde. Moi je n'y
vois rien à redire mais les autorités, les bien-pensants, les
religieux pourraient décider qu'il vous faudrait choisir un
autre nid qu'un chevet de cathédrale chrétienne voué à la
Très Sainte Vierge !

Pour se faire pardonner sa sortie, Marguerite tapotait les
épaules d'Osiris en riant gentiment tout en nous glissant de
vaches clins d'œil, l'air de dire : « Je l'ai fourré dans ses petits
souliers, ce satané Osiris. »

Osiris prit le parti d'en rire en un ruisselet léger, abstrait,
qui gommait toute aspérité, tout sentiment précis. Et moi,
soudain, je me fendis d'un commentaire pénétrant et psy. Je
mordais à Freud tout nouvellement...

— Entre Vierge et verge, au fond il n'y a qu'une petite
voyelle, que la pointe d'un i. Il y aurait à étudier ce détail. La
Vierge est dure de son hymen intact. Elle n'est pas une
femme profonde. L'ange est passé comme un courant d'air.
C'est une garçonne à sa façon.

— Tout de même, elle a accouché du Christ ! Et son
hymen a décanillé, lança Margot, humoristique.

— Oui, mais dans l'imaginaire, elle reste la Vierge invio-
lée, lisse, à l'écart du cycle de l'habituelle féminité. Elle se
place du côté des anges, c'est évident : le Gabriel de
l'Annonciation. On voit bien qu'elle n'est pas dans la norme,
qu'elle a des fréquentations miraculeuses avec tout ce qui
tombe du ciel et d'ailleurs.

— Et c'est ce qui nous aimanterait ? demanda Osiris, l'air
tenté.

— Oui, pourquoi pas ? La Vierge dans l'odeur du grand
fleuve noir, les feuillages de la rive, le bestiaire hybride et la
légion des anges immaculés. Ce n'est pas rien ! C'est rare !

— On voit qu'il fait des études ! C'est envoûtant, s'exclama

146

Osiris. Et la crypte pendant que vous y êtes, salace et gauloise, un trou d'anguille !

Osiris osait. Il avait bu, on avait bu. Mlle Poulet se tordait de rire, oubliant qu'elle était vierge elle aussi ou parce qu'elle le revendiquait soudain, identifiée aux madones aberrantes et aux anges précieux. David et Maurice ne bronchaient pas, discrets, souriants, un tout petit peu gênés, sans plus.

— La religion, c'est pas ce qu'on pense ! conclut Marguerite songeuse...

Tard dans la nuit, quand tout le monde fut au lit, je me relevai pour pisser et tombai sur Margot qui avait la même envie. Cela ne tournait pas rond, elle se plaignait de sa digestion.

— Je gonfle ! Je gonfle ! C'est pas possible, regardez !

Elle m'avait déjà fait le coup du « je gonfle ! ». Et chaque fois, j'étais dérouté par l'inflation du ventre de Margot. Un ballonnement prodigieux qui débordait vers l'épigastre. L'ennui, c'est qu'au lieu de s'en tenir à l'énoncé intellectuel, elle me priait de vérifier le symptôme. Il fallait que je glisse un doigt entre son abdomen et sa ceinture, que je calibre le mal, sa démesure. Alors, elle me regardait d'un air sournois. Je retrouvais cette Marguerite secrète, ses rêves, une soif d'idylle avec un étudiant casse-cou. Moi, je me défilai, je dégageai le doigt pincé entre son bide et sa ceinture. Nous étions face à face, de très près. Je la revois raide, mal plantée, bancale à cause du bras, le menton en galoche, le visage revêche et poché, la destinée saumâtre, en panne de romantisme. Par bonheur, Anny était couchée dans la chambre voisine. Marguerite n'aurait tout de même pas insisté. Elle ne le fit jamais, d'ailleurs. Rien de précis. Une rêverie... en

147

pointillés... au-delà de minuit, sous le coup des somnifères, dans l'hypnose diffuse. Elle oubliait le réel et ses limites. Elle vacillait d'un chouia : « Je gonfle ! Je gonfle ! touchez ! mais touchez donc... » Moi, je me dégonflais presto.

Toutefois, je dois avouer que lorsque j'avais consulté les fiches des chambres d'étudiants au service universitaire, j'avais sans doute un peu rêvé, moi aussi, à une Marguerite L. de trente-cinq ans, veuve ou divorcée, sans enfants ou alors un vraiment tout petit et fantomatique. Une Mme de Rênal en somme, Mme Arnoux douce et sensuelle. On se serait croisés tard dans la nuit dans le couloir des W.-C. Elle discrète, élégante jusque dans ses petits besoins pressants, moi timide, fasciné. Je l'aurais entendue pisser de ma chambre... un tintement contenu, fine musique en fraude, puis le froissement fluet du papier sur le pubis. Tandis que Marguerite lâchait d'un coup un torrent cacophonique. Elle s'essuyait sans art, à l'arraché.

Oui, une jeune logeuse sortie à peine du deuil, harcelée secrètement par un retour du désir, que j'aurais frôlée à minuit dans le couloir, en chemise de nuit fine sur les seins qui bougent. Moi tendu dans un réveil halluciné, m'empalant sous le retroussis du linge. La belle oubliant son veuvage, saisissant ma bite adolescente et dure, me baisant la bouche, la poitrine tandis que je palpe ses bouts, ses fesses mouvementées d'amour. Et je pénètre en elle comme en rêve. Sa main goulue me caresse les couilles et moi je touche son beau cul vierge depuis un an, son globe moite et fendu qui se contracte dès qu'elle se plante à longs coups sur ma tige raide à mourir d'étudiant plein d'angoisse, de ferveur et qu'elle s'en gorge à fond, à satiété, en émettant des chapelets de phrases obscènes sur ma queue droite et crue de jeune homme qui l'émeut, à peine émergée des larmes du deuil. Elle s'agenouille soudain pour mieux la contempler, la

148

humer, la couvrir, la napper si étroitement de ses lèvres que j'en sens la pulpe convulsée et la moindre nervure sur mon frein, sur mon gland, la scrute et la regarde encore tel un cierge vivace qu'elle se fourre et refourre dans son sexe baigné de plaisir et qui sent bon, si fort. Et moi, et moi ne sachant plus où plaquer mes doigts, à la racine de son cou délicat incliné dans l'orgasme, sur le gonflement de sa gorge, sur l'anus qui palpite à chaque coup de ma lance... oui, veuve et vouée à la résurrection tandis que sa chemise fluide, abandonnée sous nos corps, se froisse et se plisse, trempée de nos sueurs, n'est plus qu'un voile musqué, matraqué par sa croupe tournée et retournée, étoffe qu'elle mord, mange et broute à pleine bouche quand je la chevauche par-derrière. Si bien que lorsque nous avons fini et que la jeune veuve relève le chiffon de chemise, le déploie, c'est l'exact suaire de son sillon, de son cul, de sa vulve sauvage, de sa bouche et de ma bite, archive de Pompéi encore souillée par les laves du volcan, qu'elle décide de garder dans son armoire, parure précieuse, lubrique et meurtrie, linge des apparitions, preuve du rut à minuit qui lui fit oublier la mort.

Mais la logeuse fut Margot ! Ce qui sauva notre amour, à Anny et à moi, de la division.

Au réveil, Anny me raconta qu'elle avait rêvé d'Anchise, le chien géant. Nous ne faisions pas forcément les mêmes songes, au même moment... Car elle aurait pu avoir, de son côté, en Lorraine là-bas, un logeur veuf, quadragénaire bien dru, quidam échevelé, nordique... Mais est-ce à moi de conter une débauche qui m'exclut... Nulle zoophilie cependant dans le rêve d'Anny. Anchise semblait encore plus grand et plus mou... Bon... Il descendait l'escalier de la

maison, sortait dans la rue, passait devant Notre-Dame.

— Je ne sais pas... mais il était lié à la mort, c'est terrible !

J'étais surpris, car Anny ne détaillait jamais ses rêves.

— Il devenait inquiétant à force de bonté, de douceur. Il y avait une menace dans son énormité trop lente. Il était d'une couleur pâle, comme un chien blond, albinos, sans structure, sans musculature précise, lisse et glabre... C'est répugnant, n'est-ce pas ?

— Mais qu'est-ce qu'il faisait ?

— Je ne peux pas m'en souvenir. Il rôdait autour de Notre-Dame, il allait vers le champ de fouilles, vers la crypte. Il descendait sous la terre... oui, je crois. Au milieu des poteries cassées. C'est peut-être ça, l'idée de mort. Il déterrait je ne sais quoi avec son mufle dégoûtant et bonasse. Il était bête et il me faisait peur. Il agissait mollement, mécaniquement parmi les dépouilles, les ossements. Le rêve a dû venir des récits archéologiques faits par Osiris ?

Le lendemain après-midi, nous franchissions le Pont-Marie quand nous aperçûmes Johann Neuzil. Il se retourna vers nous et nous annonça qu'il avait pris sa décision et qu'il voulait nous accompagner là-haut. Anny tenta de l'en dissuader.

— Mon cœur est bon, les enfants ! Et mon orteil ne peut souffrir dans cette ascension, bien au contraire, ça l'irrigue et le fortifie. J'ai bien dormi, je me sens d'attaque !

Johann nous suivit. Nous sommes entrés d'abord dans l'aura de Notre-Dame. C'était un périmètre magnétique que créait la seule présence de la cathédrale. Dans la rue étroite qui bordait le flanc nord, le monument pesait, pressait de toute sa puissance, de ses efflorescences gothiques en gros

150

plan puis, sur le parvis, l'impression s'élargissait et l'on pouvait savourer la magie des lieux. La cathédrale trônait au centre de l'île où elle déployait un sentiment d'ouverture et de joie. On pouvait aller et venir, s'asseoir, se promener. Elle était toujours là, revêtant chaque parcelle du terrain d'une intensité singulière. On était pris dans son attraction religieuse et sereine.

Anny commentait l'escalade. Neuzil au milieu et moi derrière. Quatre cents marches. Il y avait peu de visiteurs en tout début d'après-midi. L'escalier nord était libre. On le suivait jusqu'à la grande galerie pour gagner ensuite l'escalier sud de l'autre côté. Et nous étions heureux, Anny et moi, d'emmener, d'enlever Neuzil vers le ciel. Anny, plus inquiète, se retournait souvent vers le vieil homme, lui souriait, l'encourageait. Mais Neuzil montait avec lenteur, à petits pas. Je voyais son corps se hausser, entraîner l'autre jambe, atterrir sur la marche suivante avec cette précaution de l'orteil au moment d'appuyer sur le sol et aussitôt sa silhouette fragile et têtue enchaînait sur un nouvel essor. Je comprenais la vulnérabilité de Neuzil car moi-même, quelques semaines plus tôt, j'avais ressenti à chaque enjambée la douleur de mon genou ardent. Les anti-inflammatoires avaient, depuis, résorbé la crise. Mais il m'arrivait, d'instinct, de dérober mon articulation comme pour la préserver d'un heurt, d'un écart brutal. J'étais frère de Johann, frère du vieux blessé qui projetait une image de moi-même au bout du temps et pourtant familière.

Toutes les vingt marches, on s'arrêtait. Anny prenait prétexte des graffiti qu'elle scrutait. Neuzil soufflait un peu. Nous lui lisions les prénoms et les noms. Tous les pays, toutes les langues... Cumba, Zulmira, Paul, Gertrud, Zina, Sue, Nazly, Fedor, Saï... tous les corps de la terre aspirés par la tour, l'Afrique, l'Asie, le Nord, tous ces hommes pétris par

l'histoire et puis ce duo dans un cercle de craie : Tayama et Yôko. On pouvait rêver à l'infini à leur destin. Neuzil murmurait : « Tous les romans du monde entier, mes enfants. » Et il respirait, ses poumons se gonflaient dans son thorax étroit. Il souffla : « Egon et Gerti auraient pu venir, seraient venus sans doute... Victor Hugo a gravi l'escalier, c'est sûr ! Avec Juliette Drouet peut-être. Goethe qui sait ? Rimbaud et Verlaine seraient montés... oui ! »

Dans le goulet, le cortège des peuples anonymes et, çà et là, la surprise d'une fée : « Rita Hayworth en col roulé, si ! si ! Ah si ! » Et Neuzil s'esclaffait... « Louise Colet et Ninon de Lanclos... Et comment ! Des pelotons de Blue Bell girls très athlétiques, les enfants... L'humanité ! Des légions... » Il se dressait, pétillait, farfadet halluciné, drogué par l'escalier des foules, des amoureux de Notre-Dame... Alors on cherchait plus avidement dans le palimpseste des noms... Une lucarne fissurait le mur par où Neuzil happait une lampée d'air frais, le reflet mat du jour faisait briller les nervures et les traces. On discernait sous la moisson des noms récents d'anciens passages et des fantômes : Amélie et Joseph... Éléonore... Hamilton et Dorian. Ça fleurissait par en dessous, en arborescences inconnues, généalogies perdues. Parfois, les noms s'enchevêtraient, mordaient à tel point les uns sur les autres que cela donnait un texte hybride et polymorphe. Aminatoko... Ludmicarlos... Le jour filtrait d'un éclat plus dense et vraiment nous apparaissaient les noms dans cet angélique halo... comme sur les tombes ou les troncs des chênes, noms des vivants, noms des morts. Avec quelque chose d'enfantin et de superstitieux dans le dessin gravé. Tous avaient nourri ce rêve que Notre-Dame allait leur apporter un peu d'éternité. Dans les plis de la pierre, tous s'étaient précipités, tous avaient voulu mêler leurs lettres aux grimoires. Personne n'acceptait de disparaître. La

madone veillerait sur les initiales et les rassemblerait, la Mère des Noms dans la lumière du Père qui sourdait de la lucarne. Le jour coulait comme le sang des siècles, vierge éternellement. Et les noms se mariaient, se miraient dans son rayon.

Vivifié, Neuzil reprenait l'escalade. Anny filait, franchissait quatre à quatre, par étourderie, une série de marches. Elle disparaissait un instant dans le colimaçon. Puis elle réapparaissait, freinait, échine cambrée et fesses lentes, écolières, bien calées dans le jean. Peut-être que cette vision aidait Neuzil. Il avait dû jeter un œil sur cette silhouette de jeune fille, Ariane aux galbes précis. Il était pris en sandwich entre l'écuyère et le chevalier, moi Tristan couvant des yeux mon amante et le vieux Marc.

Neuzil grimpait. Son souffle s'accélérait un peu. Il s'arrêtait plus souvent, en convenait, mais il savait qu'il arriverait là-haut coûte que coûte, soutenu par nous, par ses anges tutélaires. Il nous regarda soudain avec amour, allégresse et nous lança :

— Allez ! Courez donc un peu ! Faites comme si je n'étais pas là, je veux vous voir, vous entendre, vous deviner dans les lacets... Décampez ! Envolez-vous pour moi, pour le plaisir... puis revenez me chercher et nous recommencerons lentement.

On lui obéit et il vit nos corps s'élancer, vifs, ailés, il entendit le galop, les rires, les souffles dans la nuit du goulet. Et nous revînmes époumonés. Il contemplait notre halètement avec avidité. Il puisait dans tout ce qui se dégageait de nous, de sueur, de soubresauts, de frémissements nerveux, un aliment étincelant qui le portait plus haut.

Neuzil fut assailli d'un doute quand, après avoir traversé la grande galerie des rois de Judée, il fallut s'engager dans l'escalier sud, sa dernière section resserrée, cabrée contre

l'abrupt ultime. On proposa à Johann de se reposer un peu, en regardant Paris de la galerie entre les tours. C'était une scène large, aérée... On avait tout le temps.

— Non... Il ne faut pas que je m'arrête trop longtemps, car si je reprends l'escalade dans un quart d'heure ou plus, je n'aurai pas eu le sentiment d'une authentique ascension. Trop de paliers auront morcelé, distendu le voyage pour qu'il garde dans mon cœur son unité et son pouvoir.

Anny, cette fois, évita de nous distancer d'un bond. On encadrait Neuzil à l'avant et à l'arrière. On ne parlait plus. Il n'y eut plus de brèche dans la muraille, plus la moindre épée de jour. Était-ce la fatigue et la crainte qui nous rendaient insensibles au monde extérieur ?... Neuzil s'arrêta tout à coup. Il me regarda. Son visage était tout délabré, démantelé de lassitude. Un reproche perçait dans les yeux d'Anny : je n'aurais pas dû exaucer le désir de Neuzil. Car Johann souffrait : un élancement dans le pied, une tenaille écrasante qui s'ajoutaient à l'épuisement. On le fit asseoir dans l'étroite vrille de pierre. On entendait des voix dans l'escalier. Un couple nous dépassa, nous contourna, enjamba deux marches avec une merveilleuse aisance et leurs voix déclinèrent. Anny, qui était un peu claustrophobe, trahit une anxiété soudaine. Nous étions bloqués dans l'infini boyau. Elle ne supportait pas cette idée d'impasse fermée sur nos corps. Je me voyais avec les deux victimes, le vieillard et la jeune fille. Aussitôt j'attirai l'attention d'Anny sur Neuzil pour la détourner de son vertige. Neuzil s'excusait d'avoir parié trop gros. On ne pouvait pas dire qu'il avouait cela en articulant les mots. C'était son hochement de tête, ses épaules effondrées qui signifiaient ce regret.

— Respirez lentement, doucement, lui disait Anny qui s'appliquait en même temps la recette.

Nous étions assis tous les trois. Neuzil au centre. Dans de

beaux draps, disqualifiés. On aurait presque pu prier la Vierge. Mais on n'osait...

— Ce n'est pas grave, Johann... Ce n'est rien, on va redescendre tranquillement.

— Non ! dit Neuzil.

Et l'homme gentil martela ce non avec une rage sourde qui nous surprit.

— J'atteindrai le sommet, soudain !

Anny et moi, en interceptant ce soudain légendaire, fûmes pris d'une ardente compassion pour Johann Neuzil. Ce soudain-là résumait le personnage, une gentillesse ingénue, extravagante. Il se redressa. On voulut, de chaque côté, le flanquer, passer nos bras sous les siens.

— Non, ce ne serait plus du jeu ! nous dit-il avec un sourire clair.

Il s'autorisait juste à prendre appui sur la rampe. Et il se hissa peu à peu. On sentait la douleur de son pied, de ses genoux, de ses cartilages, de ses reins brisés, de ses muscles sans force. Il s'arrêta pour tenter de nous rassurer et nous dit en soufflant :

— Le cœur est bon... ayez confiance, je vous le jure.

Et il gravit ainsi les dernières marches, d'une escalade très lente et sans accroc. Dans l'ombre de l'escalier, la lumière naquit comme un germe vivant, puis s'étira, se déploya et ouvrit le monde, avec la corolle de ses bruits, le bleu du ciel où le vent ensorcelait les nuages. On en était tout décoiffés d'azur. Et la ville s'étalait, s'aiguisait, fourmillait dans cette avalanche de jour violent. Elle se multipliait autour de l'arbre de Notre-Dame. Elle était plate, infinie, taillée en damiers, en quartiers monochromes comme du calcaire grisâtre. Un grondement montait, confondu à la rumeur du vent. Cela rendait une exhalaison dynamique et formidable, un souffle immense plutôt qu'un bruit, un bourdonnement épique,

pulvérisé. Nous étions saouls sur notre montgolfière. Anny ressuscitait. Je voyais ses yeux briller, picotés par l'air. Neuzil se rétablit peu à peu. Enfin il se dressa et cette fois glissa ses bras sous les nôtres.

— Je me sens comme une jeune mariée ! Faites-moi faire le tour de ce cosmos nuptial !

Nous étions un peu étonnés de la métaphore. Mais contents de la victoire. On lui montra le toit de plomb et la constellation grouillante des noms, avec une station attentive pour Ehra et Wolf. Le visage de Neuzil s'épanouissait malgré l'empreinte de la fatigue. Des ondes claires naissaient de ses traits ravinés et ses rides ruisselaient d'un désir imprévu.

— Je ressens peut-être trop une impression de toute-puissance. Ce n'est pas bien ? Est-ce de l'orgueil et du triomphe ?

— C'est l'euphorie, dit Anny.

— Oui, c'est exactement cela, ce n'est donc pas un sentiment de domination mais d'expansion, n'est-ce pas ? On se dilate à l'infini. On est sur la couronne de Notre-Dame, dans les fleurons de sa gloire. On navigue tout là-haut. On cingle, n'est-ce pas ? sur la dunette ou la hune ! Je ne sais plus. On dirait que le ciel est une voile hissée. Et notre proue fend la Seine, bouge les îles. C'est comme ça ? Soudain !... Comme c'est ample. On s'échappe par le haut, n'est-ce pas ? C'est le vœu de l'homme que de s'exalter dans le vent.

L'air des cimes enivrait Neuzil. Il paraît que les grands saints sont allègres et folingues. Il s'exclama :

— On a envie d'aller sur l'autre tour, hein ! Maurice m'a révélé qu'Osiris profitait tout à son aise de la tour nord, qu'il se la réservait en somme !

— Mais il n'y a rien à voir... dit Anny.

— Ça dépend ! Les noms que vous voyez ici existent certainement de l'autre côté. Cette tour a dû être ouverte aux visiteurs dans le passé. Ce serait surprenant qu'elle ait

toujours été interdite. Les noms doivent s'arrêter brusquement à une année précise. C'est étrange... à moins qu'elle ne soit vierge de tout signe. Un jour, ils ont créé ce circuit à sens unique. C'était pratique. Et ils nous ont escamoté une des tours. Mais vous, si vous le désirez, vous pourriez demander une faveur à Osiris et découvrir la tour sœur... la jumelle du nord.

Nous avons contourné le toit de plomb en direction de l'Orient et sommes tombés sur l'enlacement d'Amador et de Rawi. Mais juste au bord des noms, il y avait un faucon mort. Il était sur le dos, la livrée coincée entre les ailes raidies, les petites pattes griffues comme rabougries. La tête maigre et morte, le bec crochu. Neuzil le prit délicatement dans sa paume. C'était comme si toutes les foudres du ciel s'étaient éteintes dans l'ovale étriqué de l'oiseau.

— C'est extraordinaire d'être en vie, dit Neuzil, c'est inimaginable ! Car tout porte à ce destin de chose figée. La vie est une incroyable folie. On est en vie, les enfants ! On est en vie ! Je n'en reviens pas ! s'exclamait Neuzil, sidéré.

Je ne comprenais que trop bien la surprise de Johann Neuzil. Moi aussi je m'étonnais de la vie qui n'était rien moins qu'évidente à mes yeux. Être en vie tenait, oui, du miracle. C'était contingent, monstrueux. On en avait presque envie de mourir pour ne pas sentir ce vertige à flanc d'abîme. Cette vie flambant sur un fil d'immensité. Et pourtant, quand nous avions débouché en pleine lumière, une joie vibrait en nous, un appel irrésistible, un désir de voir, d'envahir, de danser. A présent, c'était fini. Je me sentis frère du faucon tué.

Maurice et David avaient soufflé cette idée de Clichy :

— Vous devriez aller faire une promenade là-bas, vous verrez, vous sentirez cela. Il se passe quelque chose à Clichy, le soir...

Obéissants, Anny et moi sommes allés dîner à Clichy. Tout d'abord l'inspiration manquait. On ignorait ce que Clichy pouvait avoir d'extraordinaire. Il devait être encore trop tôt. Personne ne se pressait vers les restaurants, les gens dînaient plus tard. Et soudain nous avons perçu l'événement, ça nous est tombé dessus d'un coup. On ne savait si la chose venait du ciel ou des boulevards. C'est apparu dans le noir, la foule a déboulé. Elle sortait de partout. Des meutes de garçons et de filles de toutes races. Les bars étaient bourrés. Les cinémas avaient de grosses files d'attente. La foule bougeait, roulait, elle moutonnait dans les ténèbres lacérées de lumières. On sentait l'énergie de son désir. Les hommes couraient comme des loups, les prolos avides d'amour. C'était le samedi et cela comptait. Les Africaines riaient, géantes et musculeuses, les Asiatiques filaient dans des collants soyeux. Les minijupes de cuir découvraient les cuisses dans l'enjambée des jeans des mecs fanfarons aux ceintures cloutées. Les filles étaient

159

fringuées avec excès ou négligées. Personne n'était neutre. Personne ne s'effaçait. Tout était arboré, cliquetait, bracelets, anneaux immenses aux lobes des mulâtresses. Parfois la chair très blanche, laiteuse, d'un décolleté de rousse. L'outrance nous émouvait, Anny et moi. Ces nippes bon marché, étincelantes. La vraie beauté des femmes et des hommes rachetait le mauvais goût. Tant de trivialité splendide balayait les pâles canons du beau. La vie faisait plus vraie, plus forte. Passaient de grands flux noirs de vie. Quelque chose de populeux, d'innombrable, une luxuriance qui n'existait nulle part ailleurs et sortait du pavé. On sentait la misère défiée, niée, la lutte, l'espoir, les chimères de la foule, ses pulsations, ses fastes bruts et sa voracité sans frein. Épaules contre épaules, par pelotons entiers, ils dévalaient le boulevard, enveloppaient la place Clichy, remplissaient les ruelles attenantes.

Sous les néons, les réverbères, c'était plus cru, à moitié nu, les loubards fonçaient en vestes de cuir enlacés à leurs filles trop blondes. La rue drainait le vrai destin des hommes arrogants... J'enviais la foule, ce rapport direct, entier, avec la vie. Ils étaient plongés jusqu'au cou dans leur samedi soir. Anny sentait que j'étais décalé. Elle ne mesurait pas à quel point. Eux, ils étaient dans la vie, au diapason, dans l'océan bruissant. Moi, c'était leur fièvre qui me fascinait. Je les regardais vivre. Heureusement, les femmes singulières me happaient. Elles déferlaient sur des talons aiguilles, dans des bottes brillantes, des tennis de couleur, des caleçons rouges, des shorts moulants sur des bas sombres, des cuissardes de skaï, des jupes de quatre sous projetant la peau nue. Ça claquait, charbonnait, pullulait avec des bouches très rouges, des yeux trop faits, des cils en bâtons de rimmel, des seins haussés, gonflés, totémisés. Même les plus sveltes adolescentes saillaient du sein. La nouvelle génération voulait ça,

les progrès des corps, un essor des silhouettes vers les sommets, la voltige des culs et des gorges protubérantes. Le métissage aidait beaucoup à ces incarnations miraculeuses. Il gagnait la partie de lui-même et *de visu*. Il imposait son devenir et ses magnificences s'étalaient. Il déclassait les sans fard et les navets. Je rêvais de me mêler à tous ces cuivres et ces ocres, ces nuances brunes et chaudes et ces pâleurs arabes et bleutées, et ces jaunes foncés du Cambodge. Je me serais volontiers baigné, trempé, chamarré dans le creuset.

Oui, j'ai senti l'amour pour mes semblables dans l'essaim des bandes du soir, leur fleurissement doré, le frôlement des races majestueuses et frénétiques. Ces négresses lentes du Bénin, bien grenées, galbées, aux grands derrières chantournés, ces Algériens véloces à pommettes, ces anguilles d'Asie dans des tissus si minces, dont les rires flûtés me pinçaient, me donnaient une envie d'enculer leur fragile beauté. Quand mon œil épinglait avec trop d'insistance un coin de chair, une harmonie, et que je me retournais sans discrétion, Anny me tançait. Jalouse, tout à coup, devant mon regard nomade et boulimique. Inquiète. Je lui expliquais que c'était un mélange de curiosité et de contemplation, pas vraiment un immédiat désir. Mais que la forme singulière d'un corps me marquait de son empreinte, comme si j'avais été photographe ou peintre.

— Tu parles d'un artiste ! ironisait Anny.

Elle avait raison, car la beauté des filles, leur galop et leur ligne opulente me décochaient dans le cœur une entaille, comme une fulguration, un charme suivi d'une perte. J'étais subjugué par une brève féerie et la fille s'engloutissait dans le remous des rues. Je n'étais capable que de cette adhésion intermittente et passionnée. Sinon, j'assistais du dehors à leur samedi. Tous s'engouffraient dans le fleuve vital. Et moi, je restais sur la rive. Anny sentait ce fléchissement de

ma volonté. Les restaurants bondés me donnaient la nausée. Alors, elle me poussait du coude et avisait l'éclat d'une fille, apparition aux jambes longues et nues.

— Tu vois, c'est toi maintenant ! Et après tu me fais des reproches, lui lançais-je, en riant.

Mais Anny, d'instinct, n'avait cherché qu'à réveiller mon appétit visuel pour me renouer au flux. Elle avait tendance aussi, par mimétisme, à s'identifier à moi, à mon désir, tout en me faisant grief de ma soif des formes.

C'était vers ces périphéries de la ville où l'on entend le vent du monde, comme l'écho de l'espace et de la création. La banlieue perce par les portes et les brèches. Toutes les couleurs, tous les courants affluent des boulevards et d'au-delà. Les cercles et les enceintes de la cité sont rompus par une poussée descendue de loin. On sent que le chambardement viendra de là, un trop-plein de vie, de fringale, la razzia du grand regain. Car la foule est formidablement précoce et féline. Sa capacité de foisonnement est illimitée, toutes ses ressources animales et divines s'épanchent dans la nuit du samedi. Par contraste, notre Quartier latin ne brasse qu'une espèce homogène, confinée, étiolée et recuite... des simagrées, du simili. Pas la Vie. Pas cette révolte, cette source gloutonne, sa sombre hémorragie pailletée de feu.

On s'écartait un peu. On remontait le pont qui enjambe le cimetière de Montmartre. Un silence venait, les passants étaient moins nombreux. On voyait luire les marbres en contrebas, toute la flottille des tombeaux. Le ciel était vaste mais tout proche. Les étoiles apparaissaient, car il y avait moins d'enseignes lumineuses et de halos. Les galaxies clignotaient sur les dédales des tombes. Un silence, un

mystère. Une trêve dans le grouillement humain. L'odeur de l'air soudain et de la terre. C'est là qu'Anny et moi nous avons ressenti l'émotion bouleversante. Sur le pont, au-dessus des marbres et des morts, sous la voûte céleste, dans ce beau havre noir, encastré dans la ville à l'écoute de son âme du soir. On entendait le battement, le pas des hommes multipliés, non loin de là, sur la place Clichy, au carrefour pathétique, illuminé. Anny se pressait dans mes bras, me regardait, me convoitait. Sa bouche voulait ma bouche dans la phosphorescence des astres et des tombeaux, à proximité de la foule déroulant, amassant ses anneaux de python. Je bandais contre le fin Levis d'Anny, je sentais sa langue et sa bouche béante. Ma chair devenait noire, avalée dans la ville noire. Il me semblait que mon sexe allait péter d'ardeur, de douceur dans la cité écarquillée, bourrée d'amants à craquer.

Toute la semaine, me hanta la foule noire constellée de corps pleins de ferveur. J'étais pris dans cette poésie, mais Margot me ramena côté cuisine. Elle préparait son quatre-quarts mensuel. Et c'était toute une échauffourée. Elle régalait de son gâteau la grande maisonnée, en distribuait des morceaux à tous les paliers. Je détestais l'odeur du quatre-quarts, ce relent de pâte beurrée, de levain douceâtre et sucré. Un dessert aussi farineux et bourratif était sans séduction. Le quatre-quarts représentait à mes yeux le degré le plus primaire du gâteau. Je préférais les flans, les mousses au chocolat... Quand Margot démoulait son quatre-quarts, elle en arborait le lingot doré comme un trésor, le découpait en tranches dont le cœur était moelleux, un peu gluant. L'appartement entier sentait l'haleine du quatre-quarts, cet amalgame d'œufs, de sucre, de beurre, de farine enflée. On

en était tout boursouflé, pâteux... Elle filait chez les voisins, toquait, provoquait des exclamations, des protestations lyriques : « C'est trop !... Non, pas tant !... Vous n'en n'aurez plus pour votre étudiant. » David et Maurice avaient deux parts, bien structurées, la concierge et son mari... Justement Margot me glissa sur ce dernier une confidence insolite.

— Il perd ses poils !

— C'est l'âge, répondis-je.

— Non, c'est plus bizarre que ça, il change, il se métamorphose... je vous dis... Il se passe des choses. Lui qui était porté sur la petite affaire, insatiable aux dires de la concierge, eh bien ! Ça diminue à toute vitesse. Moins de ressort, des paresses, des lenteurs à la détente... Vous vous rendez compte, qu'est-ce qu'il a ?

Je devais rencontrer, peu après, le mari de la concierge. Il parlait dans la rue avec cette jeune crémière qui, de temps à autre, venait prendre une douche chez Margot. Je l'observai à la dérobée. C'est vrai qu'il s'était modifié, plus glabre, plus onctueux, assez dégoûtant à regarder. La métamorphose n'affectait nettement aucune partie du corps mais se diffusait par en dessous, sournoise. L'homme semblait tout amorti de l'intérieur, comme ramolli.

— Il paraît qu'il ne bande presque plus ! me confia Margot, quelques jours plus tard. La concierge, d'une certaine façon, ça l'arrange ! Elle n'aimait pas beaucoup le faire... Mais cette évolution insidieuse l'inquiète, vous comprenez. Elle ne sait pas ce que c'est, elle sent cette chose vague... floue, comme elle dit ! Ce n'est pas un mot qu'elle employait avant. Elle possède peu de vocabulaire. Cette histoire l'oblige à trouver des mots ambigus. C'est toujours ça ! Moi j'ai essayé de lui fournir l'adjectif insidieux qui convient bien à la situation. Mais c'était trop pour elle...

164

Le quatre-quarts de Margot ne pouvait pas en être la cause, c'était plutôt l'effet des anti-inflammatoires que j'ingurgitais pour calmer mon ménisque. Mais j'avais l'intestin en flammes, une vraie cavale intempérante. Margot essayait de rester discrète. Mais ce n'était guère dans sa nature. Elle me voyait aller et venir sans cesse de ma chambre au cagibi des toilettes. Souvent je lui passais sous le nez ou occupais les lieux quand elle se pointait à son tour. Alors elle me dit :

— Vous avez la...

— Oui... lui répondis-je, un cataclysme...

— Vous voulez du Pernod ?...

Je sursautai, ne saisissant pas le rapport.

— Si ! du Pernod, c'est le meilleur remède, c'est connu, ça bloque !

Elle chercha une bouteille de Pernod, mais l'échantillon lui manquait et aussitôt, sans crier gare, la voilà trissée dans l'escalier, les paliers, cognant à toutes les portes. C'était le soir, les couples étaient là, elle quémandait partout du Pernod. Je crus l'entendre distiller en catimini, intime et grivoise : « C'est mon étudiant ! Il a la courante ! » Mais Margot disait pire, triviale : « Mon étudiant a la chiasse. » Voilà ce qu'elle divulguait à toute la maisonnée, jouissant du mot, de la chuintante si expressive et de la sifflante finale en geyser scatologique. Elle recommençait pour Neuzil, la concierge qui avait d'autres chats à fouetter, pour Mlle Poulet qui posait des questions, émettait des hypothèses scientifiques à partir de ce que j'avais ingurgité. Margot me galvaudait sans égard pour ma timidité, mon amour-propre encore adolescent. Elle attentait à mon pouvoir de séduction et me ramenait au ras de la tripe, du destin viscéral. J'étais

165

rouge de honte et tout monté de haine. Je l'entendais galoper, infernale et frénétique… friande de colporter la rumeur, clignant les yeux, lubrique, complice, chuchotant : « Mon étudiant a la chiasse, vite du Pernod ! » Et tous détournaient leur regard du poste de télé où l'on commentait un voyage officiel de Pompidou, pour rigoler, se passionner de ce caca universitaire. Ça les faisait pouffer. « Mais qu'est-ce qu'il a mangé ? »… « C'est l'anxiété, ses études, la peur de l'avenir ! » disait David plus intérieur. « Ah vous croyez !? » répondait Margot, brutale et sceptique. Elle revint, empoignant un fond de bouteille jaunasse qu'elle me fit avaler sans me laisser le temps de négocier. Elle se versa une petite rasade en cas de contagion. Le remède agit rapidement, mais j'étais ivre et l'odeur d'anis me soulevait le cœur. J'avais peur de restituer cette fois par le canal buccal l'alcool qui me brûlait.

— Ah non ! Vous n'allez pas vomir maintenant !

Elle me toisait, hésitait. Je redoutai soudain qu'elle ne fuse derechef dans les profondeurs de la baraque pour réclamer un antivomitif. Mais elle n'en fit rien. Lorsque, le lendemain, je croisai dans l'escalier les voisins, les fins psychologues ne firent nulle allusion à mes désordres. Mais la concierge, elle, me riva un œil torve : « Ça va mieux la… » Et, vulgaire, elle mimait d'une giration lente de sa main blanchâtre, au niveau du ventre, un odieux tourbillon. Je me sauvai sans répondre. J'avais perdu mon prestige auprès des locataires. Il me semblait qu'ils ne considéraient plus ma personne, mon être, mon essence indicible et spirituelle, mais ma seule réalité organique et grotesque.

Osiris parut un dimanche pendant le petit déjeuner que nous prenions Anny et moi, plutôt délavés et laminés par nos

étreintes. Osiris nous flairait, nous sondait. Nous étions encore mal réveillés, mal campés dans notre identité. Et c'est notre mollesse qu'il savourait, un arôme que nous ne pouvions gommer. Anny et moi étions en pyjama, ce qui aggravait l'impression de relâchement. Les étoffes imprégnées de notre chaleur étaient cotonneuses et comme ensommeillées sur notre chair. Osiris, lui, se dressait splendide, clairement délimité dans l'espace. L'œil droit et planté sur nous. Anny le convia à s'asseoir. Ainsi il se plierait un peu et n'exercerait plus sa domination. Il s'exécuta, rapprocha sa chaise de nous, familier... Le thé chaud propageait sur le visage d'Anny un voile de rougeur, une légère résille de sueur. Moi aussi, je baignais dans une vapeur indéfinie. Le petit déjeuner est un passage, il permet d'entrer dans la vie en douceur. C'est un seuil plein de tiédeur enfantine : beurre, sucre, laitage, petits pains... Osiris profitait de notre régression aux commencements puérils pour nous manger des yeux. Il désirait cette adolescence douillette et bouffie des sucs de la nuit. On en était encore tout mélangés l'un à l'autre, mal incarnés, solubles. Et lui brillait roide de plaisir.

— Vous êtes trop jolis comme ça ! Je suis bien obligé de vous le dire, encore tout brouillés des choses du sommeil...

Il était passé pour bavarder avec David et Maurice. Puis l'idée lui était venue de nous dire bonjour, car il nous aimait beaucoup. Anny se ressaisit et lui déclara soudain :

— Quand nous faites-vous visiter la tour nord ? Ça nous changerait un peu !

— En principe, elle est interdite aux visiteurs...

— Oui, mais on la voit, toute seule de l'autre côté, déserte. Alors on a envie d'y aller.

— Vous désirez être là où vous n'êtes pas, quoi ? Ailleurs

c'est toujours plus beau qu'ici, déclara Osiris à l'adresse d'Anny comme si elle était une petite Emma Bovary.

— Non ! Pas moi...

— Tiens ! tiens ! dit Osiris en me regardant... Alors c'est lui l'instable...

— Je n'ai pas dit ça !

— Il s'intéresse à la tour jumelle, voyez-vous ça...

J'avouai ma curiosité :

— Oui, à la tour sœur, comme dit Neuzil !

— La formule est jolie ! reconnut Osiris, plus pure et moins suspecte que votre fameux cadeau « obi et branlerie d'amour... »

Nous n'avions pas envie qu'il nous resserve ça, avec son air intime et provocant. Il nous regardait, essayait de nous deviner, notre couple, ce qui s'amorçait entre nous, les connivences et les failles discrètes, ce qui nous unissait et nous diviserait, ce qui nous comblerait et nous ferait souffrir. Il sentait que cette curiosité de la tour sororale était ma lubie beaucoup plus que la passion d'Anny. Elle n'avait abordé la question que pour distraire Osiris de sa contemplation dévorante. Tout à coup, il prit sa décision.

— Habillez-vous vite, je vous emmène là-haut !

— On n'a même pas le temps de faire un bout de toilette ? demanda Anny.

— Rien qu'un petit bout !

Et Osiris nous entendit, nous écouta bouger dans notre chambre, ouvrir les placards et les robinets. Les slips enfilés vite, l'aspersion des visages. Notre précipitation, nos exclamations étouffées, nos courses et nos zigzags. le crincrin des brosses à dents. Il jouissait d'avoir semé cette gentille panique. Il aurait voulu assister à la scène. Ils n'auront pas le temps de se rincer intimement, dut penser Osiris qui nous préférait parfumés par la nuit.

Et nous voici devant lui, cheveux trempés, l'air retapé, tout un revif. Il repéra une fraîche gouttelette dans le cou d'Anny.

On prit l'escalier habituel, le nord. Mais au lieu de le quitter, d'obliquer dans la grande galerie, de la traverser, de rejoindre le dernier escalier de la tour sud, Osiris continua tout droit. Une petite porte fermait l'accès. Il la déverrouilla et la rabattit derrière nous. Et nous poursuivîmes l'ascension vers le sommet de la tour interdite. Nous étions dans le corps inconnu de Notre-Dame. Dans son silence. Nous avions l'air d'anges furtifs. Personne au sommet, le toit bombait son éminence calme. Il était sillonné d'inscriptions anciennes. Et les noms frottés par les vents, les pluies, les poussières s'étaient usés, décolorés dans l'alchimie du plomb que décapait aussi les chiures des pigeons et des faucons. Osiris se taisait et nous laissait parcourir la terrasse à notre aise. Un grand ciel uni et blanc nous cernait. Tout à coup, je vis le nom, entaillé de frais, en lettres capitales : EHRA.

Osiris s'approcha et attendit que nous parlions.

— Vous avez donc amené Ehra ici ? lui demanda Anny.

— Non, je suis venu un soir avec Wolf. Et c'est lui qui a gravé le nom de sa sœur.

Au-dessous du nom, sous le rebord du toit, s'embusquait un trou. Il était frangé de souillures plâtreuses. Osiris nous dit qu'un faucon, chaque printemps, faisait son nid à cet endroit :

— Je l'ai baptisé « le faucon d'Ehra ».

Nous sommes redescendus. Osiris referma la porte de la tour comme sur le secret de la sœur et du faucon.

Je suis entré dans la chambre de Marguerite. Je voulais vérifier un mot dans son cher Larousse dont les volumes s'étageaient sur une chaise. Toufflette, la chatte tigrée, était couchée sur le bord du lit, la tête appuyée contre la tranche des dictionnaires. Elle semblait encore plus sournoise et agressive que d'habitude. Tout à coup, Anchise, le chien de David et de Maurice, se mit à aboyer dans la demeure et ses appels hérissèrent le poil de la chatte qui détestait l'énorme chien pacifique. Mais j'étais impatient. Il me fallait feuilleter le Larousse encyclopédique, je voulais lire l'article consacré à Horus, le faucon solaire. J'étendis doucement la main vers le bouquin au sommet de la pile, sans toucher la tête de la chatte. En un éclair, la garce me mordit. Je m'étais méfié de ses griffes, pas de ses dents pointues. Je vis ma main saigner et, d'un mouvement brutal, je repoussai la bête. Mais elle se rebella, sa griffe m'agrippa le bras qu'elle lacéra. Elle était convulsée, boule de nerfs et de poils hérissés sur l'échine. Ramassée, monstrueuse, palpitante, gondolée de furie, sif-flante. J'eus peur qu'elle ne me bondisse à la face, alors, d'un coup de pied, je tentai de la faire valdinguer plus loin. Elle sauta sur mon pied, s'y accrocha, s'y noua, tout entière, les

171

quatre griffes plantées, la chaussure me protégeait un peu. Je secouai le pied. Elle ne lâchait pas prise, émettait des miaulements hystériques et commençait à m'entailler la cheville. De l'autre pied, je la percutai. Elle tenait, grappe velue, concentrée, cabossée de haine et se mit à hurler d'une criaillerie intense et continue, tel un piaulement atroce de bébé, d'enfant brûlé. Et soudain elle me sauta dessus, je sentis sur mon torse le paquet griffu qui me labourait. Saisi de terreur, je poussai un cri tonitruant, ma voix de gorge, de stentor, soutenue par une brutale libération du souffle. La chatte comme matraquée se rétrécit, lisse de panique, elle se laissa tomber sur le tapis et déguerpit d'un trait dans la pièce voisine.

Je tremblais, je n'en revenais pas du pugilat, de cette décharge de hargne, d'entêtement meurtrier. J'étais haletant, j'aurais pleuré de stupeur et d'angoisse. J'aurais foncé dans l'appartement pour traquer la bête et lui faire rendre gorge, la balancer par la fenêtre, l'écrabouiller sur le pavé. Je restai ainsi longtemps abasourdi. Je n'entendais rien de l'autre côté. Et une curiosité, une convoitise suicidaires naquirent en moi, c'était plus fort que moi. Je quittai la pièce, traversai la salle à manger en scrutant chaque recoin. Oui je la cherchais, je voulais la retrouver, la voir, assister à sa défaite, la terrasser de mon regard. Une violence plus houleuse mais plus lente montait en moi, en vrilles, amples tourbillons de lucidité. Mon souffle se soulevait. J'étais carré dans ma poitrine, mon cou... Mes mains et mes chevilles saignaient. Ma chemise était percée. J'avançais dans l'appartement, ce dérisoire, cet exécrable décor de Margot. Cette pourrissante baraque qui allait m'étrangler, m'étouffer, si je ne réagissais pas. Je poussai une nouvelle porte. La douche se dressait, enveloppée de son rideau de nylon transparent. D'un coup, j'écartai ce voile. Et je la vis sur l'émail blanc et froid. Rencognée dans

un angle, la fourrure morcelée de bosses tétanisées, la petite gueule pétrifiée. Elle ne criait plus, elle ne chuintait plus, ne s'échappaient de ses dents qu'un mince feulement, un sifflement de gaz. La tête se renfonçait, vissée à l'intérieur du cou gonflé, le corps semblait un emboîtement de boules gigognes. Et la sensation de la bête, de toute la bête, de la bestialité pure et sauvage, sans masque, à l'état brut, m'assaillirent, m'hypnotisèrent. La peur d'une bête que l'instinct recroqueville et rapetisse, tire-bouchonne de terreur dans son trou. Mais les yeux qui guettent encore, du fond de l'épouvante et de l'horrible déformation du corps. Je mesurai l'énergie folle de cette peur. C'était là, concentré, palpable, comme une fulmination rentrée. Je regardais. Je ne pouvais plus me détacher de cette vision. Et j'aimais, j'admirais cette vie, cette violence de la vie. Il y avait dans cette chatte l'incroyable instinct de vie rétracté, bouclé sur lui-même, tous les neurones et les tendons et les circuits bandés dans un cercle de fer. Cela, au milieu des choses, à côté de la machine à laver, non loin du buffet Henri II et du linoléum. La vie avait surgi, tendue, totale, paroxystique. La vigilance magnétique, l'effroi, l'œil incendié, parmi les matières passives, les meubles, les appareils ménagers. La vie avait jailli au travers. Et elle grouillait dans son coin, velue, griffue, galvanisée de sang et de feu.

Je tirai le rideau et quittai les lieux. Ma colère avait fui. Un émerveillement secret m'habitait. Je désinfectai mes plaies et les dissimulai. Je ne voulais rien dire à Marguerite. Le soir, quand elle revint, la chatte n'accourut pas derrière la porte. Marguerite s'interrogea sur ce comportement inattendu. Je lui expliquai qu'Anchise avait aboyé toute la journée.

— Mais elle n'a jamais redouté ce con de clebs !... Non ! Je crois qu'elle est patraque. Ça arrive... elle est un peu maladeuse...

Je m'étais arrangé pour parler à Marguerite dans une pièce où la chatte n'était pas. Car elle aurait manifesté sa haine et sa peur, et j'aurais été démasqué. Je racontai à Margot que le pansement qui recouvrait ma main était dû à la blessure que je m'étais faite en me servant d'une paire de ciseaux. Elle savait que j'étais maladroit et n'en demanda pas plus.

Tôt le matin, j'entendis le vacarme, une dégringolade dans la douche. J'arrivai à toute vitesse. Mais déjà Margot se redressait lentement. Nue...

— J'ai eu un étourdissement... Ça n'est pas bon, j'ai déjà eu ça.... C'est grave, c'est le cœur.

Je n'osai regarder Marguerite. La trouille lui avait ôté toute pudeur. Certes, elle n'avait jamais été bien inhibée sur ce plan... Je voyais ses seins rosâtres et tombés, son bedon mou, ses cuisses grassouillettes et torses, avec une sorte de fraîcheur de peau malgré tout, ce quelque chose d'enfantin qui persiste dans toute chair en dépit de l'âge, hormis sur le visage ridé. Elle s'enveloppa d'une serviette, s'assit par terre, l'air d'un guignol déchu. Puis elle me commanda d'appeler les pompiers. Elle voulait aller à l'hôpital sans tarder.

Marguerite avait une confiance totale en l'hôpital public. Il représentait pour elle presque un garant d'immortalité. Le fourgon des pompiers l'emmena à la Salpêtrière. Les spécialistes diagnostiquèrent une thrombose, le taux de cholestérol était élevé. Je me retrouvai seul dans l'appartement avec la chatte que Mlle Poulet venait nourrir chaque jour, car Margot avait pressenti que j'étais inapte à cette charge.

Le week-end suivant, Anny et moi lui rendîmes visite. Mon cœur se serra à la vue de la grande bâtisse terne et jaunâtre. C'était l'hosto, le vrai, celui des urgences, des cas

174

désespérés, celui du tout-venant de la souffrance. Les néons éclairaient les couloirs d'une lueur verdâtre. La grande salle du service médecine contenait vingt lits fréquentés par une majorité de vieilles et de vieux très abîmés. Margot trônait dans son lit, fiérote, mutine. Contente de se donner en spectacle et de montrer aux voisins qu'elle avait des visiteurs juvéniles. Car nombre de malades restaient seuls, sans parentèle, certains agonisaient sans qu'on leur prenne la main... Juste en face de Margot, une vieillarde avait sombré dans le coma.

— C'est un cancer, nous dit Margot. Hier, elle s'est vidée d'un coup de son sang, par le bas... L'odeur était épouvantable.

Je retrouvai Marguerite de la mort et de la nuit. Elle avait atterri au milieu des cancers et des cardiaques en fin de course. Et cela aurait dû l'inquiéter. Elle semblait partagée entre la curiosité malsaine de la mort des autres et la peur de trépasser à son tour. Mais elle espérait. Elle ne croyait pas à l'imminence de sa mort. On lui faisait des tests, des examens. Ses coronaires étaient sclérosées. Mais avec un régime, des anticoagulants, une surveillance régulière, son cas, dans l'immédiat, n'était pas qualifié de fatal. Elle pouvait durer ainsi des années, comme elle disait. Et cette idée de durer des années malgré sa maladie la requinquait. Déjà elle emménageait dans cette survie indéfinie. Elle s'était fait une copine : la soixantaine, une malade pourvue d'un avenir, elle aussi. Au fond, Margot et son amie étaient les deux sursitaires du service médecine. Elle nous raconta que, depuis six jours, il y avait eu déjà deux décès. On apportait alors un paravent qui entourait le lit du mort. Mais Marguerite et sa copine, profitant de l'absence d'une infirmière, trottinaient vers le rideau qu'elles écartaient pour épier le cadavre. C'était un jeu, un exorcisme et, chez Margot, l'essence de sa personna-

lité. Elle devait voir ! Elle voulait voir cela, surtout, la mort des autres. Elle sentait que la question la concernait de très près et en même temps elle regardait les cadavres à distance, comme le ferait une personne en bonne santé. C'était le mystère de Margot. Son ambivalence. Elle habitait les deux rives, au diapason du fait vital et de l'événement de la mort. Je ne doutais pas que, par bouffées, elle ne se crût alors immortelle, mais, avec la même force, elle avait la conviction de finir assez tôt. Elle parlait souvent de son testament, du sort de Toufflette si elle mourait. Elle ne se cachait pas la vérité. Elle avait déjà prévu une somme pour son enterrement à Chatou. Mais la vie scintillait encore au fond d'elle, une brûlante vivacité. Marguerite nous avoua aussi que, saisie d'une angoisse pendant la nuit, au milieu des agonisants, elle avait appelé son amie. Et l'autre, comme si elle n'avait attendu que ce signal, avait accouru, s'était fourrée dans le lit. Les deux femmes s'étaient serrées l'une contre l'autre, contre la mort, en sanglotant.

Anny et moi, nous n'en menions pas large, à peine si on osait regarder alentour. Avant d'entrer dans la vie, il nous fallait sans doute cette révélation de la Salpêtrière, de ces lits où gisaient les dépouilles et les naufrages. Certains vieillards avaient un regard rentré et faible, comme tourné vers le dedans, mais un dedans sans densité ni chaleur : le vide. C'était un regard maigre sans révolte, un peu grincheux peut-être, un regard ingrat surtout, l'ultime regard qu'on porte sur soi et sur les autres quand l'issue est là. On ne peut plus rien désirer, rien dire, rien voir, on est ramené aux limites de son corps navré. Et l'œil se fane, honteux plutôt qu'implorant, dans le visage ruiné. Un regard creux dans la cage de l'orbite. Toute la vie semble niée, comme si elle n'avait pas valu la peine d'être vécue, c'était ça le pire, comme si elle n'avait été qu'un piège. Les vieillards ne paraissaient pas avoir de

souvenirs. Ils restaient absolument sans lumière... Moi, je m'imaginais déjà dans ces lits de vieillesse. La chose m'arriverait puisqu'elle leur était arrivée. Il suffisait d'accélérer un peu le film et tout finissait de la même façon, dans ces limbes qui n'étaient plus la vie mais pas encore la nuit définitive. L'hosto, c'était cette région sinistre, ce demi-jour lugubre où ils attendaient sans attendre.

Certains avaient encore la force d'aller pisser aux cabinets. Quelle ne fut pas ma stupeur de découvrir que ces derniers étaient situés sur un palier balayé de courants d'air frisquets. Certains malades attrapaient une bronchite qui leur donnait le coup de grâce et libérait leur lit encore plus vite. Margot se méfiait du palier. Ayant eu l'intuition fulgurante du péril, elle réclamait à tue-tête le bassin pour uriner et pour déféquer. Elle prétextait un rhumatisme, un vertige... Elle se soulageait sans honte, à la barbe des voisins.

On entendit un battement véloce d'hélicoptère. Avec une jeunesse imprévue, Margot jaillit du lit pour voir. Un hélicoptère rouge et mignon atterrissait sur une piste d'urgence dans l'enceinte de la Salpêtrière. Toute une escouade du personnel se précipita au-devant du malade déjà enveloppé de tubes, de fioles, d'un appareillage dramatique. Margot buvait des yeux ce malheur plus grand que le sien. Elle hochait la tête d'un air critique. Il s'agissait peut-être d'un accident de la route, d'un grand brûlé... à peine un soupçon de souffle dans un thorax troué. La fascinait ce théâtre soudain. Le tonnerre des pales, l'hélicoptère cramoisi, le cortège à la rescousse. Celui-là agonisait avec un certain faste. Sa mort paraissait anormale, exceptionnelle par comparaison avec les corps qui jonchaient les lits du service médecine, moribonds sans lustre ni pompe, demi-cadavres ordinaires et fainéants qui trépassaient peu à peu mais sûrement, sans perturber la routine de la mort.

177

Dans la rue, Anny et moi, nous avions peine à adhérer. Même Anny grelottait, très pâle. Elle en paraissait fluette et sans forces. L'angoisse me submergeait par vagues, une tornade de peur clairvoyante. Cette prémonition d'une menace et d'une fatalité, qui s'était insinuée en moi dès que j'étais entré dans l'aire de Marguerite L., m'envahissait sourdement. Je m'en défendais, je la trouvais absurde, superstitieuse. Mais je sentais que ma vie, ma capacité de vie, mon élan vital étaient en jeu et que la manchote, plus ou moins consciemment, me mettait à l'épreuve avec son espèce de regard creux, presque hypocrite, quand elle épiait le destin, son regard faux. L'œil de ma mort. Ce serait elle ou moi. Je trouvais l'alternative monstrueuse. Mais elle me hantait. Margot allait me survivre, comme elle l'avait fait avec l'étudiante qui m'avait précédé et qui était morte dans la drogue et la déchéance. Ou bien je serais vainqueur... La maison de Margot, dès le début, m'avait paru un théâtre un peu maléfique, prison, dédale moisi et cabossé mais, en même temps, elle recelait dans ses profondeurs une exubérance secrète, une foi acharnée. Je ne pouvais trancher. Maison gentille, prodigue, tremplin ou trappe ?

Je me sentais si souvent posthume et révolu dans l'œuf. « Tout ce qui doit finir est déjà fini. » C'était une citation du *Roi se meurt* de Ionesco ! Une maxime essentielle et qui résumait bien notre affaire d'hommes. Mais quand mon appétit pointait de nouveau, le sexuel surtout, qui résistait de lui-même, une autre citation faisait contrepoids au verdict d'Eugène, celle-là vitale et phallique : « Le faucon du désir tire sur ses liens de cuir », de Saint-John Perse, épique en diable ! Mais c'est juré, je ne citerai plus personne. Je ne suis pas un homme de citation ni de repartie courte. Je crois aux longs sketches, aux séquences jusqu'au bout, aux riches sagas jusqu'à la lie. Toutefois, pour l'absolue panade et l'épopée

torride, j'avais quelques auteurs dans le collimateur. La littérature peut aider en cas de crise, la prose des grands ancêtres soutient un peu leurs rejetons fragiles. Ils se sentent moins bêtes devant cet engrenage meurtrier du monde que les artistes totémiques ont su traduire dans la brillance du beau.

La douche dont s'enorgueillissait Marguerite devenait le théâtre d'événements imprévus. J'y avais débusqué le grouillement venimeux, effaré de la chatte. Marguerite s'y était écroulée, frappée et thrombose. Et chaque midi, depuis qu'elle séjournait à la Salpêtrière, la crémière du faubourg Saint-Antoine venait l'utiliser. Elle faisait tout un raffut dès qu'elle entrait dans l'appartement, sous prétexte de parler à la chatte, de vérifier que les lieux étaient bien en ordre. En fait, elle m'avertissait de la séance de nudisme. La crémière était jeune, fraîche et trapue mais sans taille ni grâce. La proximité de l'étudiant l'électrisait. Elle s'exclamait en se douchant, oubliait toujours sa serviette, filait ruisselante à travers les pièces pour en chercher une dans un placard. J'étais informé minute par minute de ses manœuvres. Un jour que je revenais de la Sorbonne, je tombai au bout du couloir qui menait à ma chambre sur la crémière douchée. Elle poussa un petit cri effarouché et se mit à glousser. Je vis le volume rosé de son corps bouger à travers le rideau de nylon. Je fonçais déjà vers ma chambre quand elle m'interpella pour me demander de lui glisser la grande serviette qui s'étalait sur le linoléum. J'obtempérai, je vis le rideau s'écarter, j'aperçus un bras dodu et une portion de hanche ronde comme un Renoir. J'entrevis l'éclaboussure noire du pubis sur son ventre nacré. Elle s'écriait : « Ne regardez pas !

Ne regardez pas ! » Mais s'arrangeait pour tout montrer. Elle s'empara de la serviette en riant et s'y enroula comme Vénus surprise. J'allais pouvoir me trisser quand elle me héla de plus belle, se lança dans un lamento sur la maladie de Margot. Elle ouvrit grand le rideau, apparut ceinte de son peplum éponge, s'assit sur un tabouret, sans cesser d'émettre craintes et trémolos sur le mal qui avait terrassé la logeuse. De temps à autre, la serviette se dénouait, découvrait le gonflement ferme et marbré du sein ou l'incarnat d'une cuisse plantureuse. Elle remontait aussitôt sa parure de star arrachée au bain, s'emmitouflait dans la texture moelleuse, se tortillait de bien-être, allongeait une jambe au mollet costaud et murmurait que Margot risquait d'y rester. L'on sentait à quel point la crémière était étrangère au trépas qu'elle évoquait. Sa face rose et rieuse pétait de santé, son corps à la fois rond et carré semblait bannir la mort. Mais du même coup, à mes yeux, il n'offrait nulle prise au désir sensuel. C'était un corps pétri dans une matière si biologique, si dense, si lisse, un tantinet porcine et sans galbes, qu'elle ne pouvait susciter chez le jeune homme que j'étais aucun trouble érotique. Il me fallait à l'époque un biais pour bander, un minimum d'ambiguïté, un secret dont mon émotion s'emparait. J'aimais la femme oblique et tentante, un peu en porte à faux, puérile encore et biseautée. Comme en coulisses de ce qu'elle me dévoilerait. J'adorais la très jeune Jane Birkin pour cette raison. Je venais de la découvrir dans *Blow Up* d'Antonioni, de profil et dénudée, se cachant pour jouer dans une sorte de penderie infinie, faufilée dans un bruissement de vêtements et de robes dont elle surgissait et où elle s'éclipsait tour à tour. Son corps n'était jamais tout à fait présent ni palpable. Elle restait insidieuse, androgyne efflanqué dont la nuance saisie de côté luisait, me poignait, me creusait, me plongeait dans l'effroi d'un désir infini et

sans nom. La crémière, elle, franche, frontale, sans fissures et saturée, était toute jouissance d'être soi, elle remplissait jusqu'à ras bord le périmètre alloué à son corps et à son être. Béate, étalée dans son contour mastoc. Elle ne m'eût pas fait bander d'un pouce. Toutefois, aujourd'hui, vingt ans après, je serais attiré davantage par ce bloc de bestialité, d'épanouissement trivial. Il provoquerait sinon cet émoi angoissé et sensuel qui est chez moi le signe d'un long désir, mais une espèce d'appétit sain. J'aurais plaisir à la palper, à la cadrer, à la prendre, à me planter dans son plein contre la mort. J'aurais tendance à m'y vautrer pour ne rien voir de manquant justement, rien de noir et d'ouvert vers la maladie et la déchéance.

Mlle Poulet se pointa sur les entrefaites pour nourrir Toufflette. La crémière se dressa majestueuse dans sa serviette et embrassa la virago. C'était soudain un va-et-vient de femelles monstrueuses dans l'appartement. Pour un peu, la formidable vierge de soixante ans eût pris une douche à son tour et se fût enveloppée d'une serviette éponge. Un ballet de géantes aurait commencé. Je serais resté toujours amorphe dans cette caverne de femmes majuscules, logé parmi des falaises de chair fraîche, car Mlle Poulet ne révélait nul signe de flétrissure. Elle était blanche avec ses bras tachetés de son. J'aurais vécu comme un enfant dans cet éden des mères aux mamelons puissants, en attendant Anny. Alors, l'influence de Margot, la fourbe qui aimait la mort, eût été conjurée.

Neuzil nous emmena, Anny et moi, le long du quai Bourbon, à la sortie du Pont-Marie. C'était un de ses itinéraires favoris. Il nous disait que le quai Bourbon était le lieu le plus parfait de Paris, qu'il n'y avait rien à redire, que tout était en place, stabilisé, rangé pour l'éternité. Et cela, sans rigidité ni froideur. Si nous n'étions pas encore tout à fait sensibles à une telle perfection, Anny et moi comprenions bien ce qu'elle signifiait pour Neuzil. Et nous étions plus fascinés par son admiration que par l'objet qui la suscitait.

Neuzil s'arrêta au milieu du quai et embrassa du regard l'alignement des façades anciennes, subtilement inclinées ou déjetées mais sans jamais déclencher une impression de désordre. Le quai était classique, un peu janséniste même. Noble et pur. Il respirait l'harmonie, l'argent placé, les passions maîtrisées, un équilibre des valeurs religieuses, militaires et bourgeoises. Les hôtels les plus prestigieux se côtoyaient : hôtel de Champaigne, hôtel du seigneur de Villars... avec leurs grandes portes de bois pourpre, leurs hautes fenêtres, leurs frises et leurs frontons. Les édifices ne péchaient jamais par un excès ou un défaut d'ornement. Ils offraient le dosage le plus adéquat d'élégance et de solidité. Des volets d'un beau vert tendre et discret relevaient la sévérité des murs dont les pierres étaient à nu. Peu à peu, sous la houlette de Neuzil, nous pressentions le pouvoir de ce site, de ce chef-d'œuvre. Le quai descendait doucement, jalonné d'arbres, petits platanes, à intervalles réguliers. Et de l'autre côté se déployaient les fastes rigoureux des belles façades contiguës. Neuzil souriait aux anges. Il restait là, inséré dans ce décor strict et majestueux, dans l'ordonnance des maisons seigneuriales, des maîtres de la finance et de la guerre, des grands administrateurs qui y avaient trouvé tranquillité, repos, qui avaient vieilli parmi des objets d'art et des textes pleins de sagesse, Sénèque, Plutarque... La mort

advenait comme l'on referme un livre sans perturber la cohérence d'ensemble.

Le quai intact sur l'île Saint-Louis. Peu de voitures. Le rideau d'arbres le séparait de la Seine. On voyait rarement les propriétaires entrer ou sortir. Ce qui enveloppait les demeures d'une aura de luxe austère et de vie cachée. Les gens qui vivaient là devaient être d'une autre essence que la nôtre, oui, ils étaient coupés de nous, de notre temps, de nos tribulations. Ils n'entraient pas dans la vie comme moi et Anny. Ils ne déambulaient plus comme Neuzil mangé par la gangrène. Ils étaient invisibles. On devinait leurs ombres au crépuscule quand les lumières s'allumaient dans les grands salons. Je les enviais de ne plus avoir à lutter, à se colleter avec l'inconnu de la vie. Ici tout était classé, nommé, conservé... Margot la manchote et l'orteil putrescent de Neuzil étaient des infirmités de passage qui ne pouvaient altérer en rien ce quai intime et solennel.

Alors une petite voiture apparut, se gara en un leste créneau contre le trottoir. Et une jeune femme en sortit. Nous avons éprouvé à sa vue, Anny et moi, une telle surprise que je ne saurais préciser de quoi se composaient nos sentiments mêlés. Nous étions pris à contre-pied. On attendait quelque sexagénaire plutôt de sexe masculin, racé, à cheveux blancs, teint bis, dans un pardessus gris foncé, de belle coupe, un homme cultivé, argenté, collectionneur de tableaux, au visage empreint de finesse et de sensuelle sérénité. Un personnage libéral et tolérant, sans préjugés, indulgent, privilégié presque malgré lui, exempté des tracas matériels de la vie sur lesquels il portait un regard de commisération sincère mais un peu lointaine, rendue abstraite par soixante années d'hédonisme sans faille et d'accord avec les êtres et les choses. Telle était notre légende... Alors surgit cette très jeune femme d'à peine plus de vingt ans, en

jeans moulants et délavés, longue, tee-shirt bleuet sur des seins fermes. Cheveux châtains, visage sans fard, peau blanche, exquise, grands yeux violets. On eût dit l'actrice de quelque théâtre jouant Camus ou Sartre ou d'un film de Godard, l'air bohème et déclassé. On l'eût imaginée à Saint-Germain, au Flore, ou bavardant avec des copains au pied de la fontaine Saint-Michel. Mais cette intruse sans apprêt entrait comme chez elle dans l'hôtel particulier. Un grand portail s'ouvrit. Elle disparut. Sournois comme des espions en planque, nous nous sommes détournés vers le quai de Seine, mais nous jetions des regards en coin sur les étages. Un salon s'éclaira. La fille passa devant les fenêtres. Une silhouette masculine et plus large émergea à côté d'elle. Était-ce notre fameux sexagnéaire calme et subtil ?

Nous ne vîmes rien de plus. Le quai Bourbon archétypal recevait la visite concrète d'une étudiante des Beaux-Arts ou de la Sorbonne. Rapide, sûre d'elle, familière des lieux. Habitait-elle ici ? L'homme était-il son père ? Ou bien venait-elle rencontrer un amant beaucoup plus âgé qu'elle, généreux et charmant ? Anny penchait pour l'hypothèse filiale, moi, prévoyant, j'inclinais pour un amour unissant le sexagénaire lettré et la belle étudiante déracinée. Je m'en faisais un roman voluptueux : elle ôtait son jean soixante-huitard, javellisé, devant le beau barbon gourmet. N'empêche que le quai Bourbon en était tout perturbé, fissuré par les désirs, les transgressions, les péripéties de la vie, ses aléas vertigineux.

Je demandai à Neuzil ce qu'il pensait de la jeune fille. Il ne partageait nullement notre embarras. Pour lui, la visiteuse se fondait avec agilité dans un décor que rien ne pouvait bouleverser. Bien au contraire, il pouvait accueillir avec équanimité des figures marginales, prostituées ou voyous, comédiennes sans rôle, modèles de peintres ou de photographes.

Neuzil nous relança avec cette merveilleuse suggestion de modèle de photographe. C'était plus cru que la peinture, sans références surannées, plus direct sous les spots, dans la décharge des flashes, les déclics de l'obturateur. Et le sexagénaire armé d'un Canon devenait plus redoutable, moins confiné dans son milieu, plus imprévisible. Elle dégageait son jean. Elle n'avait pas de slip. Quoi de plus beau que la fripure d'un pantalon baissé par à-coups et torsions sur une pilosité de fille sertie dans la peau vierge des aines. Son amant, entre l'hôtel de Champaigne et l'hôtel de Villars, la visait d'un objectif noir et cannelé. Il n'avait plus tout à fait soixante ans, je lui en donnais cinquante, soudain. Cela concordait mieux avec l'art de la photo, le voyeurisme intact, la convoitise et la passion des corps, le démon de midi ou quoi ? Quai Bourbon, entre un photographe avide, beau et friqué et une nomade curieuse et désargentée.

De retour chez Margot, l'impulsion de l'étreinte me saisit. J'étais fouetté d'un feu, d'une soif plus grande que moi, qui embrassait le quai Bourbon, l'avenir et ses légendes promises. Dans mon cœur, Paris foisonnait d'histoires de désir et d'envoûtantes amours. Mais Anny fut un peu piquée de cette boulimie qui m'avait été instillée par la belle fille du quai. Une moue se dessinait sur son visage poupin. Elle était allongée sur le lit en chien de fusil, presque boudeuse. Elle n'avait pas envie. Voilà ! Moi, je ne savais pas encore résister à un désir, le dépasser, en faire mon deuil. Ce refus ne faisait qu'aggraver de façon hystérique l'urgence de l'amour. Il me semblait qu'Anny ne m'aimait plus si elle ne partageait pas la spontanéité de mon élan. J'avais une vision de l'autre tout en symbiose avec moi-même. Je n'avais pas encore démêlé Anny

de moi. Je n'avais pas compris en quoi elle différait de moi. Cette différence m'eût effrayé. Aimer l'autre indépendamment de soi et pour lui-même, dans son histoire qui ne recoupe pas toujours la nôtre, dans son fantasme et son désir qui ne coïncident pas en tout avec le nôtre et peuvent même se situer aux antipodes de notre narcissisme —, je n'en fus vraiment capable qu'aux abords de la quarantaine. J'y ai donc mis du temps, un graduel renoncement à l'emprise fusionnelle et cannibale, surtout un oubli de la peur. Mes rivages furent enfin délivrés. Une femme pouvait passer, me dire qui elle était, ce qu'elle désirait sans me mentir ni se modeler sur mes faiblesses et mon désir. Je la suivais ou non mais sans lui faire procès de son être...

Au commencement, avec Anny, je ne concevais l'amour que rond, lisse et rempli comme une pomme, sans décalage ni différence. Elle se prêtait à cet engloutissement mutuel. Nulle révolte en elle ne perçait encore. Elle possédait cette sorte de souplesse et d'aisance intérieures comme de l'argile tendre qui se moulait sur mes creux et sur mes redents... Mais il lui arrivait de se buter comme après notre promenade quai Bourbon. Jalouse oui, exclue par ma rêverie qu'elle sentait trop imaginative. Cette étudiante en jeans qui rencontrait son amant dans un hôtel particulier m'avait entraîné loin, m'avait ouvert à des images, à des scènes, à des possibilités variées dont les facettes s'imprimaient dans ma tête comme des obsessions. C'étaient, oui, des visions d'une précision douloureuse. Anny, au fond, avait accepté de bon cœur la fusion et l'unité, mais elle pressentait que j'étais capable, tout en la voulant, de la trahir, de filer au-dehors, de réclamer d'autres scènes, d'autres silhouettes... J'étais avide, j'étais sans frein, mon cerveau galopait, s'alimentait des perceptions les plus fugaces. J'étais insatiable... Devinait-elle déjà que je ne me contenterais pas de fusionner avec elle mais

que je serais poussé par le délire de posséder toujours plus, de me repaître d'une totalité jamais atteinte, toujours visée ? L'infini me manquait, me plongeait dans l'abîme d'un désir vaste, sous l'aiguillon du regard et de l'angoisse. Et ma folie donnait au monde un relief prodigieux, comme un paradis convoité et multiplié.

Anny, ce jour-là, crut qu'elle n'était que le substitut d'un objet du désir quasi illimité. A l'époque, je n'aurais pas su lui expliquer que si cet objet était justement sans limites, il n'avait pas de consistance ni de correspondance dans le réel, qu'il n'était donc qu'un vide, qu'une brûlure en moi, qu'elle n'avait pas de rivale particulière, qu'il n'y avait pas d'autre incarnation véritable pour combler ma frénésie, et que la seule personne que je connaissais dont la vie et le visage prenaient greffe en moi, c'était elle.

Mais Anny était couchée en travers du lit, repliée dans son Levis noir, fermeture Éclair close entre les parenthèses des hanches exquises. Je me heurtai à ce quant-à-soi brusque. Elle rejetait ce désir qui n'était que le ricochet d'un autre. Elle était plus naturellement fusionnelle que moi, à sa façon, plus cohérente. Elle n'avait besoin de rien d'autre que nous-mêmes. Et moi qui la réclamais toute, il me fallait l'univers jusqu'aux étoiles, aux grands trous noirs, jusqu'aux quasars, jusqu'aux objets célestes encore inconnus. C'est vers cette nuit mouvante, étincelante, que mon désir volait, cet océan immense et constellé.

Mais je ne le savais pas vraiment. Je n'avais pas encore bien mesuré la maladie. Si bien que, de très bonne foi, je ne voyais pas pourquoi Anny me résistait... Alors je m'approchai doucement d'elle. Je m'agenouillai. Je me mis à caresser son visage. Elle ne pipait pas, mais elle écoutait. Je sentais son ouïe écarquillée. Elle fut toujours sensible à mon ramage bariolé. Elle voulait des mots, beaucoup de mots tendres

d'amour, une intensité dans mes paroles qui me monterait du cœur, naîtrait du fond de moi. Voilà, il fallait que je colmate la brèche, l'échappée désastreuse du quai Bourbon. Il fallait que je me fasse pardonner, que je mérite ce pardon par une surenchère de mots, de prières, de protestations vraies. Elle m'entendait prononcer mes phrases de plus en plus ardentes et sincères. Elle voulait que cela prenne racine au centre de mon amour, de ma peur de la perdre, de mon besoin absolu d'elle. Car elle me voulait soudain tout à elle et transi, totalement éperdu. Quand je fus au bord des larmes, elle avança ses lèvres vers mes deux mains qu'elle unit dans les siennes et sur lesquelles elle déposa des baisers fervents. Ce geste me bouleversa, me combla et me fit peur, car il ne lui ressemblait pas. Elle n'exprimait jamais son amour comme je le faisais, de manière démonstrative et paroxystique. Elle me laissait venir et dire. Elle n'en rajoutait pas. Elle répondait par son regard et son corps, sans parler, sans commentaires. Elle était là. Et la seule douceur était cette évidence. Mais elle venait de me surprendre d'un geste d'adoration presque puérile. Elle ne voulait pas que je pleure. Elle m'embrassait les mains d'avoir été sur le point de le faire. Elle ne savait pas encore qu'elle me verrait pleurer dans l'avenir et que ce serait pour elle l'expérience qui la désarmerait le plus. Et moi aussi, j'ignorais qu'elle pleurerait et que je ne supporterais pas ses larmes dont je serais la cause, et qu'elle serait la seule femme dont je pourrais vraiment dire : ses larmes me donnent envie d'expier, de tout donner.

... On ne savait rien encore. Les couples jeunes se forment ainsi toujours sur l'ignorance, une incroyable absence d'assise, d'appréciation de soi, de son désir...

Pressentant la montée d'un sanglot, d'instinct, elle me devança, me saisit les mains pour m'empêcher de céder à

cette chose effrayante... cette dislocation du monde : le chaos des larmes.

Elle m'offrit ses lèvres très charnues, à l'abandon, portant en creux dans leur moindre nervure l'attente du complément des miennes. Et pour son corps offert, ce fut de même, libéré de ses vêtements sans hâte mais avec une sûreté du geste, une détermination hypnotique. Anny n'était plus lucide, elle se dénudait dans cet état de clairvoyance seconde, car elle était déjà entrée dans notre étreinte. Elle se déshabillait mais son corps, son désir, son âme la précédaient, faisaient l'amour déjà. Et moi j'adhérais à cet enchaînement, à cet engrenage halluciné. Elle colla son corps contre le mien. Elle était fine, tiède petite fille, très douce, ardente. Elle m'absorbait, elle s'absorbait en moi. Et cela venait d'une région nocturne d'elle, béante et totalement rendue. Comme si je faisais l'amour avec la face intérieure de son être et de sa chair. Cet amour, je le sentais aveugle, lancinant. Anny se mariait à moi en profondeur. Elle ne cherchait pas à savoir. Moi, je ne me fondais pas comme elle par le dedans, par cette vague ouvrante et brûlante qui nous happait. Je m'enfonçais en elle en la regardant toujours, en la buvant des yeux, en me laissant glisser dans cette vague ouvrante... Je plongeais mon membre et pressais en même temps contre mon torse les seins que mes poils rougissaient, cette chair comme moite et meurtrie, les flancs tout attendris qui s'évasaient vers une nuit plus chaude, plus noire, cette face intérieure de son être qui n'en finissait plus de s'ouvrir. Ma propre lucidité s'éteignait. Je coulais à l'intérieur de cette nuit, par la fente étroite, océanique mais dont la vague s'élargissait. La bouche était ouverte en même temps, au même rythme, et produisait le même sentiment d'avalement. Je ne voyais plus rien. Je brûlais. J'étais trempé de sueur. Nous n'étions plus ni de chair, ni d'os, ni de nerfs mais d'un alliage fluide, mouvant,

de couleur noire, oui, noire écarlate comme la lave qui sort des entrailles de la terre. Ce magma, c'était nous et nos mots le mangeaient, car nous ne cessions de gémir et de chanter dans cette catastrophe étoilée qui nous engloutissait... avec cette sensation torride soudain, ce franchissement indicible, cette échappée vers l'immortalité, ce cri doré qui dansait tout au fond de moi. Et elle, baignant dans le même or fluide, reprenait notre cri rouge sombre, le modulait en une gamme plus large, plus profonde où elle se dissolvait, avalée, évanouie loin de ses rives, alanguie dans un murmure où elle gisait, mourante, adulée par les dieux du dedans, immortali-sée, là, sous mes yeux.

Dans la nuit, elle dormait. Et je repensai à Neuzil qui avait un jour insisté sur ce que tout le monde savait : ce sentiment d'immortalité dans la jouissance. Oui, c'était la vraie ques-tion. La chair mortelle et ce déchirement immortel qui traverse le corps, qui le transcende, nous fait déferler de l'autre côté dans cette surabondance dorée où transparaît notre être divinisé.

Dans son sommeil, Anny posa sa main sur ma hanche comme ça lui arriverait toujours, quoi qu'il arrive au cours des nombreuses années, même le pire. Elle avançait sa main sur la hanche de son homme qui ne dormait pas. Sans quitter le sommeil, elle le faisait, unie parfois contre son gré, au plus profond, là où on ne peut plus choisir, où tout est scellé depuis les serments de l'enfance... Et c'était comme si elle me disait alors... Je dors, oui, mais ça ne m'empêche pas de voir que tu ne dors pas et d'être là, avec toi, malgré tout, malgré tes trahisons, malgré le temps... Ce n'est qu'à condition de dormir ainsi que je puis oublier, te retrouver, te pardonner et

voyager, aimante, endormie auprès de toi, comme au fond de la mer, jusqu'à la mort.

Nous étions entrés dans la vie par les portes profondes. Nous étions pris dans un piège insondable. Nous ne le savions pas.

C'est le lendemain de cette nuit qu'Osiris nous contempla longuement et nous dit : « Venez voir ! » Osiris ne résistait jamais à notre odeur d'amour. On avait beau se laver vite mais bien, il flairait nos réminiscences lubriques. Cela flottait sur le visage engourdi et gommé d'Anny, son air flou, ses prunelles poudrées d'ivresse. Osiris nous entraîna vers la tour sud, dans la salle du grand bourdon Emmanuel. Nous revîmes la carcasse formidable des poutres gothiques où dort dans sa corolle le battant lesté de trésors et du phallus.

Les visites étaient plus rares en cette fin d'automne. Osiris expédia un paquet de touristes et ménagea une pause pour nous. Il nous prit par la main et nous conduisit à l'extrémité orientale de la salle. Le plancher continu cessait, il y avait une rambarde et, de l'autre côté, un entrelacs de poutres recommençait, si serrées que l'on pouvait se glisser sur leurs passerelles. Osiris nous découvrit une niche à la croisée de deux poutres comme des branches. Dans un amas de paille, nous aperçûmes les touffes pelotonnées et les museaux enfouis. Je m'y connaissais en bêtes depuis l'enfance et pourtant je calai. Quels étaient donc ces hôtes inconnus de la tour ? Osiris nous laissa chercher. Et nous restions penchés sur cette crèche inattendue dans la membrure de Notre-Dame. Les poils étaient d'un beau gris doré.

— Ce sont des loirs, dit Osiris.

Je n'avais jamais vu de loirs et leur apparition m'émerveilla. Ils dotaient la cathédrale d'une présence animale et profonde, plus intime que celle des faucons. Car les loirs immobiles dormaient, hibernaient comme dans le ventre de Notre-Dame.

— Ils ne sont tout de même pas venus naturellement ?

— C'est un couple de loirs qui nichait à l'extrême bord du jardin du Luxembourg dans le fameux verger interdit aux visiteurs. L'un des jardiniers qui est un ami me les a montrés. Ils se nourrissaient d'insectes et de fruits. J'ai ressenti pour eux une vraie toquade et je n'ai eu de cesse qu'il me laisse les emmener. Un hiver, je les ai transportés dans leur sommeil, au fond d'un gros sac, car ce sont de beaux spécimens de vingt-cinq centimètres de long ! Et je les ai installés dans cette nouvelle tanière, au sein de la charpente, dans cette partie déserte. Au printemps, la nuit, ils s'éveillent, passent de l'autre côté à travers l'ogive, vers le toit de la nef, galopent le long des arcs-boutants et vont manger des insectes dans le jardin de l'Archevêché. Là, je dispose des fruits exprès pour eux. Puis ils remontent et se cachent le restant du jour dans le berceau des poutres. Ce sont mes pensionnaires, mes animaux fétiches.

Anny et moi, on n'en revenait pas de ces loirs endormis. Ils étaient la plus belle histoire d'Osiris, la plus vraie. Toute la cathédrale prenait un nouveau sens, comme si elle était bâtie aussi pour loger, envelopper ces fourrures dorées. Les hautes ogives palpitaient de cette présence vivante.

— Avez-vous d'autres secrets, Osiris ? demanda Anny.

— A l'infini... répondit Osiris en souriant.

— D'autres animaux ?

— De grandes bêtes d'or innombrables... Notre-Dame est une forêt sous la lune, bourrée de souris, d'effraies, de

hulottes, d'araignées. Il y a la cathédrale nocturne qui n'est plus celle des faucons solaires mais des bêtes de nuit. Il y a des scarabées et des coléoptères. On pourrait nourrir là-dedans un boa sans que jamais personne ne le sache. Il suffirait de lui apporter une souris de temps à autre.

— Vous n'avez pas fait ça, Osiris ?! Un serpent dans cette cathédrale chrétienne...

— J'ai dit qu'on le pouvait, qu'il y aurait toute la place et les facilités... plein de trous, de soupentes, de recoins, de réduits. Un boa doux et tranquille, béat dans le giron de la Vierge, lui suçant le sein éternellement !

— Vous ne l'avez pas fait ! Osiris. J'ai besoin de savoir si c'est vrai ou faux ?

— Je ne peux pas répondre à tout, sinon il n'y a pas de rêverie...

— Dans quel trou l'auriez-vous fourré ?

— J'aurais choisi la tour nord, l'interdite, celle d'Ehra bien sûr, la tour sœur.

— Si vous l'aviez fait !

— On ne peut pas tout raconter, Anny, tout épuiser, laissez-moi encore du champ ! des réserves où pêcher ! Alors, un jour, de nouveau je vous dirai : « Venez ! » Et vous vous inclinerez sur un boa cerclé de noir et d'or, lisse et lové sur le large d'une poutre dans les bras de la Vierge.

— Ce serait horrible, Osiris ! J'ai horreur des serpents.

— Oui, mais vous seriez fascinée !

— Méfiez-vous Osiris, un jour votre boa se carapaterait, traverserait la grande galerie, attiré par le sang chaud des loirs et hop ! il les avalerait. Vous auriez l'air malin !

— Un boa bien nourri dans les bras de Notre-Dame dort plus ravi qu'un Bouddha.

— Vous mélangez les religions, Osiris, vous métissez à mort.

— A vie ! Anny, à vie !

Marguerite rentra à cinq heures... Elle alerta les voisins, battit le rappel, se propagea pour secouer par son tintouin le fardeau de la mort. Elle passa une heure à adorer sa chatte, en des mamours auxquels Toufflette restait froide. Mais Margot persistait à la trouver sensible et si intérieure !

— Vous comprenez, elle a raison de bouder un peu. Je l'ai délaissée pendant des jours. Elle me le fait savoir ! Je l'ai blessée dans son amour.

Puis Margot alluma la télé, écouta des disques et chantonna, trottinant partout, allègre et de guingois, son moignon au vent... Elle bloqua un bol de thé entre l'épaule et son menton en trempant une tartine de sa main libre. Et son œil malicieux me toisait en mâchant le pain. Soudain elle eut très chaud. Je n'aérais jamais, j'étais trop frileux, elle ouvrit grand la fenêtre. Elle se déshabilla, courut à travers l'appartement, en combinaison miel. Elle renaissait, c'était la vie encore, multiple et savoureuse. Pourtant, le soir, au moment de dîner, avec une mimique d'ironie, elle me montra le semis de pilules auprès de son assiette. Il y avait des comprimés pour fluidifier le sang, pour fortifier les artères et puis surtout un médicament euphorisant.

— Vous vous rendez compte, un euphorisant ! Un comprimé pour être comique ! Pour amuser la galerie jusqu'au bout !

J'étais soudain inquiet de ce moment de lucidité. Je croyais que Marguerite était repartie dare-dare et spontanée, mais non ! Elle avait quand même besoin d'une chiquenaude chimique. La Salpêtrière et ses visions laissaient des traces et des hantises qui ne se diluaient pas en un jour. On dîna tous les deux en regardant la télé.

— J'aurais très bien pu ne pas revenir...

— Allons... allons... — je protestai —, malgré tous vos petits accidents malheureux, pour tenir si bien le coup, cela prouve que vous avez une santé de fer !

Je lui servis la phrase splendide qu'elle m'avait dite un jour sur le métal indéfectible de sa santé profonde qui résistait aux assauts de toutes les maladies.

— De fer, de fer ! C'était le moral qui était en fer, mais le corps il a toujours été à la traîne.

La télé donnait un document sur les déserts.

— Je ne le connais pas celui-là !

J'étais interloqué :

— Qu'est-ce que vous ne connaissez pas ?

— Ce désert-là... Je n'y suis jamais allée !

J'ai cru un moment que le cerveau de Margot était mal irrigué. Je relançai, plein de crainte :

— Mais quels déserts connaissez-vous ?

— Des tas de déserts !

Et Marguerite se redressa, l'œil malicieux, fière, attisée par ma surprise :

— Je connais les déserts du Niger, de Lybie, un peu le Sahara et le sud de l'Irak, bien l'Arabie saoudite...

Marguerite en Lawrence d'Arabie juchée sur un dromadaire. Elle faisait son voyage d'Orient comme Flaubert. Les euphorisants la faisaient-ils divaguer ? Elle rêvait au grand soleil pour conjurer l'ombre mortelle de la Salpêtrière. Elle explorait les dunes très blondes, les oasis, les palmeraies. Elle voyait de grands Touareg bleus. Nomade en somme ! Elle cinglait vers les mirages.

— Je ne rêve pas ! Je ne suis pas cinoque ! Je connais les plus grands déserts du monde !

Et Marguerite gloussait, se trémoussait. Ravie, l'esprit bien net, l'œil rivé sur son étudiant.

— Voilà ! Voilà ! Ma fille — et pourtant je vous en ai parlé —, ma fille a épousé un ingénieur dans le pétrole. Alors, au fil des années passées, ils m'ont invitée là où ils étaient en poste. J'ai débarqué comme ça dans pas mal de dictatures du désert d'Afrique ou du Moyen-Orient. Je dois vous dire que ce n'était pas exaltant mais monotone, malodorant : tous ces relents de fuel et ces fumées sur les dunes. Pas une herbe, rien, le vide... Avec de discrètes nuances d'un désert à l'autre, pour un œil exercé, des variations de l'ocre au beige, les épineux et la rocaille ou la poussière grisâtre et nulle. Et les puits, les formidables pompes, la mécanique démesurée. Mais j'étais plus jeune, je m'enivrais de l'idée de partir. J'annonçais à la cantonade que j'allais au Niger, en Lybie. C'était grandiose. Les copines m'enviaient, imaginaient des exotismes, des palmeraies. Moi-même, je finissais par m'en convaincre... C'est tout juste si j'ai entrevu un bédouin, une caravane, un pasteur et ses biques. Pourtant, à chaque nouveau voyage, la même griserie m'illusionnait d'aller là-bas, même si je savais qu'il n'y avait que du sable encore et encore. J'avais la cinquantaine. Le vide n'est jamais le vide. Mon enthousiasme le fleurissait, voilà !

Et Marguerite parla de sa fille et de son mari, des dîners qu'ils organisaient pour leurs collaborateurs et associés dans le pétrole. Mais Margot était amère. Car elle devait rester, ces soirs-là, dans la chambre à garder les gosses. Or, elle aurait aimé participer aux agapes en robe du soir, gracieuse et volubile, mondaine oui, évoluant d'un invité à l'autre. Elle eût tendu sa main pour qu'on la baise en buvant du champagne. Mais jamais, pas une seule fois, sa fille et son gendre n'avaient consenti à exaucer ce désir des Mille et Une Nuits. Tout à coup, dans un sanglot, elle m'avoua :

— Ils avaient honte de moi, de ma prothèse, oui ! Honte de leur mère, honte de mes manières. Pourtant, je peux tenir

196

une conversation. Mais non ! Ils avaient peur qu'on parle de l'enfance, de la baraque là, la prison de la Force, du papa maçon, ivrogne, du contexte peu reluisant. Je sais, je sais qu'ils avaient honte. Alors, moi qui avais élevé ma fille, qui m'étais battue, veuve et toute seule pour qu'elle réussisse, eh bien ils me planquaient de crainte d'une dissonance, de la fausse note...

Un jour, de dépit et de tristesse, je suis partie comme ça dans le désert, à pied, sous un parapluie contre le soleil. J'ai marché le long d'une piste, c'était tout droit, tout plat, parsemé de petits cailloux. Je n'ai pas rencontré âme qui vive, pas une chèvre, pas un berger, pas un insecte. Rien. La nullité immense. Mais je ne sais, une fulguration me traversa, comme une joie. Je me répétais que j'étais très loin et toute seule, à l'aventure dans un monde hostile et sauvage. Eh oui ! La joie m'a inondée. Je me suis mise à chanter et à ramasser les petits cailloux... Venez voir !

Marguerite m'entraîna vers un placard, elle fouilla dans ses tiroirs, extirpa un petit sac bourré de pierres minuscules...

— C'est des cailloux du Niger, du Sahara, de Lybie...

Elle les fit rouler sur la table. Ils étaient incolores et sans attrait. Opaques et muets. Elle les entrechoquait comme des osselets, comme les reliques de son rêve.

L'orage assombrit ma fenêtre. J'ai envie de Notre-Dame sous le ciel noir. Je sors, je franchis le Pont-Marie, je suis les quais jusqu'à la grande île. Et Notre-Dame m'apparaît dans une lumière d'apocalypse. Un rayon blême perce le ciel, droit sur les tours. Je pense soudain : Victor Hugo. Le nom se détache absurde, énorme dans ma tête, se dresse, se carre dans la stature du H. Et la forme de chaque tour répète la verticale et la harpe du H. Hugo deux fois. Deux grands Hugo droits. J'ai peur de la folie. La cathédrale s'obscurcit, taillée dans son roc gothique, comme la hanche de Hugo, comme la vieille hure de Hugo, sa gueule de gargouille barbue. Notre-Dame d'Hugo. Grâce aux ténèbres, au souffle du vent, à la tempête, voilà la cathédrale des Goths ressuscitée. Les siècles giclent de ses pierres, fourmillent en surface comme des écailles de dragon, des grumeaux magnétiques. Elle est chargée d'ombre et de coulées de sang. Chaque roulement de tonnerre sort d'elle comme une voix. Elle a cessé d'être la cathédrale de la Vierge. Elle est trop vieille tout à coup. Vieillarde, oui... Marie si noire, immémoriale. Mère éternelle percluse de rhumatismes, de grands arcs-boutants et toute cornue d'ogives et de flèches flétries. Le

199

monde a mué en un éclair. Le ciel s'ouvre, bouge, rabat sa dalle funéraire. La Seine redevient un fleuve mauvais, au débit courroucé. Les gens fuient pour se mettre à l'abri. La poussière s'envole soudain sur le parvis. Et je vois la rosace comme la prunelle d'Hugo, bouche d'ombre béante sur l'abîme. Autour de Notre-Dame, la pluie crépite, bouillonne. La cathédrale émerge, telle la proue d'un gros galion sur l'océan empanaché.

Les faucons tremblent dans l'orage et se rebrousse la fourrure des loirs... Toutes les statues de monstres, les meutes de singes, loups, vautours qui se cabrent à l'angle des tours, tout le bestiaire gluant suinte, s'ébroue, bave. Notre-Dame hausse ses deux hennins qui chavirent et qui fument. Les apôtres et les saints, les Vierges des portails se noient dans cette nuée remuante. Les traits de l'averse gribouillent, chiffonnent la façade, brouillent ses arcs et ses piliers. La cathédrale réapparaît dans les trêves. Entière soudain, intacte. Avec ses deux têtes d'Hugo, ses orbites, sa trogne, son poitrail et son Verbe. Puis elle est submergée par de nouvelles rafales de pluie et de remous.

Seule, la haute et longue ogive d'une tour découpe sa meurtrière noire. Une gargouille étincelle dans un rai d'argent. Je désire qu'il tonne et qu'il rage ainsi jusqu'à la nuit pour interdire Notre-Dame à la foule. Pour qu'elle se retranche loin de nous sur son récif tel un phare dans la colère et la tempête. Pour qu'on la perde, qu'elle se détache de nos regards, de notre emprise vulgaire. Pour qu'elle rompe son lien et qu'elle appareille sur son île, qu'elle s'en aille, qu'elle dérive, cabossée, hérissée, hugolienne... Quelque part très loin de nous, avec ses anges, ses faucons et ses loirs, ses vitraux éblouis, ses rosaces fleuries dans la nef déserte où règne seule la Vierge du XIVe siècle, celle du chœur, celle qui donne son nom au sanctuaire, la très fine, l'intime, si

botticellienne, si peu gothique, toute de grâce, frêle fiancée, comme ravie par le pirate Hugo hurlant dans ses tours, bombant son râble et ses arcs-boutants. Le père terrible et rieur, grand rapace de Marie. Madone fléchie de biais, si juvénile dans sa chair rose, son visage puéril. Elle entend le boucan tout autour, au-delà des murs. Elle écoute le grondement qui cogne et les roulis. Elle sourit, timide dans son voile que traverse le halo des cierges tandis que les hautes tours font face aux razzias de l'orage qu'elles repoussent, altières, tenaces, bigarrées d'éclairs, éclaboussées. Le vaisseau de la Vierge dans la grosse main d'Hugo. Notre-Dame de l'Ogre, dans le velu de cette grande paume pleine de pâte et de mots, sous son œil étonné, son sourcil neigeux, arqué, dont les mèches se vrillent dans le vent. Ce tout petit reflet, fétu de Vierge fendue qui trône dans l'œil du Vieux.

Quand je revins de ce vertige, j'aperçus l'ambulance au 9, rue Pavée. On emmenait Neuzil. La fièvre avait monté d'un coup, une douleur horrible dans l'orteil. Il fut amputé le soir même.

Neuzil reposait dans son lit, fragile. Les draps propres l'éclairaient. On l'avait rasé le matin et sa peau semblait douce. Il ne souffrait pas. On lui avait administré une overdose contre la douleur. Marguerite était à côté de moi, curieuse, contente d'inverser les rôles. Elle conseillait Neuzil, vieille connaisseuse de l'hôpital. Je voyais dans ses yeux qu'une seule chose l'obsédait : l'orteil... Où était-il passé ? L'avait-on conservé dans du formol ? Ça la cuisait, ce pouce

manquant. Elle qui avait perdu tout un bras. C'était bien pire. L'orteil de Neuzil n'était qu'une broutille, même si l'artérite et la gangrène menaçaient de grimper plus haut.

— C'est le bassin, peut-être, qui est gênant ? le pistolet, tout l'arsenal pour les besoins, pas vrai ?

Marguerite aimait s'enquérir de ces détails sordides. Neuzil était digne, il ne devait pas apprécier la cuvette glissée sous les reins et l'aide-soignante qui vient empocher le colis.

— Cet orteil empirait, Johann, c'était une charge inhumaine, il n'avait plus figure d'orteil... Maintenant vous êtes libre, tout neuf ! Regardez, moi, sans mon bras, j'ai des ailes !

Et Marguerite faisait l'oiseau. L'homme gentil la regardait.

Au retour, un grand trouble régnait dans la maison. La concierge nous apprit que la porte de Neuzil avait été forcée par des voleurs. Marguerite se rua dans la brèche, moi à ses trousses. Les pièces étaient sens dessus dessous, tiroirs vidés, papiers répandus. Et le linge de Neuzil, ses slips de vieux, longs et jaunasses, s'étalaient sur le sol, avec une sorte de bande herniaire avachie sur le tapis.

— Les salauds ! répétait Margot, très stimulée par le désastre.

Elle lorgnait tout, elle filait, elle se retenait de toucher les vêtements pêle-mêle, les liasses de papier, elle dévorait le chaos des yeux. Je me demandais ce qui pouvait l'exciter à ce point. Elle débaula dans la chambre de Neuzil. Il avait un lit étroit d'ermite ou d'enfant. Une photo de sa mère, Wally Neuzil, s'offrait dans un cadre sur sa table de chevet. Elle portait un chapeau. On ne lui donnait pas d'âge. Ce n'était pas la jeune fille que j'avais imaginée, nue, dix-sept ans, posant pour Egon Schiele, lascive, écartant ses bas pourpres afin de lui montrer le sexe. Une grande robe l'enveloppait. Elle faisait démodée. Schiele l'avait rêvée, transfigurée. On le découvrait, lui, sur le mur, en face du lit, un autoportrait

découpé dans un album de peinture. Les cheveux noirs et courts, le visage pointu, l'œil sombre. Une pose de dandy fulgurant. Elle et lui, les parents de Neuzil? Elle, la mère, sans doute. Mais Schiele? Le mystère demeurait. On avait peine à croire que ce peintre juvénile et tourmenté, plein d'élégance et d'arrogance, était le père du vieux Neuzil. On eût dit son fils secret. Et puis, derrière un paravent, dans un angle, sur une table de travail, je découvris le faucon empaillé, le faucon mort de la tour sud. Je le reconnus avec stupeur. Le faucon qui gisait sur le toit de plomb dans la constellation des noms. Il exhibait son bréchet clair et moucheté, entre ses longues ailes brunes. Exact et mort. Je n'aimais pas ce cadavre d'oiseau incorruptible. Ce plumage d'apparat pour rien.

— Je ne savais pas qu'il avait ce moineau! s'étonna Margot, moi je ferai peut-être empailler Toufflette si la mignonne... oh! je préfère ne pas imaginer!

Tout à coup, je pensai au dessin. Comment avais-je pu oublier le dessin! Nous nous étions précipités avec l'idée d'un vol d'argent... C'est Marguerite qui avait lancé l'idée :

— Peut-être qu'il avait accumulé des économies, Neuzil, soudain... le saint?

A présent, Marguerite me toisait du regard :

— Ils auraient volé ça?... son machin érotique?

Comment pouvais-je savoir s'ils l'avaient pris, puisque j'ignorais où Neuzil l'avait rangé. Je lui téléphonai à l'hôpital. J'entendis sa voix amicale et lasse. Le dessin était dans le placard du couloir séparant la chambre des toilettes, posé tout en bas. Je quittai la chambre, ouvrit le placard. Il n'y avait rien. Je repris le téléphone, lui demandai de préciser encore. Il répéta les mêmes renseignements. Alors je l'assurai que cela ne voulait pas dire grand-chose, qu'ils avaient tout vidé, transporté, dispersé, qu'on pouvait très bien

retrouver le dessin ailleurs dans le fatras, et Neuzil me dit :

— Ne vous en faites pas... Ce dessin est en moi.

Mais moi, cette idée qu'on avait volé l'étreinte d'Egon et de Gerti m'était insupportable. La révolte me brûlait. Impuissant, je tournai en rond en répétant que c'était dégueulasse, que c'étaient des monstres !

— Il ne faut pas exagérer, corrigea Margot... des petits voyous, ça oui ! Mais des monstres ?

— Des monstres ! m'écriai-je dans un accès de rage.

— Ah ! Ne hurlez pas ! Ne recommencez pas le coup de la colère que vous m'aviez faite le jour où j'ai eu le malheur de contester la sainteté de Neuzil ! J'espère seulement que vous n'aurez jamais affaire à des monstres ! des vrais qui vous charcutent et vous torturent et tuent tout ce qui bouge, comme on voit dans la presse ! des sadiques ! avec des rasoirs et des coupe-choux ! C'est ça des monstres. Mais, eux, ce sont des voleurs, plutôt connaisseurs, voyez-vous, puisqu'ils sont venus piquer son espèce de chef-d'œuvre...

Et Marguerite disait ça avec un air de soupçon, un doute sur la portée de l'œuvre en question.

— C'est un chef-d'œuvre unique, absolu ! oui ! Sans faille ! Indubitable. Massif ! A se mettre à genoux devant... Et moi ça me torture, ça me charcute oui et ça me tue de savoir qu'ils l'ont volé, c'est pire qu'un meurtre ! C'est moins banal, c'est plus vicelard !

— Vous déraisonnez ! C'est le côté qui me heurte en vous, qui me bloque. Vous perdez le juste sens des choses pour un dessin tout à coup... Et moi, j'ai failli crever, non ? Et Neuzil, on lui a tranché un bout, comme ça, allez ! hop ! Je te coupe ! Et vous bramez parce qu'il s'agit d'art ? Mais Neuzil, il se fiche bien du beau maintenant !

Deux flics arrivèrent pour le constat, l'état des lieux. Marguerite aimait les hommes et surtout les gendarmes. Elle

aurait préféré des inspecteurs de police, de fins limiers du Quai des Orfèvres. Mais il ne fallait pas trop demander. Elle plaisantait avec les types, leur expliquait Neuzil, la maisonnée, l'ancienne prison, la dépendance de la Force. Elle cherchait à leur extirper d'autres histoires de voleurs, plus corsées, avec violence, un crime rare même...

— Moi, je me défendrais ! Je crierais ! Je crierais ! Et je me débattrais ! J'ai de la force ! Je suis capable d'un sursaut !

Puis elle eut l'audace de leur parler du dessin, en suggérant le thème.

— C'est très cru ! très cru !

Elle ajusta une moue :

— Moi, je préfère les impressionnistes... Monet... *La Pie* ! Hein, *La Pie* ! Vous connaissez *La Pie* ?

Ils ne connaissaient pas de pie. Elle me glissa un clin d'œil, sous-entendant qu'ils n'avaient pas de culture. Bien sûr ! C'étaient des hommes d'action, jeunes et robustes. Des jeunes, des jeunes ! Ils n'avaient pas le temps, ils couraient d'un meurtre à l'autre, d'une filature à un hold-up... Elle était indulgente. Ils la distrayaient. Elle aurait bien pris comme locataire un étudiant en matières criminelles. Mais ça n'existait pas. Un type avec un revolver, un P quelque chose, Magnum et tout... Les armes la fascinaient. Brandies d'un coup, noires et nickelées, pan ! pan ! C'était légal. Elle aimait le mot noble et froid.

Mlle Poulet survint :

— Te voilà mon Petit Poulet ! lui décocha Margot d'entrée, avec une insolence pour les poulets, bien sûr...

Elle regarda les flics, sérieuse, soudain objective :

— Elle s'appelle Poulet, c'est son nom.

Puis la concierge rappliqua, à son tour, accompagnée de son mari. Elle n'avait que des soucis. C'est que son homme poursuivait sa mystérieuse métamorphose. Il perdait toujours

205

ses poils et ses ongles. Ça lui donnait un air honteux et démuni. Une expression suppliante, comme si nous avions tous dû nous cotiser pour lui faire recouvrer sa virilité.

— Ce n'est peut-être qu'une forme un peu poussée d'andropause, me chuchota Margot en rigolant. Mais il ne bande plus d'un chouia, c'est la concierge qui me l'a dit... C'est l'hallali...

Je regardai le mari. Il sentit mon regard. Je détournai les yeux. Il était aux abois. Et cette alarme brusque déboussolait son visage, sa silhouette pathétique et ramollie.

Quinze jours plus tard, Neuzil revint. Il reprenait un peu de force, juste une pincée. C'est lui qui me parla du dessin. Il perçut ma colère.

— Non, ne vous en faites pas, je suis un peu détaché de l'objet même... Je vous l'ai dit, le dessin est en moi depuis longtemps. Ce que je souhaite, c'est que les voleurs ne le détruisent pas. Or, ils n'ont pas intérêt à le détruire. Ils veulent le vendre à un collectionneur, à un musée quelque part à l'étranger... Alors Egon et Gerti ne sont pas menacés. Ce n'est plus pour moi une question de propriété. J'aurais préféré transmettre le dessin, le donner... choisir... Mais l'essentiel, c'est qu'ils aient pris conscience de sa valeur. Le vol en est la preuve.

Je me taisais. Je comprenais un peu Neuzil, mais moi, ce vol m'eût arraché les tripes. Neuzil reprit :

— Je n'ai plus rien soudain... C'est mieux ainsi. Je suis tout à fait délivré. Je puis me laisser flotter. Vous ne devez pas accepter ça, vous, maintenant ! Surtout pas ! Il vous faut prendre, toucher, tenir. C'est normal, ça vous nourrit, ça vous donne des repères et des racines. Il vous faut du

concret, du solide, des jalons... Ça donne du corps, hein, et du cœur à l'ouvrage, à la vie ! Et c'est merveilleux, vous ! Mais moi... je me déprends, c'est l'inverse, je restitue, je fais le vide. Mon dessin, je le leur donne. J'aurais dû le donner depuis longtemps. J'ai eu tort. Il ne fallait rien garder.

Abandonné dans son fauteuil, Neuzil avait une expression douce et rêveuse. Comme il semblait frêle ! La peau même pas épaissie, parcheminée, boucanée par le temps mais transparente vers les tempes, trop fine. Les veines affleuraient en tortillons verdâtres et douloureux. Neuzil ne portait pas ce masque des vieillards mythiques, aux fripures d'éléphants cartonnées. C'était un petit homme soyeux. La vieillesse l'avait frotté, poncé jusqu'à la trame la plus diaphane.

— Mon dessin voyage, après tout. Il commence d'exister, il est comme vous. Et c'est très bien qu'il lui arrive l'aventure de la vie.

Marguerite se lança dans des hypothèses :

— On est bien obligés... me dit-elle, avec une mine hypocrite. Ce n'est ni Maurice ni David. Je les exclus... bon ! Mais ils ont parlé. Eux seuls connaissaient l'existence de son dessin, en dehors de vous et moi. Ils ont parlé à leur ami Osiris. C'est lui la pièce maîtresse. Hein ! le pion gagnant... Vous y avez pensé comme moi. Osiris ou un copain d'Osiris auquel il en aurait parlé. C'est par lui que ça passe ! Bien sûr, ce n'est pas moi qui vais le vendre aux flics !

Et Margot, avec un air intérieur, complaisant :

— Ça reste intellectuel...

Anny et moi, un autre jour, on rencontra Osiris dans la rue. On alla boire un chocolat chaud tous les trois. Et je dis :

— Ils ont volé le dessin de Neuzil, c'est révoltant !

— Je sais... Je sais... Il y a des vols tout le temps et partout. C'était un dessin très singulier, très sensuel, je crois ?

Tout à coup, d'une impulsion, d'un bloc, j'ai lâché :

— J'ai pensé que le voleur vous connaissait, Osiris, et que c'était un ami auquel vous aviez parlé du dessin.

Osiris fut touché de plein fouet par mon audace. Il se tut un instant, se ressaisit et me coula un regard long, immensément curieux, quelque chose de profond, de sinueux, de spirituel dans sa prunelle, qui l'éclairait du dedans, comme s'il découvrait mon paysage intérieur, mes possibilités...

— Je n'ai jamais parlé de ce dessin, à personne ! Jamais. Ça ne m'intéresse pas. Je n'aime que les photos... les photos de garçons asiatiques et nus !... Le genre bonze des temples, du Cambodge, leur ivoire lisse. J'adore leur crâne parfait, vert de jade, leur visage rond et leurs fesses, voyez-vous, leur couleur exquise, inimitable, leur matière incorruptible.

Je me sentis légèrement rougir. Il avait frappé fort et réussi à détourner l'enquête. Il souriait. Il regardait Anny. Il était lent, moelleux dans sa façon de savourer sa victoire. Il se dandinait doucement, alléché, alangui. Un beau soleil dorait la salle. Il étendit la main, caressa cette lumière comme l'encolure d'un cheval nu.

— J'aime le soleil, beaucoup... la vie, tout ce qu'elle permet ! Est-ce que vous sentez tout ce qu'elle autorise ?

Il était dans un bon jour, Osiris, cela se voyait. Il était invincible. Puis il se mit à briller d'un élan de désir démoniaque.

— Peut-être qu'un jour, les enfants, je vous dirai :

« Venez ! » pour vous montrer, dans la tour, caché dans la tanière des loirs et protégé par leur pelage doré, le chef-d'œuvre d'Egon Schiele... Mais, en échange, il faudra me donner énormément !

Nous préférâmes, Anny et moi, ne pas l'interroger sur la nature de ce don démesuré. Il était trop en forme. Il n'avait plus d'entraves. Il était sans bornes. C'était son jour, en raison du soleil roux qui vernissait notre table et parsemait d'étincelles chaudes le bas sur la cuisse d'Anny.

Osiris nous entraîna en conversant le long de la Seine derrière l'île Saint-Louis, sur la rive gauche. Le quai s'élargissait et une flottille de péniches était amarrée flanc à flanc. Tout un village avec ses pittoresques, ses coloris, ses anecdotes, linge qui sèche, gris-gris, objets hétéroclites. Une population vivait là, sédentaire à même le fleuve.

— Wolf et Ehra habitent ici.

C'était, oui, un bon jour pour Osiris, il abattait toutes ses cartes et ses atouts en plein soleil.

— J'ai rendez-vous avec eux... Il faut que je vous quitte.

Il ébaucha un geste évasif et voluptueux, puis il nous regarda avec malice :

— Je ne vais pas vous faire un dessin... Souvenez-vous de votre formule, du talisman : « obi et branlerie d'amour ».

Osiris franchit une passerelle et s'éclipsa dans la longue péniche pansue. On n'aurait pas dû lui inventer ce talisman, il avait cristallisé dedans tous ses vices, et il nous laissait en plan !

C'était la péniche où Ehra amassait tous les signes qu'elle moissonnait dans la ville, slogans du sexe ou de rébellion, les jurons du métro, les paraphes des chiottes, les noms magi-

ques, les sobriquets et les courroux. Elle enfouissait la cueillette dans le ventre de la péniche. Parfois, elle recopiait les plus belles sentences, les plus noires, sur des feuilles de papier dessin qu'elle punaisait autour d'elle. Cette fresque du langage, elle l'observait, la désirait, comme si elle n'avait exploré son bruissement souterrain et tabou que pour y découvrir le chiffre de sa destinée. Il lui était arrivé de graver dans le bois même du vaisseau des maximes violentes, des surnoms très crus, des imprécations de rage, des outrages, cris de convoitise ou de colère, des mots majuscules écrits dans des langues étrangères : HATE ! HASS !... d'autres qu'elle ne connaissait pas ou seulement des signes, des graphes, des dessins expressifs, allégoriques, grossiers symboles de fécondité, de coït sur les flancs de sa grande péniche tatouée...

Lorsque Osiris frappa à la porte, c'est Wolf qui lui ouvrit. Ehra ne se montra pas. Wolf était nu. Il portait toujours le bandeau. Sa peau était si vierge qu'elle semblait presque phosphorescente. Osiris en ressentit une sorte d'effroi. Wolf l'attira dans une salle basse au ras des eaux. Il s'allongea sur une banquette, le long d'une unique fenêtre. Et une langue de jour imbibée de Seine noire éclaboussa la peau de Wolf, plus livide encore. Il y avait dans cette blancheur celle de sa sœur. Ehra qui fascinait Osiris mais lui faisait peur. Depuis que son œil était mort, Wolf se sentait traqué. Il avait gardé le modelé de ses muscles qui fluaient en tresses nerveuses de la nuque aux reins. Mais il avait perdu ses façons arrogantes. Wolf blessé avait peur. Et son angoisse envahissait son œil unique dont le bleu jadis si glacé avait mûri, s'était creusé de doutes et d'ombres. Osiris adorait l'épouvante de Wolf, cette

panique sourde qui assombrissait l'œil bleu. Wolf s'accouda sur la banquette, le corps un peu détourné de côté, exhibant la hanche et l'arrondi de la fesse en faucille renflée. De temps en temps, il jetait un regard sur les eaux noires dont l'odeur de croupi se diffusait dans la pièce. Alors, Osiris ne voyait que l'œil aveugle et masqué, le cou saillant, si délicat, la pomme d'Adam outrancière, l'arête du nez de prédateur, la bouche charnue, goulue, protubérante, pareille à celle d'Ehra, l'envergure des épaules bosselées dont les tendons et les fuseaux s'enchâssaient dans les biceps d'ivoire, les côtes visibles comme celles d'un flagellé, et toujours cette région plus ample, plus douce, le moyeu de la hanche, la fesse plus épanouie. Osiris désirait Wolf dans cette mare de lumière lugubre qui renforçait la pâleur de sa chair. Wolf se renversa sur le ventre. Et son dos, ses reins s'incurvèrent jusqu'au rebond des fesses pinçant entre leurs globes un sillon qui avait la nuance noire du fleuve. Puis Wolf se releva de côté vers Osiris pour lui montrer qu'il bandait. Il esquissait un sourire fat :

— C'est le contact de la banquette de velours qui me fait bander...

Osiris scrutait la verge obscène, opalescente jusqu'au gland mauve.

— Osiris... Tu as le droit de sortir la tienne, tu n'as pas le droit de la toucher. Je n'ai pas envie d'autre chose pour le moment, tu me regardes, je te regarde.

Osiris dégagea son membre lourd et brun que le désir avait allongé sans le braquer.

— On ne peut pas dire qu'on se ressemble comme des frères ! dit Wolf.

Il bascula de nouveau, fit jouer l'avalanche de son dos, de ses reins jusqu'aux deux roues fessues, coupées de noir. Il remua et la chair bougeait. Osiris vit la douceur de sa pâte

immaculée, le frémissement de son grain dans le jour de Seine.

— Ton cul, c'est de la semoule... dit Osiris.

— Ne gâche pas tout avec des métaphores cocasses et culinaires ! Regarde ! Ces conneries te font déjà débander. Osiris, tu pends !

Osiris, beau joueur, émit un gloussement de rire.

— Si tu me permettais de la prendre et de la caresser doucement, en ta présence, la situation serait rétablie illico !

— Tu n'as pas le droit de mettre la main au bâton. Je veux le voir, je ne veux pas que la main cache son beau galbe brun...

Ce discours flatteur imprima un lent redressement au membre d'Osiris. Et Wolf, coquet, se retourna sur le flanc, s'offrit de face et exhiba son sexe dressé dans l'arceau de sa hanche.

— Moi, je peux me la prendre...

Wolf se branla lentement. Osiris darda avec force. Alors la porte du fond s'ouvrit. Wolf vit Ehra s'approcher.

— Ne te retourne pas, Osiris, c'est un commandement !... Te voici pris en tenaille entre moi et elle. J'espère que tu n'en mènes pas large ! Non ! Ne te retourne pas. Elle vole sur ses pieds nus, elle est presque contre toi. C'est ma sœur très sportive et très blanche. Osiris, ne débande pas si vite, tu es trop versatile. Il nous faut donc tout reprendre par le menu... Regarde-moi, oublie-la. Je me branle, nous sommes dans la péniche d'amour sur les eaux noires... Ehra, caresse-lui doucement les fesses, très doucement. Ne crains rien, Osiris, nous sommes tous frères et sœurs aujourd'hui. Tu es le mouton noir, notre frangin adultérin, notre frère des îles, notre oiseau des tropiques... Pelote-lui bien les globes, Ehra ! Il les arbore noirs et musclés. C'est de l'or et du rhum. Glisse-lui ton doigt très blanc... oui... desserre cet amas, ce

monceau de chair et de sangles. Ça n'est plus un cul c'est un boomerang. Et raconte-moi...

Ehra parla d'une voix basse et secrète, très douce :

— Mon frère bien-aimé, c'est vrai, ce grand Noir est pudique. Il ne s'entrouvre pas vite. Je ne puis forcer l'entrée de ses talus verrouillés par les muscles.

— En caressant très doucement... S'il pense que tu es ma sœur et que je suis ton frère, et que vraiment la scène me durcit jusqu'à la douleur, je crois qu'il devrait lâcher la bride et ouvrir le gousset.

— Ça y est ! Il m'engloutit le lobe d'un coup...

— Comment ça fait... ?

— C'est profond, cerclé d'anneaux veloutés et vicieux.

— Remue ton beau doigt blanc au tréfonds de sa trousse.

— C'est ce que je fais depuis un bon moment.

— En effet ! Je crois bien que ça relève son pilon... Il s'érige comme un arbre, il est bouffi d'orgueil. Il aime le doigt d'Ehra et l'œil de son frère posé sur sa queue. Est-il bien ouvert ?

— Luxueusement...

— Amène-le sur la banquette... Couche-toi sur le ventre, Osiris...

Et Wolf grimpa sur le dos d'Osiris et s'enfonça dans le fourreau préparé par sa sœur.

Ehra n'aimait pas ça. Elle connaissait le rituel. Mais cet épisode l'excluait. Elle réprouvait cette gloutonnerie de Wolf convulsé. Pourtant, elle lui flattait le dos à chaque saccade. Et par éclairs, il tournait vers elle son visage fervent. Il se dégagea, écarta Osiris. Il coucha Ehra sur le ventre à la place du mulâtre et la prit dans sa fente de fille, en lui empoignant les fesses à pleines mains, en faisant boursoufler leurs joues entre ses doigts.

— Osiris... tu peux te branler tant et plus... et même

t'emmancher un peu, juste le gland !... Pas plus... tu es trop gros !

Osiris s'agenouilla au-dessus de la grappe des corps, les fesses de Wolf s'immobilisèrent dans leur élan pour faciliter l'accrochage.

— Pas plus Osiris... Juste ce que je t'ai dit.

Osiris regardait les longues outres nerveuses des fesses de Wolf. Il ne pouvait déjà plus se retenir. Ces fesses remontaient vers lui dès que le frère reculait dans la sœur avant d'y replonger encore. Osiris se penchait tout à fait de côté, au cours de la chevauchée, pour tenter de voir le harpon de Wolf s'enfoncer dans le sexe, sous l'anus d'Ehra. Osiris voyait trop de luxuriances brunes. Il avança sa main et prit entre ses doigts, sans le serrer, le faucon de Wolf qui allait et venait dans le sexe de sa sœur... Il remercia dans son cœur Wolf et Ehra de lui donner tout ce paradis de plaisir. Il gémissait et, dans son chant, il entendait « obi et branlerie d'amour », le talisman des deux adolescents. Soudain, le corps de Wolf se raidit d'un seul tenant, son membre s'enfonça brutalement entre les cuisses d'Ehra et y resta fourré, agité de décharges et de sursauts. Wolf poussait des cris goinfres à pleins poumons comme un nageur qui plonge dans un bain glacé, s'ébroue, halète d'effroi et de bien-être. C'est ainsi que Wolf jouissait, à grand tapage bestial et sonore. Osiris en profita pour sombrer d'un coup entre les deux fesses blanches et se délester tout à trac en émettant une mélodie très douce.

Ehra sentit l'affalement des corps, le gong des cœurs, la sueur du frère et le musc du Noir agglutinés sur elle, bras mélangés. Ce fardeau frémissant et trempé, ce naufrage de muscles à l'abandon et de membres repus, ces têtes échevelées aux faces qui pendaient comme celles des suppliciés... le visage bleu de Wolf et celui d'Osiris tuméfié, congestionné de délices. Elle voyait leurs gorges renversées où les carotides

battaient entre les tendons, leurs prunelles vidées, hagardes, leurs dépouilles de Géricault. Et ce trop-plein de chamade, de chair sabordée, souillée sur le radeau de son corps, lui ouvrit tout à coup un grand trou, un rêve, un cri rauque. Son ventre se tordait, se bombait en avant, secouait l'amoncellement des corps fraternels et démantelés dont jaillissaient des relents d'aisselles, de fourches pubiennes, de bites, d'anus et de bourses remuées. Elle laissa de nouveau tout retomber et peser sur elle... Elle attendit, huma longuement, contempla les cheveux ruisselants, les goules médusées, les lèvres gonflées sur un murmure de volupté, les flancs moites et pantelants. Puis elle cria soudain et coula... Elle jouissait. Ils s'effondraient autour d'elle et leurs verges raides encore, panachées de sperme, battaient sa hanche et son ventre. La sœur les saisit dans son délire comme des rames d'amour.

Wolf et Osiris s'étaient assis sur la banquette en buvant de l'eau. Osiris avait passé le bras sur les épaules de Wolf. Cet enlacement fraternel apaisait Wolf. Ehra les regardait. Ils souriaient, complices, buvaient dans le même verre. Une encoche de colère la perça au cœur. Elle aurait enfoncé ses ongles dans l'œil unique de Wolf pour qu'il fût tout à elle. Osiris saisit ce regard acéré. L'effleura l'idée que le faucon de Wolf n'était autre que la griffe de sa sœur. Aussitôt il chassa le pressentiment et se rallia à l'hypothèse du rôdeur sadique, armé du couteau qui cloua l'œil bleu. L'imagination d'Osiris était intarissable dans la malice sensuelle, toutes les arborescences du désir. Mais dès qu'il s'agissait de violence criminelle, son esprit se fermait. Il était sans ressources pour la mort et ne pouvait soutenir longtemps cette scène où la sœur...

La porte était restée entrouverte. Anchise, le grand chien con, fut poussé par l'unique lubie de sa vie, la soudaine impulsion de sortir, de visiter le monde, loin de ses maîtres, Maurice et David. Quand un désir si vaste de liberté naît dans la cervelle d'un berger allemand dont on avait depuis longtemps oublié le naturel combatif, nul ne peut le contenir. Anchise le savait-il lui-même ? La truffe plongée dans la cage géante de l'escalier, il en inhalait le relent de moisi, de peinture écaillée, de poussière noire. Il reniflait aussi l'air du dehors monté par le porche du rez-de-chaussée qui bâillait sur la rue. Et cela faisait grand bruit sous son crâne de chien. Toutes les senteurs de la ville, toutes les fragrances de pisse, de macadam tatoué de merde, toutes les saloperies, toutes les ordures mêlées de Paris, portées à ses narines dans des bouffées. Le musc des rats dans les égouts, les caniveaux et les pigeons et les mémés mal torchées, tous les cabots et le dédale des boutiques, triperies, boucheries, effluves de sang, d'entrailles... Anchise en oubliait ses maîtres et son amour. Une envie océanique le submergeait, réveillait en lui ses instincts de bête. Il avança sur le palier, puis descendit l'escalier pour arriver à l'étage de Margot dont la porte, elle

aussi, était restée entrouverte, car la logeuse venait de descendre sa poubelle et elle n'était pas encore remontée.

Soudain, la chatte appâtée par la couardise d'Anchise, par son indolence habituelle, jaillit sur le palier, chuintante et griffes dehors. Elle ignorait la métamorphose du chien, ces grands courants de convoitise qui déferlaient en lui. L'odeur de la chatte s'interposa entre le museau d'Anchise et l'immensité. L'odeur lacéra la chair du chien comme un coup de dague. Il crut perdre le monde, sa promesse sauvage comme un fleuve. Et d'un coup, il bondit, tomba sur Toufflette, l'énorme gueule s'ouvrit, cassa les reins de l'ennemie dont le cri s'arrêta net dans les mâchoires du chien qui la secouait en grondant, lançait en l'air sa fourrure sanglante, la rattrapait, l'éventrait, en dévorait les tripes. Anchise lâcha prise et fila à toute vitesse, croisa Margot en bas de l'escalier qui hurla :

— Anchise ! Qu'est-ce qui te prend, reviens !

Margot n'avait pas vu le sang qui souillait le museau d'Anchise. Elle remonta avec sa poubelle vide jusqu'au palier où elle tomba sur la chose, ce qui restait de l'idole déboyautée. Elle hurla, les bras levés puis rabattus sur son visage, car l'infecte Toufflette était le tout de Margot, son amour de chaque jour. La vision de ce déchet rougi décocha dans le cerveau de Marguerite un flash, une rumeur... Elle vit le train véloce dans le tunnel de l'enfance. Elle sentit le relent de métro noir et chaud. Elle entendit son cri de ventre, son cri bestial quand la machine redémarrant l'emporta, ce hurlement d'entrailles et d'épouvante qui recommençait. Mais Toufflette n'émettait nul bruit. Haillon de pelage, sans tête et sans corps. Margot crut qu'elle allait mourir, car son cœur s'arrêta, un vertige l'aveugla. Elle tituba, tomba à genoux, puis bascula à même le palier, grelottante, les genoux repliés sur son ventre comme une enfant. C'est ainsi

218

qu'alertée par le hurlement Mlle Poulet trouva son amie. Elle la souleva, l'entraîna dans sa chambre, appela le médecin.

J'arrivais de la Sorbonne quand le médecin sortit après avoir administré une piqûre calmante. Margot sombrait dans une léthargie, un délire doux où elle murmurait des mots d'amour. Le médecin, avant de partir, conseilla qu'on se débarrasse au plus vite de la dépouille informe du chat. Il fallait éviter que Margot ne fasse enterrer la bête dans un cimetière spécial. Alors, elle ne ferait plus jamais son deuil de Toufflette et cela installerait le délire. David qui était arrivé sur ces entrefaites emporta les restes dans un sac. J'appris plus tard qu'il s'en trouva bien embarrassé. Il partit vers le quai et jeta la saloperie dans le fleuve. Puis il chercha Anchise. Mais du chien, nulle nouvelle. David était partagé entre la douleur d'avoir perdu la bonne bête, la meilleure de la nature, et l'étonnement devant sa conversion criminelle. Avant de sombrer, Margot avait dénoncé le chien. Elle l'avait vu passer. C'était lui ! De son côté, Mlle Poulet avait entendu un aboi court, un aboi fou.

Margot réclamerait la tête d'Anchise devenu féroce. David décida de donner le chien à un ami sûr dès qu'il le retrouverait. Car Anchise ne pouvait pas avoir changé vraiment. L'horrible Toufflette avait dû le provoquer, l'agresser comme d'habitude.

Quand Margot revint à elle, on eut droit à des lamentations extraordinaires. Sa douleur prit sur-le-champ un tour excessif, quasi littéraire, qui ne laissa pas de me surprendre. Je m'attendais plutôt à un accablement muet. Mais Margot réagit beaucoup mieux, si l'on peut dire, par un sursaut, un déchaînement de requiem lyrique. Elle chantait sa Toufflette adorée. Elle joignait les mains avec une mimique transie comme si la Vierge Marie lui était apparue. Mais c'est

Toufflette qu'elle priait, qu'elle revoyait dans leur intimité, leur complicité de chaque jour. Elle célébrait l'intelligence, la beauté de la chatte, de sa toison tigrée, la bonté de la chatte toujours présente, accourant dès que Margot rentrait du boulot, l'accueillant par une fanfare de miaulements allègres.

Mlle Poulet et moi assistions ébahis à ce débordement d'extase.

— Ça la soutient, me souffla la demoiselle, c'est comme la croyance, c'est ça ou la dépression. Elle a toujours eu une nature exaltée.

David revint. Margot le vit. Elle s'arrêta de délirer et lança :

— Anchise !

— Il a disparu.

— Anchise ! répéta Margot sur le même ton péremptoire et sans merci, elle ajouta : Alors, je vais moi-même me mettre à sa recherche et le tuer !

Elle réagissait de mieux en mieux, mêlant les genres, épique après son thrène, prête à bondir dans les rues, hache à la main. Margot, la manchote vengeresse.

Mais elle répéta d'une voix faible :

— Anchise...

Et l'on appréhenda une chute brutale dans la déprime. Heureusement le sédatif la submergea d'une nouvelle vague de somnolence. Margot bafouilla et s'endormit deux heures durant.

Nous attendions à son chevet, Mlle Poulet, David et moi, et je chuchotai à David :

— Vous n'êtes donc pas à la recherche d'Anchise ?

Il me répondit qu'en revenant de jeter Toufflette à la Seine, il avait vu le chien sur le quai, assis, penaud, assailli par les odeurs, les bruits du fleuve. David l'avait appelé et

Anchise s'était rendu, bon enfant, remuant la queue, si docile qu'on avait peine à croire qu'il avait commis un carnage. Aussitôt David avait porté le chien à Osiris qui avait promis de le remettre à des amis.

Quand Margot se réveilla, elle réclama encore la tête d'Anchise.

— Anchise !

David était parti et je lui dis qu'Anchise avait disparu, qu'un chien errant dans Paris était ramassé par la fourrière et exécuté dans l'heure.

— Où avez-vous été pêcher ce feuilleton ! me lança Margot courroucée. Ce sont les pédés qui se liguent pour sauver la Bête !

Jamais Margot n'avait insulté ainsi Maurice et David. Les deux hommes, bons bricoleurs, lui rendaient mille services. Et puis Margot, dans le domaine sexuel, était plutôt libérale, c'est sur le terrain politique qu'elle avait tendance à serrer la vis.

— Des pédés zoophiles, me dit-elle en hachant bien l'adjectif, en le faisant briller comme une obscène et diabolique joaillerie. Cet Anchise en était tout abruti, dégénéré, oui !

— Vous ne pouvez les accuser de ces horreurs...

— Vous ne connaissez pas la vie, vous !

Cette repartie m'atteignit et me parut profonde. C'était ore la question de la vie qui déboulait, intempestive et mystérieuse. En pleine crise. Je ne connaissais pas la vie. Je ne tenais pas tant que cela à la connaître. La vie, pour Margot, c'était la convulsion, le carnage, les deuils d'affilée, son bras, son mari, sa chatte. Et toujours dans des circonstances bien horribles. Elle vit que sa phrase m'avait mouché. Alors elle la reprit, plus calme, ouvrant un horizon de méditation.

— Vous ne connaissez pas la vie...

La vie, la vie... C'était trop vaste, tout à coup, et trop sombre. Margot la connaissait. Dressée sur son séant, elle la sondait, se souvenait de ses péripéties mémorables. Elle remâchait la chose, sa destinée, celle des autres. Et son coup d'œil n'augurait nulle féerie. Mais je sentais qu'elle reprenait tout de même de l'assurance à me surplomber ainsi de toute son expérience fatale. Je la voyais, oui, tendue et comme plus haut, plus loin que moi, sur une sorte d'invisible terrasse, enveloppée de ténèbres, où elle toisait la vie, la voyait bien en face et en même temps dans ses détails et ses coulisses où elle semblait enfoncer des regards longs et lucides. Elle était le Capitaine de la noirceur universelle... qui en respire l'exhalaison avec une gravité tranquille, presque froide. Elle n'était plus émue par les horreurs de la vie. Elle n'était pas résignée non plus. Elle était simplement au diapason du réel, de la vie réelle. Elle regardait cette vérité. C'était sans maquillage. Elle était digne soudain. Et presque belle et forte. Car elle ne trichait pas mais voyait les choses mêmes. Puis elle eut une reprise d'imperceptible cruauté :

— La vie, vous la connaîtrez, tout le monde un jour la connaît. On ne sait pas quand. Ce n'est pas forcément tôt dans le temps. On la connaît chacun dans des circonstances différentes. Mais un jour, on la connaît et on ne peut plus douter de son vrai visage. Elle vous regarde droit dans les yeux et on ne peut plus les baisser.

Je tentai de résister :

— Je la connais tout de même un peu... Je sais regarder autour de moi.

— C'est pas autour, c'est devant vous, c'est vous !

— Mais qui vous dit que...

— Vous n'avez ouvert que des livres, vous n'avez rencontré que des mots. Le jour où la vie viendra, tous vos livres

seront fermés. Ils ne serviront à rien. Ils seront chose morte. Votre littérature ne sauve que des gens en pleine forme...

Dans un ultime sursaut, bouleversé, je m'exclamai :

— J'aime Anny !

Elle marqua un court étonnement :

— Ça ne suffit pas... pas pour l'instant ! L'amour, c'est à la fin qu'il peut signifier quelque chose, pas au commencement, pas quand c'est tout neuf, adolescent, plein d'illusions !

Je vis tout de suite le coup que je pouvais porter :

— Qu'est-ce que vous en savez, vous, de l'amour ?!

— Oh ! Ne vous emballez pas !... C'est vrai... Je ne peux pas dire que j'aie été comblée en amour et que mon mari mort m'ait manqué...

— Alors ?

— Alors, j'ai une fille que je ne vois presque jamais, qui est partie très loin pour fuir ses origines. Il ne faut pas oublier ça, c'est très important ! Et j'ai des petits-enfants que je ne vois jamais non plus et dont je rêve, voilà...

Elle se tut puis, fatiguée, elle ajouta :

— Ma Toufflette est morte.

Et elle pleura. Elle perdit d'un coup sa démesure et sa beauté sévère. Elle pleurait comme une vieille et recommença de dégoiser des sornettes sur les vertus merveilleuses de Toufflette.

Ce qui sauva Margot de la dépression, ce fut de retrouver des photos de Toufflette. Elle avait même gardé la pellicule dont elle fit tirer des agrandissements. Un soir, je rentrais de la Sorbonne quand, à ma stupéfaction, j'aperçus dès l'entrée, sur les murs, puis partout dans l'appartement, un raz de marée de portraits de la chatte. C'était Margot, ce siège, ce

défi. Son triomphe. Toufflette morte ressuscitait en trente photographies que Margot saluait au passage, bénissait, inondait de louanges, comme si Toufflette au fond demeurait toujours là. La vie me sembla impossible dans l'atmosphère d'une telle obsession. La chatte sur les photos était remarquablement morne. Elle regardait, c'est tout. Avec son air un peu souffreteux et rentré et son œil que le flash faisait briller drôlement comme du verre, une matière privée d'âme. La fourrure, elle-même, était rapetissée, aplatie par la lumière... La chatte cernée d'un côté par l'ombre projetée et très noire semblait factice, vaguement dédoublée.

Un phénomène de tristesse étrange arrivait à Margot, de temps en temps. Cela se produisait toujours aux toilettes qu'une paroi séparait de ma chambre. Margot pleurait aux chiottes. L'endroit réveillait d'un coup toute sa douleur. Je l'entendais gémir. Je me demandais pourquoi donc la crise la prenait là. J'en parlai à Anny, puis à Neuzil, qui ne surent me répondre. Même Neuzil qui connaissait la vie aussi bien que Margot. C'est tout seul que je devais expliquer la chose. En lisant des bouquins qu'on pourrait qualifier de freudiens... Margot avait beau dire, les livres recelaient aussi de vastes pans de connaissance profonde sur la vie. Comment m'y prendre... Bon ! Margot pleurait aux chiottes, parce qu'elle y faisait l'expérience d'une solitude et d'une rupture. Elle se séparait de ce qui la lestait. Et cette défécation réveillait en elle des idées d'abandon presque infantile. Le sentiment de deuil pouvait, oui, se loger là, à l'origine, dans ces cabinets minuscules et verrouillés. Margot était soudain submergée de mélancolie. Elle se vidait, perdait son objet, tirait la chasse d'eau et ce rituel était triste. Telle fut ma conclusion extraite de la seule force de mes lectures et de ma réflexion. C'est ainsi que je pris, moi, le dessus ! Si j'avais tenté d'expliquer le mécanisme à Margot, elle m'aurait, à coup sûr, qualifié de

vrai dingue. Je comprenais donc une chose de la vie qui échappait complètement à Margot, sur sa vie à elle pourtant ! Une chose subtile, retorse et secrète. Une vérité enfouie, peu accessible. Donc Margot ne connaissait pas toute la vie, elle avait vécu mais elle n'en avait pas maîtrisé toutes les significations et les échos imprévus. Tandis que moi, inexpérimenté, encore très jeune, j'avais fini par deviner le sens des pleurs dans les W.-C., la mélancolie des sanglots de Margot, de ses larmes sur toute perte et sur le vide d'amour. Les chiottes, c'était la cérémonie de l'adieu !

Souvent, je rendais visite à Neuzil qui remarchait un petit peu dans l'enceinte de sa chambre. Lui ne gémissait pas sur le vol du dessin et sur la perte de son orteil. Quand j'y repense, vingt ans après, l'angoisse m'envahit. Je la retrouve bien sauvage et bien noire. Il y avait dans cette baraque de la rue Pavée une concentration anormale de malheurs dont je n'avais pas encore saisi les dessous extrêmes. Je revois Marguerite et Neuzil comme les héros d'une épopée roturière et cachée. La sorcière et le saint. J'ai tort pour le premier qualificatif, même si Margot me sembla souvent maléfique, dans des espèces de flashes... Mais sur cette intuition effrayante, aussitôt un couvercle se rabattait. Margot ne montrait plus alors que sa vitalité, son fond de gaieté pugnace. Quant à la sainteté de Neuzil, elle fut la grande aventure de ce temps-là. Elle se relie étroitement à mon amour pour Anny, quoique je ne sache pas encore par quel jalon profond. Je ne cherche pas forcément à tout savoir. Mais je recevais de Neuzil un effet de lumière et de rayonnement. A moins que ce ne fût le contraire et que la source de cette sainteté s'enracinât dans mon amour d'Anny

et s'élargît vers le vieillard comme sur un personnage paternel et divin. Aller et retour miraculeux... Je ne dois pas oublier la cathédrale, Notre-Dame-des-Anges-et-des-Faucons. Car dans l'amour se reflètent et s'entrechoquent nos figures secrètes. Je n'épuiserai jamais ce théâtre invisible où se ramifient, autour d'Anny et de moi-même, la Madone, le Saint, les faucons, sans oublier Egon et Gerti Schiele étreints et nus. Il y a ce flot de lumière sur le fleuve et dans le ciel de la cathédrale. Ce serait l'origine... Surgissent les faucons de feu. Le vieillard Neuzil passe devant Notre-Dame, s'arrête et la contemple. Anny et moi le savons. Puis Egon et Gerti combinent leurs corps voraces et sensuels sur quelque frise ou tympan des porches. Phallus et fente dans une fringale solaire. Les tours s'élèvent au-dessus de la rosace des corps. La tour sud entièrement recouverte de noms et de signes, et l'autre tour vierge et nue, toute dévouée au nord, à la sœur. Je peux varier les angles, retourner les perspectives, les permuter en divers sens. Toujours une lumière belle et blanche baigne la cathédrale du fleuve. Les faucons tournent dans le ciel calme. Margot est nichée dans son trou, allègre et funèbre. Anny et moi, nous nous embrassons, au sommet de la tour, dans la constellation des noms de l'amour.

Je fréquentais toujours le restaurant des malades. J'étais attiré depuis quelques jours par un nouveau couple. Un jeune barbu oriental, de la même souche que ses confrères si vaillants et si actifs, était accompagné d'une jeune fille très pâle et voilée. Elle, pour de bon, semblait fragile et introduisait dans cette société de mâles, d'escrocs, de comploteurs, une vision tendre. Le voile surtout me subjuguait. Je m'arrangeais pour m'installer non loin du couple. Un

midi, je fus en face d'elle. Le type à côté de moi ne pouvait pas m'observer sans tourner la tête et m'alerter. Moi, je buvais des yeux la jeune fille farouche. Elle eut un bref regard sur moi qui me parut brillant et noir dans la blancheur de la cornée. J'admirais les arcs de ses paupières comme de minuscules bols renversés. Le front était lisse. Les lèvres pleines. Les oreilles délicates jusqu'à la translucidité. On ne devinait rien de son corps planqué dans une longue robe droite, couleur marron, qui partait du cou et se boutonnait devant comme une soutane de curé. Elle devait, là-dessous, être longue, avec des seins assez gros et des fesses charnues. J'eus l'intuition de sa beauté. Affluaient dans ma tête des idées indiscrètes et précises. En coups de sonde vifs... On disait qu'elles étaient épilées. Où avais-je lu cela ? Était-ce une légende ? J'aurais adoré regarder, caresser et lécher le sexe imberbe et modelé de la jeune captive... quoiqu'elle parût consentante et soudée à son type qui avalait une grosse pâtée de hachis Parmentier. Elle boudait un peu le hachis. Je m'intéressai à sa façon d'absorber l'aliment. Elle prenait la purée en petites portions, par les bords. Décalotté de son tégument gratiné, le hachis fumait. Elle observait cette brutale effusion de vapeur. Puis elle picorait des grains de viande à l'intérieur du cratère ardent. Elle s'amusait plus qu'elle ne mangeait. Elle recommençait l'opération ailleurs, soulevait une croûte et libérait la fumée. Mais elle cachait ce jeu dont l'aspect enfantin ne devait pas lui sembler très convenable. Elle portait la purée à sa bouche qui s'ouvrait sur des dents nettes et nacrées. Je voyais le bout de la langue.

Soudain, mon espionnite la gêna. Elle ouvrit moins les lèvres pour ingérer des bribes de nourriture plus minuscules encore. Un appétit d'oiseau... la formule jaillit dans mon esprit et m'excita sans que je sache bien pourquoi. Quel oiseau ? Colombe muette sous le voile ou rossignol prompt à

s'égosiller dans un chant d'amour... Son type la prenait-il avec des formes ou d'un coup ? Il avait l'air d'un pillard autoritaire et glouton. Il devait baiser comme il bouffait. Elle était nue pour lui. J'imaginais le sortilège. Sans doute eût-elle aimé qu'on la prît par préludes et par les bords comme elle-même effrangeait sa nourriture, allumait des alvéoles de feu dans les falaises du hachis. Savait-elle seulement qu'on pouvait procéder ainsi en amour ? Avec qui en eût-elle parlé ? J'aurais voulu qu'elle se masturbe sans le dire à son maître. En jouissant de toutes ses aises, dans des manœuvres lentes et subtiles. Les yeux fermés, longs cils, paupières totalement bloquées sur leur courbure d'ivoire. Oui, elle se délectait, bien au-dedans, à volets fermés. Sous le voile... belle et branlée. Elle était devant moi, toute sa vie dont je ne savais rien... C'est ainsi qu'on devient romancier, aimanté par le mystère des portes closes, happé par un désir infini de voir, de connaître... Seize, dix-sept ans, oui, très jeune... d'une apparence froide et lisse. Tant elle avait appris à dérober ses pensées ou ses braises. Je ne pouvais tout de même pas lui faire du pied. Ce n'était pas le genre d'audace dont j'étais capable. Elle eût ôté le pied vite fait, en immobilisant sa bouchée, au seuil de ses lèvres, sans me regarder, tout se passant sous l'auvent, à huis clos...

Il fallait que j'attire son attention. C'était le moment, l'autre était lancé dans une discussion avec son voisin. On sentait que c'était politique et convaincu. Je vis soudain le pichet de lait. Son verre était vide. Avec un peu de chance, elle allait allonger le bras et se servir. A ce moment-là, il me faudrait agir de même. J'attendis quelques minutes et le prodige eut lieu. La colombe avait soif, elle étendit la main, la mienne décolla, furtive, au ras de la nappe et sur l'anse nos doigts se touchèrent. D'un geste sec, elle retira sa main. Elle ne put s'empêcher de me jeter un regard. Sans rien dire, je lui

fis signe que je la priais de m'excuser de ce contact inopiné, un peu comme deux personnes qui se bousculent en se croisant sur un trottoir. Je lui souris, infusant dans ma mimique le maximum de courtoisie, de gentillesse mais de grâce aussi, de séduction pudique et voilée. Un très léger sourire affleura sur ses traits, un sourire si secret qu'il éclaira un tout petit peu sa face sans étirer ses lèvres. L'ennui, c'est que personne n'avait pris le pichet. Je voulus lui signifier de se servir sans peur et que cette fois ma chair n'attenterait pas à la sienne. Mais comment faire? Elle ne me regardait pas. C'est à cet instant que l'autre attrapa la cruche et se remplit un verre. Il pensa distraitement à sa compagne tout en continuant de discuter, elle tendit son verre et il versa une rasade de lait écumant sans faire gaffe, en débordant. Une flaque trempa la nappe. Le type n'y prêta nulle attention et poursuivit sa conversation. Mais le verre de la jeune fille était si plein qu'elle ne pouvait pas le lever vers sa bouche sans provoquer un indécent déluge. Alors, elle me coula un mince coup d'œil. J'eus l'instinct d'esquiver ce regard, de faire comme si je n'avais rien vu. Elle se décida donc à baisser les lèvres en direction du verre. Je la dévorai des yeux. Elle ne pouvait plus relever les siens vers moi. Elle pompa le lait par gorgées agiles, acrobatiques, en avançant les fronces de sa bouche, comme on le fait avec un liquide trop chaud. Elle était exquise. Elle se redressa et me vit tout entier carré, planté dans ma contemplation. Elle rougit. Des gouttes de lait souillaient ses lèvres qu'elle essuya. Mais une bavure restait comme une salive blanche accrochée au menton. Elle n'en n'avait pas encore senti l'humidité. Elle eut un autre regard en coulisse, je lui fis signe d'essuyer son menton en mimant le geste de ma main. Rapide, elle obéit.

... Cela se corsait, tout un feuilleton sentimental ou presque. Stendhal... Certaines épopées du désir ne préludent

guère sur des prémices plus lourdes. On trouvera que depuis un moment je socratise un peu les libellules, mais l'aventure fut vécue avec intensité. Il me semblait que de proche en proche, pour peu que le repas se prolonge, que le type bavarde encore et encore, que le dessert arrive... que l'après-midi s'achève, que le crépuscule tombe, que nous soyons obligés les uns et les autres, pour des raisons exceptionnelles, cyclone, émeute, attaque aérienne intempestive — ces choses-là finissent toujours par arriver... nos pères les ont vécues jusqu'à l'enfer —, que nous soyons acculés donc à la nécessité de bivouaquer dans le resto... Et voilà comment on se retrouve alignés en rangs d'oignons sur des matelas de fortune ! Certes, le type serait plus vigilant, mais la situation brouillonne mêlerait les hiérarchies, fléchirait les convenances et les pudeurs.

... Le type serait couché d'un côté de la jeune fille et moi, par hasard, dans le désarroi général, justement de l'autre côté... bon, c'est l'histoire de Perrette et du pot au lait que je vous narre. On commence par un verre, des doigts effleurés, des œillades interdites, des annulaires nomades... J'aurais l'avantage de ma capacité d'insomnie de poète. Le mec, au bout d'un temps, sombrerait dans un sommeil de bête, de militant, d'homme d'action, de poseur de bombes qui récupère sur le tas. La saga commencerait pour de bon... ma progression de renard sous la lune... oui, seulement la toucher là, imberbe, donc parfaitement nue, exhibée dans sa plus fine nervure, aux lèvres tendres... Hélas, nulle guerre en vue, nul tremblement de terre, nul coup d'État contre Pompidou... En vain rêvais-je d'un putsch, d'un couvre-feu, c'est le cas de le dire. Le couple se leva. Je la vis en pied, taille haute pour une Orientale, un mètre soixante-sept ou huit, séquences de dunes absolument vierges piquetées d'oasis, puits du désert, aiguille d'eaux vives. A force de fixer

sa robe informe, je crus deviner un invisible remous que confirma une glissade providentielle sur le sol gras du resto. Elle perdit l'équilibre, se courba d'un coup, la robe plaquée sur la rondeur brusque de sa croupe. Elle avait un cul, oui, d'une opulence adolescente encore, mais bien amorcée dans son argile. Le beau me tue, me cloue... En sortant, elle dut se retourner pour rabattre la porte. Elle me regarda. Je lui souris franchement. Et le même sourire que tout à l'heure l'embua à son tour d'un rayonnement qui me parut plus chaud, plus intime, plus dédié, plus volubile, pourtant je n'avais bu que du lait... Et cela fumait de son corps dont j'avais saisi la maturité promise, la sève, la palmeraie, l'ombre duvetée.

Avais-je trompé Anny par la pensée ? Était-ce l'annonce d'un engrenage qui mettrait des années à se déployer mais qui naissait, là, dans la perception pure, l'éblouissement des yeux ? Avais-je des regrets, des scrupules ? Me posais-je ces questions ? Je crois que j'avançais sur plusieurs chemins à la fois. La vie devant moi, Anny, et ces contre-allées voilées, fourmillantes... inconnues. Marguerite avait raison. J'ignorais la vie innombrable. La fille avec son voile n'avait suggéré que l'infini de ces contrées que je ne pouvais pas voir encore.

En rentrant justement chez Margot, j'appris la vérité sur le mal dont se plaignait le mari de la concierge. Marguerite n'en revenait pas de l'incroyable explication :

— C'est que la concierge ménopausée depuis des mois souffrait d'une sécheresse de muqueuse très douloureuse.

Je redoutais le pire, l'expérience de Margot, ses détails dans le vif du sujet, bien terre à terre, encaisse et médite, mon étudiant !

— Alors... le médecin lui a prescrit une pommade aux hormones, un produit qui réactive la féminité si vous voulez, qui remet la machine en route, enfin qui l'entretient... Mais l'autre, le mari, l'idiot, obsédé comme il était, ne cessait de faire l'amour et, du même coup, il s'imprégnait des hormones lui aussi. C'est ainsi qu'à la longue il perdit ses poils et sa force. Quand il ne pouvait plus du tout, que, déprimé, il n'essayait même plus pendant longtemps, sa puissance évidemment lui revenait. Et hop! il recommençait, loustic, mais ne faisait que réveiller le mal en absorbant le poison, il redégringolait donc et ainsi de suite. N'était-ce pas un cercle infernal? C'est à Mlle Poulet qu'elle a raconté cette histoire d'hormones. Mon petit Poulet m'a tout répété... ça l'épate, elle, la vierge, ces péripéties, ce dard tout en dos d'âne...

Margot se tut, puis tout à coup :

— Vous savez, l'autre jour, je vous ai dit que je n'avais pas eu d'amour, d'aventure d'amour avec mon mari que l'on m'avait fourré comme ça et que j'avais accepté sans chipoter à cause de ma... — du menton, elle montra sa prothèse. Mais j'ai tout de même eu ensuite un amant, véritable et choisi de mon gré !

Marguerite allait m'avouer peut-être une grande histoire d'amour. Mais je me demandais pourquoi elle s'était tue si longtemps sur des événements si doux. De fil en aiguille, elle me tissa son idylle. Cela commençait par un coup de foudre, une attirance physique comme elle disait. Elle avait la cinquantaine et lui soixante. Bel homme. Un comptable. Mais les choses se gâtaient peu à peu ou plutôt ne démarraient jamais pour de bon. Elle m'avoua d'abord que le type avait un défaut, il était pingre. Sa bagnole était démodée, il ne la changeait pas par économie et la lavait lui-même, le dimanche, à grandes eaux sur le trottoir pendant des heures. « C'est un peu agaçant, même quand le grand amour vous

aveugle. » Ils partaient en vacances une semaine. Ils pique-niquaient plutôt que d'aller au restaurant, toujours pour éviter le gaspillage. Margot eût raffolé d'un tête-à-tête romantique dans un joli resto à chandelles. Parfois même — et décidément la chronique empirait —, il s'arrangeait pour éviter l'hôtel et dormir dans la bagnole, sièges rabattus. « J'étais amoureuse mais, petit à petit, cela portait une ombre sur notre lune de miel. »

Puis Marguerite hésita... Je me demandai ce qui pouvait détériorer davantage la seule histoire d'amour de Margot.

— C'est gênant à dire, mais le mari de la concierge m'y fait penser, l'ennui, donc, avec Marcel, c'est qu'il ne pouvait plus beaucoup... Il essayait, mais on ne peut pas dire qu'il excellait, qu'il faisait ça bien longtemps. Il durait même très peu, voire pas du tout... Il était avare de tout, en sorte. Alors mon amour est devenu amer. Et puis on s'est brouillés, on s'est disputés et je lui ai lancé qu'il n'avait qu'à bander ! Mais voyez-vous, il aurait pu se venger, être cruel, m'imputer la chose. Eh bien non ? Il s'est tu, il n'a rien dit, n'a pas ironisé. C'est le meilleur souvenir que j'aie de lui. Il me disait aussi que j'avais de belles cuisses. Il me les caressait, remontait la main doucement. Alors, vous comprenez, je ne suis pas de pierre, mais il en restait là, c'était la nuit, dans sa bagnole, dans des zones un peu désolées, à la sortie des villages, au bord des bois, vers la Loire, on n'allait guère plus loin. J'aurais aimé une auberge et qu'il me fasse tout et longtemps, comme font les amants, passionnément. Mais je l'ai aimé pendant plusieurs mois. Il était cultivé. Il était abonné à *Historia*. C'était un spécialiste de Napoléon ! Il était savant jusqu'au bout des ongles. J'ai beaucoup appris avec lui. Mais ça ne suffisait pas, les dates, les victoires, la famille impériale, Joseph, Pauline et Laetitia : « Pourvou que ça doure... » avec l'accent corse ! Puis la déconfiture, la Bérézina. C'est peut-

être pour cette fin que Napoléon lui plaisait, la débandade, à dire vrai... Waterloo, Waterloo, morne plaine... me répétait-il avec insistance, mélancolique soudain. Je recevais bien le message, mais c'était tout de même dommage, pour une fois que j'avais un amant.

C'était *L'Amant* de Marguerite... la version pauvre, *Assommoir* et dérisoire, le contraire de l'Autre, la Grande, que je devais rencontrer beaucoup plus tard, vingt ans après, une longue virée le long de la Seine à partir de Trouville, des Roches Noires. Margot, la célèbre, avait eu des amants de haute volée, des résistants pendant la guerre, des littéraires, elle en avait même chipé un à Simone de Beauvoir, un soir de Noël, comme elle me l'avoua, malicieuse. Elle détestait Beauvoir : « Chez elle, tout traînait... les serviettes sales... Quel manque d'élégance ! Comment avoir une écriture, après ça ! » Tel quel !... Marguerite avait des rancœurs de Cosette devenue reine...

J'ai eu affaire à moult Marguerite... La première, ce fut ma grand-mère paternelle, une personne énorme, obscène et démoniaque. Un ouragan. Elle engueulait la terre entière et tout petit me fredonnait des chansons lubriques... Elle aimait le mal avec une spontanéité candide et radieuse. La seconde Marguerite fut la meilleure amie de ma jeune sœur. Quinze ans, belle, grande, brune, typée, longs cheveux de sauvageonne, artiste et trouble. Une nuit — j'avais quatorze ans —, je vis son derrière nu en rêve. Somptueux et secret. Beau, brun, comme allumé de l'intérieur, animal, humain, planétaire. Une sorte de prémonition donc, d'augure sur toute ma vie, mes enchantements lyriques. Je lui avouai ce rêve bien des années plus tard quand elle devint sculpteur et obtint le prix Bourdelle. Aujourd'hui, à cinquante ans, elle vit avec un vieil aristocrate nonagénaire sur le rempart de mon village. Elle fut toujours originale.

La troisième, ce fut Margot la manchote et son manque d'amants, mon héroïne, ma logeuse. Et la quatrième, Margot majeure, Margot-Mékong, la reine, la Chinoise, la romancière, pilotée en 605 Peugeot par son amant jeune, intelligent et beau. Elle me montra l'estuaire de Seine et lança : « La mer est lasse, c'est la fin de la terre »...

C'est pour l'excès que je l'aime, pour ses outrances au débotté et ses oukases grandioses. Je lui déclarai ma passion, tout carrément au téléphone quand elle m'appela, la première fois, à propos d'un bouquin. « Vous êtes ma Vraie, ma Toute, ma grande Chouchoute ! Je prends tout, je ne chipote pas, moi, car vous êtes un style ! » Elle fut quand même estomaquée, Margot d'Hiroshima, par ma tirade de Normand saoul. Enfin, une autre fois, vers minuit — elle téléphonait très tard : « L'écriture c'est une fatalité, n'est-ce pas ? » Réveillé entre deux hypnotiques, interloqué, je balbutiai : « Oui, bien sûr... » sans piger sur le coup. J'ai compris le lendemain. Elle voulait dire seulement qu'on ne choisissait pas, qu'on n'y était pour rien et voilà tout. Modeste en plus !

Mes quatre Marguerite furent toutes des filles démesurées, un colossal quatuor. Je vous chante, Margots de choc et d'estoc... Margot ma grand-mère immense et orgiaque qui sentait la suie et pissait debout sans culotte à même la terre sous un grand cerisier écarlate. Et Margot, l'adolescente fessue, féline qui m'imprima en songe sa marque, son mirage et son musc. Puis Margot de mes vingt ans, Éros et Thanatos, à la porte de la vie, terrible et gaie, ma logeuse miraculeuse et mortelle... Et toi, Margot la Pythie, Margot majeure, de la Manche et du Mékong !... J'ai effeuillé tous vos pétales à la folie. Amen et adieu mes belles ! Voici ma stèle. Votre pollen m'illumine.

Je revis la beauté au jardin du Luxembourg... Soudain, là, devant moi, au bord des tennis. La jeune Juive inclinait son visage sur un livre. Elle n'était plus revenue suivre des cours dans l'école que j'apercevais de ma chambre. Je pensais qu'elle était perdue pour toujours, partie dans un autre quartier, une autre ville. Et puis là, intacte, précise et calme. Elle lit *Madame Bovary*. La lumière est limpide... De temps en temps, elle relève la tête et sourit à une amie qui joue sur le court d'en face. Les balles claquent avec leur bruit mol et talqué ou sec dans la volée. Comme rassurée, l'adolescente replonge dans son roman. La scène me fascine. Je l'adore. Je voudrais avoir écrit le livre qu'elle lit et qu'elle préfère à son amie, au tennis, au jardin qu'elle ne contemple pas. Elle est prise dans la beauté des phrases. Elle regarde Flaubert. Elle est attentive comme mes élèves préférées, plus tard. Complice du livre. Tout intérieure, dans le halo du livre. Sur son île. Je la regarde longtemps de biais. Je suis superstitieux. Je ne veux pas qu'elle me voie. J'ai peur de la troubler, de la décevoir, qu'elle perde le fil du livre et qu'elle n'ose pas me regarder, me sourire. Je m'en vais. Je reviendrai.

Le soir, Neuzil et moi, avons parlé de la beauté. Et lui qui s'était interrogé déjà sur le sentiment d'éternité dans la jouissance, aborda une nouvelle question, du même genre, une évidence qui, pour lui, n'en était pas une justement, mais ne laissait pas de l'étonner :

— Pourquoi la beauté nous fait bander ? Enfin je parle de l'homme en général. Pour moi, c'est terminé. Je n'ai pas besoin de vous le préciser. Hein ! Pourquoi ? Les animaux ne bandent pas pour la beauté. Ils accomplissent le coït avec des partenaires choisis sur des critères biologiques. Mais nous, il faut qu'il soit beau, qu'elle soit belle, ou qu'on les trouve tels... En tout cas, le mieux, c'est de bander pour une très belle. Mais il n'y a rien en soi de bandant dans la beauté... Voyez-vous l'énigme ? On devrait désirer un musc, un sexe de femme, je ne sais pas... La chair sans distinction. Et l'esthétisme vient affiner le jeu. Certes, on devrait reconnaître la beauté, la célébrer, l'admirer pour des raisons d'harmonie, sans doute, mais de là à bander, à désirer physiquement une forme qui est d'un ordre culturel, spirituel, comment ça nous est venu ? Le sens esthétique, bon, petit à petit, autour des idées d'équilibre, de rythme, peut naître sans doute. Mais l'érection pour la beauté ? Cette envie de baiser la beauté et de la féconder par-dessus le marché !

Neuzil était irrésistible quand il traquait les fameuses évidences. Il reprit :

— Soyons clairs, un sexe est un sexe. Il n'y a pas de différence intérieure. Il suffit de fermer les yeux. Que voit-on d'ailleurs au plus fort du désir et du coït ?... Mais nous bandons pour la beauté, pour des variétés d'enveloppe. Pourtant, c'est bien le sexe que nous pénétrons... ou bien avons-nous l'illusion de pénétrer la beauté et en quoi est-ce

bandant ? Ça l'est, je sais bien ! Mais pourquoi entrer charnellement dans la beauté est bandant ?

— Parce que c'est la chair, c'est charnel et profond justement...

— Mais non... La beauté n'est pas la chair, c'est la forme qui l'organise et la cisèle qui fait la beauté. Nous bandons pour une forme, alors que nous devrions bander pour la chair, le sexe, pour la matière, le substantiel, le fond en somme ! Nous bandons pour des lignes ! C'est de la décadence par rapport aux bêtes !

— Ou un progrès justement, une élévation !

— Je parlais de décadence de l'instinct purement viril... L'homme a d'abord bandé en vertu de facteurs sexuels, hormonaux, génétiques, puis il s'est mis à sélectionner, à quintessencier, à bander pour des symboles ! C'est le mot que je cherchais ! On baise avec un symbole ! C'est un peu fort, ça finira comment ? Si ça continue, telle ou telle représentation du beau, peu à peu dépouillée de son fond charnel, nous fera éjaculer, ce serait le bouquet ! Éjaculer pour une belle idée mathématique, vous voyez le genre, pour un soleil couchant et encore... je suis optimiste ! Pour une phrase trop belle... pour un style ? Pour un meuble design ! Un carré monochrome et minimaliste ! Il n'y a plus de limites. On finira par ne plus pouvoir se reproduire. Il n'y aura plus de déclic pour le corps à corps organique et grossier. La beauté et ses avatars vont nous entraîner si loin de nos bases.

L'originalité de Neuzil ne resplendissait jamais si bien que dans ses élucubrations où il ne répugnait pas au langage cru. C'est parce qu'il se posait ces questions avec intensité et naturel que Neuzil était angélique et lucide. Et puis il était drôle. Il s'échauffait, tout chiffonné par ses énigmes. Il cherchait une porte, une solution. Bander pour la beauté, et ce sentiment d'éternité quand on jouit, ces deux faits

devaient se rejoindre et fournir la grande explication totale !

Neuzil se calmait tout à coup. Il redevenait le vieillard serein, puis lassé. Les questions l'abandonnaient. Il n'avait plus d'étonnement. Je savais que la gangrène avait repris, lente et têtue... Elle remontait.

— Il faudra lui amputer tout le pied, me dit Margot. J'ai connu un cas comme lui !

Et Marguerite me faisait tomber de l'extase du Beau, très bas dans l'horreur.

Plusieurs mois ont passé depuis la nuit où Wolf perdit son œil. Mais cette nuit-là nous hantait tous, Anny, moi, Osiris, David et Maurice... Wolf la raconta à Osiris. Plusieurs fois. Avec des variantes, des lacunes ou des rajouts. Osiris à son tour nous confia des fragments de la nuit de Wolf... Je pouvais à présent la revivre point par point. Je la voyais...

La cathédrale régnait dans la lumière égale des spots. Grand objet orangé. Mais, dans le jardin de l'Archevêché et ses prolongements, des nappes d'ombre existaient sous les arbres. La lumière se plaquait sur l'éventail des arcs-boutants comme sur les pattes d'un crustacé géant et détaillé. Wolf rôdait. Il s'arrêtait, jetait un regard circulaire. Les jeunes types vagabondaient comme lui. C'était la ronde autour de la Mère, sur l'île, tout près du fleuve noir. Wolf adorait cette région sacrée. Les bancs propices aux baisers, les plates-bandes désertées par les promeneurs du jour. On pouvait escalader les grilles et passer dans le jardin de l'Archevêché, son aire étroite et longue, au flanc de Notre-Dame... Ou bien sa balade le conduisait là-bas vers la poupe du vaisseau de l'île, vers les ponts, vers les quais, un autre pont, des quais plus larges, plus désertés... C'était une autre ville du soir, un

autre espace plus sombre qu'il connaissait d'instinct, un labyrinthe qui l'aimantait parfois jusqu'à l'aurore... Quand soudain la cathédrale s'éteignait et que les premiers ors du soleil prenaient le relais des spots, affirmaient la vraie magie cosmique... La cathédrale émergeait, cernée d'un bain de brume rougie, les rais du soleil dardaient sur son échine, sur ses vertèbres, sur son coccyx de pierre... Chaque gargouille, chaque vitrail, chaque pinacle semblait poindre entre ombre et lumière, avec une densité, un poids, un mystère. C'était là le moment vrai de Notre-Dame. Montagne bombée de substance, taillée, sculptée par la foi des hommes anciens.

Cette nuit-là, Wolf n'avait pas encore assisté à la renaissance aurorale de Notre-Dame. Mais il se promettait de rester jusqu'au matin... Sa chasse n'aboutissait à rien pour le moment. Les proies qu'il croisait le laissaient un peu indifférent. Il préférait flâner, flairer, se dérober et susciter des pôles de désir dont il se détachait. Il rejoignit le point le plus noir du jardin pour s'y enfouir, y respirer l'odeur d'automne sous les arbres. Wolf sentit un glissement derrière lui. Il ne craignait rien. Il se garda de se retourner. Il laissa venir le chasseur ou la proie. Il joua à attendre jusqu'au dernier instant. Il se dit que l'autre reculerait, découragé par sa silhouette raide, son autonomie presque menaçante. Puis Wolf n'entendit plus rien. Et ce silence l'émut. Car l'autre était là. Il le sentait sans le voir ni l'entendre. L'autre devait attendre, mesurer à distance ses intentions, sa volonté d'être seul encore... Puis Wolf perçut un bond léger... un bruit souple, animal, dont le rythme l'enchanta. Il ne se retourna pas. Il ne voulait pas voir pour préserver le rêve intact. Wolf entendit alors un bruissement un peu au-dessus de lui. Il fut surpris par l'axe, la hauteur insolite du froissement, comme si l'autre avait volé vers lui. Wolf fut envahi d'une joie paradisiaque. Il se retourna. Dans la même fulguration, la

brûlure l'atteignit aux yeux et il entendit ce bruissement déployé d'ailes ou de chevelure. Un parfum fugitif l'effleura. Wolf éprouva dans son cœur une perte démesurée. Et la douleur physique s'enfla, exista avec un relief féroce. Wolf porta ses mains à son œil bleu. Il sentit le sang affluer sans le voir. Et ce sang invisible était horrible. Wolf courut dans le jardin d'amour, les paumes contre son œil dont la vie avait fui... Il appela. On vint. Il dit qu'il avait perdu son œil bleu. Et cette phrase hanta toujours l'adolescent qui la reçut, prit Wolf par la main et l'entraîna hors du jardin.

On sait que, plus tard, Wolf racontera qu'un faucon avait fondu sur lui pour lui crever l'œil bleu. Il se souvenait du bruissement merveilleux d'ailes ou de cheveux et de l'effluve plus suave encore d'oiseau ou de sœur... Le coup fut porté. Le bec ou le couteau entaillèrent l'iris et tuèrent l'azur de Wolf.

Il ne sut jamais s'il s'agissait d'ailes, de cheveux, de quelle odeur perdue... Sa douleur fut immense et morale, bien avant ce feu de brûlure coupante qui s'acéra, puis gonfla, térébrante jusqu'au cerveau, comblant le manque sans fond où Wolf avait perdu le monde.

Les jours suivants il posséda la douleur et fut moins seul. La douleur apaisée par les calmants le berça comme une sœur. Et sa convalescence dura longtemps dans la péniche, sur le bruissement des eaux. Ehra était là.

Je suis retourné plusieurs fois dans le jardin du Luxembourg, avec l'envie de la revoir. Et bientôt mon espoir fut exaucé. Mais la jeune Juive n'était plus assise sur le banc pour lire. Sa mère l'avait remplacée à la même place, toujours belle, opulente, chevelure noire, tandis que l'adolescente

jouait sur le court de tennis. La mère ne lisait pas. Elle contemplait sa fille avec un sourire légèrement étonné, baigné d'une bienveillance où perçait un peu de tristesse. La mère semblait partagée entre ses sentiments. Elle stabilisait sur son visage la tendresse et l'amour, mais la beauté de sa fille, comme révélée d'un coup, lui causait une blessure diffuse sur laquelle l'amour aussitôt versait comme une nouvelle couche. La mère se tenait, genoux serrés sur le banc, le torse dressé en avant, courageuse, érigée vers sa fille, le visage tendu.

Et l'adolescente courait sur la terre rouge. Tout ce rouge fumait dans le vent, contre ses longues jambes nues. Quand elle démarrait, stoppait net, des traces plus claires s'ouvraient dans le rouge. Son visage débordait de vigilance et de joie conquérante. Elle fonçait sur les balles comme sur un fruit. Son bras s'allongeait, elle frappait la pomme du désir et la raquette obéissait à la jeune fille, rendait un bruit claquant et rond à chaque coup. La jeune fille adorait ce bruit rond. Elle le centrait, le renvoyait à sa comparse qui s'entendait à le lui restituer intact. La balle, les raquettes étaient les outils, et le bruit l'effet, la plénitude de leur bonheur. Les jambes de la jeune Juive étaient plus formées, modelées que je ne l'aurais imaginé, les cuisses étaient longues, lisses, juste épanouies dans la jeunesse du muscle. La chevelure se déployait au moindre essor. Noire. Il y avait de la sueur sur le visage de l'adolescente. Le cou, les épaules, les bras étaient empreints d'une grâce, d'une clarté. La jeune Juive semblait née, comme neuve. De temps en temps, elle lançait un regard à sa mère et poussait un rire comme un aboi de gorge presque animal et triomphant, à chaque coup réussi. On ne peut pas peindre ce cri glorieux qui se forgeait dans les poumons de la jeune fille et plus profond dans son corps, qui jaillissait de son corps de plaisir, de son corps de gloire... Il y avait tant

d'ivresse dans ce rire qu'il restait un instant engorgé dans le cou par l'effort, l'essoufflement, se reprenait et se délivrait, éclatait, aspergeait la jeune Juive comme un jet déréglé. J'aurais voulu me placer sous ce rire, ses soubresauts haletés, qu'il roule sur mon visage et sur mon corps, que sa cascade me vivifie.

Béat, j'assistai à l'épiphanie de la jeune Juive aux jambes pures, et dont la chevelure noire s'envolait à chaque bond sur la balle. Sa jupe se froissait et retroussait sa corolle dans le vent. Je vis la cuisse entière jusqu'à l'amorce d'une fesse charnue et plus pâle. La bourrasque releva, plaqua d'un coup tous ces pétales blancs, haut sur la taille et dévoila l'angle d'amour pour la première fois. Dans le soleil du soir, je vis ce linge étroit de jeune fille qui s'ouvrait au bonheur et provoquait enfin sa mère trop belle.

Heureusement que j'eus cette vision de la beauté avant l'effroi. D'abord ça me prit à la gorge. Une sensation de brûlure. Tout le fond du pharynx était cramoisi. J'avais de la fièvre. Je prévins Marguerite. Elle me conseilla de rester dans ma chambre. Elle m'observait avec curiosité, intéressée déjà, c'était mon tour peut-être... son étudiant subissant la première vague d'un assaut qui annonçait une bataille ample et décisive. Je téléphonai aux amis qui avaient des relations dans le domaine médical et m'avaient déjà recommandé le fameux Dr P. Devais-je aller le revoir ? Ils m'incitèrent à lui préférer le Dr. F., car mes angines récidivantes et virulentes relevaient d'un génie moins éclectique que celui de P. mais d'un grand spécialiste.

J'arrivai dans les beaux quartiers : longue rue semée d'immeubles anciens ornés de frises et de balcons cossus. On

me fit entrer dans une salle d'attente exceptionnellement vaste, un salon plutôt, au parquet luisant, aux tapis luxueux, au papier d'un bleu discret et doré. F. apparut. Il était grand, jeune, nerveux. Ses yeux étaient cernés. Son visage exprimait beaucoup de lassitude. Il m'introduisit dans son cabinet qui contrastait avec la salle d'attente par son extrême étroitesse. On eût dit un étui d'aspect froid et technique. F. me fit ouvrir la bouche, n'hésita pas une seconde et me prescrivit des piqûres de pénicilline. Pas de dialogue. F. semblait impatient, travaillé par autre chose. Cet étudiant ne l'intéressait pas. J'étais fasciné par cette incuriosité, cette fébrilité de F. hanté par quoi, quelle angoisse, quelle passion ? Déjà j'imaginais le roman de F., dans les salons somptueux où se nichait ce cabinet minuscule et glacé. F. avait des yeux verdâtres, la figure comme légèrement tuméfiée par l'insomnie et ses cernes surtout me frappaient, bruns et froncés. Cet homme avait d'autres chats à fouetter qu'une angine. Les grands spécialistes évitaient finalement les traitements sophistiqués. Pénicilline pure et dure. Et mon affaire serait réglée. F. ne prit pas la peine de me prescrire de l'ultralevure. C'était un homme qui allait droit au but et soignait les hommes comme des chevaux, sans compléments futiles. La consultation était très chère. Elle épongea une partie de mes fonds de boursier. Mais F. était un as, cela valait le coup.

Marguerite, à mon retour, me conseilla pour les piqûres de faire appel à Mlle Poulet qui, comme on sait, avait été infirmière pendant la guerre et après, et dont elle-même utilisait les services en cas de besoin. Margot courut avertir « son petit Poulet ». J'achetai la pénicilline. Le soir même, je débarquai chez Mlle Poulet, je frappai. Elle me dit d'entrer. D'abord, je ne la vis pas. Son appartement peu éclairé était couvert de papier bleu et fleuri, je perçus comme un mouvement du papier. Une masse avait bougé, bleue et

fleurie, elle aussi. Très vite ma perception rétablit la réalité objective. Mlle Poulet portait son éternelle blouse à fleurs et je l'avais confondue avec le revêtement mural. Aussitôt, mon regard se focalisa sur un nouvel objet, une grosse seringue d'aspect archaïque qui, seule, tranchait sur l'ensemble mouvant et fleuri dont elle jaillissait. Mlle Poulet me somma de baisser mon pantalon : « Baisse ton froc ! » La vierge parlait cru, elle tutoyait sans façons. « Allez ! Amène ton cul ! » Elle aspira la dose d'une ampoule dans la grosse seringue qui datait de la guerre et me planta l'aiguille haut sur la fesse, pas loin du nerf sciatique. Car Mlle Poulet non seulement était frappée de légers rhumatismes déformants aux mains, mais elle était assez myope. J'appris bien plus tard, quand je montrai les traces des piqûres, que sa technique était sommaire et périlleuse. La douleur me poigna. Car « mon petit Poulet » enfonçait l'aiguille lentement comme un pieu et pas d'un coup leste comme on doit le faire.

A part cette rudesse, Mlle Poulet était bonne. Sa mine était sereine, son teint bis. Elle me tapa sur le cul : « Hop ! tu peux te rhabiller, mon gars ! » C'était comme à la guerre. Elle reprenait du service, me piquer la rajeunissait. Pendant plusieurs jours, la même scène se répéta. Je frappais, je distinguais une énorme sphère fleurie bouger sur le fond du papier dont la seringue sortait, métallique et redoutable. Puis la bonne tête de Mlle Poulet, ses cheveux blancs suivaient avec un petit décalage. « Baisse ton froc ! » ou « Montre tes fesses ! ». Et elle plantait sa lance de vierge guerrière. Était-ce une vengeance ou un vice ? Elle me faisait cruellement mal à chaque fois. En vain je tentais de bloquer ma sensibilité, de me fermer comme cela me réussissait pendant mon adolescence quand j'exécutais mes loopings de kamikaze dans les escaliers. Mlle Poulet se trémoussait de rire et s'exclamait : « Allez ! Remballe, mon gars ! »

Anny était là quand les premiers symptômes apparurent...
Si rapides, si extraordinaires. Ma gorge fut d'abord piquetée
de quelques minuscules ulcérations qui ressemblaient à des
aphtes. Le lendemain, elle en était criblée. Je pulvérisais là-
dessus des litres de collutoire, croyant toujours avoir affaire à
une angine. Là-dessus, j'eus droit à une nouvelle rasade de
pénicilline. Je refusais de montrer ma gorge à Anny. J'avais
honte d'être malade. Toutefois, nous fîmes l'amour comme
d'habitude. Cet instinct-là résiste à tout. On dut bander sur
La Méduse jusqu'au bout. Je dirais même que l'angoisse et la
fièvre me donnèrent plus d'ampleur, d'acuité, d'intériorité,
plus de passion... Notre étreinte fut dramatique et farouche.
Anny à quatre pattes sur le lit qui grinçait, et moi la
chevauchant, gorge écarlate, pantelant, quarante de fièvre,
halluciné comme un Peau Rouge par le peyotl.

Anny repartit, soucieuse de ma mine délabrée et de ma
voix ébréchée, affaiblie, presque inaudible. J'avais hâte
qu'elle s'en aille pour lui dérober le marasme. Une diarrhée
me prit, étrange, sans me tordre les tripes, une colique d'un
genre inédit, lente, continue, sans convulsions. Un bruissement, comme si un bavardage indiscret échappait de mon
cul. C'était une matière abstraite, un froissement de pape-
roles proustiennes... Je chiais des archanges. Je compris plus
tard, quand le diagnostic tomba, qu'il s'agissait de ma flore
intestinale. Le mot est printanier et luxuriant. La flore
déguerpissait, chuintait, toutes mes forêts intérieures,
humus, violettes, anémones de mes viscères. Je me vidais de
cette chose impalpable, innombrable. Cela dura tout un jour.
La nuit vint. La fièvre atteignit un soudain paroxysme. Ma
gorge était une plaie. Marguerite en alerte voulut regarder. Je
refusai. Je ne sais pourquoi, je ne fis pas appeler un médecin
ce soir-là, je n'avertis pas le Pr F. J'avais peur de déranger cet
homme délicat et susceptible dans sa passion, ses tracas, son

narcissisme, son bel appartement sans fin. Peut-être que je ne mesurais pas mon mal. Je pensais qu'il allait diminuer de lui-même puisque j'étais bourré de pénicilline. Celle-ci ne devrait pas tarder à faire effet. Ou bien, une autre raison plus profonde, plus inconsciente œuvrait-elle en moi ? Comme un désir de sombrer, d'aller au bout de la douleur, de fuir dans une maladie sans retour plutôt que d'entrer dans la vie.

Je me couchai. Margot entrouvrit ma porte vers onze heures du soir, alluma l'électricité et m'observa avec son mauvais œil, son air de renifler la mort. Je vis ce visage ingrat. Il me semblait que je le connaissais depuis toujours, ce regard creux... morne. Je compris sa pensée : « Il ne va pas me claquer chez moi, comme ça ! » Je marmonnai que ça allait. Elle attendit. Fée Carabosse, menton en galoche, chemise de nuit, toute déboîtée par la prothèse. Elle n'avait pas de tendresse. Cela ne m'étonna que plus tard. Elle ne vint pas me passer la main sur le front, me parler doucement. Elle s'enquérait, c'était tout, m'observait avec son œil torve, cette attirance horrible aussi, ce mélange de curiosité pour la mort et de volonté de n'encourir aucune responsabilité. Elle ignorait la démesure du mal qui me ravageait les muqueuses. Mais elle humait la catastrophe, d'instinct. Du couloir, elle me glissait son regard sournois. C'était donc le grand soir. Margot m'apparaissait, dans l'embrasure de la porte et le délire de la fièvre, spectrale et lugubre. Elle hésitait. Je lui marmonnai encore de me laisser. J'allais dormir... Et c'est vrai que les somnifères que j'avais ingurgités obscurcissaient ma pensée. Je ne pouvais plus parler, saliver, je me changeais en pierre de souffrance, en monolithe ardent. La seule issue était de tenir dans cet atroce carcan, d'attendre avec une patience qui devenait invraisemblable que la pénicilline enfin fît effet... Margot me regarda une dernière fois, moche elle referma la porte.

La pénicilline agissait en effet, la superbe. En pleine action même, une razzia. C'était elle, la cause de l'horreur. Mais je l'ignorais encore...

Soudain, dans la nuit, je me réveillai. Ma gorge n'était plus qu'un galet massif et déchirant. Je ne pouvais plus déglutir, je ne pouvais plus bouger. J'entendis quelque chose... un bruissement dans ma chambre. Et je la vis : Margot immense, immobile, yeux morts. Elle était laide mais cette laideur me parut transcendante, bien plus imposante que la beauté. J'étais pris, soumis... J'allais me résigner à la reine, à sa loi qui me condamnait. Mais tout à coup, au fond de moi, jaillit un sursaut. D'abord, je me suis arc-bouté contre le galet brûlant. J'ai eu le sentiment de grandir par rapport à lui, de le dominer, de le retourner, et je me suis retrouvé couché sur son roc hérissé. Une extraordinaire tension intérieure me galvanisa dans la fièvre. Je ne sentis plus ma douleur. Je me suis mis à genoux, tout braqué en avant. Alors je criai à Margot de ma mort :

« Tu ne m'auras jamais ! »

Oui, je m'étais redressé sur le dos du grand galet. J'avais hurlé à la face de Margot mon refus. Sous l'épaisseur du galet, j'avais puisé à quelque source qui subsistait encore... là où vivait toujours le meilleur de moi-même : le visage d'Anny, la sainteté de Neuzil et Notre-Dame adolescente, ce sentiment d'éternité et de beauté dans la jouissance étoilée. Je suis sûr que c'est de ce tréfonds intact que j'ai extrait l'énergie de crier à Margot qu'elle ne m'aurait jamais ! Jamais ! Et cette scène, je sais maintenant qu'elle répétait un combat plus originel encore, une douleur ouverte, hérissée par un gros caillou tranchant, dans mon poumon, dans mon ventre d'enfant tout petit. Entre vie et mort. Avec le même improbable sursaut, la même révolte animale... Ce même cri inouï jailli de mon moi aveugle.

249

Le lendemain, j'appelai le Pr F. Je ne sais comment je réussis à parler. Margot me dit de prendre un taxi. J'obéis. J'arrivai chez F. Il m'entraîna illico dans l'étui du cabinet, m'ouvrit le bec, jeta un œil, referma, déclara ;

— C'est un muguet, arrêtez immédiatement la pénicilline.

Il me prescrivit une masse d'antifongiques. Il ne prononça pas d'autre phrase, la visite dura cinq minutes. Le Pr F. était aussi fulgurant dans l'administration de l'antidote que dans celle du poison. Il tournait casaque en un éclair. Il n'hésitait jamais. Je me retrouvai dehors. Je revoyais l'expression de F. en me quittant, son air impatient et las, une seule obsession dominait sa pensée, une affaire toute personnelle : jalousie, rupture... quelque chose de cette eau.

Muguet est un joli mot de mai, c'est une fleur d'amour... dont les clochettes fétides envahissaient pharynx, larynx, menaçant les autres muqueuses, le poumon, l'anus, tout le dedans, par les deux bouts ces floralies allaient se rejoindre et me saturer. Je sus plus tard qu'un risque d'invasion totale existait. Toute la muqueuse mitraillée, déchiquetée, qui grouille d'une plaie pullulante, immaculée, d'où le nom de muguet. Mais F. avait l'œil, il avait calculé en deux secondes la course de vitesse entre les derniers effets de la pénicilline et les premiers de l'antidote. Il en avait conclu à la victoire de ce dernier. Il ne m'avait pas fait hospitaliser. Peut-être qu'il avait voulu se venger sur moi de ses déboires d'amour, qu'il avait pris ce risque par vertige, par sadisme, contre cet étudiant juvénile, ce garçon qui méritait de payer pour un autre.

Il est des moments où l'on croise la mort. Des circonstances, des hasards, des complaisances, des fatalités nous y

conduisent. Je crois à Thanatos, à la pulsion de mort, à son combat avec Éros, à leurs liens abyssaux. Le sadisme du Pr F., mon masochisme d'alors, Margot qui aimait la mort, tout concourait au piège, à la trappe.

Pendant trois jours, si la fièvre diminua, la douleur resta la même. Je ne pouvais rien avaler. Anny m'appelait de Lorraine et sa voix me rassurait. Puis le muguet proliférant devint plus gras, plus velouté, et ce fut le début de la guérison.

Quand Anny revint, quelques jours plus tard, la bataille était gagnée. J'avais maigri. J'étais pâle. Anny me prit la main et l'embrassa. Je regardai son visage enfantin et rose, ses grands yeux bleus qu'elle fermait. Sa bouche se posa sur ma bouche en plusieurs baisers lents où elle mettait tout son amour. Et je me demandai pourquoi j'avais presque failli me laisser mourir. Entre Margot et Anny, j'avais balancé, un soir, quelques heures... Mais l'amour lui aussi était pour moi une angoisse immense, peur de ne pas être à sa mesure, peur de le perdre, peur de la vie qui est amour sur la rive de la mort. Peur de tout, de ce monde colossal, ouvert, splendide, impossible. Peur de ne pas le rejoindre, et désir de retourner au lit, aux limbes, au linceul de ma chambre, à minuit, sous l'œil avide de Margot.

La double nature de Marguerite, je la vivais sans me l'expliquer. J'en subissais l'effet avec excès. Je le dis et le redis, car c'est toute la question d'alors, et c'est la question même : elle était la vie et la mort, au maximum. Mais pourquoi ? La vie, je puis le comprendre, cet instinct de vie brûlait en moi. Mais la mort... Cette Margot maléfique, oui, mauvaise, et qui me faisait peur, d'où avait-elle surgi ? Sans

doute avait-elle vécu l'horreur de son bras arraché, avait-elle été méprisée, rejetée, ce qui justifiait son intimité avec la mort. Il y avait toutes ces histoires de mort qu'elle semblait attirer, son mari exhumé, l'étudiante suicidée qui m'avait précédé. Je le sais. Je l'ai dit souvent. Il me semblait que Margot portait malheur. Mais je devinais une couche plus profonde, plus immobile, plus morne encore, le vrai sédiment de l'horreur, sans pouvoir le désigner. Partout, au cours de ces pages, on pressent l'abîme sans que j'arrive à l'identifier. C'est Johann Neuzil qui m'éclaira là-dessus. Dans cette période de ma convalescence, il me révéla, tout à coup, que la rue Pavée où était sise la maison de Margot avait été, en 1942, un des théâtres les plus cruels de la rafle du Vel' d'Hiv. La traque y fut massive et sans merci. Alors, je compris mieux mes intuitions, mon angoisse. La rue et la maison m'étaient souvent apparues comme les lieux d'une horreur diffuse et profonde. Brusquement, Margot me remplissait d'effroi et je ne savais pourquoi montait cette grimace du mal. Souvent, en marchant dans la rue, j'avais senti la ténèbre tomber sur moi. J'avais perçu le long des murs une ombre, une grande empreinte noire, comme un cri pétrifié. La foule me faisait peur, certains jours de presse, de tumulte. Comme une folie qui remontait de la rue. Mon lien à la jeune Juive, fait de joie menacée, de contemplation fragile sur fond noir, c'était ça. La cause s'enracinait, là-bas, dans la cendre. Il y avait eu cette violence noire. Familles traquées, chassées, groupées, poussées dans la rue. Les gorges nouées, les yeux béants. Les torches de la terreur. Et je savais surtout que si Margot avait habité là, elle aurait regardé sans agir, regardé à satiété. Si son regard me faisait horreur, l'avidité de ce regard dont je n'ai cessé de parler, c'est qu'il avait vu cela, qu'il aurait pu le voir. Margot avait alors trente-cinq ans. Je ne voulais pas savoir si elle habitait

déjà dans la rue, au 9, ou à un numéro voisin. Je pense que oui. Aurait-elle trahi, dénoncé ? Je ne veux pas le croire. Mais je suis sûr de sa passivité curieuse et monstrueuse. Elle, oui, penchée à sa fenêtre et regardant l'horreur. Sans pitié, vorace. Avec quelque chose d'anonyme dans la voracité, de plus vaste, de plus veule.

Un souvenir me confirme ce pressentiment. Une fête avait eu lieu, quelques mois plus tôt dans la rue Pavée, devant la synagogue : Le Yom Kippour. Les gens s'étaient donné rendez-vous vers le soir et parlaient d'abondance en attendant, je crois, la fin du jeûne. Et Margot regardait par la fenêtre. Elle ne pipait pas. Elle ne commentait pas. Elle ravalait sa chique. Mais je voyais ses yeux, sa mimique, quelque chose de mauvais, de rentré, de lointain, de macéré, de savouré. Se souvenait-elle de la rue ? de la nuit noire ? de la rafle ? J'avais senti quelque chose, elle remâchait un secret, une vision... Puis Johann, des mois plus tard, me révéla la rafle dans la rue même. Je compris que l'horreur qui émanait parfois de Margot avait rapport aussi au gouffre. Pas seulement l'horreur de son histoire à elle, mais une horreur immense et sans fond de l'Histoire qui anéantissait toute l'Histoire et cassait le temps. Marguerite, les jours de peur, incarnait comme la figure d'une vieille déesse cannibale, oui, dévoreuse, par le seul regard, l'avidité de son regard... avide et morne.

Mais Marguerite était redevenue inoffensive, allègre... heureuse de ma guérison. Elle nous inondait, Anny et moi, des ritournelles de « son Dédé Dassary ». C'était le vrai mystère de Margot, cet or amalgamé au minerai noir de la mort. Elle avait fait cuire un poulet, indubitable signe de

festivité, elle servait son vin guilleret. Elle trinquait, elle gloussait, volubile, elle s'écoutait parler... Margot la vive... Et la nuit, je crois que Marguerite pensait avec plaisir à ce que nous faisions Anny et moi, à pleine bouche... Toute la chair soyeuse et brûlante d'Anny comme pressée, gonflée sur ma verge, affluant dans ma gloutonnerie. Et moi plongeant dans son fleuve, m'abreuvant de lui à satiété, me pâmant comme la bête du bonheur entre ses cuisses, dans nos sueurs, bercé par notre chant d'amour... ces « je jouis ! je jouis !... je jouis... » intenses et sublimes.

Neuzil se traîna dans l'appartement de Margot pour me voir. Il savait que j'avais été très mal. Il ne se pardonnait pas de n'avoir pu venir plus tôt, mais son pied le clouait chez lui. Il avait affreusement changé. C'était un vieillard harassé, même sa sainteté s'était éteinte sous la griffe de la douleur. Il était accaparé par elle, par ses progrès, la menace d'une nouvelle amputation. Johann Neuzil avait perdu son rayonnement. Il ne pouvait plus sourire avec bonté. Son sourire était pauvre. Il parvenait tout de même à parler de moi. J'eus honte de lui raconter l'accident causé par la pénicilline, j'en écourtai le récit puisque maintenant j'allais mieux. Je n'osais pas lui demander des précisions sur son diabète et sa gangrène. Il le vit dans mes yeux. Il ferma doucement les siens en hochant la tête pour me signifier qu'en effet l'on s'était bien compris et qu'il n'était plus nécessaire de parler de cela, qu'il n'y avait plus rien à ajouter, à espérer là-dessus, que c'était fini. J'aurais voulu protester, mais la lucidité de Neuzil ne me laissait aucun recours, nul moyen de mentir, de bêler dans l'optimisme à toute force. J'aurais déçu Neuzil. La seule chose que je pouvais lui apporter, c'était le souvenir

brûlant de ma douleur. La nuit de l'angoisse, voilà ce qui nous unissait, cette rencontre avec l'extrême. Il en voyait l'empreinte sur mon visage. Et cela suffisait.

C'est alors qu'Osiris entra. Il évita toute esbroufe, toute manœuvre de séduction forcée. Osiris était calme et vrai. Il s'assit devant la table avec nous. Je craignis de devoir raconter encore les tribulations de la pénicilline. Il savait tout. D'instinct, en voyant Neuzil, il évita de revenir sur la douleur. Osiris jeta un regard circulaire et lent sur la salle à manger de Margot, le buffet Henri II, le linoléum, le poste de télé, les objets démodés... Il nous sourit, nous fit mesurer l'étrangeté de notre connivence en ce lieu, en ce jour. 9, rue Pavée, chez Marguerite la manchote, pourquoi ? Petit à petit, il se mit à parler, mais très doucement, sans théâtre... de proche en proche, il aboutit à Notre-Dame dont le sujet nous ravissait, Neuzil et moi. Osiris connaissait l'escalade de Johann jusqu'au sommet des tours. Et il parla des Vierges :

— La Vierge la plus belle n'est peut-être pas celle du porche Sainte-Anne, celle qui trône en majesté, la déesse romane, cardinale et cosmique... pour reprendre vos mots, dit-il en me regardant, je n'oublie jamais vos mots... Bon ! Je sais que vous avez un faible pour celle du XIVe siècle, celle du chœur, la très douce, la coquette, la mignonne, l'Italienne... Non, la plus invraisemblable est celle du transept nord, celle du XIIIe siècle, avec son expression si naturelle, si familière, son air mi-madone, mi-matrone de fille rencontrée au lavoir ou aux champs. Je n'exagère pas ! On la dirait surprise dans une occupation triviale. C'est peut-être la plus belle, car la plus séculaire, la moins sublimée, la moins esthétisée. Presque sans code ni canons, la plus audacieuse c'est elle, la Vierge incroyable, celle du nord, du froid, de la rue étroite, celle que personne ne vient jamais voir. Et elle s'en passe bien ! Mais voyez-vous, et c'est là l'histoire...

Osiris prit son air gourmand. Et je compris qu'il allait se lancer dans un nouveau récit plus ou moins historique, apocryphe, accommodé à sa fantaisie. C'était l'Osiris des loirs dorés, celui du phallus du grand bourdon. J'avais soif de son imaginaire luxuriant. C'était pour moi la meilleure médecine.

— Oui, le tragique de la Vierge du nord, c'est qu'elle croit que son fils est mort.

Même Neuzil marqua une surprise. C'était le pouvoir d'Osiris que d'accrocher notre attention en abordant son histoire sous un angle immédiatement saisissant. Osiris ménagea un long silence pour que la phrase accomplisse tout son effet, la rime! Vierge du nord et fils mort.

— Elle ne porte plus son fils dans ses bras, c'est clair... La version officielle le considère volé, détruit pendant la Révolution, comme les autres statues, les évangélistes de la grande galerie... Elle reste donc là, debout, au nord, amputée de son fils.

Osiris ne recula pas devant le verbe. Il savait ce qu'il faisait, malgré Neuzil et justement à cause de lui. Le mieux était de parler juste, sans détours, de dire vrai.

— Mais je vous demande ce qu'il est devenu, le petit Jésus!

Et Osiris nous fit sourire par cette chute impertinente qui tranchait tout à coup sur le ton général. Il reprit :

— Je ne crois pas qu'il ait été détruit. Il a été volé, oui! Un vol, c'est plus vivant...

Osiris nous regarda avec audace. Il était beau, intense. Il savait bien que nous pensions au dessin d'Egon Schiele, que Neuzil ne pouvait que sursauter, frappé par l'idée du vol. Et moi qui manquais un peu de repartie immédiate par rapport à Osiris, même si dans mes bons moments je le dominais par la variété, le choix, la sonorité des mots, je ne le lâchai pas sur cette évocation du vol. Je voulais le tenir un peu.

— Pourquoi est-ce plus vivant, un vol ?

— Mon petit, si le petit Jésus est détruit plutôt que volé, vous n'allez pas me dire que c'est plus vif !

— Oui, mais vous avez laissé entendre que le vol, en lui-même, était vivant.

Osiris m'observa, comprit que je n'allais pas céder.

— Je ne peux pas expliquer toute la chose. Il y a peut-être aussi le vol des faucons. Hein ! C'est le même mot de liberté... Mais cet enfant volé à la mère du nord ouvre une aventure. Il se cache bien quelque part. On a retrouvé plus tard les têtes des évangélistes de la grande galerie. On peut découvrir demain le Jésus du transept nord. Car il n'est pas détruit, je le sais !

Osiris savait, mais nous sentions tout de même qu'il s'envolait dans ses légendes.

— Il est où ?

— Ah, je ne sais pas ! Mais je ne crois pas qu'il ait été détruit. On l'a mis quelque part où il attend, où il règne.

— Pourquoi dites-vous : règne ?

— Parce que c'est beau, et ne faites pas la bête, « mon étudiant » !

— Osiris, où le voyez-vous, ce Christ enfant ?

— Dans la terre.

On s'attendait à tout sauf à la terre.

— Enterré ?

— Oui, comme un arbre éternel.

— Mais rien ne pousse, Osiris !

— Qu'est-ce que vous en savez ? Je vous dis qu'il est enterré... intact, coupé de sa mère gothique. Debout, tout droit dans la terre, comme une racine de pierre.

C'était l'histoire du Christ du transept nord, la plus simple d'Osiris, la plus pure. L'enfant perdu, planté dans la terre,

loin de la mère mais vivant. Il n'y avait rien à comprendre et tout à écouter. Le visage de Neuzil s'éclairait enfin.

Johann nous quitta. Osiris lui offrit de le raccompagner et il m'annonça qu'il redescendrait pour me dire au revoir. Osiris revint au bout d'un assez long moment. Je m'interrogeais sur la conversation qu'il avait eue avec Neuzil. Osiris n'ignorait rien de ma curiosité.

— J'ai mis un peu de temps à redescendre, c'est vrai que nous avons parlé de choses essentielles.

— Et je n'y ai pas accès...

— Vous êtes assez fin pour deviner. Il ne faut jamais tout dire. Il faut laisser vivre ce qui n'est pas encore dit.

— Il s'agissait du dessin d'Egon Schiele ?

— Sans doute... je vous l'avoue, sans doute. Car Neuzil va mourir.

Osiris dit cela d'un air grave, sans emphase. Et il le répéta très doucement :

— Il va mourir, l'homme gentil.

Je me tus. Et je me mis à pleurer soudain. Osiris se tenait tout droit, frémissant. Il attendait. Je me ressaisis et je dis :

— Osiris... J'ai toujours senti comme une évidence que Johann Neuzil était un saint, mais je n'ai jamais pu faire partager mon intuition. Personne ne m'a suivi. Un saint, c'était quand même trop.

J'insistai :

— Osiris ! Neuzil est un saint, n'est-ce pas ?

Osiris me regarda avec autorité et martela :

— C'est un saint.

Puis il ajouta :

— Un saint d'une étonnante pureté dans notre monde, très simplement.

Comme j'aimais Osiris d'adopter un ton si beau, si convaincu. Il méritait toute Notre-Dame. Il était le gardien des songes. C'était son fils noir et son ange d'Afrique. En partant, Osiris me dit :

— Comme cadeau de convalescence, quand il fera très beau, bien chaud, je vous introduirai sur la tour et vous pourrez, Anny et vous, y passer toute la nuit. La cathédrale sera pour vous.

Vinrent les orages, les pluies violentes et printanières. La Seine enfla. Dans toute la ville on parla du fleuve. A la télévision, on suivit la montée des eaux. Il n'y avait rien à faire. On ne pouvait pas lutter. Et j'aimais cette victoire des éléments sur la cité de pierre. Bientôt les quais furent inondés. Certaines voies bloquées. On se promenait, Anny et moi, tout au long du débordement marqué par des palissades métalliques, des sens interdits. Le dessin normal de Paris, de son centre vivant, fut brouillé, morcelé, dévié, semé d'avertissements, d'alertes. Et Notre-Dame baignait presque dans le fleuve gonflé. Nous montions à la tour et contemplions l'ampleur de cette crue. La Seine s'étalait hors de son lit, là-bas, dans le dédale jusqu'à la Concorde et plus loin. Il y avait des mares, des franges d'eau noire, des bras qui s'avançaient sur les quais. La Cité redevenait navire, étrave et proue cernées par le flot. Et les faucons voyaient venir les eaux. L'odeur du fleuve montait vers nous. La péniche de Wolf et d'Ehra oscillait sur la Seine débondée. La moisson des signes accomplie par Ehra s'enfouissait au fond de la coque pansue, coupée de la ville inondée. Le frère et la sœur ne pouvaient plus atterrir sur le

quai sec. D'abord, on installa des passerelles. Puis il fallut des barques et des petits Zodiac pour desservir la flottille des péniches. Toute la largeur du grand quai sud, au-delà de l'île Saint-Louis, fut envahie par la Seine, comme un étang. Wolf regardait l'eau douce et noire qui se répandait. Quand Osiris ramait vers la péniche, les deux garçons poussaient des éclats de rire. Wolf demandait à Osiris de se mettre nu et de nager ainsi vers l'arche d'Ehra. Le frère et la sœur auraient aimé sortir de l'eau cette grande anguille d'Osiris noir.

Un jour, Anny et moi, nous vîmes un type qui pêchait, installé sur le muret qui sépare de la Seine le flanc sud de la cathédrale. Là s'épanchaient les grappes de lierre vert. Et le pêcheur lançait sa ligne. Nous avions déjà vu ses confrères agir plus haut, en amont ou tout en aval, au-delà du pont Alexandre-III, mais jamais un type n'avait osé se percher là, à califourchon, sur la muraille aux lierres, juste en dessous du grand transept sud, celui de la rosace du Christ. Tout à coup, sa ligne se tendit, se courba. L'homme s'arc-bouta et sortit à la force du bras un énorme brochet... tous les passants accoururent. Le poisson se tordait et sautait sur le sol, nageoires écarquillées, écailles étincelantes, et sa gueule s'ouvrait dans le vide. Il avait cette belle tête archaïque et longue de torpille que renforçait l'implantation de ses nageoires à l'arrière du corps. Les mâchoires protubérantes claquaient sur le fil enfoncé dans la gorge. Le pêcheur ébloui prit le brochet dans ses bras. Il promena ainsi sa belle largeur brillante et se retrouva devant les porches frontaux de Notre-Dame. Une cohue s'était formée, avide. Le pêcheur posa sa proie sur le pavé comme une offrande faite à la madone, à toute la cathédrale des faucons. Il me sembla que le Christ du portail central, celui du Jugement dernier, si campé, si carré, si adulte et qui n'a plus l'aspect du Fils mais le visage du Père, et qui lève ses deux bras tout droits, de chaque côté,

comme un chef du ciel... il me sembla donc que cette statue de triomphe saluait la pêche miraculeuse du brochet. Toutes les rangées des apôtres, des saints et des anges paraissaient poser le pied sur le ventre du poisson.

J'ai passé l'écrit du grand concours, pendant cette période. Même si je n'en parle jamais. Car ce n'est pas ce qui demeure le plus fort d'alors. Je triplai les doses d'Imménoctal pour dormir et, comme je l'ai confessé, c'est en planant que je vécus l'épreuve, dans une ébriété précise, une hallucination extralucide. On ne peut pas dire que je m'étais tué de boulot acharné. La galère était mon entrée dans la vie, tous ces sas qu'il avait fallu traverser, trappes et supplices, du ménisque au muguet, via Margot. Je m'étais contenté de travailler mes textes au corps, dans le concret de chaque page, de chaque mot, attentif au relief des phrases, sans m'embarrasser des théories, des thèses de seconde main. J'avais scruté jusqu'à la volupté l'intime des textes, de leur tramé. Ainsi je connus le terrain sans trop de mal. Toute ma peur se réservait pour ce qui allait se passer de l'autre côté, dans la vie des hommes sérieux... jusqu'à la mort. C'était là le véritable grand examen, tandis que le concours n'était qu'une petite porte dérobée dans un coin de la grande, ouverte sur l'infini.

L'oral n'aurait lieu qu'en juillet et je vivais mon dernier mois d'adolescence, de nudité. Me dévorait une angoisse étincelante sous le ciel cru. C'était toujours la même terreur traversée, hérissée de joie fulgurante. J'étais offert au gouffre. J'ai toujours eu cette impression que ma peau, comme ma pensée, n'était qu'une île fragile menacée par le néant. Vivre, c'était cette vigilance épouvantée, lyrique, et qui ne tenait qu'à un fil d'abîme. Et je ne peux pas décrire ce vertige

acéré, cette sensation de fosse béante et cosmique où mon être projetait une flamme d'effroi.

La première semaine de juin fut dorée, le niveau des eaux diminua. Je rappelai à Osiris sa promesse et il nous permit à Anny et à moi de passer une nuit sur la tour. C'était facile. Le gardien redescendrait après sa dernière fournée de visiteurs et de touristes et nous oublierait là-haut. Notre bonheur eût été complet si nous n'avions appris la nouvelle hospitalisation de Johann Neuzil. Il fallait lui trancher le pied et cette vision d'horreur, nous l'expulsions de toutes nos forces juvéniles, nous ne la laissions pas s'incruster dans nos têtes. Lâchement, nous avions refusé de la regarder. Mais le martyre de Neuzil diffusait par en dessous l'impression d'un péril dont l'atrocité hantait le monde.

Osiris nous a laissés au sommet de la tour vers dix-neuf heures. Notre-Dame est à nous, pour une nuit. Ce cadeau est si extraordinaire que nous restons sans bouger, dans un coin... superstitieux, intimidés. Fiancés de la cathédrale, amants de la Madone. Pourtant ce n'est qu'une chose minérale et sculptée, autour de nous. Un toit de plomb nervuré de paraphes et de noms que nous connaissons bien. Quand nous jetons les yeux plus bas et plus loin, sur le long toit de la nef, nous prenons conscience du caractère sacré de Notre-Dame. La flèche fuse dans le ciel et les statues vertes des apôtres et des saints s'échelonnent majestueusement dans leur descente, le long de la croisée. Ce vert végétal et lumineux qui jaillit du transept, à l'intersection de ses forces, incarne la promesse printanière. Il nous suffit d'aller et de venir d'un bord à l'autre de la tour pour surprendre de nouveaux angles, pour deviner l'énorme volume déplié du sanctuaire. Plus bas encore, les

contreforts, les piliers de soutien et l'éventail des arcs-boutants dont on sent à l'arrière l'étalement sans le voir, car la cathédrale pousse sa charpente au-dedans de nous. Costaude, calée, animale et monolithique, caverne creusée d'ogives et de jambages sveltes, hérisson colossal aux ossatures saillantes et brandies au-dehors, bras, mains, pieds de mille-pattes. Avec les hautes prunelles des vitraux comme ceux des poulpes, juchés au-dessus des tentacules, des éperons. Nef, forteresse embrassant toute la robe de ses chapelles secrètes, de ses autels et de ses tabernacles. On sent le grand dallage intérieur et silencieux, l'allée qui conduit à la Vierge, au chœur et au Christ. On se dit ça tout bas, Anny et moi, sans le prononcer. On a un peu peur du sacrilège, d'être de trop, d'avoir violé le temple de la Mère. Alors on se fait tout petits comme les loirs et les faucons, faune de la cathédrale, petits poussins de Dieu. On n'est rien. On ne veut rien. On prie la Mère de nous pardonner, de nous accepter, de nous porter haut dans ses bras, dans le ciel… Anny me souffle qu'on n'aurait pas dû rester. Je lui dis que la cathédrale est le berceau des hommes, un navire d'humanité, qu'elle ne peut nous en vouloir, il suffit de nous nicher et d'écouter le soir.

— On ne fera pas l'amour ? demande Anny… ce n'est pas confortable et pas tellement indiqué !

— Non !… Quoique, tu sais, la cathédrale se fiche bien de cela. Je dirai même que l'étreinte amoureuse concorde avec la vocation d'amour des lieux.

— Tu vois, tu prépares déjà le terrain…

Le plus étonnant, c'est que tous ces scrupules venaient soudain d'Anny qui était bien plus athée que moi, d'un athéisme entier, d'un matérialisme impeccable et naturel. Moi, je n'excluais jamais une présence possible, une transcendance voilée, un autre monde, des principes secrets. Elle ne croyait qu'à ce qu'elle voyait. Il n'y avait rien derrière ou

dessous. C'était un athéisme sans colère, sans révolte, sans dépit, au diapason de la terre et des astres. Elle ne croyait pas en Dieu et c'était simple. Le monde est là, tout entier, voilà tout.

La ville fait grand bruit dans les soirées de juin, une rumeur roulée jusqu'au lointain, pulvérisée, ponctuée çà et là d'une inflation sonore, klaxons, sirènes. Mais cette vie nous paraît loin, hors de portée, tant la puissance de la tour et de ses soubassements nous habite. Nous nous sentons abandonnés. Comme si cette Mère était trop vaste pour nous, trop robuste, trop altière quand la ville là-bas nous appelle de ses voix innombrables et tendres... clameurs d'hommes qui vont, viennent, remontent la Seine, parcourent les avenues, flânent sur les ponts, travaillent ou paressent. On pourrait se promener sur le Pont-Marie, s'embrasser place Dauphine. Traîner à la terrasse d'un café. Ils le font tous en ce moment, des milliers d'hommes normaux. Même Osiris est rentré chez lui. Dans la péniche là-bas, Ehra et Wolf jouissent du calme soir. Mais nous, il faut que nous soyons là-haut, dans le ciel, coupés de la terre, fourvoyés dans le formidable et le sacré. Alors, Anny et moi, on regarde de nouveau les choses telles qu'elles sont, le toit de plomb, son bourrelet familier, l'aspect de la pierre si vieille et si bonne... Ça et là, tout autour, ce ne sont que des pinacles et des aiguilles, des gargouilles fabriquées par les hommes, des statues de saints et d'anges naïfs. La cathédrale posée sur son île est la même depuis toujours. Demain, le jour se lèvera sur elle, sans rien changer. Et nous serons partis et tout continuera. Nous nous arrêterons sur le parvis. La grande façade, les trois portails se dresseront sous notre regard. Avec ou sans nous, qu'importe ! Nous ne comptons pas. Nous aimerions compter un

peu... sans peser ni enfreindre. Nous ne savons pas ce que nous voulons. Notre désir est exaucé mais nous n'arrivons pas à le vivre dans la transparence du bonheur.

Les faucons reviennent des bois de Boulogne et de Vincennes. Ils ont tué des rongeurs. Ils nourrissent leurs petits dans les nids. Cette image-là nous calme. La mère penchée sur sa marmaille, lui donnant la becquée... la criaillerie soudaine, extrême, épileptique des petits corps sans plumes, tout crus, affamés. Les faucons vivent dans la cathédrale sans problème, défèquent sur ses dentelles, copulent et pondent, s'envolent et chassent, tuent, gravitent dans le ciel. Une grande ronde d'innocence et d'oiseaux. Cette cathédrale-forêt nous apaise. Rien ne l'exclut du cycle vital. Les prédateurs ne s'y trompent pas. Ils logent dans la madone leurs meurtres, leurs ruts et leurs nids.

La lumière rougeoie à l'Occident, du côté de Saint-Cloud, là-bas, du mont Valérien, dans une vaste région empourprée où la ville se noie. Le ciel est orangé, violine, limpide encore dès qu'on écarte le regard du globe solaire. C'est un ciel de juin comme infini, où la nuit vient dans la chaleur et la beauté, sans causer de rupture. La lumière décline en laissant intacte la pâleur et la pureté de la voûte céleste. Les martinets en éventail foncent et crient vers la Seine, tombent en piqué. On les entend, maintenant que s'atténue la circulation des voitures et des bateaux. Juin, le beau mois de l'espoir et des étés précoces, avant qu'on ne soit pris dans l'élan de juillet, d'août, de leurs nuits qui déjà s'écourtent. Juin en prélude, à part, pas encore pris dans la précipitation du temps. Juin tout doré, ardent pour Anny et pour moi. La cathédrale brûle doucement. C'est une madone d'été, grande ouverte dans la

nuit qui s'annonce si peu nocturne, si peu profonde, en passerelle dans le ciel.

Nous nous sommes penchés, Anny et moi, au-dessus du parapet pour voir la Seine scintiller, serpenter, prendre des pourpres et des ors sous les ponts... là-bas. La tour Saint-Jacques, rehaussée par sa statue, offre sa silhouette gothique, alchimique et rougie encore, tout près de nous, sur notre droite... Elle s'assombrit. Les monuments s'éclipsent lentement. C'est la belle loi des jours et des soirs.

Soudain, ils ont allumé les spots. Nous avons senti l'explosion de clarté qui a découpé des losanges lumineux dans la galerie de la tour sud. Mais nous nous trouvons au sommet, abrités au revers de l'enceinte, dans l'ombre portée du petit clocheton d'angle où débouche l'escalier. Nos regards sont tournés à présent vers le ciel où le faisceau des projecteurs s'épuise... Sur le toit jumeau de la tour nord, le nom d'Ehra ouvre à la nuit son entaille solitaire, juste au-dessus du nid du faucon...

Une première étoile, puis une autre dans le bleu sombre. Ce ne sera jamais la nuit. Le rouge se ramasse en ouest, plus dense, de plus en plus paisible. Ce n'est pas un soleil qui meurt, il descend de l'autre côté de la planète, son disque se dessine encore. Rien ne nous quitte, les étoiles se multiplient. C'est la chance d'un soir immense et lucide. Anny passe son bras autour de moi et je l'enlace à mon tour, joue à joue, nous sentons la démesure et le secret des choses. Nous n'avons plus peur, nous sommes au cœur. De la ville, ne subsistent que des reliefs sombres ou des arêtes d'or frêle, puis des masses plus douces, estompées, couchées sur la terre en troupeau. C'est le ciel qui se déploie, frémissant de nuit. Je souffle à Anny que les faucons dorment sur leurs couvées repues et que les loirs d'Osiris ont jailli de leur tanière pour galoper hors de la tour, en dessous de nous, sur le toit, puis

les arcs-boutants... vers le jardin de l'Archevêché. Partout les bruits sont plus évocateurs, dotés d'un écho de mystère, même celui des automobiles, des bateaux sur la Seine... des bruits intimes et qui nous parlent de nous-mêmes.

J'embrasse Anny sur les lèvres qu'elle me donne et je la serre mieux dans mes bras.

— Tu sais... je crois... que je vais dormir quand même...

Car Anny dort toujours et partout. Ses yeux ne voient déjà plus du monde qu'un reflet dans un rêve d'étoiles englouties. Son amant est une ombre recueillie dans ses songes. Elle se réveille parfois, retrouve sa vigilance, voit le ciel, entend... puis sombre de nouveau. Je la sens dormante contre moi sur le vaisseau de Notre-Dame, enveloppé de feux précis. Cet infini qui n'est visible que par les nuits d'été, la galaxie présente, éployée dans sa gerbe qui brille. Alors, je sens Notre-Dame comme je ne l'ai jamais sentie, haute, ample, noire et profonde, ses deux tours dressées, à l'écoute, naviguant dans la pureté du cosmos. Je me fais tout mince contre le mur qui supporte le toit de plomb... La constellation des noms luit sous la Voie lactée, sous le grand triangle d'or d'Altaïr, de Deneb et de Vega... Les foules immenses se sont couchées dans les immeubles près de la terre. Des millions d'hommes et de gisants. Je ne sais si Notre-Dame veille sur leur sommeil. Il me semble plutôt qu'elle écoute les courants majestueux du ciel, surhumaine et candide à minuit. Grande madone seule au monde, est-ce bien toi la mère des choses ?...

Je m'assoupis moi aussi, je me confonds, je m'absorbe... J'émerge un peu, puis tout à coup, là, dans la fraîcheur océanique, au grand large des étoiles, je me vois, minuscule visage tourné face au ciel. Plein sud, Saturne brille. La cathédrale tranquille découpe sa noirceur bleutée sur les losanges et les fuseaux plus clairs engendrés par les spots. De

la ville montent encore des bruits confus... Elle ne se tait jamais complètement. Elle végète et chuchote comme un flot sur la plage, comme un feu dans l'ultime bourdonnement de ses bûches. Elle nous protège de l'absolu silence, elle fourmille, trouée par un éclat ou tel grondement plus sourd, puis sa rumeur d'écumes la reprend et la dilue.

Anny dort, je m'approche de sa bouche et j'entends son souffle. Mon amante dormante emmenée là, vers les étoiles. Si gentille quand elle dort, enfantine, entrouvrant ses lèvres, vivant au secret d'une vie close et lente comme dans une coquille d'œuf, pas tout à fait étanche cependant, mais légèrement poreuse... Ainsi elle bouge dans un songe, me parle, me houspille, émet un rire, me touche, me repousse, m'oublie, revient, s'abandonne sur mon épaule. Elle n'est plus dans la cathédrale, elle est dans son sommeil de chaque jour.

... Je me rendors et me réveille avec toujours un sentiment d'inconnu, de surprise, une peur brusque, avant d'avoir identifié les lieux de notre exil. Parfois, c'est très difficile. Il fait plus froid. Je n'arrive pas à penser, à nommer. Et je reste, les yeux ouverts, dans le corps de la cathédrale, en répétant : « Notre-Dame... Notre-Dame... », ce nom énorme et vide, sans savoir ce que c'est, où je suis, ce qui nous arrive à Anny et à moi... quel voyage dans cette nuit de pierres et d'étoiles ?

Tôt le matin, avant l'aube, nous sommes aux aguets, et nous avons vu naître la première pâleur de l'orient... Oh, peu de chose encore, peut-être une chimère, une phosphorescence fantôme, un pas de neige... puis deux... Jusqu'à ce que l'aube blanchisse un horizon plus large où la grande ville grise bombait sa membrure de momie. C'était un moment timide et suspendu. Mais rien ne pouvait endiguer la vague de l'aurore dont la crête rosie perçait déjà, empourprait les

clochers, leurs aiguilles et la tête des tours de Montparnasse et du front de Seine. Alors le soleil réapparut dans sa braise et sa belle courbure sur le ciel sans vapeurs. Il y eut des bandes violines, des mauves, des royaumes orangés, mais tout cela germait, naissait, limpide et nacré, avec une vénusté, comme le cœur d'un coquillage frais, agrandi, qui renvoyait les échos sonores du matin. Ainsi vint le jour, un tressaillement nous saisit jusqu'aux larmes, ce jour nous émouvait encore plus que le couchant. Nous ne savions pourquoi. Car c'était le premier rayonnement du monde. Les spots avaient lâché la cathédrale, et elle baignait dans la vraie lumière. C'était une Notre-Dame matinale dont nous sentions la vigueur dans toutes les forces de la ville et de la Seine, qui se dénouaient, s'élançaient... On vit l'astre tout entier, levé comme l'hostie du monde, d'un feu intense et moins pourpre... déjà lavé de ses songes, flambant clair sur Paris, sur Notre-Dame et sur nous.

Je serrai fort Anny contre moi. Nous nous jurâmes tout sans le dire, le serment infini de l'aurore. Et les premiers faucons s'envolèrent. Osiris apparut. Il s'arrêta, nous découvrit et nous fit un baiser d'adoration en posant seulement, de loin, sa longue main sur sa bouche.

Johann Neuzil survécut cinq jours à son amputation... Le sixième jour, Marguerite revint plus tard de son travail. Elle avait fait un détour et une visite à l'hôpital et elle m'annonça en entrant qu'il était mort devant elle.

— Vous ne savez pas ce qu'il a dit, ce bon Neuzil... je vous le donne en mille !... Il a dit : « Soudain, je meurs. »

C'était une des rares fois où il avait utilisé l'adverbe de façon adéquate. L'homme gentil était mort. Son grand dessin d'Egon et de Gerti avait disparu. Et le mystère de sa sainteté restait entier. J'étais floué. Le vieillard me manquait. J'avais besoin de sa présence, de sa sagesse, de son sourire stoïque pour m'accompagner au seuil des choses. De ses leçons d'amour, d'éternité, de ses délires sur la beauté. Je n'en savais pas assez sur Wally Neuzil sa mère, sur Egon Schiele son père supposé et sur Gerti, la petite sœur amoureuse du peintre nu, du peintre rouge. J'étais privé de la tribu. Il fallait donc entrer dans le monde sans bouclier ni béquilles. C'est ainsi que Margot avait agi, la fameuse nuit de mon agonie. Pas un baiser, pas un geste. Débrouille-toi ! Tu es seul. C'est à toi de franchir le pas. Si tu en as la force, tout au fond de toi, s'il te reste une goutte du génie de la vie. Sinon

pars, abstiens-toi... Tu n'es pas bâti pour ça. Je crois que lorsque Marguerite perdit son bras, à dix-sept ans, elle fut seule, sans recours, sans espoir, et que c'est au fond de sa nuit qu'elle puisa l'étincelle de combat et de survie. Elle le savait. Me caresser le front, me bercer de boniments eût été m'affaiblir, m'inciter à sombrer dans le sein maternel. Elle me laissa tout seul par instinct de vie et de mort. Il fallait que je subisse à mon tour ce que le sort lui avait infligé, et que j'en tire les conséquences, tout seul. Je ne dirais pas qu'elle désirait que je meure, ce serait trop exclusif, trop partiel. Mais Margot, depuis l'accident de ses dix-sept ans, devait aimer survivre et compter tous ceux auxquels elle survivait. Cependant, elle m'aimait beaucoup, même très fort, dans une région de son cœur. Elle me coucha sur son testament, comme je devais l'apprendre plus tard. Je fis partie des quelques noms qu'elle cita en pensant à sa mort et en prenant ses dispositions dernières. Alors, Margot... que me voulais-tu ? Souffle-moi enfin la réponse... Tu me voulais deux choses ensemble, deux choses mêlées, toujours. Deux désirs, deux vœux de mort et de vie. Tu avais deux étudiants, le maladif, le mortel, l'apeuré, le jumeau de l'étudiante qui l'avait précédé et qui était morte d'une overdose. Puis l'autre, le vital, l'euphorique, l'exalté, celui qui te ressemblait bien davantage. C'était à moi de choisir, *in fine*, cette nuit-là, de trouver mon camp...

Johann, lui, était mort. Il était dans les âges de Margot. Et elle avait marqué un point décisif. Pour me faire plaisir et comme une concession, elle me dit :

— Vous aviez peut-être raison. Johann Neuzil fut une manière de saint.

Je me tus, cette reconnaissance était tardive, et je sentais qu'elle manquait de conviction véritable. Je n'allais pas rallumer le débat. Margot comprit que je n'étais pas dupe.

Elle se tut, courut chercher du vin dans la réserve. Et nous bûmes beaucoup, ce soir-là, Margot et moi, jusqu'à devenir flous, attendris, diffusés dans une euphorie qui brisait les barrières entre les choses, ruinait la frontière entre vie et mort. Il suffisait donc d'être saoul.

La nuit, je n'arrivais pas à dormir. L'alcool faisait battre mes tempes. J'attendis un peu et j'absorbai une forte dose de barbituriques. Le bonheur vint comme au-devant de moi. Il descendit de mon ciel mental. Soudain il m'enleva sur ses ailes. Le paradis se déployait, émerveillé. Neuzil était partout, son sourire et sa bonté sans bornes. Egon et Gerti s'étreignaient, s'amourachaient, se reprenaient sans fin, engloutis, élargis, dans l'infinie fusion. J'avais envie de rencontrer la jeune Juive et de lui faire l'amour. Il me semblait qu'Anny me l'eût volontiers pardonné. Elle nous eût même encouragés et se serait jointe à nous. Je divaguais dans des amours multiples qui ne faisaient qu'un, où tout le monde contribuait à la ferveur, à l'extase.

Pour un peu, j'aurais pu tourner hippie, bien shooté. Je ne sais ce qui m'en a empêché. Peut-être une conception de la poésie qui ne pouvait simplement s'abandonner à la bonté, à l'amour, à la communauté. Un sens violent de la solitude et une avidité de langage individuel. Cette nourriture pour moi seul, qu'il me fallait d'abord ruminer en moi et transmuer dans l'alambic du désir, dans la matière des mots dorés, sonores. Cela ne pouvait se fabriquer dans les rondes, les fleurs et les effluves. Ce n'était pas la Californie du bonheur, non, c'était un Eldorado plein de colère et d'or perdu où je naviguais seul, à la boussole des livres aimés et des fièvres. Il n'y avait jamais de réconciliation ni d'unanimité, j'entrevoyais des rivages, des trêves, des écrivains, des lecteurs me faisaient signe, c'était l'Arche et le Radeau. Noé tenait dans sa main la colombe, elle était blanche et nue, mais ne portait

nul message d'amour universel, elle n'exaltait que la beauté de son vol singulier.

J'eus des palpitations à la mi-juin, le myocarde broyé par des tenailles. Je le sentais poignant, effaré comme faucon pris au piège. Il faisait très beau, très chaud, l'hypocondrie me poussait à me tâter sans cesse le pouls, à écouter le tambour de mon cœur. Un jour, je pris la résolution de me mettre à l'épreuve pour savoir, enfin, vivre ou crever.

Le test consista pour moi, à midi, en plein soleil, à courir le long de la Seine un trois cents mètres accéléré, et à voir si le cœur allait lâcher. Je m'élance héroïque et suicidaire. A l'arrivée, je suis pantelant, une grosse chamade me coupe le souffle. J'attends la douleur térébrante, la panne brutale, la mise à mort. Rien... Ma respiration revient assez vite. J'en conclus d'abord que le cœur est bon. Hélas, un doute s'immisce bientôt. Le cœur était peut-être fiable avant la course, à condition de le ménager, mais maintenant que je l'ai soumis à un stress furieux, il a dû perdre le peu de potentiel, de marge qui lui restaient. Il est fêlé, au bord de l'abîme. Pour être sûr de sa résistance, il me faudrait courir un nouveau trois cents mètres en plein soleil. Ce serait alors convaincant. Et me voilà reparti pour un tour. Je cours le long de la Seine en pleine canicule. Notre-Dame en a ses deux têtes dressées de stupeur. Je m'effondre à bout de souffle, ruisselant, le cœur dans la bouche... Une jeune femme assise sur un banc me regarde. J'ai honte du spectacle que je donne. La vie revient, je ne suis toujours pas mort. Je serais rassuré si le cycle infernal ne m'inspirait pas l'idée suicidaire de poursuivre, puisque j'ai peut-être, lors de cette seconde course, réellement épuisé la pile de mon cœur et qu'à

partir de cet instant le moindre effort me sera fatal. Je comprends que je délire avec cette logique absurde. La douleur nerveuse et crispée du myocarde a disparu. La course a imposé un tel surmenage à la machine qu'elle ne peut plus répondre par un pincement névrotique d'arrière-garde...

Je reste allongé au bord du fleuve. Un faucon plane au-dessus de Notre-Dame. J'enlève ma chemise. Le soleil cuit ma sueur sur le front et sur le torse. C'est ainsi que l'on renaît et se cuirasse à midi. J'étais parti pour rencontrer la mort et je finis par bronzer sur les quais. La femme du banc garde sa tête à l'ombre d'un feuillage mais offre jambes et cuisses au soleil. Elle a relevé discrètement sa robe, elle me regarde en douce pour s'assurer que je ne suis pas un satyre. Au fond, elle est contente que je sois là, avec mon air d'étudiant inoffensif, cinglé de la course à pied, ce qui n'est pas sexuel, donc peu dangereux pour elle. Nous formons une sorte de couple à distance, sans rien dire, moi découvert jusqu'à la ceinture, elle très retroussée, les yeux fermés maintenant, visage bien détendu en offrande mystique pour éviter les rides.

J'ai prévenu Anny depuis longtemps. Le jour du solstice, nous irons à Notre-Dame, car la cathédrale de la Marie chrétienne demeure, au tréfonds, un temple du soleil. Telle était ma conviction, à contempler la ronde de l'astre, de l'automne au printemps et la disposition des rosaces...

Ce 21 juin, vers onze heures, le temps hélas était encore brumeux. Nous nous sommes donc retrouvés à la croisée du transept, juste à l'entrée du chœur, au pied de la statue de Notre-Dame. Une lumière vague encore coulait par le vitrail,

loin de la Vierge pourtant. C'était plutôt une clarté ambiante et faible, car Notre-Dame reste sombre dans son transept profond. Nous regardions la Vierge du XIVᵉ, l'adolescente, la délicieuse, à la couronne fleuronnée et au botticellien visage. Je ne sentais pas Anny aussi passionnée que moi. C'était comme pour Neuzil et sa sainteté... On ne partageait pas forcément mes croyances...

A onze heures et quart, nul changement. Le ciel bouché par une vapeur d'orage ne lançait nul feu sur nous. J'étais désespéré. Anny s'inclinait contre mon épaule pour compenser d'avance ma déception. J'étais tout de même un peu étonné et conscient qu'elle m'accompagnait partout, sur les théâtres de mes folies, en confiance, comme si cela allait de soi. Jusqu'où ne m'eût-elle pas suivi, Anny? Jusqu'au bout de quels dérèglements, de quelles révélations? Je crois qu'elle aimait être précipitée dans ma nervosité, elle qui était si matérialiste et si tendre. Il lui fallait l'aiguillon d'un amant frénétique, mes péripéties la happaient dans un sillage de transe. Un jour, je lui découvrais la sainteté de Neuzil, le lendemain mes amygdales saisies par un muguet phénoménal. Avant de me connaître, elle ignorait tout de l'existence du ménisque et du staphylocoque doré. Elle s'instruisait en somme, découvrait les mœurs de la Sainte Vierge et des faucons et puis, d'un coup, je lui avais promis le soleil, en plein chœur. Alors elle attendait avec une certaine curiosité calme.

Soudain je me suis avisé que les spots qui éclairaient le chœur et la Vierge annuleraient d'avance notre aventure. L'électricité tuerait la vraie lumière. Je ne pouvais me résoudre à cet échec. Et je suis allé voir un prêtre qui venait d'achever une confession dans une des chapelles attenantes. Je lui ai expliqué que le soleil du solstice allait éclairer la Vierge, mais que si les spots restaient allumés, l'événement

ne serait pas perceptible. Il m'a regardé avec surprise. J'ai insisté. Il fallait suspendre les spots pendant une demi-heure seulement... Je crois l'avoir supplié. Alors, il a compris la beauté de ma demande. Il a disparu. Un peu plus tard, les spots se sont éteints et la grande cathédrale a retrouvé sa lueur originelle.

C'est venu vers midi moins le quart. Une percée de lumière a fleuri la rosace du sud, a touché le ventre de la cathédrale sombre... un soudain sortilège. Nous frissonnons, Anny et moi dans l'ombre qui blanchit. Le soleil avance comme une présence. On l'attend, le désire, et son approche grandit... le pas d'un Dieu. Puis l'embrasement monte continûment. On assiste à cette grande embellie de la lumière. A midi pile, je le jure saintement, un rayon d'or traverse le centre de la rosace, son dernier cercle où siège le Christ roi, et c'est l'aura du Christ qui flambe d'un coup, darde son trait sur la statue de la Vierge. Notre-Dame baigne dans la lumière du Fils. Son visage et sa robe s'illuminent. Anny et moi sommes pris dans cet amour intime et grandiose du Fils et de la Mère divine, adolescente, unis par le soleil du solstice. Le grand brasier s'accroît, toute la rosace flamboie. L'intérieur de la cathédrale s'éclaire et la croix du transept s'épanouit dans ces rayons de résurrection. La Madone brûle dans la main du Fils.

Nous sommes restés, ivres de joie, bouche bée. J'aurais applaudi, tant les glaives et les gloires pleuvaient sur la Vierge du solstice, mon Isis sainte et première. La lumière déployait ses ailes d'Horus et de faucon. L'allée n'était plus qu'un pavage de halos et de roses ardentes. Et la Vierge tournait dans le soleil, dans l'éternel feu de la lumière du monde.

Deux ans plus tard, nous sommes dans la vie, Anny et moi. Entrés oui, tout de bon. Le téléphone sonne dans notre appartement de banlieue. Une voix m'annonce la mort de Marguerite. Son étudiant noir l'a retrouvée, à genoux, la tête inclinée sur la poitrine. Terrassée... C'est la fille de Margot qui me parle. Dans son testament, Margot a écrit : « Prévenez P. » Moi, son étudiant, le vrai, le seul, celui dont elle fut fière, qu'elle aima à la vie à la mort. Trois mois plus tôt, Margot était venue nous voir en banlieue. Nous nous étions promenés après le déjeuner, elle longeait les pavillons et les verdures, elle s'écria dans une prière, ce ravissement qui la prenait pour le grand escalier du Palais de justice ou pour l'impressionnisme à Chatou : « Ah, si seulement j'avais un jardin avec des roses !... »

La fille de Marguerite me dit que je pouvais venir. On avait lesté le corps de sacs de glace. On ne l'enterrerait que dans trois jours. Ce détail sordide me représenta Marguerite exactement. Je la vis morte. J'attendis un jour, deux jours... Une dépression me prit, m'assombrit, le néant engouffré dans ma poitrine. Je ne pouvais y aller et contempler Margot la mort. Je ne pouvais pas. Je ne sais pas encore tout à fait

pourquoi. Je n'étais pas alors au diapason de la mort, en tout cas pas de celle de Margot. C'était trop fort, cela me submergeait. Il me sembla aussi que si je m'étais montré, la fille et les petits-enfants m'auraient scruté, moi, l'inconnu, l'étudiant du testament. J'aurais été la cible de leur curiosité. Et je ne voulais pas pleurer devant eux. Je ne voulais pas revoir Margot ni les découvrir eux, vivants, obscènes, venus du bout du monde, tandis que nous étions restés là, Margot et moi, dans la crise, en face à face au cœur des choses. La dépression m'ensevelit. Le troisième jour, je sus que c'était fini, qu'elle était enterrée à Chatou.

Pendant vingt ans, je ne suis pas allé voir cette tombe... Mais aujourd'hui, avec Anny, maintenant que j'ai achevé le livre, il faut que nous y allions car je ne me suis jamais pardonné ma défaillance et mon absence quand Marguerite mourut. Elle aurait tant aimé que je vienne, que je m'incline sur son lit. Au milieu de ses enfants. Son étudiant qui venait de publier son second roman. Ainsi, j'aurais fait la nique à la famille. Elle avait trouvé mieux que ces fuyards du bout du monde. Mais c'est moi, cette fois-là, qui devais fuir.

Nous avons consulté un plan de la banlieue. Il y avait deux cimetières à Chatou. Anny supposait que le second, à la périphérie de la ville, était récent, moins probable pour Margot qui reposait dans la tombe de sa famille. On se souvenait qu'elle parlait de cette tombe où tout finirait dans la beauté de Chatou. Le cimetière en question s'étale dans un quartier paisible, au milieu des maisonnettes, des jardins, des rues muettes et des pelouses. En effet, Margot ne pouvait rêver d'un plus chic séjour éternel. Quand nous sommes entrés, nous avons un peu désespéré de la retrouver. Une

allée partait droit devant, bordée de conifères, elle partageait les lieux en deux grands carrés de tombeaux. On allait errer dans ce damier des morts. Une frange de tombeaux séparés longeait la totalité du mur d'enceinte. Et juste sur notre droite, dès l'entrée, quatre rangées de tombes étaient amarrées. Jolie flottille de biais. Je ne sais pourquoi, l'instinct me poussa dans cette direction. On commença d'éplucher les noms taillés sur les dalles. Ce n'était pas facile, car beaucoup étaient effacés. Certains tombeaux se bombaient, opaques avec leur croix prise dans la pierre, sans nom. Comme de vieux galions tristes. Parfois, on déchiffrait tout de même les inscriptions usées. Le pire, c'étaient ces colonnes comprenant plusieurs membres d'une même famille, la descendante qui avait changé de nom en se mariant pouvait ne paraître qu'en dernier. Aurait-on retrouvé Marguerite planquée ainsi, tout en bas de la liste ?

Une rangée, puis deux, on ne cherchait que depuis dix minutes, on revenait vers la porte d'entrée quand je m'exclamai : « La voilà ! C'est elle... » Oui, c'était Margot, son visage me regardait. Elle était photographiée dans un cadre ovale et sous verre, rivé à une grande plaque où s'épanouissait cet hommage : « A Marguerite, Notre Amie. » Et Margot souriait un peu de côté, rétive et coquette... C'est cette œillade en plein tombeau qui m'avait fait soudain sursauter. Nous ne l'avions pas revue depuis vingt ans. Nulle photo d'elle ne nous était restée. Mais son visage avait survécu intact dans nos mémoires. Margot indubitable. Nous nous tenions tout gauches devant sa demeure noire. Sa fille et ses petits-enfants n'avaient laissé aucun message sur la dalle, seuls les amis de la grosse maisonnée et Mlle Poulet, David et Maurice... ses collègues de travail s'étaient cotisés pour la plaque et la photo. Elle eût aimé cette marque d'affection et cette idée d'éterniser son visage. Au bout d'un moment, mon

regard fut attiré par une agitation, juste de l'autre côté du cimetière, au sommet d'une maison en construction. Les maçons se bousculaient pour lorgner Anny en décolleté et jeans moulants. Éros ainsi nous faisait signe dans l'enceinte des morts. Et ce duo était bien dans l'esprit du passé, de notre première chambre.

Vous pouvez venir contempler mon héroïne, à Chatou, le coin est agréable, on revient par Le Vésinet, on se promène dans le jardin des Ibis. Il y a des lacs minuscules, des ponts, des cygnes, des arbres, et des couples s'embrassent sur les pelouses. On s'est arrêtés au soleil, Anny et moi, pas loin de Margot. C'était le mois de juin et nous avions retrouvé notre amie.

La nuit, le livre fini, beaucoup d'images me revinrent de Notre-Dame et de Margot, de mon entrée dans la vie. J'ai fait un rêve, il m'a semblé voir le dessin volé d'Egon Schiele, au sommet de la tour nord qui se dressait au-dessus d'un mélange bizarre de cathédrale, de pyramide, de mausolée... Le dessin était enfoncé dans un trou, juste sous le nom d'Ehra. Devant lui, un faucon veillait sur l'étreinte et le nid des amants.

IMPRIMERIE SEPC À SAINT-AMAND-MONTROND
DÉPÔT LÉGAL : JANVIER 1994. N° 20604 (2299-2439).

Les Anges et les Faucons. Il a vingt-trois ans et vient achever ses études à Paris. Il lui faudra bientôt passer de l'autre côté, chez les adultes, et le désir autant que la peur d'entrer dans la vie l'obsèdent.

Marguerite, sa logeuse manchote, se dresse au seuil de sa destinée : le jeune homme sent qu'une partie serrée va se jouer entre eux. Car Marguerite, qui a connu tant de malheurs, balance entre une vitalité tapageuse et une curiosité, presque une avidité pour la mort. Les présages fastes ou funestes, les épreuves cocasses et cruelles se multiplient. Marguerite serait-elle maléfique ?

Cependant, Anny, l'amante, Johann, un vieil homme lumineux qui pourrait être un bâtard du peintre Egon Schiele, et Osiris, le guide un peu mythomane de Notre-Dame de Paris, se révéleront secourables.

Notre-Dame rayonne au cœur de ce roman, habitée par les anges et les faucons qui nichent dans ses tours et chassent dans ses jardins nocturnes. Aiguillonnés par la découverte des signatures fascinantes de Wolf et d'Ehra sur le toit de plomb de la tour sud, Anny et son amant vont nouer avec la cathédrale une relation passionnée.

Photo John Foley © Seuil
ISBN 2.02.020604-8 / Imprimé en France 1-94

110 F